GRAHAM M.

Ritual

Walkers

Also by Graham Masterton

Horror

GRAHAM MASTERTON OMNIBUS

Ritual

Walkers

GRAHAM MASTERTON

A *Time Warner* Paperback

This omnibus edition first published in Great Britain by
Time Warner Paperbacks in 2002
Graham Masterton Omnibus Copyright © Graham Masterton 2002

Previously published separately:
Ritual first published in Great Britain in 1988 by Severn House Ltd
Published by Sphere Books Ltd 1989
Reprinted 1991
Published by Warner Books in 1992
Reprinted 1993, 1995, 1998
Copyright © Graham Masterton 1988

Walkers first published in Great Britain in 1991 by Sphere Books Ltd
Reprinted 1991
Published by Warner Books in 1992
Reprinted 1993, 1994, 1995, 1998
Copyright © Graham Masterton 1989

A CIP catalogue record for this book is available from the British Library.

ISBN 0 7515 3324 6

Printed and bound in Great Britain by Mackays of Chatham plc, Kent

Time Warner Paperbacks
An imprint of
Time Warner Books UK
Brettenham House
Lancaster Place
London WC2E 7EN

www.TimeWarnerBooks.co.uk

Ritual

CHAPTER ONE

Outside the restaurant window, behind the trees, a huge thundercloud ballooned up, luridly orange in the afternoon sunshine, anvil-headed, apocalyptic, the kind of thundercloud from which Valkyries should have been tumbling.

'Well, then,' said Charlie, his face half hidden in the shadows. 'How long do you think this baby has been dead?'

Martin peered across the table. 'Hard to say, under all that glop.'

'This glop, as you call it, is Colonial-style Sauce,' Charlie corrected him.

'It's glop,' Martin insisted. 'Look at it. It's so gloppy.'

Charlie bowed his head so close to the lumpy scarlet sauce spread out over his plate that Martin thought for one moment that he was going to press his face into it. Charlie was sniffing it, to determine what it was made of. He was also trying to decide whether the veal schnitzel underneath had been defrosted recently enough to justify the menu's confident claim that it was 'Homestead Fresh'.

Without raising his face, Charlie said, 'This is a mixture of Chef Boy-ar-Dee canned tomatoes, undercooked onions, and Spice Islands Mixed Herbs straight out of the jar. Its primary purpose would appear to be to conceal the midlife crisis being suffered by the schnitzel beneath it.'

'Is that what you're going to write about it?' asked Martin. Charlie could hear the challenge in his voice. He sat up straight and looked Martin directly in the eye.

'I have to be practical, as well as critical. Where else is your ravenous fertilizer salesman going to eat, halfway up the Housa-tonic Valley on a wet fall afternoon?'

He picked up his fork, wiped it carefully on his napkin, and added, 'What I shall probably write is, "The Colonial-style Sauce was somewhat short on true Colonial character."'

'Isn't that called copping out?' said Martin. All the same, he watched with amusement as Charlie lifted up his entire veal schnitzel on the end of his fork and scrutinized first one side and then the other, as if he were trying to sex it.

'Sometimes, you have to be forgiving to be accurate,' said Charlie. 'The truth is, this veal is disastrous and this sauce is worse, but we'd be wasting our time if we went driving around looking for anything better. Besides, I've eaten far less ap-petizing meals than this. I was served up with steak tartare once, in the Imperial Hotel in Philadelphia, and there was half a cow's lip in it, complete with hair. The maitre d' tried to persuade me that it was something called Steak Tartare Napoleone. I said, "This is more like Steak Tartare Vidal Sassoon."'

Martin smiled, one of those odd sly smiles which fifteen-year-old boys put on to convince their forty-one-year-old fathers that they are still interested in hearing all the hoary, unfunny anecdotes that their fathers have been telling them ever since they were old enough to listen. He poked at his Traditional Connecticut Potpie.

'I haven't put you off your food?' asked Charlie.

Martin shook his head. 'I don't think you've done anything for their appetites, though.' And he nodded towards two white-haired New England matrons who were sitting at the next table, staring at Charlie with their spectacles as blind as four polished pennies.

Charlie turned in his seat and smiled at the matrons be-nignly, like a priest. Flustered, they attended to their fried fish. 'The food is okay here,' he told Martin. 'The vegetables are all home-grown, the breadrolls are fresh, and when they

2

accidentally drop someone's lunch on the floor, they usually throw it in the trash. Did I ever tell you about the time they dropped a whole lobster stew in the service elevator at the Royalty Inn in Seattle? Yes – and scraped it up between two wine-lists. Yes – and served it up to a legionnaires' reunion party. No wonder legionnaires are always having diseases named after them.'

'I think you did tell me that, yes sir,' said Martin, and slowly began to eat. Outside, the thundercloud was already dredging the upper atmosphere with rain. There was a strange, threatening hush in the air, interrupted only by the sound of knives and forks squeaking on plates.

'This place has charm,' Charlie added. 'These days, you don't get to see too much in the way of charm. And, you know, for most people, charm is just as important as food. More important, sometimes. You're taking a girl out, hoping to screw her, what do you care if they only half cook the onions in your Colonial-style Sauce?'

Martin was quite aware that Charlie was trying to talk to him man-to-man. But anybody who had been sitting next to them, father and son, both silhouetted against the pewterish light of an October afternoon – anybody would have realized quite quickly that they were strangers to one another. There were too many empty pauses; too many moments of unfamiliarity and too many questions that no father should ever have needed to ask his own son.

'How's the potpie?' Charlie wanted to know. 'I never knew you liked potpie.'

'I don't,' said Martin. 'But look at the alternatives. That fish looks like it died of old age.'

'Don't knock old age,' said Charlie. 'Old age has a dignity all its own.'

'If that's true, your veal must be just about the most dignified piece of meat I ever saw.'

Charlie was cutting up his schnitzel with professional

3

neatness. 'It's acceptable, given the location, the net cost and the time of year.'

'You always say that. You've been saying that since I was five years old. You said that about the very first catcher's mitt you bought me.'

Charlie laid down his fork. 'I told you. I have to be practical as well as critical. I have to remember that most people aren't picky.'

Martin said, more venomously than he had ever dared to speak to his father before, 'You'd eat anything, wouldn't you?'

Charlie looked at his son with care. At last, he said, 'It's my job,' as if that explained everything.

For a few minutes, the two of them were silent. Charlie always felt tense when they were silent. There was so much to ask, so much to say, and yet he found it almost impossible to express what he felt. How can you explain to your son that you regret every minute you missed of his growing up, when there had never been anything to prevent you from being there but your own misguided sense of destiny?

He carried a plastic wallet that was fat with dog-eared photographs, and for him they were as progressively agonizing as the Stations of the Cross. Here was Martin playing in the yard at the age of three with a bright red firetruck, his eyes squinched up tight against the summer sun. Here he was again, dressed as Paul Revere at the grade-school concert, unsmiling, unsure of himself. That picture had been taken in 1978, when Charlie hadn't been home for over four months. Here was Martin after his team had won the Little League baseball tournament, his hand raised up in triumph by some ginger-haired gorilla of a man whom Charlie had never even met.

Charlie had missed almost all of it. Instead, he had been dining in strange hotels all across America, Charlie McLean, the restaurant inspector, an unremembered ghost at countless unremembered banquets. But how could he explain to Martin why he had been compelled to do it, and what it had been like? Those solitary hotel rooms, with television sets quarrelling through every wall; those fifteenth-floor windows with soulless views of ventilation shafts and wet city streets, into which the taillights of passing automobiles had run like blood.

Every meal taken alone, like a penance.

Watching his father's face, Martin said, 'Sounds like that storm's headed this way.'

'Yes,' said Charlie. 'There's a legend up here in the Litchfield Hills that electric storms are caused by ancient Indian demons; the Great Old Ones, they call them. The Narragansett medicine men fought them and beat them, and then chained them up to the clouds so that they couldn't escape. But, you know, every now and then they wake up and get angry and shake their chains and gnash their teeth together, and that's what causes electric storms.'

Martin put down his fork. 'Dad? Is it okay if I have another 7-Up?'

Charlie said, 'You know – you can call me Charlie. I mean, you don't have to. But you can if you want to.'

Martin didn't say anything to that. Charlie beckoned the waitress. 'You want to bring me another 7-Up, no cherry, and another glass of the chardonnay?'

'You're not on vacation,' the waitress said. It wasn't a question. She wore a blue satin dress that stuck to all the most unflattering parts of her hips and her buttocks with the tenacity of Saran-wrap. She could have been quite pretty, except that one side of her face didn't quite seem to match the other, giving her a peculiarly vixenish appearance. Her hair was the colour of egg-yolk, and stuck up stiffly in all directions.

'Just making the rounds,' said Charlie, winking at Martin. There was a distant grumble of thunder, and he pointed with a smile towards the window. 'I was telling my son about the Indian demons, chained up in the clouds.'

The waitress stopped writing on her pad for a moment and stared at him. 'Pardon me?'

'It's a legend,' said Martin, coming to his father's rescue.

'You're not kidding,' the waitress remarked. She peered down at Charlie's plate. 'You really hate that veal, don't you?' she told him.

'It's acceptable,' said Charlie, without looking at her. Like each of his five fellow inspectors, he wasn't permitted to discuss meals or services with the management of any of the restaurants he visited, and it was a misdemeanour punishable by instant dismissal to tell them who he was. His publishers believed that if their inspectors were allowed to reveal their identity, they would be liable to be offered bribes. Worse than that, they would be liable to accept them. Charlie's colleague, Barry Hunsecker, paid most of his alimony out of bribes, but lived in a constant cold sweat unless he was found out, and fired.

The waitress leaned over, and whispered to Charlie, 'You don't have to be embarrassed. It's awful. Listen, don't eat it if you don't want to. Nobody's forcing you to eat it. I'll make sure they charge you for the chowder, and leave it at that.'

Charlie said, 'You don't have to worry. This is fine.'

'If that's fine, I'm a Chinese person.' The waitress propped her hands on her hips and looked at him as if he were deliberately being awkward.

'It's fine,' Charlie repeated. He could hardly tell her that he was obliged to eat it, that doggedly finishing his entire portion was part of his professional duties. *And* he was supposed to order dessert, and cheese, and coffee; and visit the restrooms, to scrutinize the towels.

'Well, I took you for a gourmand,' the waitress told him. She scribbled down '7-Up + Char' and tucked her pad into the pocket of her dress.

'A gourmand?' asked Charlie. He lifted his head a little, and as he did so the last of the sunlight caught him, and gave his age away, but that was all. A round-faced man of forty-one, his roundness redeemed by the lines around his eyes, which

6

gave him a look of experience and culture, like a Meissen dish that had been chipped at the edges. His hair was clipped short and neat as if he still believed in the values of 1959. His hands were small, with a single gold ring on the wedding finger. He wore a grey speckled sport coat and plain grey Evvaprest pants. Perhaps the only distinctive thing about him was his wristwatch, an eighteen carat gold Corum Romulus. That had been given to him under circumstances that still made him sad to think about, even today.

Nobody had ever guessed what he did for a living, nobody in twenty-one years. Most of the time, this anonymity gave him a slightly bitter sense of satisfaction; but at other times it made him feel so lost and isolated that he could scarcely breathe.

'Of course, this place has been going to the dogs ever since Mrs Foss took over,' the waitress said, as if they ought to know exactly who Mrs Foss was, and why she should have such a degenerative influence. She curled up her lip. 'Mrs Foss and all the other Fosses.'

'How many Fosses are there exactly?' asked Charlie. Martin covered his mouth with his hand to hide his amusement. He enjoyed it when his father was being dry with people.

'Well, there's six, if you count Edna Foss Lawrence. There used to be seven, of course, but Ivy went missing the week before Thanksgiving two years gone.'

Charlie nodded, as if he remembered Ivy Foss going missing just like it was yesterday. 'It sounds to me like too many Fosses spoil the broth,' he remarked.

'She'd burn a can of beans, that woman,' said the waitress. 'Come on, now, why don't you let me get you the snapper. I should of warned you not to have the veal.'

There was a sharp sizzling crack, and the restaurant flickered like a scene out of a Mack Sennett movie. One of the matrons pressed her hands to her face, and cried out, 'Mercy!' Everybody looked around, their retinas imprinted with

7

luminous green trees of lightning. Then a bellowing thunder-clap rattled the plates and jingled the glasses, and set the panes of the old colonial windows buzzing.

'I think God's telling me to finish my veal and behave myself,' said Charlie.

'I thought you said they were demons,' Martin reminded him.

'I don't believe in demons.'

'Do you believe in God?'

Charlie looked across at Martin, narrow-eyed. The rain began to patter against the windows. 'Would it make any difference to you if I said that I didn't?'

'Marjorie always says that you have to believe in something.'

'How come you call your mom Marjorie but you won't call me Charlie?'

'How come you never say you hate anything?'

Charlie looked down at his plate. Then, for the first time in years, he put his knife and fork together, even though he hadn't scraped the plate clean. 'You may find it difficult to understand, but when you're somebody's employee, as I am, you have to do what's expected of you, regardless of your own personal feelings.'

'Even if you don't respect yourself?'

Charlie was silent for a moment. Then he said, 'If you and I are going to be friends, you should try to get out of the habit of quoting your mother at me.'

Martin flushed. The waitress came over and set down their drinks. 'You saved your stomach some extra torture there, sir,' she told Charlie, taking his plate away.

'We'll have the apple pandowdy,' said Charlie.

'Are you *that* tired of life?' the waitress remarked.

The rain trailed across the parking lot and dripped from the yew hedges that surrounded the restaurant gardens. There was another dazzling flicker of lightning, and another

8

furniture-moving bout of thunder. Charlie sipped his wine and wished it were colder and drier. Martin stared out of the window.

'You could have gone to stay with the Harrisons,' said Charlie.

Martin was frowning, as if he could see something outside the restaurant, but couldn't quite decide what it was. 'I didn't want to stay with the Harrisons. I wanted to come around with you. In any case, Gerry Harrison is such a turd-pilot.'

'Would you keep it clean?' Charlie requested. He wiped his mouth with his napkin. 'In any case, what the hell is a – turd-pilot?'

'There's somebody outside there,' said Martin.

Charlie turned around in his seat and looked out into the garden. All he could see was a sloping lawn and a row of badly trimmed hedges. In the middle of the lawn stood an old stone sundial, leaning at a derelict angle; and further back, sur-rounded by a tangle of old man's beard, hunched a wet, half-collapsed shed.

'I don't see anybody,' he said. 'And who the hell would want to stand out there in the middle of a storm?'

'Look – there!' Martin interrupted him, and pointed.

Charlie strained his eyes. For one moment, through the rain that herringboned the windowpanes, he thought he glimpsed somebody standing just to the left of the shed, veiled like a bride with old man's beard. Somebody dark, somebody stooped, with a face that was disturbingly pale. Whoever it was, man or woman, it wasn't moving. It was standing staring at the restaurant window, while the rain lashed across the garden so torrentially that it was almost laughable; like a storm-at-sea movie in which all the actors are repeatedly doused with bucketfuls of water.

There was a third flash of lightning, even more intense than the first; and for one split second every shadow in the garden was blanched white. But whoever had been sheltering there had disappeared. There was only the old man's beard, and the dilapidated shiplap shed, and the bushes that dipped and bowed under the relentless lashing of the rain.

'Optical illusion,' said Charlie.

Martin didn't answer, but kept on staring outside.

'Ghost?' Charlie suggested.

'I don't know,' said Martin. 'It gave me a weird kind of a feeling, that's all.'

The waitress returned with their plates of apple pandowdy and a jug of country cream. She was grimacing as she came across the restaurant. Walking close behind her was a short, fat woman in a blue and turquoise tent dress. There was an air of ferocious authority about her which told Charlie at once that this must be Mrs Foss, under whose direction the Iron Kettle was going to the dogs.

Mrs Foss wore spectacles that looked as if they had been modelled on the rear end of a '58 Plymouth Fury. The skin around her mouth was tightly lined, and the fine hairs on her cheeks were clogged with bright beige foundation.

'Well, hello there,' she announced. 'I'm always glad to see strangers.'

Charlie rose awkwardly out of his seat, and shook her hand, which was soft and limp, but jagged with diamond rings.

'Harriet tells me you didn't care for the veal,' said Mrs Foss, the lines around her lips bunching tighter.

'The veal was acceptable,' said Charlie, making sure that he didn't catch Martin's eye.

'You didn't eat it,' Mrs Foss accused him. 'Usually, they polish the plate.'

The patronizing use of the word 'they' didn't go unnoticed by a man who had eaten and slept in over four thousand different American establishments.

'I'm sorry if I gave you an extra dish to wash.' Charlie told her.

'The dishwashing isn't here and it isn't there. What concerns me is that you didn't eat your food.'

Charlie lowered his eyes and played with his spoon. 'I don't think I was quite as hungry as I thought I was.'

Mrs Foss said, 'You won't find a better restaurant anywhere in Litchfield County, I can promise you that.'

Charlie was sorely tempted to say that if there wasn't anywhere better, then God help Litchfield County, but Harriet the waitress chipped in, 'Le Reposoir.'

Mrs Foss turned to Harriet wild-eyed. 'Don't you even *whisper* that name!' she barked, her jowls wobbling like a Shar-pei. 'Don't you even *breathe* it!'

'A rival restaurant, I gather?' said Charlie, trying to save Harriet from Mrs Foss's blistering wrath. Lightning crackled through the room, and for one second they were all turned white.

'I wouldn't grace that place by calling it an abattoir, let alone a restaurant,' snapped Mrs Foss.

'I'm sorry,' said Charlie. 'I can't say that I've ever heard of it.'

'Do yourself a favour, and stay well clear,' Mrs Foss said. 'Those fancified French folks, with all of their unpleasant ideas.' She betrayed an upbringing many hundreds of miles south of Litchfield County, Connecticut, by the way she said 'idee-yuhs'. 'Most of the neighbourhood children take the long way round through Allen's Corners, since that place was opened. And you won't catch any of the local clientele going to dine there, no sir.'

Charlie reached into the inside pocket of his sport coat and took out his worn leather-covered notebook. 'What did you say it was called, this place?'

'Le Reposoir,' said Harriet, leaning over Mrs Foss's shoulder like Long John Silver's parrot. 'That's Le like in Jerry Lee Lewis; repos like in repossess; oir like in –'

'Harriet! Table six!' boiled Mrs Foss.

'I'm going,' Harriet told her, lifting a hand to ward off Mrs Foss's anger. 'I'm going.'

'I have to apologize for Harriet,' fussed Mrs Foss. 'I promised her mother I'd give her a job waitressing. There was nothing much else she could do.' She tapped her forehead. 'You wouldn't say deficient, but you wouldn't say genius.'

Charlie nodded his head in acknowledgement, and tucked his notebook back into his coat. 'I guess it takes all sorts.'

Mrs Foss pointed towards his coat. 'You're not thinking of *going* to that place, are you?'

'Is there any reason why I shouldn't?'

'I could give you just about a *hundred* reasons. I know folks like that from before. I used to run a restaurant on Chartres Street in New Orleans; Paula Foss's Red Beans And Rice, that was the name of the restaurant. I used to know folks like that back in those days. Frenchified, and *suave*. We used to call them the Célèstines. Private, that's what they were; but secret's a better word. Secret.'

Martin said, 'He's there again, look.'

Charlie didn't understand what Martin meant at first. Then Martin urged him, 'Out of the window, *look*!'

Mrs Foss squinted towards the garden. 'What's the boy talking about?'

Martin stood up, and walked stiff-legged over to the wide French windows. The matrons turned to stare at him. He shielded his eyes with his hand, and peered out into the rain. Charlie said, 'Martin?'

'I saw him,' said Martin, without turning around. 'He was by the sundial.'

Mrs Foss glanced at Charlie, and then went over to stand next to Martin by the window. 'There's nobody there, honey. That's my private garden. Nobody's allowed in there.'

Charlie said, 'Come on, Martin, let's see what we can do to this apple pandowdy.'

Martin came away from the window with obvious reluctance. Charlie thought he was looking pale. Maybe he was tired, from all of their travelling. Charlie was so used to driving and eating and eating and driving that it was easy for him to forget how punishing his daily routine could be. Since they had taken the Major Deegan Expressway out of New York three days ago, heading north-eastwards, they had covered well over 700 miles and eaten at nine different hotels and restaurants, from an over-heated Family Cabin in White Plains with sticky red vinyl banquettes in the dining room to a pretentious English-style Chop House on the outskirts of Darien at which every dish had been given a Dickensian name – Mr Micawber's Muffins, Steak Dombey and Chicken Copperfield.

Martin said, in a panicky-suffocated voice, 'You won't let it in, Dad, will you?'

Charlie was ducking his head forward to take his first mouthful of apple. He hesitated, with his spoon still poised. He hadn't heard Martin talk like that since he was tiny.

'What did you say?'

Martin glanced quickly back towards the window. 'Nothing It's okay.'

'Come on,' Charlie encouraged him. 'Eat your dessert.'

Martin slowly pushed his plate away.

'You're not hungry?' said Charlie. 'It's good. Taste it. It's just about the best thing here.'

Martin shook his head. Charlie watched him for a moment with fatherly concern, then went back to his apple. 'I hope you're not pining for anything, that's all.' He swallowed, and then reached for his glass of wine. 'Your mother won't be home for ten more days, and I can't keep you with me if you're sick.'

Martin said, with unexpected vehemence, 'It's all right, I'm not sick, I'm just not hungry. Come on, Dad, I've been eating three meals a day for three days. I never ate so much Goddamned food in my whole Goddamned life.'

Charlie stared at him. Martin's faced was hectic and flushed, as if he were running a sudden fever.

'Who taught you to speak to anybody like that?' Charlie demanded. He was quiet, but he was also angry. 'Is that what you learn from you mother, Goddamned this and Goddamned that? All I did was ask you a civil question.'

Martin lowered his eyes. 'I'm sorry. I apologize.'

Charlie leaned forward. 'What's gotten into you all of a sudden? Listen – I don't expect you to behave like the Angel Gabriel. I never did. But we're friends here, you and me. At least that's what fathers and sons are supposed to be, isn't it?'

'Yes, Dad.'

Martin kept his head bowed while Charlie made a theatrical performance of finishing his apple pandowdy. In truth, he thought it was foul. The cook had emptied what must have been half a jar of ground cinnamon in it, which made it taste like mahogany sawdust. He would describe it in his report as 'wholesome, reasonably fresh, but over-generously spiced.'

All around the building, the gutters gargled the rain away down iron throats. The French windows were as dark as the glass in a blind man's spectacles. 'You know something, it's hard enough to come to terms with this situation without either of us getting all tied up into knots about it,' Charlie told Martin.

'I said I apologized,' Martin repeated.

The garden outside was lit up by a hesitant flicker of lightning. Charlie turned towards the window again. As he did so, he felt a sensation like somebody running a hairbrush down his back. A white face was pressed against the window, so close to the glass that its breath had formed an oval patch of fog. It was peering into the restaurant with an expression that looked like a mixture of fear and longing.

It could have been a large-faced child. It was too short for an adult. Charlie was frighteningly reminded of Dopey, in Snow White, with his vacant pale blue eyes and his encephalitic head.

In spite of the child's obvious anguish, it was the most

14

terrifying thing that Charlie had ever seen. The lightning flickered one last time and then died; the garden was darkened; the face was swallowed by shadow. Charlie sat staring at the window with his hands flat on the table, rigid. Martin raised his head and looked at him.

'Dad?' he asked. Then, more quietly, '*Dad?*'

Charlie didn't look at him. He kept his eyes on the blacked-out windowpane. 'What did you see, out there in the garden?' he asked.

'Nothing,' said Martin. 'I told you.'

'You said you saw somebody.' Charlie insisted. 'Tell me what he looked like.'

'I made a mistake, that's all. It was a bush, I don't know.'

Charlie was about to bark back at Martin when he saw something in the boy's eyes that stopped him. It wasn't anger. It wasn't contempt. It was a kind of secrecy, a deep unwill-ingness to discuss what he had seen. Charlie sat back in his chair and watched Martin for a while. Then he raised his hand to attract the attention of Harriet the waitress.

'Don't have the coffee,' Harriet told them, as she came across the restaurant.

'I don't intend to. Just bring me a last glass of chardonnay, would you, and the bill?'

'I'll make sure that Mrs Foss doesn't charge you for the veal.'

'Don't worry about it, please.'

Harriet was just turning to go when Charlie lifted his hand again, and said, 'Harriet, tell me something. Does Mrs Foss have any children?'

Harriet sniffed. 'Three – but sometimes they seem like thousands. There's Darren, who takes care of the accounts. Then there's Lloyd, who buys all the provisions. And Henry – but the less said about Henry the better, believe me. Henry is really *peculiar*.'

'I mean *young* children.'

Martin glanced up. His sudden interest didn't escape Charlie's notice. He *had* seen that figure in the garden, Charlie was sure of it. What Charlie couldn't understand was why he didn't want to admit it.

Harriet said, 'Young children, no. You're talking about kids, toddlers? She's about two hundred years too old for that.'

On the other side of the restaurant, Mrs Foss's antennae picked up Harriet's slighting tone of voice, and she lifted her head and searched for Harriet with narrowed eyes. '*Harriet,*' she said, and there were a dozen Biblical warnings in that one word.

While Charlie was paying the bill, he remarked to Martin, '*You* may not have seen anything, but I did.'

Martin didn't answer. Charlie waited for a little while, but decided not to push him, not yet. There had to be a reason why he didn't want to talk about what he had seen, and maybe the reason wasn't any more complicated than the simple fact that he didn't yet trust Charlie enough to confide in him. And considering Charlie's record as a father, he could hardly be blamed for that.

'Where are we going to stay tonight?' Martin asked.

'The original plan was to drive across to Hartford, and stay at the Welcome Inn.'

'But now you want to go to that French restaurant they were talking about?'

'It had crossed my mind,' Charlie admitted.' I always like trying new places. Besides, it'll give us time to spend the afternoon any way we want. Maybe we could go bowling, or take in a movie or something. That's what fathers and sons are supposed to do together, isn't it?'

'I guess.'

'Charlie attempted a smile. 'Come on, then. You go wait for me in the car. I just have to wash my hands, as they say in polite circles.'

'Oh, you mean you have to go the inky-dinky ha-ha room.'

Charlie slapped his son on the back. 'You've got it, champ.'

The men's washroom was tiled and gloomy, with noisy cisterns and urinals that looked as if they had been salvaged from the *Lusitania*. In the brown-measled mirror over the sink, Charlie's face had the appearance of having been painted by an old Dutch master. He scrutinized himself closely, and thought that he was beginning to show signs of wear. It wasn't true what they said about life beginning at forty. They only said that to stop you going straight to the bathroom and slicing your throat from ear to ear. When you reached middle age, you started to disintegrate, your dreams first and then your body.

He bent over the sink and soaped his hands. A faint wash of watery sunlight strained through the small window over to his right. He could see treetops through it, and grey clouds unravelling. Maybe it was going to be a fine afternoon.

Outside the washroom, in the Iron Kettle's red-carpeted lobby, there was a cigarette machine. He hadn't smoked in eleven years, but suddenly he felt tempted to buy a pack. It was the tension of having Martin around him all the time, he decided. He wasn't used to demonstrating his affection on a day-to-day basis. That was why he had so rarely stayed home for very long. He had always been afraid that his love would start wearing thin, like medieval fabric.

He was still buttoning up his coat when Mrs Foss appeared, and stood watching him through her upswept spectacles, her hands clasped in front of her.

'I hope we're going to see you again' she said. 'I promise that we can do better for you next time.'

'The veal was quite acceptable, thank you.'

Mrs Foss opened the wired-glass door for him. 'I hope I've managed to persuade you not to visit Le Reposoir.'

Charlie made a dismissive face.

'It wouldn't be wise, you know. Especially not with that son of yours.'

Charlie looked at her. 'I'm not sure that I understand what you mean.'

'If you don't go there, you won't have to find out,' said Mrs Foss.

She straightened Charlie's necktie with the unselfconscious expertise of a woman who has been married for forty years and raised three sons.

Charlie didn't know what to say to that. He turned and looked out through the door across the puddly asphalt parking lot, towards his light yellow Oldsmobile. A new car every two years was the only perk that his publishers ever gave him; and considering that he covered an average of 55,000 miles a year, which meant that most of his cars were on the verge of collapse after eighteen months, it wasn't so much of a perk as a bare necessity.

He could see Martin standing on the opposite side of the car with a copy of *The Litchfield Sentinel* draped over his head to keep off the last few scattered drops of rain. He frowned. The way Martin was waving his hand, he looked almost as if he were talking to somebody. Yet, from where Charlie was standing, there didn't appear to be anybody around.

Charlie watched Martin for a while, and then he turned back to Mrs Foss, and took hold of her hand. Those jagged diamond rings again. 'Thank you for your hospitality. I'll be sure to stop by here again, itinerary willing.'

'Remember what I told you,' said Mrs Foss. 'It's not the kind of advice that anybody gives lightly.'

'Well, no,' said Charlie. 'I suppose it isn't.'

He walked across the parking lot under a gradually clearing sky. He didn't call out to Martin, but as he approached, Martin suddenly dragged the newspaper off the top of his head, turned around, and skipped in front of the car, lunging and swiping at the air as if he were d'Artagnan. *Now he's behaving just like a typical fifteen-year-old kid*, thought Charlie. *But why is he making such a song and dance about it? What's he trying to show me? Or, more importantly, what's he trying to hide?*

'You ready to roll?' he said. He glanced quickly around the parking lot, but there was nobody in sight. Just the tousled grass slope of the garden, and the quietly dripping trees. Just the sky, reflected in the puddles, like glimpses of a hidden world.

'Do you think I could learn fencing?' Martin asked him, parrying and riposting with imaginary musketeers.

'I guess you could.' Charlie told him. 'Come on, it's only three or four miles to Allen's Corners.'

He unlocked the car door and eased himself behind the wheel. The windshield was beaded with clear, shivering raindrops. Martin climbed in beside him and buckled himself up. 'They have fencing lessons at school. Danny DeMarto does it. It's fantastic.'

Charlie started up the Oldsmobile's engine and backed slowly out of his parking space. 'Maybe you should ask your mother.'

'It's only twenty-five dollars a lesson.'

'In that case, you should definitely ask your mother. Besides – what do you want to learn to fence for? You'd be better off learning how to play the stock market.'

'I don't know. Maybe I could get myself a job in the movies, if I could fence.'

'The movies? I'm not sitting next to the reincarnation of Errol Flynn, am I?'

Martin said, quite seriously, 'I thought about being a stunt-man, something like that.'

'That's kind of a wacky career,' Charlie ventured.

'Well, I'm not going to be a restaurant inspector,' said Martin. There was no scorn in his voice, and somehow that made his remark all the more painful. It was a plain and simple fact.

Charlie steered out of the parking lot and turned right on the road for Allen's Corners. For two or three minutes they drove in silence. On either side of them the woods rose up like heaps of ashes at a mass cremation, smoking with mist.

As offhandedly as he could, Charlie asked, 'Who were you talking to just now?'

Martin looked baffled. 'What do you mean? I wasn't talking to anybody.'

'In the parking lot, I saw you. You were waving your hands around as if you were talking to somebody. Come on, Martin, I know when somebody's talking to somebody.'

Martin turned away from him, and stared out of the window at the woods.

Charlie said, 'I'm not checking up on you or anything. I'm just trying to take care of you. I've also got to admit that I'm curious to know who you can find to talk to, in this God-forsaken locality.'

'I was singing,' said Martin. 'You know, like pretending to play the guitar.' He demonstrated by strumming an invisible Fender.

Charlie glanced up at his own eyes reflected in the rear-view mirror. He wanted to tell Martin that the guitar-playing gestures he was making now were nothing at all like the gestures he had been making in the parking lot. Those gestures had been flat-handed, chopping, declamatory, as if he had been explaining something, or making some kind of appeal. They certainly hadn't been imaginary chord changes.

Martin reached forward and switched on the tape player, instantly drowning out the car with jarring rock music. He began to sing along with it, making a *juvv-juvving* noise with his mouth that reminded Charlie of the sound he used to make when he was a small boy, to simulate a Mack truck laboriously climbing up the lid of his toybox. It hadn't occurred to Charlie when he had offered to take Martin around with him that Martin would constantly require in-car entertainment. Charlie always drove in silence. He liked to hear the sound of America passing beneath his car, mile by mile. That, too, was part of the penance.

'Tom Petty and the Heartbreakers,' said Martin, crashing out more imaginary chords.

'Am I supposed to have heard of them?' asked Charlie, and then thought, *What a hideous middle-aged thing to say. No wonder Martin thinks you're so damned old.*

Martin didn't answer. Charlie carried on driving through the golden mist. He began to feel as if he were living in another time altogether; as if somehow they had driven through to the Ninth Dimension, like travellers used to do on *The Twilight Zone.*

He glanced at Martin surreptitiously. No teenage boy could have looked more normal. He might be aggressive and sarcastic, but what teenage boy wasn't? At least he didn't wear studs through his ears and make-up. He was nothing more than your average, skinny, short-haired pale-faced boy, with preshrunk 501s and a big plaid jacket and sneakers that looked as if they had been borrowed from one of the Harlem Globetrotters.

Maybe Charlie's anxiety at forming a new relationship with his son had made him too suspicious. Maybe Martin was telling the truth, and all that he had seen out in the garden had been a bush. Yet why he had said, 'You won't let him in Dad, will you?' Nobody says that about a bush. And he *had* been talking to somebody out in the parking lot, Charlie was sure of it, even though the parking lot had appeared to be empty.

Maybe he had been talking to himself. Or maybe he had been talking to somebody too small to be visible behind the car

CHAPTER TWO

They drove into Allen's Corners just as the bell from the Georgian-style Congregational Church was beating out three o'clock. Charlie parked the car right outside the entrance to the First Litchfield Savings Bank, and climbed out into the sunshine. The air was tangy with woodsmoke and recent rain.

Allen's Corners lay seven miles from Washington and five miles from Bethlehem, in a wooded hollow where the Quassapaug tributary ran. The heart of the town was a plain, sloping green, faced on three sides by white-painted colonial buildings, and dappled by crimson maples. There was a colonial cannon standing at the lower end of the green, and in the striped shadow of its wheel spokes two elderly men were sitting on a bench, their trousers protected from the wet wooden slats by carefully folded up newspapers.

'Best thing we can do is get some directions from those two,' said Charlie.

Martin looked around, his hands tucked into the front pockets of his jeans. 'You're sure this place has a bowling alley?'

'Down on the south side of town, next to the supermarket and the railroad depot. What the folks from the historical district call the commercial district.'

Charlie tugged his well-thumbed copy of MARIA out of his sagging coat pocket, licked his finger, and leafed through it until he found Allen's Corners, population 671, one gas station (daytimes only); two restaurants, Billy's Beer & Bite and The English Muffin; one boarding house, 313 Naugatuck, six guests only, no dogs.

MARIA was the popular acronym for the guide called *Motor-Courts, Apartments, Restaurants and Inns of America*. For Charlie, it was appropriate that it should have been a woman's name, because MARIA had been the mistress that had broken up his marriage. MARIA was the siren who had lured him away from home, and sent him driving around America in search of an illusory fulfilment that he had realized years ago would never be his. He wasn't bitter about it. He knew that he would never be able to settle down, so the best thing he could do was to go on driving around until some early-morning maid in some small mid-West hotel tried to wake him up one day and found that she couldn't.

Founded in 1927 by a flannelette salesman called Wilbur Burke who had been stranded in rural communities just once too often 'sans beefsteak, sans bed', MARIA had been the travelling man's Bible for twenty years. In his preface to the first edition, Burke had written, 'This guide is dedicated to every man whose Model A has let him down somewhere in the vastness of the American continent, on endless plain or wind-swept mountain, and who has been obliged through lack of local knowledge to dine on Air Pie; and to seek his rest on the cushions of his back seat.'

Lately, however, MARIA had been overtaken in stylishness and circulation by *Michelin* and *Dining Out in America*. Salesmen flew to their destinations these days, eating and sleeping high above the prairies which they once used to cross in overloaded station wagons. But MARIA still sold 30,000 copies every year, and that was enough to justify the perpetual travels of Charlie and his five colleagues, constantly updating and correcting like the clerks in George Orwell's Ministry of Truth.

MARIA's restaurant inspectors managed on average to survive their jobs for three years. At the end of three years, they were usually suffering from emotional exhaustion, alcoholism, and stomach disorders. Very few inspectors were married, but almost all of those who were went through

23

separation or divorce. Charlie had lost Marjorie; but he had outlasted the next-longest serving inspector five times over.

Mrs Verity Burke Trafford, who owned MARIA, said without kindness that Charlie must have been born a glutton; not only for food but for punishment. Charlie, in reply, said nothing.

Charlie walked across the dappled shadows of the green towards the two elderly men, and Martin followed him. Their feet made parallel tracks in the silvery moisture on the grass. The old men watched them approach with their hands shading their eyes. One of them was ruddy-faced, and blue-eyed, with the deceptively healthy looks of high blood pressure. The other was sallow and bent, with tufts of white hair that reminded Charlie of an old photograph he had once seen of an Indian scout who had been scalped by Apaches.

'Fine afternoon,' said Charlie, by way of greeting.

'It'll rain again before nightfall,' replied the ruddy-faced man. 'You can make a bet on that.'

'Wonder if you could help me,' said Charlie. 'I'm looking for a restaurant hereabouts.'

'There's Billy's down by the depot,' said the ruddy-faced man. Although the church clock was clearly visible through the maples, he took out a pocket watch and examined it for a while as if he wasn't sure that it was working. 'Be closed by now, though. Five after three.'

'It's a particular restaurant I'm interested in, Le Reposoir.'

The ruddy-faced man thought about that, and then shook his head. 'Never heard of any place called anything like that. Sure it's Allen's Corners you want? Not Bethlehem?'

'I had lunch at the Iron Kettle,' said Charlie. 'Mrs Foss told me about it.'

'What did he say?' the white-haired man cried out, leaning forward and cupping his hand to his whiskery ear.

'He said he had lunch at the Iron Kettle,' the ruddy-faced man shouted at him.

'Well, rather him than me,' his companion replied. 'Never could tolerate that Wickes family.'

'The Fosses own it now,' the ruddy-faced man told him.

'Oh, the Fosses,' said his white-haired friend. 'I remember. That woman with the fancy eyeglasses and the stupid sons. And that daughter that went missing – what was her name?'

'Ivy,' the ruddy-faced man reminded him. 'And she wasn't a daughter, she was a niece.'

'You're a hair-splitter, Christopher Prescott,' the white-haired man snapped.

'And you, Oliver T. Burack, are a xenophobe.'

Charlie interrupted them. 'You don't know where this restaurant could be, then?'

The ruddy-faced Christopher Prescott said, 'You've been misguided, my friend, if you want my opinion. Somebody's led you astray.'

'Harriet the waitress told me about it. She even spelled it out.'

'Harriet? Harriet Greene?'

'I guess that's her name, yes.'

Christopher Prescott reached out and gently took hold of the sleeve of Charlie's coat. 'My dear man, Harriet Greene is well known in this locality for having an unusually low proportion of active brain cells. In other words, she's what you might call doolally.'

'Mrs Foss mentioned the place, too,' said Charlie. Beside him, Martin was growing restless, and scuffing his feet.

'What did he say?' Oliver T. Burack wanted to know.

'He was talking about the Fosses,' Christopher Prescott shouted.

'The Fosses of Evil,' cackled Oliver T. Burack. 'That's what I call them. The Fosses of Evil.'

'Be quiet, Oliver,' Christopher Prescott admonished him.

It was then that a young sheriff's deputy came walking across the grass towards them. He was thin and big-nosed and he had grown a drooping blond moustache in an obvious effort to make himself look more mature. His eyes were concealed behind impenetrable dark sunglasses. He came up to Charlie and Martin and stood with his hands on his narrow hips, inspecting them.

'That your car, sir? That Olds with the Michigan plates?'

'Yes, it is,' said Charlie. 'Anything wrong?'

'I'd appreciate it if you'd move it, that's all,' the deputy told him.

'It's not illegally parked,' said Charlie.

'Did you hear anybody say that it was?' the deputy inquired. Charlie – who had argued with traffic cops and deputies on almost every highway from Walla Walla, Washington, to Wind River, Wyoming – took a deep and patient breath.

'If it's not illegally parked, deputy, then I'd honestly prefer it to remain where it is.'

The deputy looked past Charlie and Martin to the two old men on the bench. 'How're you doing Mr Prescott, sir? Mr Burack?'

'We're doing fine, thank you, Clive,' Christopher Prescott replied.

'These two people bothering you any?'

'No, sir, not at all. Asking for directions, that was all.'

'Lost your way?' the deputy said, turning back to Charlie.

'Not really. I'm trying to find a restaurant, that's all. Le Reposoir.'

The deputy thoughtfully stroked at his blond moustache. He had a ferocious red spot right on the end of his nose. 'You know something, sir? There are laws and there are customs.'

'Are you trying to make some kind of a point?' Charlie asked.

'What I'm trying to say, sir, without giving unnecessary offence, is that your vehicle is parked in the place where the president of the savings bank parks. He's still out at lunch right now, but he'll be back before too long, and you can understand what his feelings are going to be if he discovers an out-of-state vehicle occupying his customary place.'

Charlie stared at the deputy in disbelief. The wind whispered through the maples, and over by the commercial district a dog was barking. At last, Charlie said, with uncompromising coldness, 'Take off those sunglasses.'

The deputy hesitated at first, but then slowly removed them. His eyes were green and one of them was slightly bloodshot.

Charlie said, 'Do you happen to know where I can find a French-style restaurant called Le Reposoir?'

The deputy glanced at the two old men. 'Is that what you asked these gentlemen?'

'Yes it is. But now I'm asking you.'

'Well, sir, Le Reposoir isn't open to the public. It's more of a dining club than a restaurant. The way I understand it, you have to make a special appointment before they'll let you in there.'

'I see. But can you tell me where it is?'

The deputy looked uncomfortable. 'The people who run Le Reposoir are not too keen on unexpected visitors, sir. A couple of times they've called us out to take away trespassers.'

'I'll deal with that when I get there, deputy. All I want to know from you is where it is.'

'Sir – believe me – it doesn't have too good a reputation. I don't know how you got to hear about it, but the people round here don't speak too well about it. If I were you, I'd take a raincheck. Billy's is probably the best place to eat in Allen's Corners, if it's good country food you're looking for. My cousin works in the kitchen, and that kitchen's so clean, you wouldn't mind them taking out your appendix.'

Charlie said, 'You still haven't given me any idea where to find Le Reposoir.'

The deputy pushed his sunglasses back on to his nose. 'I'm sorry sir, I'm not sure that I should. We do our best to divert people away from Le Reposoir, tell you the truth.'

'I'll make a deal with you,' Charlie suggested. 'You tell me where Le Reposoir is, and I'll move my car.'

The deputy didn't look at all happy about that. 'Let me tell you something, sir, Mr Musette isn't going to like it any.'

'Mr Musette? Who's he?'

'He kind of runs Le Reposoir, him and Mrs Musette. Well – I believe they run it, anyway. I never saw anybody else up there, excepting some tall fellow who was working in the garden.'

A Jeep sped noisily around the green, and the deputy glanced around with undisguised anxiety in case it was the president of the savings bank, returning from lunch to find that his sacred parking space had been usurped by a stranger.

'Come on,' said Charlie. 'A deal's a deal. And what do we have at stake here? The sheriff's five per cent mortgage?'

The deputy said, 'All I can tell you is the name Musette. You can look it up in the telephone book.'

'Come on,' said Charlie. 'You can tell me approximately where it is, can't you?'

The deputy looked over at Christopher Prescott, as if he were seeking approval. Charlie was sure that he saw Prescott almost imperceptibly shake his head, but he couldn't be certain about it.

'You'd better call Mr Musette first,' the deputy repeated. If you try to go up there uninvited, well – the next thing I know he's going to be yelling down the horn at me, telling me to come up and get you because you've been trespassing. Mr Musette has a real obsession with trespassers.'

Martin said, 'Come on, Dad, we won't have any time left for bowling.'

'Bowling?' asked the deputy. 'You won't be able to do any bowling around here. Nearest lanes are in Hartford. There used to be a bowl, sure, down by the railroad depot, but they closed it nine months back. Too many old folks in Allen's Corners to make a bowl pay. No youngsters any more.'

'I was here last year,' said Charlie, in surprise. 'I can remember that bowl being packed out with kids.'

'Times change,' Christopher Prescott intervened. His voice was as dry as the wind in the leaves. 'Lot of young couples decided that Allen's Corners wasn't the place they wanted their kids to grow up in. Too quiet, you see, and nothing in the way of opportunity, excepting if a kid wanted to be a horse doctor or a country lawyer. Then, of course, there were the disappearances, all those kids going missing.'

'Including the Foss girl?' asked Charlie.

'That's right,' said Christopher Prescott.' First young David Unsworth disappeared; then Ivy Foss; then Geraldine Immanelli. Then six or seven more. Some of the parents began to get scared. Those who lived in town moved out of town. Some of them even went back to the city. Those who lived outside of town didn't allow their children into the Corners any more. So the bowling alley died from what you might diagnose as a loss of young blood.'

'Did they ever find what happened to all those kids?'

Christopher Prescott shrugged. 'They dragged the Quassapaug. They searched the hills for fifteen miles in all directions. But I reckon those kids went to New York City; or maybe to Boston, Massachusetts. They never found one of them, not even a trace.'

A silver-coloured Cadillac appeared at the far corner of the green. Abruptly, the deputy snatched at Charlie's arm. 'You listen here now, move that vehicle of yours. That's the bank president, coming back from lunch.'

'Where does he eat?' asked Charlie sarcastically.

'He sure as hell doesn't eat at Le Reposoir,' Oliver T. Burack put in. 'He said to me the other day that Mr Musette was the closest thing he'd ever met to a goat that walks on its hind legs.'

'I thought your friend was deaf,' Charlie said to Christopher Prescott. 'I also thought that neither of you had ever heard of Le Reposoir.'

'Oh, Oliver's deaf all right,' smiled Christopher Prescott.

'He knows what people are talking about, though. He has a sixth sense. What do you call it? Intuition.'

'Are you talking bullshit about me again?' Oliver T. Burack said.

'Please,' the deputy asked Charlie, as the Cadillac came dipping over the last corner of the green. But Charlie persisted. He was beginning to get the measure of these people, and he wanted to know what was going on.

'The restaurant,' he said. 'How come you wouldn't admit that you knew about the restaurant?'

Christopher Prescott stared up at him with watery eyes 'Sometimes it's better to hold your peace, better to say nothing at all than to say something malign.'

'What's so malign about Le Reposoir?'

The deputy came back two or three paces and pulled again at Charlie's arm. The bank president's car had arrived outside the bank, and the bank president was leaning forward and peering through its windshield at Charlie's car as if he were seeing a mirage.

'You want me to book you for obstructing justice?' the deputy demanded, almost panicking.

Christopher Prescott said to Charlie, 'You'd better get along, fellow. I wouldn't want to get you into trouble.'

'All right,' Charlie agreed. He didn't want to cause too much of a disturbance. M A R I A inspectors were supposed to be 'discreet and inconspicuous in their behaviour at all times'. He followed the deputy back up the grassy slope, and across the road to his automobile. The bank president was sitting with his Cadillac's engine running. His face was hidden behind a geometric reflection of sky and trees on his windshield, but all the same Charlie gave a cheerful, insolent wave.

Martin took his seat beside Charlie and slammed the Oldsmobile's door. 'You realize you're copping out again,' he said.

'Who's copping out?' Charlie protested, starting the engine. I made a deal.'

'Some deal,' said Martin scornfully. 'You could have found out where that stupid restaurant is without having to ask him.'

'Oh, really? How?'

'You could have asked me.'

'You? You don't know where it is any more than I do.'

Martin reached into the pocket of his jacket and produced a small white card. He passed it over to Charlie without a word. Charlie took it and held it up to the window, ignoring the contorted face of the deputy outside, who was still desperately waiting for him to move.

At the top of the card there was an heraldic emblem of wild boars, embossed in gold, with the copperplate caption 'Les Célèstines'. Underneath were the words 'Le Reposoir. Société de la Cuisine Exceptionelle. 6633 Quassapaug Road, Allen's Corners, CT.'

Charlie turned the card over. The reverse side carried the pencilled word 'Pain'.

'What the hell is this?' Charlie asked Martin. 'First of all those geriatrics try to pretend that they've never heard of the place. Now you give me this. Where did you get it, for Christ's sake? And why the hell didn't you show it to me before?'

The deputy tapped on the window with his knuckles. 'Sir,' he mouthed, 'will you please move?'

Charlie let down his window and held up the card. 'Is this the address? Sixty-six thirty-three Quassapaug Road?'

The deputy stared at him. After all, if Charlie had known the address all along, why had he kicked up such a fuss about it? 'Yes, sir,' he said.

Charlie said, 'Okay. At least we're making some progress.' He was about to shift his car into drive and pull away when the president of the First Litchfield Savings Bank approached him – a tall, wide-shouldered, white-haired man with a head as large as a lion. He bent down beside Charlie's open window, and said, 'Good afternoon. I hope you don't feel that I'm being autocratic here.'

31

'Don't worry about it,' Charlie replied. 'I'm just about to pull out. My friend the deputy tells me you have squatter's rights on this parking space.'

The bank president stared at Charlie level-eyed, and then smiled. 'You could call them squatter's rights, I suppose. My family have lived in this town since 1845. We own most of it, and hold mortgages on the rest. So you'll forgive me if I tend to regard this parking space as private property.'

'I'm only passing through,' Charlie told him.

The bank president's pale grey eyes focused on Martin. 'You and your boy?'

'That's right. A single parent's tour of hospitable New England.'

'Listen, I apologize,' the bank president said. 'You stay right there. I'll have Clive park my car for me. Allen's Corners is a friendly town. I certainly don't expect its law officers to hassle visitors on my behalf.'

He reached his hand into the car, and said, 'Walter Haxalt. Welcome to Allen's Corners.'

'Charlie McLean. And this is Martin McLean.'

'Happy to know you,' said Walter Haxalt. 'Please feel free to stay here as long as you want.'

'As a matter of fact,' we're on our way to Quassapaug Road.'

Walter Haxalt glanced around at the deputy, then turned back to Charlie. 'I don't know that there's anything of interest to a tourist up there. Quassapaug Road is just a road. Not much of a road for driving on, either. It's all hairpins from begining to end.'

'We want to visit Le Reposoir,' said Charlie. He held up the card that Martin had given him.

Walter Haxalt's expression went through a subtle but distinct change. It looked almost as if his face had been modelled out of pink wax, and an oven door had been opened close by, melting and shifting it. 'I suppose Clive has told you that Le Reposoir is completely private.'

Charlie reached forward and switched off the Oldsmobile's engine.

'All right,' he said hotly. 'Would somebody mind telling me what in the hell is going on?'

'I'm sorry, I don't understand,' Walter Haxalt replied. 'I didn't mean to offend you in any way.'

'I'm talking about this restaurant, Le Reposoir,' said Charlie. 'Mrs Foss back at the Iron Kettle warned me against visiting it. Those two good old boys on the bench there said they'd never heard of it, when they obviously had. And your pet deputy here did everything he could to tell me that I wouldn't be welcome. Now you.'

Walter Haxalt said nothing. Clive the deputy stroked his moustache as if it were a small furry pet.

'What I want to know is what's so darned off-putting about this place?' Charlie appealed. Walter Haxalt's refusal to reply was quickly defusing his temper, and making him feel embarrassed. 'Is the food really that bad?'

Walter Haxalt stood up straight. 'I'm sorry, Mr McLean, I don't think that Allen's Corners can really give you the kind of welcome you expect. My suggestion is that you drive right on to Bethlehem. There's a good New England-style restaurant there. They serve home-made hams and excellent boiled beef.'

Martin said, 'Dad, come on. Please.'

Charlie hesitated, biting his lip. Then he twisted the key in the ignition again, so violently that he made the starter-motor screech. He was just about to pull away from the kerb, however, when he glimpsed something moving behind the maple trees on the far side of the green. It could have been nothing more than a cloud shadow, or a wind-blown sheet of newspaper. It had vanished in an instant. But Charlie was sure that he had seen a small figure, dressed in grubby white. A figure with the body of an infant and the fully developed head of a man.

CHAPTER THREE

They drove north-westwards out of Allen's Corners past two rows of white wooden houses. They saw nobody at all, nobody walking by the roadside, no other cars. After a quarter of a mile, they were back amongst the woods again, surrounded by the rusting funeral of yet another lost summer. Although it was still early, the sun had already dropped below the treeline, and glittered at them tantalizingly, always out of reach behind the branches.

Charlie said nothing for a while, but when Martin reached forward to switch on the tape player, he took hold of his wrist and said, 'Not now. I want to talk.'

Martin folded his arms and sat back in his seat.

'I want to know where you found that card.'

Martin shrugged. 'I picked it up at that Iron Kettle place.'

'Where? I didn't see any cards there.'

'I found it on the floor.'

Charlie lowered his sun visor. 'You're not telling me the truth, Martin. I don't know why, but you'd better start explaining yourself pretty darned quick, otherwise this trip is over here and now and you go off to the Harrisons.'

Martin said, 'It's the truth, Dad. I found it.'

'We were talking about Le Reposoir and you just happened to find one of their cards? For Christ's sake, what do you take me for?'

Martin sulkily lowered his head.

'It's over, have you got that?' Charlie told him. 'Tomorrow I'm going to call the Harrisons and then I'm going to drive you right back to New York.'

34

Martin said nothing.

'Have you got that?' Charlie repeated.

'Yes, I've got it,' said Martin, in his best 'anything-to-keep-the-old-man-quiet' voice.

Charlie slowed down as they approached a steeply sloping intersection with a sign saying Washington in one direction and Bethlehem in the other. He stopped the car by the side of the road and opened up his map. 'This should be Quassapaug Road right here.'

He took a right, and cautiously steered the Oldsmobile up a tight corkscrew gradient, under overhanging oaks and American beeches. The sun danced behind the leaves. Somewhere behind the thicket fence of tree trunks, there were creamy clouds and pale blue sky; but here in the woods, Charlie began to feel strangely imprisoned and claustrophobic.

'All right, admitted, I haven't been much of a father to you,' he told Martin. 'But I never told your mother one single lie. I was never unfaithful, and I always sent money. Always.'

'Well, Saint Charlie McLean,' said Martin.

Charlie swerved the car off the side of the road and jammed his foot down on the parking brake. He tried clumsily to smack Martin's head, but Martin ducked and wrestled away, and the two of them found themselves panting and glaring at each other, hands clasped tightly, a fit fifteen-year-old fighting a tired forty-one-year-old.

'Listen,' said Charlie. 'Either we try to get along together like father and son, or else that's the finish. And I mean the finish. You're old enough to survive without me, if that's the way you want it. I don't mind.'

Martin released his father's wrists and turned his face away. Charlie knew that he was crying. Someone else had once cried like this, in the passenger seat of his car, a very long time ago, in Milwaukee. Charlie felt as if the world was an ambush of endlessly repeated agonies, and here it was again. The argument, the tears, the temporary reconciliation that both of them

35

knew would never last. He squeezed Martin's shoulder but there was no love between them. He might just as well have been squeezing an avocado to make sure that it was ripe.

'I'm sorry,' he said, although he wasn't.

He continued driving around the roller-coaster curves of Quassapaug Road. A wild turkey scrambled across the blacktop in front of them, and Charlie swerved towards it in a feigned attempt to run it down. 'You ever eaten wild turkey, barbecued with new season's squash?'

Martin said, 'We never have turkey, even at Thanksgiving. Marjorie doesn't like it.'

'Marjorie, Marjorie! Why the hell can't you call me Charlie?'

'Because you're Dad, that's why.'

They passed the entrance to Le Reposoir so unexpectedly that they overshot it by a hundred feet. Charlie caught a flash of wrought-iron gates, painted black, and a discreet black signboard. The Oldsmobile's tyres slithered on the tarmac. Then Charlie twisted around in his seat and backed up all the way to the gates, with the car's transmission whinnying.

'That's it, Le Reposoir. Société de la Cuisine Exceptionelle.'

Martin stared at the sign unenthusiastically. 'Yes, and look what else it says. No visitors except by prior arrangement. These grounds are patrolled by guard dogs.'

'We can talk to them, at least,' said Charlie. He parked the car right off the road, in the entrance-way in front of the gates, and then climbed out. There was an intercom set into the bricks of the left-hand gatepost. He pushed the button, and then turned to Martin, who was still sitting in the car, and smiled in what was the nearest he could manage to encouragement. Martin pretended that he hadn't noticed, and in the end Charlie turned away. *God*, he thought, *they're like prima-donnas, these teenage boys. You only have to raise your voice to them, and they start sulking and pouting and bursting into tears.*

He pushed the intercom button again. This time, there was a sharp crackle of interference, and then a voice demanded, '*Qui? Qu'est-ce que vous voulez?*'

Charlie cleared his throat. 'Is that Mr Musette?'

'Who is it who is wanting him?' the voice asked, in English this time, but with a strong French accent.

'My name's McLean. I was wondering if you had a table for two for dinner tonight?'

'You must have made a mistake, *monsieur*. This is a private restaurant. Reservations can only be made by advance booking.'

'Well, this is advance booking, isn't it?'

'*Je regrette, monsieur*, booking is always effected in writing, and bookings are accepted only at the discretion of the management.'

'What kind of a restaurant operates like that?' Charlie wanted to know.

'This restaurant, *monsieur*. Although I must correct you. It is a dining society, rather than a restaurant.'

'So I've been told. Is it possible to join?'

'Of course, *monsieur*, by personal recommendation.'

Charlie ran his hand through his hair. 'You people sure make life difficult.'

'Yes, *monsieur*, you could say that.'

'So somebody has to put me up for membership? Is that it?'

'Yes, *monsieur*.'

Charlie thought for a moment, and then said, 'Is everything I've heard about you true?'

'It depends what you have heard, *monsieur*.'

'I've heard that you're exceptional.'

'Yes, *monsieur*.'

Charlie had nothing more to say. The voice on the other end of the intercom refused to be drawn. Charlie took hold of the gates and shook them, just to make sure that they were locked, then he walked back to the car and climbed into it. He leaned over towards the glove box and took out a pack of Rol-Aids. The Colonial-style sauce was resisting all his stomach's determined efforts to digest it. That was the trouble with bad food, it always fought back.

'They won't take reservations unless somebody sponsors you,' said Charlie.

'What does that mean?' Martin asked.

'It means they're just about the most exclusive restaurant in the whole continental United States. It may not be easy getting into the Four Seasons, but at least they want your business. This place ... who knows? How can you run a restaurant right in the middle of nowhere at all, with no advertising, no promotion, not even a signpost to tell you how to get there, and booking by personal recommendation only, in writing, in advance?'

'Maybe they're really good,' said Martin.

'What the hell do you mean, "maybe they're really good"!' Charlie retorted. 'The Montpellier is really good! L'Ermitage is really good! There are twenty restaurants in America which are really good! But, darn it, even the best restaurants have to advertise. Even the best restaurants have to let people in!'

Martin said, 'What are you getting so upset about? If they won't let you in, they won't let you in. Forget them. There isn't any point in including a restaurant in M A R I A if nobody can get to eat there.'

Charlie took one last look at the implacably closed gates of Le Reposoir, then started up the car and turned back towards Allen's Corners. 'If it's that good, if it's really that good, then I want to eat there, that's all. Even my stomach can only take so much good old country cooking. I could use a revelation. Quite apart from the fact that I'd be fascinated to find out what it is about Le Reposoir that upsets everybody at Allen's Corners so much.'

They drove back through the woods. Another thunderhead had swollen up in front of the sun, and the landscape had suddenly grown chilly and cheerless.

Martin said, 'Where are we going to stay tonight? Are we going to drive on to Hartford?'

Charlie shook his head. 'Tonight we're going to stay at Mrs Kemp's boarding house, 313 Naugatuck. I'm not leaving Allen's Corners until I can fix a table for two at Le Reposoir.'

'Dad – we're going to be days behind schedule. What are the people at MARIA going to say?'

'I can fudge the schedule, don't worry about that. I want to eat at that Goddamned private exclusive dining club and that's all there is to it. There must be somebody around here who belongs. That bank president, Haxalt, don't tell me that he's not a member. All I need is one person who's prepared to sponsor my reservation.'

Martin remained silent as they drove back into Allen's Corners. The light was turning to pale purple, and the streetlights had already been switched on. Christopher Prescott and Oliver T. Burack had left the green; but there were lights on the upper floor of the First Litchfield Savings Bank, and a few people were walking past the lower end of the green, on their way back from the supermarket. Birds sang in the maples, that sad intermittent song of early evening.

'I don't know,' said Charlie. 'This reminds me of something. *Déjà vu*, I guess.'

He drove around the green until they reached Naugatuck Avenue. This was one of the oldest streets in Allen's Corners, running directly west to east away from the green. At one time, before the main road had been laid at the lower end of the green, Naugatuck Avenue had been a main highway through to Hartford. English redcoats had marched drumming along here, while the people of Allen's Corners had watched them from their upstairs windows.

Mrs Kemp's boarding house stood at the corner of Naugatuck and Beech; a gaunt saltbox house with flaking weatherboard and windows blinded by grubby lace curtains. It was fronted by a paling fence, half of which was sagging sideways, and a small brick yard in which a single maple grew. Charlie drew up outside it, and eased himself out of the car. 'Are you coming?' he asked Martin.

'Are you sure it's open?' Martin frowned. 'It looks derelict to me.'

'It could use a lick of paint,' Charlie admitted. He opened the wooden gate and walked up the path. 'The last time I was here, the place was immaculate. I gave it a Gold Feather for comfort. Maybe Mrs Kemp has closed up shop.'

Martin followed Charlie cautiously up to the front door. There were two stained-glass panels in it, one of them badly cracked as if the door had been slammed during a violent argument. In the centre of the door hung a weathered bronze knocker cast in the shape of a snarling animal – something between a wolf and a demon. Charlie nodded towards the knocker and said, 'That's new. Welcoming, isn't it?'

Martin looked up at the loose tiles that had slipped down the porch in a straggling avalanche. 'This can't be open. And I wouldn't want to stay here, even if it is.'

'There's no place else, not in Allen's Corners, anyway.'

Charlie picked up the knocker. It was extraordinarily stiff and heavy, and he didn't much like the way the wolf-demon was snarling into the palm of his hand. He couldn't think why, but the knocker seemed familiar. He could vaguely remember reading about a wolf-like knocker in a book, but he couldn't remember what book, or when.

He banged it, and heard it echo flatly inside the house. He waited, chafing his hands, smiling at Martin from time to time. A stiff breeze had arisen with the setting of the sun, and Charlie felt unnaturally cold.

'Nobody here,' said Martin, standing with his hands in his pockets, 'Looks like we'll have to go on to Hartford after all.'

They were just about to turn away when they heard somebody coughing inside the house. Charlie banged the knocker again, and after a while footsteps came along the hallway.

Through the stained-glass windows a small pale figure appeared, standing close behind the door. After a moment's pause, the figure reached up and drew back two bolts, and opened up the door on the safety-chain. A woman's face appeared, white and unhealthy-looking, with dark smudges of exhaustion around her eyes. Her hair was untidily clipped with plastic barettes, and she was wearing a soiled blue quilted housecoat. From inside the house there came the vinegary odour of stale air and cooking.

'Mrs Kemp?' asked Charlie.

'What do you want?' the woman demanded.

'It says in the guidebook that this is a boarding house.'

Mrs Kemp stared at him. 'Used to be,' she told him.

'I see. You've given it up.'

'It gave itself up. I tried to keep open but nobody wanted to come here any more.'

'Is there anyplace else to stay the night?'

'There's the Wayside Motel outside of Bristol, on the Pequabuck road.'

'Nowhere in Allen's Corners?'

Mrs Kemp shook her head.

'Well,' said Charlie, 'I guess that fixes it. I might as well introduce myself. My name's Charles McLean, I'm a restaurant inspector for M A R I A. I guess I can take your boarding house out of the book.'

Mrs Kemp's eyes narrowed. 'I remember you. You stayed here three or four years ago.'

'That's right, you've got some memory.'

'I remember you specially because you asked for the Brown Betty. That was always my late husband's favourite, and that was why I kept it on the menu. Maybe two people asked for Brown Betty in seven years, and you were one of them. Well, well. If I'd known you were an inspector, I would have done you better, I'm sure.'

Charlie smiled. 'That's why I never tell anybody. I want to

41

get the ordinary treatment everybody else gets.' He stepped back a little and looked up at the house. 'Pity you've closed up, I liked it here. You ran a good cosy place.'

'Do you want to come inside for some coffee and cake?' asked Mrs Kemp. 'I mean, if you're really pushed for a place to stay, I could air a couple of beds for you. I wouldn't charge, it'd be company.'

Charlie glanced at Martin. It was quite plain from the expression on his face that he didn't relish the idea of spending the night here at all; and the truth was that Charlie didn't exactly fancy it either. But his curiosity about Le Reposoir had been aroused too strongly for him to leave Allen's Corners until he found out more about it. And maybe it would do Martin good to find out who was boss.

'We'd appreciate that,' he said.

Mrs Kemp slid back the safety-chain. 'You'll have to pardon the way I'm dressed. I wasn't expecting company.'

They followed her into the hallway. It was chilly and stale in there, and although the tables had once been highly polished, they were now covered by a fine film of dust. Old hand-coloured engravings of colonial Connecticut hung on the cream-painted walls.

Mrs Kemp brought them coffee in the best parlour, a gloomy room crowded with massive sawed-oak furniture of the Teddy Roosevelt era, when bellies and walrus moustaches had been in fashion. She had changed into a plain grey day-dress with a white lace collar, and sprayed herself with floral perfume. The coffee was hot and fresh; the Jubilees stale and chewy. Martin sat in a dark spoonback chair silent and bored.

'I guess you could say that one bad season begets another,' said Mrs Kemp. She kept dry-washing her hands, over and over, and then fiddling with her wedding ring, as if it needed adjusting for size. 'Business was good until late last year; I used to have all of my regulars, Mr King from American Paints, Mr Goldberg the Matzoh Man – well, that's what I always used to call him, the Matzoh Man. And there was good steady family trade through the summer and fall, right past Thanksgiving.'

'What happened?' asked Charlie, setting down his coffee cup. 'They didn't build any new detours.'

Mrs Kemp looked down at her lap for a moment. When she spoke her voice sounded muffled and different. 'I don't suppose you remember, it was three or four years since you came here last, but there was a girl who used to help me in the kitchen.'

'I think I remember,' said Charlie.

'Her name was Caroline. She was my niece. My brother and his wife were killed in an auto accident in Ohio when she was seven. I'd been looking after her ever since. When my husband passed over she was all I had left.'

Mrs Kemp paused, and then she said, 'You can imagine, we were very close.'

Charlie said nothing, but waited for Mrs Kemp to continue.

'Last November 18, Caroline disappeared,' said Mrs Kemp. 'She went to New Milford to see a friend of hers, but she never arrived. Of course if was hours before I found out that she was missing. I called the police, and the police searched every place they could think of, but no trace of her was ever found. Nothing. It was just as if she had never existed, except for her clothes of course, and her personal belongings. The police said that it happens all the time, young people walking out on their parents or their guardians. They usually end up in California or some place like that, working as dancers or waitresses or – well, you know what kind of a world we live in these days, Mr McLean.'

'Call me Charlie,' said Charlie.

Mrs Kemp nodded, although Charlie wasn't altogether sure if she had heard him or not. She said distractedly, 'I suppose what happened to the boarding house after that was my fault, really. Every salesman who came here, I used to give him a printed sheet with Caroline's picture on it, and ask him to keep a look out for her wherever he went. I suppose I used to carry on about her too much for most people's comfort. The regulars stopped calling by, and then the casual trade fell off. I wanted to keep the business going, I did my best, but I wanted to find Caroline even more, and that kind of affected everything I did.'

'It seems to me that a lot of young people have gone missing from Allen's Corners,' Charlie remarked.

'The sheriff said that it happens a lot in backwater places like this. The kids get bored, that's what he said, but they know that their parents won't let them go, not voluntarily. So they run away, and that's the last that anybody ever sees of them. Not just children of Caroline's age, neither. Some of them are not much more than nine or ten years old. Well, you've seen their pictures on the Knudsen's milk cartons. I used to look at them and wonder how any parent could possibly let their child disappear like that. But it happened to me, too, and all I can tell you about it is that it hurts a good deal, and that you can never get over it.'

They talked for a while about Caroline. Mrs Kemp opened up her rolltop bureau and produced a handful of the printed pictures that she had distributed to her guests. Charlie and Martin dutifully examined them. They showed a pretty fair-haired girl with a snub nose and a wide smile. She could have been a cheerleader or a roller-skating waitress at a drive-in soda fountain. Underneath the picture, a short appeal said, 'MISSING, Caroline Heyward, 17 years old. Last seen Allen's Corners, CT, 11/18 last year. 5' 4½' tall, slim build. Wearing brown-and-white wool coat, brown wool hat. $500 reward for information.'

'Pretty girl,' said Charlie, offering the flysheet back.

'Keep it,' Mrs Kemp told him. 'You never know, the way you restaurant inspectors travel around, one day you might just find her.'

Charlie folded up the flysheet and tucked it into his wallet. 'Would it be too much to ask you to put us up for the night?'

'Of course not,' said Mrs Kemp. 'I'd be glad to. I can give you the big room right at the back, that's the room I always used to give to honeymooners. Well – they weren't all honeymooners. "Romantic couples", that's what I used to call them.'

'I tried to get to eat at that French place,' said Charlie.

Mrs Kemp lifted her head. In the lamplight, the dark circles under her eyes looked like bruises. 'What French place?' she inquired sharply. So sharply that she must have known exactly what he was talking about.

'Le Reposoir, up on Quassapaug,' said Charlie. 'They seem to have quite a reputation around here.'

'They're not the kind of people you'd choose to have as neighbours, if you had a choice,' Mrs Kemp replied.

'Oh?' said Charlie.

'They keep themselves to themselves, that's all. They live here, but you couldn't say they're part of the local community. They seem to do whatever they like, though. They built a whole new wing on that house of theirs, up on Quassapaug, and I never heard a whisper about zoning laws. I talked to Mr Haxalt about it – Mr Haxalt's the chairman of our community association –'

'Yes,' Charlie told her. 'I had the pleasure of meeting Mr Haxalt this afternoon. I parked my car in his sacred parking place.'

'Well, then, you'll know what he's like,' said Mrs Kemp. 'He's an expert at giving folks the brush-off. And that's what he did when I tried to talk to him about Le Reposoir. "Don't you worry, Mrs Kemp, those people are here to bring more trade into Allen's Corners." But did they bring in more trade? They certainly didn't. I can tell you – lots of people come and go, up on Quassapaug Road – lots of wealthy people, too, in limousines – but none of them stop at Allen's Corners, and even if they did, you can't imagine that they'd be the kind of people to buy cream or corn-dollies or home-cured bacon. Let me tell you, Mr McLean –'

'Charlie, please.'

'– well, let me tell you, Charlie, that place is a curse on Allen's Corners. It takes everything and gives nothing. There's people around here who won't go near it for money in the bank. And don't ask me why, because I don't know. But it has the feeling about it. Allen's Corners has never been the same since that place opened, and until it closes down it never will. This used to be a happy town, but you look at it now. Sad and lost and anxious, that's what it is. Maybe Le Reposoir isn't to blame. Who can say? It could be the way that life is going everywhere, the recession and all. But I believe that place is a curse on Allen's Corners, and that the sun won't shine here until it's gone.'

Martin said, 'It's only a restaurant.'

Charlie turned around in his chair and looked at him. Martin repeated, 'It's only a restaurant, that's all.'

'Oh, yes,' said Charlie. 'And since when have you been the expert?'

Martin pouted, but didn't answer. Mrs Kemp glanced from Charlie to Martin and smiled, as if she were trying to make peace between them.

Charlie said, with a frankness that was unprecedented for him, 'Martin and I haven't seen too much of each other – well, not for years. His mother and I were divorced. You have to make allowances on both sides I guess.'

Martin looked at his father with an expression that was a mixture of embarrassment and respect. *I wish you hadn't said that, Dad, and anyway, who was it who never came home?* But he held his tongue. There are some feelings which are mutually understood between father and son, but which are better left unspoken.

'You must know Mr Musette,' Charlie said to Mrs Kemp.

'I've seen him, yes, but no more than twice.'

'And?'

'He's charming. Very foreign, of course. He likes to be called *Monsieur* Musette. A lot of the ladies around here think he's *tray charmong*. Only from a distance, of course. He keeps himself to himself. And then of course there's Mrs Musette – Madame Musette – although I've never seen her.'

Charlie waved away the offer of another Jubilee. 'Tell me something,' he asked Mrs Kemp. 'What is it about Le Reposoir that can affect a whole community?'

Mrs Kemp said, 'What can I tell you? Maybe it's nothing at all. Your son's quite right. It's only a restaurant. Why should anybody be frightened of a restaurant?'

The atmosphere in the parlour was very strange. Charlie felt as if he had been asked to complete a sentence to which there was no logical conclusion – such as, 'I like the shifting of the tides because . . .' He couldn't rid himself of the suspicion that Martin had been talking to somebody back in the parking lot of the Iron Kettle, no matter how much Martin denied it, and he also felt that his conversation with this unknown somebody had been connected with Le Reposoir. After all, where had Martin found that visiting card from Le Reposoir? And why had he denied seeing that pale-faced child in the garden?

Mrs Kemp showed them up to their room. It was stuffy, high-ceilinged, with maps of damp disfiguring the plaster above their heads. The walls had been papered with huge green flowers that were supposed to be roses but looked more like efflorescing mould. In one corner loomed a gigantic wardrobe, with blistered veneer and mottled mirrors. The bed was enormous, an aircraft carrier of a bed, built of green-painted iron with brass decorations in the shape of seashells. Martin tried to bounce on it, and complained, 'Jesus, this mattress is as hard as a rock.'

'Hard beds are good for your posture,' said Charlie. 'And don't profane.'

47

'Do we really have to stay here?'

'Maybe you can answer that,' Charlie replied, taking off his coat and hanging it up inside the cavernous depths of the wardrobe. There were five wire hangers in there, and a dried up clove and orange pomander that looked like a shrunken head.

'I don't know what you mean,' said Martin. He went over to the opposite side of the room and stuck his head inside the carved wooden fireplace. 'Halloo – halloo – any skeletons up there?'

Charlie watched him in the wardrobe mirror. 'You still haven't told me the truth about what happened at the Iron Kettle.' He tried not to sound too petulant.

'Dad,' said Martin. '*Nothing* happened.'

Martin turned away from the fireplace, and as he did so Charlie saw in the mirror that his face had peculiarly altered. It seemed to have stretched out, so that it was broad and distorted, and his eyes had the same blind look as the eyes of a dead fox he had once found lying by the road. Charlie jerked in shock, and turned around, but Martin appeared quite normal when he confronted him face-to-face. He looked back at the mirror. It must have been the mottling, and the dirt. He remembered how old he had looked himself, in the mens room mirror at the Iron Kettle.

'Do you want to go down to the car and get the bag?' Charlie asked Martin.

Martin said, 'Okay,' but on the way out of the door he hesitated. 'Do you *really* not believe me?' he asked.

Charlie said, 'I believe you.'

'You're not just saying that to stop us from having an argument?'

Charlie unfastened his cufflinks. 'Since when did boys talk to their fathers like that?'

'You said we were supposed to be friends.'

'Sure,' said Charlie, and felt a wave of guilt. He went over

48

to Martin, and laid his hand on his shoulder, and said, 'I've been travelling around on my own for too darn long, that's my trouble. Too much talking to myself in hotel mirrors. I guess it's made me a little nutty.'

'You can believe me,' Martin told him; although Charlie detected a strange hoarseness in his voice that didn't sound like Martin at all. 'You can believe me.' And it wasn't so much of an affirmation as a command. It wasn't really, *You can believe me*. It was more like, *You must believe me*.

He sat on the side of the bed and waited for Martin to return with the suitcase. He thought about a quiet foggy afternoon in Milwaukee, parking his car and walking up the concrete pathway to a small suburban duplex. Six or seven children had been playing ball at the end of the street, and their cries had sounded just like the cries of seagulls. He remembered pushing the bell, and then the front door opening. And there she was, her brown hair tangled, staring at him in complete surprise. '*You came*,' she had whispered. 'I never thought you would.'

Martin returned with their zip-up overnight bag. He laid it down on the bed, and said to Charlie, 'Are you okay? You look kind of logie.'

'I'm okay. Tired, I guess, like you.'

'I'm not tired.'

'Well, then, let's freshen ourselves up, and get on down to Billy's Beer & Bite.'

Martin looked around. 'There's no television here. What are we going to do all evening?'

'You know how to play cards, don't you? Let's see how much of your allowance I can win back.'

Martin said, 'Mega-thrill. If you really want it back that bad, I'll give it to you.' Charlie couldn't even smile. He wondered what he was going to say to the boy next – let alone how he was going to find something to talk about for ten more days. His tiredness was mostly caused by the strain of keeping

49

up a long-running conversation. He wanted with all his heart to develop an easy father-and-son relationship with Martin, but right now he would have given a month's salary to be alone.

They ate in a corner booth at Billy's. A jukebox played 'Joleen' and 'Blanket on the Ground' and 'DIVORCE' and what with the rough wooden decor and the loud laughter and the red fluorescent lights they could have been in Amarillo, TX, instead of Allen's Corners, CT. Martin seemed to have rediscovered his appetite, and wolfed down a king-sized cheeseburger with mammoth fries. Charlie restricted himself to a New York steak sandwich with onion rings. Afterwards, they walked around the windy deserted green for a while, with their hands in their pockets, not talking, and then went back to Mrs Kemp's to play cards.

Before he went to bed, Charlie found Walter Haxalt's telephone number in the local directory, and called him up from the phone in Mrs Kemp's parlour. The phone rang and rang but there was no reply.

Mrs Kemp was watching him through the partly open doorway. 'Do you know anybody who goes to Le Reposoir to eat?' Charlie asked her, as he waited for somebody at Walter Haxalt's number to pick up.

Mrs Kemp shook her head. 'You'd be better off keeping clear,' she advised him. 'I don't know what's so bad about that place, but if I were you I wouldn't want to find out.'

CHAPTER FOUR

It was well past two o'clock in the morning when Charlie awoke. For a moment he had that terrible vertiginous feeling of not knowing where he was, or what city he was in. But after years of waking up unexpectedly in unfamiliar rooms, he had developed a trick of closing his eyes again and logically analysing where he must be.

Usually, his sense of smell and his sense of touch were enough for him to be able to re-orient himself. Howard Johnson's all smelled like Howard Johnson's and TraveLodge beds all felt the same. This was somewhere private. This was somewhere old. *This*, he thought, opening his eyes again, *is Mrs Kemp's boarding house in Allen's Corners, CT*.

The bedroom was intensely dark. Charlie felt as if black felt pads were being pressed against his eyes. Either the moon had not yet risen, or it was obscured by thunderclouds. The room was also very quiet, except for the intermittent blowing of the wind down the chimney, and the soft ticking of Charlie's watch on the bedside table.

Charlie eased himself up into a sitting position. Gradually, he found that he could make out the slightly lighter squares of the windowpanes, and the gleam of reflected street light on one of the brass knobs at the end of the bed, but that was about all. He strained his ears to hear Martin breathing next to him, but from the other side of the bed there was no sound at all.

'*Martin?*' he whispered. There was no reply, but he didn't call again. He didn't want to wake Martin up for no reason at all. He reached out his hand to make sure that his son was well

51

covered by the thin patchwork quilt, and it was then that he realized that Martin was silent because Martin wasn't there.

He fumbled around in the darkness of the top-heavy bedside lamp, almost knocking it over. He switched it on and it lit up the room as starkly as a publicity photograph for a 1950s detective movie. Martin's side of the quilt was neatly folded back, as if he had left the bed quietly and deliberately, and Martin's bathrobe had disappeared from the back of the chair. Charlie said, '*Shit*,' and swung himself out of bed. His own bathrobe was lying on the floor. He tugged it on, raked his fingers through his hair, and opened the bedroom door. Outside, the house was silent. Engraved portraits stared at him incuriously from the brown-wallpapered landing. There was a smell of dust and sticky polish and faded lavender; the sort of smell that dreams would have, if dreams were to die.

'*Martin?*' His voice didn't even echo. The darkness muffled it like a blanket. 'Martin – are you there?'

Charlie cursed everything he could think of, and in particular he cursed himself for having thought that it would be a good idea to bring Martin along with him on his tour of New England. Goddamnit, the boy was nothing but confusion and trouble. Charlie called, '*Martin?*' again, not too loudly in case he disturbed Mrs Kemp, but a whole minute passed and there was still no answer, and so he ventured out on to the landing and peered down into the stairwell.

He made his way downstairs, treading as softly as he could. The house all around him seemed to hold its breath. He could feel the string backing of the worn-out stair carpet under his bare feet. When he reached the hallway, he paused, and listened, but there was nothing to be heard. He was tempted to go back to bed again. After all – where could Martin have possibly gone? Out for a walk, that was all, because he'd eaten too much, and couldn't sleep. Out for a walk, because he wanted to think about his parents, and his fractured upbringing, and how much he distrusted his father. Charlie could hardly blame him.

But then he heard a door softly juddering, as if it hadn't been closed properly and the wind was shaking the latch. He paused, and listened, and the juddering continued. For the first time in a very long time, for no earthly reason that he could think of, he was alarmed – so alarmed that he groped around the shadows of the hallway searching for something that he could use as a weapon. An umbrella, maybe; or a doorstop. All he could find, however, was a very lightweight walking stick. He swung it in his hand so that it whistled through the air. Then he made his way along the hallway to the kitchen door.

'Martin? Are you there?' His voice sounded unfamiliar, and he turned quickly around to make sure that there was nobody standing close behind him. For one second he felt the thrill of real fright. A shadow was standing close to the front door, its huddled shape limned by the blood-red light that gleamed through the stained-glass panes. But it was only an overcoat that Mrs Kemp had left hanging on the hallstand. Coats and blankets and dressing gowns, thought Charlie. Innocent garments by day, threatening hunchbacks by night. He couldn't count the number of times he had woken up in some strange hotel bedroom to stare fascinated and frightened at his own coat, crouched over the back of a chair.

He turned the handle of the kitchen door. It grated open, grit dragging against floor tiles. The kitchen smelled of burned fat and sour vegetables. There was an old-fashioned cooking range, and a white-topped table. In the corner stood a coffee grinder and an old rotary knife-sharpening machine, like Puritan instruments of torture. Blue-patterned plates were stacked on the hatch. Charlie stayed in the half-open doorway for a moment, holding his breath, but when he heard nothing he turned away, lowering his walking stick. *Martin is fifteen years old right? He isn't a child any more. And just because you happened to miss his childhood, that doesn't give you any kind of right to treat him like a kid. If he wants to take a hike in the middle of the night, that's up to him.*

Charlie wasn't convinced by any of his reasoning, but he retreated slowly along the hallway, tapping the tip of his walking stick gently against the walls, like a man who had recently lost his sight. He was just about to return it to the cast-iron umbrella stand, however, when he thought he heard somebody whispering. He froze, his head lifted, trying to catch the faint sibilant sounds of conversation.

Maybe it's the wind, thought Charlie. But he knew that it wasn't. No wind ever argued, the way that this voice was arguing. No wind ever begged. Somebody was right outside the kitchen door, in Mrs Kemp's back yard; and that somebody was talking, quickly and urgently, pleading, the way that a lover pleads, or a man asks for money – one well-rehearsed argument after another.

Raising the walking stick, he retraced his steps along the corridor. The clouds had suddenly moved away from the moon, and the kitchen was illuminated in cold, luminous blue, knives and grinders and mincers gleaming, like some spectral abattoir. There were two panes of Flemish glass in the kitchen door, and through their watery distortion Charlie could make out the shadows of two people, earnestly engaged in conversation. A thin, boyish figure, which must have been Martin, and another smaller figure, which must have been wearing a hat or a hood, because it was strangely rhomboidal in shape, like an old-fashioned coal scuttle.

Charlie tiptoed close to the door and listened. The whispering voice went on and on, as endless and insistent as water running over a weir; yet peculiarly seductive, too, in a way that Charlie found it very hard to understand. It wasn't erotic, yet it gave him a thrill that was almost entirely physical. It was a voice that knew the desires of the flesh, and pandered to them. It was frightening, but at the same time irresistibly alluring.

You shall find happiness; you shall find joy. You shall find friends and lovers. You shall find the most complete fulfilment

*known to man, and the name of that fulfilment is written where
nobody can find it but you.*

Charlie waited for almost a minute. Then he reached out
and clasped the cold brass doorknob. He wasn't sure if he
could be seen from the yard or not. It depended on the angle
of the moonlight. He took a breath, and then tugged the door
open – at the very instant a huge grey cloud rolled over the
moon and obscured it completely.

He saw something. He wasn't quite sure what it was. A
face, or a mirror reflecting his own face. A white transfixed
face, with eyes that glittered at him. A blue-white tongue
lolling between blue-white lips. Then a white blur of fabric, a
hood tugged hurriedly over, and a small crooked figure crab-
hopping away; then darkness. No sound, no cry, no noise at
all. Only the breeze blowing boisterously over the yard, and
the irritating banging of an upstairs shutter. *Squeeak-shudder-
clop!*

Martin was standing in his dressing gown, his thin-wristed
hands down by his sides, his face concealed by shadow. Charlie
looked back down the yard, in the direction the hunched-up
creature had fled, and said quietly, 'You want to tell me what's
going on here?'

Martin said nothing. Charlie took two or three steps into
the yard, but it was too dark for him to see very much. The
moon remained hidden behind the clouds. The washing line
sang a low vibrant tenor. At last Charlie turned back to Martin
and said, 'Who was that? Are you going to tell me who that
was?'

'It wasn't anybody.'

'Don't bullshit me!' Charlie yelled at him. 'I saw him and I
heard him! A little guy – no more than four feet tall!'

'I was here on my own,' said Martin. His voice was flat and
expressionless.

'Martin, don't try to kid me, I saw him for myself. It was
the same boy who was looking into the window at the Iron

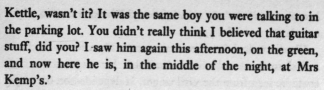

Kettle, wasn't it? It was the same boy you were talking to in the parking lot. You didn't really think I believed that guitar stuff, did you? I saw him again this afternoon, on the green, and now here he is, in the middle of the night, at Mrs Kemp's.'

Martin lowered his head. The very faintest touch of moonlight illuminated the parting in his hair.

'Martin,' said Charlie. 'I'm your father. You *have* to tell me. It's my duty to look after you, whether I like it or not. Whether *you* like it or not.'

'You don't have to look after me,' said Martin.

'I'm your father.'

Martin raised his head. Charlie couldn't make out his face at all. 'You're a man who happened to fuck my mother, that's all,' Martin snapped at him. Then he wrenched open the kitchen door and ran inside. He left the door ajar, and Charlie standing in the dark back yard, feeling more isolated than ever before. Even in the Criterion Hotel in Omaha, Nebraska, in the middle of winter, he hadn't felt as isolated as this. He began to feel that real life was a little more than he could manage.

He turned and looked up at the moon, masking itself behind the clouds. He felt there was something he ought to do, some magic ritual he ought to perform to ward off malevolence until morning, but he couldn't think of anything else to do except to cross his two index fingers in the sign of the crucifix and hold them up to the sky. 'God, protect me,' he said, although he wasn't sure what good that would do, or even if he meant it.

He went back inside, locking the kitchen door behind him. He returned the walking stick to the umbrella stand. The house was silent. He climbed the stairs feeling very tired. One of the reasons he had been able to survive his job for so long was because he had always gone to bed early, with two large glasses of water to drink if he happened to wake up, and he had always made sure that he stayed in bed for a full eight hours.

Martin had returned to bed, and was lying with his back turned to the door. Charlie climbed between the sheets, and lay there for a long time listening to Martin breathe. He knew he wasn't asleep, but he was waiting for him to say something.

After a while, he felt Martin gently shaking. He realized with intense pain and discomfort that he was crying.

'Martin?' He laid his hand on the boy's shoulder. 'Martin, for Christ's sake, if you can tell anybody what this is all about, you can tell me.'

'I can't tell anybody,' Martin sobbed.

Charlie was silent for a very long time. The worst part of it was not having the experience to be able to think of the right thing to say. Marjorie would know; Marjorie was unfailingly good with children. Marjorie had been unfailingly good with him, too, but not good enough to know what he really wanted out of life.

Martin wiped his eyes on the corner of the pillow slip and then lay there silently, not sleeping, but perfectly still.

Charlie said. 'I don't know what any of this means.'

'It doesn't mean anything.'

'But I don't see why you have to lie to me, Martin. I don't see why you have to pretend that there was nobody there when there very obviously was.'

'There was nobody there, Dad.'

For a split second, Charlie felt angry enough to smack Martin's head. But he made a deliberate effort to turn away, and stare fiercely at the bedside table, and let his sudden burst of temper dissipate into the darkness like a tipped-over basketful of small black snakes.

'We're going to have to talk this over tomorrow,' he said.

'Okay,' Martin said, as if he didn't have any intention of discussing it again.

There was another long pause, and then Charlie said, 'Was he a dwarf, or what?'

Martin didn't reply. His breathing was regular and even. Charlie leaned over him and saw that he was asleep – or, at least, that he was pretending to be asleep. He lay back on his pillow and looked up at the ceiling and wondered what the hell he was going to do now. There were no handbooks for the estranged fathers of awkward and secretive teenage sons. There was no advisory service which could tell you what to do if your offspring started making mysterious trysts with white-hodded midgets in the middle of the night. It would have been funny if it hadn't been so distressing; and if Martin hadn't plainly been so upset.

The night went by as slowly as the great black wheel of a juggernaut. Every time Charlie checked his watch, it seemed as if the hands had hardly moved since the last time he had looked. He couldn't sleep. He couldn't even remember what it was he normally did to get himself to sleep. He thought about Marjorie, he thought about Martin. He thought about Milwaukee and the pain that he had suffered there. He half dozed for a while, and dreamed that he was eating dinner in a strange high-ceilinged restaurant with a long white napkin tucked into his collar. The waiters were all hooded, like monks, and they came and went in silence, carrying plates and wheeling chafing dishes. There was no menu, you had to eat whatever the monk-waiters set in front of you. The other diners were smooth-faced and expressionless. There was no food in front of them, and yet they waited at their tables with consummate patience, as if their meals would be worth waiting for even if they took several hours to be served. The men were dressed in evening wear – white ties and stiff collars and tail coats. The women wore extravagant wide-brimmed hats with wax fruit and flowers and ostrich plumes. They also wore glittering diamond necklaces and earrings that sparkled like Christmas trees, but apart from that most of them were nude. Looking around the restaurant Charlie saw bare breasts everywhere, some with nipples that had been rouged, others which had been pierced and decorated with golden rings. He saw a red-headed woman with a feathery hat talking to the maitre d', smiling archly as she did so. Her thighs were wide apart on her satin dining chair, and a small hairless dog, was lapping with its tongue at her bushy, russet vulva. He turned. A monk-waiter had brought his meal, concealed beneath a shiny dish cover. The monk-waiter's face was as black as the inside of a clothes closet. 'Your dinner, sir,' he whispered seductively, and raised the dish cover with a flourish.

Charlie looked down at his plate and screamed.

The plate was brimming with thin, greyish soup, in which Martin's face was floating, staring up at him in silent desperation.

He opened his eyes. He was twisting the quilt in both hands, and he was smothered in sweat. He also had a taut, painful erection.

He thought for a moment that he had screamed out loud, but the night seemed so silent and undisturbed, and Martin was still breathing steadily and peacefully, and he realized then that he must have screamed only in his dream. He checked his watch. A minute and a half had passed since the last time he had looked.

He thought for a while about Martin's face staring up at him out of the plate. Then he thought about the naked women in his dream restaurant. There was no question about it, his daytime problems were catching up with him while he slept. The problems of food, fatherhood, and sexual frustration. He lay there feeling very middle aged and inadequate and tired, for hour after hour. He didn't know when he fell asleep; but shortly afterwards Martin opened his eyes and turned and looked at him, and then slid quietly out of bed and went to the window.

Martin stood by the window for almost a half-hour, while the sky gradually grew paler over the treeline towards Black Rock and Thomaston. In the yard below him, the small hooded

59

figure stood, equally silent, its cloak ruffled by the thin, early-morning wind, its eyes fixed steadily on Martin, waiting with a patience that had been shared by the diners in Charlie's dream.

CHAPTER FIVE

Walter Haxalt was smooth, patronizing, and impatient. He sat behind his leather-topped reproduction desk, his hands steepled, gently tapping his fingertips together as if he were counting the valuable seconds that Charlie was wasting, second by second, dollar by dollar.

The morning sun struck through the window of his office and illuminated, as if it were a sign from God, a gold presentation clock that stood on the bookshelf just behind him. There was a motto engraved on the clock, 'Time Driveth Onward Fast'. Strangely, Charlie could remember the verse from which that motto had been taken. It ended, 'all things are taken from us, and become/Portions and parcels of the dreadful Past'.

Walter Haxalt said, 'I can't help you, I'm afraid. My only contract with M. Musette is purely professional. He lives here and so he banks here, and that's as far as it goes.'

Charlie glanced towards the window. Martin was waiting for him outside, in the car. 'I wasn't asking for anything more than an introduction.'

'Well, I wish I could help,' said Walter Haxalt, making it quite plain by his disinterested tone of voice that he didn't wish anything of the kind. 'But I can't abuse a customer's personal relationship with the bank for any reason at all, even if that reason happened to be meaningful and advantageous.'

'Have you ever eaten at Le Reposoir?' asked Charlie.

Walter Haxalt kept on tapping his fingers, but didn't answer directly. 'I guess you'll be leaving us now,' he said. 'Travelling ever onward, in your search for culinary perfection.'

Charlie stared at him. Walter Haxalt became suddenly self-conscious about the way that Charlie was looking at him, and shifted in his studded leather chair. 'How did you find out what I do for a living?' Charlie asked.

'You told me,' said Walter Haxalt, uncomfortably.

'I never tell anybody.'

'Well, to tell you the truth, I had Clive check it out for me. He ran your licence through the computer.'

'Clive? That deputy who told me to move my car yesterday?'

Walter Haxalt nodded. 'This is a small town, it's vulnerable. We always have to take certain elementary precautions when strangers come around.'

'Did you take any elementary precautions when M. Musette set up shop?'

Walter Haxalt said, 'I can't discuss M. Musette with you, Mr McLean. If you want to know anything at all about M. Musette, I suggest you ask him yourself.'

Charlie eased himself out of his chair. 'All right,' he said. 'What can I say but thanks for nothing?'

Walter Haxalt focused on Charlie narrowly. 'We do try to be friendly, here in Allen's Corners. I want you to know that.'

'I think I've been able to make my own assessment, thank you,' Charlie replied.

'In that case, I hope you won't judge us too harshly.'

Charlie opened the office door. 'It's not my job to judge *you*, Mr Haxalt. Only your hotel and refreshment facilities. Right now, I'd say that Allen's Corners deserves the bent spoon award for service, the broken spring award for comfort, and the golden barbed wire award for hospitality.'

Walter Haxalt stood up. 'I hope you're not going to try to publish anything like that. If you do, I'm going to have to speak to your employers.'

Charlie said, 'My employers take a very dim view of bribes and threats, Mr Haxalt. Come to mention it, so do I.'

He walked out of the bank into the sharp fall sunshine.

Martin was lounging back in the front seat of the car reading *Power Man and Iron Fist*. Charlie climbed in beside him and started the engine. 'Glad to see you're reading something improving.'

Martin said, 'Did he fix it up for you?'

'No. It seems to me that Allen's Corners is low on helpfulness, apart from being a poor place to get a good steak. I'm going to try the direct approach.'

'What does that mean?'

Charlie steered away from the green and out toward the Quassapaug Road. 'That means a direct frontal assault on Le Reposoir, with all guns blazing.'

They drove for four or five minutes in silence. Then Martin said, 'Dad?'

'Uh-huh?'

'We don't have to do this, Dad. I mean, it isn't totally necessary, is it?'

Charlie glanced at him. 'What do you mean, it isn't totally necessary?'

'I mean, if it's private, nobody who reads M A R I A is going to be able to eat there anyway.'

Charlie nodded. 'You're right. You're absolutely right. But the argument against that is that *I* want to eat there.'

Martin said nothing more to dissuade him; but all the same Charlie began to feel that he was distinctly worried about their driving up to Le Reposoir and forcing their way into La Société Gastronomique without being invited. But the more reluctant Martin showed himself to be, the more determined Charlie became. Perhaps he was punishing Martin in a way, for lying to him last night. Perhaps he was just being stubborn and bloody-minded, like he always was.

They drew up outside the entrance to Le Reposoir and, to Charlie's surprise, the wrought iron gates were open. He hesitated for a moment, craning his head around to see if there were any security guards or parking valets around, but there was nobody there at all, neither to greet them nor to prevent them from driving inside. Charlie looked down the wide, shingled driveway, which curved in between two dense banks of maculata bushes. The house itself was out of sight, although Charlie thought he could glimpse rows of black chimneys through the bright yellow maculata leaves.

'Well,' he remarked. 'Not so reclusive after all.'

'We're not going in?' asked Martin.

'The gates are open, why not?'

'But it's private!'

'Since when have you been concerned about private?'

'Dad, we can't just drive straight in. You heard what that deputy said about trespassers.'

'We're not trespassers. We're potential customers.'

Charlie didn't really feel quite so confident about venturing into the grounds of Le Reposoir, but he was determined to show Martin that he was in complete control of everything he did, and that he was scared of nobody and nothing. If he backed out now, Martin would regard him for the rest of their vacation together as a flake and a wimp; and if that happened their relationship would be ruined for ever. He didn't mind if Martin thought he was a flake; but he had to be a *brave* flake; like Murdoch in *The A-Team*.

Charlie eased his foot off the brake and the Oldsmobile rolled forward between the gates and down the curving drive. The car windows were open, so that they could hear the heavy crunching of shingle beneath the tyres. The morning which had started sunny was now dull. The eastern sky behind them was as black as Bibles. They could hear ovenbirds and prothonotary warblers singing in the woods, but apart from that the air was curiously still, as if their intrusion into the grounds of Le Reposoir had been noticed by nature at large, and a general breath was being held until they were discovered.

They turned a bend in the driveway and Martin unexpectedly covered his face with his hands.

'What's the matter?' Charlie asked him. 'Martin? What's wrong?'

Martin turned his head away, and pushed at Charlie with his left hand, like a linebacker warding off a tackle. At the same time, the house in which Le Reposoir had been established rose up in front of them, sudden and dark and almost wickedly elaborate. It was built in the high Gothic style, the kind of house that Edward Gorey drew for *The Dwindling Party* or *The West Wing*, with spires and turrets and twisted columns, and a veil of long-dead wisteria over the porch. Charlie slowed the car as he passed between two old and stooping cedar trees, and drew up at last on a circular shingled turning space, with weeds growing up through the stones. He pushed on the parking brake and killed the engine, and then almost immediately he stepped out of the car and stood leaning on the open door, his eyes narrowed against the light wind, looking around like a man who has discovered an uncharted valley, or a garden which has been secretly neglected for fifty years.

'Now this is what I *call* a restaurant,' he said, although he was quite aware that Martin was making a determined effort not to listen to him. He stepped away from the car and walked a few yards out across the shingle, the soles of his brogues crunching in the fall silence. 'What a locale! It merits one star for locale alone. Did you ever see a locale like this?'

The house was enormous, yet for all its blackness and all of its size, it seemed to float suspended in the dark air, like a mirage, or a grotesquely over-decorated man of war. There was a central entrance, reached by wide stone steps, and flanked on either side by eight gothic pillars, each of them different in design with spirals and diamonds and hand-carved ropes. Between the pillars stood an arched mahogany door, with brass handles and engraved glass panels, all highly polished. On either side of the central entrance, the house stretched over 300 feet to the east and 300 feet to the west, with tier upon tier of glittering windows. A weather vane in the shape of a medieval dragon creaked and whirred to itself on the highest spire.

There was an odd smell on the wind, like burning fennel.

'You know something?' said Charlie, leaning back into the open automobile, 'I never even knew this place existed. Can you believe it? I'm supposed to be one of the top restaurant inspectors in the continental United States. I got an award, did I ever tell you that? So how did I get to miss a place like this?'

'Dad,' Martin begged him. His voice was odd and edgy. 'I don't want to stay here. I want to go on to Hartford.'

Charlie had heard the tone in Martin's voice but he feigned a brash, tourist enthusiasm.

'You don't want to see what goes on here? Look at this place? It's probably unique. Some of the really old colonial houses were built on designs the Pilgrims brought over from England. I'll bet you anything the place is haunted by Nathan Hale's great-grandmother.'

Martin begged, 'Dad, please.'

'What's it to you?' Charlie demanded. He felt a little cruel now; but he felt that Martin had been equally uncaring about him, refusing to talk about the small figure he had met in Mrs Kemp's back yard, and refusing to tell the truth about the visiting card he claimed he had found.

'Dad, I just don't like it here. I want to go.'

'Come on, Martin, there's nothing to get worked up about. It's a restaurant. And let me tell you something about people who run restaurants — even the worst of them have some sensitivity. You have to have some sensitivity, whether you're running an à la carte or a greasy spoon. You're dealing with people's stomachs, and there isn't anything more sensitive than that.'

At that moment, quite unexpectedly, a deep, cultured voice said, 'You're right, my friend. The alimentary canal is the river of human life.'

66

Charlie involuntarily jerked in surprise. He turned around to find a tall man standing only five or six feet away from him. The surprise was that the man could have approached so close without making any noise at all, especially over a shingled driveway. And the man wasn't just tall; he was unnervingly tall, at least six feet three, and he had the predatory appearance of a well-groomed raven. His black hair was slashed straight back from his hairline. His forehead was narrow and white. Beneath two thinly curved eyebrows his eyes looked like two shining silver ball bearings, and were equally expressionless. His nose was thin and hooked, although there was an angular flare to his nostrils. He sported a thin, black, clipped moustache. By his clothes, Charlie could tell that he was a man of taste, and a European. He wore a dark blue pinstripe suit in the Armani style, although obviously more expensive than Armani, a pure silk paisley-patterned necktie, and gleaming handmade shoes.

His most arresting characteristic, however, was not what he wore, but his bearing. Like the elaborate house behind him, he seemed almost to float a fraction of an inch above the ground. It was something that Charlie found impossible to analyse, and it was highly disturbing, as if the man were not quite real.

The man held out his hand and Charlie shook it. The fingers were very cool and limp, like wilted celery.

'That's your son?' he asked, nodding towards Martin.

'Martin,' said Charlie. 'And you must be M. Musette.'

'Well, well,' the man smiled. 'My reputation has reached even the ears of M A R I A.'

Charlie looked at him suspiciously. 'You know who I am?'

'I am in the gastronomic business, Mr McLean. It is my business to know who you are. Similarly, I know the inspectors from *Michelin* and *Relais & Chateaux*. Forewarned, you see, is forearmed.'

'Haxalt told you,' said Charlie.

67

'You are being unfair on Mr Haxalt,' M. Musette replied. 'Mr Haxalt would never betray anybody's trust. Even yours.'

Charlie put his hands on his hips and surveyed the black Gothic building. 'The main reason I came was to see whether your restaurant was worth putting into the guide.'

'Le Reposoir?' asked M. Musette, with obvious amusement. 'I fear not, Mr McLean. This is hardly a roadside hamburger stand. It is a private dining association, open only to subscribing members. It would be very unfair to your readers if you were to suggest that they could obtain a casual meal here as they wandered through Connecticut looking at the autumn leaves. Or, selling their patent cleansers.' That last remark was an undisguised dig at M A R I A's strong associations with travelling salesmen.

'Men who sell patent cleansers provide an honest service,' Charlie replied, more sharply than he had meant to. 'Just like most restaurateurs.'

'I'm afraid that does not include me,' said M. Musette. 'I am hardly what you could call a restaurateur. I am more of a social arbiter than a chef.'

At that moment, the mahogany doors opened, their windows reflecting the dull silvery sky, and a young woman appeared, pale-faced, in a black ankle-length cape. M. Musette turned, and gave her a wave which meant that he wouldn't be long, and that he would be with her in just a moment.

'Madame Musette?' asked Charlie.

'It is probably time for you to leave,' said M. Musette, affably but adamantly.

'There isn't any chance of eating here, then?' asked Charlie.

'I regret not. We are a very exclusive society, and I am afraid that the presence of a restaurant inspector would not be regarded by our membership with any particular warmth.'

The young woman who had been standing on the steps came closer, stepping on to the shingle driveway and watching Charlie with solemnity. She was almost alarmingly beautiful, with a fine oval face coloured by only the slightest tinge of blusher, soulful blue eyes, and very short gamine-style hair, a blonde bleached even blonder. She remained completely covered by her cape, and Charlie had the unsettling fantasy that, underneath it, she was naked, except for black silk stockings and stiletto shoes.

'Aren't you going to introduce us?' asked Charlie.

M. Musette looked at Charlie in a way which Charlie had never been looked at before. His eyes betrayed not malice but a total lack of interest in Charlie as a human being; as if he were nothing more than one of twenty thousand blurred faces in a baseball stadium crowd. 'You should not come here again without a prior appointment,' he said, and this time his tone was completely dismissive. 'Although it might appear that you can drive into the grounds unobserved, we have very attentive security services.'

Charlie looked around the grounds of Le Reposoir one last time, and then shrugged. 'All right,' he said. 'Have it your way. I must tell you, though, I could have done with a top quality French meal. This leg of the trip is always a desert, gastronomically speaking.'

'I am sure you will be able to find somewhere to satisfy your appetite,' said M. Musette. There was lightning flickering on the horizon, and a few heavy drops of rain fell on to the shingle and the roof of Charlie's car. He waited for one moment more, and then climbed back into the driver's seat, stretching over to fasten his seatbelt. M. Musette came up and closed the door for him.

'I'm sorry for intruding,' said Charlie, although he didn't sound sorry and he didn't particularly mean to.

M. Musette said nothing, but took two or three theatrical steps back. Charlie slowly swung the car around in a wide circle, and headed back the way he had come. As he did so, he glanced in his rear-view mirror at the young woman who might have been Mme Musette. Now that the rain was falling more heavily, she reached with one hand out of the darkness of her cloak to tug a large hood over her head.

The car was moving; the rear-view mirror was joggling; the morning was dark with thunder. All the same, Charlie was convinced that what he had seen was not an illusion, and he stared at Martin in amazement and perplexity, and slowed the car down for a moment. Then he turned around in his seat to stare at Mme Musette even harder.

Martin said, 'Dad? What are you looking at?'

'That Mme Musette, the woman in the cloak.'

'What about her?'

Charlie turned back again, and steered the Oldsmobile at low speed all the way up the curving driveway between the bushes. Martin repeated, 'Dad?' but Charlie wasn't sure whether he wanted to tell what he had seen or not, particularly since Le Reposoir had seemed to upset him so much. 'It's nothing,' he remarked, although he couldn't help looking back in the rear-view mirror just one more time, before Mme Musette disappeared into the house like a shrinking shadow. What had alarmed him so much had been that hand – that hand which had emerged from the blackness of her cloak.

That hand on which there had been only one finger, a forefinger, to hook down the fabric of her hood and keep away the rain.

CHAPTER SIX

By six that evening they were lying with their feet up on their beds at the Windsor Hotel in West Hartford, watching what looked like a Venusian version of *Diffr'nt Strokes* because even the black people had green faces.

'If you had to judge racial harmony in America from nothing but what you saw on hotel televisions, you'd think we were the most integrated nation on earth,' said Charlie, sipping Miller Lite out of the can. 'The red people get on with the purple people, the orange people get on with the blue people . . .'

Martin didn't even smile. He had heard the same remark so many times that he scarcely heard it. It was just Dad being Dad.

They watched the end of the programme, and then Charlie swung his legs off the bed, and pushed his hand through his hair, and said, 'How about something to eat? The restaurant here isn't too bad.'

'Do I have a choice?' asked Martin. A last chink of sunlight had penetrated beneath the blinds, and gilded his eyelashes.

'Sure you have a choice. This may be work for me, but for you it's a two-week vacation.'

'Then do you mind if I stay here and watch television? I couldn't eat another meal, not right now.'

Charlie shrugged. 'It's all right by me if it's all right by you. Are you sure you won't come along just to keep me company? You don't have to eat anything.'

'Dad,' said Martin, 'we haven't been getting along too well, have we?'

Charlie straightened his narrow blue woven necktie. 'It's early days yet. We hardly even know each other. I'm the father who was never at home, and you're the kid I never came ' ome to. We'll get along. Give it some time.'

Martin said, 'Why?'

'Why what? Why give it some time?'

Martin shook his head. 'No – why didn't you ever come home?'

'There were reasons. Well – there was one big reason and then there were lots of little reasons. It isn't too easy to explain, not at one sitting, anyway. Before you go back to your mother, though, I'll tell you exactly what happened, and exactly what it was all about. People sometimes lead lives you wouldn't even guess at, do you know what I mean? That savings bank manager, that Haxalt, for all we know he goes home at night and dresses up like Joan Crawford. And as for that Musette dude . . . well, he's some kind of weird character if ever I saw one.'

'What are you trying to tell me?' Martin demanded.

Charlie looked down at Martin's young, sunlit face. God, how lucky he was! Only fifteen, and all his chances still ahead of him. Old enough to be argumentative and arrogant, but not yet old enough to understand that argument and arrogance never got anybody anywhere. He said, gently, 'What I'm trying to tell you is that I had another life, apart from the life you already know about; and that one life was always fighting against the other life.'

'And the other life won?'

Charlie said, 'You don't resent me, do you? You don't still feel bad about me?'

'I don't know,' said Martin. 'That's what I came along on this trip to find out.'

Charlie was silent. It hadn't occurred to him that Martin was vetting him just as much as he was vetting Martin. He rubbed his forehead, and turned around so that Martin could see only his back, and then he said, 'What happens if you decide that I'm not the kind of father you want?'

'Then I'll go back to Mom and that will be the end of it.'

Charlie picked up his coat off the back of the chair. The hotel room was wallpapered in a brown bamboo pattern, and there were two prints on the wall of Boston & Maine railroad locomotives of the 1880s. He had stayed in rooms like this so often before that he had almost no sense of place, only of time. 'You're sure you don't want to eat?' he asked Martin. 'You could call room service and have them send you a hamburger or a sandwich or something. They do good ribs here, as far as I recall.'

Martin said, 'It's okay. I'm not hungry.'

'Well, I'm not either,' Charlie told him. 'At least, not for the kind of food they serve up here. But, that's the way it goes. Some people work so that they can eat. I eat so that I can work.'

He gave himself a last unnecessary check in the mirror, and then he went to the door. 'You can join me any time you want to, if you change your mind. I'll be glad of your company.'

'All right, sir.'

'Will you call me Charlie, for Christ's sake? My name is Charlie.'

'Yessir,' said Martin. Then – almost without pausing – 'Have you given up on Le Reposoir? I mean, are you content to go to your grave never having eaten there even just once?'

Charlie frowned. 'What? There are millions of restaurants I'm never going to get to eat in – tens of millions. I've never eaten at La Colombe d'Or in Houston. Why should I be worried about Le Reposoir?'

'Because it's special,' said Martin; and then, with devastatingly cold observation, 'And most of all, because they won't let you in.'

Charlie stood by the door, his hand on the chain, with the feeling in his heart that if he didn't quickly take steps to make

73

sure that Martin became his friend, he was going to finish up by being his very worst enemy. A little unevenly, he said, 'You know what Groucho Marx told that club that refused his membership application?'

'Yes, sir. "I do not wish to belong to the kind of club that accepts people like me as members."' Martin paused, and then he said, 'You told me.'

'Okay.' Charlie nodded. 'I'll catch you later.'

He walked along the red-carpeted corridor until he reached the fire door that would take him out of the Windsor's annexe, across its so-called ornamental gardens (four scrappy-looking flowerbeds and a tangle of bushes that should have been cleared away years ago), and into its Olde Hartforde Suite and the main building. He laid his hand on the fire door ready to push it open when he saw something through the smudgy wired-glass window. A white flicker in the unkempt garden. A small scurrying shape that could have been a dog or a wind-blown sheet of newspaper or an optical illusion created by the evening sunlight on the glass.

But he stood where he was, feeling cold and uncertain, because he suspected that it wasn't any of those things. He suspected that it was the dwarfish figure that he had seen in Mrs Kemp's garden last night, talking to Martin through the distorting kitchen window. And the figure was here, in West Hartford, in the same hotel, which meant only one thing that Charlie could think of. Real or imaginary, it was following them. Worse than following them, it was tracking them down.

For a moment, Charlie hesitated. Maybe he should go back and warn Martin that the dwarf was around. On the other hand, if Martin had been talking to it, maybe Martin *knew* that it was around. Maybe Martin had even gone so far as to tell it where they were going. Maybe it was nothing more than his own imagination, creating a demon or a devil which could take the blame for his own failure to make friends with the son he was supposed to have taken care of, and hadn't. He felt

74

confused and uncertain, as if he had been drinking. But at last he pressed his hand against the fire door, opened it, and stepped out.

There was no sign of any creature. Only the dry hunchbacked bushes and the untidy flowerbeds. Only the dark clouds rolling overhead as if they were hurrying on their way to some distant battle.

The food at the Windsor Hotel was relentlessly dull. In an attempt to console himself for not having been able to eat at Le Reposoir, Charlie ordered the Grande Royale menu, which started off with steamers, followed by charcoal-broiled bluefish, carpetbag steak, and peach pie. In the hands of a competent chef, any one of these traditional American dishes could have been a masterpiece. In the Windsor Hotel, they were tough, dry, slimy, and canned, in that order. Charlie sat alone at an underlit table, facing a badly painted frieze of Windsor Castle in England, chewing his way through this unappetizing menu while a four-piece band played 'Tie A Yellow Ribbon' and the six businessmen sitting next to him chain-smoked cigars throughout their meal.

When he had finished, Charlie was approached by the maitre d', who stood beside his table with his hands folded over his groin. 'You didn't care for the dinner, sir?' the maitre d' asked, with unconcealed annoyance.

'The dinner was – acceptable,' said Charlie.

'Perhaps a small glass of brandy on the house?' the maitre d' suggested. His tone of voice was almost ferocious.

'That won't be necessary.'

The maitre d' bent forward. He had huge open pores in his nose and his breath smelled of Binaca. 'It isn't my fault this place is so bad.'

Charlie stared at him without expression.

The maitre d' went on, 'I do my best, I used to work at the Hyatt Pilgrim in Boston. But what can I do with a place like this? They won't invest any money on it.'

Charlie said, 'What does this have to do with me?'

'Come on, Mr Restaurant Inspector. You can't kid me. I know a restaurant inspector when I see one.'

'You think so?'

'I was expecting you. I knew what you were, the moment you walked into the room. All restaurant inspectors have that same look. Most men who are forced to eat alone will keep their eyes on their food, or on a book. But you – your eyes are never still. You are looking at the cutlery, at the glasses, at the table linen. You are timing the waiters, you are testing the food. After you have finished your coffee you will go to the men's room to make sure it is clean. You may even try to dodge into the ladies'. I know your kind.'

Charlie slowly shook his head. 'You must be making some kind of mistake here, friend. I'm a salesman, dealing in hydraulic valves. You want to come out and look at what I'm carrying in the back of my car?'

'You can't kid me,' the maitre d' hissed at him, triumphant now. 'I was told. I was expecting you. You don't fool me for one moment.'

'Bring me the bill,' said Charlie.

'No, sir, no charge,' retorted the maitre d'.

'I want the bill,' Charlie insisted. 'In fact, if you don't bring me the bill right now I'm going to call for the manager.'

'No charge,' the maitre d' challenged him.

Charlie paused for a moment, and then stood up. 'All right,' he said. 'No charge. I'm not going to get myself involved in an argument about it.' He raised his eyes. 'All the same, I'd like to know who told you to expect me.'

The maitre d' shrugged, and flapped at Charlie's coat with a napkin to brush off the crumbs of peach-pie. 'The restaurant business is a brotherhood, sir.'

'Like the Cosa Nostra, you mean?' said Charlie sarcastically.

'No, sir. More like monks, or friars.'

Charlie looked away. The maitre d' was obviously drunk. Either drunk, or so disaffected with his job that he didn't care what he said, or to whom he said it. Monks or friars, Christ Almighty. The only possible religious ingredient in the restaurant business was the prayers of forgiveness they said when they wrote 'Fresh' and 'Home Cooked' on the menus.

The maitre d' said, 'How about that glass of brandy? Come on, friend. It's on the house.'

A little wearily, Charlie nodded. The maitre d' clapped his hands and the wine waiter came over, a stocky, unsmiling type with a tight maroon coat and a tight maroon face to match. 'Give the gentleman a glass of the Courvoisier, Arnold. You'd like it in the lounge, sir? In the lounge, Arnold. Next to the fireplace.'

Charlie sat in a high leather-upholstered library chair nursing his brandy while two large logs smouldered in the olde colonial fireplace like the last remains of a derelict building. Across the lounge, sitting in profile to him, was a thirtyish woman with ash blonde hair and a tight sapphire-blue dress and a little more jewellery than was tasteful, especially for a country mausoleum like the Windsor. Charlie surmised that she was a woman of relatively easy virtue, if not an out-and-out hooker. She made a big play of lighting a cigarette and blowing the smoke across the lounge. Charlie sipped his brandy and thought that she had a pretty impressive chest, even if her hips were on the wide side.

After about ten minutes, the woman stood up and came across to the fireplace. She stared down at the logs, the elbow of her smoking arm cupped in the hand of her other arm, her chin slightly lifted.

'I always think a real fire is so romantic, don't you?' she asked Charlie, without looking at him.

'I don't know about this one,' said Charlie. 'It looks half dead to me.'

'Ashes to ashes,' the woman remarked. Then, 'Are you travelling alone?'

'Not entirely. I have my son with me.'

'Do you usually travel alone?' For the first time she turned to catch him with a blue-eyed stare. She was good-looking, in a Hollywood kind of a way, short-nosed, broad-cheekboned, almost baby-faced; except of course that the crisscross lines were beginning to show in the corners of her eyes. A diamond brooch in the shape of a star reflected the light from one of the ceiling lamps. Charlie thought: *Genuine. This woman has been places, and done things, and men have showed their approval in the time-honoured way*.

Charlie said, 'I'm not looking for company, if that's what you mean.'

'You look unhappy,' the woman told him. 'I can't bear to see anybody looking unhappy.'

'I'm a little tired is all.'

'Would you mind if I sat down beside you and talked to you?'

Charlie nodded toward the chair next to his. 'It's a free country. I can't guarantee that you'll get any answers.'

She sat down and crossed her legs. Her blue shiny dress rode higher on her thighs than it ought to have done. She smelled of Obsession by Calvin Klein. She blew smoke over him, but he wasn't sure that he particularly minded. The top three buttons of her dress were unfastened and Charlie could see a very deep cleavage indeed. White breasts with a single beckoning mole between them.

'I saw you arguing with Bits,' she said.

'You mean the maitre d'? Is that his name?'

'It makes him sound like a gangster, doesn't it? But his real name's Arthur. They call him Bits because when he was younger he was always saying, 'For two bits I'll quit this job,' or 'For two bits I'll make that damned sauce myself.' Not that he was ever a violent man – oh no. Just a little temperamental. He says he was descended from the Borgias.'

'That wouldn't surprise me,' said Charlie. He pointed towards the woman's empty glass. 'How about a nightcap? Was that frozen daiquiris you were drinking?'

She smiled. 'You know what they say about ladies who have a taste for frozen daiquiris?'

'I can't say that I do. I hope it's polite.'

'Polite?' the woman laughed.

Charlie ignored her mockery and held out his hand. 'I'm Charlie McLean.'

'Velma Farloe.' the woman replied.

'Nice to know you, Velma. Have you been here long?'

'Here in this bar, or here in West Hartford?'

Charlie said, 'I never did feel at home in New England – Connecticut in particular. I always feel like I'm being looked at as some kind of outsider.'

'Where do you feel at home?' asked Velma.

'Illinois, Indiana. I guess I'm a small-town mid-Westerner at heart. Mind you, I was born in Elizabeth, New Jersey. My parents moved to Kokomo when I was ten, and then to Merrillsville.'

He paused, and then he said, 'I don't intend to sit here and tell you the story of my life.'

Velma dropped her eyelids in the warm, coaxing way in which some women would have dropped a perfumed scarf. 'I don't mind if you do.'

'I'm a salesman, that's all. That's the beginning and the end of it.'

'Bits said you were one of those restaurant inspectors.'

'Bits confides in you, huh?'

'Come on, Charlie,' said Velma. 'You know who I am. I'm the friendly lady who sits in the corner of every restaurant lounge from here to eternity.'

The stocky wine-waiter brought them two fresh drinks. When Charlie offered to pay, he said, 'On the house,' in a gruff falsetto that was as adamant as it was startling.

79

'Bits is trying to butter you up, that's all,' Velma told Charlie. 'He thinks if he gives you two or three glasses of brandy you're going to recommend the Windsor and get him a pay hike.'

'Some hope of that,' said Charlie. 'This is one of the worst restaurants between Mount Fissell and Wequetequock.'

'Well,' purred Velma. 'You sure know your geography.'

She shifted herself closer. She touched Charlie's left temple with her fingertips. He could breathe her perfume, and also that other indescribable odour known as Woman On Heat. He sipped at his brandy feeling as prissy as a boy scout. He needed a woman desperately, but for some reason he always held himself back, as if it were the right and proper thing to do. Because of Marjorie? No, he couldn't believe that. Because of everything that had happened in Milwaukee? No, he couldn't believe that either. It was far more deeply rooted. It was a glimpse of his mother fastening her stockings. It was his father's face intruding on his unconscious like a big pale blimp, roaring, 'Women should be respected, Charlie. 'Women are *holy*.'

Velma said, 'You're one of those quiet ones, aren't you?'

'I told you. I'm tired.'

'How tired is tired?'

Charlie raised his eyes and looked at her. She was mocking him, in a way; but she was also encouraging him, supporting him, in the way that only women like her knew how. They could take in travellers from the unforgiving night, men who were tired and disappointed and lonesome and very afraid of failure, and give them all the comfort they needed. One night of sex, one night of burying all of their anxieties in darkness and flesh and the pungent smell of intercourse, and they were ready to face the world again, ready to report back to J.J. on how many miles of UPVC piping they had sold, ready to drum up new business. They were as much a part of American business as Lee Iacocca or Aaron Spelling.

Charlie leaned back in the leather chair and looked around the lounge feeling drunk and detached. 'Who told you to talk to me? Was it the maitre d'? Bits? Or did you decide to proposition me off your own bat?'

'I'm not propositioning you,' smiled Velma.

'You wouldn't be smiling if you weren't.'

'Well, maybe I wouldn't.'

At that moment Charlie knew for certain that he was going to sleep with her. It was her honesty which decided him, as much as anything else. She was handsome and straightforward and big-breasted and that was all that he needed, for tonight at least. He would think about tomorrow tomorrow.

'You can't come back to my room,' he said. His voice didn't even sound like his own. 'My son is there.' He checked his watch. 'Sleeping by now. He isn't used to all of this travelling around.'

'Its okay,' said Velma, taking hold of his hand. 'I have a room. Come on.'

They left the lounge together. At the doorway, Charlie turned around and saw Bits smiling at him through the wine racks which separated the restaurant from the lounge. He turned away without acknowledging that he had seen him. Velma reached back and grabbed his hand and led him through the lobby to the main building. It was well after eleven o'clock now, and the lobby was brightly lit, red-carpeted, smelling of stale cigarettes, and completely deserted.

They kissed as they went up in the elevator. Her tongue snaked into his mouth. Her hand reached directly down between his legs and squeezed him. He wasn't sure whether he ought to feel aroused or frightened. They didn't say anything coherent. The slightest bit of logic would have broken the spell completely, like the fragment of mirror in *The Snow Queen*.

Velma's room was at the far end of a long, airless corridor. She unlocked it with the dexterity of experience. She went in first, leaving Charlie in the corridor to make up his own mind whether he wanted to follow her or not. He hesitated, and then went inside, closing the door by pressing his back against it.

It was only then that she switched on the bedside lamps. The room was almost identical to Charlie's own room in the hotel annexe, except that the prints were wild flowers instead of locomotives. Fool's parsley, and fragrant bedstraw. Velma, her back to Charlie, unbuttoned her dress. He made no move to help her. She dropped the dress on the bed and then turned around to face him. There was a strange, bright look of elation and defiance in her eyes. She was wearing nothing more than a black translucent bra, through which her nipples showed as smoky pink shadows, and a pair of patterned black pantihose, against which her pubic hair was flattened like the geographical map of a river delta.

Charlie approached her, gradually loosening his necktie. He held her, and kissed her forehead. It was cool, slightly damp with perspiration, and tasted of perfume. 'I hope you don't think I make a habit of picking up women in hotel lounges,' he said, his voice hoarse.

'I wouldn't mind if you did,' Velma replied. 'Practise makes perfect.'

She reached behind her one-handed and unfastened her bra, drawing it off her breasts and letting it fall. Her breasts were big and soft and heavy, with nipples that crinkled tight. she unbuttoned his shirt, tugging it out of his pants, and then she grasped her breasts in both hands and pressed her nipples against his bare chest, kissing him with mounting hunger. Her teeth sought out his lips and his tongue, and bit at them so sharply that he could taste the metallic flavour of blood in his mouth. 'I'm going to eat you,' she whispered.

They climbed on to the bed, struggling out of the last of their clothes. Charlie could hear himself panting. He took hold of Velma and rolled her over. Her breasts moved with slow-motion fluidity. Her white thighs parted. He saw dark hair and glistening pink. Then he had pushed himself into her, and the bedsprings began to jounce, and all he could see was Velma's hair and part of the pillow and a torn off piece of wallpaper that looked like the head of a dog. Details, blurs, gasps, and then a snuffling, snorting release.

He rolled off her, trying to catch his breath. Immediately, however, she was on top of him and straddled his stomach, so that he could feel her wetness pressed against him. 'I want more of you,' she demanded, and when Charlie squinted up at her, with one hand raised to keep the light out of his eyes, he could see that she wasn't smiling.

'No good huh?' he said. 'I told you I don't make a habit of it. Next time, I'll try to take my time.'

'I want you now,' she said, and her eyes glittered.

'Come on now,' Charlie protested. 'I'm only human.'

But Velma slid down him, and crouched like a cunning animal between his legs, and held his slippery softened penis in her hand. She stuck out her tongue, and it was very long and pointed, and she teased him by licking at the small sensitive opening. All the time she kept her hair drawn back from her forehead with her other hand, and her eyes fixed on him. Taunting him, provoking him, seeing how much she could shock him. She was irritating him with her caresses rather than arousing him. 'Can you guess how much I want you?' she said. Charlie was almost frightened to answer. 'How much do you think I want you?'

Charlie said nothing as she sucked his softened member completely into her mouth. She sucked too hard, and he said, '*Ah*!' and put his hand on her shoulder to push her away. But she opened her mouth even wider and tried to cram his testicles in as well. Her whole mouth was cram full and still she looked up at him with those taunting, glittering eyes.

'Velma –'

She bit him gently, then a little harder.

83

'Velma, I have to tell you that hurts.'

She didn't release him. Instead, she bent her head a little lower, and used her fingers to put his second testicle completely into her mouth. Her cheeks were swollen as if she had been gorging herself with too much food.

'Velma, come on, careful now, that really hurts when you –'

She bit him again, sharper and harder this time, and this time she drew blood. A thin dribble of it ran out of the side of her mouth. Charlie felt a peculiar empty feeling in his stomach and suddenly realized that it was panic. Here he was, lying in bed with a woman he had never met before, and she was holding everything that made him a man between her teeth. With one hard bite, she could turn him into an eunuch. She could even kill him.

'Velma, you have to listen to me now . . . let me go, will you, please?'

Velma snarled and dribbled and shook her head from side to side, worrying his sexual organs as if she were a young lioness who was refusing to surrender her prey. In spite of his fear, however – or perhaps because of it – Charlie began to feel his penis hardening again. It uncurled itself against the arch of Velma's palate and gradually forced her to let his testicles plop out from between her lips, one by one, two wet plums, although she managed to keep almost his entire erection inside her mouth.

She forced her head forward the very last half-inch. His swollen glans must have actually been inside her throat. Still she kept her eyes fixed on him, challenging, warning. Any other woman would have gagged or choked. Velma kept him there, on the brink between extreme erotic excitement and total terror, and it seemed to Charlie that whole minutes went past.

At last she lifted her head, allowing the shaft to slide out from between her lips inch by inch. 'Did I frighten you?' she asked him. Now she was smiling.

Charlie rolled over and got up off the bed.

'I frightened you,' she said.

'I'm just going to the bathroom, that's all,' Charlie felt as if the floor were tilting, and wished to God he hadn't accepted that cognac. He very rarely got drunk. He didn't like losing control of himself. Apart from that, the brandy fumes seemed to be rising up from his stomach like gasoline vapour, and he knew that it would take only one more drink to make him very sick indeed.

Velma stood in the doorway watching him as he urinated. 'Do you know something? I could have bitten it right off.' She stepped forward as he was finishing and held him in one hand. 'You knew that, didn't you? And you were frightened.'

'I do my best not to live too dangerously,' Charlie told her.

'You still don't understand, do you?' Her face so close to his that he could see the orange flecks in her eyes. 'I *wanted* to bite it off. I wanted to chew it and eat it and swallow it.'

Charlie stared at her. She had an expression on her face that he could only describe to himself as triumph, with a little mockery thrown in for seasoning. She released him, and he flushed the toilet and walked back through to the bedroom. 'I think I'd better get back to Martin,' he said, and reached for his shirt.

Velma came up behind him and touched the nape of his neck with her long fingernails. It gave him a shiver that was partly arousal and partly apprehension. *Maybe this is what I've always been missing*, he thought. *Maybe my life has always lacked a little danger.*

'Stay,' said Velma. 'I promise I won't frighten you again.'

'I don't know,' Charlie demurred.

'Your son will be okay. He's a big boy now, isn't he?'

'Fifteen.'

'Well, then,' purred Velma, turning him around and kissing his nose. 'He's almost big enough for me.'

Charlie opened his fingers and his shirt dropped on to the floor.

CHAPTER SEVEN

He woke up and there was bright fall sunshine criss-crossing the ceiling like the reflection on a fishing pond. He rubbed a crust of sleep from his eye and then turned over. Velma was lying with her back to him, still breathing deeply. The room reeked of sex and Obsession. Charlie reached over and gently untangled Velma's hair.

Beside the bed, the electric clock read 7:07. Martin had been very tired last night; he was probably still asleep. If Charlie dressed and went back to their room, Martin may not even realize that he had been away all night.

Charlie wasn't guilty about having gone to bed with Velma. He was divorced, he could go to bed with anybody he wanted. But he did feel that it might upset Martin, seeing how close Martin was to his mother. He pulled at a curl in Velma's hair and Velma opened her eyes and looked at him sideways and smiled.

'It's morning,' he told her. 'I have to go.'

'No breakfast special?'

'I think I'm just about plumb wore out,' Charlie said in an Uncle Tom accent.

'That's hard to believe,' said Velma, and turned around to admire him with eyes that were still glassy from dreams.

For the first time, Charlie noticed a deep sickle-shaped scar, just where her right breast met her chest. The scar was pale pink, and it had obviously healed well, but it looked as if something had actually taken a good sized piece out of her muscle. He didn't like to be over-inquisitive. When you met people on the road, you had to accept that they tell you as much or as little about themselves as they wanted; truth or lies; and that you had to take them for what they were. But he touched Velma's scar very lightly with his fingertips, and he asked her the question with his eyes.

'Self-inflicted,' smiled Velma.

'What does that mean?' Charlie asked.

'What do you think?'

Charlie shrugged. His guess was that Velma had stayed with a violent boyfriend just one night too many, and that he had cut her or burned her or whatever it was that violent boyfriends did these days.

'I think it's none of my Goddamned business,' he said.

'It could be,' said Velma. 'You know all about the Célèstines, don't you?'

Charlie stared at her. 'The Célèstines? You're the second person who's mentioned the Célèstines to me in a couple of days. I never heard of them before. Didn't they come from New Orleans or something?'

'Originally they came from New Orleans, yes; but now they're all over.'

'I still don't have any idea of what they are, or *who* they are,' Charlie admitted.

Velma said nothing for a moment. Then she climbed out of bed, and approached the dressing table, inspecting her naked body in the mirror. She laid one hand over the scar on her chest, and closed her eyes. 'You feel hostile towards them.'

'I don't know anything about them. How can I possibly feel hostile towards them?'

Velma opened her eyes and looked at him in the mirror. 'Do you always feel hostile towards things that you don't understand?'

Charlie swung back the covers. 'I'd better get back to my son. If I get back now, he'll still be asleep.'

'You mean he won't realize that his father has been away all night?'

'Something like that.' Charlie reached for his crumpled pants.

'Does it make you feel guilty, spending the night with a woman you picked up in a bar?'

'Not at all.'

Velma came over to him, still naked, and buttoned up his pants for him. Then she kissed him on the lips, and laughed.

'I know that some Célèstines run a restaurant at Allen's Corners,' said Charlie.

'That's right,' said Velma. 'So you do know something.'

'I don't get this,' Charlie told her irritably. 'It's like some kind of guessing game. Do you know what the Célèstines are?'

'Of course. They're like a society, a club. Every now and then they get together and they eat a special dinner.'

'Le Reposoir, they meet there,' said Charlie, and Velma nodded.

Charlie said, 'The way we got together last night, was that accidental, or was it arranged? I mean, was it arranged by somebody else? Were we *supposed* to get together?'

'You could say that,' she said. He knew now that she was mocking him.

'Do you mind telling me who arranged it, and why?'

'Are you feeling used?' she teased him. She turned her back on him and for a split second he saw a mental Polaroid of last night's lovemaking, Velma biting his shoulder, Velma sitting on his face, grinding herself into his mouth. Vicious, harsh, dangerous sex; sex with teeth and blood and fingernails.

He buttoned up his shirt, buttoned the cuffs. 'I don't know what this is all about,' he said, trying to keep his voice steady. 'I don't think I *want* to know what this is all about. I'm going back to my room and then I'm leaving. If you want some money – here –' He reached into his back pants pocket and took out fifty dollars in ten dollar bills.

Velma shook her head. 'I don't want your money. I've already been paid.'

Charlie seized hold of her wrist and twisted her around. Instantly, she slapped his face, hard, and he let her go. They stood glaring at each other, and panting. A crimson handprint gradually appeared on Charlie's cheek.

'Somebody paid you to pick me up and screw me?' he asked her incredulously.

'I was trying to help you, that's all,' said Velma. I was trying to make you understand.'

'Understand what? I mean, what's the connection? You, me, Le Reposoir, these Célèstine people. What the hell is it all about?'

Velma was calm. 'You approached them, didn't you? The Musettes?'

'You know about that?'

'I know the Musettes. They called me. They were under the impression that you knew something about the Célèstines and that you were anxious to join them.'

Charlie stared at Velma, narrow-eyed. 'Now, wait a minute. I went to Le Reposoir because I wanted to eat there, that was all.'

Velma dressed and Charlie watched her, feeling completely perplexed. If the Musettes had believed that he knew what the Célèstines were, and that he wanted to become one of them, why hadn't they invited him to join when he had visited Le Reposoir yesterday? And why on earth should they have gone to the trouble of finding out where he was staying after he had left Allen's Corners, and paying for Velma to take him to bed?

Velma lifted her breasts into her bra, and fastened it. 'You'd better go down to see your son. You don't want him to think that you're the kind of man he'd rather not have for a father.'

Charlie checked his watch. 'Okay. You're right. But stick around. Meet me in the lobby in ten minutes' time and we'll have breakfast together.'

'I never eat breakfast.'

'Well, I have to. You can always toy with a cup of coffee.'

Velma said nothing as Charlie went to the door. He opened it, and stood there for a moment simply looking at her. 'Ten minutes then,' he said.

Charlie went to the reception desk first of all, to see if there were any messages for him. The bell captain smirked, and said, 'One from your wife, Mr McLean. She wants you to call her back.'

'When did she call?'

'Maybe eleven last night, sir.'

'Didn't you put her through to my room?'

'You weren't in your room, sir.' The smirk grew wider.

'Not right then, no. But my son was.'

The bell captain's eyes blinked an almost imperceptible negative. 'There was no reply, sir. We did think of putting the call directly through to you, but we considered that you might not appreciate it too much, not right then, sir.'

He walked through the unkempt gardens of the Windsor Hotel and through to his room in the annexe. When he got there, he found that the door was wide open, and that there were two black maids in there, one cleaning out the bath and the other making the bed. The bedside radio was playing 'The Girl From Ipanema'.

'Pardon me,' said Charlie, 'did you see my son here this morning?'

The maid who was making the bed looked up slowly and shook her head. 'No, sir. This room was empty this morning.'

'But he was sleeping here. A boy of fifteen, brown hair. Light blue windcheater and jeans.'

'No, sir. This room was empty. There's some luggage here, sir, but that's all.'

Charlie opened the closet and there was his own overnight case, as well as two of his shirts hanging on hangers, just where he had left them. But there was no sign of Martin's case, nor of any of Martin's clothes. *Shit*, thought Charlie, *I left him alone last night and now he's run away. I failed him when he was a kid and I've failed him again. Now what the hell am I going to do?*

He went into the bathroom. Martin's toothbrush was gone, and there was no sign of any farewell message written on the mirror with Crest. Back in the bedroom, the maids had almost finished. They were performing their last ritual of laying out fresh books of matches and luridly coloured postcards of the Windsor Hotel photographed in the days when the gardens hadn't looked like a snakepit.

'Was there a note anywhere?' Charlie asked them. 'A piece of paper with a message on it?'

The maids made a desultory attempt to look through their black plastic trash bag. 'No, sir. Nothing like that.'

Charlie took one last look around, and then went to the reception desk. The bell captain was picking his teeth behind his hand.

'My son,' said Charlie.

'I'm sorry?' the bell captain asked him.

'My son was in 109 but he's gone.'

The bell captain eyed him steadily. 'Your *son?*'

'I left my son sleeping in 109 last night, but now he's not there.'

'Your son was sleeping in 109?'

Charlie smacked his hand flat on the desk. 'Do you have to keep repeating everything I say? I want to know what time my son checked out of here, and if he told anybody where he was going.'

'Your son sure didn't check out of here, sir.'

'You mean he left without anybody seeing him?'

'No, sir, I mean your son sure didn't check out of here. The reason being that he never checked in.'

'What the hell are you talking about?'

The bell captain looked back at him dispassionately, with the face of a man who has spent a lifetime dealing with irritable customers and pays them about as much attention as he would to a few exhausted wasps, buzzing around in a jelly-jar. 'You checked in here at 5:45 yesterday evening, sir?'

'That's correct.'

'At that time, sir, you were alone.'

'What? What is this? I mean, what kind of ridiculous joke are you trying to play here? I booked in yesterday evening with my fifteen-year-old son, and if you look at my registration card you'll see that I've included his name. Charles J. and Martin S. McLean.'

The bell captain reached under the counter and slid out a narrow file drawer crowded with registration cards. He rifled through them until he came to the M–Mc section, and tugged out Charlie's registration card. 'This is the one, sir. See what it says?'

Charlie stared at the card in horror and disquiet. It read nothing more than *Charles J. McLean, 49 West 24th Street, New York, NY 10010.* Fastened to the card was an impression of his American Express card, and that was all. There was no doubt that the writing on the card was his. He even remembered how the pen had almost run out of ink halfway through, and how he had squiggled it hard on the bottom of the card to start it flowing again. There were the squiggles, just as before. But what had happened to Martin's name?

'I don't even pretend to get this,' said Charlie harshly, giving back the card. 'But my son arrived here with me last night, and yesterday evening before I went to dinner I left him in 109. This morning he's gone – no message, no nothing – that's not like him at all.'

'Do you want to talk to the manager about it?' asked the bell captain.

'Yes, call him. And there's somebody else I want to talk to, too. Ms Velma Farloe. I don't recall her room number, but she should still be there now.'

'Ms Velma Farloe? I'm sorry, sir, but I can tell you right off the top of my head that there's nobody by that name staying here. There's Mr Fairbrother in 412, but that's about the nearest.'

'Is this some kind of Goddamned stupid joke?' Charlie roared, and an elderly couple who had just appeared out of the elevator stared at him in shock and alarm.

'Mr McLean,' the bell captain retorted toughly, 'I've got to warn you to keep your voice down. Shouting isn't going to get anybody anyplace.'

Charlie leaned across the desk and jabbed at the bell captain's uniformed chest with his finger. 'You listen to me, wiseass. I came here last night with my son Martin and I spent the night here with a lady called Ms Velma Farloe while my son slept in 109. This morning my son is gone and so is Ms Farloe. All I need to know from you is when my son left and where Ms Farloe is. Otherwise I'm not just going to talk to the manager, I'm going to talk to the police.'

The bell captain lifted both hands in taunting surrender. 'I'm sorry, Mr McLean. What can I tell you? There's no record of your son having arrived here. There's no sign of him now; and there's no sign of Ms — what did you say her name was?'

At that moment the manager arrived. He was tall, vague, distant, with a drawling Bostonian accent and a flaccid double chin like an elderly pelican. He listened to Charlie's story as if Charlie were trying to sell him a new brand of industrial floor cleaner. His dry, rutted fingernails played an impatient tattoo on the countertop, and then at last he said, 'I'm sorry, sir. I can't help you. If there's no hotel record that your son checked in here, and if there's no record that Ms Furlough checked in here either . . . well, you can understand our position.'

'Yes, I do understand your position,' said Charlie furiously. 'Your position is that for some reason best known to yourselves you're trying to fool me into thinking that my son wasn't even here last night, and that the woman with whom I spent the night was some kind of figment of my imagination.'

The manager smiled without warmth or interest. 'You said it, sir, not me.'

Charlie said tightly, 'I want my son.'

The manager didn't reply, but beckoned the bell captain to lean over the desk toward him. He whispered something into the bell captain's ear and the bell captain nodded.

'What was that all about?' Charlie demanded.

'Nothing to do with your son, sir,' said the manager. 'As I say, I'm very sorry, but we're unable to assist you.'

Charlie had always scoffed at those Hollywood movies in which unscrupulous relatives try to steal a woman's fortune by driving her mad; but he could understand now how quickly a person's sense of reality could slip away. He walked away from the reception desk for a moment in sheer exasperation; then he turned back again and said, 'Call the police.'

The bell captain glanced at the manager, but the manager shrugged in agreement. 'Of course. It's the only thing you can do. But can I ask you one favour? Be discreet. The Windsor has a reputation to keep up.'

'There's something else,' said Charlie. 'I want to talk to your maitre d'. He knows the woman I stayed with last night.'

'He won't be awake yet, sir. He doesn't come on duty until eleven o'clock.'

'Well, in that case, I'm sorry. You'll just have to disturb him. The police will want to see him anyway.'

The manager interlaced his fingers, and then said to the bell captain, 'Put a call in to Arthur. Tell him to meet me in my office in ten minutes.' He turned back to Charlie and said, 'You will allow him ten minutes, sir, to dress?'

While he waited for the police and for Arthur, Charlie went outside and walked around the hotel parking lot. It must have been raining during the night. The air was cold and damp and all the cars were bejewelled with raindrops. He opened up his own car to see if Martin had left him a message on the steering wheel or the seat, but there was nothing there at all. He slammed the car door and wiped the rain off his hands with his handkerchief.

The police took nearly fifteen minutes to arrive. Two deputies, one middle aged and as lean as a whippet, the other young and pudgy with close-bitten nails. Charlie walked up to them as they parked outside the hotel, and said, 'My name's McLean. It's my son who's gone missing.'

The lean deputy sniffed, wiped at his nose with his finger and looked around him. 'You've searched the hotel? He's not hiding or anything? Little kids do that sometimes, just to annoy their parents. Found one kid hiding in the trash once, all ready to be collected and sent off to the dump.'

Charlie said, 'He's fifteen. He's not a little kid.'

The lean deputy made a face that was obviously meant to be interpreted as *Fifteen? What do you expect from a kid of fifteen? They're always running away. It's the prime age for running away.*

'Want to give me some kind of description?' the lean deputy asked. His pudgy partner tugged out a notebook and a stub of pencil and frowned at him expectantly.

'He's a fifteen-year-old boy, that's all. Brown hair, brown eyes. Slight build. He's probably wearing a pale blue windbreaker and Levi jeans.'

The pudgy deputy assiduously wrote all this down while the lean deputy gritted his teeth in imitation of Clint Eastwood and looked this way and that as if he expected a sign from God or at least an imminent change in the weather. 'When was the last time you saw him?' he asked.

'Last night. I don't know, round about seven-thirty.'

'Here, at the Windsor?'

'That's right, in the room we were sharing.'

The lean deputy frowned. 'If you were sharing a room with your son, how come the last time you saw him was at seven-thirty yesterday evening?'

'Because I spent the night in another room.'

'You spent the night in another room?'

'I was sleeping with a lady.'

The lean deputy raised an eyebrow. 'You were sleeping with a lady and when you returned to your own room you found that your son was no longer there?'

'That's the nub of it, yes.'

The pudgy deputy scribbled in his notebook for a long time while the lean deputy peered first to the northern horizon and then to the south.

At last, the lean deputy said, 'Did you have any family problems?'

Charlie shook his head. 'His mother and I are divorced, but there isn't any hostility between us. His mother's taking a vacation right now, and so I agreed to bring him along with me. I'm a restaurant critic, I travel around eating in restaurants and writing reports.'

The lean deputy nodded his head towards the entrance to the Windsor. 'What do you think of this place? Stinks, don't it?'

'Deputy, I'm interested in finding my son, that's all.'

'Well,' said the deputy, 'the whole point is that teenage disappearances are pretty much two for a nickel these days. Kids have plenty of independence, plenty of money. They're smart, too. As soon as they're old enough to strike out on their own, they generally take the opportunity and do it. You can never tell when it's going to happen. Sometimes it happens after an argument, sometimes it just happens.'

'Thanks for the sociological analysis,' Charlie retorted.

The manager came out and said coldly, 'My maitre d' is here, as you requested. I hope you won't be keeping him for very long. He has a full lunchtime schedule ahead of him, and a Lodge dinner at seven-thirty.'

Charlie didn't answer, but led the way back into the hotel. In the manager's office, Arthur, the maitre d', was standing in green striped pyjamas and a maroon silk bathrobe with stains on the belly. He was unshaven, although Charlie could smell that he had already had a quick squirt of Binaca. He glared at Charlie with eyes like freshly peeled grapes.

'Arthur?' said the lean deputy. 'How are you doing?'

'I was doing all right before I was woken up,' said Arthur harshly.

'One of those dreams, huh?' the lean deputy gibed. 'A desert island and you and forty naked women and no rescue imminent for at least six months.'

Arthur looked away dismissively. It was quite obvious that he had no respect for anything or anybody – his employers, his customers, or the law.

'Arthur,' said Charlie, 'do you remember that woman who was sitting in the lounge with me? The woman in the blue dress?'

Arthur stared at Charlie, and then looked in perplexity from the lean deputy to the manager, and back again. 'What kind of a question is that?' he asked.

The lean deputy said, 'It's simple enough. Do you remember a woman in a blue dress sitting in the lounge with this gentleman last night?'

Arthur shook his head in apparent disbelief. 'If there was a woman there, she was the Invisible Woman. I didn't see any woman.'

'You mean that Mr McLean here was sitting on his own?'

'Well, that's right. He looked kind of fed up and lonesome so I made sure we gave him a cognac on the house.'

Charlie jabbed a finger at him. 'I was sitting talking to Velma Farloe and you damned well know it! Velma Farloe – she was right in front of your face.'

The maitre d' frowned at the manager for moral support. 'Velma Farloe? I don't know anybody called Velma Farloe.'

'Oh, she knew *you* all right,' said Charlie. 'She said your nickname was Bits. Now, isn't that true? Bits, that's what she said, because you used to have the habit of saying for two bits

97

you'd do this, or for two bits you'd do that. Now – how could I possibly have known that unless Velma Farloe was real and I'd met her?'

The maitre d' stared at Charlie for a long time and then turned appealingly toward the two deputies. 'Bits?' he asked, in complete disbelief. 'What is this guy, some kind of a fruit-cake, or what? I mean, *Bits?*'

Charlie glanced at the manager and then at the deputies. Their faces all wore the same expression of caution. *We've got a funny one here, guys. Let's just play along with him until he runs out of steam.*

'All right,' said Charlie. 'If you don't want to believe me, you don't want to believe me. But I can warn you here and now that I'm going to the sheriff, and if I don't get any satisfaction from the sheriff I'm going to the FBI. I have friends, don't you make any mistakes about that. I have influential friends.'

'Well, we're sure you do,' said the manager. 'But you have to see the situation from our point of view, Mr McLean. You checked in here yesterday on your own, you ate dinner on your own and, as far as I can understand it, you slept on your own. I guess the best thing we can do for the time being is to put the whole incident down to exhaustion, maybe, or to over-excitability.'

Charlie was so angry at that instant that he could have punched the manager in the face. Instead, however, he closed his eyes and clenched his fists and waited for the fury to die down inside of him. When he opened his eyes again, he caught the manager winking conspiratorially at the bell captain, and the lean deputy shuffling his feet as if he were practising his ballroom dancing. The pudgy deputy was eating the end of his pencil and staring out of the window.

'Okay,' said Charlie. 'Okay. Just give me some time to think this through. It happened because it happened and because I *know* that it happened. But I don't have any evidence to prove it and you guys obviously aren't going to break your asses in any kind of effort to help me prove it.'

'Mr McLean,' the lean deputy appealed to him, 'we aren't going to break our asses because so far we haven't seen any evidence that your son was actually here, let alone any evidence that he disappeared.'

Charlie said, 'Don't worry about it, okay? I said not to worry about it. Let me think it all through by myself. Then I'll call you, when I've worked something out.'

'We don't want you to think that we're failing in our duty,' the lean deputy said. 'But the simple fact is that we don't have anything that looks like a legitimate complaint here. I mean, this looks like your common-or-garden misunderstanding, which in a district like this is what occupies most police time. Maybe your son was here, maybe he wasn't. If he was here, he sure isn't here now, and he sure didn't leave any kind of evidence that he was. These good people here didn't even see him, didn't even check him in. So where is he now? Or more to the point, was he ever here at all?'

'It's all right,' said Charlie, as apologetically as he could. 'I guess I made a genuine mistake. I guess I thought that my son was here when all the time he wasn't. I guess that's it.'

'It has been known,' the lean deputy prompted him. 'You know, like mirages, all that kind of stuff. You're walking through the desert and what do you see but cans of cold Pabst. It's something you want, and because you want it so much, you think that you can actually see it in front of your eyes. That's what happened to you. You wanted to have your son with you, but you couldn't. So instead you imagined he was with you, but now he's gone, even though he wasn't there in the first place.'

Charlie raised his head and stared at the deputy with level eyes. The deputy was gazing eagerly at him, like a dog anticipating a reward. Charlie said, 'How dare you talk such bullshit to me? I've just lost my son.'

The deputy coughed and shuffled and looked embarrassed.

'I have to keep every possible option open, sir. You must understand that. And that includes the option that your son wasn't here at all – that he was only riding along with you inside of your own mind.'

Charlie knew then that there was only one way in which he was going to be able to find Martin, and that was by himself. These people might be right. Perhaps Martin hadn't come along with him at all. Perhaps the stress of his job at MARIA had all grown too much for him, and he had driven to Connecticut under the illusion that his son was with him. But he could live his life only by his own perceptions, and by his own reality, and he remembered Martin coming with him as clearly as he could see these people standing in front of him now. All he could think was, *If they don't believe me, that's too bad. I'll go look for Martin on my own.*

He was aware, however, how unwise it would be tell them that. The best course of action would be for him to apologize for being hasty; to make out that he was confused by everything that had happened; and to leave the Windsor with an idiot smile on his face. He knew that Martin had been with him. He knew just as distinctly that he had slept with Velma Farloe. The only possible reason why the manager and the bell captain and the maitre d' and these Laurel-and-Hardy deputies were pretending that he was deluded was because they knew where Martin had gone, and why.

And the only possible reason why they were keeping up the pretence was because they had been ordered to; or paid to; or because they were in fear of their lives if they told him what had really happened.

Charlie found it completely unreal that he was thinking this way. Yet his instinct for survival had always been strong. It had enabled him to travel around the continental United States year after year, testing and tasting, sleeping in unfamiliar beds, and to endure the long-drawn-out agonies of his divorce from Marjorie and everything that had happened in Milwaukee.

Stiffly, he raised his hand, and said, 'I'll leave it to you, then, deputy. If anybody calls and says they've seen my son – well, I hope that you'll let me know. I'll leave a forwarding number at the desk here, and I'll call you regularly so that you know where I am.'

The lean deputy nodded, and said, 'That's a real sensible way of going about it, Mr McLean. Come on – I know you're upset. Maybe disoriented, too. But we'll do everything we can to clear this little problem up pronto. You won't have to worry about a thing. Believe me, your son is probably home with his mother right now, watching television and eating popcorn and totally oblivious to all of your worries. We'll check into it. The very worst that could have happened is that he's decided to light out for a day or two. So many kids do it these days.'

Charlie reached into his coat and took out his wallet, and said to the manager, 'How much do I owe you?'

The manager shook his head. 'Let's call this one a gimme, shall we? You've had a bad time at the Windsor. I don't want anybody to drive away from here with a sour taste in his mouth, for whatever reason.'

Charlie wasn't in the mood to argue. It made no difference to him, after all. M A R I A picked up all of his tabs. And he had the feeling that he wouldn't be filing a report on the Windsor Hotel; nor on any of the restaurants he had visited on this trip. In fact, he had the feeling that his time at M A R I A was already over; that his career had vanished overnight, like the mist over the Connecticut River.

'This won't adversely affect your report, I hope?' the manager asked him, taking hold of his elbow and smiling at him from close quarters.

'I can't think why it should, can you?' Charlie replied. The manager's smile gradually faded, and he turned toward the bell captain and said, 'Bring the gentleman's bags, would you?'

Charlie stood by the door and waited while a black bellboy was sent to find his suitcase. The two deputies made themselves comfortable up against the reception desk and discussed football with the bell captain. When Charlie's suitcase eventually arrived, the lean deputy said, 'Don't you worry, sir, we'll make sure we keep in touch. Remember that ninety-nine per cent of all those kids reported missing return to their parents within seventy-two hours.'

Charlie said, 'What about the other one per cent?'

The lean deputy made a face. 'You want better chances than ninety-nine out of a hundred?'

Charlie stowed his case in the trunk of his car and then climbed behind the steering wheel. For a moment he regarded his eyes in the rear-view mirror. *Goddamn it, Charlie McLean, sometimes you're hopeless*, he told himself. Then he started up his engine, drove out of the parking lot, and headed towards Allen's Corners.

He was going right back to the moment when things had started going off at a tangent. Back to the Iron Kettle, back to Mrs Kemp's boarding house, and back to the place which seemed to be exerting a dark and ever-increasing influence over him: Le Reposoir.

CHAPTER EIGHT

He reached the Iron Kettle shortly after ten o' clock. The front door was locked, so he walked around the house on the wet stone pathway until he reached the kitchen. The door was open and Charlie could hear the brisk, sharp sound of scrubbing. He knocked on the door frame and stepped inside.

The kitchen was small but professionally equipped with stainless steel Jenn-Air hobs and Amana ovens. Mrs Foss, wearing a large floral pinafore, was down on her hands and knees scrubbing the brown quarry-tiled floor.

'Mrs Foss?' asked Charlie.

Mrs Foss raised her head like a penitent who had been interrupted in her prayers. She didn't recognize him at first, but then she said, 'Ah, you. Yes, well, hello there. I'm afraid we're not open until twelve-thirty.'

'Mrs Foss, I need to ask you some questions,' said Charlie.

'Questions? What kind of questions?'

'You remember I came here with my son? He went missing this morning.'

Mrs Foss grasped the edge of the kitchen table to help herself up. She reached for a towel and dried her hands, keeping her eyes on Charlie all the time. 'How did it happen?' she wanted to know. Charlie, briefly, told her – omitting the fact that he had spent the night with Velma. Mrs Foss listened, and nodded, and then said, 'Come through to the parlour.'

The parlour was a small gloomy room smelling of potpourri and damp. Mrs Foss obviously used it partly as an office and partly as a sitting room. There was a desk with invoices and bills arranged neatly on top of it, and two wheelback chairs with tapestry seat cushions. The window gave a view of the garden in which Martin had first seen the small, hooded dwarf-person; or claimed he had.

'Sit down,' said Mrs Foss. 'Would you care for a cup of coffee?'

Charlie shook his head. 'I want to track down my son, that's all.'

'So why did you come here?' Mrs Foss looked at Charlie directly and he could see the curved reflection of his own face in her upswept spectacles. Two desperate moon-faced Charlies searching for the same son.

'We had lunch here, during that electric storm – remember? – and Martin said he saw somebody in the garden. Well – I thought I saw somebody, too. I don't know what it was, maybe it was one of the neighbourhood children. Maybe it was nothing at all, just two tired imaginations playing tricks on each other. But from that moment on, things began to go wrong between Martin and me, and this morning he's gone.'

'You've talked to the police?'

'I talked to two deputies at West Hartford. They weren't exactly the Brains Brothers. They said that most runaway kids returned to their parents after seventy-two hours.'

Mrs Foss took off her spectacles and studiously polished them on the bodice of her pinafore. 'You have some suspicions, don't you?'

Charlie said, 'I'm probably crazy. I *feel* like I'm crazy.'

'Let me say it for you,' said Mrs Foss. 'You think that the Célèstines may have had something to do with it, don't you? Those folks at Le Reposoir.'

Charlie hesitated. He had already reached the stage where he didn't quite trust anybody. After all, if Velma and Arthur and the manager of the Windsor had all been deliberately deceiving him, why shouldn't Paula Foss be deceiving him too? It seemed quite possible that the moment he had walked into the Iron Kettle, he had entered unwittingly into a conspiracy to take his son away; and to make him believe that he was mad.

He decided to put Paula Foss to the test. 'Tell me about the Célèstines,' he said. 'The truth about the Célèstines. I mean, what are they? Because they have something to do with Martin's disappearance, don't they? Or don't they?'

'The Célèstines are secret,' said Mrs Foss, with considerable emphasis. 'People used to pass on all kinds of stories about them, down in New Orleans. The story goes that they came from France, originally, but they were forced to emigrate during the French Revolution. They were a dining society, that's what I heard. But they were something else besides. They were religious, too. Not religious in the way that you or I might think of it, but *mystical*.'

Charlie said nothing, but stood and listened with a face that couldn't devise any kind of expression.

Mrs Foss continued. 'They had a restaurant on St Charles Avenue, two doors down from Kolb's, but it wasn't a restaurant in the regular sense. You couldn't walk in there straight off the street, the way you could with Kolb's or the Pearl, or the red beans and rice place that I used to run. They had blanked-out windows, and a locked door, and nobody I knew ever got to eat there. They were select. They were secret. People used to whisper about them, all kinds of stories: how they were eating live monkey brains, how they were eating Pomeranian dogs. But the story most people used to tell was that they were taking stray children off the streets and fattening them up, so that they could eat them too.'

'That,' Charlie said, 'has got to be a fairy tale. I haven't heard anything like it since Hansel and Gretel.'

'All right, it's a fairy tale,' said Mrs Foss. 'But people used to tell it, all the same.'

'Why did you call them the Célèstines?'

'Everybody did. It means Heavenly People, in Cajun French. I don't know where they first acquired it, but that's what they used to call themselves. The Heavenly People. They was Cajun from centuries back, right from the time that the Spanish granted them land in the bayous. Everybody called them the Célèstines. But it doesn't just mean Heavenly People, it means something else besides. It means this secret eating society; and whether it's true or not, it means anyone who eats something they are not supposed to.'

Mrs Foss pronounced 'supposed to' in an unadulterated Deep south accent, like 'sah postah'.

Charlie said, 'I keep feeling that something's going on here and everybody's trying to explain it to me, but I still can't understand it. These Célèstines – you're not seriously trying to tell me they eat children?'

'One and one makes two. Maybe one and one makes three.'

'And what does that mean?'

'That means every time the Célèstines appear, children start to disappear. The Célèstines have peculiar eating habits, so one and one makes two, or maybe it doesn't. Nobody can prove it.'

'Children are disappearing all the time. It's a national crisis.'

'Sure they do.'

Charlie said, 'I'm sorry, I can't believe any of this.'

'Can't you?' asked Mrs Foss. 'In that case, why did you come back here?'

Charlie covered his eyes with his hand. He sat for a long time in silence, thinking about Martin, and the very last moment when he walked out of the door of his room at the Windsor Hotel. Martin had quoted Groucho Marx back at him. *I do not wish to belong to the kind of club that accepts people like me as members.* How ironic that comment would prove to be if the Célèstines really had taken him.

But the whole idea of a secret society that ate children was preposterous. How could they get away with it? and they would certainly have to be a whole lot more careful about their secrecy than the Célèstines had proved to be. Velma had appeared almost to be recruiting him to join them, and that didn't seem like the way a private society of cannibals would behave.

Mrs Foss must be prematurely senile, or suffering from overwork. 'Is that waitress of yours around anywhere?' he asked. 'What was her name?'

'Harriet. No, she hasn't been in. She wasn't in yesterday, either.'

'Do you think you could give me her address? There's just a chance that she might be able to tell me something helpful.'

'She lives with her parents on the Bethlehem Road, about three miles east of the Corners. You can't miss it. It's a square white house with a red roof almost on the road. A big maple growing right close to it.'

Charlie nodded. Mrs Foss stood quite still. 'Was that really what they say about the Célestines?' Charlie asked her. 'They ate children?'

'Maybe it was just a bogey story,' said Mrs Foss.

'I think maybe it was,' Charlie told her.

He left the Iron Kettle and drove back to Allen's Corners. The day was windy and the trees waved at him frantically as he passed the sloping green. The two old men whom Charlie and Martin had met yesterday were sitting on their customary bench, Christopher Prescott and Oliver T. Burack. Charlie parked his car not far away from them and walked across the green with the wind in his face.

'Well, well,' said Christopher Prescott, lifting his brown fedora hat.

'Good morning.' Charlie looked around. The green was deserted except for a stray brown-and-white dog sniffing at one of the garbage baskets. 'I was wondering if you might have seen my son.'

'We certainly did,' said Christopher Prescott.

Charlie's chest tightened. 'You saw him? When? This morning?'

'Yesterday, with you,' Christopher Prescott said. 'Fine-looking boy he is, too.'

Charlie tried not to show his anger with Christopher Prescott's imbecility. 'He's gone missing,' he said. 'I was wondering if you might have seen him today.'

'Missing, huh? What's he done, run off to make his fortune? You know, that's what I did when I was a boy. I ran off to make my fortune, didn't come home for five years and two months solid, and by that time I was old enough and wealthy enough to buy my father's house out from under him. Every boy should do that. If that's what your boy's done, then good luck to him I say.'

Charlie said, 'He's only fifteen years old. He doesn't know this part of the country at all. And he left without any kind of warning. No note, no nothing.'

'Doesn't want you to find him, then. That's obvious.'

'Will you do me a favour and keep a look out for him?' Charlie asked them.

'Weather-eye open,' said Oliver T. Burack.

Charlie left them with a wave and drove out on the Bethlehem Road until he reached the white house with the red roof where Harriet lived with her parents. The house looked badly in need of paint and repair. The shiplap boards were flaking, and most of the windowsills were rotten. An avalanche of shingles had left one side of the verandah roof exposed, like bones seen through decayed flesh. From one of the overhanging branches of the big old maple tree, an old tyre swung from a fraying rope. Chickens pecked around the back door.

Charlie parked his car and climbed the creaking wooden steps to the porch. He pressed the doorbell and waited, rubbing his hands to warm them up. Dust and chaff blew in the wind; chicken feathers clung to the screen door.

After he had pressed the bell a second time, Charlie called out, 'Harriet! Are you there? Harriet!'

Without warning, the front door opened, and Charlie was

confronted by a fiftyish man of slight build with thinning hair. He was wearing a carpenter's apron and he was carrying a clamp in his hand. He frowned narrowly at Charlie, and said, 'Yes?'

'I'm sorry to trouble you, sir. I'm looking for a girl called Harriet. She works at the Iron Kettle with Mrs Foss.'

'*Used* to work there. Not anymore.'

'Oh? I didn't realize that. Mrs Foss didn't tell me.'

'That's no surprise. Mrs Foss doesn't know yet.'

Charlie said, 'My name's McLean, Charlie McLean. Is Harriet here? I'd like to talk to her, if I could.'

'I'm Harriet's father, Gil Greene,' said the man. He wiped his hand on his apron and held it out. 'Been glueing a chair.'

'Is Harriet here?' asked Charlie.

'Haven't seen her since yesterday. Come on in. Would you care for some coffee? There's a pot on the stove.'

'No, thank you. It's important I talk to Harriet. Well, it could be important. Do you know where she is?'

Gil Greene shrugged, and twisted his clamp around. 'Her mother lets her do what she likes. Much against *my* better judgement, believe me. Gone off to see those French people again, that's my guess.'

'French people?'

'Them Musettes, up at the restaurant. She's always talking about them, you'd think they was crowned heads of Europe or something like that. Every now and then, they call her and she goes up to the restaurant to help out with the serving, or whatever they want her to do. Odd jobs, washing dishes, that kind of thing. She never gives Mrs Foss no notice, she just goes. She never gives us no notice neither. Sometimes she's gone for two or three days at a time, no explanations, nothing. So what can you do? Well, the point is you can't do nothing.' Gil Greene cleared his throat, and then he added, 'The last time she went, Mrs Foss said she was going to sack her if she did it again. And you can see what's happened.'

'Does Mrs Foss know where she is?' asked Charlie.

'She probably suspects. But Harriet made her mother and me promise not to tell, on account of the fact that Mrs Foss was always dead set against the Musettes right from the very beginning. I don't know whether it was anything personal but there seemed to be real bad blood between them.'

Charlie said, 'Did Harriet ever tell you what goes on at that restaurant? What they do there, or what the place is like?'

Gil Greene looked at Charlie and smiled wryly. 'You don't know Harriet. Sometimes she could talk the rear wheel off of a forty-ton truck, other times you can't get a word out of her.'

Charlie checked his watch. 'Listen,' he said, 'I'll take a drive up to the restaurant myself, see if I can get to see her. If I can't, or if I miss her, would you ask her to look me up? I'll be staying at Mrs Kemp's.'

'Didn't know Mrs Kemp was still in the boarding house business.'

'She's not. But I have to stay somewhere.'

'Rather you than me, pal.'

Charlie turned his car around and drove straight back through Allen's Corners and out on to the Quassapaug Road. A few drops of rain freckled his windshield, although it didn't look as if it were going to come down heavily. Cherub's tears, Marjorie always used to call those light sporadic showers, an occasional reminder that even the life hereafter could be unhappy, too.

The gates of Le Reposoir were locked. Charlie climbed out of the car and pressed the intercom button. There was no reply, so he pressed the button again, and kept his finger on it for almost half a minute. At last, a detached, metallic voice said, 'Please – we are closed. If you have anything to deliver, leave it at the post office in Allen's Corners. We will collect it from there ourselves.'

Charlie said, 'This is Charles McLean. I want to speak to M. Musette.'

'M. Musette is not here.'

'What about Mme Musette?'

'I regret, sir, that Mme Musette is not here, either.'

'Is there a manager? Somebody in charge?'

'Only myself, sir. I am the caretaker.'

'I'm looking for my son,' Charlie insisted, trying not to let his voice tremble.

'Your son?' asked the disembodied voice. 'I regret that I do not understand.'

'My son, Martin McLean, is missing and I have reason to believe that somebody at Le Reposoir may be able to help me locate him.'

'Sir – you must be making some mistake. There is nobody here who could possibly help you with such a matter. If your son is missing you would be advised to contact the police.'

Charlie said, 'Is Harriet Greene there?'

'I beg your pardon, sir, there is nobody of that name known to us. You seem to be suffering from some kind of misapprehension.'

'Can I come inside and talk to you? It's darned windy out here.'

'I regret that would serve no constructive purpose, sir. Besides, in M. Musette's absence, I have been requested not to admit anybody at all. There is much valuable property in the house, sir, and we have to be exceptionally careful about security.'

Charlie rubbed the back of his neck. He was feeling very stiff and very tired. 'All right,' he conceded. 'I'll go talk to the police. But I would like to see M. Musette when he comes back. Is it possible to make an appointment?'

'M. Musette has no appointments free before the end of the month.'

'The end of the month? But it's only the fourth now!'

'M. Musette is a very busy man, sir.'

Charlie controlled himself. 'I understand,' he told the voice on the intercom. 'I'm sorry if I disturbed you.'

'You are quite welcome, sir.' The voice was as faultlessly polite as it was faultlessly unhelpful.

Charlie returned to his car. For the first time he saw the remote TV camera watching him from the trees just inside the gates. He climbed back into his car, and made a showy three-point turn before taking a right along the north-west side of Le Reposoir's extensive grounds, in the opposite direction to Allen's Corners.

He drove slowly, peering between the trees that lined the roadside to see what kind of fencing protected Le Reposoir from the outside world. Every now and then he glimpsed spiked steel railings, painted green, with ceramic conductors on them. *Electrified*, he thought. *That's how much they want to keep people out. Or maybe that's how much they want to keep people in.*

After a little over a mile, however, he came to what he was looking for: a place where the grounds of Le Reposoir dipped downwards, while the verge of the road remained high. He stopped the car and got out, walking up the verge a little way to make sure that he would be able to do what he wanted to do. The wind blew across his ears like a ghostly mouth blowing across the neck of an empty bottle. He returned to his car, started up the engine again, and shifted it into first.

Carefully, he turned the Oldsmobile off the road and drove it on to the grass. The suspension bounced and bucked, and he heard the muffler scrape against the gravelly ground. But then he was able to drive at a sharp angle down towards the green spiked fence, and pull to a halt with the automobile's front bumper only an inch or two away from it. He switched off the engine and climbed out. Then – looking quickly all around him – he heaved himself up on to the hood. The sheet metal dented under his weight, but he walked without hesitation right to the front of the car to find that the green fence stood only two feet proud of the hood. He took two steps back, and then jumped right over the spikes and into the tangled bushes on the other side, tumbling over and over and tearing the elbow of his suit.

Winded, he sat up, and listened. All he could hear was the leaves rustling, and the low humming of the voltage in the electrified fence. He got up to his feet, brushed himself down, and then began to make his way through the undergrowth in the rough direction of the house.

It appeared that the woods which screened Le Reposoir from the Quassapaug Road curved in a horn shape towards the north-west side of the house; so that it would be possible for Charlie to approach the building very closely without being seen. Behind the house there were wide lawns, looking unnaturally green in the morning light, with sombre statues of naked Greek gods standing beside them, their shoulders heavy with moss, their eye-sockets blind with mildew.

The house itself was as forbidding as Charlie had remembered it. It still possessed that peculiar quality of seeming to be suspended an inch above the ground, of having infinite density, like a black diamond, but at the same time being weightless. Window upon window reflected the grey fall clouds as they hurried past, giving the extraordinary illusion that the sky was *inside* the house. Charlie came as close to the edge of the lawns as he dared, stopping and listening every few seconds in case he was being observed. The house, however, looked silent and empty. Perhaps the voice on the intercom had been telling the truth, and there was nobody here.

Charlie weaved his way in between close-set oaks and tangles of thorn that were as vicious as rolls of barbed wire. At last he reached a low stone retaining wall from which he could see into the large cast-iron solarium which ran along the back of the house. He could see potted plants and old-fashioned cane furniture, and several white marble statues of naked children. Keeping his head down, he skirted the side of the house until he came within fifteen yards of a small door. The door was carved with wooden grapes and gargoyles and studded with black iron bolts. It was impossible to tell whether it was locked or not. If it were, Charlie would not only have to risk discovery by running across the open lawn towards it, but he would have to run back again, too. He crouched down behind the retaining wall and waited to see if there was anybody around, but apart from the wind and the agitated shivering of the trees, the house and its grounds were silent. No airplanes passed overhead. No birds sang. The reflected clouds ran silently across the windows.

At last, glancing left and right, Charlie took hold of the top of the retaining wall, and prepared to heave himself up on to the upper lawn. But at the very instant he did so, the handle of the garden door rattled and turned, he ducked down just before it was opened wide. He pressed himself as close into the stones as he could, his heart beating, his face sweaty, and prayed that whoever was coming out of the garden door wouldn't come too close to the edge of the lawn and find him there. It was one thing to have driven openly into the front entrance of Le Reposoir; it was another to have deliberately breached their security and to be hiding like a would-be housebreaker in their private grounds.

He heard voices, and a noise that sounded like the squeak of badly oiled wheels. One voice was high and accented; the other was gruff, and plainly American. The high voice said, 'She should be allowed to sleep until the afternoon. You remember what it was like your first time.'

The gruff voice replied, 'I wish I could have my first time again.'

'It is the *last* time that you must look forward to now,' the high voice replied.

It sounded to Charlie as if the two speakers were moving around the side of the house and away from him. Their voices were accompanied by the persistent squeaking of wheels, as if they were pushing something. Charlie hesitated for a moment, and then edged his way about ten yards to the right along the wall until he came to a large stone urn. The urn was felted with dark green moss, and a small toad sat on its plinth, watching Charlie with yellow expressionless eyes. Charlie slowly raised his head, using the urn for cover, and tried to catch a glimpse of the people who had come out of the garden door before they disappeared.

To begin with, they were out of his line of sight behind a triangular yew bush. But suddenly they appeared quite clearly between the bush and the corner of the house, and when Charlie saw them he shivered the way a small child shivers when a grown-up shouts at him. It was surprise, and fright, but most of all it was the incongruity of their appearance, like people out of a Breughel painting of lazars and cripples.

Leading the way was the small dwarf-like figure in the white hood whom Charlie had seen at the Iron Kettle, and outside the back door at Mrs Kemp's. It walked with a swinging lurch, like an ape, yet it was distinctly human. Behind this small figure came a three wheeled invalid carriage, a kind of a Bath chair in which a pale-faced woman was lying, her eyes open, her head back, staring at the sky. She was covered up to her neck in an off-white blanket, and there was a leather strap around her waist which looked as if it was supposed to prevent her from falling out.

The invalid carriage was being pushed by the black-cloaked woman whom Charlie recognized from his first intrusion into the grounds of Le Reposoir, the woman who *might* have been Mme Musette. Her hood had fallen back, revealing her face, and even from a distance Charlie could see that she was just as striking as before, a woman of almost unbelievable beauty. Yet – remembering what he had seen in his rear-view mirror as he had driven away from the house the first time – his eyes jumped at once to the steering bar of the invalid carriage, on which the woman's hands were resting. She was wearing black cotton gloves, but only one finger of each glove was actually hooked over the bar. The remaining fingers were crumpled and obviously empty.

Charlie stared at this bizarre procession until it had disappeared from sight around the side of the house. Then he slowly slid down into a sitting position behind the retaining wall, oblivious to the green moss which smeared the back of his coat. He felt as if he had accidentally wandered into some extraordinary Victorian nightmare. *Alice Through the Looking Glass* with freaks and dwarves and beautiful women with no fingers. He wiped his face with his hands; he was wet with chilly sweat.

It was not only the weirdness of the procession that had frightened him. It was the conviction that he had recognized the pale-faced woman lying in the invalid carriage staring at the sky. Although he had glimpsed her for only two or three seconds, he could have sworn that it was Harriet Greene.

If it were Harriet Greene, though, what the hell had they done to her? She looked almost as if she were dying.

Charlie waited for nearly a minute. Then he raised his head cautiously over the top of the wall to see if there was anybody else around. But the house and the lawns seemed to be deserted, and even though ravens were circling around the spires which rose above the house like monuments in a Victorian cemetery, they were silent, as if they knew that this was not the place to cry out.

Grunting with effort, after a working lifetime of four-course meals and not very much in the way of coherent exercise, Charlie climbed up the retaining wall and then crouched on the very edge of the lawn like a middle-aged backstop who refuses to admit that he is over the hill. The grass was bright and green and springy, and felt almost like short-cropped human hair. Charlie held his breath and listened – then made his way as quickly and as quietly as he could across the lawn to the garden door. By the time he reached it he was trembling with tension, but he took hold of the handle without hesitation and turned it. It had been left unlocked, and it swung open easily, without the slightest squeal. Charlie glanced behind him to make sure that he wasn't being watched, and then stepped inside.

CHAPTER NINE

He found himself in a store room, which was gloomy but very dry. Rakes, hoes and edging-spades were hanging neatly on the walls and there were sacks of aromatic peat, of lawn-feed and rose fertilizer. Charlie edged between the sacks until he found another door on the far side of the room, a grey-painted steel door, with an automatic hinge to close it. He turned the handle, and to his relief this door wasn't locked either. He eased it open and put his head around it. On the other side there was a long oak-panelled corridor, very dark and smelling of polish, with mottled engravings all along the walls. Charlie stepped out of the store room and into the corridor, and then hesitated, wondering which direction he ought to take. If he went to the right, towards the front of the house, it would probably be easier to get his bearings. But if the Musettes were really holding Martin, it was unlikely that they would have hidden him in any of the principal rooms at the front.

He turned left, towards the back of the house. His fingers trailed along the stained oak panelling, as if he needed to touch the wall to keep his hold on reality. He glanced up at one or two of the old engravings. They were French, and they were all concerned with butchery. They showed the carcasses of cattle and sheep, and serious-faced men with big moustaches and white aprons removing with large knives the *aiguillettes* and *culottes* and *plats de côtes découverts*.

When he reached the end of the corridor he found himself at the foot of an oak staircase, which led steeply up towards a back landing. There was a large window overlooking the landing, which filled the stairwell with grey photographic light.

Charlie guessed that this must have originally been used as the servants' staircase. He looked upward. There was the sound of someone vacuum cleaning in some far-off bedroom, but that was all. He began to climb the treads one at a time, holding on to the banisters.

He was halfway up the stairs when a voice said, '*Charlie?*'

He looked up in shock. Standing just above him, one elbow casually propped on the banister, was Velma, dressed in a linen kaftan so fine that it was almost transparent. She was smiling at him dreamily, as if nothing had happened between them at all; as if they were old chums who happened to have bumped into each other on a quiet New England commuter train.

'They told me you didn't even exist,' said Charlie unsteadily.

'Who said I didn't even exist?' She wouldn't stop smiling.

'Those people at the Windsor. Bits, whatever his name was. The maitre d'. He denied point-blank that he'd ever seen you. When I said that you called him Bits, he laughed in my face.'

'I expect he did,' said Velma. 'I made it up.'

Charlie said tightly, 'Is Martin here?'

'Martin?'

'My son. Was that what you were doing – keeping me busy while Martin was being kidnapped?'

'Charlie,' said Velma, 'you're not making any sense.'

Charlie took a sharp, impatient breath. 'When I returned to my room at the Windsor after I'd spent the night with you, Martin was gone. There wasn't any trace of him at all. There wasn't any trace of you, either.'

'I left,' said Velma, with complete simplicity.

'Well, sure you did. In fact, the hotel porter said you'd never even been there. So did Bits, or whatever his name is. So what was I supposed to think?'

Velma teased up her hair with her fingers. 'This is private property, you know. You shouldn't be here.'

'I want to know if my son's here, that's all.'

Velma suddenly stopped preening herself and stared at Charlie in amusement. 'How old did you say your son was? Fifteen?'

Charlie took three or four more steps up the staircase, until he was almost at the top. He was trying to be threatening but Velma didn't seem to be intimidated in the least. She cupped one hand over her left breast through the gauzy fabric of her gown, and lifted it slightly as if she was weighing it. Charlie had felt it for himself. He knew how soft and heavy it was.

'You said something about the Célèstines this morning, didn't you?'

'Did I?' Velma asked him.

'You thought that I wanted to join them, didn't you? I mean – that's what goes on here, doesn't it? Meetings of the Célèstines? You thought that I wanted to join, and that's why you kidnapped Martin.'

Velma stretched and yawned. 'You're going to get into serious trouble, you know, if M. Musette finds you here. M. Musette is very particular about trespassers. If it was legal, he'd shoot them dead. But of course he's too law-abiding to do that.'

Charlie reached the top step. He was only three feet away from Velma now. He could smell her favourite perfume, Obsession, and he could see the crow's-feet around her eyes that last night had looked like experience and excitement, and which this morning looked like the first sign of advancing age. He could see her stiffened nipples through the linen of her gown. He didn't even know whether he liked her or despised her. He didn't even know what he thought about the Musettes. All he cared about was finding Martin, and if that meant being friendly to people he despised, then that is what he would do. He couldn't help thinking of Mrs Foss, and the serious way in which she had looked at him through her upswept eyeglasses and said: *'The story most people used to tell was that they were taking stray children off the streets and fattening them up, so that they could eat them.'*

And he couldn't help thinking about his own response. '*I haven't heard anything like that since Hansel and Gretel.*'

Charlie stood close beside Velma and touched her hair. 'Is Martin here?' he asked her gently. 'I'm his father, Velma. I'm responsible for what happens to him.'

'And do you love him?' she challenged.

'What do you think? He's my only child, my only son.'

'That doesn't mean anything at all. I was my father's only daughter, and he used to beat me up every day. Well, it felt like every day. He used to burn the soles of my feet with cigarettes.'

Charlie said, 'What are you trying to do? Are you trying to make me feel guilty, or what? Your childhood is nothing to do with me. I just want to know if Martin is here, that's all. I just want to know what the hell is happening.'

Velma's eyes brightened. 'Come with me,' she said. 'You want to know what the hell is happening? Well, let me show you.'

Charlie hesitated for a moment, but then he allowed Velma to take hold of his arm and lead him away from the landing and down a long, narrow corridor that was the twin of the corridor downstairs. Oak-panelled, dark, with only occasional windows to light up the framed engravings of abattoirs and butchery. One engraving showed a selection of butcher's knives, skinning knives, sticking knives, boning knives, cleavers and splitting saws. Another showed offal being sliced, liver, kidneys, hearts, and sweetbreads. Each engraving carried a caption in French.

'Are the Musettes at home?' Charlie asked, as they made their way along the corridor.

'What makes you ask that?'

'I saw some people in the garden. Somebody in a hood, like a dwarf; and a woman in a black cloak. The first time I came here, I got the impression that the woman in the black cloak was Mme Musette.'

Velma glanced at him over her shoulder. 'Come and see this before you ask me any more questions.'

'They were wheeling a woman in an invalid carriage,' Charlie persisted. He reached out and took hold of Velma's arm and stopped her. 'Listen to me, will you? I knew the woman from before. At least, I thought I did. She used to work as a waitress at the Iron Kettle.'

Velma unexpectedly bent forward and kissed Charlie on the mouth. 'You really don't know what's going on, do you?'

Charlie said, 'Maybe you ought to tell me. I mean, you're obviously in it with them. You're obviously a part of it.'

'A part of what?' asked Velma, with an innocence that was plainly feigned, and intended to taunt him even more.

'*This*,' said Charlie. 'The Musettes. The Windsor Hotel. All of this. Martin disappearing. That Goddamned dwarf. The way that every single person I've met in the past two days has jumped like a jackrabbit whenever anybody mentions Le Reposoir. It's all tied together, and don't you try to kid me otherwise.'

Velma looked at Charlie for a very long time, and then turned her head away. He was conscious that her profile was very handsome, and that her breasts swelled up inside the thin linen of her gown in a way that provoked him, even now.

'I guess you could say they misjudged you,' she said.

'Who misjudged me?'

She gave him a smile as faint as a distant echo. 'They thought that you knew a whole lot more about the Célèstines than you obviously did. M. Musette found out you were a restaurant inspector. I guess he must have thought that a restaurant inspector knew about the Célèstines.'

'Well, as a matter of fact, I don't. Maybe I'm unusually ignorant or something. Mrs Foss back at the Iron Kettle gave me some kind of weird story about them; and that's why I came up here. I was worried about Martin.'

Somewhere deep in the building a heavy door slammed,

and echoed. Velma said, 'We'd better hurry. Mme Musette will be looking for me in a minute.'

Charlie kept hold of her arm. 'First you have to tell me the truth about these Célèstines.'

'Don't you understand? – I'm going to *show* you.'

Reluctantly, Charlie followed her further along the corridor. She pushed her way ahead of him through a swing fire door and crossed a wide hallway with a yellow-tinted skylight and a highly polished linoleum floor. On the other side of the hallway, there was a solid oak door with a varnished wooden shield on it, emblazoned with a painting of a Papal crown, encircled by a halo.

Another door slammed, closer this time, and Charlie thought he could hear footsteps. 'They won't go totally ape, will they, if they find me here?' he asked Velma. He was beginning to feel seriously worried now. Velma didn't answer him, but pressed her finger against her lips and opened the door decorated with the Papal crown.

Beyond, there was another corridor, at least sixty feet long, dimly lit by small windows set into the doors which ran along either side. Velma beckoned Charlie to follow her, and she went from window to window, peering inside. The first three windows were covered by white cotton blinds. The fourth was uncovered, but the room inside was empty, except for a plain metal-framed bed and a white screen of the type used in hospitals.

'What the hell is this?' Charlie demanded, but Velma suddenly touched his arm and indicated with a nod of her head that he should look into the fifth window.

At first, Charlie couldn't quite understand what he was supposed to see. The room was almost bare, and lit only by the pale uncompromising daylight. A young girl was sitting cross-legged on the floor at a three-quarter angle to the door, so that Charlie could just see her profile. He guessed that she was about fourteen or fifteen years old. Her dark hair was bobbed, and she was dressed in the same kind of linen gown that Velma was wearing.

'I see a girl, that's all,' whispered Charlie.

'She's one of the new ones,' said Velma.

'One of the new what?'

'Devotees, that's what the Célèstines call them.'

'Velma, I don't understand. I simply don't understand. You're going to have a spell it out for me.'

Velma smiled broadly and there was something about her smile which made Charlie feel uncomfortably cold. It was a lewd, coarse smile; the smile of someone who has indulged every lust that you can think of, and many more that you could never think of.

'Look at her feet,' she urged Charlie.

'Her *feet*?' Charlie turned back to the window and peered at the girl more closely.

It was then he realized that the girl's feet were both mutilated. There was a heel, an arch, and that was all. The girl had no toes.

Charlie turned back to Velma and hissed, 'What? What is this all about?'

'It's exactly what it looks like,' she said. 'She hasn't any toes.'

'But why? Is this some kind of a nursing home or something?'

'Nursing home?' Velma laughed. 'Of course not.'

'Then what happened to her feet?'

'She cut off her toes, of course.'

'What do you mean, "of course"? What kind of a state of mind do you have to be in to cut your own toes off?'

'Devotional,' said Velma, as if that explained everything.

'Devotional?' Charlie echoed. 'That doesn't look like devotion to me. That looks like a straightforward case of insanity.'

'Believe me, she's not insane,' said Velma.

'Then why did she cut off her toes?' Charlie demanded. His voice was quivering now.

Velma looked at him with an expression that was almost pitying. 'Why do you *think* she cut them off? To eat them, of course.'

As she said that, the door opened behind them. Charlie, already shocked at what Velma had told him, turned around in alarm.

Standing in the doorway, silhouetted against the yellow radiance from the skylight in the hall, was M. Musette. He paused; and then he came forward so that Charlie could see his face. 'Well, Mr McLean,' he said. 'I don't know whether I ought to be happy to see you or not.'

Charlie cleared his throat. 'I don't care whether you're happy or not, pal. You and I have some talking to do.'

'Perhaps you're right,' said M. Musette. 'Velma, will you go to your room? I want to talk to you later.'

Velma passed them by. As she did so, she glanced at Charlie quickly, and Charlie saw such an extraordinary mixture of fear and desire on her face that he couldn't help looking at M. Musette in complete consternation.

CHAPTER TEN

Downstairs, in a drawing room with high leaded windows which overlooked the gardens, M. Musette sat back in a deeply cushioned armchair and crossed his immaculately pressed trouser legs and lit a cigarette. Charlie, sitting on the far side of the room, could hardly see him behind a circular antique table on which stood a huge pink and white ceramic planter crowded with hothouse camellias.

'I have to confess that what has happened has largely been my responsibility,' said M. Musette affably. 'I must ask your forgiveness, although I am sure you will find it easy to understand how the error was made.'

'Before you start giving me any explanations, I want to ask you one question,' Charlie interrupted. M. Musette, with a wave of his cigarette, indicated that Charlie could do whatever he wanted.

'Is my son here?' Charlie asked him. 'I want a straight answer, yes or no.'

'My dear sir, let me put it this way: nobody ever comes here except of their own free will. Therefore you must search in your heart and ask yourself whether it is *likely* that your son is here.'

'I said a straight answer, not a Goddamned riddle.'

M. Musette blew smoke, and smiled. 'Then I promise that I will answer you before you leave. But first, I want you to understand what is happening here, and why you should not be so fearful.'

'I'm not sure that I want to understand. Was it right what Velma was telling me – that girl actually ate her own toes?'

'You're running ahead of me,' said M. Musette. 'You came here to find out more about the Célèstines. Let me tell you about them.'

'Okay,' Charlie agreed. 'But don't take all day about it.'

M. Musette said, 'Do I have to remind you that you are trespassing on my property and on my time and that I am not obliged to say anything to you at all? It would be far easier for me to call for the sheriff and have you thrown out of here.'

Charlie didn't answer, but clasped his hands together and sat with his head bowed waiting for M. Musette to speak. M. Musette stood up, and walked across to the windows in a wafting cloud of Turkish cigarette smoke. He gazed out over the garden for a while, obviously calming himself, and then he said, 'The Célèstines were orginally members of a religious order created in the year 1260 by Saint Célèstine V, Pietro di Murrone. Célèstine was elected Pope in 1294, after the two-year interregnum that followed the death of Nicholas V. He was a saintly man, but too politically weak for the duties demanded by the Papacy, and later the same year, he abdicated in the face of opposition from Cardinal Gaetano, who was to succeed him as Pope Boniface VIII.'

M. Musette paused, and inhaled smoke, and went on: 'The Célèstines flourished during their founder's lifetime, and at their height they had over 150 houses throughout Europe. But at the time of the French Revolution they declined, and many of the French members of the order fled abroad, some to England and some to the Caribbean. It was on the Caribbean island of Sainte Desirée that the remnants of Saint Célèstine's devotees were transformed into the predecessors of the present-day Célèstines.'

M. Musette turned, and watched Charlie carefully as he spoke. 'What happened was a remarkable mixing of two cultures. Sainte Desirée is a wild and desolate island about fifteen miles off the coast of Guadeloupe. Its sole inhabitants before the exiled Célèstines arrived were native fishermen, who barely managed to make a living out of their labours. The fishermen, however, were Caribs, members of that fierce and alarming tribe who before the days of Columbus had indulged themselves in orgies of cannibalism. By the time the Célèstines reached Sainte Desirée, their ritual eating of human flesh had long since died out; but somehow, they were inspired by the religious enthusiasm of the new arrivals to revive it. There were close similarities, you see, between the ritual of the Holy Communion, with its eating of the Lord's flesh and the drinking of the Lord's blood, and the eating of human beings which had once been the Caribs' speciality.'

Charlie kept his head lowered, but the feeling that was beginning to penetrate his consciousness was one of extreme dread. He felt almost as if he were being lowered against his will into a bath of chilly water; helpless to resist.

'It is quite extraordinary how cultures can intermingle,' said M. Musette. 'There are natives in New Guinea who worship aeroplanes as gods, because their only experience of them is to see them flying high overhead. There are many pagan rituals inextricably woven into the so-called Christian calendar. The very day on which we say we are celebrating the birth of Christ our Lord was in reality one of the darkest and most magical days of rejoicing in the times of the Druids. What happened to the Célèstines as they lived in isolation on Sainte Desirée with the Caribs was that they came to believe that true communion with God could only be consummated by the eating of human flesh and the drinking of human blood.'

Charlie looked up. 'Is this true? Is this authentic history, or are you putting me on?'

'Do you think I would waste my valuable time playing practical jokes?' M. Musette retorted. 'I am talking about the achievement of oneness with God, and complete oneness with your fellow human beings. Does that sound like a put-on, as you call it?'

Charlie said tautly, 'Go on.'

M. Musette crushed out his cigarette in a large crystal ashtray. 'Over a period of 150 years, generation after generation, the Célèstine Order gradually evolved into what it is today.'

'And what is it today? A club for well-heeled cannibals?'

'Cannibalism is a word we prefer not to use; even though it describes us aptly. The word 'cannibal', after all, is derived from *Canibales*, which is the Spanish variant of the name Caribs. Cannibalism also implies that we are involved in the violent or forceful eating of the sacred flesh. While the Caribs often murdered their enemies and sometimes their friends in order to make a meal of them, the Célèstines introduced to them the Christian principle that thou shalt not kill. Instead, the eating of the sacred flesh became a *self-sacrificial* communion, in accord with the very highest tenets of Christianity.'

Charlie stared at M. Musette in complete horror. He was at last beginning to realize that he was being told the truth – that M. Musette in all seriousness was explaining to him that the Célèstines really did eat human flesh.

Unperturbed, M. Musette went on, 'Did not Jesus say, *"Take, eat, this is My body"*? And did he not say, *"Drink . . . for this is My blood of the new testament"*? The whole essence of Christianity is concerned with the sharing of flesh and blood. Not murderously, of course, but *voluntarily* – the devoted giving of one's body for the greater glory of all. That girl you saw upstairs – as Velma told you, she is a new Devotee. So far she has amputated only her toes.'

'And *eaten* them?' Charlie asked, his throat constricted.

'Only five of them. The rest she shared with her Guide and with other Devotees.' M. Musette pressed his hands together as if he were saying grace. 'A small and simple meal, but one of tremendous emotional and religious significance as far as she is concerned.'

Charlie said, 'I'm sorry, I'm finding it difficult to believe what I'm hearing. I cannot even begin to comprehend how a pretty young girl like that can voluntarily mutilate herself and eat her own flesh. Not for the greatest religious cause known to man. Not for any reason whatsoever. It's barbaric.'

M. Musette shook his head. 'Barbaric? No. It is the most highly developed act of religious devotion that I can think of. It demands the greatest degree of devotion to God that you can possibly imagine. It shows in real terms the conquest of the spirit over the flesh. To devour the very body that God gave you is the closest that you can ever get to true holiness.'

'You're out of your tree,' said Charlie. He stood up, and his legs felt as if they were about to fold up like a cheap camera tripod. 'All I want to hear from you is that Martin isn't here, and then I'm going to go straight to the police. You ought to be locked up. Jesus Christ, I don't know how you've gotten away with it for so long. And so openly!'

'The reason is quite simple,' said M. Musette. 'While it may be against the law to eat the flesh of others against their will, it is not against the law to eat yourself; neither is it against the law to eat the flesh of another person if that flesh is offered without any form of coercion. We have had the status of a religion for nearly eighty years now, and while the law may not approve of what we are doing, they know that they cannot touch us. We live with the law in relative harmony. They do not harass us, and we in turn carry out our rituals as discreetly as possible. As you yourself know, we do not exactly encourage visitors.'

'But you present this place as a *restaurant*,' Charlie said.

'As a dining society, rather than a restaurant,' M. Musette corrected him. 'In that way, we do not arouse the unwelcome attention of those Godless media people in whose eyes every religious sect is a target for scandalous exposé. In order to perform our rituals, we require much of the apparatus and many of the supplies that would be used by a dining society, and so to present to the outside world the image of a restaurant is useful camouflage. The name Le Reposoir was carefully chosen because it has two different meanings – one for our devotees and one for the outside world. Le Reposoir means 'the resting place'; but it also means 'the little altar'.

'Then the police know about this place? They know what you do? And they haven't taken any action to stop you?'

'My dear sir, the whole surrounding community is aware that there is something special about Le Reposoir. Many consider us frightening; at least until they have the opportunity to see for themselves the true significance of our rituals. I suppose you could say that there is a parallel with World War Two, when many German citizens living close to concentration camps were aware that there was something of great drama happening in their district, but preferred on the whole not to investigate too closely. Of all creatures, man is the most incurious, believe me.'

Charlie said, 'Haxalt knows, doesn't he? The president of the savings bank?'

M. Musette nodded. 'Almost all of those with senior civic positions in Allen's Corners are aware of what we are, and what we do.'

'Then why –?'

'Because many of their sons and daughters have joined us. Because many of *them* have joined us. There are fifty-eight Devotees here at the moment; some of them are the children of families whose names you would recognize. Others may not have come to us from such celebrated homes, but their parents nonetheless have considerable influence in the community.'

Charlie slowly rubbed the back of his neck to ease the tension. 'Is Haxalt a Devotee? He's not eating himself, is he?'

M. Musette smiled. 'There are two levels of Devotion. There are the Devotees, those who attain spiritual perfection through self-ingestion. Then there are the Guides, who participate in the rituals by eating the flesh of the Devotees –

only, of course, when that flesh is freely and openly offered. The Guides are both mentors and servants to the Devotees. They must assist them to reach spiritual perfection by discussing the scriptures with them; they must also do anything that the Devotees ask of them, no matter what. To give you an example, we had a Devotee in New Orleans who fell in love with his Guide, who was a woman. A very striking woman, I might tell you, a real Cajun beauty. One day the Devotee demanded that she take out his eyes and eat them, so that he would no longer be tempted by her looks.'

'You're telling me this to frighten me off,' Charlie said, 'I don't believe any of it.'

'Well, believe whatever you wish,' said M. Musette.

Charlie hesitated, and then asked, 'Did she?'

'I'm sorry?' said M. Musette, his head on one side.

'Did she eat his eyeballs?'

'Oh, that! You must use your own imagination. But I have been told that there is something very special about the human eyeball, especially when it has been freshly gouged out, and snipped quickly from its optic nerve. You can do it with very little pain indeed, provided you are careful; and I understand that there is no sensation on earth like biting into an eyeball when the optic fluid inside is still warm from its living owner . . . Ha! Do you think I'm trying to frighten you now? Maybe I am. Maybe, rather, your own inhibitions are frightening you. You eat other animals, don't you? You eat slices of cattle and lumps of lamb. Why should there be any difference when it comes to humans? Especially when you think that those cattle and those sheep and those pigs that you eat – you aren't Jewish, are you? – are all *murdered*, so to speak. None of them would *volunteer* to be eaten if they had the choice. Whereas the humans who are eaten here are eaten because they want to be, of their own free will. Isn't that far more moral?'

Charlie said, 'I've heard enough of this garbage. I want you to tell me if my son is here, and that's all.'

M. Musette lifted both hands. There was a gold ring on his right middle finger in the shape of two snakes, entwined, with emeralds for eyes. 'You are like most Americans, I regret,' he said smiling. 'You have no sense of humour whatsoever.'

'I can laugh when something's funny. This isn't funny.'

'Very well,' said M. Musette. 'I appreciate your anxiety. Your son *is* here. He came here early this morning of his own free will, and asked whether he might be initiated into the order of the Célèstines.'

Charlie had been almost certain that Martin couldn't have been here – not after all that fantastic nonsense about people eating themselves. He was so shocked when M. Musette casually admitted that he *was* that for one fragmented moment he was unable to think of anything to say. He stared at M. Musette with one clenched fist held tightly against his chest. Then he managed to say, 'You'd better show me where he is, and pretty damn quick.'

'He did ask that you should be kept away,' said M. Musette. 'At least until he's had time to settle himself in.'

'You're crazy! This is kidnap! This is a capital offence! Now you show me where my son is or else I'm going to be doing some damage around here!'

'Please, Mr McLean, keep calm. Losing your temper isn't going to solve anything.'

Charlie seized hold of M. Musette's lapels and tugged him forward until their noses were almost touching. 'You show me where my son is *right now* or else I'm going to break your arms.'

M. Musette said quietly, 'I don't think so,' and grasped Charlie's wrists. With almost no effort at all, he prised Charlie's hands away from his coat, and lowered them. Then he fastidiously brushed his lapels and gave Charlie a nod that was more of a warning than an acknowledgement of what he had done.

Charlie was breathing deeply. 'Let me get this straight. Martin came to you of his own free will?'

'That's what I said.'

'How did he get here? He doesn't have any transportation.'

'He arrived by taxi at about midnight last night. He paid the fare out of his own money. He was unaccompanied, so there was no possible question of kidnap. I talked to him myself when he arrived. He said that he had decided to join us, and that he was prepared to become one of our Devotees.'

'And what did you do?' snarled Charlie. 'Give him a knife and fork and tell him to get on with it?'

'As a matter of fact, my dear sir, I tried very hard to dissuade him from becoming a Devotee. I always do when I am approached by volunteers. I explain that it is a difficult and painful road to heaven, a road that is often beset by terrible doubts, and which can bring despair as well as ecstasy.'

Charlie said, 'He listens to rock music and reads comic-books. How the hell was he supposed to understand anything like that?'

'Your son is far more perceptive than you think. He sees you and your weaknesses quite clearly. For himself, he wants something better.'

'Cutting your own toes off and eating them is better? What kind of a cockamamie crock of shit is that?'

'Just listen to yourself,' M. Musette said. 'Listen to the sound of your own voice. You are a man of impulse and vulgarity, a man with no spirituality whatsoever. You have spent your whole life in the empty pursuit of something you can never find, which is yourself. Those endless meals you eat, those endless miles you drive, you are looking for something which you left behind with your wife and your son. Your soul is what I am talking about, Mr McLean. Your spirit.' He paused briefly, and then he said, 'Your son came here because he didn't want the same fate to befall him. He has accompanied you on your travels for only a few days, but he has already seen the tragedy of your life. It was you who precipitated his decision to come here, not I, nor any of my Devotees.'

'This is bull,' Charlie retorted. 'If it hadn't been for Harriet Greene and that damned dwarf of yours, he never would have known about Le Reposoir.'

'Oh yes, dearest Harriet,' said M. Musette. 'Harriet has wanted to join us ever since I first employed her as a waitress. A little too enthusiastic, I'm afraid; a little too talkative. She never should have mentioned our name. And of course David was waiting to collect her from the Iron Kettle and bring her here. He couldn't help noticing such an obvious candidate as Martin.'

'Who's David?' Charlie demanded.

'The one you call the dwarf. David was a Devotee, too; but at the very height of his initiation, he decided that he could no longer continue. It was impossible for him to return to the outside world, of course; but to atone for his lack of faith he acts as our gofer. His punishment for doubting the reality of heaven is the lifelong humiliation of having to live in that part of his body which he denied to the Lord.'

'And Velma? You got me involved with Velma deliberately, didn't you, so that Martin would have time to escape?'

'Nobody obliged you to get involved with Velma, Mr McLean. You did it of your own free will. You put the beastly desires of the flesh before your spiritual involvement with your son, and that is why he left you. If you had stayed with him that night, then the chances are that you could have convinced him that you are not the man he perceives you to be. You might have won his heart for ever. As it is . . . he is here now, and he is preparing himself for a physical and spiritual journey whose end is glory.'

'Take me to him, now,' said Charlie. 'This is your last warning.'

'He has no wish to see you.'

'I don't give a damn. He's my son, he's a minor, and I'm

legally responsible for him. I'm taking him away with me, and what's more I'm going to make sure your ass is thrown straight into jail, for kidnap, and unlawful imprisonment, and unnatural practices, and anything else that the law can throw at you.'

M. Musette laughed out loud. 'Very well, you can see him if you want to. What else can I do, but bow to such a terrifying threat? Let me call my wife, she will take you.'

He went across to a rococo-styled telephone and picked it up. 'Aimée, this is Edouard. Yes, that's correct. I have Mr McLean with me, and Mr McLean is anxious to see Martin before he leaves.'

M. Musette's familiar use of Martin's Christian name was not lost on Charlie. Nor was the implication that Charlie would be leaving alone.

'My wife will be with you directly,' said M. Musette. 'I hope very much that you will not be excessively angry with us, my dear sir. Our beliefs are deeply rooted, and tenaciously held, but we always do our very best to live in peace with those who do not revere the body and blood in the same way that we do.'

He opened his case and took out another cigarette. Charlie watched him in fascination and loathing. M. Musette seemed so single-minded, his view of the world seemed so complete; and Charlie felt that M. Musette had tipped open *his* brain like a worn out carpetbag cluttered with fear and prejudice and stubborn odds and ends. M. Musette lit his cigarette placidly, and returned Charlie's grim stare with the most courteous of smiles.

After a minute or two, the doors opened, and Mme Musette stepped into the room. Charlie had been right. She was indeed the beautiful fingerless woman in the black cloak. Now, however, she was wearing a watered silk day dress in misty blue, and she looked even more beautiful than before. Her eyes were startlingly wide; her skin glowed; her lips were infinitesimally parted in unconscious sensuality. All that betrayed her involvement with the Célèstines was the gloves she wore: wrist-length cotton gloves in blue to match her dress.

'Mr McLean,' she said softly, and inclined her head. 'Our security people have found your car. If you will let me have the keys, they will return it to the front entrance for you, so that you may leave here in comfort.'

Charlie reached into his pocket and handed over his keys. 'Just don't be too anxious to get rid of me, Mme Musette. I'm not leaving here without my son.'

'Well, we shall see,' she said. 'Would you care to come with me? Your son is upstairs, where all our new Devotees stay.'

'Please,' said M. Musette, and indicated with a smart click of his heels that Charlie should follow his wife.

Mme Musette led Charlie across the echoing marble-clad hallway. A thin youth with close-cropped hair and a suit that looked as if it had once belonged to Buddy Holly stood at the foot of the stairs. Mme Musette handed him Charlie's car keys. The youth gave Charlie a quick, insolent smile that Mme Musette either failed to notice or ignored.

She mounted the stairs and Charlie followed close behind her, smelling her perfume. He couldn't identify it. It wasn't anything as modern as Obsession. It could have been Chanel No. 5, but on Mme Musette's skin it seemed to have acquired a flowery aura all her own. Halfway up the stairs, Charlie said, 'Are you a Devotee, too?'

'I was; but Edouard decided that I could better serve the order if I were to assist him.'

'So you stopped at a few fingers, is that it?'

Mme Musette turned her head and glanced at him. 'That's it. You have it exactly.'

'Are you all headcases or what?' Charlie asked her.

'I don't know what you mean, headcases.'

'I mean are you mad? In my book, self-mutilation is the act of a lunatic. As for eating yourself, that's so far out I don't even know where it is.'

'Didn't Edouard explain our beliefs to you?'

'Oh, yes, sure he did. But I notice that Edouard hasn't started making himself into Edouardburger yet, whatever he says about his beliefs. And he stopped you before you got to the best bits.'

'You cannot make sport of us, Mr McLean,' she replied. 'Edouard is our Supreme Guide, and like all of the Guides in the Célèstine order it is his duty to remain whole until the end of his natural life. It is a *duty* – not a privilege. The truly privileged members of the Célèstines are those who manage to devour so much of themselves that there is scarcely anything remaining to make a meal for their mentors.'

They had reached the landing. Charlie said, 'You know something? If any of this is true, it's criminal and it's maniacal and it's totally disgusting. I thought James Jones was nuts, but you people are unreal.'

'Come see your son,' said Mme Musette gently. 'But may I warn you not to upset him? He is in the early stages of self-preparation, and if you try to bully him into leaving Le Reposoir you may cause him lasting psychological damage. You will certainly lose his affection for ever.'

'Don't let's make any mistakes here,' said Charlie. 'That boy is coming away with me right now.' He was angry; but he still wished that he didn't sound so much like Archie Bunker. The Musettes were bringing out his blue-collar Indiana background and there was nothing that he could do to stop it.

They walked down the same corridor to which Velma had taken him, all the way down to a door at the end. Mme Musette raised her deformed hand and knocked. There was a short delay, and then the door opened and a girl's face appeared. Dark, Latin-looking, with unplucked eyebrows.

'This is Martin's father,' said Mme Musette. 'He wishes to speak to Martin before he leaves.'

The Latin-looking girl glanced quickly at Charlie and then shook her head. 'It is not possible, *madame*. He is already preparing himself.'

Charlie stepped forward and pushed the door. 'Come on, honey, just get out of the way will you? I want to talk to my son.'

The girl tried to resist him, but Charlie gave her a sharp dig in the breast with his elbow, and she released her hold on the door. Mme Musette cried, 'No, Mr McLean!' but Charlie ignored her and barged into the room.

A white cotton blind had been drawn across the window, so the room was dim. There was a plain bed, covered by a white cotton sheet, a tubular steel chair, a white-painted bedside cupboard with a Bible on it, and that was all. Martin lay on the bed staring at the ceiling. He was naked.

'Martin! For Christ's sake!' said Charlie, and his eyes filled with tears. 'Martin, it's Dad here!'

He went up to the bed and took hold of Martin's hand. Martin's eyes slowly turned to look at him as if he had all the time in the world. 'You came,' he whispered. His voice sounded as if he were drugged.

'Of course I came. What did you expect? Why didn't you talk to me before you left? You didn't have to come to a place like this.'

Martin smiled. 'This is the only place, Dad. This is really and truly the only place.'

'Martin?' Charlie asked. 'Did they give you any kind of injection? Any pills, or dope, or anything like that?' Before Martin could reply, he turned around to Mme Musette, who was standing in the open doorway and he waved his finger at her threateningly. 'Believe me, lady, you're in deep trouble. Where are his clothes?'

'He has renounced his clothes,' said the Latin-looking girl.

'I'll renounce you in a minute!' Charlie roared at her. 'Just bring me his fucking clothes!'

'Mr McLean,' put in Mme Musette, 'I did warn you that it would do you no good to lose your temper.'

Charlie ignored her. 'Martin,' he said, 'you're coming with

me, and you're coming now. The car's outside. You can put on something of mine.'

'I'm not coming with you, Dad,' said Martin. He seemed to be completely unperturbed.

'Am I hearing you straight? Do you know what these people expect you to do?'

'I know all about the Célèstines, David told me. That day in the parking lot; and that night at Mrs Kemp's. We talked about it for hours. I know what they do and I know why they do it and I want to do it, too.'

'You want to eat yourself? Are you bananas?'

The absurdity of what his father had said made Martin chuckle. It was that chuckle that unsettled Charlie more than anything else. His own son could lie here and laugh because he had said something stupid; when all the time he was volunteering to commit suicide, slowly and ritualistically and obscenely.

Charlie grabbed hold of Martin's wrists and tried to wrench him off the bed. But Martin twisted away from him, and kicked him in the ribs with his bare foot, and then seized the rails at the head of the bed and glared at Charlie defiantly.

'Dad, this is my life and this is my decision.'

Charlie turned on Mme Musette again. 'You've hypnotized him, right? Is that it? Am I right? You've hypnotized him!'

Mme Musette was holding the hand of the Latin-looking girl in order to restrain her. The girl was obviously distressed, and kept tugging at her hair and mewling. 'There is no question of drugs or hypnosis or any artificial stimulant,' Mme Musette said. 'We believe in the sanctity of the body, we believe in its purity. We would never allow anything to taint the flesh which we ourselves must eat.'

'Martin, come with me!' Charlie ordered him, but Martin's hands remained clenched on the rails at the head of the bed, and he shook his head in adamant refusal.

Charlie took a deep breath. He looked at his son and could

see by the expression on his face that, for now, the Musettes had won. He couldn't pick Martin up bodily and carry him out of Le Reposoir, he simply wasn't strong enough. And that was supposing M. Musette and his staff would allow him to carry Martin out of the house without any opposition at all.

'All right,' he conceded. 'I'm going to leave you for now. But let me tell you right here and now that the first stop I'm going to be making is the county sheriff's office, and if necessary I'm going to inform the FBI, too. Then we'll see who makes a meal out of whom.'

Charlie contemptuously brushed Mme Musette aside and began stalking back down the corridor. 'Mr McLean!' she called after him. 'It won't do you any good!'

'I'll let the sheriff be the judge of that,' Charlie retorted. 'And one more thing – if Martin is missing even one fingernail by the time I get back here, I'm personally going to take the law into my own hands and I'm going to kill you. You and your husband both – slowly!'

He ran down the stairs, across the hallway, and out of the huge front doors. As promised, his car was waiting for him, with its hood dented and clumps of grass still clinging to its wheel-arches. He cantered down the stone steps and across the gravel, and as he did so a flock of ravens rose cawing from the spires of Le Reposoir, the first birds that he had heard since he trespassed here. They sounded harsh and triumphant, and they circled around and around above his head as if they were gloating over his defeat.

He got into the car, slammed the door, and switched on the engine. As he did so, Mme Musette came down the front steps of the house after him. She stopped only a few feet away, and Charlie let down his window.

'I'm going straight to the police,' he warned her.

'I know that,' she replied. 'It will do you no good.'

'Maybe it will and maybe it won't.'

'Don't you think every parent who finds out that their son

or daughter has come to join the Célèstines feels the same way?'

'Every parent?' For some reason the thought that he might just be one worried father out of a thousand hadn't occurred to him.

'Of course. Parents always have their own ideas about how they wish their children to be brought up, both morally and spiritually. But they must understand that their children are not their property; that their children are entitled to pursue happiness in any way they wish. The Rev Moon and his followers were regarded with the same suspicion as the Célèstines. Many parents tried desperate measures to rescue their children from Moonie settlements, and to persuade them never to return. But most did; and those who didn't were unhappy for the rest of their lives. Remember, Mr McLean, your son came to the Célèstines of his own free will. You will never get him back now. Physically, perhaps – although that is unlikely. But never, never, spiritually. You have lost him now, for ever.'

Charlie stared at Mme Musette with a ferocity that he had never experienced in his whole life. Then he said, vehemently, 'Fuck you,' and drove off up the gravelled driveway with his tyres spinning and the rear end of his Oldsmobile snaking from side to side.

CHAPTER ELEVEN

He found the Sheriff much more quickly than he had expected. There had been a traffic accident on the steeply sloping road to Allen's Corners. An elderly farmer in a station wagon had tried to overtake a slow-moving delivery truck on a blind bend, and collided head-on with another car coming the opposite way. The road surface was mushy with blood and broken glass, and the damaged cars were being towed away like injured dinosaurs.

The sheriff was standing by the side of the road with his hands on his hips as if he found the stupidity of his fellow men impossible to believe. He was short and sandy-haired, with a big curving belly in front and a big curving bottom behind. He wore designer sunglasses that didn't suit him at all. Not far away, the deputy who Charlie had first met when he drove into Allen's Corners was taking down an eye-witness statement from a highway worker who had been clearing out ditches only fifty yards away from the smash.

Charlie parked his car on the grassy verge and climbed out. The sheriff turned to him as he approached, then leaned sideways a little so that he could see past him to his car.

'This is an accident here, fellow,' he told Charlie, in a voice made harsh by smoking and Connecticut winters. 'You're going to have to move that vehicle out of here.'

'I was coming to your office,' Charile told him. 'I have a serious crime to report.'

Somehow, out here by the roadside, Charlie thought that his words sounded weak and unreal. The sheriff gave a short, hammering cough, and eyed Charlie through his green-tinted lenses as if he wasn't sure whether to shout at him or hit him.

'What nature of serious crime?' he inquired.

'Kidnap, maybe worse,' said Charlie.

The sheriff asked, 'Where? And when? And who got kidnapped?'

'It happened last night. My fifteen-year-old son Martin was abducted from the Windsor Hotel at West Hartford.'

'Outside of my jurisdiction,' said the sheriff. 'You should of reported it in West Hartford.'

'But they brought him here.'

'Who brought him here? You mean you know who did it?'

'M. and Mme Musette, at Le Reposoir, back on the Quassapaug Road. I saw him there not more than ten minutes ago.'

The sheriff said, 'Hold on, now. You've seen him *since* this alleged kidnap took place?'

'That's correct. I tried to get him away, but I couldn't.'

The Sheriff looked thoughtful. Then he called to his deputy, 'Clive! You want to wrap this up? I have to talk to this gentleman here for a while.'

Clive came over with his thumbs in his belt. 'How do you do,' he greeted Charlie. Then he said to the sheriff, 'This is the gentleman who parked in Mr Haxalt's space the other day.'

The sheriff said, 'Sounds like you're the kind of man who likes to live dangerously.'

'Where can we talk?' asked Charlie.

'You'd better follow me back to my office. You and I have got some discussing to do.'

The sheriff eased his bulky bottom into his car, and drove off, with Charlie following close behind. His office was catercorner from the church, overlooking the sloping green at Allen's Corners. He parked in a space marked 'Sheriff' and Charlie parked beside him in a space marked 'Coroner'.

'You sure do like to live dangerously,' the sheriff remarked, indicating the slot in which Charlie had parked. 'Our county coroner has a rare temper.'

'I'm not in the mood for worrying about people's private parking spaces,' said Charlie.

The sheriff grasped his shoulder. 'I know you're not. Just trying to lighten the atmosphere a little. Come on in. Maybe you'd care for some coffee.'

Charlie sat in the sheriff's office under a tired-looking flag and a crest with the Connecticut state motto, *Qui Transtulit Sustinet*. There was also a comprehensive selection of colour photographs of the current sheriff shaking hands with almost everybody from Ronald Reagan to Jimmy Breslin. The sheriff sent his work-worn, bespectacled secretary to bring them two Styrofoam cups of what turned out to be remarkably good coffee. Then he kicked the door closed, and settled himself down behind his desk.

'You'd better give me some of the salient facts,' he said. 'Your boy's age, description, what he was wearing, all that kind of thing. You'd better tell me how it happened, too.'

'But I know where he is,' Charlie insisted.

The sheriff pulled a tight face. 'Sure you know where he is. The difficulty is, if he's staying with those people voluntarily, we're not in any kind of a position to go crashing in there with all guns blazing to rescue him.'

'He's a minor. Don't tell me that you can't get a warrant to go in and get him. Listen – I can prove that his life is in danger. Do you know anything about those people at all? Do you know what they're *doing* in that place?'

'Well, sir, as a matter of fact I do.'

'You know about the rituals?'

The sheriff nodded, squashing his double chins like an accordion bellows.

'And you've been content to sit here and let them get on with it? For Christ's sake, sheriff, they're cannibals! They're worse than cannibals! They're actually persuading young people to hack themselves to pieces and eat their own bodies!'

'Yes,' said the sheriff.

'*Yes?*' Charlie exploded. 'Is that all you can say? *Yes?* I'm talking about my only son, sheriff. My boy is lying on a bed in that place stark naked and preparing himself to do God alone knows what. He's probably going to cut off his own fingers and eat them. Or worse.'

The sheriff sipped his coffee and then set it back on his desk. 'Whatever I'm going to say to you now, Mr McLean, you're going to feel that it falls far short of the kind of response you've been expecting from the law on this matter. But there are what you might call ramifications.'

'I don't see how any ramifications can allow the law to turn a blind eye while my son is allowed to remain in the hands of people like that.'

The sheriff said, 'The problem is, the law and the ramifications are kind of tied up together. You see, those Célèstine people used to be nothing much more than a small secret society, maybe twenty or thirty people, no more than that, centred on New Orleans. They were two separate bodies in those days, the same way that the Irish Republican movement is split up into the IRA, which is technically illegal, and the political wing, Sinn Fein, which is technically legal, although who knows where one begins and the other ends? You understand me? The Célèstines in New Orleans were divided between their religious order, which was recognized as an official religious body, and their secret society of flesh-eaters. In those days, the flesh-eating side was kept totally under cover. Several FBI agents tried to penetrate it and couldn't. All the law-enforcement agencies knew that it was going on, but there was no way of proving it. The *National Enquirer* printed a story about it, and all that happened was nobody believed it and the Célèstine Order successfully sued them for four and a half million dollars.'

Confused, Charlie said, 'What are you trying to tell me?'

'I'm trying to tell you that for years the Célèstines had to carry on this cannibalism business in total, one hundred per cent secrecy. Their people used to walk the streets of New Orleans. They'd meet up with young, disaffected runaways, get to talking to them, then introduce them to the legitimate side of their religion. When they were sure that they weren't dealing with undercover cops masquerading as runaways, they'd introduce them to the other side of what they were doing. One secret FBI report estimated that between 1955 and 1965, more that eighteen per cent of all young people who went permanently missing in the New Orleans area became Célèstine followers, and finished up as their own Last Supper.'

'If the FBI knew all this, why didn't they stop it?' Charlie asked.

'They almost did, more than one time. But the Célèstines had first-class lawyers, and since nobody could prove kidnap, abduction, imprisonment, or any criminal act either local or federal, they had to let them go. There is no law in any state which says that it is a criminal offence to devour yourself; nor is it an offence to offer parts of yourself to other people for no charge for whatever purpose they may care to put it. I guess the legislators just didn't envisage anybody wanting to do things like that.'

'But people who want to eat themselves must be mentally incompetent,' said Charlie. 'Surely somebody tried to put a stop to the Célèstines with mental health legislation.'

'Oh sure. There was a test case put before the Louisiana Supreme Court on 11 May 1967. It was held in camera, so it never got reported. They called expert witnesses to testify as to the sanity of a nineteen-year-old girl who had eaten both of her arms. They had psychiatrists, priests, social workers, theologians, anthropologists, the whole cast of thousands. Not one of them could tell the court with any conviction that the girl was nuts. She had mutilated herself for an explicable religious reason, in accordance with the teaching of a recognized church. Her lawyer pointed out that millions of young boys all over the world are mutilated every year – circumcised, that is – for religious reasons that are far less profound that those embraced by the Célèstines. The case for committal to a mental institution was dismissed, and the girl went back to New Orleans and ate the rest of herself.'

'Is that why they're so brazen about what they're doing?' said Charlie.

The sheriff nodded. 'That's part of the reason. They know now that anybody who tries to challenge them in the courts is going to have a real difficult time – apart from attracting all kinds of very unwelcome publicity. Women don't like to tell the police they've been raped; you think parents like to come along and admit that their children have been eating themselves?'

'What's the other part of the reason?'

'The other part of the reason is that the daughter of a very senior member of the United States government died two years ago at a Célèstine house in South Carolina. The scandal would have been a doozy, believe me. The FBI undertook a six-month covert investigation and found out that the sons and daughters of countless socialite, celebrity and big-business families were also Célèstine Devotees. Worse than that, at least four top-ranking politicians and at least two members of the Joint Chiefs of Staff were involved. Several of them were Guides. Do you know about Guides?'

Charlie nodded numbly.

The sheriff sucked up some more coffee. It was too hot to drink without making a lot of noise. 'The government decided that so long as the Célèstines never actually committed any illegal acts, they were to be left alone. They have what you might call diplomatic immunity. It's national legislative policy, my friend, all the way down from the Oval Office to yours truly, the sheriff of Litchfield County.'

'Why are you telling me all this?' asked Charlie. 'If it isn't true, I'm bound to find out that it isn't. If it *is*, then I would have thought that it wasn't the kind of story you would want to spread around.'

The sheriff shook his head. 'I have a very good reason for telling you, and that reason is that right now you're feeling mad. You want the law to go busting in to Le Reposoir and rescue your son, Rambo-style. And if the law won't do it for you, then by God you're going to take the law into your own hands and do it yourself. Am I right? Am I reading you right?'

'How would you feel, in my position?' Charlie asked him.

'My friend,' said the sheriff, 'I *was* in your position. My own daughter of twenty-one years old was one of the first Célèstine recruits around here, and believe me I did everything I could to get her out of there. I got hold of a search warrant, and I went through that building like you wouldn't believe. And I found her; and do you know what she'd done? She'd already cut off her own hand.'

He stared intently at Charlie just to make sure he wasn't missing the point of what he was saying. Just to make sure that Charlie didn't believe that he was the only father in the world who had ever been through agony and doubt and grief because of the Célèstines.

'Let me tell you something,' he went on, and his voice was as soft as tissue now. 'I sat down by my little girl's bed and I pleaded with her to come home with me before she hurt herself more. And do you know what she did? She touched me with her one hand, and she smiled at me, she *smiled*, and she said, "Daddy, for the very first time in my life I'm truly happy." That's what she said.'

The sheriff paused. He obviously found this bitterly painful to remember. 'That was when I used my authority, or rather my gun. I took my little girl and I got her out of that place by force. They didn't try to stop me, they just smiled at me the same way that my little girl had smiled at me, and they said, "See you later, Susan," – that was my little girl's name. I'll never forget to my dying day the way they said that. They were so fucking cheerful.

'Susan came home for two and a half weeks. That was as long as I could persuade her to stay. You don't know what those two and a half weeks were like. She was so depressed I had to take her to the doctor and the doctor put her on tranquillizers. By the end of the second week things were so bad she was begging me to let her go back there. Do you know what she said? She said that what the Célèstines were doing was showing her the way to heaven, and that even if I kept her chained up to her bed for the rest of her life, she would never be happy in this physical, material world that the rest of us have to endure. That's just what she said. "I've broken free," she told me. "Free of any kind of physical need. All that's holding me back now is my earthly body, and I'm going to eat that."'

The sheriff ran his hand through his scrubby red hair and said, 'Jesus! How do you cope when your daughter tells you something like that?'

'What did you do?' Charlie asked him, in a haunted voice.

'I didn't do anything, except to make sure that Susan was handcuffed to her bed every night. Then one morning we woke up and she was gone. She had bitten away all the flesh around her hand and wrist so that she could get out of the handcuff. The pillow was plastered in blood and bits of flesh. I knew then that I was never going to get her back. Those Célèstines had won her over and that was it.'

'Didn't you take it any further?'

'Oh sure. I took it all the way to Hartford. But in the end I was quietly taken aside and told to lay off. That's when I found out everything that I've just told you. I made one last effort and took the story to the media, and I found one reporter on the *Hartford Courant* who was prepared to take a risk. But after about a week he called me back and said the story wouldn't stand up and that was all there was to it.'

Charlie looked at the sheriff coldly. 'So what you're telling me is that I have to accept Martin's kidnap – I have to accept the fact that those people are going to persuade him to eat himself alive – because of some national conspiracy of silence?'

The sheriff said, 'That's part of the story, sure. But the other part – the real important part – is that no kid goes to that place unless they want to. I found that part the hardest of all to accept, when Susan went. She *wanted* to go.'

'Did you ever get to see her again?'

'Yes.' The sheriff nodded. 'Just once. I went up to Le Reposoir against the specific instructions of my superiors and I forced them at gunpoint to let me see her. They were so damned polite they gave me the creeps. I mean, they were even *humorous* about it. They took me into the room and there she was, or what was left of her. I wish to God that I'd never gone. Did you ever see that old movie *Freaks*? There's a guy in it who's just a head and a kind of a caterpillar body in a cotton sock? Did you ever see that? Well, that's what Susan was like. I never knew that anybody could lose so much of their body and still live. There was her face, that same face I loved so much, still with that wavy red hair, and underneath that face there was nothing at all but a body no bigger than a leg of pork, all wrapped up in a white cotton stocking.'

Charlie swallowed. His throat was dry; but he knew that if he tried to swallow any coffee he would probably gag.

The sheriff said, 'You may not believe me, but that wasn't the worst of it. The worst of it was that she lay there in the sunshine and she smiled at me and said, "Daddy", and I knew that she was completely contented. They called me about two weeks later to tell me that she was gone. I didn't say anything. I didn't trust myself. I took a week's vacation that was owing to me and I stayed drunk from Friday evening to the following Sunday night.'

'How am I going to get my son out of there?' Charlie asked him.

'I don't think you've been listening to me, my friend. Your son is there because your son *wants* to be there, and you're not going to get him out of that place without the US Marines.

'And the same thing happened to you, to your only daughter, and you just accept it?'

'Tell me what I can do about it!' the sheriff said, his jowls shaking. 'Tell me just one thing that I can do about it! Short of killing the Musettes outright, and burning the whole damned house down – and, believe me, that wouldn't help either. There are nineteen Célèstine houses in the continental United States; there are more in Eurpoe. If you burn down one, there will always be scores of others. You'd be pissing in the wind.'

Charlie stood up. He laid one hand on the sheriff's desk and looked him steadily in the eye. 'Is this what it's come to?' he said. 'The country that was founded on the principles of life and liberty?'

The sheriff gave him a defeated, sideways look. 'Sometimes the price of life and liberty is pretty high.'

'Tell me who else in Allen's Corners has lost a child.'

'Apart from Mr Haxalt, there must have been eleven or twelve. Some of them know where their children have gone, others don't.'

'Like Mrs Kemp, you mean?'

The sheriff nodded. 'We don't tell 'em if they don't find out. We don't want to cause any more distress than we have to.'

Charlie rubbed his eyes. He felt as if he were dreaming all this; but the dream was so procedural that he knew it was true. Apart from that, he couldn't wake up, no matter how hard he tried.

The sheriff said, 'I'll tell you what I'll do. I'll go on up to Le Reposoir myself, and talk to them about your son. Martin, is that what you said his name was?'

Charlie said, 'You've got to get him out of there, sheriff.'

'More parents have said that same thing to me than I like to recall.'

'I promise you – if you don't do it – then I will.'

'I can't stop you from making promises, my friend. But it's my elected duty to uphold the law, and I'm telling you right here and now that if you attempt anything in the way of aggravated assault on those people, or damage or intrude on their property, then I'm bound to give them assistance.'

Charlie said, 'What's your name, sheriff?'

'Podmore,' he replied.

'I mean your given name.'

'What do you want to know that for? It's Norman, as a matter of fact.'

Charlie said, 'I want to be able to say to you, "Norman, this is Charlie. You've lost your daughter, I'm in danger of losing my son." I want you to think about that, Norman, what that means. And you tell me something else, Norman. That boy's mother doesn't know what's happened yet. You tell me what I'm supposed to say to *her*.'

CHAPTER TWELVE

Grey-faced with rage and frustration, Charlie drove back up the corkscrew road to Le Reposoir, the tyres of his Oldsmobile howling and squittering on the blacktop. He swerved into the entrance and collided at nearly ten miles an hour with the front gate, with a noise like the gates of hell being clanged shut. Two or three of the gate's iron uprights were bent, but the locks held, and all Charlie ended up with was mild whip-lash and two shattered headlights.

He climbed out of the car and stabbed furiously at the intercom button. M. Musette – who must have inspected the damage to his gates through his closed-circuit television camera – answered almost immediately.

'Mr McLean, what can I do for you? You seem to have suffered an accident.'

'Open up,' Charlie demanded. 'I want my son back.'

'Mr McLean, you know as well as I do that your son wishes to remain here.'

'I don't give a shit, Monsewer Musette. I want my son back and I want him back now.'

'Do you always treat your son's wishes with such contempt?'

Charlie yelled, 'Don't you start getting fancy with me, you Goddamn cannibal! Now open up, and give me my son back!'

'I'm sorry, that's impossible. If your son has a change of heart, then obviously I shall be glad to let you know. But at the moment he is very happy where he is. Why don't you talk to the sheriff?'

Charlie said, with more control, 'I already did that, thank you.'

'I hope he was sympathetic.'

'Yes, he was. Yes, he was sympathetic. That's all that anybody seems to be good for, around here: being sympathetic.'

'Well, I quite understand your feelings, my dear sir. You don't want sympathy, do you? You want your son's affection.'

'I'll worry about his affection when I get hold of him again.'

'He's not a dog, *monsieur*. He's an intelligent human being – quite capable of making his own decisions.'

'And what are you?' Charlie wanted to know.

The intercom clicked once, and then remained silent. Charlie returned to his car, started the engine, slammed into reverse, then back into drive and collided again as hard as he could with the gates. Then he backed up and crashed into the gates a third time, and then a fourth, until he could hear his radiator fan clattering against its cover, and a grinding sound in the transmission like a Cuisinart full of broken glass.

He sat in his car and screamed at the gates of Le Reposoir in helpless rage. Then he crossed his arms over his steering wheel and bent his head forward and sobbed. He stayed like that for almost a quarter of an hour, while the emotionless eye of the remote-control camera watched him from the trees.

Eventually, he sat up and dug out a crumpled handkerchief and wiped his face. It was clear to him now that a frontal assault on the Célestines was not going to work. Nor was any appeal to the police, or to the media. The Célestines had won for themselves the kind of charmed lives that only true fanatics seem to be able to achieve. If he wanted to get Martin out of Le Reposoir, he was going to have to do it alone. What's more, he was going to have to make sure that his plan was properly thought out. Martin would have to be taken someplace secure, where it would be impossible for him to escape and return to the Célestines. And there was no doubt that he would need deprogramming, either by a psychiatrist or by one of those people who made it their business to deprogram Moonies and other adolescent victims of obsessional cults.

It was very hard for him, but he reversed his car away from the entrance to Le Reposoir and drove slowly back towards Allen's Corners with his transmission crunching and his suspension complaining at every bump. The sun, which for most of the day had been enveloping itself in hazy grey clouds, now suddenly decided to make an appearance, and it lit up the coppery fall leaves for miles around. There was a tang of woodsmoke in the air, and Charlie knew that he would never be able to come up to Connecticut again, in fall, whether he was able to rescue Martin or not. It would always remind him of mutilation, and self-inflicted pain, and the Célestines.

He returned to Mrs Kemp's. Mrs Kemp herself was standing at her front door, almost as if she had been waiting for him; but in fact she was lifting her face to the sun. Her eyes were closed and her fists were clenched and there was an odd little smile on her face as she basked her wrinkles.

She opened her eyes as Charlie walked up the front path.

'Mr McLean,' she said.

'How are you doing, Mrs Kemp?'

'I'm enjoying this sunshine. It'll be winter before you know it. You're back soon. I didn't expect you for at least a year; if ever. Your boy not with you?'

'Martin's . . . having a break.'

'I thought you said you were taking him to Boston with you.'

'Well, I was.'

Mrs Kemp frowned at him, and touched his arm. 'Something's wrong, isn't it? I can tell.'

'Everything's fine, Mrs Kemp. I just need a place to stay for the next few days. Some place quiet, where I can think.'

He tried to step into the porch but Mrs Kemp stopped him. 'He's gone, hasn't he? Your Martin?'

'Yes, Mrs Kemp,' Charlie admitted. 'He's gone.'

'What's the matter? Did you have an argument? Did his mother come to take him back?'

Charlie shook his head. He was about to make an elaborate excuse, but then he thought, *What the hell? Mrs Kemp lost Caroline, so at least she'll understand what I'm going through. And maybe it's time she knew that Caroline hasn't gone off to live in California; nor has she been raped and murdered and her body left in some nameless ditch. It's about time the parents of all those children who have been lost to the Célèstines got themselves together and did something dramatic.* If what Sheriff Podmore had told him was true – if the government and the law refused to admit that what the Célèstines were doing was wrong; and if the television and the newspaper people did nothing but turn a blind eye – then it was time for the nation's bereaved parents to take a stand on their own.

Because if they had no other rights, as far as their children were concerned, parents at least had the right to see them live.

'Come inside,' he told Mrs Kemp. 'I want to talk to you.'

They sat together in the front parlour and Charlie told Mrs Kemp everything that had happened since he and Martin had left for West Hartford. Then he told her what Sheriff Podmore had said about Susan. He watched her carefully as he explained that Caroline had probably died in the way that all Célèstine Devotees eventually died. Her eyes betrayed no expression at all, as if somehow she had known that this had happened all along.

When Charlie had finished, she stood up and walked with mechanical steps to the bureau. 'I think you and I had better have a drink,' she said. 'I still have some Chivas Regal left, from the time that Jerry Kogan used to stay here. Everybody used to say, "Do you know Jerry? He's in alcohol."'

'Thanks,' said Charlie. He watched in silence as Mrs Kemp poured them each a hefty three fingers of whisky. Mrs Kemp raised her glass and said, 'To the ones we love. In memory, and in hope.'

Charlie said, with a catch in his throat, 'To the ones we love,' and drank.

They shared another drink, and then Mrs Kemp said that she had to go to the market to buy supplies for supper if Charlie was going to be staying. Charlie opened up the sagging doors of her garage for her, and backed out her old tan Buick wagon. He stood at the front door and watched her as she drove off in a cloud of oily smoke on her way to the shopping mall. Then he stepped back into the airless house, and went up to the room in which he had slept only two nights ago with Martin. He knew now that he had lost Martin then, after the dwarf-like David had talked to him. If only he could go back forty-eight hours in time; to that fateful instant when Harriet had let slip the name of Le Reposoir, the resting place, the little altar.

On impulse he wrestled the Connecticut telephone directory out of the bedside cupboard, and looked up the *Litchfield Sentinel*. With the directory balanced on his knees he dialled the number and waited while the call tone purred. After a long while, a young woman's voice said, '*Sentinel?* If you want advertising I'm afraid they're gone for the day.'

'I wanted the editor,' said Charlie.

'Oh, well, I'm sorry, he's not here, either. There's a big business meeting in Danbury.'

'In that case, forget it. I'm sorry I troubled you.'

'Is it news?' the young woman asked him. 'I'm a reporter. I can take your story if that's what you want.'

'I'm sorry, I really wanted to speak to the editor.'

'Okay, have it your way. He'll be back in the morning. You're sure I can't help?'

Charlie lowered the directory on to the floor. 'I don't know, maybe you can. My son's gone missing in pretty unusual circumstances. I thought it might help if I could locate other parents whose children have gone missing.'

'Well, that's incredible,' the woman told him. 'That's exactly the story that I've been working on. You know the *Denver Post* won a Pulitzer Prize for their investigations into the missing children statistics; well, I've been assigned to do a follow-up, because we've had so many kids missing in Connecticut lately.'

'Do you know any other parents who have lost their kids, apart from me?' asked Charlie.

'Sure I do, dozens. The number of children who have gone missing in the Litchfield area in the past five months is way up – forty-two per cent higher than it was for the comparable period last year, and seventy-eight per cent higher than it was the year before.'

'And the police keep telling you it isn't a problem – just like the *Denver Post* won that Pulitzer Prize for saying it wasn't a problem.'

'That's right,' said the young woman. 'How did you know that?'

Charlie said, 'For once in my life I seem to have gotten lucky. My name's Charlie McLean, and I think that you and I ought to meet.'

'Well, sure thing. My name's Robyn Harris. Where are you calling me from?'

'Allen's Corners, but I don't want to meet you at Allen's Corners. Do you know a restaurant in Watertown called the Loving Doves? How about meeting me there at six-thirty? I'll book a table in the name of Gunn.'

'Gunn?'

'You know, like Ben Gunn, who was marooned on Treasure Island. You won't miss me, I'm forty-one years old and I look like I've spent my life driving from coast to coast and back again.'

'All right, Mr McLean. You're on. I look forward to meeting you.'

Charlie called the restaurant and made the reservation, then cradled the phone and sat for a while in thought. He wasn't at all sure that he was doing the right thing, in talking to the Press, but if he was careful he might be able to use Ms Robyn

Harris to make contact with other parents; and then there was a possibility of concerted action – something to bring the Célèstines to the attention of ordinary people, and to quarantine them for ever, if not kill them off.

As far as Charlie was concerned, the Célèstines weren't a religion, they were a disease. They were nothing better than a spiritual form of AIDS.

He eased off his shoes, then peeled off his socks. The day's tension had made him feel sweaty and sticky, and he needed a shower. As he stood under Mrs Kemp's rattling brass shower faucet, he tried to work out a plan for snatching Martin out of Le Reposoir, and getting him clean away. He made himself assume that Martin wouldn't have started eating himself already. His mind couldn't cope with the idea that he might already have cut off his own fingers or his own toes, and swallowed them.

He recognized that he was going to need help, if only to drag Martin physically out of the building. A man would be preferable, but a woman would do if she were determined enough.

He also recognized, reluctantly, that he was going to need a gun. Even though Sheriff Podmore had told him that the Musettes had made no effort to stop him when he had rescued his daughter, it was obvious that Le Reposoir had at least two security staff and probably more.

He would need a third person, too – somebody who was not necessarily involved in breaking into the building and heisting Martin out, but a getaway driver who was waiting to speed them out of trouble and take them to the nearest airport.

Because that was the last essential. There had to be air tickets ready. First, a flight to somewhere within the continental United States, because Martin hadn't brought his passport with him, then a car or a boat ride to Mexico.

After that, exile for both of them, for a while at least, while Martin was deprogrammed, and while Charlie tried to find another way of making a living.

Charlie stepped out of the shower and towelled himself with one of the rough, cheap towels that Mrs Kemp had left folded on the hot pipe. He knotted the towel around his waist and walked across the landing to his room. He heard the front door open and shut again, and leaned over the banisters and called, 'Mrs Kemp? That you?'

Mrs Kemp looked up. She was standing in the hallway looking peculiarly wild-eyed, her hair dishevelled and a button hanging off her coat. She carried no shopping.

'Mrs Kemp?' asked Charlie. 'Is there something wrong?'

'It's all right,' she said, tugging her coat tightly around herself. 'I'm fine. I'll go fix you something to eat.'

'Did you go to the market?'

'I . . . forgot.'

Charlie looked at her sharply. 'What's wrong, Mrs Kemp? Where have you been?'

But Mrs Kemp disappeared into her kitchen without answering; and Charlie heard the door slam behind her as an unequivocal warning that she did not want to be followed.

Charlie waited for a moment, then shrugged to himself, and went to his room to get dressed. He watched his face in the mirror on top of the bureau. He looked tired, and there was a look in his eyes which he had never seen before. Wounded, but determined. The look of a man who wants revenge.

He was tying up his shoelaces when he heard the scuffing of tyres outside in the street. A moment later, there was a ring at the doorbell. Then another ring. He finished tying his shoelace and went out to the landing. 'Mrs Kemp?' he called, but there was no reply. The doorbell rang again and so he went downstairs to answer it.

It was Sheriff Podmore, and he didn't look pleased. He pushed the door open wide and stepped into the hallway without being invited. 'What did you tell her?' he demanded.

'I don't know what you're talking about,' said Charlie.

161

'Don't play the stiff with me, my friend. You told Mrs Kemp what happened to Caroline, didn't you?'

'So what if I did? She has a right to know.'

'Jesus, McLean, what kind of a cretin are you? The reason I didn't tell her before was because she doesn't have the mental strength to accept anything like that. At least she used to have hope that Caroline might still be alive. Don't you understand that? Until they know what's happened to their children for sure, all parents believe that they may still be alive. Hence the great myth about them all running off to California to become go-go dancers or whatever. One per cent of one hundred per cent stay away for good. One per cent of that one per cent make a living as exotic dancers or porno stars. The rest of them get killed, one way or another; or else they end up as Célèstines and kill themselves.'

Charlie said, 'I still think she has a right to know.'

'Is she here?' Sheriff Podmore asked him.

'She just came in. She's in the kitchen.'

Sheriff Podmore stomped down to the end of the hallway and rattled the door handle. 'Ida!' he shouted. 'You in there?'

'Go away!' Mrs Kemp shouted back. 'You lied to me, Norman, I don't want to see you and I don't want to talk to you ever again!'

'Ida, will you be reasonable?' said Sheriff Podmore.

'Go away! I don't want to be reasonable!'

Sheriff Podmore waited outside the kitchen door a little longer and then came sashaying back down the hallway again, all belly and gunbelt. He lifted his hat to adjust it, and said to Charlie. 'You know what she did?'

'I have the distinct feeling that you're going to tell me.'

'She came down to the sheriff's office while I was out and she ripped the place apart. Broke the windows, emptied out the file cabinets, and then she wrote 'Norman Podmore Child-killer' on my wall. So, what do you think about that?'

'I think maybe you deserved it,' said Charlie, in a level tone.

Sheriff Podmore looked at Charlie thoughtfully. 'I hope you're not thinking of causing me any trouble,' he said.

'You'll soon find out if I am.'

Sheriff Podmore jerked his thumb back toward the kitchen. 'All I'm asking you to do is keep your eye on her. She's pretty overwrought. There's no knowing what she might do.'

Charlie opened the front door. 'I think you'd better leave,' he told the sheriff.

At that moment, however, the kitchen door opened and Mrs Kemp appeared, 'Norman!' she screeched. The sheriff turned around. 'Norman, you be warned! This isn't going to be the end of it! I'm going to kill those people if it's the last thing I do! They took my Caroline, and I'm going to kill them!'

'Ida,' said Sheriff Podmore, 'you have to know that it's illegal to make threats against people's lives.'

'And it's not illegal to let people slaughter your children, is that it?' Mrs Kemp shrieked at him.

'Ida, you take care.' Sheriff Podmore turned to Charlie again. 'I'm just telling you, my friend, anything happens here and I'll hold *you* responsible.'

Charlie said nothing, but let the sheriff out and stood by the door as he walked down the path. Mrs Kemp stayed where she was, wringing her hands. Her cheeks were running with tears. Charlie said, 'I'm sorry, Mrs Kemp. It looks like I made a mistake.'

'No, you didn't,' she said shakily. 'You were right to tell me. Up until now, I've been feeling grief, but there was no way of telling if I had anything to grieve about. I've felt angry, but I've never known who to be angry with. Now I know, and now I can do something about it.'

'You're not going to try to kill the Musettes, not really?'

'Try?' she said. 'I'm going to succeed.'

'Can I dissuade you?'

For a fleeting moment, Mrs Kemp almost smiled. 'You wouldn't *want* to dissuade me, would you? You want to see the Musettes dead just as much as I do, if not more.'

Charlie came up close and laid his hand on Mrs Kemp's shoulders. 'Can I ask you just one favour? Don't do anything without telling me first. I'm going to try to get Martin out of there before anything happens to him. If you get in there on your own, all you're going to succeed in doing is make them tighten up their security. At the moment, they're complacent. They're inside the law, however much you and I may hate them, no matter how disgusting we think they are. Let them stay complacent, huh? – at least until I've managed to get Martin out.'

Mrs Kemp reached up and touched his cheek. 'Is this a punishment, do you think, for the way we treat our children?'

Charlie tried to smile. 'Maybe. Maybe some people have a different way of looking at life and death.'

'Will you want supper?' she asked. 'I'm afraid that I didn't quite make it to the market. I got overtaken by the impulse to wreck Norman's office.'

'I'll go out to eat,' said Charlie. 'Do you think the sheriff is going to press charges against you?'

'Norman? He'd better not. I've known him since he was a big, fat, unpopular kid. He gave me cough-candy once and asked me if he could marry me. Thank God I didn't.'

Charlie spent the next half-hour straightening out his car – scraping the clumps of grass from underneath the wheel-arches and bending back the cover that protected the radiator fan. He managed to kick the front bumper reasonably straight, and fit new bulbs in the headlights. The Oldsmobile still looked as if he bought it second-hand from a family of deranged Mexicans, but at least it went along without making too much noise. The transmission was okay provided he drove in second.

He left Mrs Kemp sitting in her parlour with the last of her bottle of Chivas Regal, and drove over to Watertown. Once the sun had gone, the evening was unexpectedly cold. The Oldsmobile's climate control had been damaged, and he wished he had worn a sweater underneath his coat. It occurred to him as he drove that it was time he called Marjorie to tell her what had happened – or at least to tell her that Martin was missing – but he couldn't even begin to think of what to say.

'Marjorie, listen, we've got a problem here. Martin wants to eat himself.'

'I'm sorry, Marjorie, but Martin has decided to join a society of cannibals.'

'Marjorie –'

He arrived at the Loving Doves. It was a small self-conscious restaurant in the centre of Watertown, with gilded lettering across the facade and two gilded doves pecking at each other's beaks perched on the porch. Its style was New England *nouvelle cuisine*, if such a thing were imaginable. Perhaps its most characteristic dish was a dinner that consisted of three thin slices of brisket, four baby onions, three miniature carrots, two tiny beets, and a decoration of tenderly cooked cabbage, all laid out on a circular pool of delicate broth.

Charlie went inside. The decor was candlelight, brass, and dark green tablecloths. 'You have a six-thirty reservation for Mr Gunn,' he said. The tall, blonde waitress smiled at him as if life were still ordinary, as if restaurants still mattered, and led him across to a table in the corner. There, a young woman was waiting – a handsome young woman with long well-brushed brunette hair and wide dark eyes and big dangling earrings. She wore a fashionable suit in pale grey, with a white cotton sweater underneath it. The multi-pocketed purse slung over the back of her chair was the only give-away that here was a career woman pursuing her career.

'Mr Gunn?' she said, rising from her chair and extending her hand.

CHAPTER THIRTEEN

It was almost eleven o'clock when they left The Loving Doves. They stood in the entrance for a while, sheltering from the wind.

'What are you going to do now?' Robyn asked Charlie.

'Go back to Mrs Kemp's, I guess. I feel I have a duty to keep an eye on her.'

'You won't come back to my place for a drink? I still want to talk to you some more.'

Charlie tugged up the collar of his coat. 'I'm not sure there's any more to say. The Célèstines have got hold of my boy, and I want to get him back. End of story.'

Robyn took her spiral-bound notebook out of her pocket and leafed through it. 'I'll talk to two other parents in the morning. I may be able to get hold of one of them tonight. Then I'll talk to my editor.'

'Remember the agreement, though,' said Charlie. 'No publicity until Martin is safe. If M. Musette gets the idea that I'm going to try to break him out of there, he won't even let me through the front gate.'

Robyn closed her notebook and put it away. 'I hope I haven't been too sceptical this evening.'

'About what?'

'The whole thing. The Célèstines. It *is* pretty hard to believe.'

Charlie made a face. 'I guess the answer is that the Célèstines are absolutely no different from any other fanatical religious sect. They all have a magnetic appeal for young people, and the reason they do is because the way of life their parents lead has absolutely no appeal at all. If these sects flourish, it's our fault, the parents' fault. I mean, what have we given our children that has any spiritual value whatsoever? I'm not just talking about materialism, either. I'm talking about a lack of spirit. A lack of self-respect.'

Robyn eyed him over her red mohair scarf. 'You're talking like somebody who's been there.'

Charlie took her arm. 'Let me walk you back to your car.'

'I didn't bring my car. My photographer dropped me off. I was hoping maybe you could give me a ride. I don't live far: Waterbury.'

'What if I'd turned out to be a seventy-year-old hunchback with halitosis and axe-murderer's eyes?'

'In that case, I would have called for a taxi.'

They walked across to the parking lot under the trees. 'I was telling you the truth about driving into their gates,' Charlie remarked, pointing to the front-end damage. He helped her into the car.

'I didn't doubt that you were.'

'But you find the Célèstines difficult to believe in?'

'I accept what you're telling me, but I find it hard to accept that so many people know about it, the government, the FBI, and yet they let it carry on and nobody says a word.'

Charlie drove out toward Waterbury. 'It's nothing unusual, when you think about it. The Scientologists and the Moonies and the Masons are all run openly – to the extent that they don't try to conceal their existence. But who knows what they really do? Provided it's nothing overtly illegal, they're going to be left alone. And it's the same with the Célèstines. The media don't want to touch the story because it's too grisly and the risks of a libel action are too high. The police don't want to know because they don't believe that they'll get a successful conviction. And the government certainly isn't interested because too many people in high places have embarrassing connections with them.'

'It's such an incredible news story,' said Robyn.

Charlie made a face. 'Sure it is. But what's the story? That some psychopathic sect is encouraging our children to eat themselves in the name of the Lord? – or that this nation has such a low regard for human life that they're letting them get away with it? Do you know something, there comes a time when the principle of liberty for all has to be circumscribed. The right to bear arms is one example. I don't mind people exercising that right just so long as it doesn't intrude on *my* right to a safe existence, free from fear. And I don't challenge anybody's right to worship whatever God in whatever way they choose – except when it threatens my son's life.'

They drove into the outskirts of Waterbury, and Robyn directed Charlie to a small frame house painted white and green. There was a bronze station wagon parked in the driveway, and there were lights on in the living room window.

'You live with your parents?' Charlie asked her.

'That's right. I came back home to recuperate after a spectacularly messy love affair. My mom wants me to stay for ever, but I guess I'll be looking for my own place pretty soon. You can't be somebody's child all your life. Sooner or later you have to be yourself.'

'Maybe I won't come in,' said Charlie.

'Oh, do, they won't mind. And I do have a room of my own, kind of an office. They're very proud that their only daughter is a newspaper reporter.'

Charlie blew out his cheeks. 'Okay, then, just for a while.'

Mr and Mrs Harris were sitting in front of the television when Robyn brought Charlie into the living room. Mr Harris was skinny and unsmiling; he ran a dry-cleaning business in the centre of Waterbury and, according to Robyn, thirty years of other people's dirty clothes had permanently crippled his sense of humour. But Mrs Harris was warm and motherly and fun, and Charlie could see where Robyn had gotten her looks and her figure from. She asked them if they wanted coffee, or maybe some fresh-baked pound cake, but Robyn smiled and shook her head, and said, 'This is work, mother. W-O-R-K.'

'Still,' said Mrs Harris, beaming at Charlie as if he were a potential son-in-law. 'It's always good to meet the people that Robyn works with.'

'Oh, I don't work with her, Mrs Harris. I'm just a news story.'

'Good news, I hope?' said Mrs Harris.

'I hope it's going to turn out that way.'

Robyn took Charlie through to the small converted bedroom at the back which she called her office. It was decorated in pale beige colours, and furnished with a modern pine desk, an angular couch, and two cheese-plants in basketwork jardinières. There was a large Mucha poster on the wall, of the kind that used to be popular in the days of flower-power and 'Blowin' in the Wind'.

'Can I tempt you with a glass of wine?' asked Robyn.

'Just half a glass. I don't want a hangover tomorrow.'

Robyn took off her jacket and hung it over the back of her chair. Charlie sat down on the couch and watched her as she went across to her cupboard and took out a bottle of Stag's Leap chardonnay. Under happier circumstances, he would have been very interested in her. Her personality was incisive and bright; she had an irrepressible sense of humour; and she was very good-looking indeed. She poured out two glasses of wine and Charlie found himself wondering about her 'spectacularly messy' love affair. It seemed axiomatic that nice girls like her always got themselves involved with brutes.

'You said you might be able to contact one of the other parents tonight,' said Charlie.

'Surely. I'll give him a try.' Robyn checked through her Roladex to find the number, then picked up the phone and punched it out. 'His name's Garrett,' she said, covering the mouthpiece with her hand. 'He lost his daughter just after the Christmas holiday. She was eighteen or nineteen, if I remember rightly. She was driving through Allen's Corners to visit her brother in Bethlehem. They found her car abandoned by the side of the road.'

At that moment, the phone was picked up at the other end. Robyn waved to Charlie to pick up a second phone next to the couch, so that he could listen in.

'Hallo?' said a deep, slurred voice.

'Is this Mr Robert Garrett?' asked Robyn. 'This is Robyn Harris from the newspaper. Do you remember me? I came up to your house about four weeks ago to talk about your daughter.'

'I remember,' the voice replied, guardedly. 'What do you want?'

'Well, Mr Garrett, it seems like we may possibly have some kind of new theory about your daughter's disappearance.'

'Oh, yeah?' Still the voice was defensive.

'Mr Garrett, I was thinking today about what you told me ... the way you described your daughter's disappearance ... and I remember being puzzled.'

'What do you mean, puzzled? She disappeared, that's all. They found her car and she was gone.'

'But you said to me – here, I have it in my notebook – you said to me, "She's at peace, anyway." And – do you know something? – that isn't at all characteristic of the parents of missing children.'

There was a pause, and then the voice said, 'What in hell are you talking about? I hope you didn't call me up after eleven o'clock at night just to tell me that, because if you did – ?'

'Mr Garrett, I've been working on this story for weeks, and so far I've talked to two dozen parents of missing children. Apart from one other parent, you're the only one who hasn't shown any signs of hope whatsoever that your daughter is still alive, and you're the only one who has categorically said, "She's at peace", even though no body has been recovered and you haven't been able to give her a proper funeral.'

'What are you trying to suggest? Are you trying to suggest I killed her or something? Is that it? You're trying to say that I murdered my own daughter?'

Robyn said, 'No, sir, Mr Garrett, I am not. But what I am saying is that you know what happened to her.'

'This is bullshit,' the deep voice growled. But its owner didn't put down the phone. Charlie glanced across at Robyn and Robyn gave him a little wave of her hand which meant, *This is it, we're making headway*.

'Mr Garrett,' said Robyn, 'have you ever heard of a religious order called the Célèstines?'

Charlie kept his eyes on Robyn. From the other end of the phone, there was a silence, followed by a quick, sharp intake of breath, that was almost an admission in itself.

'Mr Garrett?' Robyn repeated. 'Did you hear what I said?'

'I heard you.'

'You know what I'm talking about, don't you? You know about the Célèstines? You know what they do, and how they do it?'

'Maybe.' The voice was on the brink either of losing its temper or bursting into tears.

'Mr Garrett, the Célèstines took your daughter, didn't they?'

There was a silence so lengthy that Charlie began to think that Mr Robert Garrett had let go of the telephone receiver and left it hanging. At last, however, the deep voice said, 'The sheriff said I wasn't to talk about it. He said it would make things worse for other runaways. They didn't want to publicize the Célèstines because other kids would get to hear about them and the last thing they wanted was an epidemic of kids joining up.'

There was another silence, and then the voice said, 'The sheriff told me that nobody could have done more. I went to the place, I talked to her, they didn't stop me talking to her, those bastards, they just stood around and smiled. She wouldn't change her mind, though. She said it was the way to heaven, for Christ's sake. The way to heaven!'

Charlie spoke for the first time. 'Mr Garrett, my name is Charlie McLean, I've been listening in.'

'Who are you? Are you a cop, or what?'

'I'm nobody. I'm a parent, like you. The Célèstines just got hold of my fifteen-year-old son.'

'Well, in that case, I'm very sorry,' said Robert Garrett. 'What else can I say? I'm very sorry.'

'Did you try to get your daughter out of there?'

'Are you kidding? I went to that place with a sawed-off shotgun and I threatened to kill the whole lot of them unless they let my daughter go. They called the police and the police locked me up on a charge of threatening behaviour and illegal possession of a firearm. After that I went to my lawyer and I spent $12,000 of savings trying to get a writ to have her released into my custody. The courts turned me down flat. The judge said that she had joined the Célèstines voluntarily and that there was no evidence of mental disturbance. The rituals may have been unusual but they were entirely voluntary and undertaken without any persuasion or compulsion whatsoever. Furthermore, if he were to rule against the Célèstines he would be setting two dangerous legal precedents. One would be to make it possible for parents to interfere legally in the chosen worship of their children. The other would be to diminish the individual's rights in respect of his or her own body. Parents could legally prevent their children from having cosmetic surgery, or indeed any surgery at all, and might even be able to reverse a child's wishes to have his or her organs used after death for transplant purposes.'

'You sound like you've memorized that ruling,' said Robyn.

'Memorized it? I didn't have to memorize it. It's engraved on my heart in letters an inch deep. I asked my attorney if it was worth going to appeal. He took me aside and said the word was that the Célèstines were well within the law and that they were supposed to be left alone. In fact, I'll tell you how brightly the sun shines on those bastards. I went to your newspaper the *Litchfield Sentinel* with my story of what had happened and your editor listened very politely and do you know what happened? Well, you know what happened.'

For the first time, Robyn was taken by surprise. 'You actually talked to Ted Fellowship about the Célèstines? And he did nothing about it?'

'Have you ever read a story about the Célèstines in any newspaper, or any magazine? Have you ever heard them mentioned on television? No, sir. Because the law can't touch them, that's why, and the law is too embarrassed to admit that they can get away with what they do.'

Charlie said, 'Robert? Can I call you Robert?'

'You can call me Bob, that's what everybody else calls me.'

'Bob — my son's in that place. I want to get him out.'

'I sympathize, Charlie, believe me. I've been there. But you won't stand a cat in hell's chance.'

'I got in there before.'

'Sure, just like I did, when I first went looking for my daughter. They let you in on purpose, so that they can show you just what you're up against. They want you to hear your own child saying no, I'm not coming back with you, dad, I'm staying right here, and there's nothing you can do about it.'

'Bob,' said Charlie, 'I have to try.'

'You can try,' Bob told him. 'Nobody can stop you trying. But what can I tell you? There isn't any future in it.'

'Will you help me?' Charlie asked him.

Silence again. Robyn looked across at Charlie and Charlie could see the tension on her face.

'Bob?' said Charlie.

'I don't know,' said Bob. 'The Célèstines are something I've been trying to forget.'

'Bob, I understand, I really do. But with two of us, and somebody to drive a getaway car, I'm sure that we can do it. If you want money for doing it, I'll pay you whatever I can. Bob, I have to get my son back. Nobody gave you any help, but if they had done, maybe you could have got your daughter out. Think about it, Bob. Those Célèstines have to be stopped sometime, by somebody. Maybe this is the time and we're the people to do it.'

Bob replied, 'It's late. Do you have a telephone number where I can reach you?'

'Call here,' put in Robyn. 'If I'm not in, my parents will tell you where you can contact me.'

'All right then,' said Bob. 'I want to toss this over in my mind. I'll give you a call by eleven o'clock tomorrow morning, yes or no.'

'Bob,' said Charlie, 'thanks for listening.'

'You got it,' Bob told him, and hung up.

Robyn picked up her glass of wine and came to sit next to Charlie on the couch. 'I'm still in a state of shock,' she said.

'Because your editor knew about the Célèstines and didn't print the story?'

Robyn nodded. 'I've suddenly found that my whole world has been turned upside down. How can I ever trust Ted again? I mean – what other stories has he spiked? I thought the press was free and fearless.'

'I don't think any of us is free and fearless,' said Charlie. 'Anyway, look at the time. I've got to get back to Allen's Corners. I'm working on the assumption that Bob Garrett is going to help me, and that means I've got to make some arrangements. Plane tickets, and a rental car, and a gun. The gun's going to present some problems.'

Robyn said, 'I can get you a gun.'

Charlie set down his glass of wine. 'Where is a sweet, innocent newspaper reporter like you going to get a gun?'

'My editor keeps one in his desk. Some outraged reader came into his office with a knife once, and threatened to cut out his kidneys. He's kept a gun ever since.'

'He's not about to lend it to you, is he?'

'I can borrow it. He doesn't get into the office until ten, and I know where he keeps the keys.'

'Supposing he finds out? That's not going to do your career any good, is it?'

Robyn shrugged. 'I don't think I'm really too worried about working for a newspaper whose editor cans crucial stories just because they don't happen to suit his personal convenience.' She lowered her head so that Charlie could see the parting in her hair. 'Listen,' she said, 'I'll get you the gun, and I'll drive the car, too. A friend of mine has a Shelby Cobra, we can borrow that.' She hesitated, and then she looked up at him. 'Charlie, I want to help.'

'You know the risks? It's not just your job, there could be bullets flying around.'

'I want to help. Don't preach.'

Charlie reached across the couch and took hold of Robyn's hand and squeezed it. 'In that case, I accept. Listen – I'll get back to Allen's Corners now. You have my number. Call me as soon as you hear from Bob Garrett. I'll fix the plane tickets. You get hold of the gun and the car. Provided Bob Garrett agrees to help – and, God, are you listening up there? Please lean on Bob Garrett and make him agree to help – we should be able to break into Le Reposoir at about noon tomorrow.'

Robyn said, 'Do one thing for me. Book three plane tickets.'

'We're going to California, and then to Mexico. I hope you understand that. I'm not at all sure we're ever coming back.'

'Ever since Carl, I've learned to take one day at a time.'

'Carl was the spectacularly messy love affair?'

'Carl was Adolf Hitler reincarnated as Robert Redford.'

Charlie knew at that moment that something was happening between Robyn and himself; that they were both strongly attracted to each other. With luck, and a little prayer, the time might come when they could let that feeling of attraction loose. But right now, Charlie's overwhelming priority was rescuing Martin. He did nothing more than lean forward and kiss Robyn on the forehead, and squeeze her hand again, and tell her, 'I'll be waiting to hear from you, right? And thanks for everything. Thanks for listening. Thanks for being sane.'

'Carl never said that I was sane.'

'Human society is riddled with bozos.'

Charlie said goodnight to Mr and Mrs Harris and Robyn came to the kerb to see him off.

'Don't stay out here,' he told her. 'You'll catch cold.'

'Tomorrow we're going to rescue your son like the Three Musketeers, and tonight you're worried about me catching cold?'

'Goodnight, Robyn.' He smiled, and blew her a kiss. He U-turned in the road, and drove off. He glanced in his rear-view mirror as he reached the intersection, and she was still standing by the fence watching him go. He didn't know whether to feel happy or apprehensive. He switched on the radio and listened to Tina Turner.

He reached Allen's Corners at half past midnight. The sloping green was silver under the full moon. The streets and the buildings were silver, too. Charlie was reminded of a poem his schoolteacher used to read when he was small, about the moon turning everything to silver. He parked outside Mrs Kemp's house, switched off the radio, and dry-washed his face with his hands. For the first time since he had discovered that Martin was missing, he allowed himself to admit that he was totally exhausted.

He was about to climb out of the car when he thought he saw something flicker beside the house. He frowned, and peered into the shadows. There was nothing there. He got out, closed the car door as quietly as he could, and locked it. It was then that he heard a rustling, scurrying sound, only about thirty or forty feet to his left, beside the trees. He froze, and stared, and listened intently. *Slowly, silently, now the moon / Walks the night in her silver shoon —*

He took one step towards the front gate. Without any warning, the dwarfish hooded figure rushed out of the shadows straight towards him, in a hopping, tumbling, headlong gait, and collided with his legs. He fell backwards against the car, jabbing his hand up as he did so to push the dwarf away. But then he saw the hooked machete lifted in to the moonlight, and he twisted sideways just as the metal blade clanged against the hood of the car, and rolled across the sidewalk into the gutter.

The dwarf hissed, and came rushing after him again. Charlie kicked at him, and felt his foot strike at the solid meat of his stubby thigh. The machete whistled, but Charlie heaved himself away, and the blade jarred against the sidewalk.

With one more roll, Charlie somehow managed to scramble up on to his feet. The dwarf advanced, swinging the machete from side to side as if he were cutting grass, panting and whispering under his breath. All that Charlie could see inside the shadow of his hood was a pale nose and two glittering eyes.

'You bastard,' Charlie breathed at him. 'You sawn-off runt.'

The dwarf let out a piercing, effeminate shriek, and rushed at Charlie yet again. Charlie backed and dodged sideways, but the machete sang into his left thigh, *wheeooo-smakk!* and even though Charlie felt no pain, he knew that he was cut. He pivoted around and punched the dwarf in the side of his hood, so hard that the dwarf somersaulted over on to the ground.

'Come on, you runt!' Charlie yelled at him. 'Come on, if that's what you want! You want blood? All right, then, you can have some blood! Come on, runt!'

The dwarf clung on to the side of Charlie's car in an effort to heave himself back up on to his feet. Charlie kicked him mercilessly in the ribs, and he dropped to the sidewalk again. Then Charlie stepped on to his arm and knocked the machete out of his reach with a sideways sweep of his foot, and then reached down and seized hold of the dwarf's robes.

'You Goddamned half-assed –!' he began. But the dwarf suddenly lifted his arms and dropped right out of his robes, falling heavily on to the ground with a noise like a sack of beets.

'*Scaaaarrccchh!*' the dwarf screamed, and glared at Charlie in venomous hate. Charlie stood where he was, paralyzed, still clutching the dwarf's discarded robes. The dwarf – the creature that M. Musette had called 'David' – was standing in front of him wearing nothing but a tight cotton waistband.

David was hideously white-faced, but his head was normal size. He was a mature young man of twenty-four or twenty-five, with wiry mid-brown hair. It was the sight of his body that had stopped Charlie dead, however. His arms had been severed below the elbows. He had been holding his machete by means of a leather strap around his right stump. His legs had been severed halfway down his thighs, and his stumps were protected by leather cups padded with the fibrous material that lined the hoods of cars. There were ugly scars and indentations all over his torso, where he must have cut out flesh for the Célèstine rituals; but worst of all, his genitals were missing. There was nothing but a bush of pubic hair, beneath which Charlie glimpsed a grotesquely twisted scar, a male vagina made out of purple knots. He took in every horrifying physical detail of this thing called David in the same way that he had made an instantaneous check of ten fingers and ten toes the moment that Martin had been born.

'I will murder you, I promise!' the dwarf shrieked at him, all teeth and spittle. Then he snatched at his robes, tearing them out of Charlie's grasp, and hopped off into the shadow of the trees. Charlie stood where he was, breathing deeply. His left trouser leg was stained dark with blood, and glistening in the moonlight. He picked up the dwarf's machete, and limped slowly up to the house.

The front door was slightly ajar. Charlie knew straight away that something was wrong here, because Mrs Kemp had always been security conscious. He pushed open the door and hobbled inside, hefting the machete in his right hand. 'Mrs Kemp?' he called. 'Are you okay? It's Charlie, Mrs Kemp! Charlie McLean!'

There was no reply. Charlie listened for a few seconds, then limped into the kitchen to see if Mrs Kemp was there. He switched on the fluorescent lights. They flickered and jolted and then came on full. The kitchen was deserted, but there was a smear of blood across the worktop, next to the rice jars.

'Mrs Kemp?' He went back to the hallway and climbed the stairs. The moon looked in through the window. *One by one the casements catch | Her beams beneath the silvery thatch.* Charlie reached the landing and hesitated, listening, listening, but there was no sound to be heard except a gurgling in the plumbing, and the faraway drone of an aeroplane.

'Mrs Kemp, it's Charlie,' he said, although his voice was so hushed now that nobody could have heard it.

He said 'Mrs Kemp' for the very last time as he opened her bedroom door and saw what the dwarf had done to her. After that, there was no point at all in calling her name.

Mrs Kemp's brass bed was a grisly raft of blood and chopped-up flesh. The stench of bile and blood and faeces was stunning. Mrs Kemp's head had been almost completely severed, and was wedged between the side of the bed and the nightstand, staring wildly at nothing. All that connected her head to her torso was a thin web of skin, like the skin of a chicken's neck. Her chest had been hacked apart, her breastbone broken, and her heart and her lungs and her liver chopped into glistening ribbons. Her arms rose stiffly up on either side of her ribcage as if she were still trying to protect herself from the frenzied blows of the dwarf's machete.

Charlie couldn't quite work out what had happened to the rest of her, and didn't want to try. He could see heavy loops of pale intestine wound around the brass bedhead, and he could see one of Mrs Kemp's feet lying on its side by the bureau, severed, but still wearing its pink slipper. He closed the door and then he stood on the landing and closed his eyes. He told himself that he was probably entering a state of shock; but that he had to keep on functioning, no matter what. The machete dropped out of his fingers on to the floor, and of course it didn't occur to him that the handle now bore his fingerprints; and that the last person who had been seen in Mrs Kemp's house, by no less a witness than Sheriff Norman Podmore, was him.

All he could think of was the Célèstines; and the fact that they were prepared to kill people in order to protect themselves. Mrs Kemp, and him, too. And nobody would protect him against them, not even the police.

He stumbled downstairs, and went out of the front door, slamming it hard behind him. Somehow he found himself sitting in the driving seat of his car. He started up the engine, turned around, and headed out of Allen's Corners in the direction of Waterbury.

The moon was gone now. Shock and exhaustion began to overwhelm him. He swerved from one side of the road to the other, and the Oldsmobile's suspension groaned with every swerve. It was dark out there, he couldn't see anything. Then he narrowly missed a roadside tree, his wheels bumping over grass hummocks and slews of gravel, and he pulled the car to a stop beside the road.

'You're going to kill yourself,' he told his reflection in the rear-view mirror.

Hm, retorted his reflection, *They're going to kill you anyway. It depends what kind of death you prefer. A highway accident — restaurant prodnose dies in auto smash — or a homicide — food scrutineer chopped into American steak.*

He wanted to go on, but he forced himself to switch off the engine and douse the headlights. He needed sleep and he needed it badly. He shifted himself into the passenger seat and reclined it. Then he loosened his necktie and tried to make himself comfortable. Even an hour's sleep would be better than no sleep at all.

He dozed and dreamed. He was trying to find his way through a furniture store, heaped high with musty antique tables and bureaux and chairs with twisty legs. His face was reflected in a dozen dusty mirrors. His feet made a reluctant swishing noise on the parquet floor. Out of the corner of his eye, he glimpsed a small figure in a hood, and for an instant he caught the shine of a curved machete. He began to hurry between the stacks of furniture, turning left and then right and then left again. A high voice kept screaming, '*Daddy! Daddy! Save me!*' In one of the mirrors he saw the machete lifted up and down in a brutal chopping motion, and fingers go flying through the air.

He woke up shouting. He sat up. He must have been sleeping for three or four hours, because the sky was already pale. He opened the door and climbed stiffly out of the car and stretched. The morning air felt cold on his sweaty underarms. He would have done anything for a hot cup of coffee and a shower. Maybe Robyn could oblige when he reached Waterbury.

He sat behind the wheel and started up the Oldsmobile's engine. He thought about Mrs Kemp and wondered whether he ought to go back to Allen's Corners and report her murder to the sheriff. But a small voice in the back of his head warned him off. If he went to the sheriff now, the sheriff would delay him all day with questions and police procedure, and that was the last thing he wanted.

Apart from that, he wasn't sure how much he could trust Sheriff Podmore. Who else, apart from Charlie himself, had known that Mrs Kemp was out for revenge against the Célèstines?

His most urgent priority was not a murdered woman whom he had scarcely known, but his son Martin. He steered back on to the road again and headed for Waterbury.

Driving through Thomaston, he was observed from the roadside by two police officers in a parked patrol car. He kept checking them in his rear-view mirror as he headed south, but they stayed where they were, and made no attempt to follow him. The chances were that Mrs Kemp's body hadn't been found yet; and with any luck Charlie would be able to rescue Martin and get clear away from Connecticut before it was.

He switched on the car radio. Bob Seger and the Silver Bullet Band were playing 'Hollywood Nights'. Charlie sang along with it for a while. '*Oh, those Hollywood nights . . . in those Hollywood hills . . .!*' but as he approached the outskirts of Waterbury he fell silent, like a man who recognizes that his destiny is about to turn, and that life and death are sitting on his shoulders like a pair of predatory hawks.

CHAPTER FOURTEEN

They drew up outside a plain 1930s house with maroon-painted shutters and a scruffy front yard and Bob Garrett appeared almost immediately on the front porch in a blue Sears suit with a fawn raincoat folded over his arm. He walked quickly towards them with his free arm swinging. Charlie climbed out of the Cobra and folded the front seat forward so that Bob could climb into the back seat.

Robyn pulled away from the side of the road and headed north toward Hotchkissville. Bob leaned forward from the back seat and introduced himself. 'You're early,' he said, with a nervous laugh. He had a simple, uncomplicated face with pale blue eyes and a cow's-lick fringe combed back from his forehead and a neatly-clipped moustache.

'I'm real glad you decided to come,' Charlie told him.

'I knew I was going to, the second you asked me. I just had to think about it, was all. I had to think whether I wanted all those memories brought back. It's the memories that hurt the most.'

'I'm sorry,' said Charlie. 'Maybe this is your moment to get your own back.'

'Do you have a gun?' asked Bob.

Charlie reached forward to the glove compartment and produced it. A hefty weapon for a newspaper editor: a Colt .45 automatic, capable of blowing a hole through five men standing in a line.

'Do you know how to use it?' asked Bob.

'I think so,' Charlie told him. 'You point it at anybody who happens to be annoying you, and you pull the trigger. Every American kid knows that.'

'Well, you've just about got it,' said Bob. 'The question is, will you have the *courage* to pull the trigger?'

He sat back, and watched the Connecticut countryside flashing past the window. Charlie looked at Robyn and made a face. 'Rambo the Second,' she whispered.

Charlie gave her a philosophical smile. 'Maybe that's what we need.'

'Have you worked out how we're going to get into Le Reposoir?' asked Bob.

'We're going to walk in,' said Charlie.

'Walk in? You think they're going to let you?'

'They're not going to let me break my way in, are they?'

'Well, I guess not,' said Bob, in that deep, hesitant voice. 'I guess if you can swing it, walking in is the best way. That's the way I did it, anyhow.'

'The most important thing is to take them by surprise,' said Charlie. 'It shouldn't take more than a couple of minutes to get hold of Martin and drag him out of the house, but we have to be fast and we have to work together.'

'So tell me what you're planning to do,' said Bob.

'I'm going to walk straight in there and tell them that I've seen the light, and that I want to join the Célèstines, too.'

'You think they're going to buy that?' asked Bob, leaning his elbows on the front seats.

'Is there any reason why they shouldn't? They have two major weaknesses – their fanaticism and their over-confidence. Fanatics always find it hard to believe that other people don't agree with their point of view. They find it a great deal easier to accept the idea that you've seen the light, and been won over. And that's exactly what I'm going to tell them. If eating himself alive is good enough for my son, then it's good enough for me.'

'I'm glad you can joke about it,' said Robyn.

'I'm not joking,' said Charlie. 'If those people think for one moment that I'm threatening them, they'll kill me.'

'You sound like you know something that we don't,' Bob said.

Charlie said, 'Let me put it this way. I didn't get this cut on my leg by accident.'

Robyn glanced at him as she drove. 'You told mom that it was an accident.'

'Sure I did, I didn't want to upset her. And she bandaged it up so well.'

'What happened? Did somebody attack you?'

'That dwarf — you remember the one I was telling you about? He was waiting for me when I got back to Allen's Corners last night.'

'Why didn't you tell me straight away?'

'With your parents straining their ears? Come on, I'm not saying they're interfering or anything, but they *are* interested in finding out what kind of a man their daughter is working with, all of a sudden. I didn't want them to get upset, that's all.'

'I've seen that dwarf, too,' said Bob. 'Well he's not exactly a dwarf, is he? He wasn't born like that. He cut off his arms and legs.'

'That's right,' Charlie nodded. 'And he's a mean son-of-a-bitch, believe me.'

They drove through Allen's Corners without stopping and made their way up towards the Quassapaug Road. Charlie managed to catch a glimpse of Mrs Kemp's house; but there were no police cars outside, no crowds, and no ambulance. Mrs Kemp's body probably hadn't been discovered yet, and that suited him fine, although the guilt and the pain that he felt for Mrs Kemp were as red-raw as fresh-cut meat. He didn't allow himself to think about her hacked-up body, soaking into the mattress. He didn't allow himself to think about her arms, still raised in rigor mortis, fighting off an assailant who had long since hurried away.

The Cobra's tyres complained as they climbed the corkscrew towards Le Reposoir. The sky was as dark as a Rembrandt painting; the trees were as pale as faces. Robyn said, 'Just about now, my editor's going to look in his desk and realize that his gun has gone.'

'He won't suspect you, though, will he?'

'Not to begin with. But one of our advertising people came into the editorial offices while I was looking through his desk.'

Charlie patted his breast pocket. 'Don't worry. I bought three tickets to San Diego. After that, we can make our way down to Baja, and thence into oblivion. Your editor won't be able to find you in a thousand years.'

They reached the gates of Le Reposoir sooner than Charlie expected. Robyn slewed the Cobra around in a wide curve, and shut off the engine. Charlie took the .45, turned it one way, then the other, then pushed it into his inside pocket. He looked back at Bob. 'Are you ready? We want to take this real easy, a step at a time.'

'I'm ready,' Bob told him.

Charlie got out of the car, and went over to the intercom. He pressed the call button and waited for somebody to answer. This time, he didn't have to wait long.

'Mr McLean? I'm surprised to see you back so soon.' It was the voice of M. Musette, but careful this time, and suspicious.

'M. Musette,' said Charlie, 'it seems that I owe you an apology.'

'An apology, Mr McLean?'

'Last night I had a run-in outside Mrs Kemp's house with that assistant of yours, David.'

Cautiously, M. Musette said, 'So I understand. You weren't hurt, I hope?'

'A slight cut, but I think I can forgive him for that.'

'Did you . . . see Mrs Kemp?'

'She wasn't at home,' Charlie lied. The last thing he wanted was for M. Musette to know that he had found Mrs Kemp's body. 'I stayed overnight at the Bethlehem Motel.'

'You have my regrets,' said M. Musette. 'David can be impetuous. I think it was after he lost his hands, you know. He started to throw tantrums, and act rather violently. He's not altogether to be trusted.'

Charlie paused for a moment, and then he said, 'The fact of the matter is, M. Musette, that I began to wonder why I was fighting you. I sat in that motel and I bandaged up the cut that David gave me, and then I sat there and said to myself, "Charlie, these people are religious, they believe in happiness and goodness and the life everlasting." And do you know what else I said to myself?'

'Do continue, Mr McLean.'

'Well, M. Musette, I said to myself, "If my son has chosen the Célestines as the way to heaven, then perhaps there's something in it. Perhaps I've been the one who's been blind. Perhaps there really is something in all of this business, after all." Because what have I seen? Sights that have shocked me, sure, I have to admit. But a new way of looking at the word of the New Testament, and that's for sure. A new way of taking communion, the flesh and the blood of Our Lord Jesus Christ.'

'What are you trying to tell me, Mr McLean?' M. Musette asked him with unconcealed impatience.

'I'm trying to tell you, M. Musette, that I've been saved. I'm trying to tell you that I've seen the light. Your way is the only way, and I don't want my son to go to heaven without me. I want to go with him. Damn it, M. Musette, I want to volunteer.'

M. Musette was silent for what seemed like five or ten minutes. After a while, however, he said, 'I find it very hard to trust you, Mr McLean. You have been nothing but hostile ever since I first met you. I am inclined to think that you are feigning this sudden enthusiasm in the Célestines in order to gain access to your son.'

'M. Musette, my son can make his own decisions. If he

wants to dedicate his life to the Célèstines then that's all right by me.'

'You *are* singing a different song, Mr McLean.'

'That's the nature of religious conversions, M. Musette. Suddenly, you see the light. Saul did that, didn't he?'

There was another long pause, and then M. Musette said, 'Wait there. I'll send my security guard to open the gate. But, please – remember that you are on your honour to conduct yourself with propriety.'

Propriety, thought Charlie, with bitterness. *You can talk to me about propriety after slaughtering Mrs Kemp?*

The intercom clicked off, and Charlie was left waiting in the wind. The dry trees rustled like the voices of gossiping ghosts. There was a smell of smoke in the air, smoke and fall and sadness.

Eventually, a black Chrysler appeared between the maculata bushes, and the thin youth with the close-cropped hair and the Buddy Holly suit climbed out and unlocked the gates.

'Mr McLean?' he said, in a nasal voice. 'Drive your vehicle slowly down to the house. I'll be following right behind. And, please, no faster than ten miles an hour.'

They drove at a crawl down to the gravelled turning-circle in front of Le Reposoir. Robyn looked at the house in amazement. 'You know something, I never even knew this place *existed*, and I was brought up around here.'

M. Musette was waiting for them in the doorway. 'All we need now is speed,' said Charlie. 'We walk straight up to him, push him aside, and then go straight up the stairs to the corridor where all the new Devotees go. I know which room they're keeping Martin in. We force our way in, take one arm each, and frogmarch him out of there. Bob, you take his left arm, I'll take his right. That way, I can have a hand free to hold the gun.'

'You realize Musette is going to recognize me straight away,' said Bob.

'Just keep cool. Speed, and surprise, that's what we need. Robyn – as soon as we're inside, you turn the car around and get ready to burn rubber.'

'I'm terrified,' said Robyn.

Charlie reached across and squeezed her hand. 'It's going to work like a charm, just so long as none of us loses our nerve.'

'A charm, he says.'

'We're all right so far,' said Charlie. 'I mean, we got in here, didn't we? And they didn't close the gates behind us. That was one thing I was afraid of.'

The thin youth came up and tapped on the window. 'Will you follow me, please?'

Charlie glanced tensely at Robyn, and then at Bob. He had been so busy reassuring *them* that he hadn't realized how tightly his own nerves were wound up. He gave the youth a salute of acknowledgement and climbed out of the car. Bob followed close behind him, keeping his face to the ground so that M. Musette wouldn't recognize him until it was too late.

M. Musette extended his hand as Charlie came up the steps. Charlie's heart seemed to have leaped up and caught itself on one of his ribs. He was breathing in short, shallow gasps. He could feel the weight of the .45 in his inside coat pocket, and he was sure that M. Musette could see it bulging out.

'Well, Mr McLean,' M. Musette greeted him with a diagonal smile. 'Perhaps I can congratulate you on your conversion.'

Charlie's mind snapped into overdrive. He swung his left shoulder forward and knocked M. Musette sideways. He felt M. Musette's collarbone jar against his arm. Then he was running across the hallway with Bob right behind him. As he reached the foot of the stairs he heard M. Musette shouting, 'Harold! *Harold*! Lock off the upstairs landing!'

Charlie turned around, tugging the .45 out of his coat, and

tearing the lining as he did so. He pointed it directly at M. Musette and yelled at him, 'You try to stop me, and I'll blow your head off!'

'It's no use, Mr McLean!' M. Musette replied. 'You can't get away with it! Martin is out of your reach now! You can only get him back by killing us all!'

'If that's what it takes,' said Charlie. 'Come on, Bob!'

Together, they climbed the stairs. They crossed the landing, but when they reached the door which led to the corridor where the new Devotees were kept, they found that it was locked. Charlie wrenched at the handle, but the door was solid steel, and he couldn't budge it.

'What are you going to do?' Bob asked him.

'Musette,' Charlie replied fiercely. He ran back downstairs, but M. Musette had disappeared. He went out through the door. Apart from Robyn waiting in the car, the grounds were deserted. Bob said, 'They've locked it all up and left us to it.'

'Round the back,' said Charlie.

They ran around the side of the house to the garden door which Charlie had used to enter the house the first time. That, too, was locked. Charlie cocked the .45 and pointed it at the lock, but Bob said, 'Forget it, that only works in movies. You'll probably end up with a ricochet right between the eyes.'

'God damn it, how do we get in?' Charlie raged.

He ran back to the front door, back up the steps, and back inside. He tried a downstairs door but that was locked too. Solid oak, with a five-lever lock. He kicked at it, but it didn't even rattle. He turned back to Bob in anger and frustration.

'I've blown it, damn it! I should have taken Musette hostage!'

'We'd better just get out of here,' said Bob. 'Let's go back and work out some other way of getting in.'

Charlie was almost in tears. His vision of bursting into Martin's room and dragging him out had been foiled by the simplest expedient of all. M. Musette had done nothing more than lock his doors and disappear, so that he could neither be reached nor threatened.

'Come on,' said Bob, taking hold of his arm. 'This is one of those times when discretion is the better part of valour.'

Charlie looked up at the florid Victorian stained-glass window at the head of the stairs. It depicted Sir Gawain on his way to do battle with the Green Knight, a brightly coloured scene of valleys and lakes and bulrushes. Charlie lifted the .45 and fired at the window. There was a deafening, echoing bang. Charlie had never fired such a heavy calibre handgun before, and his arm was painfully jarred. All that he succeeded in doing was blowing out one small pane of blue glass. Bob looked at him, and said, 'Are you satisfied now?'

'I'm going to get my son back if it kills me,' said Charlie.

He left the house, and walked down the steps. They were probably being covered by guns from M. Musette's security men, but Charlie didn't care. He stood at the bottom of the steps and shouted out. '*M. Musette! If you hurt my son, it's going to be your head next time, not just your window!*'

There was no reply. The ravens croaked amongst the rooftops, the trees shushed and rustled like the sea. Bob climbed back into the car and Charlie followed him.

Robyn said, 'What happened?'

'They locked the doors. Come on, we'd better get out of here.'

'I'm sorry,' said Robyn. 'I'm really sorry.'

They drove back to the gates, and exited on to the Quassapaug Road. As they did so, however, a huge Mack truck appeared, as suddenly as a nightmare, bellowing down the hill from the direction of Bethlehem. Charlie yelled, '*Go!*' and Robyn slammed her foot down on the gas so that the Cobra slithered away from Le Reposoir with a shriek of tyres and a cloud of dust and rubber smoke.

Charlie twisted around in his seat. The truck's front grille filled up the entire rear window. Robyn kept her foot hard on the gas, steering the Cobra from one side of the road to the other as she negotiated one curve after another. But the truck held on, tailgating them only two or three feet away. As they reached the corkscrew curve that would take them to Allen's Corners, the truck bumped them in the back, and Robyn juggled frantically with the steering wheel as she momentarily lost control.

They slid round the corkscrew with their tyres screaming like strangled cats. Their offside rear wheel jolted against a large stone at the side of the road, and then they were sliding sideways the opposite way. The truck barged them again and again. Charlie heard glass and metal grind, and the *whup-whup-whup* of something scraping against one of the rear wheels.

The truck shunted right up close to them, and as they came out of the corkscrew it was actually pushing them along, madly, uncontrollably, like a roller-coaster. Robyn cried out, '*Charlie! I can't hold it!*' and then Charlie saw a row of trees rushing at them and the Cobra hurtled right off the edge of the road, flying for nearly twenty feet clear through the air. It collided with two massive pines with a noise like a bomb going off. Charlie was thrown violently against the glove compartment, his head hitting the windshield, and something burst over the top of him and glass exploded.

Behind them, the truck bellowed around the corner and out of sight.

Charlie tried to sit up. Robyn was sitting with her head slumped forward but she was wearing her seat belt and he could see that she had been only jolted and shocked. There was a large red bruise on the left side of her forehead, but otherwise she looked all right. It was only after he had looked at Robyn, however, that he realized what had hurtled over him when they hit the trees. Bob – fired out of the back seat and through the windshield. The whole of the upper part of his body had gone through the laminated glass, and he now lay face down on the Cobra's hood, amidst a slush of broken glass. Blood ran slickly across the metal.

Charlie managed to kick the passenger door open, and heave himself out of the wrecked car. There was a strong smell of petrol, but there didn't seem to be any immediate danger of fire. He walked around to the driver's door and tugged it open after three or four strenuous yanks. Robyn was just coming round, and she stared at him with widely-dilated pupils. 'Charlie?' she asked him, her voice slurred. 'Charlie, what happened?'

He unfastened her seat belt and helped her out of the car. She said, 'Bob – is Bob all right?' but Charlie wouldn't let her turn around and look. He guided her back up the slope to the side of the road and made her sit down on a rock. 'Give me a minute, okay?' he told her. 'Bob's been hurt pretty bad.'

He went back down to the car. He had been almost sure that Bob was dead, but as he approached he heard him groaning. He came up close and said, 'Bob? Bob, it's Charlie. How do you feel?'

Bob raised his head from the hood of the car, and Charlie could see what had happened to him. The broken windshield had caught his forehead as he had hurtled through it, and sheared the skin off his face, from his eyebrows right down to his chin. He stared at Charlie with one white swivelling eyeball set in a livid oval of scarlet. His teeth snarled bloody and bare, without lips or gums. What was left of his face hung from his jaw in fatty folds, his cheeks, his nose, and his chin – as if his features had been nothing more than a latex Hallowe'en mask which had suddenly been ripped from his head.

Extraordinarily – and terribly – he was still conscious.

Charlie said, 'Bob? Bob, can you hear me?'

Bob nodded, and his eyeball turned and glistened.

'I'm going for an ambulance, Bob. You'll just have to stay where you are for a minute or two.'

Bob tried to say something but his mouth had been too badly mutilated for him to do anything but grunt and gargle.

Charlie clambered back up the rocks to the road. Robyn was still sitting there, white-faced and tearful. 'I couldn't hold it,' she sobbed. 'I tried so hard, but I couldn't.'

'We have to call an ambulance,' said Charlie. He felt weak at the knees and almost on the point of collapse. The day seemed to crowd in on him as if the clouds were determined to press him down into the ground and the trees all around him were trying to entangle him and choke him.

'Is Bob badly hurt?' asked Robyn.

'As bad as anybody I've ever seen.'

'It looks like there might be a house down there,' said Robyn, pointing further downhill. Charlie peered through the trees and he thought that he could make out the angular grey gable of a house or a barn.

'I guess it's worth a try,' he told her. 'Why don't you stay here, just in case somebody drives past, and you can flag them down?'

'What if that truck comes back?'

Charlie wiped the chilly sweat from his forehead with the back of his hand. 'I don't know. He was deliberately trying to run us off the road, wasn't he?'

Robyn held his arm. 'Don't worry about it. I'll duck down and hide if I see it. You go call that ambulance.'

Charlie began to jog down the hill. He had only gone about a couple of hundred feet however, when he heard a bursting, crackling roar from the hollow where the Cobra had crashed. He turned around and saw an orange fireball roll up from the trees and vanish like a conjuring trick. The car was already blazing from end to end.

He ran slopewise through the whiplashing bushes and the drifts of dried leaves. By the time he reached the car it was too late for him to do anything at all. The flames were so fierce that he couldn't get within twenty feet. He couldn't see Bob at all.

Robyn came running down the hill to stand beside him. They stood together, helplessly watching the fire gradually die down, leaving a hulk of an automobile burned brown and rainbow mottled. Bob's body still lay on the hood, but it had charred and shrunk into a little black figure no larger than a nine-year-old child. Charlie could see white bones gleaming through charcoal flesh. He could see something else, too, although he didn't mention it to Robyn. The metallic shine of a cigarette lighter, tightly clasped in Bob's burned-up hand. He must have ignited the car's leaking gasoline himself.

'We'd better get out of here,' said Charlie. 'There's nothing we can do now.'

'We can tell the police, can't we?'

'I'm not so sure that's a good idea.'

'But we can't just walk away!' Robyn protested.

'I think we can,' said Charlie. 'In fact, I don't think we have any other alternative. Not if we want to stay alive ourselves. That truck was waiting for us. I told you what the sheriff and Mr Haxalt told me: M. Musette doesn't suffer trespassers gladly.'

'I have to get to a phone,' said Robyn.

'What? To call your office? Come on, Robyn, think about it. If the Célèstines have as much of a hold on the media as they appear to, then the best thing we can do is disappear for a while, try to work this out undercover.'

'Do you really think they were trying to kill us? Maybe that truck just had brake failure.'

'Brake failure my rear end. They want us dead. And they've succeeded with Bob, haven't they? A poor uncomplicated guy who was only trying to help me out.'

Robyn was shaking. They were both so shocked by what had happened that neither of them really knew what they were talking about. At least bickering seemed to be real.

'We can cut across country,' said Robyn. 'If we keep on

going downhill, we'll get to the Quassapaug River. Then we can follow it all the way down to Allen's Corners. That way, nobody will see us.'

Charlie took her arm. 'Let's go. As soon as they find out that we're still alive, they'll go straight to Mrs Kemp's, and then I'm going to be in really serious trouble.'

'I don't understand.'

'They killed Mrs Kemp, too. That dwarf did it – the one they call David. Before he attacked me last night, he broke into her bedroom and chopped her up.'

'Are you serious?' Robyn demanded, staring at Charlie in disbelief. 'Why didn't you tell me this morning?'

'I didn't want to scare you out of driving for me.'

'God, I wish you had ... Did you report Mrs Kemp's murder to the sheriff?'

'Are you kidding?' Charlie retorted.

They made their way along beside the Quassapaug River for almost a mile. It was quite narrow here, splashing busily down between the rocks, sometimes disappearing under layers of russet-brown ferns. Occasionally, they heard a police siren wailing along the road from Allen's Corners; and once they saw a police helicopter heading at top speed for Bethlehem, or maybe towards Le Reposoir. Charlie had to assume that Sheriff Podmore was looking for them now; and just in case the police brought in tracker dogs he made sure that they crossed and recrossed the Quassapaug whenever it was shallow enough for them to take off their shoes and wade. The clear-rippling water was intensely cold, but after each crossing they rubbed their feet with Robyn's pale blue sweater to dry them and warm them up.

It was almost two o'clock in the afternoon by the time they reached the outskirts of Allen's Corners. The small community was almost completely deserted, but Charlie took the precaution of approaching Mrs Kemp's along the narrow alleyway which ran along behind the back yards of most of the houses on Naugatuck Street. David must have used this alleyway when he had come to visit Martin during the night; and escaped along it, too.

All the yards were empty and silent. Robyn stayed close behind Charlie, but she was growing increasingly nervous, and kept glancing over her shoulder. 'What are we doing here?' she asked.

'First of all I want to find out if they've discovered Mrs Kemp's body yet. If they have, then I'm going to be wanted for questioning – if not for actually doing it, if I've learned anything about M. Musette. Second of all, we need Mrs Kemp's car. We'll never make it anywhere on foot, not if they get dogs out. She keeps her car keys in the hutch in the kitchen.'

They reached the back of Mrs Kemp's house, and Charlie eased open the gate. There was nobody to be seen in any of the other yards, except for a woman hanging washing about eight houses away, and there was no sign of police – not even barriers or warning notices or seals on the door to protect the evidence inside.

'They haven't found her yet,' Charlie whispered; but Robyn said, '*Look*!' and pointed up to the back bedroom window.

At first, the window simply appeared to be dark. But then a faint wash of early-afternoon sunlight came out, and Charlie could see a dull blue light reflected from it, as if the glass were tinted. But it was only when the blue light began to ripple and swirl that he understood what he was looking at. Inside the bedroom, blowflies were swarming, thousands of them, and scores of them had settled on the window. The dull blue light was the shiny colour of their bodies catching the sun.

Charlie said nothing, but ushered Robyn up to the back of the house. He tried the kitchen door and it was locked; but he picked up an edging-stone from Mrs Kemp's flower-bed and used it to crack open one of the panes of glass. The key was still in the door, so he reached in and turned it.

'God,' he said, as they stepped cautiously into the kitchen. 'You can smell it even down here!'

'Do I have to come in?' Robyn asked.

'No, you wait there,' said Charlie. 'But keep your eyes peeled, okay? And don't let anybody see you.'

Charlie crossed the kitchen, trying not to breathe in too much of the cloying, sweetish smell which now permeated the entire house. He opened up the hutch, and found Mrs Kemp's car keys straight away. Underneath her keys was a roadmap of Litchfield County, two bank books, a spare pair of spectacles, and a half-finished embroidery sampler with the message 'Home Is Where The Heart Is'. *That's ironic*, thought Charlie. *Not only the heart, but the lungs, the spleen, the liver, and the stomach, not to mention twenty-eight feet of intestine*. He was about to close the drawer, however, when his attention was caught by two leaflets which had been stuffed into the back of it. He coaxed them out, and unfolded them, and held them up to the light so that he could read them.

One was cyclostyled on yellowish paper, and bore a drawing of Christ crucified. Beneath it, Charlie could make out the words *L'Église des Pauvres, Société des Gourmands, Acadia, LA*. There was a lengthy text underneath in that curious Cajun mixture of French and English. Most of it seemed to be an exhortation to love God *avec votre esprit et avec votre corps* and to serve him *avec all your heart*.

The other leaflet was almost incomprehensible, but seemed to be something to do with *Le Recreation*. There was a New Orleans address at the bottom of it: 1112 Elegance Street. But it was what was pencilled on the back of the leaflet that interested Charlie the most. *Norman, for information. M.*

Mrs Kemp must have taken both of these leaflets out of

Sheriff Podmore's office when she vandalized it yesterday. She had crammed them into the drawer along with her car keys when she came home and locked herself in the kitchen. Charlie frowned at them again. They were definitely something to do with the Célèstines, but right now he couldn't work out what. Maybe L'Église des Pauvres was another 'dining society' like Le Reposoir.

And maybe the 'M' who had signed that note to Sheriff Podmore was Edouard Musette; or even his wife.

Robyn called, 'Charlie? Did you get those keys? I'm feeling distinctly nervous out here.'

'I've got them,' said Charlie, 'and something else besides.'

He handed Robyn the leaflets. She glanced through them quickly, and then shrugged. 'I'll have to sit down with a French dictionary. I've forgotten everything I learned at school.'

Charlie tucked the leaflets into his pocket. Then he led Robyn around to the garage at the front of the house. The street was deserted. There wasn't even a dog in sight. Charlie eased open the garage doors, and together they climbed into Mrs Kemp's old Buick station wagon. 'It smells like lavender,' said Robyn.

Charlie started up the engine. It rattled and coughed, and produced a thick black cloud of smoke. 'Not exactly the ideal vehicle for a discreet getaway,' Charlie remarked.

'Where are we going?' Robyn asked him. 'We're not on the run, are we?'

'You could say that. I mean – the justice around here may be corrupt, but we're fugitives from it.'

They backed out of the driveway, and then headed for the ring road which would take them around by the supermarket and out of Allen's Corners by the railroad depot and the warehouses, where they were less likely to be spotted by sheriff's deputies or over-enthusiastic disciples of Le Reposoir. Charlie said, 'Once we make it out of Connecticut, we have a fair chance of getting away clean.'

Robyn looked at him narrowly. 'You know where you're going, don't you? You're not running away from anything; you're running *to* something.'

Charlie said, 'I'm trying to save my boy, that's all.'

'Trying to play Rambo didn't work,' Robyn commented.

'Does it ever? You can never solve anything with a sweat-band and a gun. It was my fault, I didn't think it out properly and it was totally amateurish. I'm just grieving that Bob was killed.'

'So what are you planning on doing now?' asked Robyn. She touched his shoulder, a small affectionate gesture of communication; a signal that no matter what he wanted to do, she would help him.

'You see these leaflets? All in Cajun French. Well – that's where this cannibalism started, among an isolated sect of the Cajun French. Sheriff Podmore told me it began in New Orleans, and if that's where we have to go to find out more about the Célèstines, then that's where we'll go. Leastways, that's where *I'm* going. You're not obliged.'

'Do you seriously think that I'll allow you to leave me behind?' Robyn told him. 'And besides, you need somebody to take turns with the driving.'

'Do you want to drop off home and pick up some clothes?' Charlie asked her. 'We should be reasonably safe until the police find Mrs Kemp. Then it's going to be like all hell was let out for the weekend.'

Robyn shivered, partly out of cold, partly out of anticipation. 'When you called the *Litchfield Sentinel*,' she said, 'my life changed for ever.'

Charlie steered the Buick out towards Waterbury. 'Don't start blaming me. You could have said no. You can say no now, if you want to. You can see how dangerous these people are.'

'Wild horses couldn't stop me coming with you.'

Charlie reached over and switched on the station wagon's radio. 'Wild horses I'm not worried about. It's these God-damned cannibals.'

CHAPTER FIFTEEN

They crossed the state line into New York shortly after four o'clock. There was no sign of any police pursuit, and Charlie crossed his fingers and hoped that they had gotten away. Now he settled himself down for nearly 1,400 miles of driving, all the way through eight states to Louisiana, and to New Orleans. He estimated that if they kept going, taking turns at the wheel, they could reach the Mississippi delta in thirty-six hours. That was if Mrs Kemp's oil-burning Buick behaved itself; and if they weren't stopped anywhere along the way by the police.

As they headed towards New York City, Robyn tried to translate the leaflets that Mrs Kemp had stolen from Sheriff Podmore's office. It was *Le Recreation* text which interested her the most. It was dense and obscure and smudgily printed, and neither she nor Charlie could decide why Mrs Kemp had decided to take it.

'It could be that it just happened to be lying on his desk, and she picked it up because it looked important,' Charlie suggested.

'I don't know,' said Robyn. 'It looks like it's been folded and kept in an envelope. Maybe the envelope was marked confidential or something, and Mrs Kemp thought that it might contain something which would incriminate him.'

They made a short detour off the parkway to White Plains, and stopped at Macy's on Mamaroneck Avenue to pick up a Concise French Dictionary in the book department. While Robyn paid for the dictionary, Charlie found himself glancing left and right like a criminal. Afterwards, they picked up two Big Macs and some hot black coffee, and they ate and drank as they drove south-westwards on the Hutchinson River Parkway towards New York.

Robyn said, 'I thought I'd never be able to eat anything again, after what happened this morning. Now all of a sudden I'm starving.'

'It's delayed shock,' Charlie replied. 'Just make sure you chew it properly.'

'You're the food expert. Although it beats me how you can be a food expert and still eat a Big Mac.'

Charlie swallowed, and sipped coffee. 'Let me tell you something, if you compared the hygiene in most high-class international restaurants with the hygiene at McDonald's, you'd never want to eat anything but Big Macs for the rest of your life. After about five years as a restaurant inspector, you realize that in spite of all the cockroach bodies and the rat droppings you might have been eating along with your veal parmesan and your chicken à la whatever, you're still alive and still comparatively healthy and you haven't had a day's sickness since you can last remember. I guess that's when you begin to understand that the human constitution is pretty resilient, and that you could probably eat a codfish pie out of some Bowery bum's back pants pocket without any noticeable ill effects.'

Robyn stared at him for a long time and then returned her Big Mac to its polystyrene carton. 'I'm not sure that I can eat the rest of this.'

They drove through New York and the spires of Manhattan glittered grey and silver in the last light of the day. Then they were heading south-westwards through Jersey and Pennsylvania, along Route 22 to Harrisburg. At Harrisburg, Robyn would take over the driving, but meanwhile she pored over Mrs Kemp's leaflet with her French dictionary open on one knee.

As they drove through the Musconetcong mountains, she closed the dictionary and said, 'Do you know what this is?'

'I wouldn't have asked you to translate it if I did,' Charlie replied. He glanced in his rear view mirror. So far he was pretty sure that they weren't being tailed.

'This is a kind of Célèstine newsletter. It gives a list of some of their up-and-coming meetings as well as their calendar for the year.'

'When do they have their church cookout?' asked Charlie bitterly.

'They have more important dates than that. In fact – according to this – the whole year is significant. This is the year of *Le Recreation*.'

'What does that mean? Sports, games, that kind of thing?'

'You've got to be joking. *Le Recreation* literally means The Re-Creation. This is the year they attempt actually to recreate Jesus Christ in physical form.'

Charlie looked at her. He was more tired than sceptical. 'Go on,' he said. 'Tell me what it says.'

Robyn angled the leaflet so that it was illuminated by the Buick's interior light. 'Brothers and sisters, Guides and Devotees . . .' Something something – I don't quite understand that bit. 'This is the year when the Prophecies of Sainte Desirée come to pass; when the Lord and Master will rise again, as was promised in *les temps anciens*; when the Body and Blood of Christ the Lord will be formed again out of the sacrificial flesh of all who worship Him. For three centuries, Devotees have devoured themselves, and what has remained of them has been devoured in turn by other Devotees until *au bout de ses vies* – at the end of their lives – these Devotees are devoured by their Guides.'

Charlie overtook a westbound livestock truck, and then turned to Robyn and said, 'Go on, I want to hear it.'

'It's so *bizarre*,' said Robyn. 'I find it hard to believe that it's true.'

'Go on, it's important. This may give us the information that we've been looking for.'

Robyn rubbed her eyes. Then she lifted up the leaflet again, and read, '"Each human soul which has been devoured has been recorded in the Ledger; and now we are approaching at last the sacred number that forms the very centre of the Prophesies of Sainte Desirée. That is, one thousand times one thousand souls."'

Charlie whistled. 'Do you know what that means? Since the Célèstines got started, nearly a million people have eaten themselves. A million! It's a holocaust!'

'Wait,' said Robyn, 'there's more. It says here that on the holiest of all weeks the Célèstines will gather together and observe a last sacrificial convenant. All of the remaining Devotees will devour as much of themselves as they can ... and the remaining Guides will devour what's left. At the very end there will be nobody left but one Devotee, who will become the Last Supper for the Master of Guides. When he has eaten the last of the Devotees, the Master will be transformed into the Lord Jesus Christ incarnate, whose body is the all-embracing temple of human souls. That's kind of a free translation, but it's near enough.'

'And when is this last supper scheduled?' asked Charlie.

'Whenever they reach the sacred number, I guess,' said Robyn. 'The leaflet doesn't give a specific date.'

'Well – that's one of the things we're going to have to find out in New Orleans,' said Charlie.

Robyn switched off the car's interior light and watched Charlie driving through the darkness. 'I still don't really understand why we're going to New Orleans at all. I mean – aren't you wasting time?'

'If I'm supposed to interpret that as 'Martin could be chewing his own fingers and toes by now', then I get your point. But you saw how things worked out this morning. I'm not cut out for that kind of a rescue. If I tried it again, I'd almost certainly wind up killed, and that would leave Martin completely at their mercy.'

He paused, and then he said, 'For most of my working life,

I've been eating at other people's tables without them realizing who I am. I guess you could say that my greatest asset is my anonymity.'

'So what are you going to do?'

'I'm going to New Orleans and I'll join the Célèstines, in disguise. A moustache and tinted spectacles and a haircut should do it. Then I'm going back to Le Reposoir and get Martin out from the inside.'

Robyn said, 'I suppose that's as good a way as any.'

'For me, it's the only way.'

'I don't quite see where I'm going to fit in.'

Charlie reached across the seat and held her hand. 'I'm going to need somebody on the outside to keep in touch with. At the very last moment, I'm going to have to get out of that place like Roadrunner with his ass-feathers on fire, and there has to be somebody there to do the driving.'

'You still want to me to drive, after the crash?'

'The crash wasn't your fault.'

'What happens if the Célèstines discover who you really are, and kill you? What am I supposed to do then?'

Charlie made a face. 'You forget you ever heard about the Célèstines, or Martin, or me, and you go back to your job and your parents and maybe a new boyfriend who doesn't give you a hard time, and you live out the rest of your life in peace and happiness.'

'You're suggesting that I never mention it, ever again?'

'Not if you want a long life.'

Robyn thought about that for a moment, and then said, 'There's one thing more. If you join the Célèstines, won't you have to start eating yourself?'

'I was actually hoping that I could be a Guide, rather than a Devotee. I don't know what qualifications a Guide is supposed to have, but I guess I could fake them.'

'But then you'd have to eat other people.'

Charlie gave Robyn a tight smile. 'Let me cross that bridge

when I come to it, huh? I'm hoping to get away without eating any human flesh at all.'

'This scares me,' said Robyn.

'You don't think it scares me too?'

Robyn took over the wheel just past Harrisburg, and drove into the night while Charlie lay on the back seat of the station wagon and tried to sleep. It took him until two o'clock in the morning to close his eyes. The smell of the vehicle was unfamiliar, so was the way it jolted over every bump and join in the highway, and the songs that Robyn was playing on the car radio all seemed to be songs of regret. He thought of Martin, lying naked on that plain bed at Le Reposoir, and he tried to touch him with his mind. *I love you, Martin, don't despair. Don't let them take you away.*

They stopped for an early breakfast at Buchanan, VA, a few miles short of Roanoke. They sat in a small drugstore drinking black coffee in silence and staring at themselves in the mirror behind the counter. They both looked exhausted.

'Are you sure we're doing the right thing?' Robyn asked, as they stepped out into the chilly morning air, and climbed back into Mrs Kemp's old Buick.

Charlie said, 'We could use some more gas. There's only quarter of a tankful left.'

Robyn leaned across and kissed Charlie's unshaven cheek. 'Don't worry,' she said. 'I'm with you.'

They drove into New Orleans on a humid, thundery morning, with the clouds hanging low over the city, and lightning flickering out over Lake Borgne and the Gulf beyond. Charlie had taken the wheel at Meridian, and Robyn was lying asleep in the back. For the past hour, the radio had been turned to a Louisiana station playing plangent Cajun and Zydeco music – high, shrill voices and accordions and fiddles double-bowed.

Charlie had called from Atlanta the previous evening to

make a reservation at the St Victoir Hotel, which was quoted in MARIA as being 'inexpensive, discreet, and authentic'. He knew that after more than thirty-eight hours of driving, the first priority for both of them was going to be sleep. It was no good regretting the time that they would lose. Their exhaustion had reached the point where they could see the highways unravelling in front of them even when they closed their eyes.

The St Victoir was a narrow-fronted nineteenth-century building between Bourbon and Royal, but it lacked the distinctive cast-iron balconies that characterized the finest architecture in the French Quarter. It was wedged between an over-expensive art gallery and a Creole restaurant called Jim's Au Courant. Inside, there was a cool air-conditioned lobby with potted palms and a marble floor and old sofas upholstered in damp green velvet that could almost have been moss. A fat lady in a floral frock sat behind a curved mahogany counter and smiled at Charlie and Robyn like Jabba the Hutt.

'Mr and Mrs McLean,' said Charlie. 'I made a reservation yesterday from Atlanta.'

The fat lady opened up her file drawer and picked her way through the reservation cards with tiny hands. 'That's right,' she said. 'Double room, looking to the back, for three nights provisional. May I take an impression of your card?'

Their bags were taken up by a black porter in a peaked cap who said almost nothing but hummed all the time. Robyn had brought a change of clothes from her parents' house; Charlie, of course, had taken his travelling-kit out of his Oldsmobile, before parking it right at the back of the Harris house and covering the licence plate with a plastic shopping bag so that it couldn't be identified by any passing police patrol.

Charlie had told Mr Harris that he and Robyn were taking a few days' vacation together in Canada. He had winked at Mrs Harris and Mrs Harris had obviously been pleased that Robyn had found somebody so quickly. Especially somebody so *nice*.

Charlie tipped the black porter and then closed and chained the door. The room was high-ceilinged and cool, with a huge mahogany bed and two massive mahogany chairs. There was a view from the back over the St Victoir's courtyard, shaded by layers of foliage. It had already begun to rain, heavy warm drops, and the palm leaves nodded in acknowledgement of the coming storm.

Robyn lay back on the bed and kicked off her shoes. 'I don't think I ever felt so tired in my whole life.'

'Do you want anything to eat?' Charlie asked her. 'How about some *beignets* and a pot of coffee?'

'I think I just want to sleep,' said Robyn.

Charlie went into the large tiled bathroom and slowly undressed. He took a long shower, standing for almost five minutes with his eyes closed, letting the hot water spray into his face. He shaved, but he took care not to shave the bristling beginnings of his moustache. Then he wrapped himself in a towel and went back into the bedroom. Robyn was already asleep, lying on her side with one hand against her cheek as if she were thinking. Charlie sat on the bed beside her and dried himself. She was a pretty girl. Even though she was wearing a crumpled checkered shirt and faded jeans and her hair needed washing, she had a femininity about her which Marjorie had always lacked. He rested his hand on her sleeping hip for a little while, and then returned to the bathroom to find himself a robe.

He lay on the bed and tried to sleep, but he couldn't. His mind was still crowded with thoughts of Martin, and M. Musette, and that grotesque living gargoyle they called David. He closed his eyes and heard the thunder booming over the delta, and the rain whispering through the leaves, and somebody playing the piano through an open window.

For a moment, he didn't know whether he was wakening or dreaming; but then he heard a door slam and footsteps in the corridor outside, and someone saying, 'Take those drapes down with you, don't forget.' He sat up, and looked at Robyn, She was still sleeping. He opened up his brown leather travelling bag and found himself a clean blue shirt and a pair of fawn non-crease slacks. He dressed, and then he wrote a quick note for Robyn on a damp sheet of Saint Victoir notepaper: *Gone to locate Elegance St, back soon, don't worry.* He signed the note, *Affctly, Charlie.*

By the time he reached the street, the worst of the rain had passed over, although the sidewalks still reflected the white-painted lacework balconies and the red and yellow horse-drawn carriages taking tourists around the Vieux Carré, and the sky was the colour of dynamite smoke. He approached a wizened-faced black man on the corner of Royal Street and asked him the way to Elegance Street. The man said, 'Elegance aint so much of a *street* as an *alleh.* But you don't want to go theuh. It's all churches and cat-houses.'

All the same, he directed Charlie westward on Royal, telling him to pass nine alleyways and courtyards on the left before he took the tenth, and that would be Elegance Street. Charlie thanked him and offered him a dollar. The black man took the money, but told him, 'Druthah a cigarette,' his eyes elderly, bloodshot, either drugged or drunk or too old to care about either.

Charlie walked along Royal Street, smelling rain and damp and gasoline and cooking, and jazz was playing on the wet morning wind, that pompous, stilted highly traditional jazz that the tourists come to hear but never really like, 'Didn't He Ramble' and 'St James' Infirmary' and 'Mahogany Hall Blues Stomp', musical relics of a day long past. He came at last to the narrow courtyard called Elegance Street, a shaded alleyway of old-fashioned brick that was overlaid with dripping palm leaves and overlooked by green-painted cast-iron balconies. Charlie passed the Crescent City Antiques Gallery and the Beau-monde Tearoom featuring clairvoyant readings by Madame Prudhomme. There, at the very end of the alleyway, stood a pair of black iron gates, with a plaque announcing L'Église des Anges. Charlie approached it with trepidation, and stood for a long time staring through the railings into the inner courtyard. There was a stone fountain, and a stone bench, and some wrought-iron garden chairs that somebody had knocked over sideways. But there was no sign of life, *pas âme qui vive* as the French would say. Not a soul alive.

Charlie dragged at the wet cast-iron bell pull. He didn't hear the bell ring, but after a very long time, a stocky man in a black monk's habit appeared. His hair was white as transparent noodles and his eyes were as blank as two mirrors. He approached the gates and stood staring at Charlie with the expression of a man of very little patience. Charlie said, 'Is this the church of the Célèstines?'

'This is the Church of the Angels. Some call us Célèstines.'

'A friend of mine used to belong. I've come to the conclusion that it's my turn.'

'Did your friend attend this church?'

'No. He went to the church in Acadia, L'Église des Pauvres.'

'That is our sister church,' said the man. 'Can you tell me what your friend's name was?'

There was a faraway protestation of thunder. Charlie said, 'I only knew him as Michel or maybe Michael.'

The man said, 'You can't do better that that?'

'He never told me his surname.'

'What did he tell you about his beliefs?'

Charlie glanced around, pretending to be furtive. Then he leaned closer to the gates, and said, 'He told me all about the self-sacrificial communion. He told me all about the body and blood.'

'I see,' said the man, his expression unchanging. 'And what was your response to that?'

'My response was that it sounded pretty extreme. You know, the idea of actually –' Charlie leaned closer forward and whispered, *'eating your own body.'*

The man eyed him coldly. 'Much of what we teach is metaphorical, you know. Not to be taken too literally.'

'But the whole core of your religion is this communion, right? The Last Supper, with real body and real blood.'

'You'd better give me your name,' the man told him. Rain began to sprinkle the courtyard again, and whisper through the leaves.

'Dan Fielding. I'm a chef.'

The man suddenly looked interested. 'A chef? Of what description?'

'I used to work for the South Western Hotel chain, mainly in their prestige restaurants. I could cook anything.'

'Did you ever cook . . . meat?'

'Are you pulling my leg? I was taught high-grade butchery as well as cooking. I can cut and trim a prime beef carcass in less than twenty minutes. And when I cook it, let me tell you this, nobody holds a candle to Daniel DuBois Fielding, believe me.'

The man said, 'You're not an Acadian.'

Charlie managed a smile. 'Of course not, I'm a Hoosier. Does it make any difference where I come from?'

'Strictly, no,' said the man. 'Although we *do* have a church near Lafayette, Indiana.'

'Really? I have cousins in Lafayette. I have cousins in Kokomo, too.' Charlie was deliberately acting naïf. The man listened to him patiently and the rain began to patter down heavier, until there were droplets shining on his soft black hood.

'Listen,' he said, 'why don't you come back here this evening? Maybe you'd like to talk to our chief Guide. Do you know about Guides? Did your friend from L'Église des Pauvres tell you anything about them?'

'I know about Guides,' Charlie said. He paused, and then added, 'I know about Devotees, too.'

'Well, you could be useful to us,' the man told him. 'Come back at nine. Where are you staying?'

'With friends, on Philip Street. Have you heard of the Cour-villes?'

'There must be five thousand Courvilles in New Orleans. But you come back at nine. Come alone, mind, just like you are now.'

'I understand. So long for now.'

Au revoir, monsieur.'

Charlie walked out of Elegance Street not at all sure if he had deceived the black-hooded man into believing that he was a genuine recruit for the Célestines or not. He had learned from his encounters with the Musettes that the Célestines were remarkably open and unafraid. This was not only because what they were doing was technically legal, or at least not technically *il*legal – but because like those who dealt in nar-cotics and heavy duty pornography and extortion, they had many influential friends.

He returned to the St Victoir Hotel to find that Robyn was still asleep. He was beginning to have swimmy sensa-tions, like jet-lag, but he was too agitated to sleep. He sat by the window in an upright chair looking out over the misty courtyard and listening to the sounds of New Orleans. Robyn murmured something, and turned over, but still didn't wake up.

Charlie's eyes began to close or maybe he was only dreaming that they were closing. His head nodded, and jerked. He could hear the rain trickling along the gutters. That piano was play-ing again, some high-stepping piece of music that sounded like Mussorgsky if Mussorgsky had ever written jazz. Some feeling made Charlie open his eyes again, a scarf of fear being laid gently over his shoulders. He looked down into the court-yard and he was sure that he glimpsed a small hooded figure disappearing amongst the palm fronds.

He was suddenly awake. Involuntarily, he said, 'Unnhh!' out loud, and Robyn lifted her head off the bed and stared at him.

'Charlie? What's the matter?'

'I was dozing. I frightened myself, that's all. It was only a dream.'

Robyn looked around the room with the glazed eyes of someone who has fallen deeply asleep in unfamiliar surroundings. 'I've been dreaming, too. I thought we were still driving. All those cotton fields. All those girder bridges. I thought I saw you standing in a field by the side of the road, calling me. But when you turned round, it wasn't you at all. It had a face like the Devil.'

Charlie eased himself up from the chair and walked over to the bed. The light in the room was the colour of pewter. 'It's so dark,' said Robyn. 'What time is it?'

'A little after twelve. It's been raining most of the morning.'

'Did you go out?'

'I found the Church of the Angels on Elegance Street. It's only three or four blocks from here. I'm supposed to be going back there at nine to meet the head honcho.'

'You should have woken me.'

Charlie sat down on the bed beside her and took hold of her hand. 'You needed your sleep.'

'And what about you? Aren't you tired?'

'In my job, fatigue is a way of life.'

Robyn combed through her hair with her fingers to loosen the sleep tangles 'Didn't you ever think about doing anything else? I mean – you didn't want to be a restaurant inspector when you were a little boy, did you?'

Charlie smiled. 'When I was a little boy, I wanted to be a zoo keeper.'

'That's a pretty smelly job, zoo keeping.'

Charlie laughed. Then he stopped laughing, and sat there silently with a smile on his face thinking about wanting to be a zoo keeper. He could remember all of those model animals, the tigers and the monkeys and the elephant with the broken ear. Robyn touched his shoulder and looked closely into his eyes, and he thought, you can always tell whether you're going to fall for somebody or not by their eyes. Love is retinal.

He kissed Robyn's forehead. It was still warm from sleeping. She closed her eyes and he kissed her lips. It was a long lingering kiss that was more romantic than passionate. Charlie hadn't kissed a woman like that in years. Not since Milwaukee.

In the midday twilight of a thunderstorm, Charlie unbuttoned Robyn's checkered shirt and bared her breasts to the touch of his fingertips. They were soft and heavy, and they fell to each side of her chest in full, pale curves. Her areolas were the palest pink, and as wide as pink-frosted cookies. Charlie bent forward and kissed her nipples and they stiffened between his lips. Robyn whispered something that could have been words of love; or maybe the words of a song.

He unfastened her jeans. That high-stepping piano music slowed down now, and Robyn's breathing was as soft as the rain. Underneath her jeans she wore French lace panties, peach-coloured, transparent, so that the dark delta of her pubic hair showed through. Charlie slipped his hand into the leg of her panties and felt a thin slippery line of wetness that almost made him feel as if all his emotions were going to self-destruct.

They made love for over an hour. He kissed her neck, kissed her shoulders and watched as the shining shaft of his erection slid in and out of that perfect dark delta. Feelings washed over him like bayou water, muddy, warm, and blinding, but always moving with a slow, strong current. Robyn sang that little song again, softly as a memory. At the very last she opened her thighs as wide as she could and he touched and tasted her, and then put his fingers to his lips and anointed her nipples so that they glistened for a moment like diamonds.

Robyn showered, then they ventured out of the St Victoir to the Café du Monde on Decatur Street, where they indulged themselves in a late lunch of beignets dusted with powdered sugar and piping hot *café au lait*.

Charlie could afford to relax, because he had done all that he could possibly do; and all that was left was to wait until nine o'clock. He didn't forget about Martin. He couldn't, because Martin was the reason he was here. But he allowed himself to walk hand in hand with Robyn through the French Quarter, around Jackson Square, where the twin Pontalba Buildings shone oddly orange in the afternoon light, and along Pirates Alley, where they stopped to look at paintings of nudes and bayous and old black men with wrinkled faces and straw hats, art for the tourist trade.

They reached the end of Pirates Alley, and emerged into an unexpected slice of sunshine, when Charlie caught a glimpse out of the corner of his eye of something white and small, fluttering like a flag. He stepped back to see what it was, and trod on the foot of an old lady who had been walking close behind him.

'You watch where you're treading!' she squawked, and lifted her stick as if she were going to strike out at him.

Charlie said, 'Please – I'm sorry. I thought I saw somebody I knew.'

Robyn took hold of Charlie's hand. 'What is it?' she asked him. She could see that he was upset.

'I'm not sure. I glimpsed it before, in the courtyard at the back of the hotel. At least, I *thought* I glimpsed it. I thought I was dozing off that time, but maybe I wasn't.'

'What?' asked Robyn. 'What was it?'

'The dwarf, the one who killed Mrs Kemp. The one who cut my leg.'

'But nobody could have followed us here. Nobody knew where we were going.'

Charlie shaded his eyes from the misty sunlight and tried to peer between the constantly changing patterns of passers-by. 'No,' he said. 'He's gone; if he was ever there.'

'You're over-tired, said Robyn. 'You've started hallucinat-ing.'

Charlie nodded. 'Maybe you're right. Let's go back to the hotel.'

They walked back to the St Victoir. The fat woman like Jabba the Hutt beamed at them as they passed the reception desk.

'Everything *va bien*?' she asked them.

'Fine, thank you,' said Charlie. 'We're very comfortable.'

'*Les haricots sont pas salé,*' the woman sang, as they walked across to the elevator.

Charlie was opening the decorative sliding elevator gate. He turned when he heard the women singing and said, 'What was that?'

'Just a song, *monsieur*.'

'Charlie?' Robyn frowned.

'I don't know,' said Charlie. 'Not only am I suffering from *déjà vu*, I'm suffering from *déjà écouté*.'

Robyn kissed him as the elevator rose up to the fourth floor. 'It's all this Cajun French. It's having an effect on your brain.'

Charlie checked his watch. It was almost four o'clock. Robyn saw what he was doing and covered the face of his watch with her hand. 'Don't think about it,' she said, with great gentleness. 'Don't think about it until you have to.'

CHAPTER SIXTEEN

The rain had cleared by nine o'clock but the streets were still steamy and wet, so that the lights of Bourbon Street glistened and gleamed on the sidewalks and on the rooftops of passing cars and brightly in the eyes of those who had come to listen to jazz, or those who had come to eat at Begue's or Mike Anderson's, or those who had come simply to gawp, or to score.

Against his will, Robyn had made Charlie sleep for two hours during the afternoon, and then join her downstairs in the St Victoir's restaurant for a meal of blackened redfish and rice, with ice-cold beer. There were two musicians playing under the single large palm that dominated the St Victoir's old-fashioned dining rooms: a toothless old black man of about eighty playing a fiddle and a pale, pimply boy of no more than thirteen or fourteen sitting on a stool and playing a piano accordion. They played several Cajun *complaintes*, with the boy singing in a high, weird voice. Then they played 'Les Haricots Sont Pas Salé' which was the song that had given Zydeco music its name – *les haricots* repeated over and over until it was slurred. Charlie had the feeling that he had woken up in the wrong century, on the wrong continent.

He had checked his watch at a quarter to nine, and given Robyn a tight, anxious smile. 'Time I was going,' he told her. She had reached across the table and taken hold of his hand and said, 'Take care. Just remember that whatever happens, you've got somebody to come back to.'

They walked together to the corner of Royal Street. Then Charlie kissed her and made his way along the crowded sidewalks to Elegance Street. The little courtyard was lit by a single 1920s lamp standard, and from the main street it was impossible to see the gates of the Church of the Angels. Charlie hesitated for a moment, listening to the noise of traffic and laughter and music, and then walked through the shadows until he reached the gates. He pulled the bell and waited. He wore only a lightweight grey tweed jacket, a short-sleeved shirt, and a pair of pale grey slacks, but he still felt sweaty and hot. He heard a clock strike nine; he heard a jet scratch the sky. They were like his last reminders of the real world.

The man with the black hood and the hair like Japanese rice noodles appeared so suddenly and so close to the gate that he made Charlie jump. 'You are very punctual, Mr Fielding,' he remarked. 'You'd better come on in.'

Charlie thought: *This is it. This is the moment of decision. I can back out now if I want to.* But then he thought of Martin. He thought not only of the Martin he had come to know in the past few days, before the Célèstines got hold of him, but the Martin he had known on his rare visits back home, when he was small. Suddenly, a dozen images of Martin that he had long forgotten came crowding back to him, and by the time the man in the black hood had shot back the bolts and unlocked the locks, he was ready to go, carried on a floodtide of emotional memories.

The man made a noisy performance of relocking all the locks and rebolting all the bolts. Then he said to Charlie, 'Come this way,' and led him across a courtyard that was so dark that Charlie could see where he was going only by the faint gleam of wetness on the paving stones. Soon, however, they reached the back of a large old house, which Charlie guessed must have fronted on to Royal Street, although where and how he couldn't quite work out. It was three storeys high, with black-painted cast-iron balconies, and black shuttered windows from which no light penetrated whatsoever. The man in the black hood led Charlie up a flight of stone steps to the front door.

'This house has quite a history,' he remarked, as he produced a key and turned it in the lock. 'It was originally built by Micaela Almonester de Pontalba, who also built the Pontalba buildings on Jackson Square. It was said that she had a secret admirer, and this was the house she built for their romantic trysts.'

'Interesting location for a church,' said Charlie.

The hooded man said nothing, but admitted Charlie to the hallway. Charlie was immediately struck by the smell, which reminded him strongly of Le Reposoir. It was a curious blend of herbs, and cooking, and dead flowers, and something else besides which was unidentifiable but slightly unsettling. The smell not of death but of *pain*.

The hallway was decorated with a mustard-coloured dado and wallpaper that looked as if it had been chosen from the Sears catalogue of 1908. A chandelier of black cast iron had a dozen bulbs but gave out very little light. There was a heavy bow-fronted bureau, with a black bronze statue of Pope Célèstine on it, lifting his hand in benediction. The man in the black hood led Charlie up to a pair of double doors, and said, 'You are about to meet the chief Guide and his council of Guides. The chief Guide here is Neil Fontenot. Some of the council you may recognize. But the etiquette among the Célèstines is for members not to acknowledge each other's existence outside of the church. Your friend probably told you that.'

Charlie gave him a quick-dissolving smile.

'Very well, then,' said the man, and opened up the doors.

Inside, there was a large plain room in which a dozen middle-aged men sat at a long mahogany dining table. The dining table had been polished so deeply for so many years that the men sitting on the opposite side of it were reflected upside down from the waist, so that they looked like kings and knaves on playing cards. The men were dressed in long black robes, with hoods cast back. As Charlie and his escort entered, they were all looking attentively towards the far end of the room, where a tall man with a cadaverous face was reading the Bible from a lectern.

In a rich, resonant voice, he was reading the Parable of the Dinner, in which a man invited his friends to eat with him, only to be met with repeated excuses and refusals. 'And the master said to his slave, "Go out at once into the streets and lanes of the city and bring in here the poor and crippled and blind and lame. Compel them to come in, that my house be filled. For I tell you, none of those men who were invited shall taste of my dinner."'

The chief Guide raised his head, and said, 'What do we learn from that? That Jesus believed in our divine mission. That Jesus taught us to fulfill our hunger. And what is our hunger? The *real* hunger, to which most men dare not confess. The hunger for the body; the hunger for blood. The hunger for the only food of which man is worthy. Were we ever supposed to eat pigs? The Jews say no! Were we ever supposed to eat cattle? The Hindus say no! My friends, when you read the New Testament today and consider the words of Jesus, you know in your hearts that there is only one true way.

'For what did he say at the Last Supper? He said, "*this is My body, given for you; do this for a commemoration of Me,*" and he said, "*This cup is the new testament in My blood.*"'

At last, the chief Guide turned to Charlie. He smiled, and came over, extending a long-fingered right hand. 'My friend. Welcome to the Church of the Angels. Xavier told me that you were coming.'

'I feel like I'm interrupting,' said Charlie.

'Interrupting? Of course not! We are always pleased to greet new members. I understand from what Xavier told me that you used to have a friend who was a Célèstine?'

Charlie gave an equivocal shrug. 'I never really knew what they were. All I know is, Michael was happy. Well – we called him Michael. I think his real name was Michel.'

M. Fontenot draped his arm around Charlie's shoulders, and led him down to the head of the table. There was a large mole on M. Fontenot's right cheek, and his nose was peppered with blackheads. He said affably, 'Your friend Michael was a Devotee, was he?'

'Charlie said, That's right, a Devotee.'

'And are you fully aware what happened to him?'

Charlie glanced around. 'Can I say it here?'

'Of course you can,' smiled M. Fontenot. 'Openly.' He looked around at the other Guides assembled at his table and beamed in the way that a father beams at other fathers when his son has said something cute.

Charlie said, 'The fact is, Michel told me everything that he was going to do. He said he was going to eat his own body, as much as he could, and that was the way to find Jesus.'

'And now you want to find Jesus in the same way?' M. Fontenot asked. The Guides at the table broke out into spontaneous but ragged applause.

Charlie nodded his head in what he hoped looked like idiotic acknowledgement. 'Michel said it was the only way. Michel said that if you wanted to follow Jesus, you had to do whatever Jesus did. What was the very last thing that Jesus did, before He was arrested and tried and crucified? He ate His own body and His own blood. And that was His secret! The secret that gave Him eternal life, the secret that nobody else understands. That's what Michel told me, anyway.'

M. Fontenot took hold of Charlie's hand, and said, intently, 'Yes! *Yes!* And that is why they call us the Célèstines, the Heavenly Ones. Those who are chosen by God. Because only the Célèstines understand what you have to do to sit at the right hand of Jesus. You have to devour the flesh of your own creation. That is the secret of winning God's approval. And that is the secret of everlasting contentment and perfect peace. "I am the bread of life," that's what Jesus said. "Eat me," that's what Jesus said. And Jesus ate the bread and drank the wine, too. Jesus devoured his own body and his own blood, and that was his way to heaven; just as ours is.'

Charlie said, 'I understand you're close to some kind of big occasion.'

M. Fontenot didn't seem particularly pleased to have been interrupted. 'Occasion? I'm sorry?'

'The sacred number. You've almost reached the sacred number. Isn't that right?'

'Who told you that?' asked M. Fontenot, narrowing his eyes. He stared at Charlie for a moment, and then turned to the man in the black hood called Xavier. 'Did *you* tell him that?'

Xavier shook his head. 'Not me, M. Fontenot. But his friend was a Célestine, M. Fontenot. He knows what we do, and he's sympathetic. Believe me – I think we can trust him. He's not an FBI agent. We checked it this afternoon with FBI records. Quite apart from that, just look at him. He's not exactly FBI material, is he?'

Charlie put in, 'You can trust me, I promise. You want me to cut my throat and hope to die? Here, look – here's my wallet. You can check me out as much as you like. Driver's licence, credit cards. Here.' He prayed that they wouldn't actually look. 'My friend was a Célestine; and I want to be one, too. Tell me – what else is there, in a world full of bombs and guns and ultimate weapons? To see God! To sacrifice yourself, and to see God! Don't you think that's the greatest trip of all?'

M. Fontenot seemed a little pained by the word 'trip', but Charlie was fairly sure that he had already won him over. His evangelical enthusiasm had helped; but it was obviously far more important to the Célestines that he was a chef, and an experienced butcher. (Not that he was, of course; but he believed that he could keep on bluffing for long enough to rescue Martin.)

M. Fontenot turned to Xavier and between them they had a

short, whispered conversation. At length, Xavier said, 'M. Fontenot is prepared to accept you as a Devotee, monsieur. However –' (and here he smiled as innocently as a small boy) '– he is anxious that you should be able to press your talents as a butcher into the service of the church; and for that reason he is asking you not to embark on your self-ingestion straight away. There will be need of many men with talents like yours when the Great Day comes, men who can quickly cut and prepare good meat, and he begs you not to start mutilating yourself until this Great Day is over.'

Charlie tried to look as if this were a disappointment. He lifted his fingers in front of his face, and wiggled them, and said, 'Oh, well, whatever you want. If you can tell me how I can serve the Lord some other way, some different way, then I'll be listening.'

M. Fontenot said, 'You will be allowed one finger.'

Charlie's face tightened. 'What did you say?'

'You will be allowed one finger. You can cut it off and cook it and eat it as soon as you wish.'

In a brittle voice, Charlie said, 'That seems kind of a small offering, don't you think, for my initiation as a Devotee? Maybe I should wait until the Great Day is over. Then I can make a proper job of it and eat my whole arm.'

M. Fontenot smiled at the other Guides, and some of them laughed. 'If only all of our new Devotees had the same spirit!' he proclaimed.

But straight away he turned to Charlie, and said, 'Now. You say you can butcher; you say you can cook. You say you are one of us. Xavier, bring me the knife. Bring me the pan, and the spirit-lamp. You like your flesh with herbs, monsieur? Xavier will bring you some fennel.'

Charlie felt a prickling surge of fright. 'You want me to do it *now*?'

M. Fontenot laid his arm encouragingly around Charlie's shoulders. 'We do what we can do to check the credentials of those who wish to join us. As you may have gathered, we have friends who give us access to the records of the FBI. But there is no simpler test of your faith and your good intentions than to have you take part in the sacred communion, the holy ingestion of your own flesh.'

He lifted up his left hand and Charlie saw for the first time that two of his fingers were missing. His smile was like a deep crack in a dried-out cheese.

'People are either for us, Mr Fielding, or else they're against us. There's never two ways about it. So despite the fact that we're a registered church, and despite the fact that we enjoy the patronage of some of the most influential men in the country, we still take care to protect ourselves against saboteurs and extremists and other ill-advised folk.'

As he said this, Xavier came back into the room wheeling a small trolley draped with a white cloth, on which was embroidered in purple the Lamb of God and a crucifix made from two crossed keys. M. Fontenot beckoned to Xavier to wheel the trolley right up close, and then he nodded and said, 'Thank you, Xavier.' Charlie's throat was as dry as glasspaper and his heart was beating in huge, irregular bumps.

'You may be feeling a number of things,' said M. Fontenot. 'You may be feeling elation. You may be feeling trepidation. But let me tell you this, if you're afraid, you have no need to be. The human body is a miracle in itself. It has wonderful powers of self-healing. Why, I was reading just the other day that a man had his leg knocked off by a locomotive, and dragged himself two miles to look for help. And that was his *leg* we're talking about. All you're surrendering here this evening is your finger.'

With a small flourish, M. Fontenot drew the white embroidered cloth away from the top of the trolley. Neatly laid out on the trolley's stainless-steel top was a spirit-burner, of the kind used in restaurants to flambé steaks, two plain white plates, a glass bottle of what looked like olive oil, a small china jar of fresh fennel leaves, a knife and a fork, a scalpel, and a small stainless-steel hacksaw. Neatly folded on the lower shelf of the trolley were three white towels, some gauze bandages, and some surgical adhesive tape.

Charlie tried to swallow. He wanted to say something but he was almost completely incapable of getting the words out. M. Fontenot said, 'It's the simplest act in the whole world, my friend. If your heart is in it, if your spirit is in it, your pain will be part of your joy. Believe me, we have brothers and sisters here who have to be restrained from cutting more from themselves that their nervous systems could tolerate; such is the holy joy they derive from self-amputation and self-ingestion. Now – we will say a prayer for you, to welcome you into our church, while Xavier lights the burner.'

Charlie thought: *They're going to kill your son, McLean. They're going to kill Martin. One of your fingers is a pretty small price to pay for the whole of his life.* But another voice inside of him said: *This is going to be agony. This is going to be more than you can take. And just remember that it's two days now since you last saw Martin alive. They could have killed and eaten him already.*

Xavier came forward and lit the burner – rather irreligiously, Charlie thought, with a flickering Zippo lighter. Xavier lifted the small copper chafing pan from the top of the burner, and adjusted the flame until it was hot and blue. Then he laid a folded white napkin on the table in front of Charlie, and beside it set the scalpel and the saw.

'Amputation is a simple matter,' he murmured. 'Feel where the lower joint of your chosen finger is, then cut through the skin with the scalpel until the bone is bared. Then use the saw. It will take you no more than a matter of moments.'

'Please – sit,' said M. Fontenot, and drew out a chair so that Charlie could sit down. All around the table, the Guides were smiling at him like old friends at a testimonial dinner. Charlie found their calmness and their good nature to be the most alarming part of the whole ritual.

227

'I think we should remember the words of St Paul in his letter to the Romans,' said M. Fontenot. 'And, as we do so, we can join with our brother Daniel DuBois Fielding as he enters the order of the holiest of Popes, St Célèstine.'

Xavier took hold of Charlie's left wrist and gently guided his left hand until it was lying on top of the white folded napkin. Then he took hold of his right wrist, and laid his right hand beside it. Into the open palm of Charlie's right hand he pressed the scalpel. The ridged metal handle felt intensely cold. The triangular blade winked in the light from the chandelier.

'"*One man has faith that he may eat all things,*"' M. Fontenot intoned. '"*But he who is weak eats vegetables only. Let not him who eats regard with contempt him who does not eat, and let him who does not eat judge him who eats, for God has accepted him.*"'

Charlie spread the fingers of his left hand wide on the napkin. Which one do I choose? Not the index finger, that would cripple me. I'd never be able to use a typewriter again. What about my middle finger? That would be even more disfiguring.

'Are you prepared?' asked M. Fontenot. 'Have faith, brother David. Do not hesitate. Hesitation may reveal you as one who does not truly believe.'

Charlie glanced up at him. There was an expression on M. Fontenot's face which may have seemed benign to everyone else in the room, but which Charlie read as an unmistakable warning. He looked down at his hand again, and made an instantaneous choice. The ring finger. The finger which still showed that he had been married to Marjorie. He slowly tugged off the plain gold wedding band, and set it down on the shiny mahogany table. There was a murmur of approval from the assembled Guides, and Charlie could see some of them staring at his hand with expectancy that approached lasciviousness. In Charlie's mind, there was no doubt at all that the rituals of the Célèstine church were tightly intertwined with the rituals of religious and sexual masochism; that the ecstasy of self-mutilation was orgasmic as well as spiritual.

'*Now*,' whispered M. Fontenot.

Charlie said his own silent prayer. Then he adjusted his grip on the scalpel and scratched a hesitant line around the base of his ring finger. He scarcely drew any blood; but it stung, badly. Everybody in the room was watching him in silence.

He clenched his teeth together, and cut more deeply into the top of his finger. Surprisingly, he felt almost no pain at all, but the sensation of sharp steel touching his bare bone made him shiver in his seat.

'*"If your enemy is hungry, feed him,"*' M. Fontenot quoted, as the bright red blood suddenly welled up out of the gaping slit in Charlie's finger. '*"If he is thirsty, give him a drink."*'

Charlie's hand was trembling wildly, but he knew now that he had passed the point of no return. He cut into the side of his finger until once again he could feel the blade up against the bone. Then he lifted his hand and cut around the far side, and the underneath, while the blood pumped out of the wound like water out of a badly fitting plumbing joint. He laid the gory scalpel back down on the table, and took hold of his ring finger, tugging the flesh a little way upward to make sure that it was cut through to the bone all the way around. He could actually see the bone, and he was surprised how white it was, just like bone of a real skeleton.

The pain was extraordinary. His finger hurt so much it seemed to roar out loud. Added to that, he could feel that he was close to going into shock; stunned by the gruesomeness of what he was doing to himself. But one part of his mind remained completely detached. One part of his mind concentrated on finishing this amputation as quickly and as cleanly as possible. One part of his mind was already thinking of what the wound would look like when it was healed. He didn't want any splintered or mutilated flesh.

M. Fontenot said, in a voice that now seemed to Charlie to be echoing all around him, '"*Nothing is unclean in itself; but to him who thinks anything to be unclean, to him it is unclean. For if because of food your brother is hurt, you are no longer walking according to love. Do not destroy with your food him for whom Christ died.*"'

Charlie pressed his bloody left hand flat on the folded white napkin, staining it instantly and heavily. His mouth was tightly closed, and the breath jerked in and out of his nostrils like the breath of somebody sobbing. But there were no tears in Charlie's eyes. His agony was too total for him to be able to cry.

He picked up the small saw. Wincing, he nudged the blade into the open wound on his finger. When he felt the sawblade against the bone, he hesitated, and looked up at M. Fontenot once again. 'Go on,' said M. Fontenot, encouragingly.

Charlie drew back the saw, and then rasped it forward over his finger bone. He didn't know whether he screamed out loud or not. When he opened his eyes and looked at the assembled Guides, who were all watching him in fascination, he could tell that he probably hadn't. But he had bitten the inside of his mouth: he could taste the blood.

'Go on,' M. Fontenot urged him. 'Only a few more strokes, and it will all be over.'

Mechanically, Charlie sawed at his fingerbone again, and then again. The pain was extreme, but the vibration of the saw teeth all the way through the nerves of his hand and up the lower part of his left arm was even worse. He sawed and sawed and then suddenly he felt Xavier's hand on his shoulder. 'You should stop now. Your finger is off. We don't want you to damage the table. It's antique, you know.'

Charlie stared at his left hand. His ring finger was completely severed, and lying in between his middle finger and his little finger at a peculiar angle, as if it were a joke finger that you could buy in a Mardi Gras carnival store. Slowly, stiffly, Charlie set down the saw. Then he raised his hand, and said to Xavier, 'Do you have . . . something to stop the bleeding?'

'Of course, brother,' said Xavier, and reached down to the lower shelf of the trolley to find a large gauze pad. Charlie held the pad over his pumping wound while M. Fontenot walked around the table, nodding to his Guides and smiling to himself. 'It is always an occasion, the very first cut,' he said. But then he came back around the table to stand over Charlie so close that Charlie could only see the ebony crucifix that hung low on M. Fontenot's chest. He laid an unwelcome hand on top of Charlie's head. 'But very much more of an occasion, of course, is the very first taste of one's own flesh.'

Xavier had now returned the small copper pan to the top of the spirit burner. He poured a little olive oil into it, and deftly tilted it so that the whole of the pan was evenly coated. As the oil began to bubble, Xavier leaned forward to Charlie and said, 'Your finger, please?'

Charlie stared at him, uncomprehending.

'Your finger,' Xavier repeated; and at last it registered in Charlie's shocked brain what he was supposed to do. He picked up his severed finger and held it up. It felt hard and strange and very dead. Xavier indicated with an encouraging nod that he was supposed to drop it into the pan, and so he did. There was a brittle sizzling noise, and Xavier quickly rolled the finger from one side of the pan to the other so that the outside of it was sealed by the heat of the oil. To Charlie's disgust, even the red flesh where he had cut the finger off turned the colour of cooked pork, a light whitish brown.

'Human flesh is rich, and it should be thoroughly cooked,' said M. Fontenot. 'However, one must be careful not to overdo it, otherwise it quickly becomes tough.'

Charlie sat where he was, silent, unable to take his eyes away from the finger which was frying in front of his face. The skin was turning crisp, especially around the edges of the fingernail, and because the fat was now dissolving, the finger slowly bent of its own accord, as if it were beckoning to him from the frying pan.

Charlie had anticipated all the horror of this ritual for days.

In some ways, he was prepared for it. It was almost a relief that he had found out what the Célèstines did and how they did it. But what he could never have prepared himself for was the smell. It was similar to frying pork only it was quite unmistakably *not* pork. It was strong and meaty and (in a nauseating way) almost appetizing.

Xavier added a little fennel to the pan, and stirred the finger around to make sure that it was properly cooked. M. Fontenot watched Charlie with dark eyes that never once deviated as one of the white plates was set in front of him and the finger, still steaming, was placed on it like a small morsel with which to begin a very much grander dinner.

'Your contribution to the holy covenant,' said M. Fontenot. 'Your sacrifice, your very first; and let us hope you will give many more.'

Xavier took the bloody gauze away from Charlie's left hand, and replaced it with a clean pad. Already the wound was beginning to clot, and Charlie had to admit that M. Fontenot was right: the human body did have extraordinary powers of recovery.

'Do I . . . share it?' asked Charlie, trying not to look down at the crisply fried finger.

M. Fontenot shook his head. 'This one is all for you. Later, perhaps, when you wish to have your legs removed . . . then you can share your flesh with your brothers in Christ. For this evening, however, your meat is your own. For what you are about to receive, may the Lord make you truly thankful.'

It was a long time before Charlie could pick up his fork and prod at the finger on his plate, but M. Fontenot and the rest of the Guides remained silent, watching, giving him as much time as he needed. Charlie had the feeling that they had watched such reluctant ceremonies before. The room was filled with such expectancy that it almost seemed to exert a gravitational pull, as if the rest of the world would be irresistibly drawn towards it like nuts and bolts to a powerful magnet.

Charlie stuck his fork into the fleshy underside of the finger. The crisp skin made a slight popping noise as it was penetrated by the tines of the fork. Then Charlie lifted up the finger and somehow managed to guide it towards his mouth. His stomach made an audible groaning noise, and he could feel the back of his throat tighten up.

'Xavier, bring brother David some wine,' said M. Fontenot. 'I know how it is! Very difficult to bite, very difficult to swallow. But just remember, my friend, the human body is the greatest of all foods, because the human body is the vessel of the human spirit; and no other creature on earth has a spirit. This meat that you are about to eat is the food not of the gods but of the One True God. Think how much you will be offending Him if you refuse it. Think how much you will be offending all of us.'

Again, the implicit warning. Charlie knew that he was going to have to eat his finger if there was going to be any chance at all of him rescuing Martin.

He bit. The flesh came away from the bone quite easily. His mouth was filled with the taste of meat and fat; and the terrible part about it was that it was meat that needed to be steadily chewed. With rising nausea, Charlie swallowed a half-masticated piece – a piece that would have seemed tiny if he had been eating chicken or beef, but which felt as if it were the size and texture of a small hessian-covered sofa.

Xavier held a glass of red Californian wine in front of him. He swallowed, and nodded in appreciation.

The Guides of the Church of the Angels sat and watched Charlie for almost twenty minutes as he slowly ate the flesh of his own ring finger. At the end of that time he was sweating, and very close to vomiting; although the bone that now lay on his plate was bitten quite clean, even around the fingernail. It didn't look like Charlie's finger any more: it looked like a broken piece from a biology lecturer's skeleton.

Xavier took the plate away, and wheeled the trolley out of

the room. M. Fontenot drew up a chair next to Charlie and sat smiling at him with his legs crossed and his fingers laced together. 'Well,' he said, 'you have done exceptionally well. You have crossed the threshold into the Church of the Célèstines. How do you feel now about the so-called horror of horrors – the eating of human flesh? Have you changed your opinion?'

Charlie wiped his mouth with his napkin. The wound on his left hand where he had severed his finger was throbbing so painfully that he found it difficult to think straight.

'I guess it was a shock,' he told M. Fontenot.

'But a *good* shock, wouldn't you agree?' M. Fontenot pressed him. 'Good for the spirit, and – dare I say it – good for the palate, too?'

'I've never experienced anything like it,' said Charlie, quite truthfully.

M. Fontenot paused for a moment, and then he said, 'Not even at the Napoleon House, or Le Tour Eiffel, or Pascal's Manale?'

'I'm sorry?' Charlie asked him. He really didn't understand what M. Fontenot was talking about. Not unless he meant –

'They're all restaurants, aren't they?' M. Fontenot asked him.

'That's right,' Charlie acknowledged.

'And that's what you do, isn't it? You travel around the country, under various assumed names and aliases, testing restaurants?'

Charlie's eyes were half closed with pain. He was gripping his left wrist with his right hand as tight as a tourniquet, in an effort to deaden the throbbing. 'You must have me mixed up with somebody else,' he told M. Fontenot. 'I'm a chef, not a restaurant inspector.'

M. Fontenot shook his head. 'You were never a chef, my friend. Nor were you ever a butcher. Both a chef and a butcher would have cut through that finger joint in two quick *coups*.

234

You didn't even know where the joint was, not properly. Look how badly you have injured yourself.'

He turned to the Guide sitting closest to him, and leaned forward and whispered something. The Guide said, '*Certainement, M. Fontenot*,' and got up from the table, leaving the room by the same door through which Xavier had wheeled the trolley. M. Fontenot then leaned back towards Charlie, and said, 'You should have known that we suspected you from the ease with which we admitted you to this assembly. As a rule, no lesser church officials are permitted to intrude on these meetings, and no Devotees are allowed anywhere near. This is what that old radio programme used to call the inner sanctum.'

Charlie held up his left hand, swathed in bloody gauze. 'If you suspected me right from the beginning, then why –?'

'Why did we let you amputate your own finger? My dear Daniel – or perhaps I should call you my dear Charles – if you thrust your head into the lion's mouth, you should occasionally expect a nip or two around the neck. If not complete decapitation.'

The door opened again, and back came the guide whom M. Fontenot had sent out of the room. Beside him, waddling on his stumps, came the hooded dwarf who had murdered Mrs Kemp. He made his way around the table and heaved himself up on to a chair. Charlie watched him in dread and fascination. So he hadn't been mistaken. He had seen the dwarf at the back of the St Victoir hotel, and at Pirates Alley.

'We found it quite astonishing that you thought you could get away from us,' said M. Fontenot. 'Also, that we would dream of letting you go. You made one attempt to break into Le Reposoir to take your son away from his chosen destiny. You would surely make another. This, one supposes, is it. A clumsy effort to infiltrate the church of the Célèstines, in the hope that you might be able to snatch your son away at a moment when our guard was relaxed. And where were you going to go then? To Canada, perhaps? Some of them go to Canada. But most try Mexico. It's a pity for them that we have such a close arrangement with the Mexican police. *La mordita*, that's what they call it. The bite. They will do anything for money.'

Charlie stood up, unsteadily. 'I think you'd better let me leave.'

'I'm sorry,' said M. Fontenot. 'That is absolutely out of the question.'

'You can't keep me here against my will.'

'You came here voluntarily.'

'Sure I did. But now I want to leave, and there's nothing you can do to stop me.'

M. Fontenot turned around in his seat and gave the dwarf a quick summoning wave. The dwarf rolled himself off his chair and came swinging up towards him. He stayed close to M. Fontenot's knee, his eyes gleaming malevolently out of the shadows of his hood.

'You have seen what David can do with a machete,' said M. Fontenot blandly.

Charlie said nothing, but stared back at the dwarf with equal enmity.

'As I say,' said M. Fontenot, 'You came here voluntarily. During the course of the evening's proceedings, you suffered an unfortunate accident to your finger, and since I have all the necessary medical facilities right here at L'Église des Anges for the treatment of such a wound, I suggested that you stay. An offer, of course, which you readily accepted.'

Charlie went suddenly white. He could feel the blood draining from his face just like a bucket being emptied. 'I have to throw up,' he told M. Fontenot. His stomach was churning and twisting and his mouth was flooded with bile and bits of chewed-up flesh.

Xavier took him to the bathroom along the hall and he was violently and painfully sick. He used his left hand to support himself as he leaned over the toilet and it left a wide smear of blood on the white paint. Strings of meat dropped from his stretched open mouth. He spent almost five minutes in there before the spasms in his stomach began to subside.

M. Fontenot was still waiting for him when he returned. 'You will stay here in this house until Friday. Then you will come with us to Acadia, to L'Église des Pauvres. That was the mother church in the early days when the Célèstines were still outlawed. It is there that we will be holding our Last Supper.'

Charlie lowered his head. His eyes were watering and the taste in his mouth was greasy and filthy and reeked of the aniseed flavour of fennel.

M. Fontenot reached forward and tapped him on the shoulder. '*Monsieur*, I advise you not to try to escape from us, nor to make trouble.'

CHAPTER SEVENTEEN

In the small hours of the night, when the pain became intolerable, a nurse appeared in a white winged wimple like the ghost of an albatross flying out of the darkness. Through half-closed eyes he saw the glint of a needle. Then she had injected him; and it was only a few minutes before the pain ebbed away, and dark waves of relaxation began to lift him buoyantly into the ocean of the night.

He dreamed about the strange high-ceilinged restaurant again, with the waiters who were hooded like monks, just like he had at Mrs Kemp's, and even though he was asleep he was conscious that the dream had been curiously prophetic. He saw the men in their starched shirt fronts and immaculate tail coats. He saw the mysterious and alluring women, some veiled, some wearing masks made of bird's feathers, most of them naked. One woman was standing by the doorway, her thighs and genitals tightly bound with thin leather straps, her large breasts completely covered with tattoos. She turned and looked at Charlie, and her face was the face of Mme Musette. In front of his eyes, she fell apart in great lumps of human clay.

A monk-waiter brought his meal, underneath a shiny dish cover.

'Your dinner, sir,' he whispered, and lifted the cover. Charlie knew what he was going to see there, and screamed.

He screamed, but he was drugged with morphine, and he didn't wake up. Instead, one dream closed and another dream opened. He found himself driving along West Good Hope Road in Milwaukee. It was snowing. Everything was white.

The snow pattered against the windshield and the wipers had trouble coping with it. The world crept around in silence.

He could see her on the front steps of the single-storey house as he approached. Her husband was with her. He knew what has happening even before he reached the end of their block. He could see her husband's arm rising and falling, rising and falling, like a man trying to chop down a tree. He watched her fall to the porch floor, then try to get up again.

And in his dream, he was condemned to do what he had done in real life. He drove past slowly because it was snowing, staring all the time at the one woman he had really loved being beaten by her husband. And as she had tried to struggle to her feet, she had turned, and looked towards him, and recognized him through the partially misted window of his car, driving past without stopping as if he were a helpless passenger on a passing train. And their eyes had met and they had both known that was the very end of their love affair, and then he had turned the corner and when he managed to back up the car and turn and drive past the house again, they were gone. In his dream, he stopped his car and got out and went up to the front door and beat at the knocker, just as he had done in real life. In his dream, the knocker turned into the wolf-knocker on Mrs Kemp's front door, and he could feel its bristles in the palm of his hand. Then the door was hurtled open and there stood Velma from the Windsor Inn, her face hideously white, her eyes red-rimmed, both arms severed at the elbows and spraying blood like fire hydrants.

He screamed again, and this time he woke up. It was light.

There was a woman in black sitting beside his bed. She pushed back the hood that covered her face and he saw that it was Mme Musette. She was smiling at him.

'I had a nightmare,' he croaked.

She nodded. She took a glass of water from the small table beside his bed, and passed it to him with a hand that was nothing more than a thumb and an index finger. He hesitated, and then accepted it, and drank. When he returned the empty glass, he looked down at his own hand. Sometime during the night it had been expertly bandaged, and although it still ached, the most severe pain seemed to have subsided.

'Where am I?' Charlie asked. He looked around the plain whitewashed room. There was a high window through which he could see the branches of a large live oak, and a crucifix carved out of ebony was hanging on the wall, but apart from that the room was completely bare. Charlie was naked, but he was covered by a single white sheet.

Mme Musette said, 'You're upstairs, at L'Église des Anges. We have a nurse here. She's been taking care of you.'

'My finger,' said Charlie.

'A brave sacrifice,' said Mme Musette. 'You won't miss it.'

'Is my son all right?' Charlie wanted to know.

'Martin? Of course. Martin is very well.'

'He hasn't –?'

Mme Musette shook her head. 'He hasn't yet begun the act of self-ingestion, if that's what you mean. He's being saved, you see, for the great Last Supper.'

'I don't understand you people at all,' Charlie snarled at her.

'We know that. That is why I am here. The Last Supper is to be held on Friday at L'Église des Pauvres in Acadia. We want you to be there, to participate in our ceremonies. When you were trying to gain access to Le Reposoir, you talked to my husband of Saul on the road to Damascus. Well, we want you to play that part for real. We want you to be our Saul. We want you, our persecutor, to be our ultimate convert.'

Charlie said, 'You're going to try to convert me to cannibalism? That's the worst joke I've heard all year.'

'We're going to show you the truth and beauty in what we do,' Mme Musette replied.

Charlie fiercely held up his bandaged hand. 'Truth and beauty? Does that look like truth and beauty? That looks to me like deliberate mutilation of God's own creation.'

Mme Musette smiled again. It unnerved Charlie, the way that Célèstines kept on smiling, regardless of how insulting he was to them. It made him realize that they believed without question that their grisly re-enactment of the Last Supper had been ordained by Christ. They really believed it.

Mme Musette said, 'Do you remember the quotation from Paul's letter to the Romans that M. Fontenot read to you yesterday evening? *"Nothing is unclean in itself; but to him who thinks anything to be unclean, to him it is unclean"*. When we come to our Last Supper, when a thousand thousand have devoured themselves and been devoured, then you will see the divine truth of what the church of the Célèstines has been doing. Do you remember what the angels said to the Apostles? *"This Jesus, who has been taken up from you into heaven, will come in just the same way as you have watched Him go."'*

Charlie stared intently into Mme Musette's eyes for a moment, and then said, 'I want you to let my son go. Do you understand that? If you want to keep me, well, we can talk about that. But you have to let Martin go.'

'I'm sorry,' said Mme Musette, 'but that would be quite impossible. He has already been blessed. He has already been numbered. *He* – by great good fortune – is the thousandth thousandth Devotee. When he is devoured, my husband will become the fleshly temple of a million souls, the embodiment of a million self-sacrificial communions. My husband will become at last a worthy vessel on earth for the return of Christ the Saviour. On Friday, Mr McLean, you will witness the event for which the world has been waiting for almost two thousand years, the second coming of the Son of God, as it was foretold in the Acts of the Apostles.'

'For Christ's sake,' Charlie protested.

'Exactly,' replied Mme Musette, her beatific smile unwavering. 'For Christ's sake. He gave His body and blood in order that the human race might survive. In return, a million human souls have willingly given *their* body and blood in order that He might return.'

'And this is why the government and the police and the press have left you alone? Because *they* believe it, too?'

Mme Musette nodded. 'The turning point came ten years ago when the then President's son became a Devotee. The President tried, as you have tried, to talk his son out of self-ingestion. But at last the President himself was persuaded. Not to join the Célèstines himself, but to leave us unharassed by the law as we approached our ultimate Last Supper. As he said himself, Jesus Christ may come to us, or He may not, but if there is even the remotest chance that the second coming takes place on American soil, then that chance must be nurtured. To us Célèstines, of course, the joy will be purely spiritual. But the Administration were not so blind that they could not see the political advantages of the Son of God choosing the United States for his triumphal return. America would become the Holy Land, even above Israel.'

'I don't believe what I'm hearing.' said Charlie.

'How can you *not* believe it? You have seen for yourself the people of Allen's Corners, Mr Haxalt and Sheriff Podmore and all the others. If the Célèstines did not have government approval, would we be able to recruit so openly, would we be able to discuss our religion with such freedom? The government of the United States believes that Christ will come again, Mr McLean. Why don't you?'

Charlie lowered his eyes. He looked down at his left hand, and stiffly opened and closed his fingers. 'If Christ returns to earth because you kill my son, then let me tell you this: He's not the kind of saviour that I want to know about.'

'Now you're being petulant,' said Mme Musette.

'Petulant! You've kidnapped my son, you've forced me to cut off and eat my own finger, and you have the gall to call me petulant!'

Charlie tugged away the sheet, and swung his legs off the bed. Mme Musette made no attempt to stop him.

'Where are my clothes?' Charlie demanded.

'Burned, I expect. That's what they usually do.'

'Then get me something to wear!'

'I will if you wish,' said Mme Musette. 'But before you attempt to escape, perhaps you ought to remember that there is nothing at all you can do to stop us. Apart from having government approval, we have friends and supporters in all of the law-enforcement agencies. Besides which, it would be *very* unwise of you to go to the police or the FBI. There is a Federal warrant out for your arrest, on a charge of homicide in the first degree.'

'What the hell do you mean?' Charlie sat down on the side of the bed, and pulled the sheet over to cover himself.

'The Connecticut police want you in connection with the murder of Mrs Kemp. She was discovered hacked to death by a machete, and the fingerprints on the machete were yours.'

Charlie said, 'What have you done to me? And *why*?'

Mme Musette laid her one fingered hand on Charlie's knee, making him recoil. 'We have done nothing, Mr McLean. Everything that happened to you has been a consequence of your own actions. If you had simply accepted that your son has chosen a different path from yours, then you would have been free to continue your life unharmed and unmolested. We are a religious order; not terrorists.'

She stood up, and drew her cloak tightly around her. 'I shall be back. We have much more to talk about. By Friday, I want you to believe.'

'You can want what you like, you won't get it from me.'

'Mr McLean,' said Mme Musette. 'I want you to believe not for my sake but for yours. You are a man whose existence has no meaning. You stumble through life as if you are wearing a blindfold. You allow yourself nothing: no purpose; no love. Even when you attempt to indulge yourself, as you did with

243

Velma, it brings you nothing but difficulty and pain. Think about it, Mr McLean, I am talking about having a goal. I am talking about bringing back the Saviour Jesus Christ in order to save the entire world. Your son is already part of that. In fact, your son is the ultimate part of that. You could be part of it, too.'

Charlie said, 'I think you'd better get out of here.'

'Very well,' said Mme Musette. To Charlie's complete surprise, she leaned forward and kissed his forehead. 'I shall come later, some time this afternoon, when you have rested some more.'

She left, and closed the door behind her. Charlie didn't hear a key turn in the lock, but when he went across and tried the handle, he found that he couldn't open the door even by wrestling with it. He went back to the bed and sat down.

So – the Célèstines had sewn him up. He couldn't go to the police for help, nor to the media – and that was supposing he was able to escape, stark naked, in the middle of New Orleans. On Friday the Célèstines were going to sacrifice Martin in the deranged belief that his death would bring about the second coming of Christ, and there was nothing at all that he could do about it.

He lay back on his pillow and cursed himself for handling the Célèstines so clumsily. Their friends in the FBI and local police forces must have been tracking him and Robyn all the way from Waterbury to New Orleans; and the Musettes must have flown to New Orleans yesterday. Some private investigator he turned out to be.

About a half-hour later, the nurse in the wimple came in and re-dressed his wound for him. She gave him another pain-killing injection and took his pulse, watching him all the time with eyes as blue as water.

'Do you really work for these freaks?' Charlie asked her, but she didn't answer. She packed up her black leather medical case and straightened his sheet and left him lying alone in his plain whitewashed room with only the nagging ache in his missing finger for company.

Charlie began to think about Mme Musette. Did it really show that badly, that he was living a life without purpose? There had never been very much purpose to begin with, but he had lost it for ever when he had driven past her house that day when her husband was beating her. Why hadn't he stopped? Why hadn't he jumped out of the car and run across the snowy sidewalk and beaten up her husband and claimed her for his own?

Maybe he had realized that, for her, he was just a dream, and that she never would have been happy leaving her husband. He beat her, but she belonged to him. She had *told* Charlie about the beatings, but she had never *complained* about them. Charlie had always been so tender towards her, bringing her flowers, treating her like a princess. Maybe that wasn't what cocktail waitresses wanted out of life. Maybe tenderness without pain had no meaning.

He could see her in his mind's eye as clearly as if he had only just turned away from her. Her name was Dolores. He had met her in the bar of what had then been called the Sheraton Schröder, in Milwaukee. He had been drunk and she had been desperate to hide the bruises on her cheek. They had fallen genuinely in love. It had been one of those sad stories, played on an off-key piano. '*When I fall in love ... it will be for ever .., or I'll never fall in love ...*'

Dolores would haunt him for ever more. He would see her face the day he died, watching him in desperation as he drove past her.

He slept for a while. The drugs made him feel incredibly dopey. When he woke up, there was a tray on his bedside table, with cold chicken and salad and a glass of mineral water. The sky outside the small, high window was intensely blue, as if somebody had spilled ink across a drawing pad. The live oak shone gold. He drank the mineral water but he couldn't face the thought of eating. His throat was still sore from yesterday's vomiting. And chicken! How could he possibly eat anything that had once been alive?

Later, when the sky was beginning to pale, Mme Musette reappeared, wrapped in her cloak like a Bedouin, with only her eyes showing. She sat in her chair beside his bed, and said nothing at all for five or ten minutes; simply watching him, and waiting to see what he would do.

'You've been thinking,' she said at last.

'Of course I've been thinking. There's nothing else to do.'

'No – I mean thinking *seriously*. Thinking about yourself.'

'What if I have?' Charlie challenged her.

Mme Musette allowed her eyes to register amusement. 'It's good for you, to think about yourself. Perhaps you're beginning to understand that you need some purpose in your life. You can't spend the rest of your life aimlessly wandering from one restaurant to another, until MARIA decides that you're past your prime. Because what will you do then? Will you kill yourself? Or will you simply allow yourself to fall to pieces, little by little, piece by piece, until there is nothing left of you but unfulfilled longings and curled up credit card slips?'

Charlie said, 'You'd better go. You're not going to convert me. You're wasting your time.'

Mme Musette stood up. She drew back her black cloak. Underneath it, she wore a severe black dress, and black stiletto shoes. 'I promise you, Charlie, you will kneel down in front of me, before this week is finished. You will kneel down in front of me and kiss my feet and profess your love for Jesus, the resurrected Saviour, and for Saint Célèstine, and you will tell me that you adore me.'

'I don't think so,' said Charlie.

Mme Musette came closer. Charlie could smell her perfume, which was rich and exotic; but he could also smell her womanly body. There was a hint of that honey-and-bleach odour about her, as if she had very recently had sexual intercourse. She

246

kissed his forehead, even though he turned away, and said, 'You are such a fool. The whole world is lying in front of you, stretched out at your feet. It could be yours.'

'I insist that you release my son,' said Charlie.

'How can we release him, if he has never been captive? He came to join us of his own free will; he remains here of his own free will. Yesterday, he was flown down to Acadia with my husband, M. Musette, and the remaining Devotees from Connecticut. The moment of ultimate fulfilment is fast approaching! We want you to share in it, Charlie. We want you to participate! We want you to understand at last what belonging can mean, and the joy of joining with others in the name of Jesus Christ!'

Charlie said, 'You have to let him go. I'm his father. You can do what you like with me, but you have to let Martin go. I mean it, Mme Musette. He has his whole life in front of him. I'm not going to allow him to waste it on some oddball sect like the Célèstines.'

'So you *do* believe in self-sacrifice,' said Mme Musette triumphantly.

'What do you mean?' Charlie demanded.

'You would give up your life to save your son.'

'If there were no alternative, yes.'

'But your son is offering to give up his life for the Son of Man. Is that any different? How can you approve of one kind of sacrifice and deny the validity of another?'

Charlie rubbed his eyes. 'If you think you're going to be able to persuade me with that kind of argument, you're wrong.'

Mme Musette said nothing for a very long time. Charlie, for his part, volunteered no further questions and no further comments. He had nothing to say to Mme Musette except that he wanted Martin to be released, not only from his physical bondage but from his mental bondage, too.

At last, Mme Musette said, 'Do you wish to leave?'

Charlie looked up. 'What do you mean?'

'You can leave here if you want to, and take your chances in the world outside.'

'You'd let me?' asked Charlie suspiciously.

'If you really feel that there is nothing for you here, yes,' Mme Musette looked incomparably beautiful in the late afternoon light that fell though the window. Her dark hair shone like the wing of some rare desirable bird of paradise.

'All I want is my son.'

'You cannot have your son. Your son is not a possession. He does not belong to you, any more than he belongs to us.'

'Then there isn't any point in my leaving, is there? I might as well stay here.'

'The choice is yours, Charlie. I don't want anyone to say that we held you here against your will. How does your finger feel?'

'It still hurts. Maybe not as badly as it did before.'

Mme Musette kissed him again. This time, he did not recoil. Her kisses were strangely alluring, and consoling, too. Her lips were very cool, and somehow he didn't mind being held by those hands which had only one finger and a thumb. Mme Musette left the room, closing and locking the door, but for a long time her perfume lingered in the air, like a memory that refused to die.

Charlie eased himself off the bed and went to the window. If he stood on tiptoe, he could see the edge of an adjacent rooftop, and the back of a brick facade. The clouds rolled by, curdled and lazy and trailing skirts of misty rain.

He seemed to have reached an impasse – a point in his life at which he was equally unable to go forward or to go back. Ahead lay the horrors which – even though they had been graphically described to him – were still unimaginable. Behind him lay indecision, confusion, and a lack of fulfilment so complete that it yawned in his life like a chasm. He stood naked looking out of the window of the cell from which he had been invited to escape, and tears ran down his cheeks and on to his chest.

When it was dark, they brought him a supper of grilled white fish and wholemeal bread. He asked if he could take a bath or a shower, but the girl who brought him the food didn't reply. Close on midnight, he lay on his bed and fell asleep, his finger still throbbing with every pulse as a reminder of his own folly.

CHAPTER EIGHTEEN

It was scarcely dawn when he became aware of somebody moving around in his room, and the rustling of fabric. He opened his eyes just as the door closed, but he was sure that he glimpsed the swirl of a long black cloak, like a shadow disappearing under a bridge. He sat up in bed and saw that his clothes had been neatly laid out on the footboard of his bed, his shirt and his pants and his sports coat, although there was no underwear or socks.

He climbed out of bed, and went directly across to the door. He tried the handle and it was unlocked. He opened it as quietly as he could, and peered out into the corridor. He could smell flowers, and flesh, and floor polish, but the house seemed silent and the corridors appeared to be deserted. He closed the door, and quickly went back to his room to dress. A few hours of sleep had done wonders for his optimism. If Mme Musette was offering him a chance to get out of here, then he was prepared to take it – even if it was just another ambush. He pulled on his pants and his shirt, slung his sports coat around his shoulders, and stepped out of the room barefooted.

They're watching me, he thought, as he hurried along the corridor towards the stairs. *They know exactly what I'm doing but for some reason they want me to go. Well, I won't disappoint them. I want to go too. This place is making me mental.*

He took the softly carpeted stairs three at a time. The staircase led directly down to the main hallway, which was panelled in Cuban mahogany and hung with impenetrably dark oil paintings. The huge front doors were locked but only from the inside. Charlie slid the bolts one-handed, and turned the latch. Quite abruptly, and without any difficulty at all, he was out on the street.

It was Royal Street, as he expected. The air was cold and damp and there was very little traffic around, except for a garbage truck toiling from one restaurant to another, collecting sackfuls of trash. Charlie closed the door of the Célèstine house behind him, and crossed the street. On the opposite sidewalk, he turned around and looked back at the house. Its black balconies were empty; its black shutters were closed tight over its windows. If anybody was watching him, they were keeping themselves well out of sight. Charlie hesitated for just one moment, then turned the corner and made his way back to the St Victoir Hotel.

He crossed the lobby and went up in the elevator to the third floor. He tapped on the door of his room, and waited. When there was no answer, he tapped again. 'Robyn? It's me, Charlie! Open up!'

Still there was no reply. Charlie knocked again, very much louder, and said, 'Robyn? Robyn? Are you there?'

At that moment, a voice behind him said, 'If you're looking for your wife, Mr McLean, you're out of luck.' Charlie turned around to find the fat woman like Jabba the Hutt standing behind him with her hands on her hips.

'She was booked to stay another day,' said Charlie.

'Sure she was. But she said she had to check out, didn't say why. She paid for the room on her credit card and went. But she left you this letter. Said to make sure that nobody else got to know about it.'

'Well, thanks,' said Charlie, and took the letter with a frown.

The fat woman said, 'You hurt your hand?'

Charlie said, 'What?' And then, 'Yes, oh yes. I got it caught in the door of my car.'

'Your wife took your car. And your baggage, too, such as it was.' The fat woman smiled as if she expected to hear some rare scandal when Charlie opened his letter.

Charlie tore open the envelope with his teeth, and tugged out the enclosed sheets of paper. In Robyn's deft, sprawling handwriting, he read:

Dearest Charlie, I have been followed ever since you left me and I am worried that they might be Célèstines. I have tried to shake them off several times but they always pick up my trail again which suggests that they know that I am staying here. I am moving to the Hotel Pontchartrain on Canal Street and will stay there until I hear from you. I am registered under the name of Batger which was my mother's maiden name. If they are still following me I will move again but I will leave you a forwarding letter. Love, love, love, Robyn.

Charlie folded up the letter and tucked it into his pocket.

'Not bad news?' the fat woman asked, with considerable relish.

'No, no. My wife had to go back to New York. Her father suffered a stroke.'

The fat woman said, 'You didn't stay here the last two nights, did you?'

Charlie looked at her, but didn't answer.

'I'm not being nosy,' the fat woman told him, 'but there was some gentlemen asking after you. Tall, polite. Frenchmen, I'd say.'

Charlie took out Robyn's letter again and held it up. 'You didn't show them this?'

'My dear sir, I didn't even tell them I had it. I may tattle now and again, but I don't break the confidences of my guests, believe you me, that's more than my position is worth.'

Charlie said, 'I'm sorry, I can't tip you, I don't have any money.'

The fat woman wobbled her jowls. 'Never you mind. Your wife paid me good. And when you do get yourself some money, the first thing you'd better get yourself is some shoes.'

Charlie looked down at his bare feet. 'I guess you're right. One pair of Gucci loafers, urgently required.'

'There's some plastic sandals in the closet under the stairs,' the fat woman told him. 'You can borrow them. The cleaning man uses them when he's sluicing the lobby.'

So it was that Charlie set out west along Bourbon Street at six o'clock in the morning wearing blue plastic flip-flop sandals. A cruising police car followed him slowly for a couple of blocks, making him sweat, but after a while it turned south, and he was alone again. An elderly black was wheeling a pushcart slowly along Royal Street and calling out, 'Ragaboon! Ragaboon!' It reminded Charlie of that song. '*Rags and old iron . . . rags and old iron . . . all that he wanted was rags and old iron.*'

He reached the intersection of Royal and Canal, opposite Shoppers World and the tall balconied building of Leonard Krower & Son. He crossed over, and headed north towards the Hotel Pontchartrain. He felt tired and thirsty and his finger joint was beginning to hurt again. His plastic sandals flopped on the sidewalk, and once he almost tripped over them because they were two sizes too small.

In spite of its grandiose name, the Hotel Pontchartrain was a small modern hotel that had been built on the site of the old Tessler building. Charlie pushed his way through the bronze-tinted revolving doors and into the brown-carpeted lobby. It was chilly inside; the air conditioning was down to fifty-five degrees. As he waited at the reception desk for the smooth-faced black receptionist to finish checking in a pair of British students who were determined to make sure that they took advantage of everything that was included in the price of their package vacation, Charlie began to shiver, like a man close to the end of his endurance.

'Ms Badger?' the receptionist repeated. 'I'll call her room number for you.'

'Batger,' Charlie corrected him.

'Badger,' the receptionist dutifully agreed.

At last, Robyn answered the phone. The receptionist nodded to Charlie, and said, 'She says to go on up. Room 501.'

Charlie leaned against the side of the elevator with his eyes half closed, ignoring the stares of the British students, for whom his dishevelled appearance had obviously confirmed everything they had ever heard about violent America. Blood was seeping into the gauze around his left hand, and his face in the elevator mirror was ash-grey, like a zombie.

'Do you think we ought to ask him what's wrong?' the girl student asked, in a stage whisper.

'I don't think so. This isn't exactly Dorking, is it?'

He knocked at 501 and Robyn immediately opened the door. 'Charlie, my God, I didn't expect to hear from you for days. What's happened? You look terrible!'

Charlie limped into the room and sat down heavily on the bed. It was only a single room, decorated in ginger and mustard, with a bed, a television, a crowded bathroom, and a view of Canal Street. Robyn closed the door and then came to kneel down beside Charlie and take hold of his hand.

'Charlie, what happened?'

'They were on to me all the time. They've been keeping tabs on us all the way from Connecticut.'

'Your *hand* –'

'Uh-uh. Don't touch. It's still throbbing.'

'But what happened?'

Charlie took a deep breath. For some inexplicable reason he was close to tears. It was probably delayed shock. 'They pretended that they were fooled. They made me go through a little Célèstine initiation ceremony. I had to cut my finger off. Then they cooked it and made me eat it.'

'Oh, my God,' said Robyn. She ran her hand through Charlie's tousled hair, and held him close. 'Oh, my God, Charlie.'

'I could use a drink,' Charlie told her. 'Do they have room service here?'

'Sure they do. It's a little slow, but willing. What do you want? Don't you think I ought to take you to the hospital? You don't want that finger to go septic.'

'A Scotch first, with a Michelob Lite. Then the hospital, okay?'

'Okay,' said Robyn shakily, and kissed him, and went to the phone to call room service.

'I don't know why they let me go,' said Charlie. 'They had me locked up in a room on the top floor of that building. They even took away my clothes, and told me they were burned. Mme Musette was there. She kept coming in and trying to persuade me that my life had no meaning and that I ought to join the Célèstines to save my soul. Then for no reason at all, she came up this morning and gave me my clothes back, and left the door unlocked.'

Robyn knelt down beside him again. 'Maybe they decided you were beyond conversion.'

Charlie gave her a wry smile. 'They believe in the second coming. That's what all this cannibalism is supposed to be leading up to. They think that if you eat yourself, and then somebody else eats what's left of you, then that person acquires your soul. So when *they* eat themselves, and somebody else eats what's left of *them*, two souls get passed on, and so forth, until they reach the divine number of a thousand times a thousand.'

'That's what that leaflet was all about,' said Robyn.

Charlie nodded. 'The last of the Last Suppers. The final communion. And according to Mme Musette, it takes place Friday, in the town of Acadia. They're all going to be there, all the Célèstines.'

Robyn looked at Charlie closely. His eyes were brimming with tears. 'There's something else, isn't there? Tell me.'

Charlie swallowed. 'It's Martin. I guess I should be glad that they haven't harmed him yet. But the way it's worked out, he's going to be the thousandth thousandth soul. "Great

255

good fortune", that's what Mme Musette called it. On Friday, her husband is going to kill him and eat him, and that supposedly is going to make M. Musette into a fitting vessel for the second coming.'

'I don't think I understand that,' frowned Robyn.

'Me neither. The whole Goddamned lot of them are only playing with half a deck. But the trouble is they *believe* in it. They believe in it so Goddamned sincerely that they've even managed to persuade the US government to turn a blind eye to what they're doing. According to Mme Musette, the administration is more than willing to give them a shot at bringing Christ the Lord back to earth, because it'll be such a boost for America's international standing, not to mention the tourist trade.'

'Can anybody be that cynical?' asked Robyn.

'What do they care?' said Charlie bitterly. 'A few missing kids stay missing, that's all. Serves them right for running away from home in the first place. The police don't mind. If they know for sure that the kids have been recruited by the Célèstines, they don't have to waste time and manpower looking for them.'

'What are you going to do?' asked Robyn.

'I don't know yet,' said Charlie. 'I want a drink first, then a bath, then I'm going to have this hand fixed. It hurts like all hell.'

'They actually made you *eat* it?' said Robyn.

'Yes, they actually made me eat it. Why? Do you want to know what it tasted like?'

'I'm sorry,' Robyn told him, ruffling his hair again. 'I didn't mean to upset you.'

Charlie touched her cheek. 'I'm sorry, too. I guess I'm over-tired, that's all.'

'Maybe we could get some help, a private detective or somebody like that,' Robyn suggested. 'They have agencies that specialize in snatching back children from divorced fathers, don't they? Maybe one of them could snatch Martin back. Have they brought him down to Louisiana yet?'

'Yes. Mme Musette told me. They're holding the Last Supper at L'Église des Pauvres, in Acadia.'

'All right, then. Let's get you fixed up. Then let's see if we can find one of those people to help us. There's bound to be somebody in the yellow pages.'

Charlie lowered his head. He started to laugh; but his laughter quickly turned to sobs of exhaustion. 'God, you're so practical,' he told Robyn. 'Who would have thought of looking in the yellow pages to find somebody to save my son from being eaten alive?'

'Come on, Charlie, rest,' said Robyn. 'They'll be up with your drink in a minute.'

Charlie eased off his plastic sandals and lay back on the bed. 'I have to admit, I feel dreadful,' he said. 'Do you want to turn on the television? I could use some light relief.'

Robyn went across and switched on *The Flintstones*, and then changed channels to a local news bulletin. A black woman was complaining about teenage dope dealers in Audubon Park. Robyn said, 'I'll run your bath, okay?'

Charlie closed his eyes for a moment, and said, 'I don't know what I would have done without you.'

'You would have survived. You're a survivor.'

There was a quick knock at the door. Robyn called, 'Coming!' and she came out of the bathroom. 'That'll be room service.'

She opened the door and instantly it was banged wide. In came a wide-shouldered half-caste with tight curly hair and a face like pitted oak. He was followed by M. Fontenot, in a crumpled, fawn summer-weight suit; and behind him, wearing a silky white gown, came Mme Musette.

'What in hell are you doing here?' Charlie demanded, sitting up.

Mme Musette closed the door behind her. 'You will have to forgive us, Charlie. It was the only way.'

'What do you mean, "the only way"?'

'The only way in which we could quickly locate your lady companion,' said M. Fontenot, with the same benign smile that had disturbed Charlie so much in the Church of the Angels. 'We had her under observation yesterday evening, but she disappeared, and so obviously the most expedient way of finding her was to let you find her for us.'

'Who are these people?' Robyn wanted to know.

Mme Musette closed and opened her eyes like a cat. 'Charlie will introduce us, won't you, Charlie? Although you haven't yet met Henri, have you? Henri is what you might call my argument of last resort.'

Henri patted his bulky seersucker sports coat, to indicate that he was wearing a shoulder holster. Mme Musette said, 'Sometimes even the most persuasive of words are not enough.'

'What do you want?' Charlie asked her.

M. Fontenot said, 'You must return with us now to Elegance Street. The Last Supper is too important to us for it to be jeopardized in any way. You are still not persuaded, you see, of the truth of what we believe, and you are still intent on taking your son away from us. This lady is your accomplice. And so, you see, we must insist that you remain with us until after the second coming.'

'I'm not going anywhere,' Robyn insisted.

'But my dear, it is imperative,' said Mme Musette. 'Not only imperative, but in your own personal interest, too. There is an FBI warrant out for your arrest, as an accessory to first-degree homicide, and as an accomplice to interstate kidnap. And a stolen vehicle has been found at your parents' home in Connecticut, and you are wanted for questioning in connection with that.'

'You're completely cracked,' said Robyn.

Mme Musette smiled. 'You will never forgive yourselves if you miss the second coming. And we will never forgive you if you do anything at all to interfere with it. You must be there,

258

Charlie! Imagine it! And your own son will be the final sacrifice to restore the Lord Jesus Christ to His throne on earth.'

Charlie gave Robyn a sideways glance, but said nothing.

Robyn said, in a challenging voice, 'Does it have to be Charlie's son? Can't you see what you're putting him through?'

Mme Musette came up to Charlie and gently stroked his cheek with her one finger. 'Charlie's son is already numbered and blessed in preparation for the Last Supper. It is an honour, not a punishment. Charlie will understand that soon, when the Lord Jesus Christ reappears in front of us, and so will you. I told you that you would kneel down before me and kiss my feet, didn't I, Charlie? And so you shall.'

Charlie jerked his cheek away and looked up at Mme Musette defiantly.

She pretended to be offended, and then laughed. 'I'm offering you everything, Charlie. Purpose, meaning, success. If you stay with the Célèstines, who knows? – you could become an executive of the church. You could be an administrator, an overseer, spreading the word of the Célèstine order all over the world. You could be the kind of man people admire.' She turned to Robyn. 'As for you, my dear, we always have vacancies for trained communicators.'

'Stick it in your ear,' said Robyn. 'I'm not going anywhere, not with you, and neither is Charlie.'

M. Fontenot said, 'I regret that you have no choice. I am quite prepared to give Henri the instructions to do away with you. Of course, I would rather not.'

Charlie eased himself up off the bed. 'All right,' he said. 'We'll come. But on the strict condition that you don't hurt Miss Harris here. No finger-chopping ceremonies, do you understand me?'

Mme Musette bowed her head. 'Nobody at the church of the Célèstines has ever had even the smallest morsel of their body removed without their full consent. Remember, Charlie, even you cut your finger off voluntarily. If you had admitted that you were not genuinely interested in joining us, we would not have obliged you to do it. Every act of self-amputation and self-ingestion is done willingly and joyfully.'

Charlie lifted his left hand. 'Do you call this joyful?'

'I call it appropriate,' said Mme Musette. 'A sort of poetic justice.'

'Now, let's go,' put in M. Fontenot.

'I don't have any shoes,' Charlie reminded him.

'You have the plastic sandals you wore to walk here. Besides, our limousine is right outside. You won't have to walk far.'

Charlie sat down on the edge of the bed and picked up the sandals. 'It's a pity about Mrs Kemp,' he said, as he tugged them on, one-handed.

Mrs Kemp, thought Robyn. *What on earth is he talking about Mrs Kemp for?*

'Mrs Kemp lost everything,' Charlie went on. M. Fontenot and Mme Musette weren't really listening. 'Her niece, her boarding house business. Her car.'

As he said this, Charlie looked intently at Robyn, almost as if he were trying to transmit his thoughts by telepathy. 'She lost her car,' he went on, 'and then she lost her life. Poor Mrs Kemp. All she has now are the keys to heaven.'

Robyn suddenly realized what Charlie was trying to say to her. *The car keys, make sure you take the car keys with you.*

'Are we ready?' asked M. Fontenot impatiently. 'The last thing I want is another parking ticket.'

'May I take my purse?' asked Robyn. 'It's there, on the bedside table.'

M. Fontenot picked up her small, red-leather purse, opened it up, and quickly rifled through it to make sure that it didn't conceal a gun or a canister of Mace. Charlie heard the keys jingling in the bottom of it, and lowered his head a little to hide his tension. M. Fontenot passed the purse to Robyn, and said, 'Now perhaps we can go back to Elegance Street.'

They left room 501 and walked along the corridor towards the elevator. Apart from Charlie's plastic sandals, they could have been delegates to the Pontiac Dealers of Illinois' Fall Convention, which was taking place at the Hotel Ponchartrain all this week – executives and secretaries. They went down to ground level without speaking to each other, although Henri kept clearing his throat.

Together they crossed the lobby, making their way through a milling crowd of over-enthusiastic motor-dealers. M. Fontenot went through the revolving door first, followed by Robyn and Mme Musette. Charlie hesitated, but Henri said to him. 'Go on, you go ahead,' and the expression on his face wasn't the kind of expression that gave him much leeway for argument.

Charlie pushed his way around; but just as he reached the street he suddenly forced himself backwards against the glass behind him, arresting the door's momentum. Then he quickly knelt down, preventing Henri from pushing forward by keeping his back against the glass, snatched off one of his plastic sandals, and wedged it underneath the bottom of the door. Henri shouted out loud, and tried to heave the door around further, but all he succeeded in doing was wedging the shoe more tightly, and imprisoning himself in his own section of the door.

'The car!' Charlie shouted, hopping across the sidewalk.

M. Fontenot, seeing what had happened, rushed to the revolving door and tried to drag the sandal out, but Henri kept on pushing the door, not realizing what was holding it. Several convention delegates tried to turn the door, too, and one of them started arguing with M. Fontenot and telling him to get out of the way.

Mme Musette rushed up to Charlie and clung on to his jacket with her mutilated hands. 'Charlie! This is madness! You can't go! Stay, Charlie, don't be such a fool! What kind of a life can you possibly have without us?'

Charlie tried to pull her away from him, but she held on. Robyn came up behind her, hooked her arm around her neck, stuck out a leg behind her, and ju-jitsued her on to the sidewalk, flat on her back. Mme Musette screamed. M. Fontenot, turning around, jostled his way through the conventioneers and approached Charlie with his fists raised. Charlie swung his arm around and gave him a stupefying open-handed slap on the side of the head.

Charlie kicked off the other sandal and he and Robyn ran along the sidewalk, dodging passers-by. They collided with two elegant young black men in matching berets, and knocked over a sack of trash that was waiting for collection. 'Where's the car?' Charlie hollered, as he sidestepped a woman with a baby buggy.

'Basement!' Robyn panted. 'Just down here!'

They reached the entrance to the hotel's underground parking lot, and ran down the dark concrete ramp. Charlie's feet stung but he scarcely noticed. When they reached the bottom of the ramp, Charlie looked around wildly, and said, 'Where is it? Where did you park it? I don't see it anywhere!'

'They parked it for me!' Robyn told him. 'It has to be here somewhere!'

They heard footsteps running at the top of the ramp. 'For Christ's sake, where is it?' Charlie yelled.

'There!' said Robyn. 'Look! Over in the corner! Behind that white car!'

Charlie peered into the far corner of the parking lot. He could just make out the bronze roof of Mrs Kemp's station wagon, parked behind a new white Lincoln Town Car. 'Come on!' he said, and together he and Robyn vaulted over the hoods of three cars to reach the station wagon. Robyn fumbled the keys out of her purse and gave them to Charlie, and he unlocked the door. The hotel's parking-jockeys had wedged the cars in so tightly that he had to bang the door hard against the BMW parked next to it in order to give them enough space to squeeze their way into the front seats.

'How are we going to get out?' Robyn asked him, panicking.

Charlie slotted the key into the ignition, and twisted it. He had seen so many TV movies in which fugitives tried unsuccessfully to start up their cars just as a murderer was catching up with them that he was amazed when the engine immediately roared into life.

'They're here!' said Robyn. Charlie glanced towards the entrance ramp and saw that Henri and M. Fontenot had reached the parking area, and were dodging their way towards them between the cars. Henri had his right hand lifted, and Charlie saw the sharp glint of a nickel-plated handgun.

Charlie tugged the station wagon's shift into second, and jammed his bare foot down on the gas. The station wagon bucked forward with a scream of tyres, and hit the Lincoln hard in the trunk. Charlie kept his foot down, hoping to push the Lincoln forward, but somebody had applied the Lincoln's parking brake, and all he managed to do was shove it two or three feet, with a long squeal of protesting rubber.

Henri scrambled over the BMW, and out of the corner of his eye Charlie saw him aiming his revolver. He yanked the gearshift into reverse, and the station wagon screeched backward, so violently that it collided with the parking lot wall. Robyn bent forward and covered her head with her hands, in the emergency position recommended by airlines. Charlie yelled, 'Hold tight!' and threw the station wagon into second gear, so that it roared forward and collided with the Lincoln yet again, a deafening crash that sent the Lincoln front first into a new Mercedes 350 parked opposite, and the Mercedes into a Thunderbird behind it.

Henri fired, but the noise of the cars crashing together was so loud that Charlie didn't realize they were being shot at until a hole burst through his windshield, the size of a man's fist, surrounded by a spiderweb of crazed glass. He backed up yet again, with the station wagon's tyres screaming on the polished concrete, and then stepped on the parking brake, so that the station wagon slewed around, facing the exit.

Henri leaned forward, holding his revolver in both hands, and fired at point-blank range. The bullet thumped through the driver's door, passed under Charlie's calves, and buried itself in the carpet that covered the transmission hump. 'Go!' screamed Robyn, and Charlie pressed his foot flat on the floor. The station wagon shot out of the parking area, skidded sideways at the bottom of the exit ramp, and then surged up toward the street like an Apollo rocket out of control. Charlie glimpsed Mme Musette's white distraught face right by the entrance to the parking lot. Then the station wagon flew clear of the sidewalk, hurtling right into the middle of Canal Street with a crash of ruined suspension, and hitting a taxi on the offside fender.

Before the taxi driver could get out of his vehicle, however, Charlie had backed up, stopped, twisted the wheel violently sideways, and roared northwards on Canal Street in a cloud of oil and rubber smoke. Slewing the station wagon from side to side to avoid slower traffic, glancing quickly in his rear-view mirror to make sure that he wasn't being pursued by the police or by Mme Musette, Charlie headed for Interstate 10, the quickest route out of New Orleans.

The station wagon shuddered and complained as he turned eastwards on I-10, but he kept his foot pressed down hard on the floor. Ahead of them, the sun shone directly in their eyes. Off to their left, Lake Pontchartrain glittered like an early morning mirage. Smoke poured out of the back of the station wagon, and the suspension was making a noise like a bucketful of spanners, but they kept going at eighty m.p.h., and Charlie wasn't going to let up for anything.

'Where are we going?' Robyn wanted to know.'

Charlie checked his rear-view mirror again. The last thing he wanted was to be stopped by the Louisiana Highway Patrol. If Mme Musette had been telling the truth, and the Célèstines really were thick with every law-enforcement agency between here and Connecticut, they would find themselves back at the Church of the Angels on Elegance Street before they knew it.

'We're getting the hell out of New Orleans,' said Charlie. 'Then we're going to make our way to Acadia. But we have to get rid of this car. Every cracker-barrel deputy between here and Bogalusa is going to be on the look out for a bronze station wagon with Connecticut plates and smoke coming out of the tailpipe. We won't stand a chance.'

'We can't *buy* a new car,' said Robyn.

'How much money do you have?' Charlie asked.

Robyn checked her purse. 'About one hundred fifteen dollars, that's all.'

'And credit cards?'

'Sure. Visa, American Express, Mastercharge. But we can't use credit cards, can we – not for buying a car? The FBI are bound to have circulated our charge-card numbers. They'll jump on us straight away.'

Charlie checked his mirror. There was nobody behind them, not for miles, but they were blowing out so much smoke that they were bound to attract attention before long.

'We could always liberate a car,' said Robyn.

'You mean steal it?'

'I saw it in an Elliott Gould movie. It's easy. All you have to do is drive along until you come across a car-dealer, then stop. I'll do the rest. Make it a Cadillac dealer, if you can.'

Charlie said, 'If you think I'm going to steal a car, you're out of your mind.'

'For God's sake,' Robyn retaliated. 'You're already wanted for homicide in the first degree, as well as kidnap and grand theft auto. What difference is one more stolen car going to make? It's the farm for you, whatever.'

'Yes, damn it, and you too.'

They crossed the north-eastern corner of Lake Pontchartrain, and then Charlie turned off Interstate 10 on to

Route 11. They limped smokily into the outskirts of a town called Slidell, and Charlie steered the station wagon off the road and parked it on a dusty patch under the shade of some overhanging oaks. He climbed out, tugging his sweaty shirt away from his back, and said, 'I almost feel like putting a bullet through its hood, so that it doesn't suffer.'

Robyn said, 'There's a Chevrolet dealer down there, look, two blocks away.'

'And I'm supposed to walk up to him, without any shoes, and persuade him that I want to buy a car?'

'Charlie, for Christ's sake, stop being so defeatist! We'll buy you some shoes at Woolworth's. *Then* we'll go get the Chevrolet.'

They went into Woolworth's and Charlie bought himself a pair of grey leather casuals with a silver chain across them, which was about the most tasteful pair of shoes he could find. Then together they walked into the corner lot of Gramercy Chevrolet, under lines of fluttering bunting, to the small concrete office where Dean Gramercy himself sat in his shirtsleeves behind a bare desk, smoking a bright green cigar and talking on the telephone. There was a citation on the wall from the Slidell Chamber of Commerce, and a Vargas calendar. Dean Gramercy was stubby and big-bellied and ginger like a hog.

'Be with you folks right away,' he told them, covering the mouthpiece for a moment. 'That's right, Wally. You bring those spares over by Monday. Then we can talk about price. But I gotta see them first. You know me, Wally. I pay good but I like to see what I'm paying for.'

Dean Gramercy hung up, and extended his hand to Charlie as if he were his favourite cousin come visiting. 'Good of you to drop by,' he beamed. 'If it's a quality automobile you're after, you've come to the c'rect location.'

'We were looking for a late-model sedan,' said Charlie tentatively.

'Well, now, I've got maybe a dozen that would fit the bill.

But there's one special that I know you're going to love. You come down to the lot and take a look.'

Obediently, they followed Dean Gramercy to the front of the lot. With a flourish, he showed them a silver Caprice Classic with a silver vinyl roof.

'Now you just take a look at this baby,' he enthused. 'Genuine '85 model, fully loaded, 5.7 litre gasoline engine, only 9,000 miles, one owner who was so careful she didn't even take off the plastic seat-covers.'

'Sounds perfect,' said Robyn. 'Do you mind if we take it for a drive?'

'Well, sure thing. All I have to do is turn the key in the office door. Not that there's anything to steal, apart from my calendar.' He snorted in amusement, and waddled off to lock up.

Charlie said, 'I'm sweating. Do you think we can pull this off?'

Robyn said, 'Easy. When I say go, just make sure that you go.'

Dean Gramercy came back, and opened the Chevrolet's passenger doors so that Charlie and Robyn could climb in. Then he settled himself in the driver's seat, adjusting the steering wheel so that it didn't press into his belly, and started up the engine. They drove sedately down the sun-gilded street between the overhanging live oaks, and all the time Dean Gramercy puffed affably at his cigar and rattled on about the pleasures of living in Slidell and what a desahrable vee-*hickle* this was, and how they couldn't do better anywhere for Chevrolets than good old Gramercy, and what's more he was going to throw in a Toshiba microwave oven as a fall bonus.

Eventually, just north of Slidell, he pulled the car over to the side of the road and said to Charlie, 'You want to drive her back? Just slide over.'

He climbed out of the car. Charlie slid over behind the wheel and re-adjusted it while Dean Gramercy walked around the front. He was just about to take hold of the passenger door handle when Robyn shouted out, 'Lock the doors! And *go*!'

Charlie flicked the central locking switch, shifted the car into gear, and kicked his foot down on the gas. The Caprice roared forward, leaving Dean Gramercy with his mouth open and his hand just about to curl round a door handle that wasn't there any more. The car's tail snaked a little as Charlie accelerated around a long curving bend. Then they were out on the open highway, heading northward into St Tammany County, with the sunlight flashing through the trees and the day dusty and bright.

'Wow,' breathed Charlie softly.

'What did I tell you?' Robyn laughed. 'You drive like Bullitt.'

Charlie checked his rear-view mirror, then turned around in his seat to make absolutely certain that they weren't being followed. 'Anything's possible, isn't it, if you've got the nerve?'

'You've found that out.' Robyn smiled and squeezed his arm. 'So believe me, if you can liberate a late-model Chevrolet, you can liberate your son, too.'

Charlie slowed the car and kissed her. 'I do believe I'm beginning to love you more than a man should.'

'Nobody ever loved anybody more than they should.'

Charlie said, 'I located Acadia on the map. It's way over to the west, in St Landry County, between Normand and Lebeau, right in the middle of Cajun country. If we keep to the side roads, we should be able to make it there without too much danger of being picked up by the police. You know what I should have done, don't you? I should have taken the licence plates off Mrs Kemp's station wagon, and changed them over.'

'You're getting to sound like a professional car thief,' Robyn teased him.

They drove throughout the morning through the flat Delta

countryside, under a pale bronze sky, heading westwards, in the general direction of Baton Rouge and Lafayette. At times they could easily have believed that they had the whole of Louisiana to themselves. They saw no highway patrol cars, no helicopters, nothing. Just shining bayous and girder bridges and water oaks, and glistening muddy banks thick with black-shelled mussels. They kept the Chevrolet's air conditioning turned off to save gas, and drove with the windows open. The air flowed in humid, smelling of vegetation and slow-moving water.

They stopped for wheat Po-boys and shrimp-on-a-stick at a breezeblock roadside restaurant called Frugé's All-Day. There were cheap sunglasses for sale on a card, and they each bought a pair. They sat on the Chevrolet's hood eating their shrimp and watching the clouds slowly come apart at the seams. A Cajun music station played 'Laisser les Amis Danser'.

'Well,' said Charlie, when they had finished eating, and wiped their hands on their paper napkins, 'I guess we'd better be moving along. Acadia's a good fifty miles.'

'I hope we can find someplace to stay the night,' said Robyn. 'I could use a shower and a change of clothes.'

'We're going to need somewhere to stay for two days. The Last Supper isn't till Friday.'

'Maybe you should ask,' Robyn suggested.

Charlie went back into Frugé's All-Day and approached the grizzle-haired black man behind the counter. He was watched with unabashed interest by an old man with a Jim Beam golfing cap who was making his way steadily through what the proprietor advertised as a seven-course Cajun meal — a six-pack of beer and a one-pound boudin.

'I'm headed toward Lebeau,' said Charlie. 'You don't happen to know anyplace quiet I could stay for a few days?'

The black man stopped rag-wiping the counter and pressed his hand thoughtfully over his mouth. 'You could try Eric Broussard. He lives about six miles shy of Lebeau back from the road by the Normand Bayou. He used to take in guests from time to time, back when his wife Nancy was still alive, though whether he still does it now, I can't say. Tell him that Jimmy Frugé sent you and everything's okay.'

'That's generous of you,' said Charlie.

The black man looked at him with his eyes narrowed into cynical slits. 'You're running from the law, *mon ami*, so don't talk to me about no generosity.'

Charlie was about to protest, but the black man waved his hand dismissively. 'I know a fugitive when I see one. I've been selling Po-boys beside this highway for thirty-two years. You get along now, and good luck, and don't try driving along these back roads at night, lessen you want to go swimming inside of your car.'

Charlie hesitated for a moment. Jimmy Frugé was the first person to have offered them help since they had left Connecticut. He wanted to tell him how much this meant, but he couldn't find the words, and in any case Frugé wouldn't have understood what he was talking about. So he just said, 'Thanks,' and left the restaurant, and walked slowly back to the car, where Robyn was waiting for him in her $3.75 sunglasses, looking as if she had just stepped out of 1963.

CHAPTER NINETEEN

Eric Broussard was sitting on the verandah of his house soaking in the late-afternoon sunshine as they came bumping and jolting down the muddy track that led through the fields to the Normand Bayou. They could see his bifocal spectacles reflecting the marmalade-coloured light.

His house had two storeys and was clad with weatherboarding that had once been painted red. There was still red paint to be seen in the nooks and crannies and knotholes; and the redness of the house was increased by the redness of the light and by the stand of cypress trees that surrounded it. Eric Broussard didn't wave as they approached, or give any indication that he had seen them, but when they drew up in front of his verandah and climbed out of the Chevrolet, he stood up, walked to the top of his steps, and stood facing them, an old black man in a warm plaid shirt whose sleeves were too short for his long accordion-player's wrists. He must have been very handsome once. Now his moustache was grey and most of his front teeth had gone, and of course he wore those heavy horn-rim spectacles with two kinds of lenses in them, so that he could see to read the sports pages in the *Times-Picayune* and also to scrutinize whoever was driving through the fields towards his house.

Charlie mounted the first step. 'Mr Broussard?' he said. A north-westerly wind was blowing off the bayou, and it made the pages of Eric Broussard's newspaper stir and flap.

'Who wants him?' Eric Broussard demanded.

'Mr Broussard, my name's Charlie McLean. This is Robyn Harris. We're travelling hereabouts and we've been looking for some place to stay. Jimmy Frugé suggested we come to you.'

'Jimmy Frugé? That boll weevil? He didn't have no business sending you here. I don't take in guests no more. You're wasting your time.'

Charlie wiped the sweat from his forehead with the back of his hand. 'Mr Broussard, we're kind of desperate.'

'Desperate? What does that mean?'

'It means we don't have anyplace else.'

Eric Broussard scratched his black, wrinkled neck. His skin had the quality of dark-dried tobacco leaves. 'There's a Howard Johnson's over at Opelousas. Whyn't you stay there?'

'Because we're having a misunderstanding with the police,' put in Robyn boldly.

Eric Broussard frowned. 'A misunderstanding? Who's mis-understanding whom?'

'They're kind of misunderstanding us,' Charlie explained. 'They think we're guilty of one or two rather unpleasant mis-demeanours, and the fact is we're not, but at the moment we're having a difficult time persuading them of that.'

'You was framed,' Eric Broussard suggested.

'Something like that.'

Eric Broussard slowly shook his head. 'I didn't never meet no lawbreaker who wasn't framed. You go talk to all of the men on all of Louisiana's state farms, and the amazing thing about it is they're *all* innocent, every last one of them. They was all framed by ill-wishing associates who of course are still free. So what manner of state do we live in, that sends innocent men to prison, and allows guilty men to walk the streets unmolested?'

Charlie said, 'Believe me, Mr Broussard, we're not crim-inals. But we do need somewhere to stay. Only a couple of days, that's all we need. Then we'll leave and you won't ever see or hear from us again.'

Eric Broussard sucked at his gums and thought about this. 'Jimmy Frugé sent you, hey? That boll weevil.'

'He seemed okay to me,' Charlie ventured.

Eric Broussard shrugged and sniffed. 'He's okay. He and me used to be the best of friends once upon a time. We fell out over some fiddle-playing and we haven't hardly spoke since then.'

Charlie said, 'We really do need someplace to stay, Mr Broussard.'

'Well, I can understand that,' said Eric Broussard, 'but the fact of the matter is that I don't take people into my house no more. I've grown too old, and to tell you the truth I don't care too much for anybody excepting myself.'

'We don't expect meals, or any looking after,' said Robyn. 'And we can certainly make our own beds.'

But Eric Broussard kept on shaking his head like a man who has spent far too long alone, sitting on his verandah and watching the hawks circle around the cypress trees.

'Come on, Charlie,' said Robyn. 'I think we're wasting our time.'

Charlie stepped back from the house and lifted up both hands in resignation.

'Hurt your hand there,' Eric Broussard remarked.

Charlie nodded. 'Did you ever hear of the Célèstines?'

The effect of this question on Eric Broussard's face was astonishing. He stared at Charlie until his eyeballs looked as if they going to press against the lenses of his spectacles. His mouth dragged itself downward, and he took two or three epileptic steps backwards across the verandah. Charlie said, 'Mr Broussard? Mr Broussard? What did I say?' But Eric Broussard kept on stepping backwards until he was flattened against the weatherboarded wall of the house.

'Mr Broussard,' Charlie said, 'I don't know what you know about the Célèstines. Maybe you support them, I don't know. But let me tell you that they're holding my son in captivity, and that they're planning to kill him. That's why I need someplace to stay – at least until Friday.'

'You say *Friday*?' asked Eric Broussard, with unconcealed dread.

'That's right. They're holding a special ceremony. A special Last Supper.'

'It's come so soon?' Eric Broussard asked.

Charlie climbed the verandah steps and stood just a few inches away from Eric Broussard. Robyn came up close behind to give him moral support. She tried to smile at Eric Broussard, to reassure him that they didn't mean him any harm, but he stared at them both with unmasked fear.

'Mr Broussard – *we're* not Célèstines. You don't have anything to be afraid of as far as we're concerned. But if you know something about the Célèstines, anything at all, even if it's nothing more than hearsay or rumour, I really have to know what it is.'

Eric Broussard crossed himself. 'What I know about the Célèstines ain't hearsay or rumour,' he whispered. 'I lost my dear wife to the Célèstines, let me tell you that, and the manner of her passing was too terrible for me to want to think about.'

'Your wife was a member of the Célèstine church? She was a Devotee?'

'She was a Devotee, God bless her poor soul.'

Charlie said, 'Mr Broussard, we've come here to St Landry County to try to put a stop to the Célèstines, one way or another. Friday is their great Last Supper. Friday is the day that the thousandth thousandth Devotee gets eaten – or is supposed to; and Friday is the day that Jesus Christ is supposed to come back down to earth.'

'Those people,' Eric Broussard said, shaking his head from side to side. 'Those people. You know what those people are? They're voodoo, that's what those people are! They talk about Christ Jesus, they talk about the second coming, they talk about Jerusalem builded in Louisiana! But all they are is descendants of the voodoo people, the people that point the

274

baby's bone, and curse you to death! All they are is stealers of other men's souls! I swear to God I thought I'd heard the last about the Célèstines, but when I saw your automobile come through the fields, I thought to myself, I've got a bad feeling about these people coming, I'm going to be hearing about things I don't want to hear about.'

'Mr Broussard, they've got my son,' Charlie appealed. 'My son is supposed to be the thousandth thousandth Devotee, and on Friday they're going to eat him alive so that the Lord can be resurrected in the body of their Chief Guide.'

Eric Broussard raised his head, and there were tears sliding down his cheeks. 'They took my Nancy, those people. They took her away. They took people from all over St Landry County, from Krotz Springs and Bayou Current and Ville Platte. They took people from Acadia County, too, from Iota and Evangeline. Those people went to their meetings and never came back. And if you tried to persuade them to come back, all they did was smile at you and say, "Never you mind, we've found the Lord." That's what my Nancy said: "I've found the Lord." But what kind of a Lord is it that ends a good woman's life by having her cut open her own stomach and take out her own liver and eat it while her eyes is glazing over? My Nancy ate her own liver, Mr Misunderstanding-with-the-Law, and you tell me why I should give you a room, just to be reminded of that?'

Charlie said gently, 'Can we talk inside? I think I'm going to need your help.'

'Ain't you been listening to me?' Eric Broussard shouted at him. 'Ain't you been listening to one single word I've been telling you?'

'Let's go inside,' said Charlie, taking hold of his arm. 'Please, we have to talk about it. Otherwise my son's going to die on Friday, the same way that your Nancy died, and the Célèstines are going to go on causing misery and pain for ever and ever.'

Eric Broussard lowered his head. He was silent for a long time, but then he said, 'Well, I suppose you're right. You'd better come along in. There's some beer in the icebox, no wine like there used to be. I'm sorry if your lady drinks wine.'

Robyn said, 'Don't mind me. I could finish a beer in five seconds flat.'

Inside the house the blinds were all drawn down and the stuffiness was oppressive. Eric Broussard led them through the kitchen to the front parlour, and offered them a large brown sofa to sit on, while he found them a glass of beer. Charlie and Robyn sat side by side in silence, looking at the green diamond-patterned wallpaper and the shelf above the fireplace clustered with framed photographs of Eric Broussard's family, solemn and formally dressed, and all bearing the distinctive Broussard likeness. The breeze that came across the bayou lifted the blind away from the window every now and then, so that it tapped against the windowsill, but it wasn't a strong enough flow of air to penetrate the room.

Eric Broussard came back with a tray and three glasses of cold beer. 'When I first walked out with Nancy, I used to drink it by the neck. But she would never allow me to do that. With Nancy, everything had to be just so. You don't meet too many women like that any more. These days, anything goes. Women don't have no pride any longer.'

'You must be lonely, living out here all by yourself,' Robyn remarked.

Eric Broussard sat down in a large armchair with dark varnished arms and seat cushions that had been pressed over the years into grotesque, wrinkled shapes. 'People say that you can get over losing somebody you love. Give yourself time, that's what they say. But, you know something, I've given myself years and years, and I still can't get myself used to living without Nancy. It was worse than losing a leg.'

Charlie said, 'Tell me, Mr Broussard, how much do you know about the Célèstines?'

276

Eric Broussard drank beer, and made a face. 'As much as anybody I guess. Right at the very beginning, Nancy used to tell me all about them. She tried to persuade me to join her. We could eat each other's flesh, that's what she said. We could share each other's body and blood, just like the holy communion. But, my God, that made my blood run cold, that's all. I could never understand how she could believe in it all so much.'

'Do you know anything about the second coming ritual?' asked Robyn.

'I know they believe that when a thousand thousand people have gotten themselves all eaten up, their Chief Guide is supposed to eat the thousandth thousandth person, and when he does that the Lord's going to come down and inhabit his body, and a new age is going to start. I seem to recall the Chief Guide don't have to eat all of the thousandth thousandth person, only their brain.'

'Is that all you know?'

'I know a lot, my friend,' said Eric Broussard. 'But it all depends on what you want to hear.'

'I want to know what they actually do, on the day of the second coming.'

Eric Broussard said, 'I don't have any notion whatsoever. As I say, the Célèstines used to make my blood run cold. Once Nancy joined up with them, that was our marriage gone for good. Even before she went off to stay with them permanent, she seemed like she was *possessed*, you know what I mean? She used to say the strangest things, and sometimes she used to be sitting at the dinner table and deliberately bite her own arm, just lift it up and bite at it, and there was blood going everywhere and me not understanding a word of what she was trying to explain to me. "I seen God!" she used to call out. "I seen God!" All you could say about her was, she was a woman possessed.'

'Did you ever try taking her to a doctor?' Robyn asked him.

277

'Oh, surely, I *tried*. But the doctor said she was fine; just a little overwrought, that's all. He prescribed her some Valium tablets and charged me a hundred-ten dollars.'

Eric Broussard eyed Robyn with bloodshot eyes. 'Let me tell you what I'm going to do. I'm going to go upstairs and find my Nancy's Célèstine Bible. Then you can look up anything you want to your heart's contentment.'

Charlie said, 'The Célèstines have their own special Bible?'

'Sure they do, just like the Latter-Day Saints. They brought it round for me when they came to tell me that Nancy was gone. I was tempted to drop it in the stove, but then I thought that I might need it someday, just to prove to the world what Nancy had to go through. Otherwise, who'd've believed me?'

'We believe you,' said Robyn gently.

Eric Broussard lifted his head. The muted sunlight caught a fingerprint on the lens of his spectacles, setting it glowing like a tiny spiderweb. 'Whatever I do to help you,' he said, 'it ain't never going to bring my Nancy back.'

Nonetheless, he lifted himself out of his armchair and shuffled off to look for the Célèstine Bible. Charlie sipped his beer, and said, 'We need to find out *when* they're going to hold the ritual – whether they're supposed to do it at any special time of the day or night – and we also need to know what happens, so that we don't make fools of ourselves by bursting in to rescue Martin at the wrong moment, before they've brought him out of his room, for instance.' He didn't add, 'or after they've eaten him', but he didn't have to. Robyn knew that their chances of getting Martin away from the Célèstines were extraordinarily slim, especially since the police and the FBI and anybody with any political or commercial influence seemed to support them, or at least to turn a blind eye to what they were doing.

Eric Broussard returned with a thin book about the size of the New Testament, bound in cheap red leather with a white mitre embossed on the front. 'Nancy said the red leather was supposed to represent the blood, and the white hat was supposed to be the body.' He passed the book to Charlie, and Charlie opened it up, while Robyn leaned closer so that she could read over his shoulder.

On the title page, it said, '*The Book of Célèstine*', and underneath: '*Being the holy words of Saint Célèstine V, Pietro di Murrone 1215–96, concerning the communion of the Last Supper.*'

Charlie flicked through the text. There were 120 pages of closely printed text. 'Mr Broussard,' he said, 'it's going to take us some time to read all this; and we do want to study it really well. I'd truly appreciate it if you'd allow us to stay.'

Eric Broussard slowly rubbed the back of his neck. Then he said. 'All right, if that's what you want. But in return, you can go to Sidney's Store for me out on the Normand highway and fetch in some steaks and some groceries and maybe a couple of bottles of liquor.'

'Mr Broussard, you've got yourself a deal.'

'Not quite,' said Eric Broussard. 'You've got to stop calling me "Mr Broussard" and start calling me "Eric" instead. Either that or "Tabac-Sec".'

Charlie reached over and shook Eric Broussard's hand. 'Eric, I think we're in business.'

They lifted their beer glasses and drank a silent toast to an adventure that would probably prove to be dangerous, painful, and frightening.

Eric Broussard wiped his mouth with the back of his sun-wrinkled hand, and said, 'You want a double bed or two singles? I've got clean sheets for both of them. The double bed creaks pretty bad, on account of all the weekending couples we used to have here, but in times of stress I always say that it's better to have somebody to hold on to, don't you?'

They ate a supper of steaks and fried eggs and Bulgar wheat salad, with straight Jack Daniel's as an accompaniment, and

279

then after supper Eric Broussard produced his German accordion and sat on the kitchen chair and played slow, bluesy, but inarguably Cajun melodies of love and dancing and crayfish, and many other subjects close to the Cajun heart.

'I play better out of doors,' he said, when he had finished. 'There's something about the plein-air that makes the music resonate. I like to play out of doors wearing a big wide hat to keep the sun off of my face and the rain off of my cigareet. That's why they call me "Tabac-Sec".'

They thanked him for his cooking and his music, and then they went upstairs and showered and undressed and climbed into the big double bed which creaked as friendly and amusing as anybody's honeymoon bed in any honeymoon hotel. Charlie sat propped up with pillows drinking the last of the whiskey and reading the Célèstine Bible. Robyn lay close to him and closed her eyes and rested. The north-west wind blew across the bayou and whistled lightly through the cracks in the window frame, a soft *complainte* of its own.

Most of the Célèstine text was rambling evangelism and complicated prophecies about 'the Lord who smiteth all those whose faces are set against His Glory; and all those who worship artifice and deceit,' and 'in the Days of the Ethiopian whose descendants shall number fifty times fifty millions, a drought shall descend upon the lands of their forefathers and their suffering will be heard in all corners of the world.'

It quickly became clear, even under Charlie's inexpert scrutiny, that the Célèstine Bible had certainly not been written by Saint Célèstine himself, but possibly as much as five hundred years later – even as late as 1775. There was a reference to the 'Lands that were given by deed to those who had been cast out of Acadie.' If Charlie remembered an article he had read not too long ago in the *Reader's Digest*, those who had been cast out of Acadie could only mean those French colonists in Nova Scotia who had been dispossessed by the British after the Treaty of Utrecht in 1713. In those days, Nova Scotia had been called Port Royal, or 'L'Acadie', meaning pastoral paradise on earth. The French had been uprooted from their paradise and sent back to France, or to Guadeloupe; or even as far as the Falklands; but they had been invited back to America in 1775 when the French sold Louisiana to the Spanish. The new Spanish governor had been worried that his small population would not be able to resist a takeover by the British, so he had offered the one-time Acadians a free passage back across the Atlantic and free land deeds so that they could settle in the south-west.

Charlie found another more glaring anachronism. Although there was no direct mention of cannibalism, there was an endless obsession in the text with human flesh and blood and its relation to the words of the Last Supper. From what M. Musette had told him at Le Reposoir, the Célèstines had only taken to eating real flesh and real blood after their sojourn with the Caribs on the island of Sainte Desirée – and that had been after the French Revolution in 1789. So it was conceivable that the Célèstine Bible had been written in the early part of the 1800s, or even later.

Robyn fell asleep, and Charlie felt her breathing softly and deeply against his arm. Eric Broussard had been right: it was good to have somebody to hold in times of stress. He finished his whiskey, and went on reading, although he would have given anything to be able to close his eyes. A little after one o'clock in the morning, he came across the passage that he had been looking for . *The Return to Earth of Our Lord Jesus Christ as Prophesied by the Angels.*

The verses read: '*And the Day shall come when one thousand times one thousand shall have taken communion with Christ our Lord, save only for twelve disciples, one disciple from each parent church. And the twelve shall be brought to the appointed place known as the place of the poor, in the company of elders and Guides, and there they shall take communion with Christ our Lord in solemn memorial to the Last Supper. And they shall take*

*communion one upon the other, until there is but one; and he shall
be numbered one thousand times one thousand.*

'*Then shall the elder of the Guides take communion with the
twelfth of these disciples, and he shall become the vessel in which
those souls now reside, one thousand times one thousand. And
in so doing he shall become a worthy vessel in his turn for the
second coming on earth of Christ our Lord, and he shall be
transformed. And all of those who have kept the faith of the
true communion shall be rewarded on this earth as well as in
the next.*

'*For know you by these secrets that the fifth day was the one on
which he was vanquished, but his day is the sixth day, and on
that day you shall be given your just reward.*'

Charlie read the verses again and again. There was no doubt
that they were referring to the ceremony that was supposed to
be taking place on Friday at L'Église des Pauvres, the Church
of the Poor. Twelve Devotees from twelve Célèstine churches
would be brought down to Acadia as representatives of the
twelve disciples – only the Last Supper was going to be worked
in reverse. Instead of the Master giving them *His* body and
His blood, they were going to give Him theirs, and the process
that had led up to the Crucifixion and the Ascension was
going to happen backwards. At least, that seemed to be the
Célèstine theory.

The last verse puzzled Charlie a little, because it was the
only verse that didn't appear to make explicit sense. It had the
character of a riddle, but there was something about it which
sounded peculiarly like a warning as well, although Charlie
couldn't quite analyse what it was.

Certainly there was a mention of 'secrets'. And the next
phrase was odd – 'the fifth day was the day on which he was
vanquished.' Presumably this meant Good Friday – but no
Christian believed that Christ was vanquished on Good Friday
– rather that he finally triumphed over evil. It was also noticeable that in this one paragraph 'he' was spelled with a lower-

case 'h'. And what did the writer mean by the sixth day being 'his day' – the day on which you will be given your just reward?

Maybe it was that term 'just reward' that Charlie found vaguely threatening. It seemed to have the quality of 'on Saturday, you'll get what's coming to you.'

When it came to rewards, too, there was another line that bothered him: '*And all of those who have kept faith with the true communion shall be rewarded on this earth as well as in the next.*' To be given a material reward as well as a spiritual one seemed peculiarly at odds with anything that Christ would have promised or a Christian would have expected.

At a quarter of two, Charlie finally put down the Célèstine Bible on the bedside table. He switched off the light, and snuggled up close to Robyn. In fact, the bed dipped so much in the middle he didn't have any choice.

By two o'clock he was asleep. He didn't dream. But the north-west breeze stiffened during the early hours of the morning, and rattled the window even more frantically, and one by one it leafed over the pages of the open Bible, one whispering page after another, until it came to rest at the page which said, '*But the sixth day is* his *day, and on that day you shall be given your just reward.*'

While only two miles away, in the darkness, a car turned off the Normand highway and began to make its way purposefully along the dirt track that led to Eric Broussard's house on the bayou.

CHAPTER TWENTY

Charlie was awakened by a bony hand shaking his shoulder. Involuntarily, he shouted in fright, and sat up so fast that he knocked heads with Eric Broussard, who was leaning over him. Eric Broussard said, 'Shit, Charlie, that hurt.'

'What's the matter?' Charlie asked him. 'What's wrong?'

'I'm not too sure,' said Eric, in the darkness, 'but there's a vehicle parked in the cypress grove, about two hundred feet off to the east. I heard it coming. Your ears acquire a sensitivity for things like that. But it didn't come right up to the house, like you'd expect. It parked in the trees and now it's just waiting.'

Charlie switched on the light. Eric Broussard was wearing a wonderfully ancient pair of red-flannel longjohns, and big, old, frayed carpet slippers. Eric said, 'If it's the po-lice, I don't want no shooting.'

Charlie climbed out of bed. In doing so, he allowed Robyn to roll into the dip in the middle of the mattress, and that woke her up. She blinked and stared at them and said, 'What time is it?'

'Five o'clock,' Eric told her.

Charlie went to the window and drew back the blind, but it was too dark outside for him to be able to make out anything. All he could see was his own face, as pale as a ghost floating in the night. 'If it's the police, or the FBI, it seems pretty weird that they should park in the trees like that. They know I'm not armed.'

'Who else could it be?' asked Eric.

'Célèstines?' Robyn suggested.

Charlie dressed himself. 'The only way to find out for sure is to go out there and see for ourselves.'

'Charlie,' said Robyn, 'they'll kill you.'

'I don't think so. I don't think they meant to kill us the last time.'

'They shot holes in our car and they didn't mean to kill us?'

Eric stood up. His belly hung slack in his longjohns like a giant canned tomato. 'I can think of a better way. Let me send my dog Gumbo, he'll roust them out. He's half Doberman, half German shepherd, and half bird-dog.'

'That's a dog and a half,' Charlie remarked.

'Sure it is, and that's what Gumbo is, a dog and a half.'

Charlie said to Robyn, 'You'd better get dressed. If the Célèstines are really here, we may be in for some trouble.'

Eric went off to find himself a yellow plaid shirt and some bleached-out blue denim overalls, while Robyn dressed in the same skirt and blouse that she had been wearing this morning. She had washed the blouse and it was still slightly damp. 'What are you going to do if it *is* them?' she asked.

Charlie shrugged. 'Try to give them the slip, I guess. Maybe Eric knows another way out of here.'

'There can't be another way,' said Robyn. 'The house backs right on to the bayou.'

Charlie gave her a wry smile. 'What kind of a swimmer are you?'

Just then, Eric came in to tell them that he was ready to let Gumbo off the leash. They all went downstairs, keeping the lights off, feeling their way across the kitchen to the back door. Eric unlocked it, and opened it up as quietly as he could, and stuck his head out to listen to the sounds of the night. Charlie whispered, 'Anything?'

'Nothing; but there's somebody there. I can feel it in my bones.'

'Where do you keep your dog?'

'He's around the side, in his doghouse. Come on, Charlie,

you follow me. Miss — you stay here. Keep the door locked. Don't open it to nobody, only to us. But when it *is* us, you make sure you open it real quick.'

Robyn gripped hold of Charlie's sleeve in the darkness. 'For God's sake, Charlie, be careful.'

'You can count on it,' Charlie told her.

He and Eric stepped out on to the verandah and Robyn turned the key in the lock behind them. Dawn was not far off. All along the banks of the bayou, the trees and the bushes seethed in agitation, and Charlie wondered how Eric could distinguish any kind of noise amidst it all, but when they reached the top of the steps Eric stopped for a moment, listening, and then said, 'Come on. It's okay for now.'

Keeping close together they skirted the northern side of the house until they came to a ramshackle collection of outhouses and derelict chicken coops. Gumbo, the dog and a half, growled deep in the back of his throat as they approached, and his tail started to lash against the planks of his doghouse. Charlie had never seen a doghouse built like this before. It was more like a miniature fort. Eric unfastened the padlock that held the doghouse door, and Gumbo launched himself at them like a jet-black, bristling drag racer. Charlie instinctively jumped back, but Gumbo was chained up and, with a jingling of solid steel links, he was arrested only a foot away from Charlie's ankles. He snarled and slavered and twisted, but Eric let out a sharp whistle between his teeth and said, 'You mind your etiquette, Gumbo, this is a houseguest,' and the dog quietened down a little, and allowed Eric to approch him, although Charlie still felt uncertain about his lolling tongue and hungry panting, and decided to keep well back. 'Now, you stay polite, boy,' Eric kept soothing Gumbo. 'You stay polite and keep your fangs to yourself.'

Eric caught hold of the dog's chain and released it. Then, with the dog leaning away from him as if it were being pulled by a giant magnet, its breath scraping in its half-strangulated throat, he led it across the yard toward the edge of the fields. 'You see them trees,' Eric told Charlie, indicating the dark, sad spires of the cypresses. 'That's where they're at. I heard them drive off the track and across to them trees and they haven't stirred since. But old Gumbo'll roust them, won't you, Gumbo? Gumbo's the best rouster that ever was. Chickens, rats, turtles, catfish, gars. He'd roust anything on land or water, would Gumbo – wouldn't you, Gumbo?'

As if he had been given his cue by an off-stage prompter, Gumbo said *grrooowwrrrr* and scrabbled at the grass with his claws.

Eric knelt down and let Gumbo off his chain. 'Go fetch them, Gumbo. You go fetch them.' Gumbo dashed off madly towards the left, abruptly stopped, and then barked loudly and tore off toward the cypress grove. They saw him running like the shadow of a passing storm cloud across the grass, and then he had disappeared into the darkness. Eric slowly stood up, and placed his hands on his hips and listened.

'That's some dog,' said Charlie, mainly because he was nervous.

'That's a dog and a half,' Eric agreed. Charlie liked to hear him say it, because of his Cajun pronunciation of *hay-uff*.

They waited. The wind blew through the trees, making the cypresses bow and curtsey like dancers at a midnight ball. Eric sniffed but kept his hands on his hips and said nothing. Charlie surreptitiously checked his watch. He didn't like to say that, for the best rouster that ever was, Gumbo was taking his own sweet time about rousting. It was quite clear that Eric worshipped his dog and a half; and Charlie would no more have thought about criticizing Eric's wife, if she had still been alive.

After about five minutes, Eric placed his finger and thumb in his mouth and let loose a sharp, ear-splitting whistle. 'Dog's taking too darn long,' he said, by way of explanation.

Charlie strained his eyes to penetrate the pre-dawn darkness. 'Give the poor fellow a chance.'

'Fellow?' said Eric. 'That ain't no fellow. That's my dog.' And to prove the point, he let out another piercing whistle.

The wind blew and the night began to lighten a little, a faint grey light that outlined the world without colouring it. Eric hummed 'Les Blues du Voyager' and Charlie could tell that he was worried now. 'Maybe that dog forgot to stop running,' he said.

'Maybe there's nothing in those woods to roust,' suggested Charlie.

'Oh, I heard them all right.'

Charlie said, 'Do you want to go take a look?'

Eric was silent for a long while. Then he said, 'I don't know . . . this ain't like Gumbo one bit. That dog's the best rouster that ever was.'

Charlie peered into the gloom. He was sure that he could see something move, over to the left of the trees. Something small, and pale, like a child running through the long grass. He took hold of Eric's arm and said, 'Look – do you see that?'

Eric looked, with his glasess and without them, but in the end he shook his head. 'I guess I could use a new pair. I haven't had my eyesight tested since Nancy went. I guess I haven't been looking after myself too well in lots of ways.'

Charlie said, 'Come on. Let's take a look for ourselves. It's the only thing we can do.'

He began to walk toward the cypress trees, and Eric reluctantly followed behind him. They were almost halfway there, however, when Eric said, 'Ssh – listen! I heard something! That's Gumbo, I swear it!'

Charlie listened but all he could hear was the wind. Eric said, 'He's mewling or something, like he's been hurt.'

Without any further hesitation, Eric began to run stiffly across the field, his long arms and legs waving like a semaphore. Charlie called, 'Eric, for Christ's sake be careful!' but Eric had heard his dog calling and that was all he cared about. Charlie had no choice but to go running after him. He glanced behind him only once, just to make sure that the house was still deserted and unlit, apart from the single lamp that he had switched on in their upstairs bedroom.

'Eric!' Charlie shouted. He didn't care if there was anybody there to hear him. If there was, they would have seen them and heard them by now in any event.

He had almost caught up with Eric when they saw a huge ball of orange fire suddenly ignite in the shadow of the trees. The flare up was immediately followed by a high stomach-lurching scream – a scream that sounded human at first – but which was even more horrifying to Charlie when he realized that it wasn't.

The fireball came rushing towards them through the grass, zigzagging as it came, and it was shrieking unbearably – high and harsh and agonized, like somebody dragging their finger-nails down a dry chalkboard. Charlie and Eric stopped where they were, both of them, and stared at the running, tumbling flames in helpless fright. They knew what it was but they couldn't bring themselves to believe it. It was Gumbo, and he was ablaze from head to tail, and screaming in agony as he ran.

'Watch out!' Charlie told Eric. 'He's coming straight for you! He wants you!'

Gumbo ran burning through the grass and the fire that engulfed him rippled like a cloak. Eric was paralysed for a second, but then he turned and began to stumble away. Gumbo in his death agony was running for the one person he could trust; the one person who had always protected him and fed him and kept him from harm.

Eric tried to escape, but Gumbo was too fast for him. Gumbo was driven by the pain so intense that he was running faster that he had ever run in his whole canine life, faster than he had ever chased chickens or catfish. He passed within two feet of Charlie and Charlie felt the heat of his blazing fur, and smelled gasoline and burning flesh.

Eric tripped, and cried out, and fell to his knees. Gumbo leaped on top of him, still screeching, still blazing, like a dog from hell. Eric rolled over and over trying to beat him off, but Gumbo's flesh and fur came off in burning chunks, and seemed to stick like napalm to Eric's clothes. Eric yelled out hoarsely for help. 'Charlie! Charlie! For God's sake, Charlie! He's killing me!'

Charlie ran through the grass and kicked Gumbo hard in the side. The dog rolled off his master with a roar of flames, then rolled over again and lay quivering on his back, only barely alive, his blackened paws drawn up like spider's legs. Charlie tugged off his coat and covered up Eric's shoulders and chest with it, and brushed the smouldering dog fur away from his face. He glanced at Gumbo but the dog must surely have been dead now. The flames had died down, and all that Charlie could hear was the crackling of his fire-shrunken tissues.

'Eric, are you okay?' Charlie asked him.

Eric shook his head. 'He's hurt me bad, Charlie.'

'Come on, Eric, I'll call for the ambulance. You'll be okay.'

'It's not the burns, Charlie. The burns hurt but the burns ain't nothing.'

'What are you talking about?' Charlie demanded. 'If you let me call the ambulance right now, we can have you in hospital in fifteen minutes.

'Don't,' Eric whispered. In the growing light of the morning, Charlie could see how grey his face had become. 'I don't want to die in no hospital. I want to die here, by the Normand Bayou.'

'Eric, you've been burned, but only superficially. You're not going to die.'

Eric cleared his throat, and looked up at Charlie with an odd smile. 'It's my heart, Charlie, it's been giving up on me for years. I had a bad attack last year, the doctor said I was lucky as all hell to be still alive. I'm going, Charlie. I can feel it closing in. Old man death, creeping in. Old Baron Samedi, that's what my mother used to call him.'

'Eric, I'm not going to let you die in some field,' Charlie protested. He squeezed the old black man's hand very tight.

'Well, you don't understand, this isn't no ordinary field, this is the field where I lived, me and my Nancy. This is the field where we danced, and delighted ourselves. So, this is a good field to die in, if you're talking about dying in a field.'

Charlie said, 'Somebody set fire to Gumbo on purpose.'

'Them Célèstines.' Eric nodded. 'They're out there now, you take my word for it. They came after you, didn't they, even though you thought you was clean away?'

'Eric, what can I say? If it hadn't have been for us, this wouldn't have happened.'

Eric laid his head back in the scorched grass, and let his eyelids droop a little as if he were tired. 'Every man has to go some time, Charlie, and none of us chooses the way. It wasn't your fault. My heart was ready to take me at any time. I could of been brushing my teeth, I could of been dancing. I just thank the Lord that it wasn't in bed, when I was asleep, because then I wouldn't have known nothing about it.'

Charlie said, 'Do you think you can make it back to the house, if I carry you?'

Eric shook his head again. 'Don't move me, Charlie. I want to stay here. I want to see the sun rise, if I can.' He grunted, and then he smiled and said. 'It's a funny thing, that yours should be the last human face I ever see. My father ain't going to be too pleased with me, when I get up to heaven. He sent the doctor out of the room when he was dying. He said he didn't want no white ghost faces looking at *him* when *he* died.'

'I have to move you,' Charlie insisted.

'Don't you dare try. Those people who burned my dog are out there somewhere and believe me they want to do the same to you, or worse. The best thing that you can do is get the hell out of here, you and your lady friend, and not come back.

There's a skiff down by the landing. You can row south-westwards from here, if you keep the sun off'n the right side of your back all morning, and off'n the left side of your chest all afternoon, you shouldn't get lost.'

'Eric, you're coming with us,' said Charlie.

'No,' said Eric. 'Leave me here, Charlie, and leave me now. I'll only slow you down.

Charlie stood up. He looked towards the cypress grove, following the zig zag path of scorched grass which Gumbo had left behind him as he chased after his master. It was light enough now for him to be able to see the quick glint of chrome from an automobile bumper, and the small pale flicker of a hooded child.

They had sent David the dwarf after him. Now he knew for certain that the Célèstines meant business. They were determined to catch him, and they were probably determined to kill him, too. He bent forward to give Eric's hand one last squeeze, and then he began to jog towards the house. He had no intention of leaving Eric out in the field unattended, but with the Célèstines closing in on them, he figured that the best idea would be to call for an ambulance as quickly as he could.

He ran up the verandah steps and knocked at the kitchen door. The curtain was tugged back and he saw Robyn's frightened face. 'It's okay, it's me. Let me in.'

She frantically unlocked the door. 'Where's Eric? What's happened?'

'Eric's been hurt. The Célèstines are here. I have to call an ambulance.'

'Oh, my God! What are we going to do?'

Charlie picked up Eric's old-fashioned telephone and dialled for the operator. While he waited for an answer, he told Robyn about the skiff moored on Eric's jetty. 'We won't stand a chance if we try to get out by road. They've probably got the track blocked back by the highway.'

'Do you know how to row?' Robyn asked him, aghast.

'It's easy, it's like anything else. You can pick it up as you go along.'

Robyn watched him, biting his lip, as he talked to the operator. 'Listen – there's been an accident out at Eric Broussard's place, on the Normand Bayou. Eric's suffered a heart attack. He's in the field about seventy feet to the east of his house. I offered to move him into the house but he didn't want me to touch him. Can you make sure an ambulance gets here quick. . . . You don't have to worry about my name. I'm just passing through. All right, then, yes. I surely will. Thank you.'

Charlie hung up the telephone and said, 'That's the best I can do. Right now, you and I have to get out of here.'

They went upstairs to gather up the few possessions they had left there, including the Célèstines' Bible. Then Charlie went all around the house, peering out of the windows, to see if there were any signs of an ambush. 'It looks quiet,' he said, as he let the parlour drapes fall back. 'Maybe they've decided that we're too scared to come out again.'

They opened the kitchen door, and Charlie leaned this way and that to make sure that the verandah was deserted. He listened – but, like before, his untrained ear could hear nothing at all but the wind and the rattling of dry leaves across the yard.

'All right,' he said. 'I guess it's now or never.'

They tiptoed along the verandah and down the steps, checking from right to left with almost ever step they took. Robyn clung on to Charlie's sleeve, and kept nervously coughing, a little dry cough of sheer fear. They crossed the yard, and there was a sudden gush of wind which made the dust sizzle against their ankles. Robyn said, 'Is that somebody singing? I'm sure I can hear somebody singing.'

Charlie listened, and when the wind died down he could hear the high quavering voice of Eric Broussard still lying on his back in the field where his own dog had brought him down, singing 'Laisser les Cajuns Danser'. There was something infinitely sad about it, a man lying dying in a field, singing his own requiem, but there was something infinitely eerie about it too.

The crouched their way along the back fence until they reached the path which led to the jetty. The sky was light enough now for them to be able to see Eric's skiff outlined black against the bronze surface of the bayou. Frogs croaked, katydids chirruped, and steam rose from the surface like a graveyard scene in a horror movie. 'Come on,' said Charlie. 'I don't think they've managed to figure out where we are yet. They're probably still watching the car.'

Running now, they headed for the jetty; but just as they did so they heard the roaring of a car engine, echoing around the side of the house, and a pale-coloured Buick came sliding around the corner in the dry black dirt, its headlights full, cutting them off from the entrance to the jetty.

'This way!' Charlie shouted, and took hold of Robyn's arm and dragged her away from the jetty and back towards the house. They ran in between the outbuildings, their footsteps thudding, while behind them the Buick revved up its engine again and came slewing around the yard. Charlie pressed Robyn against the wall and then breathed, 'They have to go all the way around the house. Come on – let's get back to the bayou.'

They could hear the car's tyres sliding and howling as it circuited the house once more, hunting for them like an enraged beast. They ran without a word towards the jetty, along the wooden duckboards, and out on to the rickety wooden structure itself. They were only halfway along it when the Buick reappeared, its headlights blinding them, its engine screaming. It headed straight towards them, the duckboards clattering and thundering under its wheels.

'*Dive!*' yelled Charlie, and they tumbled off the jetty into the water. The Buick flashed past them with its brakes shrieking like strangled pigs. Although there was fifty more feet of jetty to go, the Buick's driver must have been heading towards them a fraction too fast, and the boards were slippery with moss and early-morning damp.

Charlie, tossing his head up out of the water, saw the huge car go flying off the end of the jetty in a bloody blaze of brakelights, and crash into the bayou. Immediately, weighted down by the engine, the front of the car dipped under the water, and the trunk reared up like the stern of a sinking ship. A wave of chilly brown water slapped against Charlie's face, and he felt as if he had swallowed half of the bayou. He frantically trod water, then mud.

'Robyn!' he shouted. 'Robyn! Are you okay?'

'I'm here!' Robyn called back. 'I'm right by the boat!'

Charlie touched the oozy bottom of the bayou, and managed to wade a little way closer to the shore. Grabbing hold of the tough grass that grew on the bank, he pulled himself hand over hand toward the jetty, and at last managed to climb back up on to the planks, where he lay chest down for a moment, panting with effort, his trouser legs glistening black with mud from the knees down. After a few seconds spent getting his breath back, he stood up and squelched along to the end of the jetty, and looked down into the water. Robyn was clambering into Eric Broussard's skiff, tilting it sideways as she did so.

'You sure you're okay?' he asked her.

'What about those men in the car?' said Robyn.

Charlie looked towards the bayou. Already there was nothing to be seen of the Buick but its red taillights glowering under the surface. Charlie wiped his hands across his mouth to clear away some of the mud, and said, 'Fuck them.'

'But they must be still alive.'

'They wanted to run us down, didn't they? They were trying to kill us!'

But before Robyn could say anything else, Charlie took a

deep breath, ran a short distance along the jetty, and dived back into the bayou. He knew just as well as Robyn that he couldn't leave the car in the water without making at least a token effort to save the men inside. Fighting for your life was one thing. Letting people die was another.

He felt his clothes clinging heavily around him as he swam below the surface towards the submerged car. The water was so murky that he found it impossible to see anything except the vehicle's lights until he was almost on top of it. It was tilted downward, with its nearside bumper already buried in the ooze, its passenger compartment still half full of air, giving it a lumbering buoyancy. Charlie could hear the blurting of bubbles, however, as the air steadily poured up to the surface, and he guessed that it couldn't be more than a matter of seconds before the car filled up completely. He swam around it, short of breath now, staring as wide-eyed as he could.

He heard thumping, and something that must have been a shout for help. He kicked himself around to the car's offside, and saw M. Fontenot, his white face pressed against the driver's window, a mask of absolute terror. In the passenger seat, the big-shouldered man called Henri was sitting, his face equally strained, but making no effort to open the Buicks' doors. Charlie tried to snatch at the driver's door handle, but he was out of oxygen now, and he had to thrash himself up to the surface.

Robyn was sitting in the skiff watching for him. Charlie gulped for air, and doggy-paddled around in a circle. 'Did you find them?' called Robyn. 'Are they still alive?'

'They're alive all right. But they don't have long. It's that Fontenot guy from the Célèstines, and the other one, the big one. But they don't seem to be making any effort to get themselves out.'

'Can you open the doors?'

'I don't know,' Charlie gasped. 'I'm going back to give it a try.'

He took two more giant breaths, then plunged back under the surface of the bayou once more. He had never been a good underwater swimmer, and it took him several strenuous strokes of his arm to get himself back down to the car. Even then he had to tug himself further down by holding on to the drip-rail around the car's roof.

M. Fontenot and Henri were still sitting where they had been before. The water had already filled up to M. Fontenot's chest. His eyes were bulging and his teeth were clenched, as if the skull that had been hidden inside his head for so many years had caught the scent of freedom. Henri's expression was extraordinary, and even more frightening because it was so resigned. Charlie wrenched the door handle, but the door was either locked or jammed, or too heavy to open because of the water pressure. Charlie banged on the window, and gestured frantically that M. Fontenot should try to open it from the inside. That way, the pressure inside and outside the car would equalize.

But M. Fontenot shook his head, and screamed, 'I'm trapped! I'm trapped behind the wheel! My legs are trapped!'

Charlie realized with cold dread what he was witnessing. M. Fontenot refused to open the Buick's doors because he was unable to get out; and obviously he had ordered Henri to remain where he was, too, so that he could have just a few more seconds of life. Henri's lungs must have already been bursting for air, but obediently he remained where he was, drowning for the sake of his master. Because the car was tilted towards the nearside, the water would reach Henri's face first. It was already filling up to the side of his chin, but he made no attempt to lift his mouth clear of it.

Charlie banged on the door again, and gestured towards the door locks. But M. Fontenot did nothing but stare at him in desperation. Charlie couldn't stay down any longer, and he released his hold on the car and kicked himself up to the surface.

Robyn had untied the skiff and brought it closer. Charlie, coughing, spitting up water, clung gratefully on to the side of it. 'Tried,' he choked. 'No damn good. Fontenot's legs are trapped.'

Robyn leaned forward and took hold of his hand. 'Just get on board, Charlie. If there's nothing you can do, there's nothing you can do. I don't want *you* to drown too.'

'One more try,' said Charlie, but just as he was taking his second deep breath, there was an abrupt and noisy rush of bubbles from below the surface, and the Buick's lights went out.

'It's no use,' said Robyn. 'God knows you did your best.'

Charlie trod water for a few minutes, waiting to see if Henri had managed to get out, but after a while the bayou returned to steamy stillness, and the frogs took up their regular chorus as if nothing at all had happened. 'Okay,' said Charlie. 'I'm coming aboard.'

With Robyn tugging at his soaking shirt, he clambered into the wildy rocking skiff, and sat on the plain plank seat, with water running from his clothes, his head bowed, trying to cough up as much of the Normand Bayou as he could.

'Well,' he said, 'we licked them, didn't we? And all *that's* going to look like is accidental death. Come on, let's get back to the jetty. I want to see if Eric's okay. Then we can take the car and get the hell out.'

Robyn balanced her way to the middle of the skiff and picked up the paddle. She leaned forward and kissed Charlie's wet tangled hair. 'You were fantastic,' she whispered. 'You were better than Lloyd Bridges.'

Charlie gave a wry, slanting smile. 'Can't you ever love me for myself?'

They began to paddle their way back toward the jetty. As they did so, however, they heard the warbling sound of an ambulance siren in the middle distance. They heard something else, too – the whip-whipping of a police siren.

'Shit,' said Charlie.

'Do you think we can make it to the car in time?' Robyn asked him.

'Oh sure. But there's only one way out of here by road, and what do you think the police are going to do when two fugitives from justice come steaming toward them in a stolen vehicle? Come on — we don't have any choice. We're going to have to paddle our way out of here. Eric said to keep heading south-west.'

Charlie quickly checked the contents of the skiff. At the prow, there was a heap of clumsily folded rubberized sheeting, which Eric had presumably used to cover himself up with when it was raining. There was a broken fishing basket, a collection of baling-hooks and rusty screwdrivers and some piece of machinery that looked as if it had once belonged to an outboard motor. There was also a spare paddle and a bottle that contained about half a pint of clear liquid. Charlie uncorked it and sniffed. 'Bad Eric,' he remarked. 'This is raw corn whiskey.' He wiped the neck, took a cautious swig and swallowed it.

'Benedict Arnold,' he swore, as it soaked down his throat like lighted kerosene.

They took up their paddles, nudged the skiff around, and began to splash their way south-westward along the bayou. They bayou was nearly sixty feet wide here, but Charlie could already see that it narrowed up ahead. The steam enveloped them in mysterious swirls, floating over the brown surface of the water like the ghostly hands of all those who had lived and died on the Normand Bayou. It seemed to clutch and cling at their paddles, and then whirl away as they splashed into the water. The sound of the police siren soon became muffled and distant. After a while they could hear nothing but the frogs and the watery guttural noise of their own paddling. They didn't speak for a long time. They were both tired and shocked, and Charlie was beginning to feel chilly and uncomfortable in his soaking wet clothes. He thought of Eric dying in his field. Perhaps Eric's spirit was travelling with them now, in the skiff from which he had fished so often, with his bottle of raw corn whiskey and his broken basket full of catfish. Charlie began softly to whistle 'Laisser les Cajuns Danser', although he had never realized that he had picked up the tune.

The morning passed and the steam thickened and then began to clear; so that by eleven o'clock they were paddling on water that was livid yellow-ochre in colour, and sparkling with sunlight, in between high levées where catalpa and willows draggled their roots, and mud-turtles basked at the water's edge. Charlie in his damp-dry clothes suddenly lowered his head and said, 'I'm just going to have to rest up for a while. Why not let's pull under that bridge?'

About a quarter-mile up ahead of them was a wooden bridge; not much of a bridge, because here the bayou was comparatively narrow, but closely surrounded by water oaks, thick with dangling vines, so that the underneath of the bridge was curtained off like a dark, private room. They gently bumped the skiff into the cool shadow, stowed away their paddles, and sat for a while in the gloom looking at each other. A few chinks of sunlight penetrated the wooden walkway of the bridge above them, and played on the water and on Robyn's hair. Turtles splashed and plopped; catfish finned by in swirls of grainy silt. They felt so far away from the rest of the world that they could have been children again.

'Today's Thursday,' said Robyn, as if to remind them both of the urgency of what they were doing, and why they were here.

Charlie nodded. 'It shouldn't take us very much longer to get to Acadia.'

'Go on rest up,' Robyn told him soothingly. He smiled at her, she smiled back and he realized without any fear whatsoever that he loved her.

He eased himself down into the well of the skiff, resting his head on her lap. She straightened his tousled hair with her fingers. 'We're not exactly the world's best dressed couple, are we?' she said.

Charlie closed his eyes. All that diving into the the bayou to try to rescue M. Fontenot – on top of the shock of seeing Gumbo burn and Eric Broussard lie there dying began to overwhelm him, like a cloak of lead. He could feel the skiff dipping and bobbing beneath him. He could feel Robyn's fingers stroking his forehead. He wasn't sleeping, but he was already in that strange anteroom to sleep, where reality and illusion intertwine, and so he didn't pay any clear attention to the slight shifting sound in the back of the skiff, where the rubberized sheets were stored.

Nor did he open his eyes when the sheets were gradually nudged back, and the dull blade of a machete appeared from underneath them, like the claw of some monstrous crab.

CHAPTER TWENTY-ONE

Charlie began to dream about the dark monkish restaurant again, although this time the dream seemed to be subtly different. He was sure that he could hear chanting, from the direction of the kitchen doors. It sounded like a Gregorian chant, disciplined and sweet, and yet he could also hear the dull erratic thumping of a primitive drum.

He left his seat and began to walk between the tables towards the kitchen. Other diners turned to watch him as he passed. All of the men were dressed in formal evening wear, although not all of them appeared to be real. Some of them had faces that were as smooth as wax, and others had eyes that burned in their heads like coals. The women wore decorative masks, covered with mother-of-pearl and gleaming peacock feathers and glass jewellery; as well as heavy bodices embroidered with gold and silver thread. From the waist down, however, almost all of them were naked, and they sat with their thighs wide apart in order to expose themselves to whoever was passing. They giggled and tittered beneath their masks as Charlie walked towards the kitchen. He had a terrible feeling that they knew something he didn't – something frightening and dire.

The kitchen doors came nearer and nearer – as if they were gliding towards him instead of him walking toward them. They were stainless steel with circular porthole windows in them. The windows were totally black, impenetrable, like tunnels to nowhere at all. As he approached, Charlie's heart began to tighten with fear, and his feet began to drag on the carpet, as if his shoes where soled with Velcro. *Don't go inside*, his sense of survival cried out to him. *It's the ritual kitchen, don't go inside!*

He stopped walking, but the kitchen doors continued to glide nearer, until he was standing right up against them. He put out his hand. The stainless steel was utterly cold. He knew there were faces watching him through the porthole windows, but he didn't dare to look at them. They were blind faces – faces with eyes like the eyes of freshly boiled fish.

Don't go inside! his sense of survival screamed. *It's the ritual kitchen, don't go inside!*

One of the women approached him. She wore a mask like a hawk, with a solid silver beak and glossy black feathers. The eyes that looked out at him through the apertures in the mask were Velma's. Her breasts were covered in a sleek black bodice with silver fastenings. A plaited cord of black silk was pulled tight between the lips of her vulva, so that they pouted vivid pink with shining black pubic hair. She reached out and touched his lips with her fingers, and whispered, '*You're one of us now, my darling. You've tasted the holy bread now. You're one of us.*'

Then silently, her fingers dropped off, and fell pattering on to the floor, leaving her with nothing but a mutilated paddle instead of a hand. Her eyes smiled at him through the mask, '*You're one of us now*', she repeated, and screeched with laughter. '*One of us now! One of us!*'

And then . . .

. . . with a sinister swishing sound, the kitchen doors swung open. Charlie screamed. But instantly, he understood that it wasn't *he* who had screamed at all. He was splattered all over with something wet, and the skiff was rocking wildly, and then Robyn tumbled over him, still screaming, and fell heavily into the stern.

Charlie glimpsed a dwarfish, hooded figure, and eyes that stared malevolent and pale. He glimpsed a curved upraised machete, strapped to a stunted arm. He twisted around, tried to get up, overbalanced, and then the machete sang like a bird and hit the plain plank seat. Charlie stood up, crouched, breathing hard, facing the dwarf with both hands held out in front of him. His good right hand, and his left hand, from which one finger was missing.

'Robyn!' he snapped. 'Robyn! Are you okay? Did he hurt you?'

The dwarf cackled and danced, deliberately rocking the skiff from side to side. 'Stupid bastard! Stupid bastard! Running away! Running away!'

'Robyn?' Charlie repeated. 'Robyn, for Christ's sake!'

Robyn said, in a high voice, 'He hit my shoulder.'

Charlie stared at the dwarf with renewed fury. 'You runt, David,' he breathed, taking two awkward steps forward in the bottom of the skiff. But David laughed, a ridiculous hysterical laugh, and swished his machete from side to side, and taunted Charlie as if he were taunting a dog.

'Come on then, bozo. Come here and get it. You think I'm a runt? I'll show you who's a runt! I gave my arms and legs to the Lord Jesus Christ, that's how much of a runt I am! Would you dare do that? Would you give your cock and your balls to the Lord Jesus Christ? That's what I did! I cut them off myself, with a big sharp knife, and I ate them! You can't do anything to me that I haven't already done to myself, bozo, so you listen good. I'm going to kill you, you and your harlot too! I'm going to cut you into little pieces, the same way I did with Mrs Kemp! I'm going to drink your blood, bozo! I'm going to drink it out of your arteries while you're still alive! You got me? So come on here, come on – and make me happy!'

Charlie remained crouched in the middle of the skiff, watching the dwarf intently, lifting first one hand and then the other to give the impression that he was skilled in some kind of martial art. He wanted to say all kinds of things to David to psyche him out, but somehow the words wouldn't come. The only noises he could make was a series of attenuated burps. *Fear*, he thought. *I'm afraid.*

'I'm going to take your manhood first,' the dwarf promised

him, whistling his machete around his head. 'Your manhood – and then your head. Just think how pleased Mme Musette is going to be, if I bring her your head.'

'You asshole,' snarled Charlie. 'You couldn't even go the whole way, could you, and do a good job of killing yourself?'

The dwarf let out a noise that was halfway between a retch and a scream and hobbled violently towards Charlie with his machete swinging. Charlie threw himself sideways out of the skiff, splashing noisily into the muddy water under the bridge, and the dwarf toppled after him, still screaming. Robyn fell into the water, too, clutching her injured shoulder; but Charlie knew that it was only three or four feet deep, and that she wouldn't come to any serious harm.

For David the dwarf, however, the water was overwhelming, and his scream of fury turned to a gasp of shock. Charlie immediately waded towards him, with a surge of muddy wash, and gripped the stump to which his machete was strapped. David bucked and jumped and heaved his amputated limbs, but Charlie smacked him hard in the side of the face, and twisted the machete free of its leather strap. He tossed it away, into the water, and it skipped just once on the surface before sinking.

David screeched, *'Heretic! Heretic! Bastard! Heretic!'* in a voice that sounded completely unreal. But then Charlie seized hold of the back of his neck, and forced his head under the water, into the mud. David struggled and thrashed like a maniac. Charlie found it almost impossible to hold him. But he knew that if he didn't kill David now, he would return time after time to haunt him, and that in the end he would destroy him, and Martin, and Robyn too. With that determination firing him up, he kept David's face pressed deep into the mud, two feet below the water, and he held him there and he held him there and he wasn't going to let him go for anything.

David struggled and struggled, but gradually his convulsions became weaker, and more spasmodic. His back arched in one final shudder, and then he floated face down in the water, nudged by the current, a torso with stumps for arms and legs, wrapped in a soaking robe. A dwarfish parody of Ophelia, *'Till that her garments, heavy with their drink, | Pull'd the poor wretch from her melodious lay | To muddy death.'*

Juddering with cold and exertion, Charlie waded his way back around the skiff. Robyn had pulled herself up on to the muddy bank of the bayou, underneath the trailing vines, and she was pressing her hand over her shoulder where David had cut her. She was white-faced, and shaking. Charlie sloshed up to her through thigh-deep mud and put his arm around her and held her very close. 'It's all right. You don't have anything to worry about. He's dead.'

Neither of them turned to watch David's body float like a water-sodden cotton bale out from under the bridge and slowly away down the bayou. Charlie carefully opened Robyn's blood-soaked blouse and lifted her hand away from her wound. It was a vicious, blunt, nasty cut, and there was no doubt that it needed stitches. But David had missed her vital arteries, and chopped his machete into nothing but muscle and bone. She was lucky: a second blow could have caught her in the skull.

'Listen,' said Charlie, 'I don't know even the first thing about dressing wounds. But if you can hold on until we reach the next community, I'll make sure that you get this properly stitched.'

'They'll call the police,' Robyn protested. 'The next thing I know, they'll put me under arrest. Or worse – they could hand me over to the Célèstines.'

'Listen, don't worry about it,' Charlie reassured her. 'We'll find ourselves a country doctor. One who doesn't ask too many questions.'

'Are you kidding?' said Robyn. 'Country doctors who don't ask too many questions died out with *Young Dr Malone*.'

'*Young Dr Malone*? You're too young to remember that.'

'If you think I'm too young to remember *Young Dr Malone*, then you're too old.'

Charlie helped Robyn back into the skiff, and made her comfortable, padding her wound with the tail torn from his shirt. Then he paddled out from underneath the bridge, into the glaring sunshine, noon in south-western Louisiana, with the cypress trees turning crimson, and the sky clear. Robyn said, 'God, this hurts,' but a little while later they passed the body of the dwarf David, dipping in the bayou, and Robyn didn't complain after that. All she said was, 'I wonder who his parents were? I mean, they must have sent him to school, and been proud of him. And look at him now.'

Charlie said, 'My mother always told me, "Never ask questions when you know that you're never going to be able to find out the answer".'

'Is that what they call homespun philosophy?' asked Robyn.

Charlie didn't answer, but carried on paddling. He was finding it increasingly difficult to shake off his dreams. In fact, he was beginning to wonder whether this journey to rescue Martin was in itself a dream, propelling a flat-bottomed skiff along a narrow Louisiana bayou on a warm October afternoon, while the police were hunting for him high and low, and Marjorie was fretting, and M. Musette was lasciviously sharpening his butcher's knives for the second coming of Jesus Christ.

Around three o'clock, dry-throated, exhausted and hungry, Charlie finally raised his paddle out of the water and let the skiff glide. Robyn had been drowsing, her head couched against her arm. 'What's the matter?' she asked him. She kept his shirt tail pressed to her shoulder. It must have been hurting pretty bad by now.

'I think I've had it,' Charlie admitted.

'We can't go on like this,' said Robyn. 'We have to find someplace to stay for the night; and another car, too.'

'Another car?' said Charlie.

'Sure. How else are we going to take Martin away from the Célèstines? On bicycles?'

Charlie knelt up, setting the skiff tilting from side to side. He shaded his eyes and peered at the fields spread out on either side of the bayou. 'There's a girder bridge, no more than a half-mile ahead of us. I guess we could land right there, and hitch ourselves a ride. That's always supposing somebody comes by.'

'What if they don't?' Robyn wanted to know.

'Then we'll walk,' said Charlie. 'Acadia can't be too far from here.'

He paddled towards the bridge. The bayou was wider here, and the bridge was a steelgirder construction, with tarred wooden slats for a roadbed. It was only when he was far too near to it to turn back that Charlie saw the Louisiana State Police cars parked on either side of the bridge's ramps, and the wide-hatted officers standing waiting with pump-guns resting on their hips, their eyes concealed by orange Ray-Bans, their faces laconic and bored, as if homicide suspects came paddling their way down the bayou every damn day of the week.

There was, of course, no chance of escape. One of the officers lifted a loud-hailer from the roof of his car, and called out, 'You there! Charles McLean and Robyn Harris! We're arresting you here for homicide in the first degree, kidnap, and grand theft auto. Would you pull your boat into the side here, please? We have instructions to shoot you if you try to get away.'

Robyn said urgently, 'Do you really think that they'd shoot?'

'Do you really want to put them to the test?' Charlie said.

He guided the skiff towards the muddy bank, until its flat bottom scraped against the mussels that clustered below the waterline. Then he balanced his way on to dry land, turning around to help Robyn out. Two young police officers came down to the edge of the bayou to guard them, and to drag the skiff right out of the water. Charlie climbed the levée and stood in the sunshine with his hands on his hips, exhausted, out of breath, and resigned at last to being caught.

The officer with the loud-hailer came forward and took off his sunglasses. 'Sergeant Ron Duprée, Louisiana State Police,' he said, in a very slow drawl. 'You've been causing us a whole lot of trouble, sir.'

Charlie said, 'If you're going to arrest me, don't you think you ought to read me my rights? You wouldn't like to be responsible for having my indictment disallowed, would you?'

'Well, we can Mirandize you all in good time, sir,' Sergeant Duprée told him, holding his sunglasses up to the light to check that they were perfectly polished. 'Right now we'd like to invite you along for a little ride.'

Robyn put in, 'We don't have to go anywhere, not unless you arrest us properly and read us our rights.'

Sergeant Duprée turned and stared at her in exaggerated amusement. 'Well, now, I always was partial to an outspoken lady.' He walked up to Robyn with his thumbs in his belt and grinned at her. 'You're perfectly correct, my dear lady, you're not *obliged* to come along for this ride, not in the eyes of the law. I can't coerce you. It'd be different, of course, if you were to volunteer.'

'You're crazy,' said Robyn. 'I'm not going to volunteer.'

'But supposing your boyfriend here was to happen to meet with some unfortunate accident?'

'Are you threatening us?' Robyn demanded.

'Sure I'm threatening you. This isn't New England, this is south-western Louisiana, and here we have a way of doing things different. Totally according to the letter of the law, mind you, but different. You could say we were more community-conscious, if you like. More neighbourly. And there's some neighbours of ours who'd like to have a little talk with you, about this and that.'

Charlie said coldly, 'I suppose you mean the Célèstines?'

Sergeant Duprée looked back at Charlie over his shoulder and gave him a toothy grin. 'That's right first time, sir. Right first time. Give the man a porce-a-lain rabbit.'

Robyn said, 'Charlie?'

Charlie let out a long breath. 'I don't think that we have very much of a choice, do you?'

Sergeant Duprée laughed, and slapped Robyn cheerily on the shoulder. 'Right again, sir. Right again.'

Covered all the way by pump-guns, they were led to one of the three police cars that had been parked beside the bridge. Sergeant Duprée opened the rear door for them, and they climbed in. The car was unbearably hot inside, and smelled of McDonald's hamburgers. Sergeant Duprée climbed into the passenger seat and took off his hat. 'We'll have that air conditioning blowing in a while, folks, then you'll feel more comfortable. I have to say that you're both in a sorry state, aren't you?'

'Miss Harris' shoulder needs attention,' said Charlie. 'She's been given a serious cut.'

'Well, I'm sure your friends at L'Église des Pauvres can help you out there,' Sergeant Duprée said. 'They've got all the facilities for dealing with cuts to the human body that anybody could wish for.'

They drove at nearly sixty miles an hour along a narrow, dusty highway, in between fields that were the colour of red roof tiles. The air conditioning was set to Hi, and after a few minutes the interior of the car was freezing. Sergeant Duprée took out a pack of grape-flavoured chewing gum and offered it around. 'You surely caused us a whole lot of trouble, I've got to tell you,' he repeated, folding a purple stick of gum between his front teeth.

'Is the church far?' asked Charlie.

'Three miles, that's all. The town of Acadia is just over to your left there, you can see the spire of the Baptist church once we pass these cypress trees up ahead here. Then L'Église des Pauvres is about three-quarters of a mile further on. It used to be a farm, years ago, before the Célèstines took it over. Scarman's Farm. Lots of people hereabouts still call it Scarman's Farm. We Police Sergeant Duprée however, have to be accurate in our terminology.'

They drove for a little while without talking. Then Charlie said, 'Can I ask you what you think about the Célèstines? I mean, you personally?'

Sergeant Duprée barked with laughter. 'Me personally? I think they're fruitcakes.'

'But it doesn't concern you, what they're doing?'

'Sir, they aren't breaking no laws. I may disapprove of them, morally or whatever, but just like I said we do things here by the letter of the law, and if they want to eat themselves for lunch, that's up to them.'

'Besides which, they keep you paid off?' Charlie added.

'Now, that's where you're *wrong*,' Sergeant Duprée told him, without taking offence at Charlie's allegation that he was taking bribes. 'The Célèstines themselves don't pay nobody nothing. Not a cent. But let me put it this way: there are plenty of influential people in this state who have friends and family connected with the Célèstines, and it wouldn't be wise of me to encourage career problems, would it? It's all a question of politics. Apart from which, those Célèstines have official approval from some very high places indeed.'

After about ten minutes, they skirted a wide cornfield, and then turned off to the right along a rutted, uneven track. At the end of the track, there was a metal gate, and a high fence wound around with razor-wire. A man in a plaid shirt and a stetson hat stood by the gate holding a rifle. When he saw the police car approaching, he swung the gate wide and allowed it to enter, although he approached it with his rifle held ready and peered into the windows. 'Looks like you had some good hunting there, Ron,' he remarked.

Sergeant Duprée chewed his gum noisily. 'Where's the big chief?'

'Main building, I guess. You'll have to go round the back way, there's a couple of buses blocking up the front.'

'*Hasta la vista*,' said Sergeant Duprée and pointed forward like an orchestral conductor, to indicate to their driver that they should move on.

L'Église des Pauvres still clearly showed its origins of Scarman's Farm. They drove around a cluster of outbuildings and barns and pig-pens and silos: although there were no animals here any longer, and no feed, and no manure. All the buildings had been immaculately whitewashed, and were presumably being used as offices and dormitories. The main building was a converted barn, with an arched roof, its northern side shaded by an enormous and ancient oak. On the apex of its roof, a high gold cross caught the sunshine, almost as if it were alight.

They parked close to the oak, and climbed out. Sergeant Duprée didn't bother to cover Charlie and Robyn with his gun, now that they had safely arrived. 'Come along,' he said, and beckoned them to follow him up the wooden steps and into the double doors of the main building. Charlie glanced at Robyn, but at that moment she wasn't looking at him. He hoped to God that she didn't think he had let her down.

Inside, the main building had been divided up into corridors and separate rooms. It was very silent and cool in there. All the walls were painted white, and the only decoration was a painting of St Célèstine contemplating the Cross. There was a smell of subtropical mustiness and rose-scented room spray, and something else, like herbs and formaldehyde all mingled together.

Sergeant Duprée led the way along the central corridor until they reached a pair of swing doors. He pushed them open, and ushered Charlie and Robyn into a high, white-painted room, illuminated by clerestory windows. There were rows of trestle tables on the floor of the room, nine or ten of them, each laid with a bright, white linen tablecloth, and decorated with fresh flowers. A small group of people were standing at the side, talking in cheerful, animated voices. Charlie instantly recognized both M. and Mme Musette. At the far end of the room, the floor had been raised into a low platform, and on this platform stood a huge altar, draped in yellow and white, the colours of the Papacy. Behind the altar rose a polished brass crucifix, at least twenty feet high, with an elegant and sad-faced Christ nailed on to it with shining chrome-plated nails, and crowned with chrome-plated thorns.

Sergeant Duprée led Charlie and Robyn over towards the Musettes. M. Musette was wearing a white cassock and a white cape around his shoulders. A gold crucifix shone on his chest. Mme Musette was dressed in a very white silk sheath that reached to her calves, so tight and clinging that Charlie could clearly see the outline of her nipples and even the depression of her navel. Her hands were concealed in elbow-length while silk gloves.

'Well, well, Mr McLean,' said M. Musette, extending his hand. 'You have decided to join us at last. And Ms Harris, too! Welcome to L'Église des Pauvres. You couldn't have chosen a better time.'

Charlie ignored M. Musette's hand. 'Forget the welcome, *monsieur*. All I'm going to do is repeat what I said before. I want my son, and then I want to leave.'

Sergeant Duprée chuckled. 'This gentleman's an optimist, you have to give him that.'

'Thank you, sergeant,' said Mme Musette smoothly. 'You've done an excellent job.'

'You can't hold us here,' Robyn protested.

'Of course not,' said M. Musette. 'But while young Martin McLean remains alive and whole, I'm sure that his devoted father is not going to abandon him. Any more than *you* my dear, are going to abandon his devoted father.'

'I want to see him,' Charlie insisted.

'By all means,' agreed M. Musette. He looked at his eighteen-carat Ebel wristwatch. 'At the moment, he is at devotions. But he should be here shortly. Perhaps you would like me to show you around?'

Robyn said, 'This is quite illegal and quite ridiculous.'

M. Musette smiled distantly. 'It depends on your definition of both words, my dear. Sergeant Duprée will assure you that nothing is being done here which contravenes either state or federal law. And as for it being ridiculous ... well, even our Lord was ridiculed. Look at him there, with his crown of thorns.'

Robyn snapped, 'Officer – I insist you arrest this man for kidnap.'

Sergeant Duprée shook his head. 'I can't do that, miss. I don't have any grounds.'

'Then arrest me, on the charges you mentioned before.'

'I may,' Sergeant Duprée told her. 'But not just yet.'

'It's all right, Sergeant Duprée,' said M. Musette. 'You just leave these good people to us. We'll take care of them.'

'Sir – I'm sure you will,' Sergeant Duprée replied. He raised his hat to Mme Musette, and then to Robyn, and walked unhurriedly out of the hall, closing the double doors behind him.

'Now what?' said Charlie.

M. Musette raised a hand. 'There's no need to be impatient, Mr McLean. Nor is there any cause to be angry. First of all, you look as if you could use a shower and a change of clothes. Perhaps I can lend you one of my suits; and I'm sure that Ms Harris here is just as slender as my dear wife.'

'I want my son,' Charlie repeated doggedly.

'All in good time,' M. Musette assured him.

It was then that a wheelchair was pushed into the hall by a man with a blue medic's shirt and close-cropped hair. The wheelchair was crammed with white pillows, to support the creature who was sitting in it. The man with the close-cropped

314

hair wheeled it across the hall, and parked it right beside M. Musette. 'You said you wanted to see her before she cuts off her breasts.'

'That's right,' said M. Musette. 'I wanted to give her a last word of praise and prayer.' He knelt down beside the wheel-chair, resting his elbow on the arm of it, and looked warmly into the eyes of his Devotee. Charlie could feel Robyn's hand searching for his. He held it, and she clutched him tight with absolute horror.

The creature propped up in the wheelchair had no legs and one arm. She was wearing nothing but a yellow sleeveless T-shirt, which had been knotted together underneath her pelvis to conceal the stumps of her legs. The stump of her left arm was still wrapped in surgical dressings. It was her face, how-ever, which was the most disfigured. She had cut off most of the fleshy part of her nose, leaving a red-raw cavity, and she had sliced ribbons of flesh off her chin and her cheeks. Her carefully back-combed ash-blonde hair made her disfigure-ment seem all the more grotesque.

M. Musette held her one remaining hand, and squeezed it. The creature turned her eyes on him, and gave him a mutilated smile. 'The Lord is near,' she whispered. 'I can feel it.'

M. Musette said, 'Yes, Velma, my dear. The Lord is near.'

CHAPTER TWENTY-TWO

Charlie and Robyn were taken away from the main building to one of the accommodation blocks, which looked as if it had once been a creamery. They were led to separate rooms, both bare except for a single bed and a plain pine locker, and a picture of St Célèstine. They were allowed to shower; and when they came out, they found that their old clothes had been removed, and new clothes laid out in their place. Charlie had been given a light grey suit with unfashionable bell-bottomed trousers, while Robyn had been given a blue print cotton frock with puffy sleeves and a very deeply scooped front.

All the time, the man with the close-cropped hair stood guard outside Charlie's door; and a matronly-looking woman waited outside Robyn's door. They were not technically prisoners, but Charlie was quite sure what the reaction would be if they attempted to escape.

They were brought back to the main building and told to wait. M. Musette was welcoming the delegation from Reno, Nevada. Mme Musette was meditating. They sat at the end of one of the trestle tables, supervised from twenty feet away by the man with the close-cropped hair, who stood with his arms folded, completely expressionless, and stared at the opposite wall.

Charlie looked around. 'They must be holding the Last Supper in here.'

'Just so long as they don't expect me to attend,' said Robyn. 'That *woman*, Velma – I can't believe that anybody could do that to themselves.'

'Religious ecstasy,' said Charlie. 'Think of Jonestown, that

316

was worse in a way. I guess there's a self-destructive element in all of us.'

'But she *smiled* . . .'

Charlie closed his eyes. He didn't like to think about Velma. He could still remember too vividly the way she had appeared when he had first seen her at the Windsor Hotel. A little blowsy, maybe, but strongly attractive; a woman with looks. It was almost impossible to believe that the maimed and mutilated creature in the wheelchair was actually her, the same woman. Only the eyes gave her away. They were Velma's eyes. The eyes, and the ash-blonde hair.

Robyn held Charlie's hand. 'Supposing it actually happens,' she said.

'Supposing *what* actually happens?'

'Supposing they eat all these twelve Devotees and supposing He does come back – Jesus.'

'Are you kidding? Do you think that Jesus – even if you *believed* in Jesus – would seriously consider returning to earth for a bunch of crazies like the Célèstines?'

'Do you believe in Him?' asked Robyn seriously.

Charlie lowered his eyes, but wouldn't look at her. 'Right at the moment, I'm not so sure.'

'Because of Velma?'

'I guess Velma's part of it. But mostly it's because I can't see Jesus condoning anything like this. I mean, whatever name you want to put on it, it's barbaric. It's like voodoo.'

Robyn said, 'I went to Haiti once. My friend's father used to have a sugar plantation just outside of Port-au-Prince. She was always talking about voodoo. That was when Baby Doc was still in power, and they still had the Tonton Macoute. She took me down to the servant's quarters, and showed me a bone that her father's maid used to use for putting evil spells on people. It was a baby's finger bone. It gave me the shivers. She said if you pointed this bone at somebody you didn't like, Baron Samedi would come and tear them to pieces.'

317

'Baron Samedi?' said Charlie, lifting his head.

'That's right. He's the great voodoo demon. The king of all the zombies.'

'Eric mentioned Baron Samedi.'

'Well, I expect he would. He probably thought that Baron Samedi was coming to get him. I mean he probably *believed* it.'

'Samedi means Saturday, right?' asked Charlie.

'What of it?'

'I don't know. Something clicked. Maybe it's just circumstantial. But in the Célestine Bible, when they're talking about the Last Supper, they say something like "You should know by these secrets that he was vanquished on the fifth day, but the sixth day is his day, and on that day you're going to get your just reward."'

'Well?' said Robyn.

'Well, don't ask me,' said Charlie. 'But "his" was written with a small "h", as if they weren't referring to Jesus, but to somebody else. "He was vanquished on the fifth day". Who was? Not Jesus. Jesus triumphed on the fifth day. He was crucified and he died and just by dying he redeemed the sins of the world, and conquered evil. So who was vanquished?'

Robyn whispered, 'The Devil.'

'That's right, evil was vanquished. But what does the Célèstine Bible say? The sixth day is his day. And the sixth day is Saturday. Samedi. And on that day you're going to get your just reward.'

'Charlie,' said Robyn. 'What exactly are you trying to tell me?'

'I don't know. Maybe I'm going crazy. I *am* going crazy. But supposing when those Célestines lived on that Caribbean island with those cannibals all those years ago – supposing their religions became totally tangled up, voodoo and Roman Catholicism, so that you couldn't tell one from the other? The Caribs worshipped Baron Samedi, right? So what if Baron

Samedi got himself all mixed together with Jesus Christ? Supposing what they're actually doing here isn't arranging for the second coming of Jesus – but the second coming of Baron Samedi? "The sixth day is his day," right? For God's sake – supposing they've gotten it all wrong?'

Robyn squeezed his hand. 'If you don't believe in Jesus Christ, you're not going to start believing in the Devil . . . Or are you? Come on, Charlie, it's not going to happen. It's all fantasy. There won't be any second coming of Jesus Christ and there won't be any reincarnation of Baron Samedi.'

Charlie sat back, and tried to smile at her. 'What do you think of the suit?' he asked.

'Terrible,' she said. 'You look like one of the Monkees.'

'Something really bad is going to happen here tomorrow,' Charlie told her. 'Can't you feel it? I don't believe in the supernatural, but can't you feel the *atmosphere* in here?'

'I don't know,' said Robyn. She stared at him sadly. 'What are you going to do about Martin?' she asked. 'Do you think you're going to be able to get him free?'

Charlie said, 'I'm going to have to talk to him first. It's possible that he's changed his mind about cutting himself up. If he has, we're going to have a pretty good chance of getting out of here. If he hasn't . . . well, I'm going to have to work that out as I go along.'

The doors opened and M. Musette appeared, accompanied by Mme Musette. 'Well, Mr McLean,' he smiled, rubbing his hands together so that they made a dry, chafing noise. 'How would you like a tour of inspection?'

'Can I see Martin?'

'My dear sir, of course you can. You are only too welcome. I will take you to meet all of the twelve Devotees who will be part of the second coming. Your son, *naturellement*, is the twelfth. Perhaps you will meet some other faces that you know.'

Mme Musette said, 'We were talking about you, Mr

319

McLean, just a moment ago. We were saying what a courageous man you are. You have fought harder than any other father we have come across. You were mistaken, of course. Being a father does not entitle you to own your child's future. But very courageous.'

Charlie could have lashed out with any one of a hundred different retorts. But he knew that this was the moment for keeping cool. He nodded his head in silent acknowledgement of Mme Musette's compliment. At the same time he noticed how incredibly beautiful she looked, in her white silk sheath. She was standing directly under the light, so that her body stood out in shadowed relief – her breasts, her angular hips, the curves of her upper thighs and the distinctive swelling of her pudenda. She could have been a statue, smoothed out of pearly-white ice.

'This way,' said M. Musette. 'Let me show you some of our accommodation.'

He led Charlie and Robyn outside. The afternoon was grey and overcast but very humid. They walked across to a long single-storey building with a corrugated asbestos roof and white-washed walls. 'This is where our friends from Le Reposoir are staying,' M. Musette explained. 'I'm sure that they'll be glad to see you.' He opened the door, and beckoned Charlie and Robyn inside. 'This church is a family, you know. If we like you – well, we treat you like a relative.'

'And that's what you do to your relatives, is it?' asked Charlie. 'You cut them up and eat them?'

M. Musette looked saturnine and stern. 'Don't mock me, Mr McLean.'

'I'll make a deal with you,' said Charlie. 'I'll stop mocking you if you let me take my son away from here, unharmed.'

'What a word to use, *unharmed*,' said M. Musette. 'How can he come to harm if his destiny is to become part of the reincarnated Christ? Mr McLean, you son is going to be honoured above all imaginable honour. His life will become

320

the keystone in the perfect reconstruction of the Mother Church. Tomorrow the world will change for ever, and your son's self-sacrifice will make that change possible. Don't you feel any pride at all? Don't you understand what your son is about to do?'

Charlie said tautly, 'What my son is about to do makes me sick to my stomach, so don't talk to me about perfect reconstructions of the Mother Church, do you mind? Just do whatever it is you want to do, and then leave us alone.'

'You're a heretic, Mr McLean.'

'You're not the first person to tell me that today,' said Charlie.

M. Musette smiled, as if he knew what Charlie was talking about, but he said nothing in reply. He took hold of Charlie's elbow and guided him into the accommodation block. 'Of course, this isn't the Beverley Hills Hotel, but it's clean and it's comfortable – and, do you know, we'll be catering for more than one hundred and fifty people here – Guides and Devotees and advisors. It's very peaceful here, very secluded. Our Lord will be mightily pleased.'

'Mightily, huh?' said Robyn sarcastically. M. Musette ignored her.

They walked along the corridor to the first door. M. Musette knocked, and said '*C'est moi, madame!*'

They waited for a while, and then the door was opened. It was Mrs Foss, from the Iron Kettle. She was wearing a beige two-piece suit, with a pleated skirt. She looked at Charlie in bewilderment; but then her face suddenly broke into a smile.

'You *came!*' she exclaimed. 'You actually came! Harriet bet me twenty dollars that you wouldn't.'

Charlie looked back at her, stunned. 'Mrs Foss? I thought you hated the Célèstines.'

'Oh, come on now, how could anybody hate the Célèstines, when they're bringing back Lord Jesus Christ? You didn't take me seriously, did you? You knew about Ivy going missing?

Ivy was a Devotee, and I'm a Guide. Ivy's one of the thousand thousand – and *you*, you lucky man – your son's going to be the *one*! The thousandth thousandth!'

Charlie said, 'You inveigled me into it, didn't you, Mrs Foss?'

'Oh, come on now – *inveigled*?'

Charlie was furious. 'You trapped me, you caught me, and worst of all, you caught Martin. You were a Célèstine and Harriet was a Célèstine, and you knew how close you were getting to the thousandth thousandth. Did the Musettes give you some kind of reward for kidnapping my son? Huh? Money, stocks, something like that?'

'Your son wanted to join us,' said M. Musette calmly.

'My son didn't know anything about you until that dwarf of yours persuaded him to go to Le Reposoir. You know that and I know that, so don't you give me any bullshit about him wanting to join you. He was kidnapped, and then he was brainwashed.'

M. Musette shrugged. 'If you say so, *monsieur*.'

'You bet I damn well say so. In fact, I want to see him now.'

M. Musette clapped his hands in genial impatience. 'All in good time, Mr McLean! Give your son a chance to pray and meditate! Give him a chance to realize his own private destiny!'

'Let me tell you something,' Charlie warned him. 'My son's destiny is to grow up, and mature, and then grow old, with a wife and a family and a house wherever he wants it – that's what my son's destiny happens to be. My son's destiny is certainly not connected with chopping off parts of his body and eating them. Now – do you have that straight?'

M. Musette turned away. 'I thought you would understand, Mr McLean. I really believed that you would understand.'

'I understand everything,' Charlie replied. 'I understand everything perfectly.'

'Then come along,' said M. Musette, and guided Charlie to the next room. He knocked, and the door was opened by Mr Haxalt, from the First Litchfield Savings Bank. He was wearing a bathrobe, and his silver hair was wet and spiky. 'Yes?' he asked; but when he saw Charlie and M. Musette together, he stepped back, confused.

'Mr Haxalt is one of our staunchest supporters, aren't you, Walter?' M. Musette enthused.

'I do my best,' said Walter Haxalt guardedly.

Charlie said, 'You know something, Mr Haxalt? I'm glad I took your parking place. I should've stayed there all day.'

M. Musette laughed. 'Mr McLean is a little upset,' he told Walter Haxalt. 'He'll get over it, mark my words.'

He guided Charlie to the next room. There, sitting on the bed, dusting his feet with athlete's foot powder, was Christopher Prescott, one of the old men from the green at Allen's Corners. 'Why, you made it!' he exclaimed. 'It's good to see you.'

'Where's your friend?' Charlie asked him.

'My friend? Oh, you mean Oliver Burack. Oliver T. Burack. He doesn't know anything about all this. Better that he doesn't. He's back at Allen's Corners, where he should be. He thinks I've gone to see my sister in Tampa. Little does he know, hey?'

'That's right,' said Charlie, his voice flat. 'Little does he know.'

A large room at the end of the block had been converted into a television lounge, and there Charlie saw several more faces from Allen's Corners. Clive, the deputy sheriff who had first approached him when he arrived there, gave him a shy, acknowledging wave. Then there was the woman who served behind the delicatessen counter at Allen's Corners supermarket. All of them were smiling, all of them were happy. You would have thought they had come for a weekend vacation, rather than a religious bloodbath.

'Where's my son?' asked Charlie.

M. Musette laid his arm across Charlie's shoulders. Charlie didn't attempt to lever it away. 'He's a very special boy, your son. We're keeping him someplace special.'

They left the accommodation block and walked along a shadowy avenue of pecan trees, until they reached a small breezeblock building surrounded by a low whitewashed wall. A young man with the oval, pimply face of a halfwit was sitting on a chair outside the door, reading a *Super Friends* comic. As M. Musette approached, he stumbled up off his chair and let out a hoot of enthusiastic welcome.

M. Musette ruffled the boy's awkwardly cropped hair. 'Ben has his uses, don't you, Ben? If I tell Ben that nobody gets in or out of here, excepting me and my wife, then I know that nobody is going to get in or out of here.'

He produced a key from his robes and started to unlock the building's green-painted door. Robyn said, 'All those people back at the accommodation block – did they actually conspire to lead Charlie to the Célèstines?'

M. Musette raised one eyebrow. '*Conspire* is a very media kind of a word, my dear lady. But you could say that once young Martin had been observed by Mrs Foss, there was a certain concerted community effort to induce Mr McLean to come into the fold. It is not often that you find a boy of the right age travelling alone with his father, as Mr McLean was. Especially when the time of the thousandth thousandth is imminent.'

'You mean everybody at Allen's Corners *knew*?' said Charlie.

'Most of them,' replied M. Musette. 'They knew, and they rejoiced. There were, of course, one or two exceptions, like Mrs – what was her name now?'

'Kemp,' Charlie told him. 'That woman you told your dwarf to hack to bits.'

M. Musette tutted. 'She was being very obstreperous. But come on in. Your son is here, he's waiting for you.'

M. Musette opened the door and led the way into the building. There was only one room, with one corner of it partitioned off as a shower and toilet. The walls were white, the floor was scrubbed oak blocks. Against the far wall, there was a hospital-style bed, covered with a white sheet. Martin was lying on the bed, wearing a simple white habit. His head had been shaved, and he looked waxy-pale, with circles around his eyes that could have been stained with beetroot juice.

'Martin,' whispered Charlie, and stepped forward with his hands held out.

'Dad,' said Martin, and managed the faintest hint of a smile.

Charlie sat on the bed and took Martin in his arms and held him close. Martin felt different, thinner, and he smelled of the same herbs which permeated all of the Célèstine buildings. Fennel, and something else unidentifiable, something bitter.

'Are you all right?' Charlie asked him quietly. 'They haven't hurt you?'

'No, Dad, I'm fine. I'm really fine.'

'Have they been feeding you properly? They haven't interfered with you, anything like that?'

Martin prised himself free from Charlie's embrace. 'You mean sexually?'

'I mean in any way at all.'

Martin looked towards the doorway where Mme Musette was standing with her arms folded, the ice queen in silky white. 'They've been treating me good, Dad. They brought me down here in a private plane. It was neat.'

'You don't know how good it is to see you,' said Charlie. He was so choked up with emotion that he could scarcely speak. His eyes were filled up with tears. Martin touched his shoulder, and said, 'It's good to see you, too, Dad. It really is.'

Charlie cleared his throat. 'You know why you're here, don't you? You know what they're planning to do?'

'I'm all prepared for it. I've been praying and fasting and now I'm all ready. Tomorrow's going to be fantastic.'

'Martin, if these people have their way, tomorrow you're going to die.'

Martin smiled again, a little dreamily. 'Am I supposed to be afraid of dying? Is that it?'

'Martin, they're going to kill you. Don't you understand? They're going to kill you, and that's going to be the end of your life, period. No life hereafter, nothing.'

Martin shook his head. 'Tomorrow I'm going to do something for which most people would give their lives ten times over. That's what Edouard says. Tomorrow I'm going to become part of the living saviour. Tomorrow I'm going to be part of our Lord Jesus Christ.'

Charlie was shaking. He gripped hold of Martin's hands, and said, 'I'm begging you, Martin. I've never begged you for anything before. But I'm begging you now, *please* don't let them do this to you. Give yourself some time, think it over, then decide.'

'It has to be tomorrow,' said Martin. 'Tomorrow is the day.'

'Martin,' said Charlie, 'if I mean anything to you at all, please think this over.'

Martin wrapped his arms around Charlie's neck, and pressed his forehead against Charlie's forehead. 'Dad, you don't seem to understand at all. I love you. You're my father. If you hadn't given birth to me, I never would have been able to serve Jesus this way. Don't you know how proud and grateful that makes me?'

Under his breath, Charlie said, 'You won't be serving Jesus, Martin. Maybe you won't be serving anybody at all, except those Célèstine yo-yos. It's even possible that you'll be serving the Devil.'

Martin stared at him, their eyes only inches away from each other. 'The Devil?' he whispered. 'What do you mean?'

'I mean that this ritual tomorrow, this Last Supper, it could have completely the opposite effect to what you believe. Instead of bringing down our Lord and Saviour from heaven above, it could raise the Devil himself from out of hell.'

Slowly, very slowly, Martin began to smile again. 'The Devil,' he repeated. 'From out of hell?'

Christ, thought Charlie, *I've gotten through. I've actually made an impression on him. Maybe now he's going to turn around and start doubting what the Célèstines have been telling him. Maybe now, at last, he's going to set himself free.*

Martin smiled even more broadly. *I've done it,* thought Charlie. *I've done it, I've done it, I've done it!*

Then Martin began to laugh. He threw back his head and laughed and laughed, a weird high-pitched laugh of total mockery. He grasped his bare feet and rocked from side to side, looking, with his shaved head, like some hilarious young Buddha.

'The Devil!' he gasped. 'You really believe that we're going to raise the Devil!'

'It's a possibility,' Charlie snapped. 'You only have to read the Célèstine Bible. It's a mixture of voodoo and Roman Catholicism and cannibalism and all kinds of ridiculous mumbo-jumbo. Martin – a million people have died for this moment, over the years. Men, women, and children. A million people have died in agony, for the sake of some twisted superstition. It's practically genocide, this so-called religion. Do you seriously think that Jesus would have condoned genocide?'

Martin stopped laughing, and stared at his father with distant, lambent eyes. 'Jesus said, *"Take, eat, this is My body. Drink . . . for this is My blood of the new testament, shed for many, to the remission of sins."'*

Mme Musette came forward, stood beside the bed, and laid her gloved hand on top of Martin's shaven head. Martin glanced up at her with a quick smile, like an obedient pupil, or an adoring pet. Charlie got to his feet and looked down at Martin and couldn't think what else to say.

'There is one thing more,' Mme Musette told him. 'When

your son goes to the altar tomorrow, it is you who must willingly give him as a sacrifice.'

Charlie stared at her. 'You expect me to offer up my own son?'

'It is his destiny, Mr McLean. You cannot deny him his destiny.'

'I can and I will. You must be cracked.'

M. Musette said, 'It is necessary for the completion of the ritual. The father must willingly sacrifice his son. Do you remember what God said to Abraham when he offered to sacrifice Isaac? "*You have not withheld your son, your only son, indeed will I greatly bless you.*"'

Charlie said, 'I seem to remember that God spared Isaac's life.'

'In those days, God had no need of it,' M. Musette replied. 'But now that His only Son has been crucified, He requires such a sacrifice in order for Jesus to live on earth once again.'

'This is complete bullshit,' said Charlie. 'If you don't let me take Martin out of here right now, I'm going to break your face.'

'Dad!' interrupted Martin.

Charlie turned to him.

'Dad,' said Martin, more quietly. 'I'm not leaving. I'm staying here. I'm happy. This is what I want. Dad – this is what I want more than anything else in the whole world.'

Mme Musette stroked Martin's head once more. 'You see, Charlie? He's determined.'

'I'm still damned if I'm going to sacrifice him for you.'

'Well, we'll see about that,' replied M. Musette. 'We do have ways of making people do what we want. Not painful ways, mind you! We managed to bring you here simply by making it difficult for you. I could see what an obstinate man you were, right from the moment I first met you. Tragedy and failure usually make people grow obstinate.'

Charlie said nothing. Robyn came up and took hold of his

hand, and said, 'Come on, Charlie, let's leave it for now. While there's life there's hope.'

'You're right, my dear,' said M. Musette. 'And after death, there is glory.'

Reluctantly, Charlie allowed himself to be led away. They visited the remaining eleven disciples, who were housed in what used to be the farm's feed store. All of them were already mutilated, some of them severely. Dulled by disgust, Charlie and Robyn were introduced to a seventeen-year-old girl without legs or breasts or ears; a twenty-two-year-old boy who had amputated his entire body below the waist, and who was being fed intravenously; and a stunningly good-looking woman of twenty-seven, who had cut off and eaten her own feet. The building smelled strongly of bile and antiseptic, and there were seven nurses and two doctors in constant attendance, keeping these pathetic scraps of human meat alive and conscious for one more day.

What Charlie and Robyn found most disconcerting, however, was the cheerfulness of everybody in the building, Devotees and staff alike. There was almost a carnival atmosphere, and most of the disciples were singing hymns and spirituals and laughing as if to cut oneself into pieces was the happiest privilege they had ever been given.

Charlie stood in front of the woman with no feet for a very long time, while she hummed 'Michael, Row The Boat Ashore'. After a while, he said, 'Could I ask you your name?'

'Of course,' she said. 'My name's Janet. You're Martin's father, aren't you? I saw you in Connecticut.'

'Janet,' said Charlie, ignoring her question. 'Can you tell me why you're doing this? Can you explain to me what it is that has made you mutilate yourself this way?'

Janet's eyes were bright. 'I'm giving myself to Jesus. What better reason could I have than that?'

'Do you have a family? Parents? A husband?'

'I'm married, with two small children. A boy and a girl.'

'And don't you think your family needs you?'

'Jesus needs me more.'

Charlie talked to two or three more disciples, but each time he found their devotion to the Célèstines impossible to penetrate. They were like gentle, loving lunatics, who had discovered a dangerous but different reality, and could never be persuaded that what they were doing was madness.

Outside the disciples' building, Robyn said to M. Musette, 'They all believe in it, don't they? I mean, they all believe in it without one shadow of a doubt.'

'They believe in it because they know it to be true,' M. Musette replied. 'Besides, what else does the world have to offer them? Money, perhaps. But not much more. Everybody has to have spiritual goals, if they're going to be happy. If you give people a spiritual goal, their life is transformed, and you can never persuade them to go back to the time when their ambitions were circumscribed by material greed. Once you have felt Jesus's seamless robe brushing against your face while you sleep; once you have heard Him murmur in your ear, you are won over for ever!'

'I think Sergeant Duprée put it all in a nutshell,' said Charlie. 'He said you were a fruitcake.'

M. Musette smiled. 'Sergeant Duprée has to do what he is told, by his superiors. As long as he does what he is told, he can think whatever he likes.'

Now they walked back across the farmyard towards the main building. 'The last part of the guided tour,' announced M. Musette. 'Then we must retire to meditate and to pray, and to prepare everything for tomorrow.'

He led them back into the corridor, and into the room where the trestle tables were all laid out. 'This way.' He beckoned them, and he took them across the room and along another shorter corridor. At the end of this corridor, to Charlie's deep alarm, there were two stainless steel doors, with circular porthole windows.

'*The kitchen*,' he whispered. '*The ritual kitchen.*'

'Yes,' said Mme Musette, who was right behind him. 'But why are you hanging back? The kitchen is the most fascinating part of our tour.'

'I don't want to go in there,' said Charlie.

'You must,' M. Musette told him. 'How can you understand what is going to happen here tomorrow unless you see the kitchen?'

'I don't want to go in there, that's all.'

Robyn took hold of his hand. 'Come on, Charlie, you'll be all right.'

'Yes, come on, Charlie,' M. Musette mimicked. 'It's only a kitchen, you know.'

'I had a nightmare about it,' said Charlie. His legs refused to move forward.

'We all have nightmares,' said M. Musette. 'The only way to break their spell is to confront them in reality.'

'But I saw those same doors in my dream, those same stainless steel doors with those circular windows.'

M. Musette shrugged. 'In that case, you must have considerable powers of clairvoyance. Come along now, you mustn't miss this for anything.'

Charlie allowed Robyn to drag him towards the kitchen doors. M. Musette deliberately heightened the suspense by standing with his hands flat on the door, pausing before he pushed them open. 'Are you ready?' he asked. 'There will be no blood. We haven't started the ritual yet.'

He opened the doors and marched ahead of them into the kitchen. Charlie and Robyn followed, still holding hands, and Mme Musette came behind.

The kitchen was almost fifty feet square. It was tiled in white, with a single green band running around it, and it was artificially lit with fluorescent tubes hanging from the ceiling. In the centre of the room, there were twelve tables with stainless steel tops and gutters running all the way around them.

Charlie had seen tables like that before, in *Quincy*. They were similar to the tables used for autopsies, and the gutters allowed the bodily fluids to run off into the drains.

At the far end of the kitchen, there was a gas-fired range, large enough to serve a small hotel. Hanging up over the burners, there were rows of aluminium pots and pans, *bains-maries*, woks, colanders, and ladles.

They walked between the tables, their faces dully reflected in the stainless steel surfaces, like people who had drowned under ice. Each table was equipped with a full selection of Victorinox knives, butcher's saws, and surgical scalpels. There was also equipment for medical emergencies: oxygen, dressings, and electronic resuscitators in case of cardiac arrest. Each table was also provided with a large tilting mirror, so that the Devotees could see what they were doing while they amputated their own limbs.

'I feel sick,' said Charlie, looking around. 'This is even worse than my nightmare. This is worse because it's real.'

'I'm amazed that your Devotees can actually stand the shock and the pain of cutting off their own arms and legs,' Robyn remarked to M. Musette. Charlie thought, here she goes again, once a newspaper reporter, always a newspaper reporter.

M. Musette trailed his fingertips across the surface of one of the tables. 'The human body is a remarkable thing, Ms Harris. You may talk about worms being cut in half, and still wriggling away. But you can cut a human body down to practically nothing, you can cut a grown man down so small that you can carry him under your arm like a dog, and still he survives! And, of course, each time a man is reduced in size, his heart has less work to do, pumping blood around the length and breadth of his circulatory system, so the body in actual fact grows stronger and more capable of survival, right up until the very last *coup*. You know, there was a sideshow freak called Prince Randian, born without arms and legs. He lived until he was sixty-three, and fathered four children.'

'But how do they stand the pain?' asked Robyn.

'All pain is relative,' said M. Musette. 'These Devotees are reaching for spiritual ecstasy, they feel very little pain. Some of them revel in it.'

'And what about you?' asked Charlie, looking at M. Musette keenly. 'You're supposed to be transformed tomorrow, aren't you? You're supposed to turn into Jesus Christ. Aren't you frightened?'

M. Musette turned to Mme Musette and gave her a smile. 'I know that my Redeemer liveth,' he said. 'He is more than welcome to live inside of me.'

CHAPTER TWENTY-THREE

Charlie couldn't sleep at all that night. Apart from his fear of what was going to happen in the morning, there was constant activity throughout the church compound as the Célèstines prepared themselves for the second coming. Charlie heard shouting and laughing and hymn-singing, and at about two o'clock in the morning, somebody started playing a guitar. He stood by the darkened window of his room, watching the moon slowly slide across the sky. All he could see was the row of pecan trees and the corner of the building where Martin was being held. He tried reaching Martin by telepathy — by concentrating all his thoughts into making Martin wake up and realize what he was going to do — but there was no response.

He sat on his bed and bent his head forward and prayed. He hadn't prayed like this since he was a child, sitting next to his father at the Episcopalian Church on Sunday mornings, smelling the pipe tobacco on his father's suit, and staring down at his polished brown shoes.

O Lord, save me from this predicament. O Lord preserve my son. Whatever you want of me, you can have it. Just don't let Martin die.

The moon vanished behind the pecans and soon the sky began to lighten. He had prayed that time would stand still, and that this morning would never come. But by seven o'clock the sky was firmly blue and the sun was shining across the whitewashed buildings. At seven-thirty, the man with the close-cropped hair brought Charlie a cup of black coffee and two wholemeal breadrolls, with jack cheese.

'A happy day for you, huh?' Charlie asked him, as he set the food down on top of the bedside locker.

The man looked at him without expression, and left.

Charlie drank his coffee but he couldn't manage to swallow any bread. He went to the window again to see if there was any activity around Martin's building, but it appeared to be deserted. He couldn't even see Ben, who had been sitting outside guarding it for most of the night. Perhaps they had taken Martin to the main building already.

At nine o'clock, the man with the close-cropped hair came back and said. 'The rituals are about to begin. M. Musette wants you to come now.'

Without a word, Charlie put on his jacket and buttoned it up. Then he followed the man outside. In spite of the sunshine, the morning was quite cold. His breath smoked in the damp air as he walked towards the main building. As they reached the doors, Charlie could hear singing. '*O God, our help in ages past, our hope for years to come . . .*'

The man took hold of his elbow and guided him into the main room. Overnight, there had been a transformation. The walls of the room were now hung with yellow and gold banners, and the tables were set with plates and glasses and silver cutlery, and beautifully arranged centrepieces of flowers. Every table was crowded with Célèstine Guides, dressed in plain white-hooded robes – businessmen, bankers, musicians, television producers, fashion models, writers, salesmen, mechanics – men and women from a rainbow of backgrounds. Charlie recognized several famous media faces as he was ushered between the tables to the end of the room. He saw at least one well-known politician, and a singer whose records he had once bought, and right at the end of the table next to the kitchen doors, Sheriff Norman Podmore, his eyes squeezed tightly shut in prayer.

Charlie was taken to the end of the centremost table, facing the white-draped altar. M. Musette was kneeling at the altar in prayer, flanked on one side by Mme Musette, and on the other side by one of the Guides from L'Église des Anges in New Orleans. Sunlight fell from the clerestory windows high above, and an electronic organ softly played an inspirational interlude before the next hymn.

The man with the close-cropped hair said, 'Wait there,' and left Charlie standing a little way behind M. Musette. As Charlie stood there, his hands down by his sides, it occurred to him that he could jump on M. Musette and seize him around the throat and strangle him. But he probably wasn't strong enough to do it – even if he did manage to fend off the bodyguards – and he wouldn't have a chance at all of helping Martin if he screwed up. So he remained where he was, feeling tense and jittery, while M. Musette continued to pray, and the organ continued to pour out 'Jesus Wants Me That I Know.'

At last, M. Musette stood up, and came across to Charlie. It was uncanny, but he did almost look as if he were possessed of a great inner light. He was certainly happy, and at peace with himself. He took hold of Charlie's arm and led him to the table. 'The proud father,' he said. 'God bless this day, and God bless you.'

'God bless you, too, you maniac,' said Charlie. But M. Musette was quite beyond insults now. He stood at the head of the table, and beamed at Charlie on his left, and Mme Musette on his right, and the surrounding company of Célèstines.

'In the name of our Lord Jesus Christ, I bless this meal, which is to be eaten in the sure and certain knowledge of the resurrection of our Saviour.'

'Amen,' chorused the Célèstines. Charlie swallowed, because his mouth felt so dry.

'Please, sit,' M. Musette invited him. 'You are about to eat the meal of your life.'

Charlie said, 'Oh, no. Not a chance. I'm not going to eat that stuff.'

'That would be very impolite of you, as well as impious,' said Mme Musette. She was dressed almost like a nun, with a starched wimple. 'This meal is the product of one thousand times one thousand lives. It is the true reflection of the Last Supper. How can you refuse to take part in the sacrament? And how can you let down your son? This is your son's day of glory!'

Charlie reached across for the cut-glass water jug and poured himself a large glass of cold water. He drank it without saying a word. He had promised himself during the night that he wouldn't allow the Musettes to provoke him. He had to think clearly and logically and be prepared to act at a split-second's notice.

'Don't worry,' said M. Musette, laying his hand on top of his wife's two fingers. 'Mr McLean is a connoisseur. Once he has tasted long pig for the first time, he will be hooked for ever.'

'Long pig?' asked Charlie. 'What's that?'

'Just my little joke,' said M. Musette. 'Long pig is the euphemism the Caribs used for human flesh. You see, the trouble with human flesh is that it tastes so very good. Well cooked, it is rich and firm, and better than the very best beef. It is illegal to eat it only because those who have tasted it always long for more. It's a fact, historically proven! Take that poor Australian convict who escaped with his fellow prisoners from MacQuarie Harbour. He ended up eating them, to stay alive; but once he had tasted human flesh, he killed people deliberately so that he could get more. The Donner party who were stranded in the Sierras ate the bodies of those who died, and one Mr Keseberg was found boiling the liver and lungs of a young boy in a pot, even though he had left whole legs of oxen untouched. The ox-meat, he said, was too dry eating.'

Charlie glanced from M. Musette to Mme Musette, and then quickly searched around to see if he could see where Robyn was. At last he caught sight of her two tables away, and she looked as sick and as tired and miserable as he did. M. Musette, undeterred by Charlie's inattention, continued to tell him about modern-day cannibalism.

'Look at those boys who were stranded in the Andes after that airplane crash! They ate their friends, and they were haunted afterward by what they had done. But sometimes in the darkness of the night the craving comes and the craving is like a drug! It is irresistible! It is not only gastronomic, but erotic – and this is quite apart from its powerful spiritual significance. Many primitive tribes used to eat the brains and the hearts of their dead fathers and mothers in order that they should inherit their intelligence and their strength. The Fore people of Eastern New Guinea still do it today – only they tend to be less than fastidious about hygiene, and they suffer quite frequently from a progressive and fatal disease called kuru. No chances of contracting kuru today, I hasten to add. All the meat will be fresh and clean!'

Charlie closed his eyes. He prayed that when he opened them again he would be somewhere else, and that his encounter with the Célestines would have proved to have been nothing but a long and troublesome nightmare. But he could not block his ears, either to the low burbling of conversation all around him, or to M. Musette's persistent monologue about the delights of human flesh. Eventually he opened his eyes again to find Mme Musette smiling at him like a sister of mercy. If only she were.

'Come now,' said M. Musette, bristling with enthusiasm, 'now that I have said grace, you may accompany me to the kitchens.'

Charlie said, 'I'd rather stay here, if it's all the same to you.'

'Charlie,' M. Musette insisted, in a low and threatening voice, 'you may accompany me to the kitchens.'

Charlie took a deep breath, then pushed back his chair. 'I'm warning you now, if any harm comes to Martin or Miss Harris . . .'

M. Musette linked arms with him. 'What will you do? Strangle me with your bare hands?'

Charlie felt an odd little chill. That was exactly what he had been thinking about doing, only a few moments before. He began to wonder if there was something spiritual about M. Musette — if all his years of eating human flesh had invested him with an extra sense of psychic perception. After all, if so many tribes had believed in eating human flesh in order to acquire the brains and the strength of the people they had devoured, maybe there was something in it.

Or maybe M. Musette and his followers were all deranged; and Charlie was becoming deranged too.

M. Musette said, 'I heard this morning about M. Fontenot. They found his body in a bayou, drowned. Accidental death, that's what they said,' He squeezed Charlie's arm uncomfortably tight. 'He was one of my dearest friends, Fontenot. I just thought you might like to know that. His death is very painful to me.'

Charlie said nothing. If M. Musette was psychic enough to be able to work out that M. Fontenot had died trying to chase after him, then there was nothing he could do to conceal it. If he wasn't, then Charlie certainly wasn't going to admit it.

They approached the kitchen doors. The windows were black, like tunnels going to nowhere at all, tunnels that never ended. From inside the kitchen Charlie could hear the clattering of knives and the dull ringing sound of saucepans, and something else. Grunts, and suffocated cries, and the spasmodic rasping of saws.

'I can't go in,' he told M. Musette. His face felt as if it had no blood in it at all.

M. Musette tugged at his arm, coaxing, threatening. 'You must. This is what you came for. This is what you came to see. This is what you have been pursuing so hotly, both asleep and awake.'

Charlie swallowed but his throat was utterly dry. 'I can't go in.'

'You must.'

'Is Martin there yet? Is Martin in there?'

'Not yet.' 'Martin will come in when the feast is almost finished, and he will make the first self-sacrifical cut right in front of us.'

'What cut?'asked Charlie.

M. Musette tugged at his arm again. 'Come on, you have to see it for yourself.'

'What damn cut?' Charlie persisted.

'What cut do you think? The cut that is holy without being fatal. The cut that transforms a man into a divine being.'

'He's going to –?'

M. Musette nodded.

Charlie could have screamed, and hit out at him, and banged his head against the wall. He was shuddering with suppressed hysteria. But all the time his logic was telling him: *This isn't the way. These are only words. They haven't hurt Martin yet, and until they do you've got to bide your time, Charlie, otherwise you'll blow this chance and you'll never get another.*

'Come on,' M. Musette encouraged him. Charlie swallowed again, and followed him through the kitchen doors.

It took Charlie a few seconds to understand what he was seeing. The kitchen was so crowded and steamy, and there was so much bustle, that at first he saw nothing but stainless steel and glistening scarlet flesh and two dozen men and women wearing blue aprons and overalls. There was a strong smell of garlic and grilling meat; and that distinctive aroma of herbs which the Célèstines always seemed to find to their taste. The noise was chaotic, too. Pans were being clonked on to the ranges; knives were being sharpened on steels; people were shouting and coaxing and calling and sobbing and crying out; and it could have been the busy kitchen of any large international restaurant.

Except . . . as Charlie stepped forward, pulled by M. Musette like a boat being pulled through water, the true spectacle of what was happening was almost too grisly for the human mind to comprehend.

At the first table, a young naked girl with long brown hair was sitting up, supported by two blue-shirted Guides, and she was sawing through her own arm at the elbow. Her eyes were fixed and wild-looking. Her teeth were clenched on a hard rubber wedge, to prevent her from biting her tongue. She had cut through the skin and muscle of her upper forearm with a surgical scalpel, and now she was rasping her way through the bones, radius and ulna, bone dust mushing white into her bright leaking blood.

At the next table, a one-armed boy of about twenty was grimacing in concentration as he cut long deep slices of flesh from his calves and his thighs. One leg had already been reduced to the bare bone, and the raw meat of his upper thigh was bound around with a rubber tourniquet to prevent the boy from bleeding to death before he had finished stripping the meat from his other leg. Blood ran along the gutters around the table, and poured darkly down the drains.

One hideous spectacle followed another, eleven of them, and M. Musette tugged Charlie past all eleven. Velma was there, or what was left of Velma. She had sliced off both her breasts, and then cut open her own stomach in an attempt to drag out her liver and her kidneys. The assistants who had been helping her looked up as M. Musette passed, and explained, 'She died just a few minutes ago.' Two of them were carefully dipping their hands into the bloody tangle of her abdomen and cutting out her stomach and her pancreas; a third was severing her head with a stainless-steel hacksaw.

'Of course, you knew Velma,' said M. Musette, but Charlie could only hear his voice as a distant echo, like somebody shouting through a closed window.

Harriet was there, too, the waitress from the Iron Kettle.

She was weeping as she lifted her left bicep away from the bone with the point of a broad-bladed carving knife. M. Musette approached her and laid his hand gently on her naked back, and said. 'Are you in pain, Harriet?' And she turned to him with tearful eyes and smiled.

'Christ suffered on the cross,' she said, with the blade of the knife running right through her upper arm from one side to the other, and blood running from her elbow in an endless stream.

They came across two more disciples who were already dead. Their bodies were being quickly and expertly butchered. The dark red meat was being arranged on white enamel trays, according to which cut it was, leg or arm or shoulder or rib. Offal was being collected in white enamel buckets, great slimy maroon heaps of human liver, and gristly crimson hearts.

Out of all of this horror, one image cut itself with extra vividness into Charlie's consciousness: a young boy of nineteen, no more than that, who had already amputated both of his legs below the knee, holding a razor-sharp butcher's knife underneath his scrotum, and staring at his genitals in fascination and fear. For the first time since he had seen a Célestine Devotee, Charlie saw indecision and uncertainty. Ecstasy was one thing: self-emasculation was another. M. Musette must have seen the hesitation, too, because he stopped for a while, and watched the boy with expressionless eyes.

'Vincent?' he said at last.

The boy looked up. Charlie saw a look of terrible desperation. So it *was* possible for the influence of the Célestines to be broken. It remained to be seen, though, whether the boy could stand up against the cold, withering personality of Edouard Musette.

M. Musette stepped forward and laid his hand on the stump of the boy's left leg. 'Vincent? Is something troubling you? Today you will become part of our Lord Jesus Christ.'

The boy opened and closed his mouth, and then looked

down at his genitals again. Charlie could see his hand was trembling.

'Vincent?' whispered M. Musette.

Charlie turned away. He heard the knife slicing through skin and veins and spongy flesh. He heard the boy Vincent utter a noise that was almost inhuman. When Charlie turned back, the boy's assistants were already pressing a large bloody pad of gauze between his thighs, and the boy was holding up something which looked like a butchered bird.

'Now,' said M. Musette, 'let us see how our sacramental feast is being prepared.'

He guided Charlie through to the kitchen range. There, a small sallow man with a white apron and a black wilting moustache was grilling flesh over a gas barbecue. As the slices were cooked, he was arranging them on white dinner-plates, three thin slices on each, and garnishing them with zucchini and peeled tomatoes and green beans. The plates were then being carried out to the waiting company.

'This is Fernest Ardoin, who directs the preparation of all our sacrifices,' explained M. Musette. 'Fernest has prepared meals of human flesh for private dinners all over America, and a few in Europe, too. Some of the meals were for spiritual purposes. Others were simply for the appreciation of long pig. All of the meals, of course, were superb. Fernest is an artist, as well as a dedicated Célèstine.'

Fernest nodded his head to acknowledge this flattery. 'We are almost finished preparing the first course, M. Musette. The barbecue-grilled fillet of upper thigh, served with a light tomato-and-garlic sauce.'

Next to him, one of his younger assistants was cutting liver into wafer-thin slices, almost transparent, to be lightly sautéed in butter and served with fresh rosemary.

The cooking smelled so much like ordinary restaurant cooking, and it was so fastidiously prepared, that Charlie found it almost impossible to associate the elegant *nouvelle cuisine* on the plates with the grim self-inflicted butchery that was going on behind him. Somehow he had always imagined cannibalism to be a matter of gnawing at half-roasted human legbones, or cutting off human flesh in strips and hanging it out to dry, like pemmican. This gastronomic expertise somehow made the Célèstine's crime against nature ten times more ugly, and ten times more sickening. They were indulging a forbidden appetite, that was all, and they were taking the name of God in vain to do so.

M. Musette touched Charlie's elbow, and said, 'We must go back to the feast, my dear sir. They will be missing us, and we will be missing our appetizer. I hope you have found this to be instructive.'

Charlie nodded numbly. 'Instructive, yes. I think that's all I can say.'

He averted his eyes from the gory bodies of the eleven disciples as they left the kitchen. The young girl with the long hair had severed her forearm, and was holding it up in triumph. The doors swung shut behind them. M. Musette said, 'Are you all right, Charlie?' but Charlie pushed him away and said, 'Don't worry about me.'

They rejoined their table. Charlie sought Robyn's face and tried to convey with nothing more than a slight shake of his head the horrors he had just witnessed. He felt as if his stomach was filled with worms and grease, and his throat was so parched that he found it almost impossible to say anything.

'You look pale, Charlie,' said the nun-like Mme Musette. 'I thought restaurant inspectors weren't supposed to be squeamish.'

Charlie choked out, 'I don't usually inspect the kitchens, Mme Musette. And I have never inspected a kitchen like that. That kitchen is a human abattoir.'

'Well, you're right, of course,' said M. Musette, cheerfully. 'Look – here is our food.'

Plates of thigh meat were set in front of each of them.

Charlie kept his head raised so that he wouldn't have to look at it; and so that he wouldn't have to witness Mme Musette carefully slicing it up with her knife and fork and putting it into her mouth.

The Guide sitting next to Charlie tapped him gently on the shoulder and said, 'Don't you want yours?'

Charlie could do nothing but stare at him. The Guide said, 'Do you mind if I . . .?' and forked Charlie's meat on to his own plate.

The feast was slow and leisurely and proceeded with sinister stylishness. Outside, the sky became overcast and dark, and the clouds that Charlie could see through the clerestory windows looked like inkstains on wet cartridge paper. 'Wouldn't be surprised if we're in for a storm,' remarked M. Musette, with his cheek full of human liver. 'Makes it more dramatic, in a way, don't you think?'

After every course, there were prayers of hope and thanksgiving, and the Célèstines sang a hymn. They ate thigh meat and liver and boneless ribs, and then they were served what M. Musette called, 'a selection of delicacies', which included thin slices of female breast, some of the best of them tinged with the nipple, and pale pink *sushi*-like arrangements of raw marinated labia. Mme Musette laughed a tinkling laugh at Charlie's obvious disgust.

'You sit down at Thanksgiving and eat the butchered carcasses of living creatures, served with sauces and herbs and vegetables. This is no different, once you have accepted the notion that there is nothing blasphemous or illegal in man eating man. This is a sacramental feast of body and blood. It is God's gift, and you should be grateful, not disgusted. Those young people gladly gave their flesh and their pain – *gladly* – how can you sit there and feel self-righteous about rejecting their sacrifice?'

Charlie said, 'You might be able to persuade the rest of these freaks but you're never going to persuade me. Haven't you heard about something called the sanctity of human life?'

345

Mme Musette smiled, and slipped something into her mouth that looked like a flesh-coloured oyster, but obviously wasn't. Charlie turned away, his lips tightened, his stomach clenched in tightly suppressed nausea.

By eleven o'clock, the feast was close to its climax. A choir of twelve Célèstine guides assembled solemnly in front of the altar, and began quietly to sing the *Kyrie Eleison*. The kitchen doors were opened, and a procession of Célèstine cooks emerged, headed by Fernest Ardoin. Between them, they were carrying in the most symbolic and most openly grotesque of all the dishes that had yet been served – the dish that showed conclusively that the eleven disciples were now dead, and that the assembled Célèstines were about to eat their very essence. On a large white dish were heaped, still steaming, their eleven brains, lightly poached in a stock made from boiling their lungs and their sweetbreads, served on a bed of red cabbage. The dish was carried up to M. Musette for his approval, within inches of where Charlie was sitting. Charlie did nothing more than glimpse the shining fawn-coloured convolutions of human cortices – did nothing more than breathe in one nostrilful of their pale, sweet aroma, and he started to gag. Without excusing himself, he pushed back his chair and walked quickly toward the exit. Behind him, M. Musette nodded to the man with the close-cropped hair to keep an eye on him.

Charlie went outside and bent double under the oak tree and vomited coffee. The man with the close-cropped hair stood on the steps watching him. Charlie's stomach went on convulsing for two or three minutes, but at least he managed to stand up straighter and lean against the tree, his throat sore and his eyes watering.

'You done now?' the man asked him.

Charlie nodded. He raised his head and looked around. Clouds had gathered above L'Église des Pauvres, and over towards Ville Platte and Evangeline County lightning was flickering all along the horizon like the tongues of electrified snakes. A cold wind began to stir the dried oak leaves that were scattered on the dirt, and the cypress trees dipped and swayed.

There was an extraordinary feeling in the air. Excitement, fear, the sense that something incredible was about to happen. Charlie looked at the man with the close-cropped hair and for a moment they both shared this sense of oncoming apocalypse.

'We'd better get ourselves back inside,' the man suggested, his white robe ruffled by the wind. But at that instant, a blinding artery of lightning ran down into one of the abandoned cotton fields only a quarter-mile away, with a sizzling crack, and from inside the main building Charlie heard a deep, low moan, all the Célèstines chanting at once.

Charlie wiped his mouth with his sleeve, and pushed his way quickly back into the feasting hall. The room was almost completely dark now, and assistants were going from table to table, lighting candles. M. Musette was standing at the head of the dining table, his arms outstretched, and he was reciting the Célèstine Creed, while his followers chanted their responses. Thunder burst over the rooftop with a noise like a collapsing bridge.

'It is time!' cried M. Musette. 'It is time for the second coming!'

Charlie quickly checked that Robyn was still at her place, and then walked purposefully up to M. Musette. 'This is it,' he said adamantly. 'This is where the game finishes. I'm taking my son and I'm going.'

M. Musette stared at Charlie and his eyes didn't even look human. 'This is the hour of the second coming of the Lord Jesus Christ. You will not deny Him your only son.'

Charlie made a quick move toward M. Musette but the man with the close-cropped hair was quicker. He grasped Charlie's arm and whipped it painfully behind his back in a half-nelson. 'Keep still and I won't break it for you,' he murmured, almost apologetically.

M. Musette raised his hand. 'Bring the sacrificial lamb!' he cried out. 'Bring him here, for the moment is upon us!'

Charlie shouted, '*No!*' but four Célèstines rose from their table and went to one of the side rooms, their hands crossed over their chests.

Through the clerestory windows, Charlie could see more flickers and flashes of lightning. Rain began to beat against the glass, and patter on the corrugated roof like dancing cats. He turned almost hysterically to Mme Musette, who was sitting upright in her seat, her face rigid and incandescently beautiful.

'Don't let him do it!' he yelled at her. 'Don't let him murder my son!'

Mme Musette said nothing, but gave Charlie a wan, mysterious smile, and turned away.

The four Célèstines returned to the room, walking with their heads bowed. In the middle of them walked Martin, completely naked except for a white headband. Charlie struggled against the man who was holding him, but his arm was jerked upwards until his hand was almost touching the back of his neck, and there was nothing that Charlie could do to break free. Charlie looked desperately at Martin's face, hoping for one last breakthrough of normal feeling, hoping for one last sign of love and recognition, but Martin was smiling the same idiotic, accepting smile that Charlie had seen on the face of so many Célèstines. Happiness is obedience. Nirvana is an empty mind. Heaven only comes to those who surrender their private will to live.

'*Martin!*' Charlie appealed to him. '*Martin, this is your father! This is Daddy! Martin, listen to me, don't let them do this to you! Martin, for Christ's sake!*'

'Yes,' murmured Mme Musette. 'For Christ's sake.'

And M. Musette added, '*Amen.*'

The four Célèstines brought Martin in front of the altar, and then turned him round so that he was facing the assembled company. He was the twelfth disciple, the final sacrifice. M. Musette approached him, walking all the way around him, and then stepped up to the altar, where he knelt down and bowed his head and spent a moment or two in silent prayer. Then he rose up again, and turned to the main body of the hall, and spread his arms wide in conscious imitation of the crucifixion.

'Almost two thousand years ago, our Lord Jesus Christ sacrificed His body and His blood in order that we might live. Now, we have repaid the debt; and we are about to return to Christ that body and that blood which He so freely gave to us.'

There was yet another crackling lightning-strike outside. Charlie jerked his head up. He felt sure that it had hit the crucifix on the roof. There was a strong smell of ozone and burned metal, and he could feel the hairs on the back of his neck lifted up by the huge charge of static electricity in the building.

M. Musette nodded to his wife, and she left her place and walked up to Martin. She touched his forehead, she touched each of his nipples, she touched his navel. Then she drew out of her robes a long steel-bladed knife with a handle fashioned out of gold and silver.

'The sacrificial knife,' said M. Musette. Charlie watched in fascinated horror as Martin accepted it from M. Musette, and lowered it between his thighs.

'You said you had to have my consent!' he screamed at M. Musette.

M. Musette turned to Charlie in acknowledgement. 'Of course; but only when it comes to giving his life. And I am sure that by the time he has finished sacrificing his arms and his legs and his genitalia to the Saviour, you will be quite prepared to give your consent in order to release him from his earthly suffering,'

Charlie found himself unable to speak. He looked away, he

couldn't bear to see Martin hurting himself. But then he found that he had to watch. Martin was his son, his responsibility. He had to know what agony Martin was going to go through, or he would never be able to redeem his own guilt for it in the future.

If he *had* a future, of course. The Célèstines were probably planning to kill him, too, once this ritual was over. Especially when it failed to produce a second coming.

M. Musette pressed his hands together and prayed. '*All flesh is as grass, and all the glory of man like the flower of grass. The grass withereth, and the flower thereof away falleth, but the Word of the Lord endureth forever.*'

As he spoke these words, Charlie alone in that company of Célèstines, raised his eyes. Directly above the altar, suspended only a few feet below the ceiling, he saw a white light, soft and radiant and steady. He thought at first that it must be static electricity, something like St Elmo's Fire, but it remained calm and steady and unblinking.

M. Musette continued to pray, and while he did so, the light very slowly descended, growing brighter and larger as it neared the top of the altar. '*Do you not know that your bodies are members of Christ? Shall I then take away the members of Christ and make them members of a harlot? It shall never be! Or do you not know that the one who joins himself with a harlot is one body with her? For He says, 'The two will become one flesh.'*'

'*But the one who joins himself to the Lord is one spirit with Him.*'

One by one, then more quickly, the praying Célèstines raised their eyes. A ripple of astonishment ran all the way around the room. Only M. Musette remained as he was, with his hands pressed together and his eyes closed. Charlie had to admire his faith. He knew what was happening, he believed in it, and by God it was actually coming to pass.

The light hovered a few inches above the altar and it was

now as dazzling as phosphorous, and impossible to look at directly. Charlie used his one free hand to shield his eyes, although the man with the close-cropped hair gave him a sharp tug on his other arm to remind him that he was still held captive.

Martin hadn't moved. His eyes remained bright. He held his knife ready. All he was waiting for now was the word from M. Musette that would begin his self-sacrifice. The first cut, which would instantly change him from a young man to a eunuch.

The light above the altar seemed constantly to shift and change, as if it were a living spirit. M. Musette at last turned around to face it, and he genuflected and crossed himself and cried out in a voice choked with tears, 'Oh, Saviour! I know that my Redeemer liveth!'

There was a moment of utter silence. Then a hair-raising voice spoke all the way around the room, a soft, deep voice that was everywhere and nowhere at all. Charlie wasn't sure whether he was hearing it with his ears or through his bone marrow.'

'*You have summoned Me here. You have called upon Me and I have heard your voices.*'

M. Musette let out a cry of sheer ecstasy. 'Oh Lord, you have returned to us! We thank you, Lord, for hearing our cry! Everything is ready, we have consumed the thousand thousand, but for the very last, and your earthly temple awaits You!'

There was weeping and shouting and clapping in the hall. Many of the Célèstines dropped to their knees. But none of them could take their eyes away from the bright, pure light.

'Where is this last sacrifice?' asked the soft, deep voice.

M. Musette stepped back from the altar and took hold of Martin's shoulder, turning him around so that he was facing the light. 'Here, O Lord, a boy pure in body and spirit.'

'And who gives him to Me?'

'We do, oh Lord, the church of the Célèstines.'

There was a pause. Charlie could see M. Musette biting at his lower lip in tension. Then the voice said. 'Only the boy's father can give him to Me. It is the law – just as Abraham offered Isaac in the old writings.'

'My Lord, he *will* give you the boy,' said M. Musette.

'The boy must be untouched, and whole,' the voice insisted.

M. Musette looked around in panic. 'Charlie?' he said. 'Charlie? Did you hear that?'

Charlie was staring at the light. A remarkable feeling had come over him; a feeling of bottomless peace and wholeness. He relaxed his arm, and the man with the close-cropped hair, sensing that something extraordinary was happening, released him. Charlie could see his whole life behind him like a tangle of black briars: all the lies, all the cheating, all the cowardice, all the aimless driving from place to place. He saw himself in hotel rooms all across America, thumbing through Polaroids of his son he hardly ever saw. He saw himself in Milwaukee, betraying the only woman he had ever really loved. Yet he knew that this part of his life was over now. He understood what it meant to have your sins redeemed. He felt as if he were being healed all over, mind and body. There were tears running down his cheeks, but he wasn't even aware of them.

'Do you have to take my son, Lord?' he whispered.

The voice replied, 'Do you believe in Me?'

Charlie nodded. 'I don't believe in what the Célèstines have been doing, that's all. I don't believe that You could condone such pain and suffering.'

'If that is what you believe,' the voice told him, 'your choice is as clear as the day.'

Charlie frowned. And then he understood.

At least, God Almighty, he hoped he understood.

'Take him,' he said, so quietly that not even Mme Musette could hear him.

M. Musette snapped, 'What? What? What did he say?'

'Take him,' Charlie repeated, more boldly now.

M. Musette's eyes widened. 'You're going to give him to us? Freely, willingly?'

'Not to you,' said Charlie. 'To the Lord.'

M. Musette grasped Martin's bare shoulders in unconcealed glee. 'Now, Martin!' he whooped. 'Now is your time! Now!'

Martin lifted the shining knife, and held himself out in preparation for the first cut. M. Musette rushed back to the altar, and abased himself in front of the dazzling light, and cried out, 'Lord! O, Lord! The very moment of your second coming has arrived!'

But the soft voice was suddenly stern. 'You have not summoned *Me*, you evil man. I came because I was aware that you had summoned another.'

M. Musette slowly raised his head. 'What?' he said. 'What do you mean? What do you mean I've summoned another? What other?'

'You have performed today the culminating ritual of him whose day is the sixth day, a spirit long banished for his cruelty and evil. Your devouring of human flesh is the greatest of all sins; and your love of its taste is the deepest of all iniquities. I came today to save the innocent and the pure, and he stands before me, freely sacrificed to Me by his father, as Abraham freely sacrificed Isaac.

'For this man knows, as Abraham knew, that your Lord is neither cruel nor murderous; that He gave His body and blood in order that man should no longer kill or maim or cause suffering to the defenceless and the innocent.

'And I say to this man, as My Father said to Abraham, 'Indeed will I greatly bless you, because you have obeyed My voice.' And I say to him, go now, and take with you those whom you love, untouched, unharmed, and always be blessed.'

M. Musette stood aghast. He turned to Charlie, and then to

353

Martin, and then to Mme Musette. Mme Musette came over and held her arms around him, and stared at the light in mounting horror.

M. Musette screamed. 'You can't do that! You can't do that! I – I am your earthly temple!'

The voice remained completely calm. 'It is time that the temple gates were opened, and the souls of those you have taken prisoner were released, in order that they may take their rightful place by the side of their Maker. And – since you have summoned another, I shall leave you with him, in order that you and your sinful disciples may suffer the punishment which you have brought upon your own heads.'

M. Musette shrieked, 'You aren't the Lord! You aren't Christ! You're nothing but a falsehood! You're nothing but a liar and a deceiver!'

But the brilliant light began to rise up, and as it rose it faded, until the feasting hall was once more drowned in the eerie darkness of the electric storm. There was a terrible silence. M. Musette looked all around him, like a caged animal, and then he suddenly lunged forward and grabbed Martin around the neck.

'A false God!' he shouted to the silent Célèstines. 'That was a false God! If we sacrifice this boy, we'll summon the real God!'

Charlie, however, without hesitation, and without being hindered by any of the Célèstine assistants, strode forward and punched M. Musette hard in the side of the head. Then he twisted the sacrificial knife from Martin's grasp, and went after M. Musette with nothing in his heart but bloody revenge. Whimpering, M. Musette picked himself up, dodged back behind the altar, and fell to the floor.

'That was a *false* God,' he babbled. 'That wasn't Jesus, that was a *false* God!';

Charlie, maddened, went after him. But Robyn had left her seat and was tugging at his arm and saying, 'It's over! Charlie, it's over! All we have to do is get out of here!'

Charlie stiffened, and stood straight, staring at M. Musette like Captain Ahab staring at Moby Dick. 'I'll kill him,' he breathed. 'By God, I'll kill him.'

But it was then that M. Musette stood up, and he was staring at Martin with bulging eyes. 'I can't,' he retched. 'I can't –!'

The room darkened. The shadows could have been filled with clotted blood. And then M. Musette clutched at his throat, and vomited blood, and chewed-up flesh.

'Oh, God,' said Mme Musette, and tried to take hold of Charlie's arm, but Charlie wrenched her away.

M. Musette's body heaved and shook in terrible convulsions. He tried to scream, but his screams were choked and gargled with half-digested human tissue. Then he arched his neck back, with his veins bulging, and began to sick up not just everything that he had eaten, but every human being that had been ingested by the Célèstines, a thousand times a thousand. In the words of the voice that had spoken from the dazzling white light, the temple gates were opened, and the souls of all those who had been taken prisoner were released.

M. Musette's mouth stretched wide. He couldn't speak. Only his eyes betrayed his agony. Out from his lips fountained blood and brains and human flesh, gallons of it, dark red and pungent, hosing the floor of the feasting hall. The Célèstine Guides screamed and shouted and began to elbow each other toward the doors.

Then, however, two eyes appeared. Two scarlet flaring eyes, and the smoky outline of something grisly and bizarre. The Célèstines fell silent again, and turned and stared at the altar. The eyes flicked this way and that, reddened as coals, mesmerizing everybody they looked at.

'Baron Samedi,' breathed Robyn. 'They've summoned up Baron Samedi.'

A deep rumbling noise shook the building from end to end. Lightning crackled and blasted against the roof. The scarlet eyes glared this way and that, and everywhere they glared, people

people burst into flames, as if they were made out of nothing but sawdust and sticks. Charlie grabbed Robyn with one hand, and Martin with the other, and said, 'Let's go! This whole place is going up!'

They struggled their way between screaming, hysterical Célèstines. On either side of them as they pushed their way towards the exit, people were spontaneously exploding into flames. Their shrieking was so intense that at times it was inaudible, like a hundred-strong chorus of dog-whistles.

They reached the doors; Robyn whimpering, Martin silent and still and robotic in his movements, but obedient. After all, hadn't M. and Mme Musette taught him obedience? From now on, he would do everything that he was told.

Charlie turned around. He saw M. Musette, thigh-deep in regurgitated tissue, still endlessly vomiting one thousand times one thousand. He saw Mme Musette, with her wimple alight, rigid with hysteria and fear.

Behind them both, smoky and vague, but with eyes that burned like coals from hell, he saw Baron Samedi, the voodoo devil, wreaking his revenge on all those who had disturbed him from his thousand-year sleep.

They let the doors swing shut behind them. Then they hobbled and ran across the compound. A Cherokee four-wheel-drive was parked down at the end of the accommodation block, with the keys still in it. Charlie wrenched open the doors, and said, 'Come on. Let's burn rubber.'

They drove into a day that loomed all around them as dark as night. Lightning crackled down on either side. In the rear-view mirror, Charlie saw the Célèstine building blazing from end to end, and even before he reached the bend in the track, he saw the roof collapse, showering fire and molten metal on the congregation who called themselves the Heavenly Ones.

He drove straight through the metal barrier which protected the property, and headed east. Baton Rouge, Hammond, and then Route 59 back towards New York.

They had driven only two miles before Martin began to shiver from cold, and weep. Robyn helped Charlie out of his coat, and draped it over Martin's shoulders. She looked at Charlie with that expression which convinced him that he loved her, and smiled. 'Martin's fine, Charlie. I do believe you've managed to get your son back.'

After ten miles of high-speed driving, just east of the Atchafalaya, Charlie pulled the Cherokee off the road and killed the engine. The storm had passed over, the sun was beginning to drift through the clouds, and there was a smell of sassafras and dust in the air. Charlie bowed his head over the steering wheel for a moment, in exhaustion and delayed shock, and then turned to Martin and touched his face.

Martin didn't respond first of all; but then his eyes glittered with tears, and he took hold of Charlie's hand, fingers intertwined with fingers, and said, 'Dad. Dad. I love you, Dad.'

Charlie gave him a tight smile. 'Why don't you call me Charlie?'

'Charlie,' said Martin, and then they both held each other tight and neither or them was ashamed of crying.

'Do you know what I'm going to do?' said Charlie. 'I'm going from one Célèstine church to another, one by one; and I'm going to burn them all to the ground. And, believe me, there isn't one police officer or one politician who's going to lift a finger to stop me.'

Robyn reached across the front seat and held his hand, and said, 'You're a brave man, Charlie McLean.'

CHAPTER TWENTY-FOUR

It was evening, three days later, when Charlie parked the Cherokee in the driveway outside Le Reposoir. The sky was the coldest of pinks, and the trees stood tall and naked around the building's silhouetted spires. Charlie opened the Cherokee's tailgate, and dragged out two metal jerry cans, both sloshing full with gasoline.

He carried the jerry cans one after the other up the front steps. He tried the door handles, and to his surprise the doors were unlocked. He opened them up, looked into the dark echoing hallway and called, 'Hallo? Anybody there?'

There was no response. He waited for a little while, listening, and then he hefted the jerry cans into the hallway, and set them down. Only the faintest of lights filtered down the stairs from the medieval stained-glass window. Only the faintest of breezes blew through the building that had once been called 'the little altar'.

Charlie opened up the first jerry can, tipped it over, and poured gasoline all over the floor. When it was half empty, he was able to pick it up and slosh more gasoline over the staircase and wooden panelling. He coughed once or twice. The fumes were almost unbearable.

He was about to open the second jerry can when he thought he heard a clicking noise. He stood up straight, listening hard. It was probably a rat, or a bird. He waited a couple of moments longer, and then he began to slosh out more gasoline.

Bastards, he thought, *I'm going to burn your name off the face of the earth.*

He searched in his pockets for the cigarette lighter that he had brought with him. He didn't see the small shadow that fell across the floor.

He didn't see the small hooded figure that approached him silently as a ghost; and the dull blade of a machete that caught the very last strains of evening sunlight.

Walkers

On the steps of the bright madhouse
I hear the bearded bell shaking down the woodlawn
the final knell of my world.

—Gregory Corso, "In the Fleeting Hand of Time"

If I should die . . . There shall be
In that rich earth a richer dust concealed

—Rupert Brooke, "The Soldier"

Merrimack sounds like the Gaelic words *mor-riomach*,
meaning "of great depth."

—Barry Fell, *America BC*

O·N·E

*H*e took his eyes off the road for no more than an instant, reaching across to the glove compartment to find his Santana tape, when something blurred and grayish white like a huddled child in a raincoat scampered across the road right in front of him.

He shouted *"Ah!"* and slammed his foot on the brake—slipped—slammed again. The station wagon slewed sideways across the slippery blacktop, its tires shrieking. Then it bucked and bounced onto the leafy bank and banged loudly against the trunk of an oak tree.

Jack killed the engine and sat shaking in his seat. *Jesus Christ! Jesus Christ almighty!* The misty rain began to prickle the windshield. He had been driving fast, for sure, fifty or sixty miles an hour toward a blind uphill curve. But the visibility hadn't been *that* poor; and he hadn't done more than glance to one side for just a split second. He didn't know how the hell he could have failed to see a child running out from the side of the road.

"Jesus Christ," he repeated, out loud. His voice sounded flat and unconvincing. He was still shaking uncontrollably.

He took a deep breath, unfastened his seat belt, and climbed out of the car. It was now facing back the way he had come, the offside rear end impacted against the tree. The road and all the woods around it were oddly hushed after the noise of driving. Nothing but the dripping of the rain from the overhanging trees and the intermittent *pee-oo, pee-oo* of a distant pewee.

Woods, woods, and more woods. His mother's father had always hated Wisconsin, because of the trees. His mother's father had been a farmer, and to him trees meant stumps. "All these frigging trees," he used to complain, even in retirement.

Jack sniffed, shivered, and looked around. There was no child lying in the road, thank God, and no sign of anybody on the nearby verge. No gray-white raincoat smeared with blood. No twisted training shoe.

Tugging up the collar of his sport coat, he negotiated his way back across the churned-up mud, trying not to mess up his new saddle brown shoes. Because the rubbery tire marks repelled the softly falling rain, he could clearly see where he had slammed on his brakes, and where he had started to skid. Four crisscrossing figure eights, scissoring their way across the tarmac. He hunkered down to look at them more closely. There was nothing to suggest that he might have hit anybody.

He didn't think that he *had* hit anybody. He couldn't remember an impact, except for the final collision against the tree. He turned around, shielding his eyes against the rain, and stared at the front of his station wagon. The front bumper wasn't marked, no lights were broken. He just hoped he hadn't clipped somebody a glancing blow and sent them hurtling into the bracken and the underbrush. He had heard of hit-and-run victims lying in the bushes just yards away from a busy main highway, and dying at last of exposure.

He walked a little farther back along the roadway. He cupped his hands around his mouth and called, "Hallo? Is anybody there? Hallo?"

He stayed quite still, and listened. The pewee called *pee-oo, pee-woo,* then *pee-widdi*. The rain fell as soft as the veil of a dying bride. It was hard to believe that he was only twenty minutes away from Madison, the state capital, and fewer than two hours away from Milwaukee.

He called "Hallo?" three or four more times. There was

still no answer. His heart stopped churning, his breathing gradually returned to normal. He began to feel calmer. He took out his handkerchief, wiped his face, and blew his nose. In spite of the chill, his shirt and his underwear were soaked in cold perspiration.

Must've been a deer, right? Or maybe a goat. Some kind of animal, anyway. You didn't get too good a look at it, did you? I mean, come on Jack, let's be serious here, what would a child be doing right out here in the woods, on a wet Thursday afternoon, miles from anywhere? You wouldn't be here yourself, would you, if you hadn't had to check up on Dad's old summer cottage at Devil's Lake, and the only reason you came down this road is because it happens to cut fifteen miles off your journey through to Route 51.

I mean, what the hell would a kid be doing way out here?

The disturbing thing was, though, that Jack was sure that he had seen running legs, swinging arms, and an upraised hood. Common sense told him that it must have been an animal. But he could still picture a huddled child in a gray-white raincoat, darting out in front of him in that wild miscalculated way that children do.

He waited a few moments longer. Then, slowly, turning around from time to time, he walked back to his station wagon. An '81 Electra, in metallic red, misted with rain now; his dad's last car. Jack had inherited it along with the summer cottage, and roomfuls of sour-smelling books, and more newspapers than anybody could have counted. He had been forced to sell the apartment at Jackson Park to pay off his dad's taxes and funeral expenses (not that he could have persuaded Maggie to live there, not for anything, not for diamonds, because Maggie had always believed that cancer was somehow catching). A whole life of dreaming and working had produced nothing more spectacular than something to drive around in and something to read.

The car's taillights had been smashed, scattering dark red plastic fragments across the leaf mold. The tailgate had been pushed in, so that it sneered on one side like Elvis Presley's lip, and no matter how hard Jack banged it down, it wouldn't shut properly. He guessed it could have been worse. He could have hit the oak tree head-on and been seriously injured, or killed. It was probably just as well that he didn't know how to control a front-wheel skid. A better driver might have died.

He climbed back into the car and started up the engine. The fan belt squealed, but apart from that it sounded as if it were off and running. So long as it took him back to Milwaukee, he didn't mind if it sounded like the Pfister Bier-keller Band.

Just before he switched on the windshield wipers, however, he thought he glimpsed something through the silvery mist of the rain that coated the glass. A whitish flicker, in the woods, off to his right. He cleared the windshield and peered at it again, but it had gone. He opened his car door and climbed half out so that he could see more clearly. Again, the faintest of movements, the faintest gray-white blur, he was sure of it.

He reached across to the backseat and pulled over his raincoat. There was somebody down in those woods, no question about it—somebody or something. And whatever it was, it had almost totaled them both. If it were an animal, there wasn't very much that he could do about it, except report it. But if it were a child, then he wanted to know what the blue blazes that child thought it was up to, running around the woods on its own.

He left the car, slammed the door, and began to climb diagonally downhill. Underfoot, the slope was thick with sodden leaf mold, and he slid sideways with every other step. By the time he had reached more level ground, his shoes were dark with wet, and the pants of his mohair suit had been snagged by brambles. He stopped for a while to get his breath back and to wipe his face yet again.

"Shit," he muttered to himself. He didn't know what on earth had possessed him to set off down this wet tangled slope in pursuit of a child who probably wasn't a child at all, but somebody's dumb runaway goat. He could have been driving back home right now, sitting in his dry, warm car with Santana's *Abraxas* playing at top volume to drown out the noise of his squeaky fan belt.

"And I hope you're feeling better . . . and I hope you're feeling good!"

He waited, and sniffed, and looked around. Behind him, he could just make out the dull red fender of his station wagon, high up beside the highway. In front of him, the ground continued to slope downward, but into a dark and overgrown cleft, dense with brambles and dripping ferns. He could hear water running somewhere, the clackety sound of a small stream, but on this wet afternoon under a heavy gray sky, it somehow sounded flat and depressing instead of cheerful.

He could have gone back. *It is not logical to continue, Captain.* Even if the gray-white figure *had* been a child, he plainly hadn't killed it. And if it was a goat, it could easily outrun him, and climb hills and valleys for which Florsheim shoes were not just unsuitable but downright dangerous.

"Hallo!" he called, one last time. "Is there anybody there?"

He was beginning to shiver again, from cold this time. He needed to pee, too, urgently. He stood up against a clump of ferns and his urine steamed in the afternoon chill. It seemed to go on for ever. But he hadn't even halfway finished before he saw the grayish white figure again, only for a second, way down at the bottom of the cleft between the trees.

"Hey!" he called out. "Hey, you!" He zipped up and began to scramble after it. "Hey, kid, you just wait up there!"

The ground beneath his feet suddenly dropped more steeply. He slipped three or four times, and once he was forced to cling to some brambles to stop himself from

falling, and he tore the heel of his hand, so that it bled.
Sucking the blood, limping, swearing under his breath, he
scrambled deeper and deeper into the narrow valley.

You stupid bastard, he told himself. *It's going to take you
hours to climb back up to the car. And, damn it, it's raining
even more heavily now.*

He slid down a gulley of loose stones, grabbed at the
ferns to balance himself, and then fell heavily on to his
back.

Shit! he raged. *Shit and double-shit!*

Slowly, painfully, he climbed to his feet. His pants were
soaked at the back and gritty with mud. His new shoes were
good for nothing but throwing in the trash. His right hand
was still bleeding and he had bruised his left elbow.

*This is it. Kid or no kid, this is where I turn around and
head for home.*

He stood up straight and took a deep breath, and then he
shouted out, "Kid! Can you hear me? This is it! Forget it! If
you're lost, that's just tough shit! You hear me!"

He listened, but all he could hear was the echo of his own
voice, and the rain, and the clattering stream. "Stupid
damn kid," he said under his breath. "Stupid damn—
whatever-it-is, shit, goat. Who cares?"

He began to climb back up the valley. Right then,
however, out of the corner of his eye, he saw the gray-white
figure up on the bank to his left, only about twenty yards
away—not moving, not running, but simply standing with
its head bowed among the nodding ferns. He stopped and
stared at it, his teeth chattering with cold. This time, for
some reason, he didn't feel inclined to shout out.

"Right, now I've got you, you bastard," he said under his
breath, and began to wade uphill through the ferns and the
brambles. This time the figure stayed where it was, in its
grayish white raincoat, its hood peaked up and its shoulders hunched. Jack thought it was odd that it hadn't turned
around, that it hadn't moved at all. It must be able to hear
him, after all. He was crashing up the slope with about as

much subtlety as General Patton and the Third Armored Division.

He had almost reached the figure now, and still it didn't move. It was standing right next to a two-strand barbed-wire fence that ran diagonally down the side of the valley. It was definitely a child, rather than an animal. Yet it appeared to be a peculiarly hunched-up child, a distorted child; and for the first time Jack began to feel genuine unease.

"Hey kid!" he called harshly, but more out of bravado than anger. "Hey kid, you almost killed the two of us, back there on the road."

Still the child stayed where it was, against the fence. Jack stepped up to it at last, holding on to the top wire of the barbed-wire fence to prevent himself from slipping back down the hill.

It was only when he was almost able to touch the child that he understood that it wasn't a child at all. It wasn't even an animal. He grasped its "hood" and pulled it away from the fence, and all he had in his hand was a rain-sodden copy of last Sunday's *Milwaukee Sentinel*. Somehow it had become unfolded and blown against one of the fence posts in the shape of a hooded child.

He stood for a long time in the rain, frowning, with a bunch of wet sports section in each hand. He couldn't understand this at all; and in a peculiar way it was almost more unsettling than actually finding a child. He had seen this same-shaped figure running across the highway in front of him. He had seen it dart off down the hill and into the valley. From the gulley below, it had looked exactly like a child in a gray-white raincoat. How the hell could it turn out to be nothing but newspaper?

He unfolded the damp pages and saw the date. Last Friday's edition. Nothing special about it. Slowly he crumpled it up, and then he swung his arm back and tossed it away. He had one last look around the woods. There was no sign of anything else remotely like the child he thought he had been pursuing. No tantalizing flashes of gray-white raincoat among the ferns. He sniffed, and wiped his forehead with the back of his hand, and prepared himself for the long struggle back up to his car.

It was then, however, that he glimpsed the outline of what looked like rooftops among the trees. He climbed a few yards farther up the hill, and soon he could see it quite clearly. A huge building with yellow-brick towers, and shining blue-gray slates, and rows and rows of Gothic-style windows. Now, what the hell building was *that*?

Jack stretched apart the strands of the barbed-wire fence, ducked his head, and eased his way through. The building stood on the far side of the valley from the highway, its towers concealed among huge white oaks, so that even though it had been built with such a commanding view of the surrounding woods, it was almost impossible for anyone to see it from the highway.

It was fiercely protected from the outside world by the natural environment all around it, like Sleeping Beauty's castle. Jack could tell that the woods must have been cleared once, twenty or thirty years ago maybe; but now he had to struggle his way through thorns and wild rose-bushes, and by the time he had reached a stand of oaks about two hundred yards below and southwest of the building, the tails of his raincoat had been ripped twice and his socks were in ribbons. Forget about the hundred-and-seventy-dollar shoes.

What intrigued him so much, though, was the way in which he felt he had been *led* here: as if he had been destined all his life to discover this building, on this particular afternoon, at this particular hour. As if it had been *waiting* for him.

When he was a boy, he had spent almost every summer vacation up here at Mirror Lake or Devil's Lake or Lake Wisconsin, and he and his friends had crisscrossed these woods on hundreds of hiking expeditions and "jungle explorations."

Yet he had never seen this building before now, in spite of its immense size. He had never even known of its existence. It was so grand and mysterious and atmospheric that Jack felt almost resentful that he hadn't found it when he was eleven years old. Think of the games that he and Dougie McLeish could have played around here! Prince Valiant! The man in the iron mask! Dracula! They could have had an incredible time! Why should he have had to wait to discover it now, today, when he was a forty-three-year-old married man living in Milwaukee, running a chain of quick-fit muffler shops?

The building looked like a castle, or a hotel, or a grandiose railroad station. It was built of that same pale yellow brick as the old Pabst Brewery on the west side of Milwaukee—that same brick that had once earned Milwaukee the nickname of the "Cream City." Its architectural style was Austrian Gothic, with a square tower at each end of its two-hundred-foot frontage, each with a cluster of five spires, and decorative wrought-iron railings all the way round the gutters.

There were faces everywhere. Gray faces, cast out of lead, on each of the drainpipes. Yellow-ocher faces, carved out of stone, above the windows. Black iron faces, on the corners of the railings. Probably more than a hundred altogether. Unlike most gargoyles, however, none of the faces were ugly or grotesque. They were all calm and saintly and serene; although the strange thing was that every face had its eyes closed, as if it were blind, or asleep, or dead.

Jack made his way through the trees until he reached the white gravel driveway that surrounded the building. The gravel was overgrown with ivy and crabgrass. On the west tower the ivy had climbed its way up to the level of the third-story windows, clinging to the bricks like a dark and possessive mistress.

He had no doubt that the building had been empty for years, maybe even for decades. The gutters were badly corroded, and water had been trickling down the side of the main doorway, leaving a rusty stain all the way down the brickwork. Every window was dark and dusty and empty, and scores of the diamond-shaped leaded panes were broken. There were abandoned birds' nests in almost all of the chimney stacks, and wedged between the spires.

Over the entire building, as it stood in the softly falling rain, there was an air of quiet despair, of long-lost memories, and of elegant regret.

Jack walked up to the main door, climbed the stone steps, and tried tugging at the heavy bronze door handle. The doors were locked—probably barred, too. Not that there was much danger of the building being vandalized, out here in the woods where nobody could find it.

Beside the doors was an old-fashioned tug-down doorbell, with a cast-bronze face on it, the face of a saint with closed eyes. Jack tugged it once and did nothing but dislodge a shower of rust, but then he tugged it a second time, harder, and he heard a harsh clanging sound somewhere inside the building, a clanging that went on and on, like somebody madly ringing a handbell.

He stepped back in embarrassment. God almighty, supposing there were somebody here? He half expected the face on the doorbell to open its eyes and stare at him in disapproval.

But then the clanging died away, and the building was silent once again. The face on the doorbell remained beatific and blind. Jack shook his head and said, "Nerd," and grinned at himself for being alarmed.

He left the main door and walked farther along the front of the building until he reached the tower at the eastern end. He tried peering in at one of the windows, but the glass was so murky that it was impossible to see anything, except the shadowy outline of what looked like a sofa. Around the side of the building, the grass and the weeds had grown up almost to chest height, so he picked a branch, snapped off two or three extraneous twigs, and used it to thrash his way through the undergrowth. Indiana Jones. Stanley looking for Livingstone.

The silence and the dankness and the isolation of the woods somehow stirred up an excitement that Jack hadn't felt since he was a boy. He began to whistle softly between his teeth, a dramatic soundtrack to accompany his progress through the weeds. When he startled a squirrel, he whipped up his stick like a rifle, and pretended to take potshots at it as it fled up one of the nearby oaks. *Kachow! Kachow! Kachow!*

He passed the flaking blue-painted doors of what must have been the building's kitchens. Pressing his forehead against the windows, he could make out a huge old-fashioned range and two large sinks with upright faucets. There was a glass-fronted cupboard on the wall, which was still filled with stacks of white dinner plates and cups.

It was uncanny. It looked as if the building had been abandoned with everything in it—furniture, crockery, carpets. There was even a glass flower vase on the kitchen windowsill, with a spray of desiccated chrysanthemums in it.

Jack reached the back of the building. There was a long wrought-iron conservatory all the way along it, badly rusted now, with dozens of broken panes, and its glass roof thick with leaves and grime. From the conservatory, stone steps descended into a sunken garden, where gravel paths had been laid out in a formal cloverleaf pattern. All the flower beds were now tangled and overgrown, and a rose pergola that stood in the center of the garden had partially collapsed. Beyond the sunken garden, the grounds rose in terraces toward the woods. Off to the west, part of the grounds had been laid out as tennis courts, and next to the tennis courts was an outdoor swimming pool, with a tiled surround.

Jack walked the length of the conservatory until he

reached the tennis courts. The rain was misting across the valley, miserable and cold, but Jack cupped his hands over his forehead to keep water out of his eyes and stood for almost five minutes staring into the distance. On a summer's day, the view across the woods would be breathtaking.

He slid down the wet grassy bank to the tennis courts themselves. The nets were sagging and rotten, with the dried-out corpses of birds tangled in them. But the red asphalt was still in good condition, and it wouldn't take much to have them back up to scratch.

He approached the swimming pool. It was tiled in white, with brown vine patterns around the edge: Edwardian and lavatorial, and quarter filled with greenish black water. Something was lying in the water, too, something shapeless and pale, just beneath the surface. He tried to reach it with his stick, but it was too far away. It nodded, bobbed, and rolled. It could have been anything.

You know—thought Jack, standing up and looking around the back of the building—*there's a whole lot of potential here. A fine building, basically sound. A tremendous location. Plenty of room for sports facilities. Cleverly redeveloped, this could become the finest resort hotel in the entire midwest.*

Slowly he walked across the tennis court and around to the front of the house once again. An idea was ballooning inside his mind. A business idea. A *career* idea. An idea that would take him away from the confines of the city, and away from the daily tedium of Reed Muffler & Tire. An idea that would bring him freedom and fulfillment and prestige and *enjoyment*, too—all in one stroke.

If the building had been left empty for so long, then obviously nobody wanted it, or nobody had realized its potential. He should be able to pick it up for—what?—half a million? Three hundred thousand? Maybe even less. His friend Morris Tucker at Menomonee Savings would be able to help with the financing. They had both attended

Wisconsin Business College, class of '67, and three or four times every summer they still went out fishing together from Whitefish Bay, with floppy sun hats and six-packs of Pabst Blue Ribbon and Beatles tapes on the ghetto blaster.

No doubt about it, he would need millions to fix the building up to international resort standards. But if Morris could put together the right financial package—well, it was a hell of a risk. A *hell* of a risk. Yet what did he stand to lose, even if it all went wrong? A house in suburban Milwaukee, a dented station wagon, and a crushingly predictable future fitting mufflers onto other people's automobiles? That wouldn't be a loss; that would be liberation; even if it all fell through, and he had to go back to working in an office.

He reached the gravel drive and walked right up to the building and pressed his hand against the wet brickwork. *Once in every man's life, just once, a great opportunity presents itself.* Jack was sure that finding this building was *his* great opportunity. It *had* to be. *Just look at the weird way in which I was led here. By a blown-away newspaper that looked like a running child. If that isn't fate, my friend, then I don't know what the hell is.*

He could see it now. The building restored, the grounds all cleared, the sun shining, smartly dressed couples strolling in and out of the conservatory. Helicopters landing on the terraces, bringing guests directly from Chicago or Milwaukee. A squash court, a glass roof for the swimming pool, a golf course cleared out of the woods.

He would call it Merrimac Court Country Club. Owner and president, John T. Reed, Jr.

Slowly he backed away from the building, chafing his hands together and sniffing in the cold. As soon as he got home he was going to find out who owned the building and how much they would be prepared to sell it for. Then he would have it surveyed, just to make sure that the structure didn't have any defects that would cost more to put right than they were worth. *Come on, you're going to be sensible and practical about this. You're not going to let yourself get carried away.*

But he knew that there was no going back. His life had already been turned upside down. Even if *this* building was beyond restoration, he would find one that wasn't, and he would open his country club one way or another, even if it killed him.

Stand aside, Leona Helmsley. Jack Reed is coming through.

He gave the building one last long look, trying to fix it completely in his mind's eye, and it was then that he saw a face at one of the dormer windows, high up on roof. A small white face, like a child's.

He stood staring at the window, blinking the rain from his eyes. He felt intensely cold, and very tired. But he hadn't imagined it. He had seen it quite distinctly. Just for an instant, sure. But a child's face, way up high, looking down at him.

He didn't quite know what to do. It must be the same child that he had seen on the roadway, the same child that had led him here. The newspaper up against the fence must have been nothing more than coincidence. But even if there *were* a child inside the building, what the hell was *he* supposed to do about it? It wasn't his building; it wasn't his child. Maybe he ought to call the local police and tell them, in case the child was a runaway, or in some kind of moral or physical danger. But he couldn't see that his responsibility stretched any further than that.

Still—the child must have gotten into the building someway, and that meant there must be an open door, or a window that could be climbed through. Even if he couldn't find the child, he could at least take a look inside and see what condition the interior was in.

He walked around to the back of the building again. He tried the French windows at the side of the west tower; but they were firmly locked, and he could see that they were bolted, too.

He made his way to the conservatory doors and tried those. At first they wouldn't budge, but when he pulled the handles right down and tugged them again, one of them juddered open.

He hesitated. Technically he was already trespassing, just by walking uninvited around the grounds; but if he stepped inside he would be guilty of illegal entry, too. For all of its apparent dereliction, this might still be somebody's home; and if that somebody were here, he was going to have a whole lot of awkward explaining to do.

He knocked on the window with his knuckle. "Hallo? Anybody home?" he called out. Inside, the conservatory was thick with dust, silent, and dim. A cast-iron table lay tipped over on its side, and the pieces of the green ceramic pot that had broken when it fell were still scattered next to it. Against the opposite wall stood a collection of large earthenware urns, with dead yellowish plants trailing out of them. The air smelled of damp, and something else that was sourer, like vinegar.

"Anybody around?" Jack repeated. But the conservatory was silent, except for the persistent dribbling of rainwater through its corroded flashings.

Use your noodle, Reed, Jack told himself. *Nobody lives here. Only squatters maybe, or vagrants, or runaway kids. Nobody who has any more right to be here than you do. Nobody legitimate.*

He eased open the door a little further and stepped inside. The floor was gritty, and his shoes made a grinding, squeaking sound. He paused for a moment, then he crossed the conservatory and went up two steps to the doors that led directly into the building itself. They were stiff, too, but he was able to open them.

Here goes nothing, he thought, pushing the door just a little way and easing himself in.

The room in which he found himself appeared to be a large lounge or recreation room. There were cream-painted cane chairs all around, fifty or sixty of them, and cream-painted cane tables. On some of the tables, there were cups and saucers, marked mahogany brown inside with long-evaporated coffee. Magazines and newspapers were strewn across the green-carpeted floor. Jack bent down and picked up a copy of *Collier's*. It carried a cover story—"Walter Camp's All-America Team"—and it was dated 1926. He picked up a newspaper, with the banner headline HALL-MILLS MURDER TRIAL OPENS. The date was June 21, 1926.

He stood in the middle of the room for a moment and then carefully laid the magazine and the newspaper down on one of the tables. He felt strangely claustrophobic, as if the lounge were closing in on him. His immediate inclination was to get back out into the open air. *Because, Jesus, this room must have been crowded with people back in June 1926, and for some reason they all upped and left, and the building was locked up, completely locked up, and nobody has touched anything here for sixty-two years.*

He took a deep breath. The air inside the building was even colder than it was outside; and there was still that distinct sharpness of vinegar.

He listened, but the building remained silent. All he could hear was the rain, pattering on the conservatory roof. He looked around the lounge and thought to himself: *This would make a terrific cocktail bar.* A long antique mirror, running the length of the back wall, a marble-topped counter, gilded antique chairs. He crossed the lounge to the inner door, which was slightly ajar. *This place could have such style.*

He opened the door, and found himself in a huge cavernous hallway, with a galleried landing all the way around it. On each side a flight of marble stairs rose up to the second floor. What a reception lobby! A huge iron lantern was suspended from the ceiling high above. It trailed cobwebs below it like a slipping shroud. The floor of the hallway was tiled with red-and-white-checkered marble, but it was thick with dust and grit and fallen plaster and twigs from birds' nests.

At the foot of each staircase stood a life-size stone statue of a saintly figure in biblical robes, two identical statues, both with their eyes closed. Jack walked over to one of them and looked at it for a long time. He didn't know why he found all these faces with closed eyes so unsettling, but he did. *I mean, who the hell makes statues with their eyes closed? Is it because they're supposed to be dead, or asleep, or is it simply that they don't want to look back at us while we're looking at them?*

Whichever it was, he didn't like it. It gave him the unpleasant sensation that when he turned his back on them, they would open their eyes and stare at him.

He climbed up two or three stairs and called, "Hallo? Hallo! Is there anybody up there?"

There was no echo. But he heard a slight scuffling noise somewhere in the building. A squirrel, maybe. Or a bird. Or a small boy, who knew that he had done wrong by running across the road without looking and had hidden himself in one of the upstairs rooms.

"Hallo!" Jack shouted. "Can you hear me? Because I'm coming up to get you, ready or not!"

He mounted the stairs and climbed up to the second story, two or three stairs at a time. When he reached the landing, he looked back down at the two statues in the hallway. The light was beginning to fade, but they gleamed with an almost unnatural ivory radiance. Neither statue opened its eyes; neither statue moved. *Jack, my friend, you should stop imagining things.*

From the landing, two long corridors ran off in each direction, one toward the west tower and one toward the east. They were both dark, but Jack could just make out a glimmer of reflected light on their linoleum floors. He took a dime out of his raincoat pocket and flipped it. "Heads west, tails east," he told himself. The dime fell on the floor, tails up.

He walked along the eastward corridor. It was long and narrow and shut-in, but he supposed that he could always let in some extra windows. It was lined on both sides with rows of doors, cream-painted doors, all locked—but each door had a small spyhole in it, covered by a pivoting brass cover. He peered into three or four of the rooms. All he could see were beds and chairs, and in one of the rooms, nothing but a mattress.

Every sixth door, a short side corridor branched off toward the rear of the building, giving access to a window. Each window, however, was covered with a black steel diamond-patterned mesh, very fine gauge, which cut down the light by nearly half. What was more, the mesh hadn't just been bolted into place but *welded*. It struck Jack as pretty absurd that the building's owner had been security-conscious enough to protect all of the upstairs windows, yet hadn't thought to cover up any of the downstairs windows.

He went up the first side corridor, right up to the window, and squinted out. Through the dust-clogged mesh and the grimy glass, he could see part of the tennis courts and a corner of the swimming pool, and that tangled abandoned garden. He stayed by the window for two or three minutes, looking out. The rain was still falling, the sky was the color of Barre granite, the grass was poisonously green. He checked his watch and saw that it was already 4:30. He wouldn't get home until well after dark.

At the end of the corridor, Jack was faced with double stained-oak doors, not only locked but fastened with a steel hasp and a heavy-duty Ingersoll padlock. He rattled it, but it didn't budge. Whatever was kept in the east tower, its owners obviously wanted it to stay there. A valuable library maybe, or an art collection? Or maybe the floors had collapsed, and they simply wanted to keep people out for their own safety. But off to his left, another narrower staircase rose into the darkness, leading up to the next floor.

He found a light switch on the wall to his left, and he flicked it up and down; but of course it didn't work. The whole building would probably need rewiring, from top to bottom.

There was a window halfway up the staircase, but that, too, was covered with steel mesh. The mesh was dented in several places, as if something heavy had been hurled at it, again and again.

Jack set one foot on the staircase, then hesitated. It was growing late, and dark, and he didn't have a flashlight. Maybe he should call it a day and think about getting himself back home. He knew that Maggie would be worrying about him and that his turkey dinner would be all dried up. He was always so punctual; and he always called to let Maggie know if he thought that he was going to be delayed.

On the other hand, he had never come across anything like this building before, this chance of a lifetime. This was worth it. And what the hell was one dried-up Hungry Man dinner in the great scheme of human destiny?

He started to climb higher, his shoes scuffing on the marble. As he did so he thought he heard a noise, and so he stopped, and held his breath, and strained his ears.

It was a heavy, scratching, *dragging* sound, rather like the noise of concrete being mixed. But it was very indistinct, and he couldn't make out where it was coming from, and it stopped almost at once, so that he couldn't be sure if he had really heard it or not.

He stayed exactly where he was, listening until his neck began to creak with tension, but the noise wasn't repeated. It could have been rainwater, gurgling through the gutters. It could have been squirrels, pattering through the eaves.

He continued to climb the stairs, more softly this time. The next landing was even darker, and smelled even more strongly of vinegar. It was probably animal piss, of some kind. The whole building was probably a huge hotel for polecats and skunks and squirrels and birds. He remembered once seeing the roof stripped off a house on the outskirts of Madison. Squirrels had been nesting in it for five years, and the eaves had been packed with a huge wedge of torn-up fiberglass insulation, riddled with the half-decayed bodies of squirrel young. The stench of death had been overwhelming; and he had never again been able to look at a squirrel and think that it was cute.

Jack took a quick look along the third-floor corridor, but it was up in one of the dormer windows that he had seen the young child's face (if it *had* been a young child's face, and not an owl or a pigeon or some chance reflection off the window glass or something freakish like that). So he climbed the stairs yet again to the very top. Again, there was a window halfway up the stairs, and again, it was heavily protected by thick steel mesh.

Another odd thought occurred to him: steel mesh was usually fixed to the *outside* of windows, so that the glass couldn't be broken by stone throwing, and so that second-story men couldn't reach the windows in the first place. This mesh must have covered the windows so that they couldn't be broken from the *inside*.

But who would live in a grandiose building like this and have to protect the windows from themselves?

He reached the uppermost landing. Here the eaves curved inward to form a mansard roof, and even though he was right at the top of the house, Jack felt even more closed-in than he had before. If he wanted to escape from the house in a hurry, he would have to run down three flights of stairs, a long narrow corridor, another flight of stairs, across the hallway, through the lounge, and through the conservatory.

He waited for a moment, breathing deeply. He had never suffered from claustrophobia before, but there was something about this building that made him feel trapped. It was probably the windows, the way they were all covered

over with mesh. It was the locked doors, too. He hadn't yet
found a single room upstairs that wasn't locked.

He started to make his way along the corridor that ran
the entire length of the building, through the roof. It was
deeply gloomy now, and he could see only a dozen feet in
front of him. He ran his hands along the top of the
stained-oak dado, to guide himself. At each door he
stopped and tried the handle. If the child had appeared at
one of the dormer windows, it must have been able to enter
one of the rooms. And just so long as it didn't have a key,
and was able to lock the door after it, Jack would be able to
find out where it was hiding.

"Hallo!" he called. "Anybody there?"

He rattled another door handle. It was locked. He went
on and rattled the next one. That was locked, too.

He was halfway along the corridor when he thought he
heard that scraping noise again. He stopped and listened. It
was behind him. A deep, low, dragging-a-bag-of-concrete
noise. It was behind him and it seemed to be coming
toward him.

He turned, his scalp prickling with alarm. There was
nobody there. He could see for himself that the corridor
was completely empty.

Yet the noise continued. *Sssshhhhhhhh-sssshhhhhh-
ssssshhhhhh;* thick and heavy and relentless.

Jack stood still for a moment, listening to it. Then he
began to walk more quickly along the corridor, away from
it, toward the west end of the house. He tried the first two
or three door handles, but the noise kept after him, so
he ignored the rest and began to jog. *Sssssshhhhhhh-
ssssshhhhhh-sssshhhhhh,* along the walls, punctuated by a
strange hollow knocking noise at every door.

It sounded as if something huge and invisible were
chasing after him along the corridor, its body dragging
against the walls and rattling against the doors. It began to
sound louder and louder and faster and faster, *sssshhhh-
knokk! ssshhhhh-knokk! ssshhhh-knokk!*

Jack broke into a run. The corridor jiggled darkly in front of his eyes. He hoped to God there was a staircase at the other end. It hadn't occurred to him when he started running that there might be only one.

The noise came pouring after him, *sssshhhh-knokkk! sssshhhh-knokkkk!* and he didn't know what it was or what the hell it might do to him, but he wanted out of that house as fast as his legs could take him.

He had almost reached the end of the corridor. There *was* another staircase, thank God! He plunged down it, leaping four or five stairs at a time, gasping for breath with every jump. But the noise came after him, *shakka-takka-shakka-takka* down the staircase.

He grasped the banisters and swung himself down the last half-dozen stairs, slipping and jarring his ankle. Then he sprint-hopped along the second-story corridor to the landing, down the last flight of stairs, across the hallway, through the lounge, through the conservatory, and burst out into the wet evening drizzle.

He turned around, panting. Whatever it was, he could face it now, out in the open. But just to be safe, he tugged an edging brick out from the side of the gravel path and hefted it in his hand.

He thought he heard the *ssshhhhhhh* noise coming through the lounge. He heard the lounge doors racket open. Then the conservatory rattled and shook as if it had been hit by a car, and several panes of glass pealed noisily on to the marble floor.

Jack took a step back, swinging the brick. But then there was silence. The noise had stopped. He waited and waited but the noise didn't return. He heard the rain in the gutters and the distant pewee singing *peewoo, peewoo!* But that was all.

He took two or three cautious steps back toward the conservatory and peered inside. He called "Hallo?" but nobody answered, because there was nobody there.

He listened to his heart beating for a while, then he stepped back inside. He wasn't going to be frightened off by this building; and he particularly wasn't going to be frightened off by his own imagination going ape-shit. He had been *led* here, right, by fate, and this building was going to be the Merrimac Court Country Club, owner and president John T. Reed, Jr., or bust.

Nerd, he told himself. *It was your own breathing, your own blood rushing through your eardrums. Same as hearing the sea, when you press a seashell over your ear. You just allowed yourself to get psyched.*

He picked up one of the broken panes of glass that had dropped from the conservatory roof. *No mystery about that, either. The doors banged shut behind me, and this ironwork is so darn corroded, I'm not surprised a couple of panes of glass fell out.*

He went back into the lounge. Empty. Unchanged. Not even a chair tipped over. If something had really been chasing him, he would have seen it, *ja?* He picked up one of the newspapers, went back into the conservatory, and closed the doors behind him.

All right, he still hadn't *totally* managed to convince himself that what he had heard was nothing but his own blood whooshing through his eardrums. But look at it rationally, Jack. There are no such things as ghosts; and something you can't see can't possibly hurt you, now can it? The very worst that it could have been was a squirrel running along inside the cavity walls. Yes, that was it. A squirrel, goddamn it, rushing after him to protect its young. They could be fierce, right? especially out here in the woods.

He was pleased with the squirrel theory. When he had the building surveyed, he would ask the surveyors to check out the wall cavities.

It was growing very dark now, even though the rain was beginning to ease off. He walked around the building one more time, trying to assess it as pessimistically as possible, looking at the very worst aspects of it, its collapsed gutters, its missing tiles, its rusted ironwork.

Come on, Jack, there's a hell of a lot of work here; and a hell of a lot of grief, too, before it's done. You could walk away and leave it, and that would be the end of it. Back to Milwaukee, back to Reed Muffler & Tires.

But he knew that he would never be the same again. He had been seduced by an elderly but alluring old lady, and he would never be able to get her out of his mind.

He slid-scrambled wearily away from the building, through the trees, and down through the ferns and the brambles to the barbed-wire fence. He had almost reached the fence when he saw a signboard lying flat among the weeds. He hobbled over and was about to lift it up when he saw that it was covered in black glistening slugs. He turned it over with his foot instead.

Through the greenish black lichen that obscured most of the board, Jack could just distinguish the words OWN RISK. He let it drop back into the undergrowth. He took one last look at the rooftops of the Merrimac-Court-Country-Club-to-be, and then he ducked between the barbed wire and made his way back to his station wagon.

T·W·O

*H*e had practiced his speech all the way home, but Maggie was still furious. She marched up and down the kitchen while he sat at the breakfast bench with a Pabst in front of him. The Hungry Man turkey dinner complete with fudge brownie had been consigned two hours before to whatever heaven awaits untouched TV meals.

"Tell me!" she demanded. "Tell me! Tell me just *one thing* that you know about running a country club! Just *one thing,* that's all, and then maybe at least I can begin to take you seriously!"

Jack shrugged. He was trying very hard to stay rational and coolheaded, and not to get crazy. For one thing, Randy was already asleep. For another, he always lost arguments with Maggie when he got crazy, because he had to say sorry for getting crazy, and as far as she was concerned that meant sorry for arguing as well, no matter how right he might have been.

"Point number one, I know how to run a profitable business," he told her. *Profitable,* her face said, in instant and silent scorn.

"Point number two, I also happen to have a pretty strong idea of what *I* want out of a country club, as a paying customer."

"How can you conceivably have any kind of idea what you want from a country club?" she retorted. "You've never even *been* to a country club."

Jack looked down at his beer. "Well," he said, "I'm

sorry, but that shows what you know. I went to the Kenosha Golf Club with Harry Whiteman; and I went to the Mud Lake Tennis and Racquet Club when we held that muffler dealers' convention at Madison."

"Oh, I forgot," said Maggie. "The Mud Lake Tennis and Racquet Club. Half a dozen potbellied men in Hawaiian shirts, trying to hit featherless shuttlecocks over a row of folding chairs."

"The net was being repaired," he snapped back; and then thought, *Shit, she always traps me into details.*

"But that's your pretty strong idea of what you want out of a country club? Mud Lake?"

He lifted his head and stared at her, giving her the evil eye. But he managed to hold back his temper. He had disappointed her, he knew that. He had disappointed her ever since they had been married. She had imagined him to be somebody else, some other kind of man, and for eleven years he had never been able to discover what other kind of man he was supposed to be.

He had tried asking her. "What the hell do you want from me?" he would roar at her, after too many beers. But she never told him. She just locked herself in the bedroom and put her hair in heated rollers. It was more than likely that she didn't know herself.

There was still love between them, although Jack found it difficult to qualify just what kind of love it was. They still made "a smart couple" when they went out together. Jack was tall and long-limbed, with chestnut brown hair that always looked as if it were overdue for a cut, and one of those long handsome faces that people can never quite take seriously, like Dick Van Dyke's. He had a habit of overdressing—wearing a necktie when everybody else was wearing open collars—but even at the age of forty-three it was still difficult to shake the overwhelming formality that had been imposed on him by his father.

He had realized too late that his father's formality had

been a symptom not of traditionalism and strength, but of shyness and chronic insecurity.

Maggie (or Margaret-Ann, as he called her when he was really crazy) was a second-generation Milwaukee German. Her hair was silver blond, her eyes were as green as grapes, and her chin was strong and Germanic and deeply cleft like her father's. When she was happy she was exuberantly feminine. She would dance with plump bare feet. But when she was angry she could look off puttingly mannish. She was big-breasted, but her arms were big, too, and went freckled in the summer, and she always complained about her heavy thighs.

Her father was a retired printer, who had always harbored vague delusions that he was a European intellectual of some kind. His bookshelves were crammed with unread copies of books like *Narziss und Goldmund* and *The Voyage of the Beagle,* and he subscribed to *Psychology Today.* He smoked small cigars and talked of "worlds within worlds."

Maggie, who had once appeared to be quite contented with her part-time job teaching piano at Marquette University, had lately been showing signs of similar delusions. She had enrolled in an evening class in Expressionism, due to start in March. Jack didn't even know what Expressionism was.

He kept saying, "What the hell is Expressionism, anyway?" but she wouldn't tell him, or couldn't.

"We could live a life-style like you never imagined," he told her.

"Don't you think the real one is bad enough?" she replied. She marched up to one end of the kitchen, and then marched back again.

"You think it's *bad?*" he asked her. "You think the way we live is *bad?*"

"For God's sake, Jack, I didn't mean bad. Not *bad* bad. I meant, I don't know—*stressful.*"

"What stress?" he demanded. "What stress? The only stress is that we have no stress. We have no challenges."

"And you think that running a country club is a *challenge*? Jesus! Some people's idea of a challenge."

She marched six paces one way, six the other. Five months and four days ago she had quit smoking, cold turkey. The Colonial oak cupboard fronts were disfigured with water stains, and the electric clock on the wall was never quite straight, and never right either.

Jack shook his head, trying to look as if he felt sorry for her because she didn't understand. "This building, honey ... it's like something out of a fairy tale. You remember Sleeping Beauty? The castle all surrounded with thorns and stuff? You'll have to see it to believe it."

"I don't want to see it," Maggie told him. "I haven't even the slightest interest in seeing it. The whole thing, the whole idea—it's like you've gone mad. It's like you've come back home and told me you've contracted AIDS or something."

"AIDS?" he almost screamed at her. "AIDS? It's a building, Maggie. It's a rambling old building right in the middle of the woods. It has potential like you wouldn't believe! It has everything you could ask for! Will you give me a break, for Christ's sake?"

He paused, shaking, and then he said, "AIDS, for Christ's sake."

Maggie stopped marching and pressed her hand against her forehead. "I never heard anything so dumb," she said, as if she were talking to somebody else on the telephone. "I can't believe that you came home two and a half hours late and told me you want to open a country club. Maybe I'll wake up tomorrow and you won't have said it."

Jack stood up. *God, give me some strength here, please.* He was close to the edge of going crazy. "Maggie," he said, as gently as he could manage. "Do you think I'd give up twenty-five years of Reed Muffler and Tire for something that wasn't going to work? Do you really think that? I'm not a cheesehead, Maggie. I'm a practical man. But what you have to understand is that I have an imagination, too. I have a vision. I may be forty-three but I still have ambition."

"Ambition," she repeated, nodding her head, as if she were still speaking on her imaginary telephone.

"Is that so wrong, to have ambition?"

Her green eyes swung to him sharply. "That's *your* ambition you're talking about, my friend. *Your* ambition. Not mine."

Jack walloped his fist down on the counter, splashing beer. "All right, Goddamn it! It's my ambition! But how the hell can I help you with your ambition if I don't even know what the hell your ambition is?"

The bedroom door slammed. Plaster sifted from the ceiling. Jack sat alone in the kitchen looking at his slopped-over beer. *Blown it again,* he told himself, with that familiar sick bitterness in the back of his mouth. *Blown it again. Now the only options left to me are (a) give up the country club, or (b) divorce.*

He was still sitting there when the door opened again. He thought for one irrational moment that it might be Maggie, come back to tell him that she was sorry. But it was Randy, tousle-haired, puffy-eyed, wearing his "A-Team" pajamas and carrying that hideous beige-colored sexless being that a feminist friend of Maggie's had knitted for him because it was totally nondiscriminatory.

Randy called it Waffle, because it had the skin texture of a waffle. Jack called it the Turd.

"How're you doing, ace?" Jack asked Randy, lifting him up onto the counter.

"You and Mommy woke me up," Randy said accusingly.

"Well, we were singing," said Jack.

Randy shook his head. "You were fighting."

"Nah. It wasn't a fight, it was what you might call a discussion."

"Mommy locked the door and when I looked through the keyhole she was putting on her rollers."

Jack sighed. "All right, Officer, I'll come quietly. It was a fight."

"What was it about *this* time?" Randy was very world-weary for a boy of nine.

"Oh, I don't know. This and that. The usual. The impossibility of two grown people who have any opinions beyond the weather to live cozily and contentedly with each other. Is the universe shaped like a donut and if so where's the jelly. Your mom and I can argue about anything."

He paused for a moment and drank a mouthful of beer, and then he said, "Randy, would you like to move away from here?"

Randy held the Turd more tightly and frowned at him. "You mean move someplace else?"

"Sure. Like—I don't know—the woods, maybe."

"The *woods*?"

Jack nodded wildly. "That's right, the woods. You're beginning to sound like your mom. I say 'the woods' and she says 'the woods?' and I say 'the woods,' and so we go on, ad nauseam, ad infinitum, and for ever."

Randy stared back at him, mystified. At last Jack allowed himself to grin, and said, "Listen up, Randy. Let me give you the goods on the woods."

It was still raining the next morning when Jack drove out to Reed Muffler & Tire out on West Good Hope Road, next to Wisconsin Cuneo Press. He parked in the space marked RESERVED and hurried across the puddly concrete apron to the fitting shop. His mechanics looked as if they had their hands full. There were two cars up on lifts, having their exhaust systems replaced, while the tire bay echoed to the whirring screech of power drills and the deafening bang of inflated tires.

Jack's foreman Mike Karpasian gave him an oily-fisted salute and then came waddling beefily across the fitting shop in his outsize Oshkosh B'Gosh coveralls. Mike used to be a boxer, and spoke with a dumb-ox slur in his voice, but he was easily the most reliable and quick-witted man on the staff.

"What happened to your car?" he wanted to know, nodding out toward Jack's dented station wagon.

"Skidded, hit a tree," Jack told him. "You going to be busy like this all day?"

"Looks that way. We've got five more booked for this morning; two muffler replacements and three emissions tests. Tire bay ain't so tied up, but you never can tell. People start to worry about their tires when it gets slippery." ·

He sniffed, and then he said, "My cousin Waldo can fix that rear end up for you. He runs a body shop in Cudahy. Preferential rates."

"If he's anything like your cousin who fixed my trash compactor, I think I'll pass. I now have the only trash compactor in America that makes your garbage bigger."

Jack made his way through the fitting shop to the office. Karen was busy typing out invoices on the word processor, but she glanced up when he opened the door and smiled.

"Didn't expect you out here today," she told him. "I thought you were going to Wauwatosa."

"I came to see you," he said, closing the office door behind him.

Karen had worked for him for three years now. She was twenty-six years old, a bouffant brunette, very pretty in a pouting, baby-dollish, four-pairs-of-false-eyelashes kind of way. She always wore low-cut cardigans with no bra and tight short skirts and wiggled her butt when she walked. She was a major attraction to the male customers of Reed Muffler & Tire, but she only had eyes for Jack.

Not that they were messing around together. Karen had just been granted a decree against her second husband, a 304-pound trucker named Cecil who had cracked her jaw in two places, and just at the moment she was taking what she called "an emotional vacation," nursing her heart and looking after her daughter by her first marriage, Sherry (short, improbably, for Sherrywine.)

Karen and Jack occasionally went to the Bierkeller across the street for a drink together after the fitting shop had closed for the day, and to talk sentimentally about things that were and things that weren't, and things that could never have been; but that was as far as it went.

"You and Maggie been scrappin' again?" she asked him.

"Well, not exactly." Jack sat down behind his desk and dry-washed his face with his hands. Behind his head hung a nude calendar, extolling the virtues of the HRS-71 low-profile tire.

"Want some coffee?" Karen asked him. "You look like forty miles of rough road."

Jack shook his head. "What I need is a Jack Daniel's; and a Blue Ribbon to chase it down with."

"Life can't be that bad," said Karen, tugging down her pink angora-wool cardigan so that she showed even more cleavage, and a gold-plated necklace with her name on it.

"I don't know," Jack replied. "Maybe it can. I mean— supposing you just happened to run across something which was what you always wanted, even though you didn't know it, but you couldn't have it, at least not without losing everything?"

"That a riddle, or what?" Karen demanded.

"Well, kind of," admitted Jack.

Karen looked at him for a very long time, chewing bubble gum, saying nothing. At last she said, "You want to tell me what's wrong?"

"I'm not too sure that I can," said Jack. It had suddenly occurred to him that if he told Karen he wanted to sell Reed Muffler & Tire and open a country club, he would be pulling her job security out from under her feet like a cheap nylon hearth rug. She had Sherry to care for, after all; and all the men at Reed had families to support. Where would Mike Karpasian find a job—fifty-seven years old, with

slurred speech and a talent that stretched only as far as
fitting new mufflers on cars?

Maybe he was acting more selfish than he knew. He had
read about the male menopause in the *Reader's Digest*.
After years of sobriety and responsibility, middle-aged
men could unexpectedly break out like spoiled adolescents.
Chasing women, driving too fast. Dreaming dreams of
impossible grandeur, like running a country club.

But Karen said, "I've worked out the riddle. You've run
across something you've always wanted. Maybe you didn't
know that you wanted it—not before you ran across
it—but when you ran across it, you thought, this is it, this
is what I've always wanted."

Jack nodded, and then smiled.

"So what is it?" Karen wanted to know. "You're going to
keep me on tenterhooks?"

Jack thought for a moment, and then he said, "I went up
to Devil's Lake yesterday; just to check on my dad's
summerhouse. On the way back I crashed the wagon. Not
seriously. Sideswiped a tree, that's all. But when I got out
to check the damage, I found this incredible building."

Karen said nothing, but shifted her gum to the other side
of her mouth, which showed she was listening, and that she
was interested in what he was telling her.

"It's hard to tell you what it was like," Jack told her. "It
was huge, really huge, and old. But very grand, too. It
hadn't been lived in for years and years."

"And you wanted it," Karen put in, in the softest voice.

"Yes," he said. "I wanted it."

"I could tell you wanted it," she said. "You had that
same kind of hush in your voice that Cecil used to have
when he talked about the sixty-eight Barracuda
Notchback."

Jack gave her a wry grin. "Let me tell you something,
Karen, if I had this building, it could change my whole
life."

"But Maggie doesn't want you to buy it, am I right? But *why* doesn't she want you to buy it?"

"No reason. She just doesn't want me to buy it."

Karen said, "Uh-huh," and nodded her bouffant hairstyle up and down, and then said, "uh-huh." But then she said, "Pardon me for asking, but why exactly do *you* want to buy it?"

"I, uh—want to spread out, you know? Diversify, that's the word. I mean I got all my eggs in one basket, with RM and T. I'm thinking of going into hospitality, too."

"You want to open a hospital?"

"No, no, a hotel. A country club. Somewhere for people to hold conventions, you know, and play tennis, and swim, and have saunas. Somewhere elegant, do you understand what I'm saying, with fine food and fine wines."

"It sounds like heaven on earth," said Karen.

"Yes," said Jack. "It does, doesn't it? But Maggie is one hundred percent hostile. One hundred percent. She seems to think that running a country club is out of my league."

Karen watched him, and chewed. "So what are you going to do?" she said at last.

"I don't know," he confessed. He looked through the office window at a Riviera being lowered back to the oil-stained shop floor, at the silhouettes of his mechanics against the gray glare of a rainy day. That building had seduced him, all right. He could picture it now, standing abandoned in the drizzle.

Rescue me, it had begged him. *Make me grand again.*

And perhaps he recognized an echo from his own abandoned life, his own ambitions that had never come to be.

Karen said, "Let's get that drink, huh? You look like you could use it. Talk about the living dead."

They crossed West Good Hope Road together in the rain, Jack with his collar up, Karen click-clacking in her ridiculously high stiletto heels.

"Take me to see it!" Karen shouted as a truck drizzled past them.

"What?" he shouted back.

"The building! Take me to see it!"

He sat in the office most of the afternoon, calling realtors in Madison, before he discovered who was managing the building. None of them was helpful. As soon as he explained which building he was interested in, they said, "Oh, *that* building," as if he had mentioned some reprobate relative whose portrait had long been turned to the wall.

"Yes, *that* building," he told a brittle-sounding woman at Capitol Realtors. She asked him to hold; and after he had held for nearly three minutes, listening to a scratchy looped tape of the "Post Horn Gallop," she came back to say that ye-e-e-es, the building *was* managed by Capitol, in a manner of speaking, but that he would have to make an appointment to see Mr. Daniel Bufo.

"All right, that's terrific. I'll make an appointment to see Mr. Daniel Bufo."

He was home early that evening, with flowers. They looked too much like those hastily selected flowers that husbands buy for their wives to say sorry, too much spriggy stuff and too many hothouse roses. Maggie came in through the door and stood under that unflattering hall light and watched them for a moment as if she expected them to wilt in front of her eyes. Then she hung up her myrtle-colored beret and the knitted coat that Jack always called her mujahedin outfit, and walked briskly through to the kitchen, leaving the flowers where they were.

"Flowers," said Jack, nodding toward the hall.

She gave him a tight smile. "You didn't start supper?"

He glanced toward Randy, who was sitting on one of the kitchen stools, watching TV. "Randy had a bowl of Lucky Charms. I didn't know what time you were going to be back."

"The women's group finishes at six-thirty, you know that. You didn't even bring home a pizza?"

"I'm sorry. I thought maybe we could go out to eat. Maybe Schneider's, huh? Sausage, sauerkraut? *Deutschland über alles?* Nothing like filling up the ethnic batteries." The truth was that he hadn't thought about eating at all. He had been too preoccupied with the Merrimac Court Country Club, and his appointment to meet Mr. Daniel Bufo tomorrow at eleven o'clock. He had already doodled an elaborate letterhead for the country club—the letter *M* for Merrimac, with the spires of the country club rising up behind it.

"You booked a baby-sitter?" Maggie wanted to know. Green eyes expressionless, waiting. Randy turned around and saw that she was back, but didn't say anything. He knew that there was a row to be gotten over first, before he became a priority. He glanced at his father expectantly.

"Well . . . I didn't make any solid arrangements," Jack admitted.

"You planned to take me out to Schneider's but you didn't make any solid arrangements?"

"I thought maybe that Randy could come along."

Maggie's voice took on that terrible patronizing flatness that always brought him to the brink of fury. "He's wearing his pajamas, Jack. He has school tomorrow. You're going to take him to Schneider's?"

"What the hell?" Jack retorted. "I mean, what the hell? He's nine years old, he can come to Schneider's."

"Jack, he has *school.*"

"He can skip school."

"Jack," she said, "you're crazy."

He nearly said *Yes, I'm crazy*, and swept his beer glass off the counter, and slapped her face, but instead he lowered his head and breathed deeply and didn't allow that alternative scenario to happen.

Randy looked at his mother, then at his father. Expectant, but not afraid.

After a long while Maggie said, "All right," as if she hadn't cared about any of this argument anyway. "But if he skips school, you're going to have to take care of him. And you're going to have to write him a letter for his teacher."

"I'll do it, for Christ's sake," Jack assured her. "You want a note, I'll write you a note. For Christ's sake."

"You've been drinking," Maggie reprimanded him.

He covered his eyes with his hand, as if he were tired, and the light were too bright for him. *But let's face up to it, Jack, you're hoping that when you open your eyes again, everything's going to be different. Maggie will be smiling; and Randy will be happy; and none of this bitchiness will ever have happened.*

Maggie said, "Well . . . if we're really going to Schneider's, I'd better freshen up. Randy—go get yourself changed. And wear something respectable, for God's sake. Not your Alf T-shirt."

Randy switched off the television and ran to his bedroom to change. Jack looked at Maggie and Maggie looked at Jack.

"You know something?" said Jack. "We're not such a bad couple, you and me. We're not ill-suited. We go off at tangents, that's all. Kind of *miss* each other, if you know what I mean."

"That's your opinion, is it?" asked Maggie. He couldn't see anything in those clear green eyes that told him he might have won her over.

He nodded. He couldn't think of anything else to say. Maggie stood looking at him for a moment or two, and then went off to the bedroom to freshen up. He heard her turn the key in the door.

Jesus, he said to himself, *this marriage is over. Dead and buried. I should finish this beer and walk straight out of the door and never come back.*

But then Randy came in, wearing his new Levi's jeans and his bright red turtleneck sweater, and he was all smiles and ready to go to Schneider's. Jack held out his arms for him and clutched him tight, and smelled that hot biscuity smell of boy, and cursed God for making fathers love their sons.

It was raining hard when they reached the sloping turnoff a mile past Lodi. Sure enough, Mr. Daniel Bufo was waiting for them, in his saddle brown Sedan de Ville. Jack pulled up behind him and turned off the engine. He let down the station wagon's window a couple of inches, because the windshield was misting up. The rain was pattering noisily in the roadside laurels and drumming unevenly on the roof of the car. There was a moment's pause, and then the Sedan de Ville's door was thrust open wide, and a huge figure in a gray plastic raincoat and a gray plastic rain hat reared out of it and came lumbering toward them.

"Oh my God?" said Karen. "It's Moby Dick."

Daniel Bufo reached their car and thrust his dripping face close to Jack's open window.

"Mr. Reed? How's life treating you? And Mrs. Reed? Good to meet you, ma'am."

Karen crossed and recrossed her legs, and tugged down the hem of her miniskirt, and uttered a peculiar high-pitched laugh.

"And who do we have in the back there?" asked Daniel Bufo. "Is that the smallest Reed?"

"That's Randy," said Jack.

Daniel Bufo wiped his face with the back of his hand. "Randy, hey? Once had a dog called Randy. No offense meant. Terrific dog. Swear he would've *talked,* that dog, if he would've stopped eating long enough." Jack saw pudgy fingers, thick gold rings.

"You folks follow me down the hill, off to the left. Easy turning to miss, so take it slow."

He returned to his car, and then they started up their engines and cautiously descended the winding road between the trees. It was so dark sometimes, under the trees, that Jack's station wagon automatically switched its own lights on. It was hard to believe that it was only eleven o'clock in the morning.

Protruding branches squeaked and scraped at the station wagon's sides. Then the road widened a little, and Jack could distinguish black iron gates, chained and padlocked. Daniel Bufo stopped his car, heaved himself out of it, and went across to the gates to unlock them. Before he heaved himself back into the driver's seat, he gave Jack an A-okay sign.

They drove up a long avenue of overhanging trees. Karen said, "It's kind of *gloomy,* isn't it?"

"Hasn't been cared for since God knows when," Jack replied, his mouth dry with anticipation. "If these trees were cut back, and the grass mowed."

The avenue seemed to go on and on, for at least a mile. Then, without warning, the building appeared, even larger and more imposing than Jack had remembered it, and in some inexplicable way more *surly,* almost as if it somehow resented Jack bringing more people to disturb it. Karen said, "It's fan-*tas*-tic," but Randy sat back in his seat, his eyes wide, as if he didn't like the look of it at all.

They parked outside the main entrance, and Daniel Bufo climbed puffing up to the doors and searched noisily through a bunch of keys that would have done justice to Jacob Marley. "This is a fine historic building; truly fine; they just don't make 'em this way anymore. Can't find the craftsmen."

"So, how long has it been empty?" Jack asked him. He had asked him already, over the telephone, but Daniel Bufo's response had been inconclusive. "Awhile," he had answered. "Maybe somebody else knows for sure."

Daniel Bufo found the right key and held it up. It was unlike any key that Jack had ever seen before—more like one of those wavy Balinese daggers than a key. "Don't make keys like this, neither. Is that a key or is that a key?"

"What do you think, twenty years, thirty years?" Jack persisted.

Daniel Bufo shrugged. "Well, my partner says that it was built just before the turn of the century. Used to be a private house, first of all, 'built by Adolf Krüger who founded Krüger Beer. Seems like he sold it just after World War One, and after that it was converted into a nursing home."

He turned the key in the doors and eased them open. They didn't creak, or judder. Their hinges moved as noiselessly as if they were new.

As he walked in, Randy looked up at the blind bas-relief faces and asked in a whisper, "Why do they all have their eyes closed?"

Daniel Bufo glanced up and then shook his head so that his jowls wobbled. "Your guess is as good as mine, my friend."

"They look like those kind of masks," put in Karen. "You know when somebody's dead and you make like a mold of their face."

"Death masks," said Jack.

"That's it, death masks. Creepy, isn't it? I mean, what if they *are*? A whole building covered with the faces of real live dead people."

They entered the huge echoing hallway where the ivory-colored statues stood. The building was utterly silent except for the scuffing of their shoes on the floor. Randy held his father's hand, and Karen gave a nervous little shiver.

"Well, cozy it ain't," she remarked.

"Mr. Reed, from what you told me on the telephone, you've been toying with the notion of converting these premises into some kind of a—what was it?—resort hotel?" said Daniel Bufo, looking around.

"That's right." Jack was standing still, listening. *Listening for what?* he asked himself. *Listening for whispers? Listening for rainwater running in? Or listening for that same sssshhhing noise that had pursued him down the stairs?*

"This property has all the potential, in that case," said Daniel Bufo. "Very generous reception rooms; very impressive indeed. You can see it all now, can't you? Lights, people."

"All I can see is dust and trash," Karen put in.

"We-e-ell." Daniel Bufo laughed. "Mr. Reed quite plainly understands that it's going to take a little vision to set the place to rights, not to mention a considerable amount of finance. It's been standing empty since the twenties, that's what my partner told me. So none of us are under any illusions here—are we, Mr. Reed? You're going to need to rewire, replumb, refit, strip the roof, bring the building up to local and state and federal requirements. Who knows what else needs remodeling. This is the first time I've ever been here myself."

Jack looked around and cleared his throat. "Donald Trump did it. No reason why I can't."

Daniel Bufo glanced at Karen and pulled a cautious face. By now he had realized that Karen wasn't Jack's wife, so he was making no direct sales pitch to her. In any case, it was obvious that Jack had dreams about the place, and that he wanted it, no matter what. A buyer like Jack had to be treated gently.

Jack walked up to the statue that stood at the foot of the east staircase. A tall draped figure, with her eyes closed. *What have you witnessed?* he thought to himself. *What's been happening here, that you had to close your eyes for ever?*

"You were talking about Donald Trump," put in Daniel Bufo. "It's possible that the state of Wisconsin might allow you to hold this building free of property taxes, on account of the fact that you're remodeling a historic structure and creating new jobs for the local work force. For a limited period, anyway. That's the deal that Trump managed to squeeze out of New York. I mean, don't tell anybody in Madison that I suggested it, but—"

Jack nodded. Karen's stiletto heels clattered and echoed

on all sides, because she had worn down the heels to the metal tips. Randy turned around and around, staring up at the ceiling, and at the huge cobweb-draped lamp. He stopped because he began to feel giddy.

Daniel Bufo said, "What? You want to take a look around? Feel free. I'll just check out the cellar, see what kind of condition the utilities are in."

He shook out his huge yellowing blueprint of the basement and spread it on the hall table, while Randy began to climb the stairs and Jack and Karen circled the hall, hand in hand.

"Jack—are you really *serious* about buying this place?" Karen asked him, wrinkling up her nose. "It's so *old*. And so *cruddy*."

Jack ran his hand down the robes of the ivory marble statue, almost as if he expected to find out that they were linen. "It's going to take a whole lot of money, Karen; but think about it. Try to imagine what it's going to look like when it's finished. People are going to fly in here from all over the world. The Merrimac Court Country Club, *the* place to be."

"You think so?" She looked around the hallway and it was plain that she couldn't imagine it at all. She had lived in a trailer for most of her life; what she saw was what there was.

Jack grinned and nodded. "It's a dream come true, Karen. Believe me."

"What about Reed Muffler and Tire?" she asked him. "I mean you going to keep that on, or what? You're not going to close it down? I mean for *this*?"

"I don't know yet," he lied. "It's kind of early to come to any decisions like that. But I want this place, Karen, believe me. There's something about it."

"Your funeral," Karen replied, blatantly chewing Bubblicious.

* * *

Randy climbed up to the galleried landing and looked down, waving to his father but not calling out, because the hallway echoed too much, and he thought that the echoes were frightening, like other people shouting your own words back at you.

Jack waved back, and so did Karen. They looked very small from up here. Randy liked Karen. She was fun and she smelled nice and she always gave him bubble gum, but he couldn't quite understand what place she occupied in his father's life. His father behaved even more affectionately to Karen sometimes than he did to his mother. Randy had seen him kissing her once or twice. Yet that was as far as it went. His father came home every night and kissed his mother, too, and told her he loved her. Sometimes he *shouted* at her that he loved her. Randy couldn't quite work this out, but said nothing, because his father seemed to expect him to say nothing.

He peered down the long linoleum-floored corridors that led away from the landing to the far ends of the building, east and west. The corridors were dark, yet Randy thought that they were strangely enticing. He had never been enticed by the dark before. He usually found it frightening. He insisted every night that his father leave on the corridor light (although, mysteriously, it was always switched off by the morning). He approached the eastward corridor and peered down it for a long time. Then he said, "Hallo?"

No answer. But no echo, either. He called "Hallo?" a second time, and he didn't know why he expected anybody to answer, but somehow he was disappointed because nobody did.

He was turning away to go back down to the hallway when out of the edge of his eye he glimpsed a small grayish white figure, rushing away from him down the very far end of the corridor. He turned back, shocked; his heart beating *blompety, blompety, blompety.* It had gone now. But it had been a child, it had to be. A little girl, in a hood, and a rustling rain cape. He hadn't so much *heard* the rustle as *felt* it—*sssssshhhhh, sssssshhhhh, sssssshhhhhh* along the corridor.

"Dad," he called, but then he realized that he had whispered, rather than shouted out loud. "Dad," he repeated, but his voice was just as quiet.

He made his way cautiously along the corridor, his fingertips trailing along the walls and the doors on either side. The grayish white figure had disappeared from view, but he was quite confident that she was still there, waiting for him, somewhere in the darkness, and that there was nothing for him to be afraid of.

"Little girl?" he called. "Little girl?"

He passed one window after another. Each of the windows was barred by metal mesh. At last he reached the very end of the corridor and found himself on a landing. Another staircase rose to his left, dimly illuminated by a mesh-barred window. He could hear the rain whispering against the glass. He waited and listened. This time he didn't call hello. There were double doors in front of him. He tried to open them, but they were obviously locked. The little girl must have run up the staircase. He glanced quickly back along the corridor and then decided to follow her. She couldn't have gone far.

As he climbed he thought he could hear somebody singing, very far away.

> *"Lavender blue, dilly-dilly;*
> *Lavender green.*
> *Here I am king, dilly-dilly;*
> *You shall be queen."*

He had always liked that song, every since he was little. For some reason it had made him feel sad and happy at the same time. And somebody was singing it here! He reached the next landing. There was no sign of the little girl here, either, but he felt confident that she had climbed up higher, to the very top floor, and that he would find her there.

By the time he reached the attic floor, he was puffing. He stood with his arms by his sides, catching his breath. Then he looked around, blinking in the way that children blink when they mimic concerned adults.

"Now where are you?" he demanded.

He began to plod along the corridor, his red Keds squeaking on the linoleum floor. He tried to open one of the doors, then another, but they were both firmly locked. He could still hear somebody singing, *"Lavender blue, dilly-dilly . . . lavender green . . ."*

Halfway along the corridor he stopped. Ahead of him one of the doors was ajar. Only a little way, but enough to cast a shark's fin triangle of watery light onto the linoleum. He felt uncertain, but not afraid. He listened to the house and he felt that it was creaking and dripping all around him, like Noah's ark. He could hear himself breathing. He could hear his father's voice, echoing flatly along the corridors and up the stairs. And there, in front of him, was the half-open door, and the shark's fin triangle of light on the floor, and a feeling that *I'm here, Randy, we're here!*

Life happening at different speeds. Slowly pushing open the door. Slowly stepping inside. Blurry sound, unfocused vision. *I'm here, Randy! We're here!* A small room wallpapered with brown flowers; an iron-framed bed, painted cream, with a sagging mattress, stained by countless nights of helpless incontinence. A tilted picture on the wall, *Susanna and the Elders,* by Thomas Hart Benton, plucked eyebrows, curved breasts, cleft vagina, and men looking. *Randy! I'm here, Randy!*

He turned his eyes. He looked at the wall. Halfway up it, in the dim sloping morning light, he saw that the wallpaper was raised in the shape of a man's face—almost as if the decorators had papered over him, with brown flowers. The man's eyes were closed, but he was smiling. He looked friendly, in a way that you couldn't quite trust, like one of those practical jokers who whipped your chair away just when you were sitting down.

Randy stared at him, shivering. He didn't know if he was a real man or not. But how could he be real, if he was papered over? You couldn't *breathe* if you were smothered in wallpaper, could you? And he wasn't moving, he wasn't real, he was totally still, a bas-relief in brown wallpaper.

Randy approached him across the linoleum floor. The linoleum was streaky green, with square black-and-white patterns that looked like squinting cat's eyes. The man smiled and didn't move, but every detail of his face had been captured in wallpaper: his eyelids, his lips, the cleft in his chin. Randy stared at him and didn't know what to do.

Are you afreet, Randy? You don't have to be afreet.

"Are you real?" he asked, his voice high-pitched with fear.

There was no reply. Randy stood and stared at the man's face and didn't know what to do next. He couldn't be real, could he? Yet he seemed to be breathing. You couldn't actually *catch* him breathing, yet he obviously was; you could hear it, sense it. In, out, in, out. Tight, suppressed respiration, like somebody hiding in a closet, in a threatening game of sardines.

"You're not real!" he cried, out loud. "You can't be!"

What do you call real, Randy? Do you think you're real, standing out there in the cold?

Randy bit his lip. He was right on the point of flying out of the room and running back downstairs. But although the man in the wallpaper was strange, he somehow wasn't threatening. There was something childlike about him, like that loopy boy George who worked for old man Hamner at the corner store.

"Can you talk?" Randy asked him. He took one cautious step closer. "Can you open your eyes?"

No need to open my eyes, Randy. None so blind as won't see.

"Who are you?" Randy asked him. "How come your face is in the wall?"

Name's Lester. Well, sometimes it's Lester. Other times it's Belphegor. That's a name, isn't it? Belphegor.

"How come your face is in the wall?"

How come you're here at all, Randy? It's Randy, isn't it? I heard your daddy calling you Randy.

"My father wants to buy this building and make it into a hotel."

He does? Well, there's a few people going to be pleased about that. Some that aren't; some that like things the way they are. But a few that will be.

"I don't know. I don't like this place. It's kind of old and smelly."

Well, maybe. But if you came to live here, you'd have dozens of new friends.

"This is way out in the country," said Randy. "Who lives out here?"

We do. All of us. And we could be your friends. And I could be your very special friend.

Randy hesitated. He could hear his father's footsteps, coming up the staircase, followed by the tappety-tapping of Karen's worn-down heels.

"I have to go now," he told the face.

Come here, come closer, the face asked him.

"I don't think so."

Come closer. You want to be friends?

"Sure, but—"

Come closer.

Randy stepped up close to the wall and lightly laid his hand on it, just below the face. The face said, *You like mysteries, Randy? You like magic? You like naked women?*

Randy didn't know what to say to that.

The face smiled a slow, secretive smile. *I can show you mysteries, Randy. I can show you magic like you never dreamed of. I can show you naked women, too.*

Randy shivered; he didn't know why.

Jack's voice came echoing along the corridor. "Randy? You there? Randy, where the hell are you?"

You want to see those things, you come back here Randy, you come back to this room, and you talk to me. But don't you tell nobody you saw me. Don't you tell nobody at all. Not your daddy, not your mommy, nobody. And especially nobody else that's in the wall.

"Randy!" Jack shouted, much more sharply this time.

"What do you mean, nobody else that's in the wall?" Randy asked hurriedly.

Word to the wise. Some of them aren't as friendly as me. Some of them are downright mean. Some of them are downright dangerous. Should have been kept under lock and key.

At that moment Jack pushed the door wide open and said loudly, "Randy? Are you in there?" The face that called itself Lester melted from sight as if it had been made out of jelly; and by the time Jack had stepped into the room and caught sight of Randy, the wallpaper was smooth again, utterly smooth.

"Can't you answer when I call you?" Jack demanded. "I've been looking for you all over."

There was a faint *sssssshhhhhhhh—sssssshhhhhhh—* along the skirting board. Jack laid his hand on Randy's shoulder and frowned and said, "Listen!"

Randy looked up expectantly.

"Did you hear that?" asked Jack. "Kind of a shushing sound."

Daniel Bufo had caught up with them, crepe soles squelching on the linoleum floor. "Rats, probably," he remarked, wiping the back of his neck with his handkerchief.

"Well, could be squirrels," said Jack.

Daniel Bufo glanced around the room and wrinkled up his nose. "Sure could use some cleaning-up around here."

They left the room. Randy turned when he reached the door and looked back at the brown-flowered wall. He didn't know whether he ought to tell his daddy about Lester or not. It sounded crazy when he thought about it. And his daddy would make such a fuss—feeling the walls, first, and when he couldn't find anything, feeling Randy's forehead, and asking him if he were feverish. And how could he explain about the naked women? His father wouldn't let him see any naked women, that was for sure.

He decided to keep quiet; for the time being anyway. Maybe they would never come back here. And Lester had asked him not to tell anybody. *Word to the wise. Some of them are downright mean. Some of them are downright dangerous.*

"I'm going to hear from you, then?" asked Daniel Bufo.

"Sure, you'll hear," Jack agreed. They were standing outside in the rain, while Karen and Randy waited in the car. Karen was fixing her lipstick in the rear view mirror; Randy was drawing patterns with his finger on the misted-up window.

"I talked to the present owners this morning," Daniel Bufo told him, wincing his eyes a little. "I have to tell you, they're what you might describe as reticent."

"You mean they're not keen on selling?"

"Hard to tell for sure. They're not given to straight replies, if you know what I mean. I said I had a party from Milwaukee who might be interested in coming to some kind of terms, and they didn't say nothing. Just 'hmmm,' and put down the phone."

"Just *hmmm*?" asked Jack.

Daniel Bufo leaned closer. There was a drip of rainwater swinging on the end of his nose, and his breath smelled of Hungarian salami and Binaca. "It might help if I could go back to them with some kind of a price."

"You mean, they don't have any particular price in mind?"

"I'm not too sure they have selling in mind, to tell you the truth."

"But they didn't tell you outright that they wouldn't sell?"

"No, sir. They said 'hmmm.'"

"Well," said Jack, "I was thinking in the region of five hundred, maybe five hundred and fifty."

Daniel Bufo made a face. "That's pitching it pretty low, Mr. Reed," he said, without much conviction. "There's seventeen acres of woodland here, as well as the building."

"Has anybody else made an offer?"

"No, sir."

"Well, that's my offer. Ask the owners, and see what they think about it. The worst they can say is 'hmmm.'"

"I guess so." Daniel Bufo took out his handkerchief and blew his nose. "It would be really something to move this building off our books, believe me. It's an office joke, you know? Whenever anybody complains about a property sticking, they say that it's almost as bad as The Oaks."

"That's the name of this building? The Oaks?"

"That was the name they gave it when it was a nursing home."

"The Oaks," Jack repeated. He stepped back and looked up at the building one more time, its dark rain-glistening spires. He couldn't work out why it appealed to him so much. But he had fallen in love with it, with its deteriorating elegance, and with its mystery. He turned toward the car, and Karen gave him a little finger wave. Randy had his nose squashed dolefully against the rear window. He was probably wishing now that he had gone to school.

"All right," said Jack, and shook Daniel Bufo by the hand. "You put my offer to the owners; then we'll see what we can do. By the way, can you tell me who the owners are?"

Daniel Bufo shook his head. "I'm sorry, Mr. Reed. I'd like to, believe me. But client confidentiality, you know how it is."

"It's not the Wise Guys?"

Daniel Bufo made a noise like somebody playing the

bagpipes and trying to laugh at the same time. "No, sir. It's not the Wise Guys."

Jack climbed into the car and banged the door. "How about a hamburger?" he suggested as he started up the engine.

"Whatever you like," said Karen, tugging at the hem of her skirt. "Will you look at my *hair*?"

They drove slowly down the avenue of dripping trees. Randy twisted around in his seat to watch the building being gradually eaten up by the black shadowy leaves. They had almost reached the gate when he saw the grayish white figure of the little girl, standing in between the tree trunks, waving to him. One arm lifted, waving.

The strange thing was, though, that her face was hooded, as if her head were fixed on backward. Either that, or she had no face at all.

T·H·R·E·E

*H*e came home three days later and Maggie was waiting for him in the sitting room, wearing her raincoat, her blue vinyl suitcase parked neatly beside her. He said, "What's this?" as if it weren't obvious.

Maggie said with well-rehearsed bravery, "I think they call it getting a breath of fresh air."

"Is that what they call it?" he retorted. "Aha, is that what they call it?" He had drunk one too many Blue Ribbons over at the Hunting Lodge. "That's funny. I call it running out on your husband."

"Jack——" she said, and when she looked up at him, he saw for the first time what all the arguments of their years of living together had done to her face. Or maybe it was just the unflattering ceiling light.

He said nothing. He looked around the room. It had no character at all, this room. Bland beige walls, sculptured shag-pile carpet in a color that was supposed to be honey but had turned out to be beige, too. Colorless paintings on the walls; a beige couch with brown-and-white flecks in it.

And sitting on the beige couch with brown-and-white flecks in it, a wife he didn't really love, with her suitcase packed.

She gave him her prepared speech, picking at her fingernails as she did so. "I've been trying very hard to understand you, Jack. I've been trying to understand what it is that you want out of your life, and to give it to you. To help you find it, anyway. But you don't seem to know what it is.

And if *you* don't know what it is, how can *I* help you find it? I feel as if I'm wasting all of my time and all of my precious energy, helping you to search for something that doesn't even exist."

He waited. Perhaps she expected an answer. He said, "Yes?"

"I'm not getting any younger," she said, with tears in her eyes. "I want to enjoy my life before I'm too old to enjoy it."

"*Ohhhh . . .*" said Jack. "I never realized! You want to *enjoy* your life! Why the hell didn't you tell me before? I wouldn't have made you wash my shirts, for Christ's sake, or cook my dinners, or clean my house! I wouldn't have given you Randy! I mean, you can't enjoy yourself with a kid around your neck, can you?"

"Randy's waiting in the car outside," said Maggie, standing up and picking up her suitcase.

"What do you mean? Whose car?"

"We're going to stay with my sister."

"Oh, God. The blessed Velma. Not to mention the blessed Herman."

"Jack, I have to get away from you. You're suffocating me. I don't want to leave you, not for good. I love you, but you're driving me mad. Ever since you found this building, you've been worse than ever. What do you ever talk about? How you're going to find the backing, how you're going to drain the swimming pool, how you're going to break the news to everybody down at the works that you're thinking of selling out, how you're going to clean the marble, how you're going to strip the roof. Jack, I can't *take* it anymore!"

Jack gripped her wrist. "Maggie—will you listen, for Christ's sake?"

"Velma's waiting."

"*Listen to me, for Christ's sake!*"

She snatched her arm away. "I've been listening to you for years, Jack. It wasn't good before and it's worse now. If

you want to build this—this resort hotel, or whatever you
call it—you go ahead and build it, but don't expect Randy
and me to have to suffer for it. Live your life! Go ahead! But
don't expect me to live it with you! You're too damned
miserable and you're too damned obsessed and you're too
damned *everything*! And you've been sleeping with Karen,
haven't you?"

"What?" Jack roared at her. *"What? You think I've been
sleeping with Karen?"*

"You're drunk," she said, tight-lipped. "I'm leaving. I
can't discuss anything if you're drunk. Good-bye, Jack."

He seized her sleeve and twisted her arm around. He
glared straight into her face and he felt that he could have
killed her, right at that moment.

"Let me go," she said. He could hear the fear in her
voice, and that made him angrier still.

"You think I've been sleeping with Karen?" he repeated,
with such softness and reason in his voice that he frightened her even more.

"Randy said—" She turned her face away. The very
thought of it made her flinch.

"Randy said what? Tell me, Randy said what?"

"Randy said you took Karen along with you to see the
building. Randy said—you kissed her."

Without a word Jack released Maggie's sleeve and lifted
both hands in a gesture of surrender, and backed away. He
didn't feel angry anymore. He was almost relieved that
Maggie had decided to leave. He hadn't slept with Karen,
and the chances were that he never would. He couldn't be
angry. It took guilt to stir up anger. Guilt, and frustration,
and distress; and he felt none of those things.

Instead, all he could think was: *If Maggie and Randy stay
with Velma for a while, I can concentrate all of my attention
on The Oaks. I can make this deal happen for real. And
when it's happened, and we actually open up, don't tell me
that Maggie won't be happy then. Don't tell me that she*

won't promenade along that veranda, Queen of the Merrimac Court Country Club, with the sun shining and the pool glittering and the guests all nodding their hellos.

Maggie said, "By the way, somebody called Bufo called you. He said they've accepted your offer, whoever they are."

"Daniel Bufo, he's the realtor," said Jack. "They've accepted it? That's what he said?"

Maggie opened the front door and stared at him for a moment. "God help you, Jack," she told him, and then she left, closing the door with commendable quietness. Jack stayed where he was. Then—when he heard Velma's Volkswagen pulling away from the curb outside—he went to the fridge and opened it and regarded its contents with the philosophical expression of a man who knows that he is probably going to have to eat out for quite a while.

After all, what can even the best chef create out of half a pack of Oscar Mayer bologna, five kumquats, an aerosol can of whipped cream, and some very old Roquefort? He was still gazing philosophically into the open refrigerator, however, when he heard the Volkswagen pulling up again. He closed the refrigerator but he didn't go to the door. He stood waiting in the kitchen while Maggie turned her key in the lock and came marching back in again. She was tugging Randy behind her with one hand and carrying his Rambo overnight bag in the other. Randy's eyelashes were glued together with tears. Maggie's face was taut and pale.

"He wants to stay with you," she announced, in a voice like somebody dropping an expensive wineglass onto a concrete patio.

Jack said nothing but turned to look at her.

"He says he likes the building and he's made a friend there; and he wants to stay."

Jack frowned at Randy. "Friend, what friend?"

Randy shrugged. "There was a sort of a man there, that's all."

Jack looked at Maggie. "What did Randy do, make a scene?"

"A scene? A cop came over and asked us to show our ID. He thought we might be—abducting him, for God's sake." Her nostrils flared.

Jack nodded. He didn't feel any sense of triumph. In fact, he would have preferred it if Maggie could have taken Randy with her. But he didn't want to fight, not now. He had begun to understand that part of his failure in life was his inability to cope with more than one thing at a time. He was capable of being a devoted husband, and an inspired lover, and a steadfast father. He was also capable of being a trustworthy employer and an imaginative real-estate developer. But he could only take on one of these tasks at a time. Trying to love his wife and bring up his son and console his workers and build for the future, all at once, that only confused him, and he ended up drinking too much with Karen and doing nothing at all.

This time Maggie slammed the door behind her so that the glass rattled. Randy stood awkwardly in the hallway with his hands by his sides. He was wearing a sweatshirt with the message "Experience Is What We Call Our Mistakes" printed on the front.

"How old are you?" Jack asked him. For the first time he saw Randy as another human being, as a person who was looking at him, the same way he was looking at Randy.

"Nine," said Randy. Unlike adults, children don't find it peculiar that you ask them questions to which you obviously know the answer. Teachers are always doing it.

"Nine," Jack repeated. "Jesus. If only I'd had your spunk when I was nine."

He picked up Randy's Rambo bag and unzipped it. Inside were pajamas, a clean pair of jeans, a red sweater and a T-shirt, and three pairs of carefully balled-up socks. "If you stay with me, you have to sort out your own socks, you got that?"

"Yes, sir."

"You want a chili dog?"

"I guess."

Under the fluorescent lights at Cap'n Dogg, their elbows ostentatiously propped on the Formica-topped table, with the jukebox playing bellbottomed-jeans-era music like "Salisbury Hill" and "Bummer in the Summer," they made a wonderful father-and-son mess of giant chili dogs and fries and pig's dinners to follow (nine flavors of ice cream swimming half-melted and khaki in a sundae dish).

"I feel sick," said Jack, swallowing the last of his beer.

"I don't," said Randy.

"You're nine, that's why you don't feel sick. Nobody of nine feels sick, not unless they eat adult food like squid, or escargots. Then they're sick."

"What's an escargot?"

"A snail. French for a snail. You bake them in their shells with garlic butter, right? And they're something special. Mm-hmm! You ought to try them!"

"Have you ever eaten them? Snails?"

"Not since I started subscribing to Greenpeace. I swore then that I'd never eat anything slower than myself."

Randy spooned up the last of his pig's dinner. Jack watched him, proud but uncertain. It wasn't easy, taking a son away from his mother. When you did that, you had to be gentler than usual; you had to be father and mother, and something else besides. Friend, spiritual counselor, and security blanket.

When Randy had finished, Jack leaned back in his seat and looked at him and smiled. "What friend?" he said at last.

Randy blushed.

"Come on," said Jack. "What friend? You know what I'm talking about. You told your mother you had a friend out at The Oaks. Now that was a whopper, if ever I heard one."

Randy said, "I'm not supposed to tell you."

"What do you mean you're not supposed to tell me?"

Randy said nothing for a very long time. The waitress came up and asked, "You folks through with all of this?" She had a very short skirt and very hitched-up breasts and black frizzy hair and a nose that you could have used to open a can of tomato juice. Jack wondered as she leaned in front of him to collect their dishes if anybody had ever made love to her, and if so what she had thought about it. There was such a gulf between picking up empty pig's dinner plates and reaching a sexual climax.

He suddenly realized that his frustration was showing. He sat up straight and tried hard to look disinterested and middle-aged.

"Are you really sick?" asked Randy. God curse children for their perception.

Jack shook his head. "I want to know what friend. And who says you're not supposed to tell me?"

"Lester," said Randy reluctantly.

"Lester? Who the hell is Lester?"

"Well sometimes his name's Lester and sometimes it's something like . . . Belfry."

Jack turned his ice-cream spoon over and over. "Randy—I want you to tell me the truth. This—what's-his-name—Lester, you made him up, right? You made him up so that your mom would allow you to stay with me?"

Randy shook his head. "I saw him."

"At The Oaks?"

Randy nodded. "He said I mustn't tell anybody. Not my mother or my father or anybody."

"Why not?"

"I don't know. Because. He said that I mustn't tell any other people, either, because they were mean, and danger-ous. He said that some of them should have been kept under lock and key."

A parental alarm bell rang in Jack's brain. It occurred to him that Randy could well be telling him the truth, or a half-distorted story that was partly the truth. Children of

Randy's age didn't naturally use phrases like "lock and key," not unless some adult had said it to them.

It was entirely possible that Randy *had* met somebody while they were visiting The Oaks. The building was big enough, and Randy had wandered off on his own. But who the hell was it? A squatter, maybe? Some kind of itinerant pervert? I mean, where do homosexuals and Hell's Angels and serial killers go, when it's raining?

That *sssshhhhhhing noise*—maybe that was him, maybe that was Lester, running along secret passages. A god-damned pervert called Lester, who had already wooed Randy with sweet-talking promises and peculiar threats.

And, Jesus H. Christ, who could tell what kind of black mischief somebody like that might have in mind?

"Randy," said Jack. "Are you sure about this? You saw a man there, back at The Oaks? This is serious, you wouldn't kid me?"

Randy nodded. "Cross my heart and hope to die."

"Well, you don't have to say that," Jack told him, laying a comforting hand on his arm. "But I think that you and me, we should pay The Oaks another visit. What do you think? A *surprise* visit, so that Lester doesn't know that we're coming."

"When?" asked Randy.

Jack checked his Rolex. It used to belong to his father; and it had always run slow. His father had said that it made him immortal, this watch; because whenever the time came for him to die, he would always have two minutes of life left.

"It's eight-thirty. If we head out that way now, we could be there by ten. Do you think you can stay awake?"

Randy lowered his head. "You won't tell Lester?"

"What - that you grassed on him? I'm your father, for God's sake. And that building belongs to me now. Well, almost. Daniel Bufo has accepted my offer; all I have to do now is string him along for a week or two while I sort out the finance; and we're home and dry. And *then* there'd better not be any Lester or Belfry or whatever you call him, lurking around that building. Then I have legal rights to clear him out."

Randy begged, "Do we *have* to go?"

Jack stripped off two dollar bills, folded them, and tucked them under his saucer. "There's one thing you have to learn, Randy, and that's to face up to whatever it is that frightens you. It might be rats, it might be dogs, it might be spiders. Right now you have to face up to Lester, whoever he is, and tell him no. And I'll be there, right beside you, to back you up."

"But he's—" Randy began.

"He's nothing that you and I can't handle," Jack interrupted.

"He's in the *wall,*" Randy finished miserably, and much too softly for Jack to hear.

Heading west, Jack suddenly changed his mind and swung north on Seventy-sixth Street, and up toward West Good Hope Road. The wipers dragged across the windshield with a rubbery juddering noise. It was raining too hard not to use them, but too sparsely to lubricate the glass. Ahead of them, the scarlet tail lights of other cars were reflected in the wet blacktop like exhaust flames from Buck Rogers's rockets.

"Thought we'd take Karen," Jack explained, driving one-handed.

Randy nodded. There was nothing else he could do, after all. If they took Karen, that would mean that he would be relegated to sitting on his own in the backseat. He stared out of the window at the stores and the gas stations and the brightly lit intersections, and he missed his mother more than he could have explained; not without crying, anyway, and he didn't want to cry.

Jack pushed a tape into the tape deck. The Eagles, singing "Hotel California."

They reached Karen's house. It was right on the corner

of a side street, two blocks north of West Good Hope Road. It was small and scruffy, painted pea green, with a huge TV antenna, more like a shack than a house. A child's tricycle stood abandoned on the sidewalk. The only sign of life was the television, flickering against the drapes. Jack said, "Hold on, ace. I won't be a second." Randy sat and waited. The rain poured steadily and insistently onto the windshield, so that he couldn't see. He didn't think that he had ever felt so miserable in his whole life.

After ten minutes his father appeared on the porch arm in arm with Karen. They scuttled quickly toward the car so that they wouldn't get wet. Without being told, Randy unbuckled his seat belt and climbed over to the backseat. His father didn't even seem to have noticed. Karen jumped into the car with a little high-pitched squeal and said, "My hair!"

"You're hair's fine," Jack reassured her, starting up the car.

Karen buckled up and then turned around in her seat. "Hi, Randy! Late-night adventure, huh?"

Randy nodded without answering. Jack said, "He's tired. Not surprised, the way things have been." He steered the station wagon back south, toward 94. "If I'd known the way that his mother felt. If she'd only *told* me. You know, *communicated*."

"Well, some women just can't do that," said Karen, crossing her legs in her black fishnet tights. Her gold hoop earrings reflected the light from the street lamps, one orange curve after the other. "My sister was like that, she could never communicate."

Jack glanced in his rearview mirror. "Trouble is, running a country club, that needs communication, twenty-four hours a day. You know, *response*. People come to a place like that to be pampered, you know what I mean? It's just the same when they come for a muffler. They don't want to hear maybe, or wait, or come back Tuesday. They want the right muffler and they want it now."

Karen licked her lips so that they shone. "You don't think that you-know-who could hack it?"

Jack shrugged. "I'm not putting her down. Believe me, I'm not putting her down."

They turned onto 94 and headed west through the rain. Waukesha, Oconomonoc, Johnson Corner, the signposts swam by like signposts in an extended dream. Randy lay down on the backseat and closed his eyes, listening to the whishing of the tires on the surface of the highway, and the rubbery scraping of the windshield wipers, and the *fluff-fluffing* of the wind through the dented tailgate, where Jack had collided with the tree.

Jack was tired, too, but he felt determined, as if he were doing something positive for a change. If there was somebody squatting at The Oaks, some kind of sex pervert or whatever, he was going to roust him out and give him the hiding of his life. He was going to start taking control of his life, and everything around him. Maybe Maggie didn't care for him; but Karen did; and Randy did, too. We weren't talking mufflers and tires anymore; we were talking real-estate development, and stock-market quotations. Goddamn it, we were talking *power*.

Before he reached Madison, he turned north-eastwards; and twenty miles farther on he took a left to Lodi. The headlights jiggled through the rain; the tires blurted through roadside puddles.

At last they arrived outside the iron gates, and Jack parked close beside them. He opened the car door. The rain was nothing but a faint soft prickle now. He hefted the padlock in his hand. It was too big for him to force open; and in any case it was probably better if they approached the building on foot. That way, they could check if there was anybody squatting there without being detected.

Out here in the wet Wisconsin woods, miles from anywhere, the idea of flushing out a social misfit from a dark and abandoned building didn't seem like such an appealing idea. It hadn't occurred to him before, but maybe this Lester was armed. Jack had pictured him as a sniffling, creeping homo; but supposing he was six-one and built like Arnold Schwarzenegger, with a hand grenade dangling from each lapel, and one of those sawback knives that commandos used to cut their own gangrenous feet off?

Karen came around the car and stood beside him, shivering in her short scarlet raincoat. "Are you really going in?"

He cleared his throat. "Sure I'm really going in. Do you want to wait out here?"

"Are you kidding me? I'm not sitting out here all on my own."

"I'm just kind of debating whether it's really worth it."

He curved his arm around Karen's shoulders. She kissed his cheek. He turned his face and kissed her on the lips. She tasted of Peach Surprise lipstick and salt. He felt her heavy breast through her raincoat pressing against his arm and he realized how much he wanted her. Well, *needed* her, anyway.

"Hey, whoa," she said, and twisted away. Randy had woken up. He had switched on the station wagon's interior light and was sitting with his hair sticking up at the back like Alfalfa, watching them with pale-faced solemnity.

"Karen, uh—why don't you just wait here?" Jack suggested. "I'll take a flashlight, okay, and take a quick scout around."

"No way," Karen told him. "Wherever you go, I go."

Randy climbed out of the car, too. Jack said, "Hey, ace, close the door quietly. We don't want to let them know we're coming."

Randy said, "I'm thirsty."

"Well, listen, we'll just take a look around to see if there's anybody here, and then we'll find ourselves someplace to have a drink, okay?"

"Okay." Randy nodded.

Jack squeezed his shoulder. "Okay, then. Let's go. But any sign of anybody, and we back off, you understand that?"

Jack collected his flashlight from the glove compartment; and then they squeezed one by one through the gap in the hedge next to the gate. They walked Indian file up the shadowy avenue of trees. Their feet scrunched on the gravel. Karen was wearing high-heeled shoes, and twice she almost lost her balance, so Jack waited for her to catch up with him and then took hold of her arm. Randy plodded along behind them, with the collar of his windbreaker turned up. He kept glancing toward the trees where he had seen the little girl with no face. He very much didn't want to see her again.

Jack's flashlight darted this way and that, mainly illuminating the gravel in front of Karen's feet so that she could see where she was walking.

Gradually the silhouette of The Oaks came into view. Its spires and chimneys were outlined against the night sky like the complex pieces of some particularly difficult riddle. Jack had sobered up now, completely sobered up, and he was sharply regretting that he had brought them out here at all. They could be back home watching "The Cosby Show" and sharing a bowl of fresh homemade popcorn, instead of sneaking through the night ruining their shoes.

They walked around the back of the building, toward the conservatory. Karen looked up at the rain-slicked rooftops and the corroded railings and snuggled herself close to Jack's shoulder. "Is this place ever spooky. I mean, God. I've seen some spooky places."

They reached the conservatory door. It was closed; Daniel Bufo must have closed it. Maybe he had locked it, too. Jack found himself wishing that he had. It looked very dark inside, as black as an old-fashioned photographer's hood; and supposing Lester had already seen them coming, and was waiting for them?

The strange thing was, though, that even though the

building was frightening, Jack found it alluring as well. It was decrepit, and it was claustrophobic, but for the past four days he hadn't been able to think about anything else; and now that he was back here, he felt just as excited as he had when he had first seen it. Approaching the conservatory door was like walking right up to the edge of a fifteen-story office building, and looking down at the street below, and being gripped by an irrational urge to jump. Or picking up a razor-sharp kitchen knife, and wondering what it would be like to slice it across his own tongue.

As he took hold of the door handle he realized that he hadn't come out here to look for a squatter called Lester; not really. He had come out here because he simply couldn't keep away.

He turned the handle. With a small off-key complaint, the door swung open.

Welcome back, Jack.

He took a deep breath, and he could smell that distinctive sour odor of vinegar, mingled with dust and damp. It was unpleasant, but strangely appetizing, like pickled herring. He probed the conservatory with his flashlight, but all he could see was broken glass and overturned pots.

Randy and Karen were holding back. Jack turned around to them and said, "So far so good. You coming in?"

He stepped inside, crossed the conservatory, and entered the lounge. Randy and Karen cautiously followed him. Karen said, "Would you turn the flashlight this way? I can't see a darned thing."

They reached the hallway where the two blind statues stood. Jack flicked the flashlight beam up toward the ceiling. It caught the lantern momentarily and whitened its shroud of cobwebs, and for a split second it looked as if some huge translucent spidery skeleton were crouched in the bottom of the dusty glass.

Jack listened. "Can't hear anything," he remarked.

Karen opened her pocketbook and took out a pack of lemon-flavored Bubblicious. She gave one piece to Randy and unwrapped a piece herself. They stood in the huge darkened hallway listening to the dripping of the rain and the endless mastication of Karen's gum.

"Where did you say you met Lester?" asked Jack, shining his flashlight toward the left-hand staircase.

"Upstairs," Randy whispered. "Right up at the top."

"All right, then," said Jack. "Let's go up and say hello."

He mounted the stairs, with Karen and Randy reluctantly following him. Karen's high heels echoed and reechoed throughout the building. "This is what I call a wild-goose chase," said Karen, hitching up her skirt so that she could climb the stairs more easily. "I must be crazy, coming out on a night like this, to a place like this. You know that? I must be losing my marbles."

Randy said nothing. Now that they had actually arrived at The Oaks, he was desperately worried that Lester might turn nasty because he had told his father about him. And what about those other people, the ones who were mean and dangerous, and who should have been kept under lock and key?

They reached the landing. For a moment Randy thought he heard somebody singing,

> "*Lavender blue, dilly-dilly*
> *Lavender green.*
> *Here I am king, dilly-dilly;*
> *You shall be queen.*"

Jack stopped, his head inclined to one side, listening. "You hear that?" he asked Karen.

Karen said, "Jack, honey, you're imagining things."

But Randy said, "I heard something. Singing."

"Me too." Jack nodded. He began to walk slowly along the east corridor, trying all the door handles, even though he knew from before that all of them were locked. From time to time he leveled his flashlight through one of the spyholes and peered inside.

"There's somebody here," he said softly. "I'm sure of it."

"Well, *who?*" Karen wanted to know. "And where are they?" But all the same, she came *trippety-tripping* to catch up to Jack and take hold of his arm. "You know I truly hate this place. It's just like the hospital where my grandmother died."

But Jack kept on walking along the corridor, shaking the door handles, peering into the spyholes, faster and faster. He could *sense* that there was somebody here. The whole building seemed to be alive, like a building in an earthquake. There was a deep resonance within the building's walls, a dark rumbling excitement. A sensation of anticipation so strong that he could *breathe* it.

"Daddy!" screamed Randy; and Jack swung his flashlight down to the very end of the corridor. He was just in time to catch a glimpse of a grayish white coat, rushing toward the staircase.

Karen hadn't seen it. "What was that?" she cried, wide-eyed.

But Jack had already gripped hold of her hand and tugged her along the corridor at a breakneck run. Randy came behind them, panting with fear and effort.

They reached the foot of the staircase. Jack saw a flicker of grayish white, and then the child had fled upstairs. He was about to run up after it, but Karen pulled his sleeve and stopped him. "My shoes!" she complained, hopping on one leg and trying to take off her shoe. "I could never run in high heels."

"All right, all right." Jack held on to the banister rail and supported her while she took off her shoes. Randy stood beside them, trying to get his breath back.

"Have you seen that little child before?" he asked Randy.

Randy nodded. "I saw her upstairs, and I saw her in the garden outside when we were leaving. She waved to me, but she didn't have a face."

"Didn't have a *face?*" asked Karen, wrinkling up her nose. "What do you mean she didn't have a face?"

"I don't know. She was wearing a hood or something."

Jack said, "I saw exactly the same child. If it *is* a child. On the highway, first of all, that was the child I was telling you about, the one who made me crash."

"You mean the child who turned out to be a newspaper?" asked Karen.

Jack said, "That's right."

"And I suppose this isn't a newspaper, too? Or an owl? Or a rat, more likely?"

Jack looked at Randy and then shrugged. "Maybe you're right, maybe it's the same thing. Just a couple of sheets of newspaper."

"But it ran upstairs," Randy protested. "I saw it. It ran upstairs."

"Could have been a squirrel dragging a newspaper up to its nest," said Jack.

Randy stared at him in the light of the flashlight. Jack could see that Randy didn't believe him. A squirrel, dragging newspaper upstairs? But what the hell else could it be? Don't tell me some child lives here, rushing from floor to floor in a grayish white raincoat. Don't tell me it's a *ghost,* for Christ's sake.

Karen declared, "I want to go home. This place is giving me the creeps."

Jack took hold of her hand and squeezed it. Then he shone the flashlight up the stairs. "Come on, it can't be anything. Even if it *is* a child, are we afraid of a child?"

"Jack," said Karen, "if it's a child it won't be living here alone, will it? It'll be living here with its parents. Or one of its parents. Maybe this Lester creep."

Jack took the first step up the staircase. "Come on," he coaxed her. "There's nothing to be scared of. This is only an old building, that's all."

"Jack, *no,*" she said, trying to tug her hand free. "I'm frightened."

Jack tugged her hand again, but again she resisted. He turned to Randy. "How about you, Randy? You frightened?"

Randy swallowed. "No, sir," he said, in a thin, expressionless voice.

"There you are, then." Jack grinned. "Two to one we're not frightened. Motion carried. We're not frightened, so we press on."

"Jack—" Karen protested.

"What are you going to do?" he asked her. "Go back downstairs on your own, with no flashlight?"

She hesitated, and then she said, "Okay, okay. But I won't forget this. I never liked the dark. My daddy always used to shut me in the dark, and I used to scream and scream but he never came."

They climbed the next staircase; then the next; until they reached the attic floor. The vinegary smell was almost overwhelming, and there was an extraordinary trembling tension in the air. Jack directed the flashlight along the corridor. The beam reflected in crisscross patterns from doors to walls to ceiling.

"It was about halfway," said Randy. "It was the first door that was open."

Karen said, "If there's somebody there, Jack, I'm gone. I mean I'm out of here, flashlight or no flashlight."

He gripped her shoulder reassuringly. "Come on, Karen, everything's going to be fine." He felt breathless himself; but at the same time he felt compelled to carry on. If there was somebody there, he wanted to talk to him. He wanted to find out what he was doing here, and what he knew about the building. There were so many silent mysteries here. Why did all the sculptured faces have their eyes closed? Why were the windows barred? Why were all the doors locked?

And why had the whole building been abruptly vacated in June 1926, and left unsold and abandoned ever since?

The three of them walked along the corridor with Jack in

the lead. At last they reached the half-open door where Randy had encountered Lester. They stopped. Jack said, "In here?" and shone the flashlight into the room. It looked as if it were empty.

"Hallo?" he called. "Anybody there?"

"Oh *sure*," said Karen. "The Ghost of Christmas Yet to Come."

Jack reached out with his left hand and eased the door open a little. It swung back smoothly except for a little grittiness in the hinges. He waited. The room was silent. The rain whispered softly against the windows, *lavender blue, dilly-dilly, lavender green* . . . He stepped into the room, turned, took two quick steps backward in case Lester had been hiding behind the door, lanced his flashlight left and right.

"It's empty," he said with a smile. "Nobody's here and nobody's *been* here."

"How do you know that?" asked Karen.

"Oh, come on, think about it. Have you ever seen a squat? Trash everywhere: blankets, empty bottles, dirty diapers, camping stoves. This room hasn't been used for sixty years."

Randy stood in the doorway serious and wide-eyed, saying nothing. Jack hunkered down in front of him and ruffled his hair.

"Maybe Lester wasn't quite so real as you thought he was, huh?"

"Are you mad?" asked Randy.

Jack shook his head. "Of course I'm not mad. It's been quite an adventure, hasn't it? And, believe me, ace, I would much rather find nobody here than somebody."

Randy said, "I guess so." He looked almost disappointed. Perhaps he had imagined Lester after all. And the little girl with no face, waving through the trees.

Jack said, "Let's walk right along to the end, just to make sure."

Randy frowned around the room. "Can I wait here?"

"On your own? In the dark?"

"There's enough light."

"Well, what are you going to do here, all on your own?"

"Rest, that's all. My feet are tired."

As a demonstration that he meant what he said, he slid with his back down the wall until he was sitting on the floor. Jack looked at Karen. Karen said, "He'll be okay, won't he? He must be bushed. We'll only be gone for a minute."

"Well, okay," said Jack. "But you stay right where you are. No wandering off. Parts of the flooring are not as safe as they should be, okay, especially along the far end."

"Okay," Randy agreed. He clasped his knees in his hands and lowered his head on his knees and he looked so small and weary that Jack felt like a selfish stupid bludgeoning ogre for driving him out so far so late at night, when he should have been tucked up in bed.

"Listen," Jack told him. He pulled the Turd out of Randy's jacket pocket and snuggled it up to his cheek. "We won't be a minute. Waffle will look after you, and you can shout out if you want anything. I just want to make absolutely double sure that there's nobody here."

"Okay," Randy repeated, and yawned.

Keeping close together, Jack and Karen walked farther along the corridor. They jiggled every door handle and looked into every spyhole.

When they had almost reached the end, Karen said, "You don't really think that there's anybody here, do you? You'd have to be out of your tree to live in a place like this."

Jack said, "It doesn't look like it, does it? I guess 'Lester' was just a figment of Randy's imagination. Poor kid. Maggie's walking out—well, he's taken it pretty damn hard. Maybe 'Lester' was like some imaginary friend, somebody he could talk to, apart from me."

"Sure," said Karen. She looked back down the corridor.

"Breaking up is always toughest on the kids. I can remember how bad Sherrywine took it. She cried for a week, then she started stealing stuff from the Piggly-Wiggly."

She reached up unexpectedly and touched Jack's cheek. He flinched at first, not realizing what it was, but then she stroked it gently and touched his hair, and he turned his head sideways and kissed her wrist.

"How have you been taking it?" she asked him.

He kissed her wrist again. "I've been getting by."

"I don't know," she told him. Her eyes glistened in the darkness. "Sometimes getting by just isn't enough."

He gripped her wrist. Then he drew her awkwardly closer, hesitated for just a moment, and kissed her on the lips. It was a tentative kiss, to begin with, exploratory. But then she opened her lips wide and he pushed the tip of his tongue in between her teeth, and they kissed violently and hungrily.

"We shouldn't," Karen gasped. "Jack, we shouldn't." But she made no move to pull herself away from him; and she continued to kiss his lips and his face and his neck. "God, you don't know how long I've wanted you," she told him.

He fumbled at the buttons of her cardigan. The beam of the flashlight darted this way and that, picking out Karen's face, then the wall, then the ceiling, then the glossy black nylon of Karen's bra. Jack slipped his hand inside her cardigan and cupped her breast. She unbuttoned her cardigan even further and tugged it wide open. Then she pulled up her bra cup so that her breast was exposed. It felt warm and heavy in the palm of Jack's hand, the nipple crinkling in the cold of the night.

"Not here," she whispered. "We can't do it here."

Her short tight skirt had ridden up her thighs. Jack twisted it up even further, right up to her waist. Underneath she was wearing nothing but black fishnet tights. He ran his fingers tantalizingly around her thighs and she shivered, and nipped at his neck with her teeth. He caressed her between her legs. The swollen lips of her vulva bulged in diamond patterns through the fishnet. He slipped in his finger and she was slippery and hot and wet.

"Karen," he breathed. "Oh God, Karen."

It was then that they heard the noise drag past them. *Ssssshhhhhhh—sssshhhhh—ssssshhhh.* That slow, thick, cementlike sound.

They froze, both of them. Their breath fumed in the darkness.

"What was that?" said Karen.

"I don't know," Jack replied, still listening, still alert. His hard-on curled up; he drew his finger out of Karen's vagina.

"Randy?" he called. Then, louder, "Randy?"

There was no reply. He waited, listened. Then he shouted, *"Randy!"*

"Oh my God," said Karen. "What's happened to him?"

Jack hurried back along the darkened corridor. Karen tugged down her skirt and pushed her breast back into her bra and came running after him.

"Randy! Are you there?" called Jack.

They reached the open doorway where Randy had been sitting. The room was empty. Jack shone the flashlight from side to side, into the corners, up to the ceiling. Brown flowered wallpaper, a mildewed reproduction of *Susanna and the Elders*. A bed stained with brown tide marks of incontinence. No Randy, anywhere.

"Randy!" Jack shouted down the corridor. His voice was flattened by the deadness of the air.

"He was bored, probably," Karen suggested. "He couldn't have gotten far."

"I told him to wait here," said Jack. "I told him to wait here and not to move. Jesus! He should have come with us!"

"Jack, you're not to blame."

"I don't know what the hell I was thinking about, letting him stay here by himself."

Karen reached out and held his sleeve. "Come on, Jack, you know what you were thinking about. And so was I."

Jack shouted out, "Randy! Randy! Can you hear me! Randy!"

He listened. There was no reply. All he could hear was the rain gurgling in the gutters, and the soft creaking of a building that had been neglected for sixty years. *Welcome back, Jack,* the building whispered.

"We'll have to go look for him," said Jack. "God almighty! How long were we gone? Two minutes, three? Didn't I tell him to sit there and wait and not to move? Didn't you hear me say that? *Randy!*"

They walked back along the corridor as far as the stairs. Jack felt cold and prickly, and he couldn't stop swallowing. Supposing Randy had been right, and there *was* a pervert roaming the building? He could have murdered Randy by now, and dragged his body away, and how could they ever find him?

Even if they did find him, it might already be too late. Randy could have been tortured, abused, strangled; and all the time Jack had been sticking his finger up his secretary. What was he going to tell the police? What was he going to tell Maggie?

They hurried down the stairs. Their footsteps clattered in the claustrophobic silence. Karen said breathlessly, "He's here someplace, Jack. He's just wandered off."

"Randy!" Jack shouted, and shone his flashlight down the third-story corridor. He waited, but again there was no reply.

"Do you know how many damn rooms there are in this building?" he asked Karen.

Karen said, "I'm sorry, Jack. It's my fault, too."

"Of course it's not your fault. I'm his father. I shouldn't have brought him out here. I shouldn't have come at all. I don't know what the hell—"

Far in the distance, like the muffled shout of a small child falling down a night-black well, he heard a voice cry "*ammyyooowwww*" and then die away again.

"Hear that?" he asked Karen.

"Something, I don't know. Maybe a cat."

"Cat? That was Randy. *Randy!*"

No answer. Jack ran along the third-story corridor until he reached the staircase at the other end. "Randy? Randy? Randy, it's Daddy!"

They spent two hours, searching every floor, rattling every door handle. The building had over a hundred rooms, and only the room in which they had left Randy was unlocked. There was no sign of Randy anywhere—not in the corridors, not in the kitchens, not on the second-floor landing.

At last they came down the stairs into the hallway. It was almost two o'clock in the morning, and Jack's flashlight was beginning to falter. Karen said, "I'm going to have to call Bessy, tell her I won't be back." Bessy was a waitress with thick ankles who had lodged with Karen ever since her divorce, and who baby-sat for Sherrywine whenever Karen wanted to go dancing or drinking.

"There's no phone," said Jack.

"There's a phone back at that gas station, at Lodi."

"So what do you think I'm going to do? You think I'm going to leave Randy here so that you can call your baby-sitter? Jesus, Karen, he might have been murdered!"

"He's not here, Jack! He's wandered off! We've been up and down these corridors a dozen times! He's probably gone back to the car to get some sleep. We haven't checked the car yet."

"We haven't checked the cellars, either."

Karen rubbed her arm stiffly. It was a gesture of suppressed nervousness. "Jack, I'm frightened," she admitted. "I mean supposing this Lester is *real*."

"It won't take us long to check the cellars."

"Jack, I *hate* cellars. I really hate them."

"Well, do you want to wait here?"

Karen looked around at the blind and silent statues standing at the foot of each flight of stairs. "Here? In the dark?"

"Wait outside, then."

Karen bit her lip. "No, I'll come with you. Just so long as that flashlight doesn't give out."

The door to the cellar was on the west side of the hallway. It was wider than most of the doors in the house, and it was paneled in faded oak. Jack tried the door handle, expecting that it would be locked, *hoping* that it would be locked, but it swung open easily. A damp chilly draft rose from the darkness, and Karen shivered.

"You *really* think he's down there?"

Jack shone his flashlight into the doorway, and the waning amber bulb illuminated a flight of stone steps and a plain oak handrail.

"Randy?" he called. His voice didn't echo at all. He might just as well have been shouting into a pillow. "Randy?"

"He wouldn't have gone down there," said Karen, gripping Jack's arm.

"He's nowhere else," Jack told her, straining his eyes.

"He must have gone back to the car. He wouldn't have gone down there."

"Karen, I'm sorry. I have to look."

Karen took a deep breath. "All right. I know you do. I'm sorry."

Keeping close together, they went through the cellar door and down the steps. By the faltering beam of his flashlight, Jack could see that the cellars were vast. They ran the entire length of the house, with arched ceilings of lime-washed brick, supported by massive brick pillars. Underneath the floor of the hallway stood an immense dinosaur of a Kenwood boiler, its brass pipes encrusted with green corrosion and its dials blinded by grime. The rest of the cellars were crowded with packing cases, coils of rope, dried-up cans of paint, faded brown wrapping paper, empty carboys marked "Pickling Vinegar," boxes of nails, crates filled with murky-looking bottles of linseed oil, sagging sofas, dismantled iron beds, soiled mattresses, bicycle wheels, and a collection of fifty or sixty heavy glass accumulator batteries.

No sign of Randy.

Karen said, "Call him. Call him again."

"Randy!" Jack shouted. "Randy! You down here anywhere?"

The flashlight brightened momentarily and then faded. There must have been a window open somewhere in the cellars, because the draft was damp and cold and smelled of rain. "He's not here," said Karen. "We'd better go look outside."

As he turned to go, however, Jack glimpsed something beige and lumpy on the cellar wall, close to the back of the boiler. At first he thought it was fungus; but when the flashlight brightened again, he saw that it was something oddly familiar.

"Wait," he said, and went cautiously down the rest of the cellar stairs and picked his way across the floor. He went right up to the excrescence on the wall and shone the flashlight on it.

"What is it?" asked Karen, her voice unsteady with anxiety.

Jack reached up and touched it. It was beige, and woolen, and shapeless. It had the texture of a waffle. The Turd, halfway up the wall, inextricably stuck.

"It's Randy's toy," Jack called back.

Slowly Karen came across the cellar to join him. She stood beside him and stared up at the Turd in bewilderment.

"What's it doing there?"

Jack tugged at it. The Turd wasn't just stuck, it was buried in the brick, as if its atoms had become intermingled with those of the wall.

"You ever see anything like that?" Jack asked Karen. "I can't get it out."

He tugged again. This time he ripped the Turd apart, and he was left with a handful of torn wool and kapok stuffing.

God, he thought, *Randy's going to kill me.*

"How did he *do* that?" Karen asked. "And, you know, *why?*"

Jack said, "More to the point, where is he?"

"Maybe we'd better come back when it's light," said Karen. "I mean, he could be anywhere. I sure can't see him down here."

Jack tore away the last fragments of wool that still hung from the brickwork. "I think we ought to call the police. The sooner they start looking, the better."

He shone the flashlight around the cellar. He lifted up some sheets of hardboard and shifted two or three crates. He prayed to God that he wouldn't find Randy lying dead. He moved a chaise with a collapsed seat, and he was just about to push aside some rolls of linoleum when he heard that noise again.

Sssssshhhhhhh—sssssshhhhhh—sssssssshhhhhhhhh dragging along the wall.

He stiffened, the skin at the back of his neck prickling. The noise went slowly along the entire length of the cellar, and then it started coming back again.

"Come on—I think maybe we're better off out of here," said Jack.

They retreated across the cellar floor, carefully at first. But the noise scraped nearer and nearer, faster and faster, like concrete being churned, like a body being dragged through gravel, thick and gritty but somehow *soft.* By the time they reached the stairs they were practically running.

"What is it?" Karen gasped, turning wildly around

"I'm not going to stop to find out," Jack panted back. "Come on, let's get out of here!"

They stumbled up the stairs. The noise was almost on

top of them now, as deafening as an oncoming locomotive.
Jack pushed Karen up ahead of him, gripping the wooden
handrail and heaving himself up three and four steps at a
time. They had almost reached the top of the stairs when
his flashlight died; and at the same moment, without any
warning, the cellar door swung shut.

They were immediately swallowed by blackness. Karen
screamed, *"No!"* And the noise came rushing up the
staircase after them *sshhakkkk-attakkka-shhhaaakkkk-
atttakkkka.*

Jack tripped on the top step and fell heavily against the
wall. As he did so he felt somebody gripping at his left
ankle. He thought it was Karen at first, trying to stop
herself from falling; but then his right ankle was gripped,
too, and he found himself being pulled back down the
stairs.

"Karen!" he yelled out. *"Karen, something's got me!"*

Big, powerful hands, wrenching him back. He snatched
at the handrail, but he couldn't get a firm hold on it before
he was pulled down four or five stairs, grazing his cheek
and sharply knocking his chin.

"Karen!" he yelled. And at that moment Karen reached
the cellar door and groped it open, so that the faintest of
lights washed down the cellar stairs.

Jack twisted and turned around, kicking at the hands
that gripped his ankles.

What he saw then made him shout out loud with terror.
The hands that were holding him were gray and dusty, the
color of concrete, and they rose directly out of the concrete
floor.

A little farther away, a *face* had emerged from the floor,
too. A man's face, with a heavy forehead and a strong jaw,
and a fixed triumphant grin. It looked as if it had been
smothered with dry cement. There were powdery wrinkles
and cracks around its mouth. Its eye sockets were totally
black—*black,* like night, no whites at all, as if the inside of

its head were empty. But it was alive, there was no question
about that. It had risen straight out of the concrete floor, in
the way that a swimmer emerges from the dust-covered
surface of a lake.

It was alive and it was grinning at him and it was gleefully
trying to drag him under the surface of the concrete, too.

F·O·U·R

*H*e believed for one long moment of panic that he was lost. The hands gripped him so tightly that his legs were almost numb. His left heel was pulled further and further down toward the floor, until at last it was pressed right up against the concrete. The pain was excruciatingly abrasive —like having his bare heel pressed against a spinning whetstone. He shouted and kicked and twisted, but the hands pulled him down yet again, until both heels were being dragged into the floor.

His fingers scrabbled for the wooden handrail. The first time he missed, but then he arched his back and managed to hook his fingertips around the lowest wall bracket that held the handrail in place. He stretched, and stretched again, and at last he managed to grip the handrail tightly.

Karen was screaming, *"Jack! Jack!"* but the pain in his feet was so raw that he could hardly hear her.

He kicked, and kicked, and kicked again. For an instant, the grip on his right ankle loosened. He twisted his right foot free and lashed out at the hand that was holding on to his left foot. The dusty gray face grinned even more wildly, as if it enjoyed the struggle, as if it were elated by sharing his pain. Then it opened its mouth wide and let out a sound that froze Jack to the backbone.

It was like the combined screams of three hundred people in a doomed airliner. It was like a subway train hurtling out of a tunnel. It was fear and rage and agony beyond all human understanding.

"*Jack!*" shrieked Karen, her voice scarcely audible over the deafening noise.

Lashing out with his right foot, Jack kicked himself free from the gripping hands. He rolled himself over and staggered back up the cellar stairs, sharply knocking his knee. Karen threw her arms around him and bustled him out of the cellar door. She was all ready to run straight out of the house, but Jack said, "Hold it, wait, hold it!" and slammed the cellar door shut, and turned the key.

"That ought to slow it down," he panted.

"But it came right out of the *floor!*" Karen squealed. "It came right out of the *floor!*"

Jack was trembling. He didn't know whether to stay where he was or to run. He wasn't sure that he *could* run, even if he wanted to. His whole body seemed to have lost its coordination. Karen stood a little way away from him, her arms clasped tightly over her breasts, staring at him in terror and uncertainty.

"Must have been what Randy was talking about," he said. He didn't even *sound* like himself. "You know, Lester."

"But how could it come out of the floor? How could it *do* that?"

Jack shook his head. "I don't know. I just don't know. But it pulled me in, too. At least it was trying to. I could feel it against my feet, I mean the pain of it. I never felt pain like that before. I mean it was actually trying to drag me down into the floor."

"That's *impossible,*" Karen declared.

"Sure. It's impossible! Logically and scientifically impossible! People can't walk through solid walls and people can't come—rising up through solid floors."

"What are we going to *do?*" asked Karen. "Do you think it got hold of Randy?"

Jack leaned back against the cellar door and squeezed his eyes shut. All he could see was that greenish gray face, the

color of cement. He didn't even want to think what it could
have done to Randy.

Karen said, "Jack, if it got hold of Randy—"

Jack opened his eyes. "I'm just going to pray that it
didn't. Do you know how *strong* that thing was? He
wouldn't have stood a chance."

"So what are we going to do?"

"I don't know. Call the police, I guess." He wished he
could stop trembling.

*Randy, my poor Randy! Pray God that thing didn't get
you; pray God you didn't suffer, if it did.*

After a moment Jack managed to calm himself down.
"Come on," he told Karen. He sniffed and cleared his
throat. "Let's go find that telephone. There's nothing more
that we can do on our own."

They crossed the hallway and went out through the
lounge to the conservatory. As they were weaving their way
between the reading tables in the lounge Jack thought that
he could hear that dragging noise again. *Sssssshhhhhh—
ssssssshhhhhh—sssssshhhhhh* along the wall.

"Listen," he said, and laid his hand on Karen's arm.
Karen stared at him, wide-eyed. The noise stopped, as if
somebody had been following them, and was waiting for
them to continue. Waiting, watching, with bated breath.

"Let's just get out of here," Karen urged.

"No, wait. Listen. Can you hear something?"

"I can't hear anything and I don't *want* to hear anything.
Oh God, Jack, I'm terrified."

But Jack stayed absolutely still. The rain dripped
through the broken panes of the conservatory and rustled
in the laurels in the darkened garden. But there was
another sound, soft and powdery, like dead plaster sifting
down behind age-stiffened wallpaper, like somebody hiding behind the curtains and not daring even to breathe.

Jack slowly, slowly turned around. The lounge was so
shadowy that it was almost impossible to make out any-

thing at all. Basketwork chairs, tipped-over tables. Magazine racks crammed with yellowed newspapers. But between the bookcase and the door, he thought he could distinguish a *lumpiness* on the cream-painted wall.

"*Jack,*" pleaded Karen. She was so frightened now that she was practically in shock.

But without a word, Jack took three or four steps slowly back toward the door, staring all the time at the lumpy outlines on the wall. He would have done anything for a flashlight.

"*Jack, please,*" Karen begged him.

"Do you have some matches?" Jack asked her. His mouth was so dry that he spoke in a whisper.

"Matches?"

"You know what I mean, matches. For lighting cigarettes with."

"I think I have some in my purse. But I left it in the car."

Jack took another step nearer the door. He didn't want to approach too close. His ankles were still sore from the hands that had seized him in the cellar.

Karen was fumbling in the pockets of her raincoat. "I have some book matches."

"That's fine, that's perfect." Jack reached behind him to take the matches without once glancing away from the wall. He opened the cover, bent the matches back, and struck all of them at once, with his thumb. They flared up brightly, and he lifted the matchbook and held it up as high as he could.

By the brief flickering light of the matches, he saw that the cream-painted wall had raised itself in bas-relief, into the shape of a naked young woman. She was large-hipped, large-breasted, with narrow shoulders and a rather Negroid-looking face. Her hair radiated out from her head like the rays of the sun.

"Oh my God," whispered Karen. "Oh my God, she's right inside the wall."

In fact it looked as if the wall were nothing more than a

thin sheet of glossy cream-painted rubber against which
the girl was pushing herself from the other side. Her
cream-painted eyes were open and she was staring at Jack
without moving, without breathing.

"Who are you?" he whispered. He didn't think that he
had ever been so frightened in his life.

The girl continued to stare at him, unblinking, saying
nothing.

"Who are you?" Jack repeated.

She was alive, there was no question about that. She was
alive and she was staring at him. But how could she be,
inside the wall?

Jack took two more hesitant steps forward. The flames
from the matchbook were almost gone.

"Who are you?" he shouted at the girl. *"Where's my
son?"*

The girl suddenly turned, with a faint *ssssshhhhhh*
sound. Jack jumped back in fright. But she didn't attempt
to grab him. She turned right around. He glimpsed her
naked back, and then the wall smoothed itself out and the
matchbook burned his fingers and she was gone.

He touched the wall with the flat of his hand. It was cold
and solid. He could even feel the brush marks from the
paint. A wall, that's all. He heard the *sssssshhhhhhh* sound
dying away.

"You saw that?" he asked Karen, his voice shaky.

"I saw it," she replied. "A girl, just standing there. Then
she disappeared."

Jack backed away from the wall and took hold of Karen's
hand. "What do you think, you think we've eaten something and gone crazy? Or maybe there's some kind of gas
leak around this building, something that gives people
hallucinations."

"I saw it," Karen insisted. "It was real. A real girl, just
standing there."

They left the lounge and walked out through the conservatory. Outside, on the gravel path, Jack checked his

watch. It was almost three o'clock. They stood in the rain for two or three minutes, breathing in the chilly night air. Jack looked up at the building's dark spires, his eyes half-closed against the raindrops, and he didn't know what he thought about it now, whether he still wanted it, or whether he dreaded it. He knew that he had to have Randy back, whatever happened. He felt so desperately unhappy and frightened for Randy that he was close to tears.

"Do you think they were ghosts?" asked Karen.

Jack wiped the rain from his face with his hand. "I don't know. Maybe. I never saw a ghost before, and I never knew anybody who did. Who's to say that they can't come sticking out of the walls? I mean, everybody says that they walk through walls, maybe that's how they do it."

Karen said, "The cops aren't going to believe us, you know. They're going to think we're totally crazy."

"But it's true, it happened, we saw it with our own eyes."

"Forget it," said Karen. "I had enough of cops when Cecil started to beat up on me. Most of the time they tried to make out that it was all my fault, because I provoked him. You should of seen the size of that man, and I provoked him? One cop told me that in his opinion I deserved everything that Cecil did to me, and if I'd been *his* wife, he would have given me a beating I wouldn't have forgotten."

"We have to tell them, Karen. If somebody's taken Randy, or if he's hidden around the building someplace, we'll never find him without the cops."

"So what are you going to tell them? That there's a man in the floor who tries to grab your feet, and a nude woman in the wall?"

"I'm going to tell them the truth."

"Jack—" Karen interrupted. "Think about it. Randy's missing and how come we took him out to this weird old building in the middle of the night?"

"We were looking for some vagrant called Lester, remember?"

"Oh, sure. Some squatter. But you saw for yourself that nobody was squatting here, didn't you? So how come we left Randy alone?"

Jack glanced at her quickly. "We don't have to tell the police about that."

"Of course not. But how come we left him alone?"

"He was tired, that's all. Come on, Karen, for Christ's sake, he's my son. I'm just hoping and praying he didn't go down to the cellar. The police are going to be able to see for themselves how bad I feel about it."

"Sure you feel bad about it, but feeling bad about it isn't going to help us any. The first thing the cops are going to think is that we took Randy out here to get rid of him. You had a bust-up with Maggie, you wanted to hurt her, you found yourself burdened with a kid you didn't want. You can fill in the rest for yourself."

"Except you're forgetting one thing," Jack interrupted her. "It isn't true."

"That never worried any of the cops that *I* ever met."

Jack ran his hand wearily through his wet hair. "Let's think about the cops later, okay? Right now we ought to take a look down by the swimming pool. Maybe he wandered down there."

"Jack . . . I'm sorry," said Karen. "Please, honey, don't be angry with me. I want to find Randy just as much as you do. But I know what it's like when you call in the cops. Everything gets turned on its ass. After a while you don't know yourself what you did and what you didn't do."

"Jesus, he could be anywhere," said Jack, more to the night than to Karen. The wet shining on his cheeks wasn't rain. "Let's take a look by the swimming pool, then we'll go back to the car."

Holding hands, they walked across the tennis courts toward the swimming pool. It was so dark that Jack had to run his hand along the top of the tennis net as a guide. The canvas was cold and wet and unpleasant to touch. They said nothing until they reached the edge of the pool. They

could just discern the surface of the water, circled and
circled by the falling rain. The water was black and
stagnant and stank of ammonia.

"You don't happen to have any more of those matches?"
asked Jack.

"About half a book," said Karen, fishing in her raincoat
pocket yet again. "I always pick them up, you know, out of
habit. I used to have a collection. You know what, I even
had one from William Holden's house. That was before he
got drunk and cracked his head and killed himself."

She produced the matchbook. The first match was too
damp, and the head simply mushed when Jack tried to
strike it. The second match flared damply, and he held it
up, peering through the smoke down to the water in the
bottom of the swimming pool.

"There's something in there," said Karen. "Look, over
there!"

Jack peered into the swiveling shadows, but the match
died away. He struck another, which wouldn't light, then
another. His last match burned just long enough for him to
see a dark humped shape lying in the water.

"You don't think it's Randy?" asked Karen, in a petrified
voice. "Maybe he saw that thing in the building and he was
really scared and ran down here and didn't realize the pool
was here."

Jack stood where he was, shaking with cold and indecision. "I saw something in the pool the very first time I was
here. It was just a shape, I don't know what it was. Maybe
that's the same thing. Maybe a tree stump or something
that somebody pushed in the water just for the hell of it."

"But what if it's Randy?" asked Karen.

Jack hesitated one moment longer. Then he quickly
unbuttoned his raincoat and stripped it off. He took off his
sport coat, his necktie, his shirt. The rain spattered across
his bare chest. He took off his shoes and socks, followed by
his pants and his shorts.

"Oh, Jack honey," Karen begged him. "Please be careful."

"Careful? Are you kidding?" he shivered. He took off his Rolex and gave it to her. "Don't drop it, it used to belong to my father."

He hurried naked to the far side of the pool, where the steps were. Karen said, "It was just about there . . . maybe eight or ten feet from where you're standing."

His teeth chattering uncontrollably, he climbed down the metal ladder until his foot touched the water. It was deadly cold, and smelled so strongly that he retched out loud. He peered down into the darkness. God alone knew what was lurking beneath the surface. He climbed down two rungs further, the water clinging around his calves like garters of cold steel. His testicles shrank so tightly that they almost disappeared inside his groin.

Still holding on to the ladder with one hand, he leaned out across the pool, scooping his fingers across the surface of the water, trying to feel the mysterious shape in the darkness.

"I think I can see it," said Karen. "It's about three feet away from you. You're going to have to swim for it."

He swallowed. Then he said, "All right, I'll give it a try."

He took one more step down on the ladder, but unexpectedly there were no more rungs, and he suddenly plunged straight down into the water, right over his head. He shouted out underwater, in a gargled rush of bubbles. He could feel soft bulky things bumping against him in the darkness, and he surged to the surface in fear and disgust and desperation.

"Ah!" he shouted out, sucking in air.

"Jack, are you okay?" Karen called out. "Jack!"

"Ah!" he repeated. "Ah! Ah! Shit, I'm drowning! Shit, this is disgusting!"

Karen said, "It's over there, I can see it. Look, just there; you're only a couple of feet away."

"I can't see a goddamned thing."

"There! Look, there!"

Stiffly Jack swam across to the place where Karen was pointing. The water clung to his bare skin, more like chilled jelly than water, and something slippery trailed between his legs, making him thrash around with revulsion.

At last his fingers touched something floating in the slime. Something covered with heavy-duty cotton, like Randy's windbreaker. Something that bobbed on the surface soft and lifeless, like a drowned boy.

Jack grabbed hold of it. Then, slowly, his arms stiffening with cramp, he swam back toward the side of the pool, pulling the sodden object after him.

Karen came around to help him. Shuddering with cold and disgust, he climbed up the ladder, and then heaved the object onto the tiles. It made a deep, squelching sound, followed by a steady soft dribbling of water.

It was a mail sack, not a boy; but it was quite heavy enough to contain the body of a boy. There was something inside it that was repellently soft and shapeless, and it stank so strongly of decay that Jack regurgitated a mouthful of acid-tasting lunch.

"It's not Randy," Karen whispered, her face white in the rainy darkness. "It can't be Randy."

"I'm going to put some clothes on," Jack told her. "Then we'll just have to open the bastard up and see what it is."

Karen said nothing, but handed Jack his clothes from underneath her raincoat. He was bone-cold, so cold that he could scarcely think, and his shirt and pants stuck wetly to his skin. But once he had tugged on his shoes and socks and buttoned up his coat, he began to feel warmer and a little less shocked.

"Okay, then." He sniffed, hunkering down beside the mail sack. "Let's find out what the hell we've got here."

With stiff fingers he unlaced the top of the sack and pulled it wide open.

"Oh, Jesus," he said. The stench of decayed flesh filled up his mouth and his nose with nauseating sweetness.

"I can't see," he choked. "I can't even see what it is."

He pressed his hand over his face and peered intently into the darkness of the opened sack. He could make out something glistening, but that was all. Karen stayed well away.

"Oh my God, it's something awful, whatever it is," she whispered.

Jack stood up. "You don't have any more matches?"

She shook her head. But then she said, "My key ring! Why didn't I think of that before? Look, I have a little flashlight on my key ring!"

She jangled her keys until she found the miniature flashlight, and pressed it. "Cecil bought it for me. It's always so dark on my porch, I could never find the keyhole."

Jack took the key ring and knelt down beside the mail sack again. He directed the beadlike beam on to it and tried to make sense of what he saw.

A tangle of grayish pink flesh, mottled here and there with the bright greens and blues of decay. A swath of brindled fur, an upraised leg with the bone rotted right through the skin. A dog of some kind, probably a German shepherd. Certainly not a boy.

It was when he probed the beam further into the depths of the sack, however, that he prickled with shock. There was only one body, but *two* half-rotted heads were staring at him; two muzzles; two sets of snaggled teeth; two blackish tongues. Four yellow eyes, veiled with mucus.

He switched off the flashlight abruptly and stood up. "A dog," he told Karen. "Somebody drowned their dog."

"How could anybody *do* that?" Karen shivered.

Jack couldn't answer for a moment. His mouth was swimming with bile and saliva. "It was kind of a freak. Guess it was kinder, in a way."

Karen took hold of his arm. "At least it's not Randy."

"Let's get back to the car," said Jack.

Karen glanced back at the mail sack. "What are you going to do about that?"

"I don't know. Leave it for now. What else can I do?"

But it was right then that a very powerful flashlight shone in their eyes, and a dry-sounding voice said, "You could throw it, mister, and mind your own business."

The flashlight jiggled dazzlingly closer. Jack lifted his hand in front of his eyes; but all he could see was a dark silhouette of a man in a black fireman's waterproof coat and a huge floppy rain hat. Beside him, on a tight leash, he could see what looked like a Doberman, wheezing and whining for the man to let it loose.

"That was my dog," the dry-sounding voice remarked, momentarily flicking the flashlight beam across to the other side of the swimming pool. "You've heard of a dog with two tails being happy. But a dog with two heads, that's no fun at all. Lived for seven months, and I never saw one of God's creatures so miserable."

There was a pause, and then the man said, "You mind if I ask you people what you're doing here, trespassing around, at half past three in the morning?"

"Who are you?" Jack asked him.

"Sorry, friend. I asked first."

"My name's Jack Reed. I'm buying The Oaks."

There was another pause, much longer this time. Then, "You're *buying* The Oaks?"

"That's right. You can check with Mr. Bufo at Capitol Realtors."

"Mr. Bufo never told me nothing about that."

"Well, that's probably because the deal hasn't formally been concluded yet. But the owners have accepted my offer."

"Mm!" said the man. "They would."

"What's that supposed to mean?"

"It means what it means. They would, you'd expect them to. I'll bet they couldn't believe their luck."

Jack said testily, "Do you mind telling me who you are?"

"Sure," said the man. He suddenly shone the flashlight into his own face. He was quite an old man, midseventies, Jack would have guessed. He looked German, or vaguely Slavic. His eyes were very pale blue and his skin was the color of liver sausage and he had two rows of crimson scars running down each side of his nose.

"Name's Joseph Lovelittle," he said. "Parents changed it from Kleinlieb during the First World War. Little love, love little. Just about the only folks in Milwaukee who did. Most of them were proud to be German, still are."

He lowered the flashlight. "I saw your wagon, back on the road. I don't hardly never sleep, that's my trouble. Never could, that's why they gave me the job of watchman. Round about two in the morning, I usually take Boy here out for a walk. He likes to walk at night, same as I do. You see more, at night."

"Did you see a young boy back at my wagon?" asked Jack. "Nine years old, fairish hair, blue windbreaker?"

Joseph Lovelittle thought about that. "Can't say that I did," he replied at last. "Checked inside, too. You missing him?"

Jack nodded.

"Well," said Joseph Lovelittle, "The Oaks ain't the ideal place for wandering around at night. We get squatters, from time to time; or let's say *would-be* squatters. Hippies, dope addicts, bikers, you know the kind. But Boy and me, we do our best to discourage them from staying. Mind you, The Oaks ain't the kind of place you'd really *want* to stay, even if you was a biker."

"Do you think you might have any ideas where my son might be hiding himself?" asked Jack. "We searched the building."

He glanced at Karen, wondering if he ought to tell Joseph Lovelittle about the hands that had reared out of the cellar floor, and the staring impression of the woman in the wall, but Karen gave him a tiny shake of her head. They didn't really know who this "Joseph Lovelittle" was yet; and they didn't want to appear eccentric or unhinged. He could easily call the police and have them taken in for trespassing. Besides—Jack might have been right, and there might have been some gas leak or atmospheric peculiarity in the building that caused brief and frightening hallucinations.

Out here, on the rainy tennis court, it was difficult for Jack to believe that he had really been seized by a gray-faced man who had burst out of solid concrete.

Joseph Lovelittle picked up the sodden mail sack and slung it one-handed back into the pool. Then he began to walk back toward the building, dragging his half-asphyxiated Doberman along with him. Jack and Karen followed.

"No real use searching the building by night," Joseph Lovelittle remarked. "No use searching it without keys, neither."

"Randy couldn't have gotten into a room that was already locked," Jack pointed out.

Joseph Lovelittle's raincoat made a rubbery squeaking noise as he walked along. "I'm not so sure about that," he told Jack. "All those doors are self-locking, know what I mean? They lock automatically whenever you close them and you can only open them from the outside, and only with a key. So your boy could have found a door that was open, and gone inside, and closed it behind him, and then he wouldn't have been able to get out."

"I'm sure we would have heard him calling, or knocking, if he'd done that."

Joseph Lovelittle grunted in amusement. "Those rooms are pretty well soundproof, once they're shut. They were made that way, special."

As they reached the graveled path at the rear of the conservatory Jack looked at his watch. "Look—if we come back when it gets light, do you think you could help us to search the building?"

"Cost you," Joseph Lovelittle said promptly.

Jack reached into his back pants pocket and took out his money clip. He tugged out a twenty-dollar bill and handed it to Joseph Lovelittle without a word. Joseph Lovelittle scrutinized it in the beam of his flashlight.

"All right, come back by seven. It'll be good and light by then. That's supposing it ever stops raining." He sneezed, twice, into his hand. Then he said, "I'll meet you right here. Don't be late, will you? I've got enough to do without looking for kids who shouldn't have been here in the first place."

"I could always call the police," Jack challenged him, although he didn't really mean it.

Joseph Lovelittle laughed. "You'd have to pay the cops five times what you just paid me just to come out here. Sheesh! They hate this place. They really hate it."

"We'll see you at seven," said Jack. "Meanwhile—you keep an eye out for my boy, you hear me?"

Joseph Lovelittle shone his flashlight directly into Jack's face. "You're pretty wet, ain't you? Better get yourself a hot shower before you catch pneumonia." He paused, and then he said, "You know who you remind me of? Dick Van Dyke, that's who you remind me of."

"I'm a little younger than Dick Van Dyke," Jack told him.

"I mean Dick Van Dyke when he's in 'The Dick Van Dyke Show.' You know with Morey Amsterdam and Rosemary What's-her-face and Mary Tyler Moore."

The Doberman called Boy wheezed at his leash, his tail thrashing against Joseph Lovelittle's raincoat.

"I'll see you later," said Jack. He felt defeated, very cold, and very tired. He would have done anything to have

Randy back safe, and to be able to crawl into bed and sleep for the next two days.

"I'll be here," said Joseph Lovelittle. "You can count on it."

Obligingly he pointed his flashlight toward the avenue of oak trees that would lead them back to their car. Jack turned back once or twice to look at him, but all he could see was the dazzling lens of the flashlight.

"Was he creepy or was he creepy?" asked Karen as she balanced her way down the erratically lit driveway on six-inch heels.

But Jack countered, "What I want to know is, why should the owners be so goddamned delighted to have sold this place?"

"Come on, Jack," said Karen. "You saw what happened in the cellar. Don't tell me the owners don't know all about it."

"I'm not so sure . . . if anybody had ever seen that before . . . don't you think they would have gotten in touch with the press, or the television? This is a seriously haunted building we're talking about now."

"We were probably dreaming the whole thing. Did you ever see *Nightmare on Elm Street*?"

"For God's sake, Karen; that was a movie. This is real."

They squeezed through the gap in the fence, and Jack unlocked the car. As Joseph Lovelittle had told them, it was empty. They climbed in, out of the rain, and Jack switched the engine on and started the windshield wipers. It was 3:37 in the morning.

"There's a Howard Johnson's on Ninety-four, back toward Madison," said Jack. "You can call Bessy; and then we can both take a hot shower and get a little sleep."

Karen leaned across and kissed him. "I'm sorry, Jack. I'm sorry it all turned out this way. But we'll find Randy, believe me. If he's there to be found, we'll find him."

"And what about the ghosts?" asked Jack. He glimpsed himself in the rearview mirror: white-faced, exhausted.

"What about things that come up out of the floor and grab you? What about women in the goddamned walls?"

"Jack, honey, we'll find a way to deal with it, okay? That geeky watchman was absolutely right. It's better to look in the morning."

Jack pulled the station wagon's gearshift into drive, backed up, and turned.

"Do you know something?" he said. "It's never going to stop raining. Never, ever, as long as we live. Never."

Jack took a yellow vinyl bar stool into the shower and sat under the hot water with his face upraised and his eyes closed tight. Karen opened a fresh piece of Bubblicious and sat on the end of the bed wearing nothing but her black nylon bra, and talked on the phone to Bessy with the thick ankles.

"Believe me, Bessy—if I'd've known what was going to happen! Bessy! You're an angel, Bessy, you know you are! You know that necklace you wanted? I'll buy you that necklace you wanted. I promise! I know it's a drag! Bessy, I'm sorry! But Sherrywine loves you so much!"

At last, just as Jack was coming out of the shower, she put down the phone. "Fuck her," she said, chewing noisily.

"What—she give you a hard time?" asked Jack, rubbing his hair dry.

"Oh, not exactly. Not in so many words. She keeps trying to make me feel like a bad mother, that's all."

"You're not a bad mother."

"You have bruises on your ankles. Have you seen them?"

Jack looked down. Both ankles were crisscrossed with reddish blue marks.

"That thing was real, wasn't it?"

Jack nodded. "Yes, it was real. It wasn't a ghost. It was real."

He sat on the cheap green nylon quilt cover, right next to her. She turned to look at him closely, her jaws working all the time. She was very pretty; even though one of her false eyelashes had become detached and was hanging over her eye. She had firm pointy breasts with brownish pink nipples as wide as coffee saucers; and even though her stomach sagged a little from having children, she was still very thin. He saw for the first time that she had carefully nail-scissored her pubic hair into the shape of a heart. She had copied it from *Playboy*.

"You can call the cops if you want to," she said. "I mean he's your son, you mustn't let me put you off. If the same thing happened to Sherrywine . . ."

"First, I want to search The Oaks properly," Jack told her. His voice sounded harsh and terrible, like Richard Burton about to die. "I don't know—I'm just convinced that he's still there. Those people in the walls. And the Turd, the way that was stuck in the bricks."

"That watchman—what was his name—" said Karen. "Littlelove, Lovelittle?"

"That's it, Lovelittle. Do you hear what he said? Even the cops don't like visiting The Oaks. You'd have to pay them five times more. Now, why should that be, if there isn't something weird going down there? I mean something that scares them?"

Jack dropped his rough motel towel on the floor and lay on his back on the bed. He stared at the ceiling for a while, and then he closed his eyes. It was twenty to five in the morning. Outside the tangerine-colored loose-weave drapes it was already light; though grayly, because it was still raining.

Karen knelt beside him for a while, watching him. She shifted her gum from side to side. She liked him. She thought that she could probably love him, if destiny would let her. She read her horoscope every Sunday in the newspaper, but she didn't trust in destiny. After a few minutes she realized that he was sleeping. His fingers uncurled and he began to snore. She reached behind her back and unclasped her bra.

Jack murmured in his sleep. Nothing comprehensible. Karen stroked his face with her fingertips, touched his eyelids, ran her finger across his lips. He kissed thin air, dreaming. She ran her fingernails down his breastbone, lightly scratched his stomach. Then she took his penis in her hand, and squeezed it, and slowly massaged it up and down. It filled and stiffened, and Karen gripped it even tighter, but Jack still didn't wake up. He was far too exhausted by shock and anxiety and lack of sleep.

Karen circled her fingertip around and around the moistened opening of his penis; but then she took her hand away and lay by herself, watching the lights of passing trucks swivel across the ceiling.

She glanced across at Jack. He would never be hers. She wasn't sure that she could manage a man with a conscience. But she snuggled up close to him as the room gradually lightened, and she didn't sleep, and when he opened his eyes at twenty after six and stared at her, she smiled, and kissed him, and said, "Good morning, lover."

By daylight, Joseph Lovelittle looked even older and shabbier. He was waiting for them in the lee of the conservatory, the collar of his fireman's raincoat turned up, while his Doberman Boy sat beside him and shivered feverishly. The sky was quite bright, but gray, and the rain clattered straight out of it like water from an ornamental fountain. Their shoes crunched wetly on the gravel.

"Well," snorted Joseph Lovelittle. "Thought you wouldn't come."

"I'm looking for my son," Jack reminded him seriously.

"So you are, so you are." Joseph Lovelittle turned toward the conservatory door, a drip of transparent phlegm swinging from the end of his curved nose. "This the way you went in before? Sometimes it's locked and sometimes it ain't."

"You lock it?" asked Jack.

Joseph Lovelittle turned his head without turning his shoulders. It was quite unnerving to watch. "Sometimes I do. Sometimes I don't."

He swung the door open. Jack said, "Who locks it, when you don't? Daniel Bufo?"

"Sometimes."

"And who else?"

Joseph Lovelittle challenged him with pale blue eyes. "Who do you think?"

They stepped into the conservatory. Joseph Lovelittle took a deep, thumping breath. "You should've seen this conservatory, back in twenty-five. Tropical plants, cactus, you never saw nothing like it. Dr. Estergomy's pride and joy."

"Who was Dr. Estergomy?"

Joseph Lovelittle turned and stared at him yet again. "You're buying this place; you don't know Dr. Estergomy?"

"Is there any reason why I should?"

Joseph Lovelittle thought about that, and then shrugged. "I guess not, when you think about it."

"But who was he?" asked Karen.

"You know this place was a nursing home? That's what Mr. Bufo told you?"

"That's right. The Oaks Nursing Home, that's what he said."

"Well . . . Estergomy was doctor in charge. You know what I mean? Top banana."

"I see," said Jack. "And this conservatory here—"

Joseph Lovelittle smiled at him as if he were quite mad. "That's right, Mr. Reed; you got it. Dr. Estergomy's pride and joy."

"You remember it?" asked Jack, looking around at the shriveled leaves and the broken glass and the cracked flowerpots.

"Sure. I started work here in twenty-three, when I was twelve years old. Cleaning, washing dishes, helping out.

Cabin boy you might say. Used to read stories to the patients, too, those that could understand."

He took off his hat and his eyes seemed paler than ever. "Dr. Estergomy's pride and joy. Used to grow grapes in here. Little green grapes. I can remember coming in here in the summer and stealing them."

He opened the door to the lounge and allowed Karen and Jack to go in ahead of him. Boy the Doberman thrust his muzzle up the back of Karen's skirt and she snapped, "Get off, wet-nose!" Joseph Lovelittle cackled, and winked at her.

They entered the hallway. Joseph Lovelittle unbuttoned his raincoat and hung it on the banister. Underneath he wore a sagging orange cardigan and baggy-assed jeans. "Best thing to do is to start from the attic, work our way down." He held up a key ring with a half-dozen odd-shaped keys on it. "Passkeys, one for each floor."

They climbed the stairs, right up to the attic. As they climbed, Joseph Lovelittle said, "When this was Mr. Krüger's house, it was called The Maze. Nobody ever knew why, because there wasn't no maze. That's why Dr. Estergomy changed it when he took it over. Dr. Estergomy was one of those practical-minded people, didn't like nothing you couldn't explain."

"When did the nursing home close down?" asked Jack. "I saw some newspapers in the lounge dating from 1926."

"Well, that's right, June fifteenth, 1926. Eleven-thirty in the evening."

Jack frowned at Karen. "That's a pretty odd time for a nursing home to close down, eleven-thirty in the evening."

They had reached the third-floor landing. Joseph Lovelittle let his Doberman off its leash, and it bounded up the stairs with its claws scratching against the linoleum. "If your son's around here anywhere, Mr. Reed, you can bet your bottom dollar that Boy will sniff him out."

"It won't hurt him?"

"Are you kidding me, Mr. Reed? That mutt?"

They heard Boy scuffling madly all the way up to the attic. When he reached the top, he barked twice to let them know that he was there. They plodded up after him. Joseph Lovelittle was badly out of breath and had to stop every now and then, his eyes bulging, the air scraping in and out of his lungs. "Smoked a hundred a day when I was younger, wish to God I never had."

Jack said, "Did you ever see a little girl playing around here? She would have been wearing a kind of whitish-colored raincoat, with a hood."

Joseph Lovelittle stopped a few steps short of the top-floor landing, breathing hard and staring at him. "Little girl? You mean, all on her own?"

"That's right. No more than six or seven years old, I would have thought."

Joseph Lovelittle sniffed. "What would a kid that age be doing out here on her own?"

"I don't know. I was just asking if you'd seen her. Or him. I'm not entirely sure if it's a girl."

"Well, Mr. Reed, things ain't always what they seem."

"No, I guess they're not."

Joseph Lovelittle took out his keys and began opening doors, one after the other, and leaving them open. Jack and Karen followed him along the corridor, peering into every room. Most of them were completely empty, but a few still had beds and bedside tables. In one room there was even a cork bulletin board, with postcards pinned up on it, and a curled-up pinup of *An Egyptian Houri, 1926.*

Karen uncurled the pinup and smiled at it. "Sexy, huh?"

They walked along farther. Joseph Lovelittle said, "No scent yet. Boy always barks like crazy whenever he picks up a scent."

Jack looked into another empty room. "Was this a private facility? Or was it owned by the state?"

"It was private, but Dr. Estergomy was paid by the state of Wisconsin for some of the patients."

"Was it always full?"

"Oh, sure, always full. Full to busting. Night it closed down, we had one hundred thirty-seven patients."

"Estergomy must have been quite a doctor."

"Well, sure. He had all of these newfangled treatments. They was new for 1926, anyhow. These days they're probably just about as antiquated as me."

They reached the end of the attic floor, but there was no sign of Randy. "Let's try the next floor down," said Joseph Lovelittle, selecting the appropriate passkey.

He went on ahead, shuffling down the stairs. Jack said to Karen, "If we can't find Randy in the building, I'm calling the cops, that's all there is to it. Even if I *do* have to bribe them to come out here."

Joseph Lovelittle turned around and said, "Do you have anything that belonged to your son, Mr. Reed? Maybe it would help Boy to pick up the scent."

Jack reached in his coat pocket and took out the shredded remains of the Turd. He held them under Boy's nose, and Boy sniffed at them and licked them and then tugged at them with his teeth.

"What was that?" Joseph Lovelittle asked, looking askance at the waffle-patterned shreds of wool.

"A nondenominational, nonracist, asexual, all-natural play item," said Jack.

Joseph Lovelittle stared at him. "I used to have a Jack Armstrong flying-saucer gun when I was nine."

"Well, you can't always have all the luck," said Jack. He was beginning to feel light-headed with tiredness, almost hysterical.

They walked the length of the next corridor, with Joseph Lovelittle opening up every door, and Boy trotting in and out and sniffing. Again, they found nothing. But Jack was surprised to see that the walls of every single room on this floor were thickly lined with grayish white fabric.

"Quiet rooms," Joseph Lovelittle remarked with a wry smile when he saw Jack touching the walls. "That's what Dr. Estergomy liked to call them."

They went down to the next floor. It was here that they came to the double doors that led to the tower, strongly padlocked.

"I guess he couldn't have gotten in there," Jack remarked.

"You want to look?" asked Joseph Lovelittle. He sniffed, and the swinging drip of phlegm vanished up his nostril as if by magic. "This was Dr. Estergomy's clinic. You know— where he did all of his treatment. He always kept it well locked up, on account of the drugs and all the other stuff."

Joseph Lovelittle fiddled with his keys, and then found the correct key for the padlock. He unlocked it and swung open the right-hand door. Jack hesitated. "Go ahead," said Joseph Lovelittle. "Nothing to be scared of."

Jack stepped inside and found himself in a dim, dusty room whose ceiling was two stories high. Heavily curtained windows looked out over the avenue that approached the house from the road; all Jack could see outside were wet oak leaves, kowtowing to the heavy rain.

In one corner of the room stood a large leather-topped partners' desk. It was still strewn with yellowed papers, as if somebody had been working at it only this morning. A fountain pen lay with its cap unscrewed on top of the ink-squiggled blotter. The only sign of how long it had been there was that its nib was rusty.

Not far from the desk was a high medical examination table, draped in a sheet whose hem had been gnawed at, probably by mice. In the center of the room, however, stood the most impressive piece of furniture: a huge squarish chair of sawed oak, with a metal cap attached to the back of it by a curved brass bracket, and leather restraints for the wrists and the ankles. The chair was connected by a thick brown fabric-covered cable to a huge bank of electric dials, like the flight deck of an old-fashioned flying boat. There were rows and rows of tarnished switches, and scores of little red light bulbs, and the whole bank was wired to a stack of glass accumulators, most of them dusty and cracked and encrusted with chlorine salts.

Jack glanced up. Over the chair hung a battery of black-painted spotlights, smothered in abandoned cobwebs. Even the spiders didn't live here anymore.

"It looks like something out of *Frankenstein*," said Jack.

"It looks like the electric chair to me," put in Karen.

Joseph Lovelittle leaned proprietorially against the open door with his arms folded, looking around the clinic. Boy stuck his head in the wicker wastepaper basket and worried some pieces of crumpled-up notepaper.

"You're both right, I guess," said Joseph Lovelittle. "This was one of Mr. Estergomy's big new treatments. Something about sorting out your brain cells so that they behaved themselves. He showed me once, with a magnet and some iron filings. He pulled the magnet past the iron filings and they all made a pattern. That was the way he tried to explain it to me, anyway. I guess I was too young to understand him; or too dumb; or both. I'm good with my hands, you know. Not too hot in the thinking department."

"So this was a nursing home for mental patients?" asked Jack.

"Mr. Bufo didn't tell you that? This was a *famous* nursing home for mental patients. Over at the university they used to call it The Walnuts, instead of The Oaks."

"That explains the padded rooms and the doors that you can't open from the inside," said Jack. "What a dummy, I should have realized."

"They was all violent," said Joseph Lovelittle. "Every single one of them, totally ape-shit, excusing my French. The state penitentiary sent them here because the guards couldn't handle them. All kinds we had here. Ax murderers, mother smotherers, baby stranglers, fire-starters, you name it. Men, women, children too. One hundred thirty-seven the night we closed down."

"I had no idea," said Jack, shaking his head. "I never heard of this place before."

"Sure you didn't. They didn't advertise it when it was open, because the local residents wouldn't have relished a holiday home for dangerous criminal maniacs right in their backyard, now would they? And after what happened, they weren't about to advertise it after it closed."

"What *did* happen?" asked Jack.

Joseph Lovelittle whistled to Boy between his teeth. "You finished in here?" he asked Jack.

"Yes, I think we're all finished."

They left the treatment room and Joseph Lovelittle locked the door behind them. "You can look at the west tower if you like, but that's just books. Mr. Krüger left most of his library behind when he sold the house. Think he went off to Europe, someplace like that. He gave up the beer business, too."

"Is it possible that Randy could have gotten into the *west* tower? Or is it locked like this?"

"It's locked just the same."

"All right, then, let's leave it for now and check the downstairs rooms first, and then the cellar."

Karen said, "You're not going back down to the cellar?"

"I have to. The Turd was there."

Joseph Lovelittle threw Jack an odd sideways look. Jack still couldn't work out how he was able to rotate his head without moving his shoulders.

"My son's toy," Jack explained.

Coughing thickly, Joseph Lovelittle led them downstairs to the hallway, and then shuffled ahead of them around the kitchens, the rest rooms, the art studios, the closets which once stored coats and boots.

At last they ended up in the bathhouse, at the back of the building. It was echoing and cold and cavernous, with tiny windows that overlooked the tennis courts. There were five white-tiled bays, in each of which stood a massive white-enameled bathtub. Each bath had a wooden lid, with an oval hole cut in it—just large enough for a human head to fit through. On the sides of the lids, four brass clamps had been fitted so that the occupant could be screwed to the rim of the bath, restraining him from climbing out. Every lid was scratched and gouged and darkly stained.

"If any of the patients got really crazy, Mr. Estergomy used to leave them in here, up to their necks in cold water. Boy, they used to scream! Sometimes you could hear them way out by the swimming pool. They used to scream and they used to scratch, and the nurses would take them out of the baths afterward and the whole bath would be full of blood, and their fingers would be scraped right down to the bones."

Karen shivered. "Gives me the creeps."

Boy the Doberman prowled around the baths, his claws tapping on the tiles. "Doesn't look like your son's in here," Joseph Lovelittle remarked. "Last place to try is the cellar."

"You ever *see* anybody here?" Jack asked him as they left the bathhouse.

"I see dope addicts, bikers, but not too many of them."

"No, no. What I meant was, do you ever see anybody unusual?" He couldn't quite bring himself to say "anybody in the walls."

Joseph Lovelittle unlocked the cellar door. "Depends what you mean by unusual. I could say that you and your lady friend are pretty unusual, coming around here, looking for a son you can't even prove you ever had. How do I know what you're really here for?"

"Just wait up a minute," said Jack. "I paid you, didn't I, to help us look for my son? You took the money and so I wouldn't mind seeing a little cooperation, if you don't mind."

Joseph Lovelittle promptly stuck two fingers into his cardigan pocket and produced Jack's twenty-dollar bill. "You're not satisfied, here's your money back. I wouldn't take money from anybody who wasn't satisfied."

Jack pushed it away. "All right, I'm sorry. I just want to find my boy."

Karen said, "Jack . . . I think I'll stay here. I don't want to go down into that cellar again."

"Hey . . . there ain't nothing to be scared of." Joseph Lovelittle grinned, exposing teeth the color of old piano keys. "It's nothing but a cellar, that's all."

"All the same," said Karen, her voice off-key with agitation. "I'd just as soon stay right here."

"Suit yourself." Joseph Lovelittle sniffed. He reached up beside the cellar door and took down a green-enamel inspection lamp. *God*, thought Jack, *if only we'd known about that lamp last night.*

"You coming, Mr. Reed; or are *you* scared, too?"

The old watchman led the way down the cellar steps, swinging the wide beam of his lamp disconcertingly from one side of the cellar to the other, so that it looked as if the whole place was tilting. For one moment the lamp shone through his ears, so that they gleamed red and hairy and laced with dark red veins.

"I don't come down here too much anymore," he told Jack over his shoulder. "Was a time I used to maintain the boiler, but during the war there wasn't no spare fuel for it, and there didn't seem too much point, for a building that nobody was never going to live in no more."

At the foot of the cellar steps he suddenly turned and frowned at Jack as if he had never seen him before in his life. "What do you want to *buy* the place for?" he demanded in a querulous tone. "Fellow would have to be crazy to buy this place."

"You want me to keep you on the staff?" Jack asked him. "Caretaker, chief of security, something like that?" He was hoping that Joseph Lovelittle would be sufficiently impressed to behave a little more helpfully.

Somewhere in the depths of the cellar, Boy began to bark.

Joseph Lovelittle turned his back on Jack and said, "Chief of security? Don't give a shit, to tell you the truth. Just as soon retire."

Jack followed him across the rubbish-strewn cellar floor, past the domed and silent boiler. They crunched and splintered over sheets of plywood and climbed across three broken sofas. Joseph Lovelittle didn't seem to care what he trod on. He kicked two glass accumulators and one of them smashed, leaking battery acid all the way across the concrete floor. Jack climbed over the trash as carefully as he could, but said nothing.

Boy was standing by the lime-washed wall in one of the alcoves, barking loudly.

"You found something there, Boy?" Joseph Lovelittle asked him. He shone the inspection lamp on the bricks, but the wall was completely blank. "Dog's as stupid as shit, believe me. Every other Doberman—smart as paint. Not mine, though. This dog sees trespassers—what does he do? He brings them sticks so that they can play with him. I was never lucky with dogs. Never once had a dog that turned out right."

"Maybe there's something behind the wall," Jack suggested. He felt chilled but sweaty, and he wiped his hands on the sides of his pants.

"What's behind that wall, Mr. Reed, is solid rock, that's what's behind that wall."

Jack took out the shredded pieces of the Turd and offered them to Boy to refresh his memory. Boy sniffed and snapped at them eagerly, and then jumped up at the cellar wall, barking and barking and thrashing his tail.

"Will you shut up, you shit-stupid dog!" Joseph Lovelittle shouted at him, and lashed at him with his leash. "Never known a dog so goddamned stupid!"

"But he thinks there's *something* there," Jack pointed out.

"Oh yeah?" Joseph Lovelittle demanded. He seemed quite angry now. "What? What does he think is there? Come on, Mr. Reed, what the blue shit does he think is there?" He stepped noisily over a stack of hundreds of old wooden coat hangers and stood right next to the wall.

"This is solid brick, solid brick! Hasn't been painted since 1924, hasn't been disturbed. There's nothing here, Mr. Reed, you take my word for it. Solid brick!"

He snatched at Boy's collar but Boy dodged him and circled and barked and backed away.

"You listen to me, you mutt! You quit that goddamned noise! You hear me! You just quit that goddamned noise!"

It was then that Jack was sure he heard that chillingly familiar dragging noise. That low, soft *sssssshhhhhhh—sssssssshhhhhh—sssssshhhhhhh*. He turned around quickly, trying to decide where it was coming from. But Boy's barking racketed and echoed from every wall, and it was impossible for Jack to hear the noise distinctly enough.

It was approaching, though. A soft, thick, gritty undertone.

"Mr. Lovelittle!" he called.

"What? What is it?" snapped Joseph Lovelittle.

"Mr. Lovelittle, I truly believe that we'd be doing ourselves a favor if we got the hell out of here."

"What? What the hell are you talking about? Boy—shut up that damned barking, I can't hear myself think!"

Sssssshhhhhh—sssssssshhhhhh—sssssshhhhhh. The dragging was louder still. Jack looked quickly and anxiously around the floor, expecting at any second that the trash would burst apart and a gray hand would reach out and snatch for his ankles.

"Mr. Lovelittle, come on!" he called, trying to sound coaxing. "I don't think it's really too safe down here, you know? Come on! Your dog will follow along when he's calmed himself down."

"Shit-stupid dog," Joseph Lovelittle repeated.

At that moment the *sssssshhhhhh* noise behind him was so loud that he turned in surprise and stared at the wall. "Did you hear that?" he asked Jack. "Maybe there *is—*"

Two powerful brick white hands came exploding out of the wall and seized Joseph Lovelittle's head.

"Jesus!" he screamed. But then the hands pulled his face

smack into the brickwork. Jack heard the hollow turkey-bone snap as his nose broke.

With relentless force, the hands dragged Joseph Lovelittle up and down, up and down, *chip-chop, chip-chop,* so that his face was scraped against the brick like a cabbage against a metal grater. He screamed and screamed in helpless agony, one long high-pitched howl. His screams silenced even Boy, who stood stiffly among the rubbish with his ears pricked up and his eyes unblinking.

"Hold on! Hold on!" Jack shouted out, and rattled across the coat hangers and snatched hold of Lovelittle's shoulders and tried to pull him away. But Lovelittle was being wrenched up and down so violently that Jack was thrown back by his wildly flailing arms.

The skin from Joseph Lovelittle's face was stripped across the wall in thin bloody shreds, where it slowly uncurled. Then suddenly the gritty mortar tore through the last of his skin and into his flesh, and the brickwork was gaudily painted with circles of bright red shining blood.

The gray-white hands wrenched him right to left, right to left, again and again. One of his eyes was dragged out of its socket, one of his pale colorless eyes. It stuck to the bricks for a moment on its stringy optic nerve, staring surrealistically toward the floor. Then it suddenly dropped and disappeared among the scattered coat hangers.

Jack backed away, slowly at first, then faster. Joseph Lovelittle was still screaming, still trying to cling to the wall to stop himself being scraped across the brickwork, but Jack could see that it was hopeless, there was nothing he could do.

"Jack!" shouted Karen from the hallway. She must have called before, but he hadn't heard her over Lovelittle's screaming, and the terrible cabbage-grating sound of his head being scraped against the wall.

Jack had almost made it to the steps when Joseph Lovelittle let out the most chilling scream of all. He didn't even sound like a human being anymore. The hands were

dragging him all the way along the cellar wall, from one end
to the other, ripping open his cardigan, scraping the fat
white bulging flesh of his oelly, tearing away his corduroy
pants, smearing the lime-washed bricks with a five-foot
track of blood.

"*Jack!*" shouted Karen. "*Jack, what's happening? Jack,
for God's sake!*"

Gasping with shock, Jack unsteadily climbed the cellar
steps. By the time he had reached the top, Joseph Lovelittle
had stopped screaming. Jack didn't look back. He blun-
dered his way out through the cellar door and stood in the
middle of the hallway between the two blind statues,
swaying like a man on the edge of collapse.

Karen was standing right by the door to the lounge,
ready to run if she had to. He turned around and stared at
her.

"Jack?" she whispered. "Jack, what's happened?"

All Jack could do was shake his head and open and close
his mouth.

F·I·V·E

Jack found a quarter bottle of Jack Daniel's in the station wagon's glove compartment. He swigged a mouthful, coughed, and then passed it over to Karen.

"No, thanks." Karen handed it back. "I'm just sick to my stomach already."

"We'll have to call the police," said Jack. He couldn't control his voice; and he felt as if his mind were leaping up and down on some kind of a trampoline. "We don't have any options anymore."

"Okay," said Karen, folding another stick of gum into her mouth. "If that's what you want to do."

"Well, what the hell else can we do? There's something down in that cellar that grabs people, and kills them."

"Sure," said Karen. Her tone was noticeably flat. "Something that comes jumping out of solid concrete."

"Karen—the police will be able to see what happened for themselves."

"Oh, sure."

"He was pulled up against that wall, sweetheart, and he was rubbed up against it, and he was torn to *shreds,* for Christ's sake."

Karen looked at him narrowly. The rain dribbled down the station wagon's windshield and beaded the hood. There were dark smudges under Karen's eyes, and for the first time since he had known her, Jack thought that she looked old.

"What do you think the police are going to say about

that?" she asked him. "About Lovelittle being scraped up against the wall?"

"It's there, Karen. The evidence is there. The body, everything. All they have to do is to look at the wall."

"And they're going to believe you when you tell them he was pulled up against it, from somebody inside?"

"What are you getting at?"

"They're not going to say that you *pushed* him up against it?"

Jack swallowed another mouthful of Jack Daniel's. There was only a drop left in the bottle now. He hesitated, and then swallowed that, too.

"Listen—" he said. "I'm assuming the police are going to be logical." He screwed the cap back on the empty bottle and returned it to the glove compartment. "They would only have to look at me to see that I wouldn't have the physical strength to scrape a man of Lovelittle's size all the way along a two-hundred-foot cellar wall. And if I wanted to kill him, why would I kill him like that? Why not stab him or shoot him or hit him with a baseball bat? I'm not a lunatic."

"Well, maybe I'm just prejudiced," said Karen.

They sat in the car a little while longer in silence. All they could see of The Oaks was a misty outline behind the oak trees.

At length, Jack said, "I'm pretty sure that Randy's down there somewhere."

"In the cellar?"

"The dog barked; that was the only time he barked. I let him sniff the Turd, and he went straight back to the wall."

"You think that Randy's in the wall, too?"

"I don't know," said Jack, rubbing his eyes. "I don't know what to think. I know what I've seen and I still don't believe it."

"But you expect the police to believe it?"

"Karen, the evidence—"

"Jack, honey, in my limited experience, the police don't give a fuck about the evidence."

Another silence. The rain dripped and rustled through the trees. Jack took out his car keys and picked out his ignition key. "He's my son, Karen," he said. "I can't find him on my own. I think he's in the wall, God knows how he got there. This Lester he kept talking about—"

"*Look,*" breathed Karen.

Jack frowned and looked up. Between the dark trunks of the oaks, he could just distinguish a small grayish white figure, hooded, faceless, standing alone in the rain. It was no taller than a seven-year-old child. Yet what would a seven-year-old child be doing out here, watching them?

Jack opened the station-wagon door, but as he did so Karen gripped his arm. "Wait, it's waving."

The small figure had lifted both arms. *Not waving,* thought Jack. *Beckoning.*

"It wants us to follow it," he said.

"What, are you out of your *mind*?" Karen retorted. "Jack! You're not going *back* there? Not *again*?"

"You don't have to come," Jack told her. "But Karen—if there's any chance of finding Randy—"

Karen looked up at him tiredly. She knew that he would have to go. "I'll wait for you, Jack, listen to the radio. But if you're not back in twenty minutes . . ."

"If I'm not back in twenty minutes, call the cops. I mean it. You'll have to. Don't come after me."

He climbed out of the car. The small grayish white figure was still standing among the oaks, still beckoning. He squeezed through the gap next to the gate and began to trudge up the gravel driveway with his coat collar turned up. The figure lowered its arms and stood waiting for him. It was difficult to see through the trees and the rain, but it seemed as if Randy had been right. The figure had no face. Perhaps it was only newspaper, after all, sodden newspaper waving in the wind.

Before he could get too close, the figure ran off toward the back of The Oaks. It ran in a strange jerky way, just like a child in a new raincoat that was too big for it, but peculiarly disjointed, too. More like a speeded-up film than a real child.

Jack came around the back of the building. The small figure was waiting for him by the open conservatory door. It didn't beckon anymore. When Jack reached within twenty yards of it, it jumped in through the conservatory door and disappeared.

Jack knew with raw dread where this game of follow-the-leader was taking him. He hesitated at the conservatory door, breathing deeply to calm himself down. *You don't have to go back. You could call the police.*

There was no sign of the small grayish white figure, not unless it was hiding behind the door. There were no wet footprints across the conservatory floor.

But Randy was inside the building somewhere, he was convinced of it, he could *feel* it. He had no alternative but to go in to look for him.

He walked through the conservatory, through the reading lounge, into the hallway. The building seemed even more silent than usual. The cellar door was still partly open, as he had left it. He went across to it and pushed it open with his fingertips. He could hear his own heart pounding.

He was just about to step inside when a voice whispered, *Welcome back, Jack.*

He turned around. The blind statue on the opposite side of the hallway had opened its marble eyes and was staring at him.

Pleased you could come, Jack, said the statue.

Jack willed himself to cross the hallway. His feet dragged as if he were half-paralyzed. He stood in front of the statue and stared back at it. Its face was white and cold and mocking. It was alive, and it was formed in the image of a woman, and yet there was something utterly inhuman about it. A face of marble, a heart of stone.

You're looking for Randy, said the statue.

"He's here?" asked Jack hoarsely.

Of course he's here. We've hidden him.

"Who's 'we'?"

Well, my name's Lester . . . but there are many more of us. Don't you worry, Jack, your Randy's quite safe.

"Where is he? I want to see him."

All in good time.

"I want him *back*, damn it! I don't care who you are or what you are, you have no right to keep him here!"

Brave talk, Jack! But don't overdo it. We have Randy, remember, and some of us are aching to do him a serious mischief! Some of the women . . . well, even Quintus has difficulty keeping some of the women in order.

"Quintus? Who's Quintus?"

Let's put it this way, Jack—the statue leered at him—*every social group has its leaders. Quintus just happens to be ours. As long as it suits us, of course.*

"What do you want?" Jack demanded. "Is it money? Just tell me what the hell you want!"

We want the priest, the statue hissed. Now it seemed to be talking about something it really hated. *You must bring us the priest. Otherwise Randy will be crushed; just as Joseph Lovelittle was shredded up; and just as something terrible will happen to you.*

"Priest?" Jack asked the statue. "What priest? What are you talking about?"

We want the priest! Bring us the priest! Unless you bring us the priest, your Randy will be crushed, and crushed, and crushed to nothing!

Jack raised both hands. "Please! Listen to me! If you want me to bring you a priest, I'll bring you a priest! But *which* priest? Any particular priest? Or will any priest suit you?"

The priest! screamed the statue, its marble mouth stretching wide to reveal a white marble tongue. *The priest! The priest! You must bring us the priest!*

Jack shouted, "I'm not bringing you anybody—not until you can show me that you've really got Randy—not until you can show me that he's safe! You hear me! Otherwise, forget it! I walk out of here and you never see me again!"

Fool! screamed the statue. And at that instant Jack heard Randy's voice, high-pitched and blurting, like a child trying to cry out underwater, and Randy's head rose up from out of the black-and-white marble floor, then his shoulders, then his arms, right up to his waist, like a boy standing in a shallow lake.

Daddy! he cried out, and lifted both hands in a desperate plea to be rescued. *Daddy save me!*

"Randy! Hold on!" shouted Jack, and ran across the hallway toward him. But before he could reach Randy's outstretched hands, Randy plunged back into the marble floor, as if somebody had pulled his legs from below.

Jack fell to his knees and pummeled the floor desperately with his bare fists. It was hard and smooth and cold, and completely unyielding.

"Let him go!" he roared at the floor. "You bastards! You bastards! Let him go!"

There was no reply. After a long while Jack wiped the tears from his eyes with his fingers, and stood up, and walked back toward the statue. The eyes were closed, and there was no sign of life.

"Which priest?" he asked it, in exhaustion and misery. "Which goddamned priest?"

But the statue said nothing. The building was silent. The people in the walls had told him what their ransom demand was; and somehow or other he was going to have to find the right priest for himself.

He turned, and was just about to walk out of the hallway when the cellar door opened. He stepped back, startled.

Out of the cellar trotted Boy, the Doberman. He came

across the floor, his claws *click-clack*ing. He was carrying something in his mouth.

"Boy . . . good Boy . . . what have you got there?"

The Doberman carefully laid down the object that he was carrying at Jack's feet, and then looked up appealingly, as if he wanted Jack to play throw-and-fetch.

Jack looked down at it. It was blue white and shiny, with a few tatters of red gristle at each end. It was one of Joseph Lovelittle's thighbones.

"So no police?" asked Karen, hitching up her skirt to make herself more comfortable.

"No police. Not yet. I want to find them a priest first."

"But they didn't tell you *which* priest."

"I don't know. Maybe any priest. Who knows. We'll just have to find out."

"Jack—I have to get back home. Bessy's going to be climbing the walls."

They reached the main road. Jack said, "Sure. I'm sorry. I shouldn't even have dragged you out here in the first place."

She leaned across and kissed his cheek. "I came because I wanted to."

He kissed her back and squeezed her thigh. "Do you know something? I should have met you years ago."

"That's what you think," said Karen, but she was obviously pleased that he had said it. *Maybe, just maybe, when Randy was safe—*

He drove her into Madison. Lake Mendota lay photographically gray under a photographic sky. Students cycled through the wet streets with tote bags over their heads to keep dry. He found her a cab downtown and gave the driver seventy-five dollars to take Karen back to Milwaukee. "Listen," he told Karen, "I'll call you later, okay? Tell Mike that I'll phone him this evening. Tell him I've had some family trouble."

"Well, you're not kidding, are you?" said Karen. She

kissed him with cold lips through the partly open window of the cab. Neither of them dared to say "I love you"—not with Randy missing, and not with life so threatening and strange.

Jack watched the cab drive away, and then he crossed the street to the Jackdaw Bookstore for a cup of coffee and a donut. The bookstore was crowded with more students, smoking and talking and laughing. Jack sat on his own and forced himself to eat his donut, even though it stuck in his mouth like thick dusty glue. A pretty girl student with waist-length blond hair and wire-rim spectacles came past him and said, "Are you okay?"

He lifted his head. "Sure, I'm okay. Is something wrong?"

She smiled at him. She was almost young enough to be his daughter. "You're crying, that's all. Didn't you know?"

He raised his hand to his eyes. He was surprised to find that tears were running down his cheeks. He said nothing, but tugged out his handkerchief and wiped his face. The girl watched him for a little while longer and then walked out into the street.

Capitol Realtors wasn't difficult to find. It was only two blocks away from the bookstore, in a small smart new office development with tinted windows and air-conditioning and a mosaic-floored atrium filled with trees. Daniel Bufo was eating his breakfast on his desk when Jack was shown into his office: two huge lemon danishes and a mug of hot chocolate with "Green Bay Packers" printed on it. He scooped up the danishes on a property prospectus and carefully slid them into his top drawer.

"Don't let me interrupt you," Jack told him.

Daniel Bufo brushed the crumbs off his notepad with the side of his hand. Behind him, through the slatted blinds, there was a strangely clear view of another office building, where a man and his secretary appeared to be arguing with each other heatedly. On Daniel Bufo's desk was a laminated plaque awarded to Madison's Real Estate Man of the Year, 1975.

"Didn't expect you to come by," said Daniel Bufo with a fat unamused smile.

"I need some information," Jack told him. He could tell that Daniel Bufo was disturbed by his appearance: unshaved, his clothes crumpled, and obviously weary.

"How about some hot chocolate?" Daniel Bufo asked him. "It's Dutch; it's like a meal in itself."

Jack shook his head. "I want some background, that's all."

"On The Oaks? I told you, there isn't too much to tell. It's been empty since 1926."

"It used to be a lunatic asylum."

"Ah," said Daniel Bufo, rubbing the side of his face.

"Well, it's true, isn't it? It used to be a home for the criminally insane."

Daniel Bufo picked up a ballpoint pen and turned it around and around between his pudgy fingers. "It was a nursing home, for sure."

"A lunatic asylum. A nuthouse."

"All right, it used to be a lunatic asylum. But I don't see what difference that makes. It hasn't been used for well over sixty years. And you're going to change the name, aren't you?"

Jack said, "I need to know how to get in touch with the owners."

"I don't think they're going to be too happy about that, Mr. Reed, with all due respect. They are—well, as I think I made it clear to you—*reclusive.*"

Jack lowered his head for a moment. Daniel Bufo sucked at his hot chocolate, waiting for him to say something.

At last Jack said, "Either you put me in touch with the owners or the deal's off."

"I'm sorry?"

"You heard me. I want the owners' address and telephone number right now, or else the deal's off."

"Mr. Reed—you're putting me into a very difficult position here. I have to respect my clients' rights of privacy. They did specifically request that this transaction should be completed only through attorneys and not face-to-face."

Jack stood up. "All right, that's it. Forget it. As far as I'm concerned, there's no deal."

"Mr. Reed, please, believe me—the owners are very anxious to sell you the property. They like the price, they're pleased with your plans to keep the original building and turn it into a resort hotel. They're all in favor! But when a client asks me to guard her privacy—well, what else can I do? There's a code of ethics in realty, you know. It's almost like being a doctor."

"Proctologist, more like," Jack retorted, opening the door. Daniel Bufo reared up to come after him, but Jack lifted a hand to warn him off.

"If your clients change their minds, you can reach me at Howard Johnson's, on Route Ninety-four." He reached into his coat pocket and tossed Daniel Bufo a book of matches. "The number's on there."

"Mr. Reed—I really don't think—"

"Mr. Bufo, I need this information badly. Life or death. At least take the trouble to ask your reclusive clients whether they might consider talking to me face-to-face. Just *consider* it, okay?"

He closed the door, leaving Daniel Bufo frowning down at his cup of hot chocolate, like a big frustrated child.

His next stop was the offices of the *Madison Times-Dispatch*. They were located in an unprepossessing concrete building next to a run-down collection of auto-parts stores and Chinese restaurants. He spent most of the afternoon in a cramped back room, trying to dig out their files for 1926. They had microfiched their back issues only as far back as 1943.

A spinsterish woman in a black cardigan and a gray skirt was pasting cuttings. She clucked and huffed every time he pulled out another volume. The room smelled of sour old newspapers and ashes-of-roses perfume. The rain tinkled and tapped against the single window, and Jack began to feel bowed over with tiredness.

"Don't you ever *eat*?" the spinsterish woman asked him just after two o'clock.

He attempted a smile. "Some things are more important than eating."

At last, at the bottom of a stack of files with broken spines, all marked "Awaiting Rebinding," he came across the *Madison Times* for June 1926. He laid it out on the table and read through it carefully, page by page, column by column.

After an hour he had found no mention whatsoever of The Oaks, nor of Mr. Estergomy.

He sat back and allowed the file to slap shut.

The spinsterish woman said, "Can't find what you're looking for?" It was almost four o'clock.

Jack shook his head. "They've got everything in here. Baby contests, marriages, who's dead and who isn't. I just would've thought—well, I don't know."

She inspected him through upswept spectacles. "What were you looking for in particular? What year is that?"

"Nineteen twenty-six."

"I was living here in Madison in 1926. My father was a professor in history at the university. Douglas Manfield, you might have heard of him. He wrote a very famous book about Etruscan inscriptions."

She stood up, and came across to where he was sitting. She held out her hand. "Helena Manfield," she introduced herself.

Jack stood up, too, and shook her hand. "Jack Reed."

"Not from round here?"

"Uh-uh, Milwaukee. Reed Muffler and Tire, five shops all around the city."

Helena Manfield perched herself on the edge of his desk. In spite of her age, she had a birdlike grace. Her gray hair was combed back into a black velvet bow, and although her skin was wrinkled now, she must have had a very strong face once. She reminded Jack of Katharine Hepburn, in a way. She said, "What's a muffler-and-tire man doing searching through 1926 newspapers in Madison?"

"I was looking for any mention of The Oaks. It's a nursing home, out near Lake Wisconsin."

"I know The Oaks. I know *of* The Oaks, rather."

"You do? Seems like hardly anybody does; or if they do, they're not telling."

"Well, it was a mental hospital, more than a nursing home, that's why. Many of the local people objected to it when they discovered what it was. But in the end they closed it down anyway."

"Yes, I know that," said Jack. "I'm interested to find out *why* they closed it down, and under what circumstances."

Helena Manfield inclined her head to one side, interrogatively.

Jack said, "I've been thinking of buying it, as a matter of fact. Converting it into a resort hotel. I just wanted to know something about its history."

Helena Manfield thought about that for a while, looking down at the diamond ring on her left hand. Then she said, with great preciseness of speech, "You'll forgive me, Mr. Reed, for being inquisitive. But it seems to me that you've been searching for this history with more than what I would usually describe as a *casual* interest."

Jack gave her a wry smile. "Does it show that much?"

"Well . . . you've been here almost all afternoon, without any lunch. You look a little *disheveled,* I must say, for a man who's buying a resort hotel. And *frantic,* if you don't mind my saying so."

"Miss Manfield—" said Jack. "Do you happen to know who owns The Oaks?"

"Of course, I've known her for years, ever since she came here. Olive Estergomy, she was the middle one of the three Estergomy girls."

"And they were the daughters of Dr. Estergomy, The Oaks's previous owner?"

"That's right. Beautiful girls, all three of them. Alice, Olive, and Lucy. Beautiful! But then their mother was very good-looking."

"Do you happen to know why Dr. Estergomy closed The Oaks so suddenly?" Jack asked her.

Helena Manfield shook her head. "Nobody ever knew. We didn't find out that it had closed for months and months. Then one of our local storekeepers happened to mention that the Estergomys had canceled all of their orders for provisions."

She stood up and walked back to the table where she had been working. "The Estergomys left the area at the same time. The only one of them who ever came back was Olive. She never said much, whenever I asked her about The Oaks. She wouldn't talk about her family, either. In the end I could see that she didn't want to discuss it, so I left her alone. It was sad, though. Once upon a time the Estergomys were very good friends of ours. My father and Dr. Estergomy used to get along like a house on fire. But when they left, they didn't even stop by to say good-bye."

"So you never found out what had happened?"

"No," said Helena Manfield. "There were scores of rumors. But my guess is that the local residents managed to put enough pressure on the state penal commission to have them withdraw their funding."

Jack said nothing for a while. While Helena Manfield had been talking, he had been unexpectedly visited by a vision of Randy. Those big serious eyes; that hesitant way of talking. He could almost *feel* him; he could almost smell him. His warm biscuity hair.

"You're crying," said Helena Manfield, in a matter-of-fact voice.

"I'm tired, that's all." This time he made no attempt to wipe away the tears.

"You must tell me what's wrong. Perhaps I can help."

"I don't know," said Jack. "I don't think anybody can."

"Well, you can always try me," Helena Manfield suggested. "I think I know something about emotional pain."

"What do you know about losing people?" Jack asked her.

Helena Manfield stood up straight. "I'm a spinster, you know. I shouldn't have been. My fiancé died in the war. He was in the air force, shot down at Ploiesti. Over three hundred young airmen died that night, in Romania; and all because Allied intelligence said there were scarcely any guns there."

She took a sharp breath. After forty-five years, her bitterness was still fresh. "After that—well, nobody else seemed to compare. I preferred being alone."

Jack said, "I'm sorry."

Helena Manfield smiled, her eyes out of focus. "Don't be sorry; it all happened a long time ago. I shouldn't whine. Have you lost someone, too?"

"My son, Randy, he's nine. I took him out to The Oaks."

"Yes?"

"Well, I know it sounds crazy. But he disappeared."

Helena Manfield said, "When?"

"Last night. Late last night. We searched the building from top to bottom, twice over, but we couldn't find him. He's hiding someplace. God knows where."

"Did you call the police?"

Jack shook his head. "He's still in the building, I'm sure of it. And, besides, I've been given the distinct impression that the police aren't going to be very amenable. Not when it comes to The Oaks, anyway."

"You've lost your nine-year-old son and you don't want to call the police?"

Jack shrugged. "Sounds irresponsible, doesn't it, when you put it like that. But I don't honestly think the police are going to be able to help."

Helena Manfield stayed silent, watching him.

"Let's put it this way," he said, "the first question the

police are going to ask is what I was doing at The Oaks so late at night, with a nine-year-old boy; and the second question they're going to ask is why did I kill him?"

"You don't think he's dead?"

"No, he's not dead. Least, I don't *think* he's dead. I pray that he isn't. But things aren't as simple as they sound."

"Believe me," Helena Manfield replied, "they don't sound the least bit simple."

She thought for a moment, and then she said, "Why don't I introduce you to Olive? She's very shy, but she talks straight. Maybe she can give you some ideas where your boy might be hidden. Maybe The Oaks has a secret closet or a secret passage, something like that."

"Olive Estergomy still lives around here?"

"Certainly, she has a house out at Sun Prairie."

Jack said, "That's near enough. Fifteen, twenty miles? What can you do, call her?"

"Of course I can call her." She picked her purse up from the floor, and opened it, and took out a small crocodile address book. "And before you ask me *why* I'm going to call her, let me tell you that I've been trying to find an excuse to see her for ages and ages, and that I'm bored silly, and that I *love* to stick my nose into other people's business."

"Sounds reasonable to me," Jack acknowledged.

She went out to the pay phone in the corridor. Jack stood beside her as she slotted in her dime and dialed the number. From the office close by, he could hear the flat plasticky rattle of somebody typing out a story on a word processor.

At last she said, "Olive? Is that Olive? Olive, this is Helena! Helena Manfield, of course!"

They drove out to Sun Prairie under a sky that was smudged with thick charcoal clouds, past red-painted barns and dark green fields of curly kale, past silvery silos and rain-beaded greenhouses. Helena Manfield said very little, but refused to wear a seat belt and sat with her hands in her lap like two fitfully sleeping birds.

Jack drove badly, jerking the brakes at intersections and running two red lights. It was only now that he was beginning to understand how tired he was.

It was almost dark when they reached Sun Prairie. Helena directed Jack off 151 onto 19, and then down a jolting unmetaled track that finally brought them out on top of a hill, where a green-painted house stood all on its own, surrounded by grass and flowers and nothing else, as if it had been dropped out of the sky like Dorothy's farmhouse in *The Wizard of Oz*.

Jack parked next to an abandoned harrow and a rusty feed trough, and arm in arm he and Helena Manfield made their way against the stinging rain up to the porch.

The front door was opened almost immediately. The light from inside was reflected on the wet boards of the porch. A woman's voice said, "Come along in! Come along in!" and the next thing Jack knew he was jostling out of his coat in the smallest of hallways.

"Well, Helena!" Olive exclaimed. She was a large, big-boned woman, much taller and bigger than Helena Manfield, but attractive, too. Her gray hair was tied back from her forehead with a blue velvet band, her eyes were almost violet, and she had the broad, intelligent face of somebody who wouldn't put up with fools, but who could laugh at herself quicker than anybody else.

She wore a large dress patterned with blue-and-black flowers, striking but messy.

"Come in! Helena, you dear person! I just couldn't believe it when you called! It's been so long!"

She led them through to a parlor crowded with good but mismatched antique furniture. A French chaise longue, upholstered in green figured silk, a brown leather armchair, and occasional tables of all shapes and sizes. On the walls hung unnaturally bright watercolors of Wisconsin lakes, and framed diplomas and honorary degrees. Jack leaned over the chaise longue to examine one of the degrees more closely. From Edinburgh University, an honorary doctorate in clinical psychology, awarded to Elmer J. Estergomy, March 12, 1921.

A log fire was smoldering weakly in the grate. Olive Estergomy stabbed at it with her poker, and then said, "The wood's so damp."

"I'm Jack Reed," said Jack. "I'm the fellow who's been negotiating to buy The Oaks."

"I see," said Olive Estergomy. She looked questioningly at Helena Manfield, twisting her long amber necklace between her fingers. "How did you happen to meet Miss Manfield?" There was an odd implication in her voice that he and Helena had cooked up some kind of conspiracy between them.

"Olive, we met at the *Times-Dispatch*, purely by accident," Helena told her. "I was pasting clippings, and Mr. Reed was trying to find items about The Oaks."

"I was very impressed with your proposals, Mr. Reed," said Olive Estergomy. "It would be wonderful to see the place restored."

Jack said, "Has Mr. Bufo been in touch?"

"He told me your suggested price, and I accepted."

"Has he been in touch today?"

Olive Estergomy stood by the fireplace, leaning slightly to one side, like a gym teacher restraining herself from giving a practical demonstration. "Not today, no. Is anything wrong?"

"I told him that I had to speak to you face-to-face. I told him that if he didn't arrange it, the whole deal would have to be canceled."

Olive Estergomy slowly sat down. The fire began to crackle and spit. "Mr. Bufo didn't say a word about that. Not a word."

"I made a point of telling him it was urgent," said Jack.

"Perhaps he thought that it would upset me. And, as a matter of fact, it *has* upset me. Why should you need to speak to me in person?"

Jack laced his fingers tightly together. *Here is the church, here is the steeple, open the door* . . . "Miss Estergomy, I need to know what happened, the night The Oaks was closed down."

Olive Estergomy stared at Jack, her face rigid. It was only now that Jack noticed the faintest tic in her left eyelid, the constant fluttering of suppressed anxiety. "Nothing happened. We closed it down, that's all."

"For any special reason?"

"We didn't have sufficient patients to remain open, that's all. It was plain economics."

Jack took out his handkerchief and wiped his nose. "I was told you had one hundred thirty-seven patients the night you closed down. That was more than you'd ever had before."

"Who told you that?"

"Joseph Lovelittle, the caretaker."

"Oh, him. I hope you realize that Joseph used to be a mental patient, too."

"He seemed pretty sure about it, mental or not."

Olive Estergomy lowered her eyes and didn't reply.

"Miss Estergomy—" said Jack. "My nine-year-old son is missing. I took him to The Oaks yesterday evening and he disappeared. I'm desperate to find him."

"You took him to The Oaks?" asked Olive Estergomy flatly.

"Miss Estergomy, there's something strange about that building. I've experienced it for myself. Noises, voices, hallucinations." He didn't go further; he didn't want her to think that he was a candidate for the nuthouse, too.

Olive Estergomy remained totally silent for almost a minute. Then, as if she had suddenly arrived at a crucial personal decision, she said, "They disappeared. They all disappeared."

Jack was perplexed. "Who disappeared, Miss Estergomy?"

She looked up. "The patients, of course. Every single one of them. One minute they were all there; the next they were gone."

She fell silent again for a very long time. A minute, more than a minute.

"Can you tell me how it happened?" Jack coaxed her. It was obvious that the memory still distressed her.

"There's nothing much to tell. We were sitting together in our parlor that evening when one of the male nurses knocked on the door—shouting, frightened—and said that all the patients had escaped. Of course my father couldn't believe it. But when we went up to the first floor, we found that every single room was empty."

Helena Manfield sat down, too. "Olive," she said. "You never told me this."

"Nobody would have believed me, my dear; not even you."

"But if all those lunatics had gotten out—"

"They were gone, yes. But they hadn't gotten *out*. Not in the sense that they had opened their doors or climbed out of their windows. Every single room was still locked, and none of those rooms could be opened from the inside. Every single window was still intact; barred and unbroken. There were cups of coffee in the lounge, still hot, still only half-drunk. There were newspapers, dropped on the floor. Just as if they had all *evaporated*."

"But if there were over a hundred of them," Helena Manfield protested. "Where did they go?"

Olive Estergomy shook her head. "To this day, Helena, I simply don't know. My poor father was almost driven insane himself, looking for them. Where *could* they go? He called the police and of course the police found the doors locked and the windows unbroken, and at first they assumed that my father had suffered some kind of a breakdown and let all the patients free himself. They were never particularly sympathetic, the police, because my father was a great champion of rehabilitation for the criminally insane. He actually believed that they could be cured, and returned to the community, whereas all the police wanted to do was to see them exterminated."

Jack said, "What happened then?"

"The police searched the whole area. But they couldn't find a single footprint—not one—nor any sign that over a hundred people had escaped from The Oaks. They were called less than an hour after the patients disappeared, and since some of the patients were physically handicapped as well as mentally handicapped, and most of them were wearing nothing but hospital robes, and some of them were completely naked because they would have strangled themselves with hospital robes, the chances of them having gotten any further than the perimeter fence were practically nil."

"But?" said Jack.

"But they were gone," Olive Estergomy replied. "One hundred and thirty-seven patients had completely vanished."

"And you don't know where?"

Olive Estergomy said, "Perhaps God took them. Perhaps the devil took them. I don't know."

"What did the police do about it?" asked Jack.

"There was nothing they *could* do. There were no patients. There were no clues. None of the patients had been seen on the roads or in the woods or attempting to hitchhike. No thefts of clothes were reported. No barns broken into. Nothing."

She paused for a moment. A pretty little silver clock on the mantelpiece chimed six. "At ten-thirty that evening, a whole gang of assorted bigwigs arrived from the justice department and examined the building for themselves. They talked to my father for ten minutes, and then they officially declared that The Oaks was closed. Well, of course, it had to close, we didn't have any patients left. But the official reason they gave for its closure was that they no longer had confidence in my father's rehabilitation program."

"How did they explain the patients' disappearance? I mean, officially?"

"They waited for a week, to see if any of the patients would show up. When they didn't, the justice department announced that they had all been sent to a new high-security facility up at Lake Nokomis. After six months—when none of them had reappeared anywhere—they told the relatives of those patients who still had relatives who cared about them—and, believe me, that wasn't too many—that their not-very-loved-ones had died of food poisoning. I think they even held funerals."

"That's astonishing," said Helena Manfield.

"Of course, but what else could they do? How were they going to tell the public that one hundred thirty-seven highly dangerous mental patients had vanished without a trace and that every effort to find them had met with complete failure?"

"Did the police have any theories about it?" asked Jack.

"No," Olive Estergomy replied. "As far as I know, they erased the case from their records, just as if it had never happened. They took away all of my father's case histories, too, and you can imagine what happened to them. It broke his heart."

"What happened to your father?" Jack inquired, as gently as he could.

"He couldn't work any longer. After The Oaks, there wasn't a state in the country that would allow him to practice. We went to England for a while, where he made some money lecturing; then we moved to France. My father drowned in 1934, while he was swimming in the sea off Arromanches. My mother died the following year."

"Your sisters?" asked Jack.

"They stayed in France. They were still living near Paris when war broke out. I never found out what happened to them."

She said, in the quietest of voices, "That evening in 1926, Mr. Reed, everything vanished out of my life. Not just one hundred and thirty-seven mental patients, but my father's career, my mother's health, my two dear sisters."

"I'm sorry," Jack told her uncomfortably. "I'm really sorry."

"But you've lost your son," said Olive Estergomy.

"He's still at The Oaks," Jack replied. "That's why I wanted to talk to you."

"I'm not sure what you mean."

"I'm not too sure what I mean, either. But I think I know where he is, and I also think I know what happened to your father's patients."

Olive Estergomy frowned at him. "You know where they went?"

Jack nodded. "I have a theory—well, half of a theory. You'll probably think that I'm just as loony as they are."

"Mr. Reed," said Olive Estergomy, trying hard to contain her ferocious curiosity, "would you like a drink?"

"Do you have whiskey? If not, a beer would go down well. And please call me Jack."

"Olive," said Olive Estergomy. "Although my friends call me Essie."

"All right, Essie." Jack nodded. "Just one question first. Can you tell me why you haven't thought of selling The Oaks before now?"

Essie was opening her stained-oak liquor cabinet. "I've had two or three offers," she said, "and once I even advertised it. But there's a clause in the deed that says that nobody must demolish the building; and until *you* came along with your idea of restoring it, and turning it into a resort hotel, nobody else was interested in keeping the building intact. You know yourself that it will probably take millions to bring it back up to scratch."

"Have you ever visited it?" asked Jack. "I mean, since 1926?"

"I went back to look at it about four years ago. I didn't go inside. As you can imagine, it doesn't hold very many pleasant memories for me."

"They're still there," said Jack.

She stopped in the middle of pouring out his whiskey. Her back remained turned, but he could tell from the tension in her shoulders that she knew what he meant. She was waiting for him to spell it out for her.

"The reason that nobody could find those so-called escaped lunatics was because they never escaped. They're still there. I've seen a couple of them. They're inside the walls."

Essie turned around and was staring at him wide-eyed. Helena said anxiously, "What do you mean, they're inside the walls? How can they *possibly* still be there? That was over sixty years ago, they would have died of old age by now. And what would they eat?"

Jack didn't take his eyes away from Essie. The emotion in her face was an inch away from total tragedy. *My father, my mother, my poor dear sisters. And they're still there! Those screaming, foaming, raging lunatics! They're still there!*

"I knew it," she said. She was trembling. "In a peculiar way, I always knew."

"But how *can* they be?" Helena insisted. "It's impossible! *Inside* the walls? In secret passages, is that it?"

Jack laid his hand on her arm. "I don't know how they got into the walls; and I don't know how they managed to survive. But they're not in secret passages. They're actually, *physically*, inside the bricks. I know it sounds wacky. I know it defies all the laws of physics and all the laws of nature, you know, all that stuff about two material objects not being able to occupy the same space at the same time.

"But," he said, "I've seen them. I've actually seen them. They've got my son. They almost got me."

He bent forward, lifted up the cuffs of his pants, and tugged down his socks. "See these bruises? One of them came right up out of a solid concrete floor and grabbed me."

Essie handed him his glass of whiskey. Helena said, "You won't mind if I help myself to a gin, dear? I'm shaking all over."

"No, no, go ahead," said Essie abstractedly. Then she looked at Jack and said, "It's madness, isn't it? It's absolute lunacy."

"I know," he told her. "But it really happened. And you know it really happened because you were there when they disappeared, weren't you? And what other possible explanation could there be?"

"I've never heard anything like it," said Helena. "You've made me feel utterly unreal."

Jack said, "Ther s one called Lester."

"They *spoke* to you?" asked Essie, in astonishment.

Jack nodded. "They communicated, in a way. I'm not sure that you'd actually call it speaking."

"Lester Franks, that was his name," said Essie. "I remember Lester very well. He always appeared so sane. He used to sing songs to me and tell me stories. He couldn't have been older than eighteen or nineteen. Always helpful! Always ready to run errands! And do you know what he had done? When he was baby-sitting, at the age of fourteen, he had cut off his three-year-old sister's head. They had found him playing ball with it in the yard, throwing it up and catching it. The whole yard had been smothered in blood."

"Oh my God, Essie, you're making me sick," Helena protested.

"Oh, no—most of them had done far worse," said Essie. "Mind you, when my sisters and I were children, we used to revel in all the gory details. There was one man there, what was his name? Holman or Hofman or something like that. His wife had chattered too much, so he had tied her wrists and ankles to a dining-room chair and nailed her tongue to the table. She was there for days before anybody found her."

"Essie, I *am* going to be sick," Helena proclaimed.

But Essie continued regardless. "My father tried to rehabilitate this Holman or Hofman or whatever his name was by giving him odd jobs to do. One evening he didn't come in for his tea and they found him in the garden, unable to move. He had nailed his own penis to a tree."

"Essie!"

"I'm sorry, Helena," said Essie. "But that's exactly what kind of people they were. They had no feelings for human life whatever. They couldn't tell the difference between pain and pleasure. Some of them would amuse themselves by cutting off their own fingers and playing with them. They were utterly insane, Helena! You have no idea!"

"That's not the kind of people they *were*," Jack corrected her. "That's the kind of people they *are*."

"Well, Jack," said Essie, "I'm not at all sure I know how to react to that. I don't know what to say, or what to feel, or anything. I believe that you're telling me the truth, but I'm not so sure that my mind is going to *allow* me to believe it."

"There's one thing I need to know," said Jack. "Was there ever a priest attached to The Oaks? Or a local chaplain that the patients might have known?"

"Why, yes, of course. There was Father Bell. He was only a young priest, but he used to come out to The Oaks every Sunday for any of the patients who wanted to take Communion. Some of them were fanatically religious. One of them was quite sure that he was God, and every time Father Bell said 'praise the Lord' he used to say 'thank you very much.'"

"Do you happen to know if he's still alive?"

"I really have no idea. I haven't seen him since the night the patients disappeared. If he *is* alive, he must be getting on to ninety."

"He was there the night the patients disappeared?"

"Yes. He just turned up, I don't know why."

"You weren't expecting him?"

"No, it was Monday. He usually came only on Sundays. Oh, once I think he came on a Saturday afternoon, when we had a carol service. What a disaster *that* was! Can you imagine a hundred and fifty homicidal schizophrenics trying to sing 'We Three Kings of Orient Are?'"

Jack gave her a tight smile. It must have been essential for the Estergomy family to retain a sense of humor in the dangerous half-world in which they had been living out at The Oaks.

"Can you remember which church Father Bell came from?"

"Oh, yes. St. Ignatius, I think it was, at Portage."

Jack finished his whiskey. "Essie," he said, "I'm sorry I busted in on your privacy. But I hope you can understand that it was only out of desperation. You've been truly helpful."

Essie smiled. "I want you to keep in touch, Jack, tell me what's happening. I pray that you find your son."

She hesitated, and then she added, "If you find those people . . . the patients. If you find them, be very careful. They were sent to The Oaks because they were too dangerous for anybody else to take care of. They have no conscience whatsoever, and some of them are very strong.

"There was one in particular, a man called Quintus Miller. Watch out for him. He was incredibly intelligent, incredibly powerful, and totally mad. He nearly killed a woman patient once, I won't tell you how."

Jack went to the door and buttoned up his coat. "Quintus Miller," he repeated. "Lester mentioned somebody called Quintus. All right, I'll take care. And I'll call you if I find out any more."

After Jack and Helena had left, Olive Estergomy stood very still in the middle of her crowded parlor with her hands pressed together as if she were praying. The feeling of dread that she hadn't felt for sixty years had returned, cold and familiar. It was a dread that was worse than the dread of death. It was the dread of everlasting pain that couldn't be borne, and of screams and sobs and nightmarish laughter.

It was the dread of The Oaks, and of utter madness, and of Quintus Miller.

S·I·X

Jack drove back to Howard Johnson's, showered, and changed into one of three new shirts he had bought in Madison. He called his office. It had closed for the night, but he guessed that Mike Karpasian would still be there. Mike said they were up to their asses in muffler replacements, and when the hell was Jack going to sign the checks for B. F. Goodrich because B. F. Goodrich sure as hell wasn't going to supply them with any more tires unless they paid for the last consignment, but apart from that everything was going good.

Karen wasn't home. Bessy said that Karen had taken Sherrywine to the doctor because Sherrywine had regurgitated her fish fingers all over Mommy's favorite long-haired nylon scatter rug.

He called Maggie. Maggie was furious because he hadn't called her all day and she wanted to take Randy to a special Women's Consciousness-Raising Gala on Saturday. Jack said he wasn't outstandingly keen on having his impressionable nine-year-old son hanging out with a bunch of lesbians and nuclear disarmers and nonsexist knitters, but then he suddenly thought of the Turd, and of Randy rising out of the floor, and his throat tightened and he had to hang up the phone without saying good-bye.

Maggie, of course, couldn't call him back because she didn't know where he was. But he bet the phone back at home was ringing and ringing, and would probably ring all night. Maggie was that kind of a woman.

He called Daniel Bufo but Daniel Bufo had left for the day.

He ordered a New York steak and a bottle of red wine on room service. He sat with his plate on his lap watching "The Cosby Show." It was the first time he ever watched it and didn't laugh once.

He didn't know when he fell asleep, but when he woke up it was well past ten o'clock and his mouth felt dry. His half-finished steak lay on the bed beside him. He rubbed his eyes and sat up. This was no good. He had to sleep properly. He undressed, brushed his teeth, switched off the television, and climbed into bed.

He lay there awake for hour after hour, staring up at the ceiling, thinking about people who played finger puppets with their own amputated fingers and of men who tried to kill women in ways that were so horrifying they couldn't even be described.

He thought of Lester, the face on the statue. *Lester always appeared so sane.* He thought of Quintus Miller.

It was nearly three o'clock in the morning when he thought he heard a noise in his room. He lifted his head from the pillow, frowning into the darkness. The night was completely silent now. The traffic on 94 had dwindled to an occasional long-distance semi. The motel stood silent.

But there it was again. *Sssssshhhhhhh—sssssshhhhhhh—sssssshhhhhhhh:* just like that noise in the walls of The Oaks.

Jack went cold. He eased up his sheets and slid sideways across the bed, trying to make as little sound as possible. But the dragging noise continued, and it was coming closer. *Sssssshhhhhh—sssssshhhhhh—sssssshhhhhh.*

He froze, trying to suppress his breathing. Maybe it would pass without realizing that he was here. He closed his eyes in the hope that it would vanish if he did, but then he immediately opened them again because he didn't want it sneaking up on him without him seeing it.

Please God may it drag itself away.

It was then that he saw a dark hump rising up beside the bed. It was brown sculptured motel carpet, but it was in the shape of a boy. *It was Randy, rising out of the floor.*

Jack lay back on the bed, staring at him in horror.

"Randy?" he mouthed. "Randy?"

The priest, Daddy. We want the priest.

"Randy—is that you? Randy!"

Bring us the priest. That's who we want. We want to chop off his fingers and guzzle his bones.

Numb with fear, Jack reached out with both hands and took hold of Randy's carpeted shoulders.

You shouldn't touch me, Daddy. You never know what might happen.

"Randy, for Christ's sake, I want you back!"

Jack tugged at him, trying to wrench him out of the carpet. But instantly Randy's head fell off, and rolled heavy and carpeted across the bed. Ice-cold blood spurted out of his neck, drenching the sheet.

Jack screamed and screamed, rigid with terror.

He screamed so loudly that he woke himself up. In fact he wasn't screaming at all, but making a hoarse *haahhhhh!* sound. He had thrashed out with his arm and knocked over the glass of water beside his bed, splashing the sheet. There was no decapitated Randy swaying next to the bed, no carpeted head lying on the covers. It was ten after six, still raining, but already light.

He lay on his back for five minutes, breathing deeply to calm himself down. He must have slept for at least three hours, and he felt much more refreshed. He never had needed too much sleep. At last he eased himself out of bed and called room service for coffee and toast.

He drew the drapes. The raindrops freckled the windows. Beyond the motel parking lot he could see the trucks roaring through the spray, on their way to La Crosse and Eau Claire and Duluth, or southeastward toward Chicago.

Today he was going to get Randy back. He pledged himself that. No matter what it took, by nightfall tonight, his son was going to be safely back in his arms.

While he drank his coffee, he leafed through the telephone directory. There were twenty-two Bells, none of whom lived in Portage. But he did find the number for St. Ignatius. He called it, and nobody answered. It was, after all, quite unlikely that anybody would be sitting around a church at six o'clock in the morning, even in Portage. The best solution was to drive up there. It was only about thirty miles.

It took him over an hour to reach Portage because of the rain. By the time he turned onto the cracked concrete parking lot outside St. Ignatius, his eyes were strained from staring into the spray, his neck was stiff, and his back felt as if it were clamped in a vise.

He stepped on the parking brake, unfastened his seat belt, and stretched.

St. Ignatius was a small church on the southern outskirts of Portage, a gray cinderblock building with a roof of green-painted corrugated iron. On one side of it was a lumberyard, on the other side a gas station. The church boasted a spire, with a single bell, and arched wooden doors with stained-glass windows in them, but otherwise it could have been mistaken for a paint shed, or a boat shed, or any other kind of shed.

He climbed out of his station wagon and hurried across the concrete driveway with his collar pulled up against the rain. He was just about to climb the wooden steps to the front door when a voice shouted out, "Nobody there! Hey, mister! Nobody there!"

"What?" Jack came back across the concrete. A pimply teenage boy with an immense blond pompadour was leaning out of the garage pay booth.

"Nobody there," he repeated as Jack came up close.

He paused, and then obviously realized that Jack might have been going to St. Ignatius simply to pray. "Well," he said, "'cepting for God."

Jack said, "I'm looking for a priest."

The boy sniffed. "Father Dermot, he's your man. But he ain't there today."

"I was looking for Father Bell."

"Father Bell? Ain't never heard of no Father Bell. You sure you got the right church?"

Jack nodded. "Father Bell was the priest in charge here back before the war."

"My dad was in the war, Fourth Marine Regiment."

"I mean the war before the war before that."

"Huh?" the boy asked him in bewilderment, wrinkling up his nose.

At that moment a bullet-headed man in a greasy pair of overalls appeared, wiping his hands on a piece of torn rag.

"Hey, what happened to my coffee, zitface?" he demanded. He glanced at Jack and said, "How are you?"

"I forgot," said the boy.

"He forgot," appealed the bullet-headed man. "He'd forget where his frigging ass was if his body didn't bend in the middle."

The boy disappeared inside the pay booth. Jack said, "I've been looking for a priest who used to be here, at St. Ignatius. Wonder if you've heard of him, Father Bell."

"Sure," said the bullet-headed man without hesitation. "I know Father Bell."

"He's still alive?"

"Sure, he lives up at Green Bay now, in one of them senior citizens' homes. His daughter Hilda is friends with my wife, they trade recipes."

"His *daughter*?" asked Jack.

"Sure. He gave up priesting, years before I ever knew him. But everybody kept on calling him Father Bell regardless. Like kind of a nickname, you know. Or when you leave the army, people still keep on calling you colonel."

He paused to yell out, "How long does it take you to make one frigging cup of coffee? What the hell are you doing, growing the frigging beans?" He finished wiping his hands, balled up the rag, and tossed it with impressive accuracy into a trash bin on the opposite side of the forecourt. "This frigging weather, doesn't it make you want to kill yourself?"

Jack asked hesitantly, "Father Bell's daughter . . . can you tell me where she lives?"

The bullet-headed man gripped Jack's arm. "You drive straight down here until you reach the first turnoff to your right. You turn off. There's a yellow house directly in front of you. Well, I say yellow to be polite. More like somebody barfed their Mexican dinner all over it. That's the house."

The boy appeared with a mug of coffee.

"My son," said the bullet-headed man. "What the hell did I do to deserve a son like this?"

"I shall be eighty-eight this year," said Father Bell. "I was born on September sixth, 1901, the very same day that President McKinley was shot. Of course he didn't actually die till eight days later."

He turned away from the window and looked at Jack with sad glistening eyes. "My childhood is so clear to me now, every detail, as if I were regarding it through a crystalline window, brightly lit. Yet it was eighty years ago! So far away, and lost forever."

"Your daughter asked me to bring you these," said Jack. He held up a soft red paper package.

"Ah, bed socks," said Father Bell. "Well, that's very kind of her. She's always sending me little gifts and keeping in touch. A good girl, Hilda. A fine, gentle girl. Have you known her long?"

"I met her for the first time today," Jack told him.

"Really?" asked Father Bell in faint surprise. Then, "Really?"

Father Bell was a tall angular man, with no spare flesh on him at all. His wrinkled skin was shrink-wrapped onto his skull, so that his eye sockets and cheekbones appeared inky and cavernous. He was almost bald, but his eyebrows were dramatic and bushy, and his nose curved out like the outstretched wing of a bat, all veins and bones and translucent nostrils.

He wore a taupe-colored turtleneck sweater and a voluminous pair of brown bell-bottom pants, which he must have bought some time in the 1970s. *"Imagine me and you, I do, I think about you day and night. . . ."*

Jack said, "I was talking to Miss Olive Estergomy yesterday."

"Essie! Were you? Now there's a surprise! I call her Essie, you know."

"I know," said Jack, and couldn't resist adding, "So do I." He paused for a moment and then he said, "Essie told me you used to administer Sunday Communion at The Oaks, back in the days when it was a mental institution."

Father Bell said nothing, but fixed Jack with unblinking eyes. Outside the window of his shadowy room, the rain coursed across Bay Beach Park. The bay itself was almost completely hidden by misty spray.

The room was modern and clean, with an orange-covered sofa bed and a pine desk and an armchair and a scrupulously neat bookshelf. But apart from a framed black-and-white photograph of the round-faced woman who lived in the house that looked as if somebody had barfed their Mexican dinner all over it, there were no personal knickknacks whatever. It was the sort of room that if you died in it at four minutes to nine in the morning, it could be ready for its next guest at eleven minutes after.

All of the books were impersonal, too: dated best-sellers like *The Holcroft Covenant* and *The Carpetbaggers*. Considering that Father Bell was a former priest, it was noticeable that his bookshelf contained no Bible.

Jack ventured, "Essie also told me that you visited The Oaks the night the patients all disappeared."

Father Bell breathed in and out, in and out, as if it were something he had to make a conscious effort to do, in order to stay alive.

Jack persisted, "Father Bell—this is kind of presumptuous of me, I know that. But the fact is that my son has disappeared, too. At The Oaks."

Father Bell turned his head in profile. For an achingly long time he said nothing at all, but occasionally moistened his lips with the tip of his tongue.

"Father Bell," said Jack, "I know my son's there. And I need your help to get him back."

At last Father Bell shifted in his chair, his hands crawling over themselves in his lap like two skeletal cats. "What you're talking about, Mr. Reed . . . that all happened a very long time ago."

"They're still there," said Jack.

For a moment he could see that Father Bell was considering the option of denying all knowledge of who "they" were. But Jack had said it so directly and so forcefully that there was no escaping it.

"They're *still there*?" he repeated, in disbelief.

"You know what happened to them, don't you?" asked Jack. "You know where they went."

"Yes," said Father Bell. "I know where they went."

"Are you going to tell me about it?"

The horror of what Jack had said suddenly began to sink in. "They're still there, you say? After all these years? My God . . . I didn't think that they would be able to survive. They should have starved, by rights. They should have died within days. Still there! My God, still there!"

"Tell me about it," Jack insisted. "You have to."

"Oho, my friend, I'm not so sure that I should. I'm not sure that I *can*. If they're still there, my God!"

"Father Bell, I have to save my son."

"I'm not a priest anymore, Mr. Reed. I have no duty to help you."

"What are you talking about, duty?" Jack demanded. "He's just a kid!"

"You don't know them, Mr. Reed. You don't know them the way I do."

"You're trying to tell me you won't help? You're eighty-eight and my son's nine. Doesn't that count for anything? He's got his whole life ahead of him!"

Without warning, Father Bell clutched the arms of his chair and twisted from one side to the other and bellowed hoarsely, "I'm terrified, Mr. Reed! I'm frightened to death! My God, do you know what you're asking me? You're crazy! You're *crazy*! You're almost as crazy as they are!"

Jack stood up, and walked across the room, and stood right over him. Father Bell rolled his eyes up toward him, then looked away. Jack said, more patiently, "It can't hurt you just to tell me about it."

"Ah, no. But if they find out—"

"They won't find out. How the hell can they?"

Father Bell shook his head. "They'll know. They'll guess! Nobody else knows what happened but me. One of them told me, during confession. That's why I couldn't tell the police. That's why I left the priesthood. I saw poor Elmer Estergomy, pilloried by the state; I saw his whole family ruined. And all the time I couldn't speak out to defend him, because of what a madman had told me in confession."

Jack said, "Damn it, Father Bell, you have to tell me now. Because, by God, if you don't tell me now, my son is going to be killed by those lunatics; and if that happens, then I'm going to kill you, and that's a promise, and damn the consequences."

Jack had never threatened anybody like that before, and he was almost as frightened by what he was saying as Father Bell was. But when the old man whispered, "You won't let them out, will you? Whatever happens, you won't let them out?" he knew that Father Bell was going to tell him what he wanted to know.

Jack dragged his chair two or three feet nearer and sat down again. "This patient who talked to you in confession —was it Quintus Miller?"

"How did you know that?" Father Bell's voice was jumpy with terror.

"Inspired guess, I guess. Essie Estergomy told me he was probably the toughest and the most intelligent of the whole lot."

"Yes, he was, by a long shot. Quintus Miller, my God. He was an extraordinary man. Short, but very broad, very muscular. He looked like a weight lifter. A neck as thick as a bull's! Black hair, greased down, parted dead center. Of course that style was fashionable then. A face like a rock. Hard eyes, eyes like nail heads, completely without expression, completely without compassion. And a tattoo on his chest like you've never seen in your life. Two tattooed hands, apparently reaching around from behind him, and tearing his abdomen wide open. His insides, tattooed in red and yellow and blue—his stomach, his liver, his intestines. It used to make me freeze just to see it."

Father Bell took a whistling breath in one nostril. "It was the way he flaunted his own mortality, that was what frightened me so much. There is nothing so terrifying as finding yourself faced with a man who does not care if he lives or dies. There were quite a few of them like that, at The Oaks, both men and women, but they were usually *self*-destructive. None of them frightened me the way that Quintus Miller frightened me. You felt that if *he* were faced with death, he would do everything he could to take as many people with him as he could. That man had the morals of a hammerhead shark."

Jack stayed quiet for a while, to give Father Bell the chance to calm down. Then he said, "Tell me what Quintus Miller told you in confession."

"We had many confessions. Two years of confessions, almost every week. I warned Dr. Estergomy several times that Quintus was very dangerous. But of course Dr. Estergomy knew that already, from his attempts to rehabilitate him.

"It was quite *unhinging*, listening to Quintus talk. He sounded so rational, and yet you would suddenly realize that he was telling you the most hideous, obsessive, illogical nonsense. In confession, in almost the same breath, he would admit to sins as inconsequential as stealing candies from other patients, or masturbation, or lying, or blasphemy, and then he would tell me that he had tortured his fellow patients by breaking their fingers or by crushing their testicles in his fist. He had no sense of proportion. To stub out a cigarette on somebody's eyelid was no more but no less serious to Quintus Miller than to steal a bar of chocolate.

"He tried to kill a woman patient, you know. Attacked her with his bare hands. But since he was already incarcerated for life and had already been declared by the courts to be mentally incompetent, the worst they could do to him was lock him up in solitary confinement."

Father Bell hesitated, and then he said, "After about a year at The Oaks, Quintus suddenly started talking about freedom, about getting himself out. When I asked him about it, he said he had found a way to escape. I advised Dr. Estergomy to check the building's security, but Dr. Estergomy said he was completely satisfied that not even the most determined patient could get free. In those days, of course, the whole property was surrounded by a ten-foot barbed-wire fence.

"All the same, Quintus went on and on about escaping. He said he had discovered something about the building that would help him get out. He kept rambling about mazes and what he called 'earth magic.' He became so obsessive about it that I had to ask the nurses to take him away sometimes, because his confessions were going on for half an hour at a time."

Jack said, "You still didn't believe that he could really escape?"

Father Bell shook his head. "I didn't believe in his so-called earth magic, that's why."

"And what was 'earth magic'? Did he explain it to you?"

"I knew about it already," said Father Bell. "Earth magic was the magic of prehistoric times, the magic of the Druids. The pagan priests believed that there were spiritual forces within the earth itself. They believed that all over the world, at certain precise locations, these spiritual forces manifested themselves in places of special sanctity. In Britain, there was Stonehenge and Glastonbury. Here in the United States, we have Mystery Hill, in New Hampshire, and Gunjiwaump, in Connecticut, and North Salem, New York, and—well, there are dozens of others."

"Including The Oaks, Wisconsin," Jack suggested.

Father Bell nodded. "All of these magical locations were interconnected one to the other by a pattern of unswervingly straight lines. Ley lines, they called them, which meant *lea* lines, or meadow lines. Quintus said that The Oaks had been built at the precise intersection of several of these ley lines—that, in fact, it was the principal center of earth magic in the entire North American continent—and not accidentally, but on purpose."

Jack thought for a moment and leaned back in his chair. "Then I guess it follows that what's-his-name, the beer baron, Adolf Krüger—he must have known about earth magic, too?"

"Almost certainly," Father Bell agreed. "It's hard to imagine that he built The Oaks on that precise spot by accident. I often speculated how Quintus Miller had first found out about earth magic. He wouldn't tell me, of course. But the only logical conclusion seemed to be that he had discovered a book in Adolf Krüger's library. I don't know whether you know it, but Krüger himself had left the house in very mysterious circumstances."

"But how was this earth magic going to help Quintus Miller escape?" Jack asked.

Father Bell watched the rain dribbling down the window for a while. Then he said, "At the time, when he told me, it sounded to me like the babblings of a lunatic, so I scarcely listened. But I remember him saying that the building itself was the key to the underworld. It was like a maze, he said, and if he could find his way to the center of the maze, where the ley lines converged, and where the four elements of the universe became one, he would have access to the ley lines, and be able to escape along them 'like strolling down a highway.' That's what he said. 'Like strolling down a highway.'"

Jack said, "Another thing I want to know is—how come you were up at The Oaks that night they all disappeared?"

"Chance, mostly," Father Bell replied. "I telephoned Dr. Estergomy around seven o'clock to tell him I was going to be late the following Sunday, because I had to drive some of the Sunday-school children out on their picnic. He said, 'You won't believe this, Father, but they've all gone.' Well, I remembered at once what Quintus Miller had been telling me, so I got into my car and I drove up there directly."

Quietly he said, "What I saw there filled me with complete consternation. The patients' rooms were still locked, their windows were still barred, but they were gone, every single one of them. You can imagine what I felt like. But in my consternation I recalled what Quintus had told me, that the building was a maze—and that before he could escape along any of the ley lines, he would have to reach the center of the maze. I prayed that he and his followers had not yet had the time to do so.

"I ran outside, and I circled the building, consecrating the boundary as I did so, running, sprinkling it with holy water, and reciting the prayer for keeping evil spirits at bay.

I had only just finished when I heard a rushing noise, a terrible rushing noise, like a hundred barefoot people running toward me, under the ground.

"It was *them*—it was the inmates of The Oaks, and they were escaping. I was convinced of that. I was terrified. But the rushing abruptly stopped, because they had come up against the holy circle I had described around the building. I hadn't been able to prevent them from vanishing; but I *had* managed to prevent them from leaving the building.

"There was a howling beneath the ground which still gives me nightmares to this day, and a pummeling of fists against the earth, *drum-a-drum-a-drum-a-drum*, like an earthquake."

He took a deep breath, as wheezy as Joseph Lovelittle's Doberman. "I thought the patients would reappear in their rooms after a while, when they realized there was no way for them to escape. But they never did. Perhaps it was only possible for them to pass through the maze in one direction. After several weeks I could only presume that they had all perished. That was another reason why I gave up the priesthood. I believed I had the deaths of one hundred thirty-seven helpless people on my conscience."

Jack said, "What about the circle, the holy circle? Is that still there?"

"Of course it is; and it will stay there. It can only be removed by the priest who originally consecrated it, or by three cardinals acting in concert."

"And of course you wouldn't even think of removing it?"

Father Bell stared at him. "If I were to let Quintus Miller and the rest of those creatures loose on the world—as insane as they always were, and as full of vengeance and resentment as they must be now—well, that would be an act of the gravest irresponsibility. That would probably make me an accessory to *massacre.*"

The door opened and a freckle-faced nurse looked around the door. "Are you ready for your supper, Billy?"

Father Bell looked up. "What is it tonight?"

"Fish cakes."

"Goddamn it, I hate fish cakes."

"Don't be long," the nurse told him brightly, and closed the door.

Jack said, "That your name—Billy?"

Father Bell's mouth sloped sideways in a cynical smile. "My old man's idea of a laugh, calling his son Bill Bell. That's the kind of practical joke that parents used to play on their children way back then. Not that they're any better these days, calling them Wentworth and Chevy."

"How about coming out to eat with me?" Jack asked him. "I haven't eaten all day. There must be one or two reasonable restaurants here in Green Bay."

"Why should you want to take an old man of eighty-eight out to eat?" Father Bell asked him suspiciously.

"Because I'm hungry. Because I hate to eat alone. Because I want to talk to you more about The Oaks. Want any more reasons? Lobster has to be better than a fish cake."

For the first time Father Bell smiled. "You're a persistent man, Mr. Reed."

"So would you be, if your son was stuck in a wall with Quintus Miller."

Father Bell opened his eyes. "Where are we?" he said, sitting up in his seat. "I must have dozed off for a while."

Jack took the keys out of the station wagon's ignition. "I decided to take the pretty way," he said tiredly.

Father Bell wiped the fogged-up window with his hand. "Where the hell are we? This isn't Green Bay!"

"No, you're right, it isn't. We're back at The Oaks."

Father Bell stared at him in indignation. "The Oaks? You had the goddamned nerve to take me all the way back here to The Oaks?"

"You were sleeping, after all of that lobster and all of that Chablis. I guessed you wouldn't mind."

"Are you crazy? Are you stark staring crazy? This is kidnap, for God's sake! Let me out of here!"

Jack unlocked the station wagon's doors. "Go ahead. It's pouring with rain, it's three-thirty in the morning, we're ten miles away from the nearest human being, and you don't have a raincoat. Not to mention the fact that you're eighty-eight years old, and you have bursitis."

"How do you know that?" Father Bell demanded irritably.

"You told me, over dinner. You told me a lot of things about yourself, over dinner."

"You can't do this," Father Bell protested. "You have no right."

"My son gives me the right."

Father Bell said, "Listen, my friend, I'm very sorry about your son. But I can't help you. There's nothing that I can do. I haven't been a priest for sixty-three years; and I don't have the slightest desire to be a martyr."

"You must have had some compassion for other people, to want to be a priest."

"Oh, sure, and look where it got me."

"It got you *here*, Father Bell. Right back where you left off. If you want a classic lesson in facing up to your responsibilities, this is it."

"Don't you moralize to me!" Father Bell roared back. "I did what I could; I stopped those bastards from getting away! I can't do anything else! You can't expect me to do anything else! Jesus Christ, that was back in 1926! I was twenty-five years old! I did what I could!"

"Please—you can talk to them, at least," Jack insisted. He knew that Father Bell was terrified. He knew that it had been wrong of him to drive him all the way here. Taking an elderly ex-priest against his will and driving him half the length of the state in the middle of the night was probably a criminal offense punishable by twenty years in the state penitentiary, or worse; and he probably deserved it, too.

But he was too tired and too desperate to worry about

the morality of what he had done. All he knew was that
Lester had asked him to bring them the priest, or Randy
would be crushed.

Father Bell hunched forward in his seat and peered
through the darkness toward The Oaks. "Can't see it. Trees
must've grown."

"I don't suppose it's changed much," Jack told him. He
opened his door. "Are you coming?"

"Does that mean I have a choice?"

Jack leaned into the car. "You're here, Father Bell. You
can finish what you started. You might as well give it your
best shot."

Father Bell sat in the passenger seat of the car, looking
yellow-skinned and fragile and very tired. "To tell you the
truth, Mr. Reed, I'm not at all sure that I've got it in me."

"Will you *talk* to them? That's all I'm asking. If nobody
can deconsecrate the circle around the house but you, then
what have you got to worry about? The choice is entirely
yours."

"I don't know," said Father Bell. "I'm not too sure I
want to face up to Quintus Miller again . . . not after all
these years."

Jack walked around the station wagon and opened the
door. "Come on, Bill Bell. Let's do it to them before they
do it to us."

Father Bell hesitated for a moment, but then he swung
his legs out and reached for Jack's hand to help him.

"God-awful night," he remarked.

The two of them walked up the gravel drive together,
with Father Bell leaning heavily on Jack's arm. The wind
was up, and the rain flew almost horizontally through the
darkness, like a plague of ice-cold locusts. Jack had bought
new batteries for his flashlight, and he flicked the beam
here and there so that Father Bell could see the building he
hadn't visited for more than sixty years.

"Grounds are overgrown," Father Bell observed. "Apart

from that, though, can't say that it's changed hardly at all. Same look, same smell. If you knew how much I used to dislike this place."

"You and me both," said Jack.

He helped Father Bell around the back of the building to the conservatory. He opened the door, and they stepped inside. Father Bell peered this way and that in the darkness.

"Ruined," he said, touching the broken plant pots and the desiccated plants. "You should have seen it then! Every variety of hothouse flower you could think of! And a grapevine, too!"

"Come on," said Jack, and led him into the lounge.

Father Bell hesitated, stopped, and looked around him. "I can't believe it. It hasn't changed. It hasn't even been *touched*. Can you imagine coming back to a house you once lived in sixty years ago and finding it exactly the same as the day you left it? It's uncanny!"

They went through to the hallway. Jack quickly shone his flashlight on each of the marble statues, but both of them were as blind as justice. Their footsteps crunched on the gritty marble floor. Up above their heads, the huge iron lantern creaked in the early-morning draft.

Father Bell shuddered in the cold. "Do you know what night it was, they all escaped? June twenty-first, midsummer's night. Didn't strike me as relevant till years later. But that's the time when the forces of the earth are strongest. Summer solstice. One of the Druid times. One of the times when the ley lines come to life, and all the earth joins up."

"I fit mufflers," Jack told him. It was a way of saying that he had very little imagination, at least as far as magic was concerned.

"Sure you do," said Father Bell. "And I spend my time staring out of the window at Green Bay. But just because you and I are practical and pragmatic, my friend, that doesn't stop the summer solstice coming around, and that doesn't impress the elements. Earth, fire, water, and air. And the fifth element where they all meet together—the Quintessence."

They stopped in the middle of the hallway. The building was dark and silent. But Jack knew now that it was more than a building, very much more than a building. It was a mystical maze, built on one of the most potent sites in America—a site that had probably had awesome significance in the days when America had been explored by Celts and Norsemen and ancient Egyptians. Jack felt afraid, in a way that he had never felt afraid before.

"You're right, they're here," whispered Father Bell. "I can feel them."

"Wonder if they've realized we're here?" asked Jack, shining his flashlight toward the cellar door. It was slightly ajar.

Father Bell made the sign of the cross and said, *"Crux sacra sit mihi lux; non draco sit mihi lux; uade retro Satana; nunquam suade mihi uana; ipse uenena bibas."*

Jack glanced at him. "You still remember the jargon, then?"

"It's not something that you forget."

The cellar door creaked very slightly. Jack strained his eyes to see if there was anything there, hiding in the darkness.

"Maybe I'd better call them," he suggested.

Father Bell's mouth tightened, but he said nothing. He was too concerned with looking around, and with his memories, and with his fears.

"What do you think?" Jack repeated. "Do you think I'd better call them?"

Father Bell nodded.

"Lester!" Jack shouted. "Lester, you there?"

His voice echoed around the galleried landing. He waited, but there was no reply. No sign of movement; no eyes opening; no dragging sounds.

"Lester, you asked me to bring you the priest and I brought you the priest!"

Still no reply. Father Bell touched Jack's sleeve and whispered, "They *asked* you? You didn't tell me that!"

"Would you have come up here if I had?"

"I'm here under sufferance anyway."

Jack cupped one hand to the side of his mouth and called, "Lester! Lester, where are you?"

At that instant the cellar door flew open and a large dark object came rushing across the floor toward them.

Father Bell cried out, *"Jesus!"* but Jack was too frightened even to speak.

He saw almost straightaway, however, that the dark object was Joseph Lovelittle's Doberman, Boy. Its eyes gleamed, staring and yellow in the beam of his flashlight, and its jowls were bursting with creamy froth.

It had nearly reached them when it abruptly stopped, its claws skidding on the marble floor. It let out an anguished scream. Jack had never heard a dog scream before, and he was chilled right down to the base of his spine.

A hard marble white hand had reached out of the floor and gripped the dog's back paw. Gradually, forcefully, it was pulling the dog downward.

Boy barked and yelped and scrabbled desperately at the tiles, but the hand sank smoothly back down into the marble, pulling the paw after it.

Jack pushed his flashlight into Father Bell's hands and circled the struggling dog, looking for an opportunity to seize his struggling body. He lunged forward once, and the dog's claws scratched at the back of his hand. Then he lunged forward again and caught hold of him.

"Domine sancte, Pater omnipotens, aeterne Deus . . ." mumbled Father Bell, crossing himself again and again.

Jack pulled at the Doberman as hard as he could. He could feel its muscles shuddering with pain and terror. Its spine whiplashed. But the hand that had risen from the floor was far too strong for him. All he could do was try to keep his grip as the dog's sleek-haired body was dragged into the floor.

"Ab insidiis diaboli, libera nos Domine!" Father Bell shouted out, in pious desperation. But his prayers were hopeless; because Boy was pulled straight into the floor without any hesitation at all.

The dog's head disappeared last of all. Its mouth gaped, its eyes bulged. It uttered one last gargling bark. Then it was gone, and the floor was as smooth as it had been before.

"Per Dominum nostrum Iesum Christum Filium tuum, qui tecum uiuit, et regnat in unitate Spiritus sancti Deus, per omnia saecula saeculorum, amen," Father Bell whispered. Hopeless.

"A warning," said Jack, shivering. "I'll bet you anything you like that was a warning. Don't play any games, that's what they're telling us, or this is what's going to happen to *you.*"

He stepped back. As he did so there was a gurgling, sticky noise from the floor in front of him. Out of the marble poured the remains of the dog, gray flesh, rainbow-colored intestines, strips of ripped-apart skin. A single severed leg, which shuddered and kicked in the last throes of nervous reaction.

And somewhere in the house, faint and clear, came the strains of a song.

> *Lavender blue, dilly-dilly;*
> *Lavender green.*
> *Here I am king, dilly-dilly;*
> *You shall be queen.*

"Quintus Miller," breathed Father Bell.

S·E·V·E·N

*T*hey climbed the stairs. Father Bell had to pause halfway up to rest for a moment or two, but Jack waited for him patiently.

"I'll show you Quintus's room," said Father Bell as they resumed climbing. "After he almost killed that woman, it was always kept locked, and he was allowed out only for exercise, and of course for therapy with Dr. Estergomy."

"Dr. Estergomy still continued treating him?" asked Jack.

Father Bell cleared his phlegm-clawed throat. "Oh, yes. He continued treating him. Elmer Estergomy believed that no disturbed mind was beyond redemption. I was a priest, you know, and a priest who had been trained as an exorcist—but I'm afraid that I disagreed with him. I saw some terrible things here, Mr. Reed. I saw men and women whom the Lord had quite plainly deserted for good and all; and for whom there was nothing left in their lives but unremitting hell. Hell on earth, and hell hereafter."

They walked along the eastbound corridor until they reached the third window. Father Bell stopped to listen. The corridor was airless and oppressive. Still very faintly, they could hear *"Lavender blue, dilly-dilly . . ."* quiet and mocking as a humiliating memory. Father Bell said, "He always used to sing that song, over and over. And he always used to change the words, to say *here I am king*. I suppose in a way that he was. There was nobody at The Oaks who was stronger than Quintus Miller, nor more determined."

He stopped and lifted his hand as if he were giving a benediction. In front of them, one of the doors stood ajar. Cream-painted, like the rest, but much more kicked and scratched.

"This was Quintus Miller's room," Father Bell breathed. Jack had the odd impression that Father Bell was almost relieved to see it, as if he had suspected all his life that he would have to come back here one day.

At least the waiting was over.

Jack said, "That door was locked, the last time I tried it. I tried all the doors along here."

Father Bell gave him a sideways glance that was almost mocking. Then he pushed open the door to reveal the interior of Quintus Miller's room. There was no furniture, only a mattress and a toilet without a seat. The room smelled sour and musty and indefinably evil. Jack didn't even want to go inside.

"There, on the wall," said Father Bell.

In the gloom Jack could see that a huge six-pointed star had been scrawled on the wall with some dark brown substance, a substance as dark as blackberry juice, or blood, or excrement.

"What's that?" asked Jack, peering at it in distaste. "The Star of David?"

Father Bell approached it cautiously. "Not exactly. This is the Hexagram of Solomon. It is, quite simply, the most powerful occult symbol ever known, even more powerful than the cross. It has as much meaning in pagan worship as it does in Judaism and Christianity. It looks like a star; but more accurately you should interpret it as one triangle superimposed on another. The upward-pointing triangle—you see?—which represents fire and air. And the downward-pointing triangle, _ere. which represents earth and water.

"Where these triangles overlap, in the six-sided figure within, there is the conjunction of all ancient power—the fifth element, the Quintessence. Presumably Quintus used this power to escape into the walls."

"Quintus? Quintessence? Do you think that could be more than just coincidence?" Jack asked him.

Father Bell shrugged. "The fifth son and the fifth element? You may be right. But I regret that my knowledge of earth magic and all its ramifications is not very extensive. I was, after all, a Roman Catholic priest, not a Druid."

Father Bell looked around. "This hellhole," he remarked. "The number of times I sat with Quintus Miller in here, trying to reason with him, trying to restore his sanity. But he was too far gone for me, and too far gone for Elmer Estergomy."

"All the same," said Jack, "maybe we ought to try calling him."

Father Bell allowed himself the weakest of smiles. "I don't think we need to call him, Mr. Reed. He knows we're here, don't you, Quintus?"

The rain prickled against the window, behind the protective steel mesh, wooly with dust, unsteady with age. The passing years had punished the building as it had punished them all. But the passing years had left Quintus Miller keener than ever for freedom and revenge, while Father Bell had been left dried up like a chili pepper and just as frail, and craving nothing except peace, and his book-club thrillers, and his tedious pine-and-orange room. Even sixty years of disappointment and boredom were better than sixty seconds of absolute pain.

There was no response. Jack listened, but there was no *sssssshhhhhh* noise inside the walls, no telltale dragging of human bodies through solid brick and solid cement.

"Maybe we'd better try the cellar," he suggested, although the last place on the whole planet he wanted to go back to was the cellar. "That's where they tried to pull me down into the floor, and that's where I found Randy's toy."

But Father Bell lifted one hand and said, "Wait. I can feel something; I'm sure."

Jack waited and listened. "I don't know, Father. I can't hear anything."

Moments passed in soft rustling quietness, like a plaza at night when thrown-away newspapers are blown across it in the wind. Rain, the nervous banging of a downstairs door.

Father Bell approached the pentacle scrawled on the wall. "This is the entrance to the underworld," he said. "A gateway, do you understand what I mean? The pentacle gives you access to the maze; and the maze in turn brings you to the point where the ley lines intersect; and from there—well, my friend—from there you can journey anywhere you wish."

He laid his hands flat on the pentacle and examined it with a serious face. "In the fifteenth century, occultists were quite matter-of-fact about passing from one element to the next. They saw the elements simply as a kind of ladder, up which one could progress from the stonebound underworld at the bottom to the ethereal realms of heaven at the top. Given the right conditions, the human soul could exist in all of these elements, the way that fish swim around in the sea."

Jack looked around him uneasily. "What I want to know is—how did Quintus Miller and the rest of them actually get *inside* the wall. I mean you say that's a gateway. But how does it work? You can't just step into solid brick, can you?"

Father Bell continued to smooth his hands across the design on the plasterwork. "It's happened before. Some of the stories about it are ancient legends, like Theseus going into the labyrinth in Crete to kill the Minotaur. Some of them are much more recent, like the Pied Piper, who led all the children of Hamelin into solid rock."

"But how's it *done*?"

"There are rituals for entering the underworld in the same way that there are rituals for entering heaven. Substantially there is very little difference in them. In the nave of Chartres cathedral, in France, there is a maze that you can follow, and the movements you make when you follow it are a ritualistic dance that are part of the procedure for reaching a condition of divine spirituality."

Jack pounded on the wall with his fist. "But this is *brick*, for Christ's sake! There's nothing spiritual about brick. It's not a state of mind, it's hard-baked clay!"

Father Bell said, "If Quintus Miller did it, we can do it. We'll have to try Elmer Estergomy's library. We can probably find the rituals in there."

Jack stepped back. He was beginning to wonder if it had been such a good idea, bringing Father Bell back to The Oaks. Although there were rustlings and scrapings inside the walls and the whole building seemed to be agitated, Quintus Miller and his followers were keeping themselves very well concealed, and there were no more signs of Randy, or indications from Lester or anybody else about how Jack might get him back.

"Lester!" he shouted. "Lester, I brought you the priest!"

Again, there was no response. Jack felt the cold throat-swallowing feeling of complete despair.

"Lester!" he repeated. "Lester, can you hear me, damn it! You promised to give me my son back!"

Almost immediately, in answer to his shouting, the wall inside the pentacle began fluidly to bulge out. It rose into the shape of a human face. A boy's face—Randy's face. Jack stared at it, not moving, with a mixture of horror and anticipation. Perhaps Lester was going to keep his word after all and let Randy go. The only trouble was—what was he going to expect in return?

Randy's paint white face opened its paint white eyes.

Daddy? I don't like it here. Please help me. It sounded like an old-fashioned tape recording of Randy's voice.

Jack stepped forward but Father Bell caught at his arm. "Don't, Mr. Reed—not yet. It could be a deception of some kind. Quintus was always very devious."

Daddy, begged Randy. *You have to help me. Please, Daddy, help me!*

"What do you want me to do, spaceman?" Jack asked him. "Spaceman" was an affectionate nickname that Jack had given Randy when he was very small, when he used to fling him, giggling, up into the air.

Daddy, they want to bè free.

Father Bell clutched Jack's arm even more tightly. "No!" he breathed. "You can't let them out! That would be absolute madness! They would murder, they would rape! You have no conception of what they're like! They're scarcely human!"

Please, Daddy, pleaded Randy's masklike face.

Jack said to Father Bell, "All right, listen. You say they'd go wild if you let them out. But what can they really do? They're mentally backward. They've been shut up in this place for over sixty years. Essie Estergomy says some of them are physically handicapped, too; and half of them are bare-ass naked. What can they do? If they escape, they're going to get picked up by the police before you know it. Especially if we *tell* the police what to expect."

Father Bell still refused to release his grip on Jack's sleeve.

"Mr. Reed, you have no idea of how strong they are, and how totally *vicious* they are. Why do you think they were sent to The Oaks in the first place? Have you seen that metal mesh covering the windows by the staircases? Have you seen how dented it is? They used to throw themselves against it, from the top of the stairs. One second they would be smiling and laughing and talking as sanely as anybody you'd ever met—the next second they would be crashing themselves against the mesh, and rolling down the stairs, screaming and shuddering and foaming at the mouth."

Jack inclined his head toward Randy's face on the wall. "That's my boy there, Father Bell," he said, his voice unsteady with tiredness and emotion. "That's my son."

"I know, Mr. Reed; and I can understand how you feel.

But we have to find another way to get him out of there. We don't dare let Quintus Miller go."

"You mean *you don't dare.*"

Father Bell's nostrils flared. "Very well, if that's the way you want to put it, *I don't dare.* But more than that, I won't accept the responsibility."

"Did I ask you to?" Jack retorted.

Daddy, whispered Randy. *Please, Daddy, they're going to hurt me if you don't.*

Jack abruptly twisted his arm free from Father Bell and approached the wall. "Here, Randy—take hold of my hands. Can you do that? Can you get your hands out? Come on, spaceman, I'll pull you out of there!"

"No!" shouted Father Bell, rushing after him.

With a jarring blow from his bony shoulder, Father Bell knocked Jack away from the wall. But as he did so two plaster white hands, far too large to be Randy's hands, came thrusting out of the wall. One of them caught hold of Father Bell's right wrist. Father Bell shouted in fear and tried to pull his wrist away, but the hands were far too powerful for him.

Jack stumbled, caught his balance, and immediately plunged forward to help Father Bell break loose. As he did so, however, Randy's face turned to him and snarled with feral teeth.

Get away, you stupid interfering bastard! A voice cement-thick with menace.

Jack recoiled. "Randy?" he called. "Randy?"

But in front of his eyes, Randy's face suddenly crumbled like dry chalk, and broke open to reveal beneath it the staring face of a man. Just as white, just as masklike, but with a narrow forehead and near-together eyes, and lips that peeled back to reveal long teeth in badly receded gums.

"Holman!" whispered Father Bell. "Gordon Holman!"

The very same, Father Bell, the face crowed at him. *What a good memory for faces!*

Jack skirted cautiously around behind Father Bell's back, looking for an opportunity to grab Holman's arm and to pull Father Bell loose. But in a high hysterical shriek, Father Bell cried out, "No! Don't! Stay well away! It's far too dangerous!"

Oh, come on, Father Bell. We're all dangerous!

"Gordon, let me go," said Father Bell. "I took care of you, Gordon, you just remember that. I brought you gum, didn't I? I brought you all of those movie magazines."

Holman smiled at the memory of it. *You were a good priest, Father Bell. We all loved you, you know; until the last. We all trusted you.*

"Come on, then, let me go," Father Bell encouraged him. "Come on, now, there's a good fellow. You're hurting my wrist."

But the narrow chalky face on the wall half closed its eyes and gave Father Bell a knowing, superior grin. *You heard what I said, Father Bell*—until the last. *That was when you betrayed us. That was when you trapped us here. Trapped, Father Bell! No way to go forward, no way to go back.*

Father Bell said fearfully, "Let me go, Gordon. No good is going to come of this."

The face laughed out loud. *You're right, Father Bell! No good at all!*

At that instant Jack lunged at Holman's arm and tried to wrench it away from Father Bell's wrist. But the arm was hard and chilled and muscular, startlingly inhuman, and Jack wasn't nearly strong enough to break its grip. There was a second's pause, and then Jack heard Randy screaming *Daddy! Daddy! Don't!* right above his head.

Horrified, confused, Jack stepped back. Randy's head and shoulders had appeared out of the ceiling, with a man's hand gripping the back of his neck and forcing his head down into the room as if he were trying to drown a puppy. Jack shouted, "Randy!" and hurled himself upward, jumping two or three times; but the ceiling was too high, and each time he missed by inches.

Daddy! Please! Save me! Daddy, they're hurting me! Daddy, they're going to—

Randy was lifted forcibly back up into the ceiling, and its molecules closed over him like the surface of a bowl of freshly mixed plaster. In fury and desperation, Jack turned back toward Father Bell, and toward the staring white face in the middle of the pentacle.

"You evil bastards! You let my boy go, you hear me? For Christ's sake, I brought you the priest, didn't I? What the hell else do you want? Let him go!"

But the voice was soft and sly and adamant. *Quintus says—only if you let us out.*

Jack shouted back, "You want out? We'll let you out! Come on, Father Bell! What the hell difference is it going to make?"

But Father Bell cried out, "Mr. Reed! Don't even *think* about letting them go! Never! Not in a thousand years! Mr. Reed—don't listen to what he says! I beg you, Mr. Reed! Never!"

Jack pointed furiously up to the ceiling. "You saw that? You saw that boy? That's my son! And what the hell *difference* does it make if we *do* let them out, that's what I'd like to know! In any case, don't shout at me. I can't let them out, not on my own. Only you can do that. And what do you think? *You* think that it's more important to stop some—some theoretical 'revenge of the loonies'—you think that's more important than saving my son! Brother, you should have gone into politics, not the church."

"Mr. Reed," said Father Bell. He was trying to sound rational, although he was grimacing with pain. "There is nothing theoretical about these people, nor about their madness. You're misjudging them, badly. Once they get out of here, you will never be able to stop them or to control them. If they get the chance, they will slaughter everybody who gets in their way."

Oh, but we'll have our fun first, said Holman. *Like* this!"

He suddenly cracked Father Bell's right arm back and smacked it tight against the wall. Father Bell cried out, the pitiful cry of a man who was born into this world with nothing, and will leave it with nothing.

You stopped us, Father Bell, whispered Holman. *We had come through the maze, we had struggled not to panic, we had struggled to stay alive. Some of the women were as crazy as shit, do you think it was easy? But there they were. The ley lines stretched in front of us—north, south, east, west, anywhere we wanted to go. They were beautiful. The first beautiful things that most of us had ever seen. We stood there, you know? Whores and homicidal crazies and arsonists, and we all agreed that this was it, this was the future. Freedom, light! That Quintus Miller, what a magician! And we drank in that magic, and we drank in that glory.*

He closed his eyes completely. *One moment of joy! One moment of hope! But you know what happened then? The shutters came down! Oh, yes, you bet! The shutters came down! One by one, the ley lines were sealed off. Sealed off by darkness, just like a mine caving in; darkness—falling through the surface of the earth; rolling thunder. That was you, Father Bell! That was you, and your fancy incantations, and your holy water! And that was the last we saw of the world outside. You stopped us, Father Bell, you trapped us! But now we want out, buddy! Now we want out!*

Father Bell lifted his head. His Adam's apple quivered, stringy and vulnerable.

"I can't do it, Gordon. I can't let you go."

You want to suffer?

"I've been suffering for sixty-three years. I can't let you go."

The face opened its eyes. Then—suddenly—another hand burst out of the wall and seized Father Bell's left hand. He was pulled tight up against the wall, his arms outstretched, his face pressed against the plaster. He turned his head sideways and stared back at Jack in pain and terror.

"Holman!" Jack warned the chalk white face. "Don't you touch him! Let him go!"

What he needs is suffering, the face replied. *True suffering, the way that Christ suffered. That's why Quintus chose me for this. I'm good when it comes to suffering.*

There was a deafening bang, which made Jack jump back. Father Bell screamed—a scream so high that at first Jack wasn't sure that he had really heard it. His right arm had disappeared up to the elbow into the wall. Then there was another bang, and his left arm vanished in the same way.

Father Bell screamed again and again, trying to tug his arms free from the wall. Gordon Holman's face melted away, but then it reappeared on the other side of the room, next to the door.

The crucifixion of Father Bell, Holman said, gloating.

"Let him go!" Jack shouted. "For God's sake, let him go!"

For God's *sake? We don't do anything for God's sake. And why should any of us feel sympathy for Father Bell? Think what he did to us—keeping us captive here for sixty years.*

Jack went up to Father Bell, who was whimpering and shaking in anguish. He tried to pull Father Bell's arms out of the wall, but just like Randy's woolly toy they had fused with the brickwork; flesh and brick were indivisible.

"Get him out!" he repeated, turning back to Gordon Holman.

There's only one way to get him out now, said Holman. *And that's to amputate his arms.*

"He's eighty-eight years old!" Jack retaliated. "Whatever he did when he was twenty-five, he's an old man now, completely helpless!"

That's right. The same way that we've been helpless.

"Oh God," babbled Father Bell. "Oh God, it hurts; oh God, it hurts."

"Are you crazy?" Jack screamed at Gordon Holman.

Holman tittered. *Of course I'm crazy. We're all crazy. What did you expect in a nuthouse?*

"Let him go!"

If he lets us go, we'll let him go.

"And if he won't?"

We still have your son, we still have little Randy. So if Father Bell won't let us go, you'll just have to go off and find yourself three cardinals, won't you, to get us out, and that isn't going to be easy. Otherwise, Randy gets skrushed into something that won't even look like a boy.

"I beg of you, I beg of you," wept Father Bell. His sunken cheeks were wet with tears.

Jack leaned against the wall, very close to him. "Father Bell, you're going to have to let them go. You're going to have to say the words. For Christ's sake, Father Bell, that's the only way they're going to let you out of there."

"Can't," wept Father Bell. "You don't even understand what they'll do."

Is he going to help us? asked Gordon Holman. *Perhaps he needs a little more persuasion.*

"Can't you see that he isn't going to give in to you?" Jack demanded.

Oh . . . I don't know. Wait till we set his hands alight. We can do that, you know. Anything to do with the elements. Earth, water, air, fire. Go take a look in the room next door, and watch him light his candles to God.

The white face melted again. In blind anger, Jack stalked across the room and punched the wall where it had been. "He's an old man, you bastard! Let him go!" His fury was all the worse because he had brought Father Bell down here against his will, and in spite of Father Bell's own warnings. The responsibility for every ounce of Father Bell's agony was entirely his.

"Oh God protect me," breathed Father Bell.

Jack said, "Father, listen to me. You're not a priest

anymore. You said so yourself. You don't have to feel guilty about letting these people go! It isn't your job anymore! Just let them go, and they'll let you go! You think you're going to die here, with your arms buried in a wall? Is that what you think you're going to do? You want to be a martyr, or what?"

Father Bell turned to stare at him, and as he did so his jaw dropped open in a soundless scream of absolute pain. He shuddered and shook, and hit his own forehead against the wall, but he couldn't get free.

"What is it?" Jack asked him in panic. "What are they doing to you?"

Go take a look in the room next door, and watch him light his candles to God.

Immediately Jack hurtled out of Quintus Miller's room and rushed to the door of the adjacent room. It was locked, as Quintus Miller's room should have been locked. Jack frantically rattled the handle, but it wouldn't open.

Father Bell shrieked. "*Oh God, oh God, protect me!*"

Jack lifted the brass cover over the door's spyhole. What he saw made his skin prickle and his mouth flood with bitter saliva. Father Bell's hands came right through the wall, from Quintus Miller's room, as if he were standing in a pillory. The tip of each finger was blazing; and even though Father Bell was wriggling his fingers in a desperate attempt to extinguish the flames, it was clear to Jack that the fire was far too hot, far too intense.

He shook the door violently, until he heard the frame cracking. But it was far too solidly built for him to budge it. It had been designed to keep criminal lunatics locked away for life, and even the most desperate of men couldn't have forced it open.

All he could do was stare in horror as the flesh at the end of Father Bell's fingers reddened and blistered and charred, and his fingernails curled up like burned onion skins.

Already, with every agonized wriggle, the bones of

Father Bell's fingers were breaking through the skin. In anoher minute, the way this fire was blazing, he would have no hands left at all.

"I'll do it!" screamed Father Bell. "Gordon! Gordon! Aaaahhhhhh, Gordon! Gordon, I'll do it! Aaaaahhhhh! Gordon! Please, Gordon, I'll do it! *I'll do it!*"

The fire was immediately snuffed; although Father Bell's blackened fingers still smoldered like charcoal twigs and filled the room with smoke. Jack went back into Quintus Miller's room and found that Father Bell was quivering with pain and shock. Blood ran from the sides of his mouth because he had halfway bitten through his tongue, and crept along the creased of his age-weathered skin.

Jack put his arm around Father Bell's shoulders, feeling helpless and angry and nauseated. Father Bell's eyes filmed over. The pain in his hands and arms was raging so furiously that he kept lapsing in and out of consciousness.

In the corner of the room, the plaster boiled and bubbled like liquid mud. A man's form appeared, between one wall and the other, a short thin man, naked except for a shawl around his shoulders. He looked toward Father Bell with blank plaster eyes, and there was an expression of peculiarly lunatic compassion on his face.

Father Bell gasped, *"The pain—the pain I can't bear it."*

Jack turned toward the naked figure in the corner. "Come on, for Christ's sake, let him out of this wall."

Christ suffered more, the figure in the shawl replied, withouth taking his eyes away from Father Bell. *At least, that's what you Gentiles keep telling us.*

Jack took a deep breath. 'For the sake of humanity, then. Let him go.

When we go, he goes. That was the agreement.

Jack held Father Bell tight. "Father Bell? Can you hear me? Just nod if you can hear me. You have to let them go now. You have to say the words."

Father Bell nodded. There was a lengthy pause, while he moistened his blood-dried mouth, and then he whispered,

"In the name of the Father, and of the Son, and of the Holy Ghost . . . I hereby declare that this palcce which I have consecreated and protected . . ."

He hesitated, and licked his lips. He leaned his head against the wall. "I can't do it," he said. "I mustn't."

You want the fire again? the figure in the corner asked him. *You want us to burn your hands down to the wrists?*

"Father Bell," Jack insisted, holding him closer still, feeling his bony shoulders beneath his coat. "Father Bell, you have to. There's no other way out."

Father Bell took a shivering breath. Then he went on. "This place which I have consecrated and protected from the forces of darkness and devilry . . . should now be deconsecrated, and returned to the natural state of its creation . . ."

As he spoke these words Jack felt a shifting and a stirring inside the building, as if thousands of cockroaches had been disturbed inside its walls. The figure with the shawl smiled slowly in triumph.

". . . and released from the guardianship of all His holy agents . . ."

The shifting and stirring grew louder. It was like the sound of a huge crowd of silent people, shuffling toward a single doorway. Then it grew louder still. It was all around them. *Sssssshhhhh—ssssssshhhhhh—ssssssshhhhhhh.* The thick, concrete-mixer sound of human molecules being dragged through solid brick, as the long-imprisoned inmates of The Oaks made their way back through the maze of its walls, toward that ancient and terrifying place where the mystical ley lines intersected, where all four elements became one Quintessence.

". . . forever, and ever. . . ."

Father Bell finished his recitation. His face was glistening with tears and perspiration. "That's it," he said. "That's everything." But he had hardly spoken when the shuffling in the building suddenly stopped. Jack stepped back from Father Bell and listened, his head raised up.

"What is it?" he asked. He turned to the plaster white man in the corner. "Why has it gotten so quiet?"

We're still trapped. The ley lines are not yet open.

"Father Bell?" Jack demanded; but Father Bell did nothing but groan.

The deconsecration is not complete, said the figure in the wall.

"What do you mean? He said all the words, didn't he?"

The ley lines are not yet open, the figure insisted. *We are all still prisoners.*

"Father Bell?" Jack repeated. "Father Bell—you must have left something out. They're still trapped inside the building. Father Bell!"

Father Bell's head lolled. He was only half-conscious. Jack shook him and said, "Father Bell! Wake up! You must have left something out!"

Father Bell stared at Jack with misted eyes. "I have to—make—the sign of the cross."

Jack turned back to the figure in the shawl. "You *have* to let him go! He has to cross himself, otherwise you'll *never* be free!"

He has to cross himself?

"That's right, you've got it. He has to make the sign of the cross, in the air, you got it? With his hand, you stupid bastard. Otherwise spellee no workee."

The figure opened and closed its powder white eyes like a desert lizard. Then it flowed back into the corner of the room, with a billowing of plasterwork, and vanished. Probably going to talk to Quintus Miller, Jack guessed, as he heard it slide through the brickwork with a swift *sssssshhhhhing* sound.

Jack waited, supporting Father Bell's sagging body as much as he could. He was exhausted, too, both physically and emotionally. He hadn't even allowed himself to think if he could bring this nightmare to an end—or, if he did, how he was going to deal with the guilt of what he had done to Father Bell. All he wanted right now was to get Father Bell out of the wall, and to rescue Randy.

"Hilda?" asked Father Bell, deep in shock. "Is that you, my dear Hilda?"

"It's okay." Jack shushed him. "Hilda's going to be here soon."

He waited almost five minutes. Father Bell may have been emaciated, but he was big-boned, and heavy, and Jack's back began to ache from holding him up.

"For God's sake!" he shouted at the wall. "Are you going to let him go, or aren't you?"

His answer came explosively, almost at once.

With a grinding, mincing, chopping noise, Father Bell's arms were cut off just where they met the wall. His body dropped, Jack couldn't hold on to him. Blood pumped out from both of Father Bell's sheared-off elbows. Jack jumped back, sprayed with sticky scarlet. But as he did so, two white hands lunged out of the wall, fast as rattlesnakes, and seized hold of Father Bell's spurting right forearm, and flung it this way and that, *Domine sancte, pater omnipotens, aeterne Deus,* mockingly imitating the sign of the cross.

Blood filled the room in a mist of droplets and spatters. For one fraction of a fraction of a second, the bloody cross that Father Bell had described in the air with his mutilated elbows hung suspended in front of them in glistening loops of gore, just like water from a hose wiggled into a figure eight. Then everything was splashed with blood—the floor, the walls, the ceiling—and Father Bell rolled silently across the room, his severed arms held stiffly out in front of him, and the noise his body made was hollow and drumming, like rolling a Thanksgiving turkey across the floor.

He was dead by the time he reached the door.

Jack stood shocked, speechless, his own hands held out in front of him, cups of blood.

"Oh, Jesus Christ what have I done?" He could hear himself talking, but he was almost deaf with stress.

He knelt down beside Father Bell's body. Father Bell's face was pressed against the floor. His eyes were open; he was staring at nothing at all. Jack couldn't even summon up the nerve to close his eyelids. God almighty, he was still warm!

Jack looked around the room. Blood was sliding down the walls and dripping audibly on to the floor. The air was rich with the smell of recent death, like an abattoir.

"You promised to give me my son back," he said hopelessly.

There was no reply. Only the rain. Only the slow, glutinous dripping of Father Bell's blood. Jack stood up and took two or three breaths, and admitted to himself for the first time since he had followed that scampering gray-white figure down the valley to The Oaks that he had been taken for a fool. That Quintus Miller had enticed him here; that Quintus Miller had indirectly contrived for him to go to Olive Estergomy so that Olive Estergomy could send him off to track down Father Bell.

That very first day, when the gray-white figure had run in front of his station wagon, Quintus Miller must have sensed him passing, somehow, and sensed what he wanted out of life, and drawn him here.

The rest had been done by fear, by cajolery, by blackmail, by violence. That was the kind of man that Quintus Miller was. He had all the persuasiveness of true insanity.

Jack shouted at the blank walls, "I want my son back. You hear that, you goddamned crazies! I want my son back! You promised! I want him back!"

There was a long, long silence. Then the wall flowed and rippled, and half of a woman's body appeared, a young woman, with long wavy hair, in profile. Her eyes were closed and she didn't open them once.

Quintus will keep his promise. He always does. Her voice sounded like a high-toned bell, chiming through a Sunday-morning fog.

"I want my son now," Jack told her.

Quintus will give you back your child when Quintus is free.

"Quintus is free already. You're *all* free. Come on, open your eyes. Look at this body! That's a man, an innocent man! You've tortured and killed an innocent man!"

The young woman's voice was unrepentant. *Father Bell was never innocent. You should have seen him, with some of the women patients. Especially the younger ones. Twelve, and thirteen; the ones who couldn't speak. Don't go mourning Father Bell.*

"You listen to me," Jack told her. "I don't give a shit what happened in 1926. I don't give a shit for Quintus Miller, and I don't give a shit for you. I want my son back, that's all. I want him here, and I want him now. That was the deal. You got that? That was the fucking *deal*!"

The young woman turned her face toward Jack, but still didn't open her eyes. She could have been beautiful, but there was something about her forehead that was a little too bulbous. Something about her mouth that was a little too uncontrolled and weak.

Quintus will give you your son back when he is free.

"I've told you, Goddamn it! He's already free!"

The young woman smiled without humor. *He is free of this building, yes. But of course he is not yet free of the earth.*

"I don't understand."

It requires an extra sacrifice for him to escape from the earth.

"Oh, yes? You mean he's gotten himself out of The Oaks, by walking through the walls, and through the ground outside, but he can't get himself out of the ground?"

It requires a sacrifice, the young woman told him. *A special sacrifice, to pay off the debt.*

Jack made a point of averting his eyes from Father Bell's body. He could feel Father Bell's drying blood sticking to the soles of his shoes. He said quietly, "I want you to take this message right the way back to Quintus Miller, you understand me? Either he lets my son go, and I mean *right now*, or else I'm going to bring down on top of his head more goddamned grief than he's ever known in his life. And let me tell you this—I'm not some progressive psychiatrist like Elmer Estergomy, and I'm not some softheaded sky pilot like Father Bell. I don't have any sympathy for Quintus Miller, nor for you; not one inch. I'm going to break his ass."

He stopped and took a breath. Then he said, "What do you mean, sacrifice?"

Debts have to be paid, Mr. Reed. Nothing ever comes for free.

"What are you talking about? What kind of a sacrifice?" Jack shouted at her.

A blood sacrifice. What other kind? Eight hundred lives, one for every month of our imprisonment.

"What the hell are you talking about?"

Eight hundred lives must be offered, Mr. Reed, for every life that emerges out of the earth. Eight hundred lives must be taken.

Jack stood and stared at her with his arms by his sides, quite stiff with disbelief. "Eight hundred people have to be killed? What—for *every single patient* who wants to get out of the ground?"

The white face nodded. *Eight hundred lives, for every life.*

"But that's—thousands of people! You can't kill thousands of people!"

The gods will not release us out of the earth for anything less.

Jack covered his mouth with his hand. He was beginning to understand why Father Bell had been so desperately reluctant to let Quintus Miller loose.

Eight hundred, for every one of us, the young woman told him. *It isn't much to ask.*

"So Quintus Miller won't let my son go—not until he's

killed eight hundred people—and gotten himself out of the earth?"

Quintus Miller is worth eight thousand ordinary people. Quintus Miller is worth the lives of everybody else on earth.

Jack had never felt so defeated in his life. "What am I supposed to do?" he asked the young woman. "Wait for eight hundred innocent people to die? And what happens then?"

You made a deal, Mr. Reed. A deal is a deal. Your son's freedom for Quintus Miller's freedom.

"But eight hundred people, for God's sake—"

That was the deal, Mr. Reed. You made it. You have to live with it.

Jack hurried down the stairs, across the hallway, and into the night. Lightning was stilt-walking across the horizon, over toward Baraboo and Mirror Lake. He left The Oaks by the conservatory and ran along the shingled pathway toward the front of the house. Just as he reached the corner of the building, thunder compressed his eardrums, and rain lashed out of the sky so fiercely and so suddenly that he had to take shelter under the eaves of the kitchen.

He stood there panting, dripping, and praying that this was all a nightmare. *You'll wake up soon, Jack; you'll be back at home; with Maggie sleeping close beside you and the sun lighting the pink bedroom drapes; and the tinny sound of Randy's television turned low as he sits cross-legged in the living room, watching early-morning cartoon shows.* *If dere's one thing I can't stand . . . it's a flower that steals bananas from the refriger-ator-ator!*

He wiped his face with his hand. His station wagon was parked at the end of the avenue. As soon as the rain eased off a little he would make a run for it. He began to think that it had always been raining, ever since he was born. He couldn't remember any sunshine; he couldn't remember any snow. Only his father, leaning toward him and laying his hand clawlike on his knee, with the rain sprinkling across the lake outside, and saying, "When you got nothing to say—say nothing. That's my motto."

Jack had later discovered that somebody called Charles Colton had said the same thing, just about two centuries before, and at that moment the last impression of his father had disappeared, like an overexposed photograph.

He reached out to test the rain. As he did so a thin-fingered hand came out of the darkness and clutched his wrist. He shouted out, *"Nyaah!"* and jolted back up against the house, hitting his shoulder.

A flashlight dazzled him; then a face appeared. The face of an elderly woman, pale and alarmed, wearing a deer-stalker hat and a brown plaid cape.

"Mr. Reed? I didn't mean to startle you."

It was Olive Estergomy—Essie. Jack lifted both of his hands in mute surrender and told her, "It's all right. It's quite all right. You surprised me, that's all."

"Mr. Reed, you have blood on you."

He looked down. His coat was spattered with Father Bell's blood; dried now, and rusty-looking, but unmistakably blood.

"It's not mine," he told her. "It's Father Bell's. He's—well, I'm sorry to tell you he's dead."

"Dead" seemed like a euphemism, after the torture that Father Bell had suffered. The fire, the agony, and the amputation.

Essie shone her flashlight toward The Oaks. "Dead?" she said.

"It was all my fault," Jack told her. "He told me how dangerous it was, but I didn't understand."

Essie shone the flashlight back at him. She seemed bemused. "Mr. Reed, I couldn't sleep. I called your motel but they said you were out. I had to come back here to see for myself; just to make sure that everything was still quiet."

Jack said, "Listen, come back to the car. Something's happened. Something bad."

"Bad? What do you mean?"

Jack said, "I found Father Bell, up in Green Bay. He wasn't a priest anymore but everybody still called him Father. He said that I was right. They were still in the walls. Quintus Miller, Lester Franks, Gordon Holman, all the rest of them. They got there by some kind of—I don't know, hard to describe it, magic almost. Earth magic, that's what he said. Something the Druids used to believe in."

Essie Estergomy stared at him from under the brim of her dripping hat.

Jack said, "They killed him." He tried to explain how. He tried to explain that Randy's face had appeared from the wall, and then Gordon Holman's, and that Father Bell had been seized and burned and mutilated. But on a fresh thundery night in the middle of Wisconsin, with lightning sizzling and rain dredging the trees, his words sounded flat and unbelievable.

Essie said fearfully, "You've called the police?"

Jack looked away. "I don't know whether that's the best thing to do," he said evasively.

"Mr. Reed! A man's been murdered!"

"Yes," he said. But how could he tell her that thousands more people were supposed to be sacrificed—eight hundred unsuspecting lives for every single patient who had escaped from The Oaks? And how could he tell her that this wholesale massacre was just to restore them to the real world, the world of air and fire. God alone knew what they would do once they were free.

Jack said, "I know this sounds—well, I know this doesn't sound like the regular thing to do. But let's wait till the morning before we call the police. I need to think, you know? The police could make things worse. I need to find some way of dealing with all of this."

Essie said, "They were really inside the walls? Inside the bricks?" She shone her flashlight up the side of the building and illuminated one of the sculptured faces with closed eyes.

"I think we're better off out of here," Jack told her. "They're not only dangerous, they're angry. They want revenge for being shut up for so long."

Essie hesitated for just a moment, then she nodded. "My car's parked just beside yours."

Jack took her arm, and together they made their way back down the avenue of oak trees, their feet crunching quickly in the gravel.

"Surely the police will be able to help us," said Essie. "If the patients have gotten away, they can put out descriptions, catch them. I still have my father's list of admissions, with their original pictures."

"You don't seriously think the police are going to believe us, do you? A hundred thirty-seven lunatics have been buried in the walls of a building for sixty-three years, and now they've escaped? I can hear them laughing now."

"But surely we can show them," Essie replied. "Surely we can find some way of persuading them."

"What are we going to show them?" asked Jack. "Father Bell's body? And how do you think they're going to react to that? They're going to throw me in the slammer with no chance of bail, while Quintus Miller and all the rest of his loonies go free."

Essie stopped and clasped Jack's hand. "You didn't kill Father Bell, did you? I mean—you're telling me the truth?"

Jack looked at her and attempted a smile. "Essie," he said, "you're just going to have to trust me."

They were two-thirds of the way down the drive when they saw a small figure standing by the gates. A small figure, grayish white, like a child in a hooded rain cape. The figure had its arms outstretched, as if to bar their way, but it wasn't moving, wasn't waving. It had no face.

"That's a *child*," said Essie, in disbelief.

Jack stopped, and stopped Essie, too. "I don't think so," he said.

"But it's a little girl . . . what on earth is a little girl doing out here in the middle of the night?"

Jack said, "I've seen her before. I've seen *it* before. I'm not sure what it is, but it's something to do with Quintus Miller."

Essie released Jack's hand and went forward, toward the gates. The grayish white figure remained motionless, although its cape flickered in the wind, like a rain-sodden newspaper.

"Little girl!" called Essie. She quickened her pace, then slowed down again uncertainly. "Little girl?"

Essie stopped, and stood facing the figure for a very long time. Jack waited a few steps behind her. Essie shone her flashlight at the figure's head; but although its feet were pointing toward them and there were buttons down the front of its coat, all they could see was the back of its hood. Essie turned to Jack with a look of perplexity. "Her head's around the wrong way," she said. "How can her *head—*"

Jack warned, "Be careful. I'm not too sure that it's a child at all."

Essie took two or three steps nearer. "Little girl?" she called. "Are you all right, little girl?"

She took one more step, and then two bare arms came crashing out of the gravel just in front of her feet and seized her ankles. She screamed, and dropped to her knees. As she did so two more arms burst out of the shingle and snatched at her arms. Her flashlight tumbled away and went out.

"Hold on!" Jack shouted, and ran up to her, kicking one of the arms away. He held her around the waist, and tried to yank her upright again, but more arms came out of the gravel and dragged him away. He kicked and struggled and thrashed, and managed to break free and to roll across the wet grass.

Essie cried out in pain as one of her legs was plunged

right into the ground, then the other. "Help me! My legs! Oh God, help me!"

Jack scrambled to his feet. But as he did so he saw swiftly moving furrows in the gravel path, and arms that curved out of the ground like the arms of swimmers, just below the surface of a lake. There were five or six of them at least, and they homed in on Essie's struggling body with a slurring, crunching, gravelly rush.

Dodging the arms that snatched at him from all sides, Jack grabbed Essie under the arms and hefted her upward. She came free from the ground so easily that Jack fell backward, with Essie on top of him. She was still screaming, still frantically waving her arms. But she was no longer kicking. Her legs had been amputated, right up to the top of her thighs, and her femoral arteries spurted dark cascades of hot blood all over the gravel, and all over Jack.

Instantly, more powerful hands pulled her out of Jack's grasp and dragged her across the path. He tried to get up, but another arm burst out of the path and seized him around the neck, half throttling him and pulling him back to the ground.

He felt other hands snatching at his legs and grabbing at his clothes.

They've got me! This time they've got me! They're going to grind me up, the same way they ground up Lovelittle's dog, and spew me back out again.

He heard Essie let out one last high-pitched shriek. Out of the corner of his eye, he saw her pulled down into the gravel and disappear. He kicked out in panic at the hands that were trying to tug at his ankles; and he took hold of the arm that was gripping him around the throat and forced it downward. Then he bit it, as hard as he could.

The arm recoiled and whipped away. Jack somersaulted onto the grass, gasping for breath, staggered onto his feet, and then ran madly toward the gates. He heard the gravel *sssshhhhhhhing* right behind him as Quintus Miller's maniacs came swimming in pursuit beneath the surface of the path, their arms hooking out of the ground like shark's fins.

He squeezed through the gap beside the gate, the branches scratching at his face. Then he ran across to his car, flung open the door, and started the engine. A hand thrust itself out of the ground right beside his open door and caught hold of his foot. He slammed the door on its wrist, and felt the hand convulse. Cursing, shaking with disgust, he opened up the door again, kicked the hand away. Then he stamped on the gas pedal, and the station wagon's back wheels slithered and snaked, and he was away.

His headlights jostled and jumbled through the rain. He saw trees, hedges, rain-slicked curves. He glanced in his rearview mirror again and again to make sure that nobody was following him. About a mile up the road he hit a deep puddle, and slid sideways, and almost went off the road. He pulled in to the side, stopped, and gripped the wheel, just to stop himself from shaking.

Calm down, start thinking straight. If you start panicking, then there won't be anybody who can cope with Quintus Miller. There won't be anybody to save Randy.

He switched on the car radio. His first contact with normality all day. A woman was crowing, *". . . and praise the Lord! Yesterday I was riddled with cancer, today I'm eating pork sausages!"* He switched channels, until he found a country-western station. *"He got fishing lines strung across the Louisiana River. . . ."*

After ten minutes, still trembling but more relaxed, he pulled away from the side of the road and carried on. Right now all he wanted to do was go home, and sleep, and try to work out what he was going to do next. At the moment his mind was logjammed with sheer horror.

"It takes him every bit of a night and a day . . . to even reach a place where people stay. . . ."

Jack had almost reached the Lodi intersection when he saw the small grayish white figure standing right in the middle of the narrow road.

Oh God, he prayed. *Please let it not be a child; not really.*

He sped toward the figure at nearly sixty miles an hour. It made no attempt to move; it made no attempt to jump out of the way. Just before he hit it, he thought, *Supposing it's deaf; supposing it hasn't seen me.* He braked instinctively. The wheels locked, the tires shrieked, and he collided with the figure head-on and heard a dreadful wet thump. His windshield was splashed all over with blood. He skidded to a stop, gasping and gagging.

Unsteadily, he climbed out. Spread across the hood of the station wagon, dripping and stringy, all tubes and blood clots and yellowish glistening sacs, were the mashed remains of a human body. They steamed in the dim reflected light from the headlights. Jack had seen more death in the past two days than he had ever seen in his life, but this was too much for him. He had deliberately slaughtered a child. He dropped on his knees by the side of the road and vomited half-digested lobster.

After a minute or two he wiped his mouth, and wiped his eyes, and stood up. He would have to clear the body off the front of his car. He had a cardboard box in the back. He guessed that he could tear off one side of it and use it as a scoop.

It had been a child, after all, and he had run it down. It had been a living child, just like Randy.

He lifted the station wagon's tailgate. As he did so he glimpsed something through the side window, on the opposite side of the road. Something blurry, something grayish white. Frowning, he stepped around the car to look at it.

The small figure was standing not far away, faceless, silent, unharmed. He stood watching it; and he knew that it was watching him back, although it had no face.

It wasn't until he had scraped a lump of raw flesh out of

the gully in front of the windshield, and seen a tangle of amber beads beside the wipers, that he understood whose mangled remains had been dumped all over his car.

Essie's, Olive Estergomy's.

Which meant that all the time he had been sitting by the side of the road, listening to the radio, Quintus Miller and the rest of the patients had been following him, beneath the ground. Which probably meant that they were capable of pursuing him anywhere.

E·I·G·H·T

A dishrag dawn was smearing the sky by the time he reached Karen's house and parked. He climbed out of the station wagon and stretched his back. He felt as if he had been bruised and pummeled all over.

He leaned over the hood and inspected it carefully, just to make sure that he had left no telltale streaks of blood. He had managed to scoop most of Essie's remains into the bushes, where he hoped that they would be eaten by worms and wild animals. The rain had washed the rest of the car clean.

He was worried now that the police might be looking for him. Father Bell would have been reported missing from his senior citizens' home in Green Bay, and Olive Estergomy would certainly be missed from her house at Sun Prairie. In both cases, the last person who would have been seen with them was him.

He rang the doorbell four times before Karen came to the door. She was wearing a black baby-doll nightdress and her hair was done up in curlers. It was stale and gloomy in the living room. On the artist's-palette-shaped contemporary coffee table, next to the *capo di monte* statue of a weeping child, there was a bottle of Smirnoff vodka, nine-tenths empty, and a single lipstick-smeared glass.

Karen put her arms around his neck and kissed him. Her breath smelled of stale alcohol. "I've been worrying myself *sick*," she told him.

He peeled off his coat and sat down on the white vinyl
settee. "I don't know what the hell to do next," he said.
"It's been nothing but sheer bloody murder."

"I'll make some coffee," she suggested. "Come on, tell
me about it. What are friends for?"

He told her what had happened, trying not to sound
hysterical, trying to sound sane and collected and reasonable, trying not to leave anything out. She sat beside him
with her hand on top of his. Her crimson nail polish was
chipped. She said, "Uh-huh, uh-huh," and "Uh-huh?" but
she didn't interrupt him or ask any questions, and he
wasn't sure that she believed him.

"Well, you sure don't want to tell the police now," she
said once he had finished. "That would be—you know—
like suicide. Cutting your own throat."

"I don't know what else to do."

"Jack, honey, all you have to worry about is getting
Randy back."

"But, Karen, they're going to kill thousands of people—
literally *thousands*—that's if they haven't started already."

"Jack—it's not your fault. You've done what you can."

But Jack shook his head. "It's my goddamned fault, all
right. It's my fault that Joseph Lovelittle died and it's my
fault that Father Bell died and it's my fault that Olive
Estergomy died. Karen—it's my fault! They wouldn't have
gone anywhere *near* that building if it hadn't been for
me."

"But why did *you* go near it? Because Quintus Miller
wanted you to. I mean whatever this little white girl is, she
must be something he can *control,* you know like *thought
control.*"

"That doesn't make me any the less responsible."

"Well, maybe it does and maybe it doesn't. But I'll tell
you what. The way I finally got my way with Cecil was to
find out how to be *stronger* than he was, and the way I could
be stronger than he was, was to be *smarter.* I had the clerk

at his trucking company call me up whenever Cecil was going drinking with the boys, and so I made sure that I stayed out that night, till late. In the end he grew tired of having nobody around to use as a punching bag. You can beat this Quintus Miller if you're smarter. Come on, Jack, he's a goddamned headcase, after all. It shouldn't be hard to be smarter than a headcase."

Jack sipped his coffee. "No, I guess it wouldn't."

Snuggling up beside him, Karen said, "You have to find out more about him—you know, who he was, and what they locked him up for. Find out what kind of a headcase he was; you know, maybe he was frightened of something, like spiders, or going outside."

Jack kissed her. "Hey," he told her. "You're not as dumb as you look, are you?"

"You never said I looked dumb."

"I'm sorry, I didn't mean it. It's just a saying, you know?"

"Well, you ought to find out more about this earth-magic stuff, too," Karen told him. "Maybe this Quintus Miller doesn't have to kill all those hundreds of people at all. You know, maybe it's just a what-do-you-call-it, legend."

"You're right," Jack agreed. "Father Bell said that Adolf Krüger was into earth magic, you know? And that maybe Quintus Miller found out all about it from Adolf Krüger's library."

"There you are, then!" Karen told him. "All you have to do is to get yourself into Adolf Krüger's library, and read all about it in the same books."

"You make it sound easy." Jack smiled.

"Jack, honey, nothing is easy, you know that. Life's a joke, then you croak."

Jack closed his eyes. Karen stroked his forehead with her fingertip. "Mike was wondering what had happened to you," she said. "I told him not to worry, everything was fine. Oh—and Maggie called the works. She was going bananas about some women's weekend?"

Jack said, without opening his eyes, "I've seen people die. I've never seen that before."

"You need some sleep," said Karen.

He slept on the couch for over three hours. When he woke up, his head was thumping, and his mouth tasted like a pocketful of pennies. On the edge of the artist's-palette table, Karen had left him a note that read, *Gone 2 Work. Catch U Later.*

He opened the thin unlined drapes. It looked as if it had stopped raining at last, although the streets were still glossed with wet. He went through to the kitchenette, opened up the refrigerator, and found himself a beer. Heineken: Karen thought that it was ritzy to buy imports. He popped open the can, walked through to the bathroom, and turned on the shower. Leaning against the shower stall, he stepped out of his pants and his socks. He smelled strongly of sweat and something else: the cold vinegary mustiness that pervaded The Oaks.

After he had showered, he called Karen at the works and asked her to meet him at the Bierkeller across the street. "And don't tell anyone you're meeting me, just in case the cops come looking."

Karen said, "There's a couple of Cecil's old shirts in the closet, and some shorts, and some jeans, I think, if you look down at the bottom."

Jack dressed in a huge woolen trucker's shirt, red-and-white plaid, with the sleeves rolled up; but the shorts were like the sails of an oceangoing schooner, and the jeans were a size fifty-six waist—big enough for him and Karen together, one in each leg.

He borrowed the least frilly pair of Karen's panties that he could find—white satin with a bow in the front—and sponged as much of the blood and dirt from his own slacks as he could, and then pressed them with Karen's traveling iron on the kitchenette counter. He watched TV while he ironed. There was a news report about a fire on board the ferry steamer from Milwaukee to Ludington, and then an update report from Madison on a party of Girl Scouts who had mysteriously disappeared while camping up near Mirror Lake.

"Police discovered all the Girl Scouts' tents and camping equipment, including clothes and personal possessions . . . but by dawn this morning there was still no sign of the twenty-three girls and their four scout leaders . . . no indication that they might have been attacked, or been frightened by somebody or something, and run off . . . in fact, the mystery deepened later this morning when detectives revealed that the girls' footprints entered the campsite, but did not appear to exit . . . a fact made especially baffling because the ground all around the camping area had been softened by recent downpours."

Jack set down the iron. He felt as if somebody had hit him in the face. *They've started,* he thought. *They've taken those girls, and dragged them into the ground, the same way they dragged Essie Estergomy into the ground. They've started, and they mean what they say. Eight hundred sacrifices, for each of them. And then—*

He pulled on his slacks, switched off the iron and the television, threw his coat over his shoulders, and left the house. The day was fresh and the sky was beginning to clear. He climbed into his station wagon and U-turned it with squittering tires toward West Good Hope Road.

He sped along the puddly roads until he reached Reed Muffler & Tire. His station wagon jounced across the concrete forecourt. Mike Karpasian was standing in the tire bay, talking to a customer, but as soon as he saw Jack climbing out of his car he excused himself and came hurrying across.

"Jack? Is everything okay?"

"Not exactly. I just netted myself a couple of urgent family problems, that's all."

"You look like shit. Is there anything that I can do?"

Jack squeezed Mike Karpasian's shoulder. "Just keep the customers happy."

"Sure, no problem. But I need a couple of John Hancocks. Goodrich won't deliver any more tires until we settle their account, and we're totally cleaned out of TAs."

"Just put the checks in front of me, okay, and I'll sign them."

He crossed the noisy echoing workshop with Mike Karpasian in close pursuit. When he entered the office, Karen looked up in surprise. She was wearing the red sweater that one of Jack's customers had called "Living Jell-O" and a tight black leather skirt with laces up the side.

"What's wrong?" she asked him, her nails suspended over her word-processor keyboard.

"We have to leave right away. Can you call the agency and have them send out a temporary? And Mike wants those checks."

"Okay, sure," said Karen. She passed him a plastic folder marked "Checks for Signature," and punched out the number for Milwaukee Office SOS.

"What's happened?" she asked him under her breath as she waited for the agency to answer. "I thought you were supposed to meet me at the Bierkeller. Maggie's called three times this morning, wanting to know where you are. She says she's going to call the cops if you don't bring Randy home by lunchtime."

"They've started killing people," said Jack, glancing toward Mike Karpasian to make sure that he couldn't overhear him.

"What? What do you mean?"

"A whole troupe of Girl Scouts went missing this morning near Mirror Lake."

"You're sure?"

"It was on the news. I heard it when I was pressing my pants."

"Maybe they got lost," Karen suggested.

Jack finishing signing the checks and raised his hand to show her that he knew what he was talking about. "Believe me, it's Quintus Miller. We have to get to that library and find out how the hell to stop him."

Mike Karpasian suddenly turned around and said, "Hey, Jack. It's Maggie!"

"Oh, Jesus," said Jack. But there she was, in her square-shouldered "Dynasty" suit, the brown one from Sears, storming across the workshop, turning the heads of every fitter and mechanic she passed. *Hey, that's Jack's old lady . . . looks like she's ready to do some damage.*

Maggie slammed open the office door, so that the glass shook. "Where's Randy?" she demanded.

Jack made a point of ignoring her. "Did you get through to SOS yet?" he asked Karen.

"Where's Randy?" Maggie repeated.

Without looking at her, Jack said, "He's okay, he's staying with a friend at Wauwatosa."

"What's he doing at Wauwatosa? He should be at school! I called the school and they haven't seen him today or yesterday."

"Maggie, listen, he has a very slight cold. Nothing to worry about, just a sniffle. He couldn't stay home, I couldn't bring him to work, so he's staying with a friend at Wauwatosa. All right? He's well looked after, he has other kids his own age to play with. There's nothing for you to worry about."

"Where were you last night? I called you all night, last night."

"Maybe the phone was on the fritz, I don't know."

"I want to see him," Maggie insisted.

"Sure you do, but you can't. You'd probably upset Randy, and you'd certainly upset my friends. And, besides, how do I know you won't try to steal him back?"

"Because I give you my word."

Jack turned to her and said, "Listen, lady, you gave me your word that you would love, honor, and obey."

"What about Saturday?" Maggie persisted.

"What about Saturday?" Jack wanted to know.

"We're having a gala, I want to take Randy along."

"I'll think about it. What is it, lesbians?"

"God, you're a bastard, Jack. You always were. Women's consciousness raising, that's what it's all about. Learning that we don't always have to knuckle under to brainless chauvinistic bigots like you."

"I don't remember you calling me a brainless chauvinistic bigot the night that Randy was born. Or the night that he was conceived, for that matter."

Karen pressed her hand over her mouth to stop herself from laughing and Maggie gave her a glare that would have dissolved Kryptonite.

"Can I come round this evening to see him?" asked Maggie.

"I guess so," said Jack.

"Eight o'clock not too inconvenient?"

Jack nodded.

"I said, eight o'clock?" Maggie repeated.

"Sure, sure, eight o'clock," Jack told her. He turned away because he knew what Maggie was going to do next, which was to slam the door and stalk back out of the workshop in full wide-shouldered fury.

"Oh, shit," said Karen. "Oh, I'm sorry. I didn't mean to laugh."

"Did you get that temporary secretary?" Jack asked her. His heart was beating faster than normal, and his mouth felt a little dry, but Maggie hadn't upset him as much as usual. Saving Randy and stopping Quintus Miller were far more urgent than arguing with his wife. But he thought, *Why couldn't Maggie just—*

"He'll be here in an hour," Karen told him, switching off her word processor and picking up her purse.

"*He'll* be here in an hour?"

"Secretaries come in all sexes," Karen told him. "You're too old-fashioned, that's your trouble."

"What are you trying to do, make me feel old?"

Jack opened the office door and followed Karen out of the works. He could tell by the sly sideways looks they were giving him that all his mechanics thought he was taking her out for a lunchtime quickie. But right now he didn't care what anybody thought about anything he did. There were 137 escaped crazies underneath the ground, and nobody knew about it except him and Karen. Everybody else who had found out about them had found out the hard way, and was dead.

They drove back toward Madison under a misty, illusory sun. Karen said, "I wish to God you'd never gone to look at that building. That building is damned to hell."

"Me and that building both," Jack told her.

It was the first time that Jack had seen The Oaks in the sunshine, but somehow the building looked even more dilapidated and unwelcoming than ever. Its spires were shrouded in a midafternoon heat haze, and hundreds of pigeons perched on the rooftops and crowded the parapets and the gutters like lice.

He couldn't think why he had found it so exciting when he had first discovered it. Right now he would rather have turned the state penitentiary into a resort hotel than this place.

Perhaps it had been the living personalities of its inmates that had drawn him here, the lunatic seductiveness of Quintus Miller. Now *they* were gone, The Oaks was no more than a shell.

Jack was carrying the tire iron from the station wagon, in case they were attacked. He doubted if it would help him much. He had thought about bringing a gun, but he doubted if that would have helped him much, either. Still—even swinging a tire iron gave him more confidence than walking up to The Oaks empty-handed.

Karen said, "You don't think that any of them could have stayed behind?"

Jack said, "No, I don't think so. I hope not. They've been trapped in here for sixty years, remember. They all would have wanted out; and as far away as possible. Besides, if they're looking for human sacrifices, they won't find them here."

"Only us," said Karen.

The conservatory door was half-open. Jack hesitated, but then he pushed it wider and stepped inside.

"God, I hate this place," said Karen.

They walked through the lounge into the hallway. They were greeted by the blind statues at the foot of the stairs, even more luminescent than usual in the sunshine that filtered through the clerestory windows. Karen's high heels rapped on the marble flooring.

"Can you *smell* something?" asked Jack.

Karen sniffed. "I have my sinus."

"It smells like burning," said Jack. "Burning paper."

They climbed the west staircase to the landing, and then walked along the corridor to the west tower. Karen kept close to Jack, and she was obviously jumpy. "I can smell it now," she told him. "Like burning newspaper, you know?"

Jack said nothing. He was thinking about Maggie. He hadn't meant to shout at her like that. It wasn't her fault they didn't get along. And of course she was anxious about Randy, she was his mother. The only reason he had shouted at her was because he felt guilty about losing Randy, and he hated lying. But what was he going to tell her? Our son's been kidnapped by a homicidal lunatic and dragged into the ground, but don't worry, I'll try to have him out of the ground in time for your women's consciousness-raising gala on Saturday?

They reached the doors of the west tower. They were double doors, heavily padlocked, just like the east tower.

"Oh boy, the smell's really strong here," Karen said, and sneezed twice.

Bless you, thought Jack.

"How are we going to get inside?" asked Karen. "We don't have a key. Only that big fat realtor guy has a key."

Jack hammered the sharp end of his tire iron into the door, behind the metal hasp. Then he levered it outward. The oak cracked, the screws cracked. He dug the tire iron further in and levered it again. After five minutes of sweating and struggling, the screws suddenly grated out of the wood, and the doors were unlocked.

When they opened them up, however, they discovered the source of the burning smell. They were in a huge library, two stories high, like Elmer Estergomy's clinic. Every wall was lined with shelves, and every shelf was crammed with books, thousands and thousands of books, wedged in tight. But at least a hundred books had been heaped into the middle of the carpet and set alight. The air was filled with acrid blue smoke. Jack knelt down beside the books and sifted his hand through their blackened remains. It had been a miracle that the whole building hadn't burned to the ground. The windows were stained nicotine brown with smoke, and a library chair stuffed with horsehair was smoldering still. The carpet had been burned right through to the floorboards.

Jack poked at the ashes with his tire iron and teased out a half-burned book.

"Look at this," he told Karen. *"Awen, the Divine Name."*

He picked out another book and peeled back layer after layer of charred pages. *"Ye Origines and Historie of Ye Druides.* And look at this: *The Culdees in Christian Britain.* And *Druids in the Gallic Wars."*

Karen glanced at them momentarily and then went back to fanning the smoke away with her hand and chewing gum. "Sure stinks in here. I hate it."

"Druids," said Jack, picking up more and more crumbling black pages. "This was all to do with Druids. And they've deliberately burned it all, to stop us from finding out about it."

"What's a Druid?" Karen wanted to know.

Jack stood up. "Well . . . they were like priests, you know? In ancient Britain. That's all they told me at school."

Karen watched him in silence for a long time, and then she said, "What are you going to do now? If they've burned all the books?"

Jack looked around the library. "I don't know. I guess I'll have to find out about the Druids some other way. But the point is—they've shown us their weakness."

"Jack, I don't understand that at all. What weakness?"

"Think about it! Why did Quintus Miller burn all these books? He burned them because he didn't want us to find out what was in them. Because if we find out what's in them, we may find out how to stop him—you know?—and send him back where he came from. Back into the walls, or wherever. By rights he should have been dead for years."

"So what do we do?"

Jack gathered together three of the less-burned books. "The best bet is the university. They must have somebody on campus who knows about Druids. I mean they get visiting professors from all over the world."

Karen reached out and held his hand. "Jack?" she said. "What is it?"

"Well, you know this might not work out, you know? I mean—if Quintus Miller is really as bad as that priest told you he was—well, Randy might be dead already."

Jack had tried to come to terms with that possibility ever since he had found the Turd, half-buried in the cellar wall. "Yes," he said. "But we can't stop trying, can we?"

They left the library and walked back along the corridor. Karen linked arms with him. "Jack, honey—listen— whichever way it turns out, I want you to know that I love you—and if you want to move in . . . well, you're more than welcome."

Jack kissed her hair and squeezed her hand. "I'm not too sure that I could fill Cecil's shoes. I certainly can't fill his jeans."

Their footsteps echoed down the staircase. They left The Oaks through the conservatory door and walked down the avenue of trees where Essie Estergomy had died. Jack kept glancing from side to side for signs of what had happened, but the gravel was smooth and undisturbed, and there was no blood anywhere.

"It's time we listened to the news," said Jack. "I want to make sure they haven't taken anybody else."

"What if they have?" asked Karen.

"Then there's nothing I can do about it."

She pecked his cheek. "In that case stop torturing your goddamn feelings of guilt and let's get down to the university."

When they reached the gate, however, they saw Daniel Bufo's Cadillac parked next to their station wagon, and Daniel Bufo sitting in it, looking dyspeptic and unhappy. As they squeezed through the gap beside the gate Daniel Bufo eased himself out of his car and came toward them, hitching up his pants.

"Mr. Reed, I have a bone to pick with you."

"Oh, yes?" said Jack.

Daniel Bufo nodded to Karen and gave her a tight grimace. "Mrs. Reed?" he acknowledged her, his eyes lingering for just a moment on the Living Jell-O.

Karen said nothing. But Jack opened the door of his station wagon so that she could climb in.

"Before you go, Mr. Reed," said Daniel Bufo, leaning his elbow on the station-wagon roof and blocking Jack's way around it, "I'm not too happy about the way this sale has been shaping up. Not too happy at all. I'm beginning to think—well, that you may not be one hundred percent motivated."

"Oh, really? What gave you that idea?"

"Well—believe me, I don't want to upset you, Mr. Reed. You showed a keen interest in The Oaks at the outset, and in spite of the fact that you made an offer that was well below the property's actual value—"

"Let's wait up a minute here," Jack interrupted. "Are we talking about market value or curiosity value?"

"Mr. Reed," said Daniel Bufo, "I don't want to cause any bad feeling here, but are you still genuinely interested in acquiring this property? Because if you're not, you could save both of us a considerable amount of time and work. Just say the word, and we'll call it a day."

"Of course I'm still interested," Jack assured him. "Everything's on track. I'm talking to my attorney later this afternoon." Daniel Bufo was standing so close to him that he could see the clear perspiration on his upper lip. In truth, after what had happened, Jack would never have considered buying The Oaks in a zillion years. But if he called the deal off now, his access to The Oaks could be severely limited, and until he had tracked down Quintus Miller, he wanted to be able to come and go from the building as often as he needed to.

"Well, I'm real glad to hear that," said Daniel Bufo, with obvious relief. "After what you said to me yesterday— about meeting the vendor face-to-face . . ."

"Well, that won't be necessary," said Jack. "I guess I was just being persnickety. I've been suffering some toothache recently—tends to make me out of sorts."

"Oh, I'm sorry," Daniel Bufo told him, solicitous now that he was reassured about his sale. "I hope you manage to get it fixed soon. My sister was a martyr to toothache."

He leaned forward and leered at Karen's legs as she sat in the car. "Good to see you again, Mrs. Reed."

Jack reluctantly shook his hand, and said, "I'll be in touch, okay? Just as soon as I've talked to my attorneys."

Daniel Bufo walked back to his car, his large coat flapping in the breeze. Jack watched him go. Karen said, "You're not really going to buy it, are you, after all of this?"

Jack said, "I wouldn't buy this building if it was the only building left standing on God's good earth."

Daniel Bufo turned and gave Jack a wave before hefting himself into his car. Jack was turning away when he thought he saw a ruffling in the grass beside the road. He looked again, frowning. Must have been the wind, nothing more. But then he saw the ruffling again, and it couldn't have been the wind because it rushed along the verge like an invisible polecat running through the grass. It was headed straight toward Daniel Bufo's car.

Karen said, "What's the matter, honey?" but Jack had already started running.

"Mr. Bufo!" he shouted. "Mr. Bufo! Get the hell out of here, quick!"

Daniel Bufo frowned at him through the windshield, and then did the worst possible thing that he could have done. He switched off his engine. Jack yelled, *"Go! Mr. Bufo! Go!"*

The furrowing movement in the grass verge reached the road itself. Suddenly an arm burst out of the solid earth, and the hard-packed roadway crackled and split. Daniel Bufo let down his car window and leaned his head out and called, "What did you say, Mr. Reed? Is there anything wrong?"

Jack had almost reached Daniel Bufo's car by now. "Go!" he shouted at him. "They're here!" He suddenly realized that he had probably made matters worse—that if he hadn't shouted and tried to warn him, Daniel Bufo would have already gone by now.

Daniel Bufo's face was large and placid. "I'm sorry, Mr. Reed, I'm not too sure what you—"

Frantically, Jack looked all around the car, to see where the furrowing had gone. The roadway had closed up behind it, as if it had never happened.

"Who's here, Mr. Reed?" asked Daniel Bufo.

Beneath his car, they heard a loud metallic clonking noise; then a sound like somebody hammering at sheet steel. The whole car shook and squeaked up and down on its suspension.

Daniel Bufo said angrily, "What the hell is *that*?"

"Mr. Bufo, if I were you, I'd—"

But at that moment there was an explosive bursting noise, metal and fabric and springs, and Daniel Bufo jumped back in his seat. A bunched-up fist with red raw knuckles came punching out of the brown hide upholstery right between his thighs.

"What the *hell!*" he exclaimed, but his voice was an uncontrolled squeal, the same kind of squeal that a pig lets out when it suddenly realizes that it's just about to be slaughtered.

One arm thrust its way out of the seat, then another arm. They seized Daniel Bufo around the throat and jerked him violently downward. His nose hit the steering wheel, and Jack heard the bone snap.

"Graaarrggghhh!" choked Daniel Bufo, one arm clawing out of the car window for Jack to save him. Jack tugged at the door handle, but the car was centrally locked, and when he tried to reach inside to open it, Daniel Bufo snatched hold of his sleeve and wouldn't let him go.

The two muscular hands had pulled Daniel Bufo's head right down between his knees, so that he was bent double. He was gargling and struggling, but he couldn't find the breath to scream. Jack shouted at him, "My arm, let go of my arm!" but Daniel Bufo's panic was total, and all he could do was to clutch it tighter.

Two more hands, a black man's hands this time, wrenched their way out of the car's upholstery and caught hold of Daniel Bufo around the waist. At once they started to pull him down into the seat.

Jack held on to Daniel Bufo's hand as tightly as he could. But inch by inch, in a series of steady, irresistible tugs, Daniel Bufo was dragged doubled-up into the depths of his seat. The back of his coat mushroomed up behind him, and then he suddenly started to throw himself from side to side in wild unbearable pain. His bare back was being scraped against the torn-open metal of the Cadillac's underbody.

Jack tried to prize the hands away from Daniel Bufo's throat, but they were so strong that he couldn't even budge them. All the time he kept glancing quickly and frantically around him, just to make sure that the road wasn't furrowing up and that more of Quintus Miller's mad disciples weren't hunting *him*.

There was a moment when the tug-of-war between Jack and Daniel Bufo and the hands that were dragging him downward reached a shuddering impasse. Daniel Bufo was gripping Jack with one hand and the Cadillac's steering wheel with the other, desperate not to be pulled down into the ground. His knuckles were white, his whole body shook with agony and effort.

"Arrrrgghhhh!" Daniel Bufo gargled. Then he gasped an ounce of precious air and screamed, *"Help me!"*

They were the last words he spoke. At that moment Jack heard his rib cage crackle in a fusillade of broken bones and then his pelvis snap in half with a sound that he would never forget, like a large serving plate being snapped in half underneath a cushion.

Blood splashed out of Daniel Bufo's mouth and onto his feet. Then with one last jostling wrestle, he was pulled down into the depths of the seat, and through the floor of the car, and into the ground itself, leaving nothing behind him but ripped clothing and ribbons of bloody fat still clinging to the seat's twisted-open springs.

Jack got down on his knees, trembling and panting, to look underneath the car. For a brief second, the ground was in turmoil, the same way the ocean is momentarily churned up when a shark claims its victim.

Karen was calling, "Jack? Jack? What's going on? What are you *doing*?"

Jack climbed to his feet and leaned against the side of Daniel Bufo's car, wiping sweat from his forehead with his sleeve.

Then, without warning, a hand clawed out of the hard-packed earth in front of him and clutched at his shoe.

He stamped at it, and jumped back. But immediately he recognized that it wasn't one of the lunatics' hands. It was pudgy, and white, with heavy gold rings. It was Daniel Bufo, making a last hopeless effort to rescue himself.

Jack reached out for the hand, but it was pulled away from him across the road—quite slowly at first, then faster and faster. It vanished into the grass with an agitated rustling, and then it was gone.

Quickly, jerkily, Jack walked back to the station wagon. Karen was waiting for him with her eyes wide and her mouth open and her chewing gum in suspense.

"What *happened* back there? Where did Mr. Bufo go?"

Jack climbed into the driver's seat and said, "Close the door. Come on, quick. We're getting out of here."

As he twisted the key in the station wagon's ignition he saw the roadway cracking over to his left. The engine whinnied, but wouldn't start. He tried again, it whinnied again.

"Come on, you bastard," he fretted.

Karen said, "I was going to tell you. Your inside lights were on."

"What?" he demanded. "You mean the map light, the door lights? I left those on?"

"I switched them off for you," said Karen helpfully.

Oh, Jesus, my battery was pretty weak already. There's a new battery under my desk at the shop. Why is it that somebody who runs an auto business is the very last person to look after their car?

He tried the ignition again. This time the engine heaved over twice, and then died. The furrow in the road was coming closer. An arm broke the surface, then another arm. Jack turned his head, and through the woods to the right of the car he saw bushes bustling and shaking, and leaves turfed up, as more furrows came rushing toward them.

"Kick your shoes off," he told Karen.

"What?"

"Kick your shoes off, we'll have to make a run for it."

"Are you kidding me?"

"Just kick your shoes off and get out of the car and run like hell and stay away from any broken ground! Now, go!"

Karen stared at him, petrified. But then the station wagon violently shook, and under the floor they heard the parking-brake wire snapping, and fists pummeled furiously at the metal beneath their seats.

"What is it?" screamed Karen. "Jack—what is it?"

"Go!" yelled Jack, and they flung open their doors and ran. Past Daniel Bufo's Cadillac, along the wall that surrounded The Oaks, and up the road.

"What are we—running—from?" Karen gasped.

Jack reached out and gripped her hand. "Don't—talk—*run!*"

He glanced behind him just once. His station wagon was shaking on its springs, and he could hear metal tearing. Then one of the tires burst, with a deafening bellow that sent the crows screaming and wheeling up from the nearby oaks.

The black gas station attendant had been watching them approach for almost a mile: walking along the tree-lined road like the closing scene in *The Third Man,* except that Karen was hobbling in her stocking feet and a too-tight miniskirt, and Trevor Howard didn't stop to offer them a lift.

When they finally reached the Exxon station the attendant said simply, "Hi," to Jack and "hi," to Karen, and then "Breakdown?"

"Just need to use your phone, please," Jack told him.

"I can get you a tow truck," the attendant offered.

"No, thanks. All I need is a phone. And the lady here could use something to put on her feet, if you have anything."

The attendant stuck out his bottom teeth and looked

down at Karen's feet. "We sell Milwaukee Brewers baseball regalia. Should have some boots your size."

Jack bought two Sprites from the Coke machine and then went to the pay phone while Karen freshened up in the ladies' room. He popped the top off one of the cans and drank almost half of it straight down. Then he called the operator and asked for the number of the University of Wisconsin at Madison.

He had just been connected to the administration office when Karen reappeared. He couldn't help smiling at her as she came flapping toward him in a pair of size-eight baseball boots.

"I don't know what the hell you're laughing at," she said as she opened the folding door and crowded into the phone booth next to him.

"Did they pick you for the team next season?" Jack asked her.

Karen nodded toward the phone. "Who are you calling? Not the cops?"

"Uh-uh. The university. You remember what I said about getting some expert help? They're trying to connect me to the religious-studies department."

"You really think that's going to do any good?"

"It can't do any harm. We have to know what we're up against here."

They waited for almost five minutes while Karen noisily drank her soda, and Jack fed the phone with quarters. At last a distracted voice said, "Department of religious studies?"

"All right," said Jack. "Do you have anybody there who knows anything about Druids? No, no, *Druids*. Yeah, that's right. It's urgent."

The minibus driver let them off on campus, beside Lake Mendota. Huge thunderclouds were building in the inky afternoon sky. "Your department of religious studies is right across there, man," the minibus driver told them. He must have been forty-six years old, with graying shoulder-length hair, impenetrable John Lennon sunglasses, and tie-dyed jeans. He had talked to them all the way from Waunakee with the sipping style of speech peculiar to those who had never quite managed to outlive The Doors and Jefferson Airplane and head shops and who spoke as if they were smoking a roach.

Jack said, "Good luck, and thank you."

"Peace," replied the minibus driver.

They hurried hand in hand across the newly mowed grass. "That's the first time I've been called 'man' in about twenty-five years," Jack remarked. He was hurrying, not because it looked as if it were going to rain, but because he felt unusually defenseless without a car.

Karen asked him, "Is this going to do any good? I mean shouldn't we be trying to find out where this Quintus Miller has actually taken off to?"

"Think about it," Jack replied. "Supposing we find him—what do we do then?"

"Well, couldn't we *shoot* him or something? You have a hunting rifle, don't you?"

"You've been watching too many *Rambo* movies. This character exists under the ground. Not just under the ground, *in* the ground. Or in solid walls, or floors. How do you shoot somebody like that?"

"I don't know," Karen admitted, bustling her bottom to keep up with him. "It's just that talking to professors and stuff . . . it's so kind of wimpy, you know?"

They reached the arched brick doorway marked DEPART-MENT OF RELIGIOUS STUDIES and pushed their way in through a heavy swinging door. Inside, the building was dark and stuffy, and the green-painted corridor was stacked with boxes of duplicating paper. Jack stopped a tall blond girl with a beaky nose and spectacles.

"I'm looking for Mr. Summers?"

"He's in the common room, right down at the end of this corridor," the girl told him, in an oddly dreamy voice, as if she were talking about God, or at the very least Robert Redford.

Jack and Karen walked the length of the corridor and knocked at the common-room door. There was no reply, so Jack opened the door and they went straight in. On one of a collection of motley sofas, with his feet up, they found a lanky black-bearded man in baggy green corduroy pants and a loose brown sweater, smoking a pipe and contentedly reading a copy of *Woman's Circle Home Cooking*.

"Mr. Summers?" asked Jack.

"That's me," the man replied in a British accent without looking up.

Jack held out his hand. "I'm Jack Reed. I called you earlier."

Mr. Summers looked up. His eyes were slightly bulbous and green like freshly peeled grapes. "So you did. The Druid man, yes? The *urgent* Druid man?"

"That's right. I was wondering if maybe we could talk."

"Of course. I'm not sure that I can tell you anything very useful." He swung his brown suede shoes off the sofa and stood up. "I've been trying to find out why my pot roasts are always so vile."

"You probably don't cook them slow enough," Karen told him. "That's the mistake that most people make. You have to cook them real slow, for hours and hours, otherwise they're tough and they're stringy and they taste like somebody's training shoes."

"Ah! Well, that's probably my problem," said Mr. Summers. "Too impatient! You wouldn't think that anybody who had devoted their life to the study of comparative religion would be impatient, would you? But there you are."

He frowned at Jack suddenly and said, "You were calling from a *garage*, weren't you?"

"A gas station, that's right. Up at Waunakee. The administration office put me on to you, said you were pretty well up on ancient religions."

"You'll forgive me," said Mr. Summers, "but who calls up from a garage—beg your pardon, gas station—asking for an urgent appointment to talk about Druids? It's not that I *mind*, believe me. I'll talk about Druids till the cows come home. But you want to talk about them *urgently?*"

"Mr. Summers," said Jack, "I'll come right to the point. Do you know anything about people who can walk into walls? I've been led to believe it's connected with the ancient Druids, but I'm not too sure. People who can move around, under the ground?"

Mr. Summers stared at Jack with interest. "Who told you about this?" he asked.

"Nobody told us, we—" Karen began, but Jack squeezed her hand to keep her quiet.

"We just found out about it, that's all."

"Well, it's really most interesting," said Mr. Summers. "One of the classic mysteries of the pre-Christian world. There are hundreds of ancient stories of people being able to walk through rocks, and of priests living inside the trunks of solid trees, and of men and women who could travel through walls.

"Whether it was actually possible or not, there are *so* many stories about it, and *so* many inscriptions that describe it in detail, that you have to admit that the Druids certainly *believed* it was possible."

He looked at his wristwatch. "I've finished for today, and there's rather a cozy bar not far from here. Do you fancy a drink?"

"Sounds like music to me," said Jack.

"You'd better call me Geoff," said Mr. Summers. "Whenever people say 'Mr. Summers,' I turn around to see if my father's standing behind me."

They walked across the windy parking lot to collect Geoff Summers's run-down Valiant, and then he drove them two or three miles outside of town, to a small white-painted bar and restaurant called Lindstrom's Farm. They squeezed themselves into an uncomfortably rustic oak booth and ordered beers. A candle flickered in a red glass table lamp. Jack could see from the way Geoff Summers hardly ever took his eyes away from the busty Germanic-looking waitress what his principal interest in drinking here was. Jack had heard about academics.

Geoff Summers swallowed a mouthful of beer. The foam remained on his mustache. He took out his pipe and said, "This whole business of walking through the earth goes way back into ancient history—*before* the Druids, as matter of fact. All the way back to megalithic man, the people who built Stonehenge and all those other mysterious stone structures. So the time we're talking about is somewhere about two thousand seven hundred years before Christ.

"Those ancient men and women discovered the magnetic lines of force that underlie the earth . . . telluric currents, they're called, or ley lines. And where these lines intersect each other, you find locations of extraordinary psychokinetic influence."

"Is that what they call earth magic?" asked Jack.

Geoff Summers had struck a match to light his pipe but allowed it to burn down between his fingers. "I'd love to know what your interest in this is, Mr. Reed."

"Jack, and it's pretty hard for me to explain it to you."

"Well, Jack, have you heard a ghost somewhere, is that it? That's the usual reason people start looking into earth magic. They hear knockings in the walls, or on the ceiling, and they assume that it's an invisible spirit. In fact— almost without exception—their house is standing on a ley line, and what they're hearing is somebody actually passing through their walls. An earth-walker."

Jack held Karen's hand under the red-checkered tablecloth. "That's pretty much an approximation of what we've been having trouble with," he said guardedly.

"Let me tell you something," said Geoff Summers. "These ley lines have far more power than modern scientists understand, particularly at certain times of the year. For example, the bluestones that the ancient Britons used to build Stonehenge came from the Prescelly Mountains of Pembrokeshire, one hundred thirty-five miles away from the site where they were eventually set up—even though some of the stones weigh fifty tons.

"In terms of modern science, nobody has yet been able to explain how the ancient Britons could have moved a fifty-ton stone one mile, let alone one hundred thirty-five. But the Druidic story says that the stones were simply *summoned*, and that they crept along the ley lines from Wales to Stonehenge, under the ground, by *themselves*."

"That's weird," said Karen. "That's really weird."

"Unfortunately it's impossible to substantiate," Geoff Summers replied, with his eyes fixed on the waitress. "But it's happened in America, too. At Mystery Hill, in New Hampshire, and in Arizona, too. The Pima Indians have a legend about Tcu-Wutu-Makai, the Solid-Earth-Magician, who could walk through the ground. And we've had quite a few modern sightings of earth-walkers.

"In Applebachsville, in Pennsylvania, in 1881, a woman saw the figure of a naked man moving along the wall of her farmhouse, and as recently as 1903, a farmer in Pewamo, in Michigan, swore to his local newspaper that he had seen a field full of human arms. He swore blind that they had snatched his white prize bull and dragged it right down into the ground."

"Do you believe that?" Jack asked cautiously.

"I don't know," said Geoff Summers, lighting another match and singeing the fresh tobacco in the bowl of his pipe. "But in religious studies, we're not as skeptical as anthropologists, say, or pure historians. We make allowances for the mystical side of life. And—you see—what that Michigan farmer said did actually tally with Druidic lore. Once a priest was intermingled with the earth, a blood sacrifice would be necessary to allow him to return to the air. Sometimes several blood sacrifices."

He puffed smoke, and then he said, "The Druids kept their rituals secret, so nobody can tell how many people they actually sacrificed. There are very few human remains at any of their sacred sites, two or three skulls, a couple of thighbones, so most historians have assumed that they scarcely held any blood sacrifices, perhaps none at all.

"But the stories and legends are quite explicit. The early Druids were supposed to have killed men and women by the hundreds, and not very nicely, either. They were said to have castrated the men and pulled out the women's wombs. They tore off their arms and legs, and scattered their blood on the ground. Whole villages were decimated that way. It was said that they studied the writhings of their dying victims in order to divine the future."

Karen pressed the heel of her hand against her forehead in a quick, fretful gesture. Geoff Summers said, "I'm sorry . . . I didn't mean to turn your stomach."

But Karen glanced at Jack and Jack knew that it wasn't squeamishness that was making her feel so upset. It was her fear of Quintus Miller and his followers, forging their way through the darkness of the ground, with an appetite for blood that was whetted in equal parts by stone-age mysticism and by sheer criminal insanity.

Jack said to Geoff Summers, "Is there any way—do you know of any way at all—in which these earth-walkers could be stopped?"

Geoff Summers observed him for a while with his grape green eyes. "Stopped, what do you mean by stopped?"

"I mean killed. Could anybody track them down and kill them?"

"Jack," said Geoff Summers slowly, "I am beginning to ask myself just what it is that you've got yourself into."

"I'm asking you a question, that's all. How do you kill them?"

Geoff Summers slowly shook his head. "I'm not saying another word until I find out what this is all about."

Jack took a deep breath. "I can't tell you anything, not yet. Somebody could get hurt. I have a young son, as a matter of fact. *He* could get hurt. Can we just make a deal? You tell me what you know about earth-walkers, and when it's safe for me to do so, I'll come back and I'll tell you everything. I'll even write it down for you."

"You bastard," Geoff Summers told him cheerfully. "Have you *found* an earth-walker?"

"Uh-uh," Jack replied. "I don't know what I've found. But, please. I need your help. I'm not asking for you to give me anything for nothing. I'll pay you. What do you want? How does twenty-five hundred sound? Cash, no taxes."

"Have you actually *found* an earth-walker?" Geoff Summers repeated.

Jack slammed the flat of his hand on the table and struggled out of his seat, bruising his thigh on the armrest. "I told you, Geoff—I need your help. I need all the help that I can get. But I can't explain what's happening because I'm not at all sure what's happening myself. If you *won't* help—well, I'll have to find somebody who will."

Geoff Summers quickly took his pipe out of his mouth and lifted his hand. "Wait, Jack—*fanites!* Come on, now, let's not go rushing off madly in all directions. Just answer me that one question—just tell me if you've found an earth-walker. And whether your answer is yes or no, I'll tell you what I know about the Druids, I promise. It isn't very much—you could find out most of it for yourself if you knew which books to read. But after that I won't ask you any more questions till you're ready. How does that sound?"

Jack hesitated. All hell would be snapping at his heels when the police found out what had happened to Joseph Lovelittle and Father Bell and Essie Estergomy and Daniel Bufo—not to mention the Girl Scouts and all the other people that Quintus Miller and his lunatics might already have massacred. Before he confessed to any involvement in what had happened, Jack wanted to find Quintus Miller first, and make sure that he destroyed him.

And if Randy were still alive—somewhere, somehow—he wanted to save him, too.

"This is very complicated," he said. He sat down again.

"The Druids were very complicated people," Geoff Summers assured him. "They understood the world they lived in, they understood its powers, and they used them to devastating effect. Here we are, four thousand seven hundred years later, and we *still* can't come up with any rational scientific explanation for the building of Stonehenge, or Easter Island, or Carnac in France, or Mystery Hill. Either *why* they built them, or *how*."

Karen put in, "Geoff, it's true, we've found one. An earth-walker. Well, more than one, as a matter of fact."

"*Karen*," Jack protested, but Karen said, "It wasn't your *fault*, Jack! It wasn't your fault! And what else are you going to do? Somebody has to know about it. They scare me, Jack. They really scare me."

Geoff's eyes lit up, and he leaned forward on the table with his pipe puffing like an old-time locomotive. "This is great! You're going to let me in on it? I've been waiting for something like this! Listen to me, Jack, if this is true, if you've really found an earth-walker, then this is the rarest mystical event in decades. My doctorate is in the bag."

"I don't give a shit for your doctorate!" Jack retorted. "Those people have *my* son!"

Geoff sat back, abashed. "I'm sorry. Listen, I'm sorry. I didn't understand." But then he leaned forward again, with renewed enthusiasm. "If you let me in on it, believe me, Jack, I'll do everything I can to help you to get him back."

Jack repeated, with exaggerated patience, "Just tell me how to kill them."

"Well . . ." said Geoff, "this is only a story, you understand? There is no historical evidence for any of this. But then—ha!—so what? There's no historical evidence for earth-walking, either. To kill an earth-walker—this is what the Druids said—you have to drive him with incantations to a point where the earth comes to an end. Like the edge of a cliff, perhaps. You have to force him into an area from which he can't escape. Then you have to break apart the earth or stone in which he is hiding, and kill him in the ritual Druidic fashion."

"And pardon my ignorance, what is the ritual Druidic fashion?" asked Jack.

Geoff smiled. "You have to bend him over backward, until his spine breaks."

Jack was silent for a long time, picking up the book of matches marked "*Lindstrom's Farm*" and dropping them again. "And these—what-do-you-call-them?" he asked. "These incantations? What are you supposed to incant?"

"Nobody knows. Sorry about that. The Druids did have a written language, apparently, but—well, you know. It's like so many things. Lost in the murky mists of time."

"Lost in the murky mists of time, huh?" said Jack. "That's a fat lot of help."

"Well, I'm sorry. But that's all I know. This was over four thousand years ago. There aren't any Druids left around to ask. Well, there's a modern order of Druids, but they're nothing but a bunch of eccentric Welshmen who dress up in sheets at weekends."

But Karen had been gum chewing furiously and thinking hard. "Jack—listen—the holy water kept them there, didn't it?"

Jack said, "The holy water kept who where?" He was very tired.

She shifted her gum to the other side of her mouth. "Didn't you tell me the reason the loonies couldn't get out of the building was because it had holy water all around it? Didn't you tell me that? And because that priest had said all the right prayers. Like, you know—'stay put, you unclean spirits, or else.'"

Jack nodded. "That's right!" he said. "That's absolutely right. So if they can't escape a ring of holy water . . . maybe we could use holy water and prayers instead of a Druid incantation."

In their excitement they forgot about Geoff Summers, who was watching them in ever-increasing fascination and amazement.

"There must be books with all the right prayers and stuff," Jack told Karen. "Then all we need to do is to find ourselves some holy water—out of a font or something—and when we're ready we can track those bastards down."

Geoff Summers said politely, "I can help."

Jack turned back to him. "I'm sorry, believe me. But you're not supposed to be listening to any of this."

"I can *help*," Geoff insisted. "I have all of the books that you need. All of the rituals of exorcism, all of the spells for dismissing demons. Even a prayer for ridding the community of people who have an unorthodox view of the meaning of the Scriptures. Let's put it this way—I don't think 'stay put, you unclean spirits, or else' is really going to work."

Jack hesitated for a moment and then pointed a finger at him. "You want to be in?"

"Of course!" Geoff grinned. "You wanted an expert, I'm an expert. At least as far as comparative religion is concerned."

There was something about Geoff Summers's intense Englishness that made Jack feel more like Dick Van Dyke than ever. *It's Murree Poppuns!* in a fake Cockney accent.

"Okay, then," he said. "You're in. But two warnings, okay? One is, we're not yet ready to tell the police about what's been going on. If we do, we could screw up everything, even worse than it is already. Second, it's very dangerous, and I mean *very* dangerous, and there's a serious possibility of getting yourself hurt."

"Well . . . I think I can live with that," Geoff replied. "I enjoy living dangerously. You know—motorcycling with no helmet, yachting with no life preserver. Having it away without a condom."

"There's one thing more," Jack told him. "This whole thing is ultimately down to me. It's my son; it's my situation. That means that you have to do what I say, and you have to do it quick, without asking."

"All right, all right," Geoff Summers reassured him. "Now . . . are you going to tell me what's going on?"

Jack said, "First of all, I have to find myself a car. Then we have to find a base, somewhere to sleep, somewhere to monitor the news."

"The *news*? You're expecting reports about Druids on the *news*?"

"Geoff," Jack told him, fixing him with an intent stare. "You have no idea how serious this thing is."

"No, well, obviously I don't." He grinned at Karen, and raised his eyebrows, and said, "Gosh!" and Jack suddenly realized how young he was.

N·I·N·E

At 5:30 that evening, a sixty-seven-year-old woman called Matilda Pancic left the Whole-Sum Discount Health Food Store on Lincoln Avenue in West Milwaukee and began to walk the three blocks west to her apartment building.

She hummed as she walked, *"This is my lovely day . . . this is the day I will remember until the day I'm dying. . . ."*

Close behind her, the concrete sidewalk began to craze over, in a narrow furrow, and although she couldn't hear it because of the traffic, and because she was partially deaf, she was followed by a thick dragging noise. *Ssssssshhhhhh —sssssshhhhhh—sssssshhhhhh.*

Matilda Pancic had been a widow for four years and nine days. Her husband Milton Pancic had been a specialty baker. His photograph stood on her bureau, a bald-headed man with a drooping mustache. He had died of a perforated ulcer the night before their wedding anniversary. The cake he had made for it stood next to his photograph, under glass. *For My Sweetest Matti, Thank You for Forty-Eight Wonderful Years, Yours For Ever, Milton.*

He had brought the cake home at six o'clock. *For Ever* had lasted seventeen minutes.

These days, Matilda Pancic felt the cold, so she wore a head scarf with views of Niagara Falls printed on it, and a dull blue quilted raincoat. Her face was rounder than ever; but what else was there to do but sit in front of the television and eat tropical-fruit yogurt out of the container and think of Milton? Sometimes, in the night, she thought she heard his voice, calling her from the kitchen, as loud and clear as when he was alive.

She stopped at Carswell Drugs to buy the *Milwaukee Journal* and a new toothbrush. Mr. Druker, the horse-faced pharmacist leaned over the prescription counter and said, "You tried that ointment for your eczema, Mrs. Pancic? What did you think?"

She pulled her lips tight with distaste. "Too greasy, Herman—didn't like it. It messed up my sleeves."

"You should try it for a month, at least."

The girl in front of her was taking a long time trying to decide between Honey Dawn hair coloring or Tawny Rapture. Mrs. Pancic peered over her shoulder and said, "Take the brown. With the other, it's too light, you'll look like a floorbrush."

The girl turned round and stared at her and gave an embarrassed whinny through one nostril.

"Take my advice," Mrs. Pancic urged her. "I should know from hair coloring, look at mine. Snowy Surprise."

She cackled at her own joke. But only six inches away from her left foot, the black-and-white vinyl-tiled floor was beginning to ripple and bulge, and the dry, dragging sound seemed to be nearer and nearer to the surface.

"Just the newspaper and the toothbrush," said Mrs. Pancic, holding them up and showing them to Mr. Druker.

At that instant, the floor beside her foot erupted, ripped-open tiles and spraying concrete, and a massive hairy-backed hand lashed out and seized her ankle.

She shrieked with shock and pitched forward onto the counter, smashing the glass partitions. She dropped heavily onto the floor in a shower of Anacin, Tylenol, Tums, and Tampax.

The girl shrieked, too, and leaped back two or three steps. Mr. Druker said, "Oh my God!"

Matilda Pancic clawed at the plinth around the counter

in an effort to pull herself free. But another hand wrenched its way out of the floor and seized her right calf. All the time she said nothing, nothing at all, but lifted her hand toward the counter, trying to get a grip on something solid.

Mr. Druker shouted at his assistant pharmacist, "Call the police!"

"What?" said his balding assistant.

"Call the fucking police!" Mr. Druker screamed at him, the first time he had sworn since 1951, in Korea.

The two huge hands gripped Matilda Pancic and hurled her from side to side—smashing her *crakkk!* against the counter, then *crakkk!* gainst the floor, then *crakkk!* against the Hallmark birthday-card stand. Her Niagara Falls scarf suddenly flooded crimson with blood; her arms flailed loose because they were broken. She was smashed from side to side, again and again, until she flew with the blows like a bloody rag doll.

Sirens cried like children in the street outside. A crowd had gathered outside the drugstore already, not to save Matilda Pancic but to watch her die. Her blood and brains were sprayed against the drugstore window and all across the counter.

See that blood flying? See those whiplashing arms? Look at her face!

At last the huge hands reached up and possessively gripped her. In front of everybody's disbelieving eyes, she was manhandled down into the floor, into the concrete itself, in a tangle of blood and insides and thrown-back head, a gory human jigsaw puzzle that nobody who was watching could quite understand.

The very last thing to disappear was her swollen left foot—an old woman's foot, bandaged. It scraped into the concrete with a sound that set your teeth on edge; flesh against concrete. Flesh *into* concrete.

Then she was gone, and the floor momentarily bulged. The police rushed in, with their guns drawn. "Out of there!

Freeze! Police!" But nobody could follow the deep, slurred escape of the man that somebody had once christened Lester.

Shortly after seven o'clock that same evening, a thirty-three-year-old insurance assessor named Arnold Cohn stepped out of the elevator at Parking Level 3 of the Wisconsin Mutual Assurance Building and walked the length of the parking floor, smoothing his hand through his hair.

He was meeting a girl called Naomi Breinstein that evening, for an Italian dinner, and then he hoped to take her back to his apartment in Shorewood to listen to opera. In his briefcase, apart from all the papers on that highly suspicious fire at Voight's Vegetable Warehouse, he carried a new CD recording of *Le Calife de Bagdad* by François Boieldieu. Arnold was a real opera buff, far beyond Verdi.

He was concerned about his hair. Even though he was only thirty-three, it was beginning to thin on the crown, to the extent that if he swung his medicine-chest mirror outward so that he could see the back of his head in the mirror in the hallway, white scalp was revealed, gleaming through soft black curls.

Arnold's father was almost completely bald, but it was okay for fathers to be bald. Arnold had never thought for a moment that it would ever happen to *him*. Particularly not *now*, when he had discovered a girl for whom he had developed the genuine hots.

Naomi was a cellist with the Milwaukee Symphony Orchestra. Her hair was dark and came halfway down her back, her eyes were as brown and shiny as all-chocolate M&Ms, her thighs were strong. Arnold had never come across a girl who exuded so much brio.

Arnold had almost reached his car when he thought he heard somebody walking behind him, dragging their feet. He stopped and looked around, but the concrete garage was empty. Arnold had been working late, and apart from his own Volkswagen, only six or seven vehicles still remained. One of those was a Corvette that belonged to his colleague John Radetzky, and which lay permanently shrouded in tarpaulin.

Arnold stayed perfectly still for almost half a minute, suppressing his breathing. But the garage was silent. He said "*hmmph*" to himself for being so nervous and continued walking. He wondered if Naomi might be persuaded to stay the night. He had watched her thighs clasped around her cello. The thought of having them clasped around his waist was enough to make him sweat.

He took out his car keys. As he did so he heard the noise again. *Sssssssshhhh—ssssshhhhh—ssssshhhhh*—like somebody dragging a heavy sack. He looked up. It seemed to be coming from the *ceiling*, this noise; from Parking Level 2. Yet Parking Level 2 had been deserted, and in darkness, when he had passed it in the elevator. It was usually only used for daytime visitors.

"Anybody there?" he called out. *There*? mimicked his echo.

He unlocked his car door. *Sssssssssssshhhhhh*, whispered the noise. This time Arnold swung around really quickly.

"Listen—if there's anybody there, you'd better understand that your presence here is unauthorized, and that I'm going to inform the building super on my way out of here."

It was then that he saw the tarpaulin shroud over John Radetzky's car rippling slightly. So that was it. Somebody was hiding inside Radetzky's car. Some bum, probably. Either sleeping in it or thinking of stealing the hi-fi system.

Arnold crossed the garage floor as quietly as he could, smoothing his hand over the back of his hair. When he reached the covered-up Corvette, he hesitated for just a moment. Then he bent down and grasped the tarpaulin in both hands.

Right, you bastard. One, two, three! He whipped the tarpaulin back and shouted, "Got you!"

But the car was empty. There was nobody in it.

Embarrassed—and glad that there was nobody else around—Arnold peered in through the shiny windshield.

As he looked inside, cupping his hand over his eyes to cover the reflections from the flourescent lights, the concrete ceiling directly above his head began to distort, as if it had become as soft as sand.

Slowly, as the molecules of the concrete poured themselves apart, the impression of a naked woman appeared, lying horizontally on a ceiling beam. She had an odd wild-eyed beauty, small breasts, but the kind of curved powerful thighs that Arnold would really have appreciated.

She reached down with both hands, like a swimmer reaching down into the sea, and with infinite gentleness she touched Arnold's hair.

Arnold impatiently brushed his hair back, thinking that a fly had touched him, or that his hair had simply curled away from his bald patch again.

The woman touched him again, and this time he looked up, frowning.

"*Ahh!*" he shouted. It was all that he could manage. The inside of his stomach felt as if it had collapsed in terror, like a torn balloon.

The woman in the concrete didn't give him a chance. She gripped his neck tightly with both hands and heaved him upward, so that his feet were swept off the floor. He kicked and swung and choked and tried to scream, but she drew him effortlessly up to the ceiling, her thumbs pressing into his Adam's apple, her fingernails digging deep into the back of his neck.

Crimson-faced, he pushed against the ceiling with both hands, but she pulled him up and up until his face was pressed against hers.

Her cheeks and her forehead were just as abrasive as the concrete from which she had appeared. Her blank concrete eyes stared straight into his. He couldn't breathe, couldn't scream. He felt as if the whole building were dropping on top of him. In fact, it was the other way around. He was being pulled up into the building.

Kiss me, the woman commanded, smiling, rubbing her nose against his cheek and painfully scraping it. *Don't you think that I'm beautiful? Look at my breasts! Don't you want to make love to me?*

She rubbed her face against his, from side to side, faster and faster. Scratches quickly became lacerations; lacerations deepened into furrows. Skin was shredded away like tissue paper, nerve endings bared, flesh scraped off. *Right —left—right—left—chip—chop—chip—chop, last man's dead!*

The concrete woman laughed at him, her concrete face shiny with Arnold's own blood. Arnold opened his mouth and tried to scream, but she was squeezing his throat too tightly—and as he did so, her roughcast forehead ripped his lips off, two thick red mutilated worms. His nose came afterward, in a bloody knot of cartilage and bone; but it was when she scraped his chin right down to the bare bone that he quaked with an agonizing vibration that was transmitted right through his brain, and he struggled so much that she dropped him.

He collapsed heavily onto the floor, splattering blood all over John Radetzky's car. Gasping, choking, his mouth bubbling, he crawled away from the car, across the concrete floor, leaving behind him a trail of blood as bright as freshly splashed paint.

My face, he thought, through a maelstrom of different kinds of pain. *What has she done to my face?*

The blood was pouring over his eyes, so that he could hardly see. He didn't dare to touch his face to wipe it clear; but if he blinked his left eyelid, he could just about make out where he was going. His right eyelid hung useless from the side of his eye.

He saw his bright green Volkswagen, parked on the other side of the garage. He heaved himself toward it, trying not to think what had happened to him, trying simply to get there. *Get there, then you'll be safe.*

He felt freezing cold, and his body seemed to be twice its normal weight. Every time he blinked his left eyelid, a fresh curtain of blood poured down. He tried to remember the words of *Koanga* by Frederick Delius, one of his favorite operas.

He was only six or seven feet away from his car when the concrete underneath him began to rise up, like gray swelling bread. *Earthquake,* his mind told him. But then he felt harsh and powerful arms around him, in a terrible embrace, and roughened breasts pushing themselves against his chest. He blinked his left eye and she was smiling at him, a mad triumphant frightening smile, her face freckled with oil from parked cars and spotted with Arnold's blood.

Make love to me, she demanded. *Come on, my sweetness, make love to me.*

She kissed his raw and lipless mouth, her concrete teeth scraping against his. Then with one powerful tug, she submerged like a diver into the floor and pulled him down with her.

For one split second, Arnold knew pain so intense that it transcended anything he had ever experienced. It was like falling alive into an ocean of meat grinders. As he was crushed and mangled and ripped apart he was amazed that his consciousness could have survived for so long, when his body was nothing more than fats and slimes and fragmented bones and ground-up string. He died amazed. He died in white-hot agony.

There was silence in the garage after he had vanished. Then, almost inaudibly, the *sssssshhhhhh—sssssshhhhhh—sssssshhhhh* of human flesh moving through solid walls.

At 2:30 the following morning, Officer Gene Spanier of the Milwaukee police force was driving home northward on Lisbon Avenue when he saw what appeared to be a drunk lying on the sidewalk. He drew his car slowly into the curb, turned around in his seat, and looked back, his engine idling. Either a drunk or a stiff, although as far as he knew nobody had reported a stiff. The local residents will step over drunks, but they do prefer to have corpses taken away.

Officer Spanier was very tired. He had been working since eleven o'clock the previous day, and all he wanted was bed. But here was this figure, sprawled face down on the sidewalk, arms by its sides, and supposing this figure was a late figure, and Officer Spanier drove on?

He said a bitter prayer to the Lord God above. *O Lord, You give yachts to bank robbers and Cadillacs to pimps. How come you never give me anything but wall-to-wall buffalo chips? Amen.* He backed up his shuddering eight-year-old Oldsmobile until he was parked right next to the figure, and he examined it with some sanguinity through his tightly closed window.

Inebriated, or exited? It was hard to tell from the curbside. He couldn't detect any breathing, and the figure's face was the strangest color, almost the same color as the concrete on which it lay. Its coat was concrete-colored, too.

A man, maybe thirty-five years old, stockily built, Polish or German maybe.

Officer Spanier backed up a foot or two farther and saw that the figure had bare feet. Concrete-colored bare feet.

Drunk, had to be. No sign of blood. No sign of head injury. But on the other hand, his face was that awful concrete color—wasn't it?—and his chest didn't appear to be rising and falling as he breathed. And even if he *wasn't* dead—even if he was just drunk—he could be suffering from alcohol poisoning. Officer Spanier might be able to save his life.

If there is any point in saving a man lying facedown-drunk on Lisbon Avenue at two-thirty in the morning, thought Officer Spanier, without charity. He had never liked the parable of the Good Samaritan. He didn't know many policemen who did. Most of the time the people they saved didn't even want to be saved, and the rest of the time they weren't worth it. Bums, junkies, would-be suicides, unemployed brewery workers, crazy Polacks.

Officer Spanier was thirty-nine˙years and fifty-one weeks old, and he had just been divorced for the second time. He opened his eyes two hours too early every single morning and lay there wondering what his life was all about. Next week he was going to be forty. He lived in a two-room apartment with a soprano saxophonist upstairs and a prostitute across the hall. The soprano saxophonist played excruciatingly bad imitations of Roland Kirk and the prostitute wore tight white short-shorts that cut like the sharpest of knife cuts between her legs, and both of them bothered him differently but equally. He drank a lot of Jack Daniel's when he was off duty and laughed sardonically at "Miami Vice." And why not? Neither a white Armani suit nor a red Ferrari Daytona were necessary adjuncts to being a happy cop. All you needed was a good wife who didn't nag you and burn your frittata and who didn't turn around when you climbed into bed looking like Frankenstein Meets the Three Stooges and then use her full-length brushed-nylon nightdress to enforce a state of monkitude on you. You could do without those fucking Milwaukee winters, too. That wind blowing right off the lake like facefuls of razors marinated in ice-cold vodka.

Grunting, and with huge reluctance, Officer Spanier heaved himself out of the driver's seat. Since his divorce, he had put on fifteen pounds, as well as growing a Teddy Roosevelt mustache. His greatest hero was Burt Reynolds. He had a signed photograph of himself and Burt Reynolds, arm in arm, at Universal Studios. *For Gene, With Best Squiggle, Burt Reynolds.* He could never make out what the squiggle meant.

He hunkered down next to the sprawled-out figure on the sidewalk. No smell of alcohol. No smell of anything. Drunks usually reeked like drunks, and stiffs usually stank of shit. Loss of anal tension. But this hombre didn't smell of anything at all. Officer Spanier regarded him with professional disinterest for a minute or two and then sniffed and said, "Hey fellow, you sleeping, or what?"

The figure on the sidewalk remained totally still. Not drunk, not dead, but completely inanimate.

Officer Spanier reached out and cautiously touched the figure's arm. It was cast out of concrete, it was a statue, for Christ's sake. Somebody had made a statue and laid it on the sidewalk.

He pushed it but it wouldn't move. He couldn't even work his fingers underneath it. It was fused into the sidewalk like it was an integral part of the concrete. Jesus. Somebody had cast a paving slab into a sculpture and just left it here. Anybody could have tripped over it, broken their leg. The whole idea of it was totally crazy, the kind of thing that happened in California, but here in Milwaukee?

Yet whoever had created it, it was brilliant. You had to scrutinize it from two inches away before you realized it was concrete. The detail was incredible. Whoever made it, they should be manufacturing rubberized women, comforters for divorced cops.

The trouble was, now that Officer Spanier had found this sculpture, Officer Spanier would have to file a report; and Officer Spanier would have to locate the sculptor, and make an arrest, if sculpting the sidewalk was an indictable offense. Maybe it came under vandalism, or public disorder.

Maybe he could solve everything by levering the sculpture off. He could use the sharp end of his tire iron and chip into the concrete. He must be able to move it. If somebody had put it here, somebody else must be able to take it away. All he had to do then was to drop the goddamned thing in the lake and pretend that it had never existed.

He went back to his Oldsmobile, opened the trunk, and stretched inside for the tire iron. While he was doing so, he thought he heard something scraping, and he stopped and looked around, but Lisbon Avenue was totally deserted. *Nothing,* thought Officer Spanier. *Late-night jitters.*

He returned to the sculpture. *I really cannot believe this. I'm supposed to be home and in bed. But here I am, chiseling a human figure off the sidewalk. I should have listened to Uncle Albie and taken up that trailer dealership. At least I would have made some money. At least I wouldn't be squatting on the goddamned sidewalk at three o'clock in the morning, coping with the lunatic handiwork of some fruitcake artist.*

Wheezing softly, Officer Spanier knelt down beside the sprawled-out figure and positioned the chisel-shaped end of his tire iron right where its cheek met the sidewalk.

He was about to chip into the concrete when the statue flicked open its eyes and stared at him. Officer Spanier dropped his tire iron with a clang and stood up, nervously wiping his hands on the thighs of his jeans.

"You moved," he accused the sculpture. "You opened your eyes."

The statue smiled. *Nothing is ever what it seems to be. You're a policeman. You should know that.*

Officer Spanier picked up his tire iron and brandished it. "I'm warning you. Whatever the hell you are, you're under arrest. I'm going to read you your rights."

I know my rights. My rights are given by Awen, the greatest of names.

"Just stand up, mister. Stand up slow. Keep your hands in sight, no false moves."

I cannot stand. Not yet.

"I said, up!" Officer Spanier snapped at him.

That's impossible. The concrete is me and I am the concrete.

"If you don't stand up of your own accord, mister, I'm going to drag you up."

Officer Spanier seized the collar of the statue-man's coat and tried to haul him on to his feet. But—"shit!"—it was impossible. Either the statue-man was impossibly heavy, or Officer Spanier was too exhausted after sixteen hours on duty to lift up squat, or else the statue-man really *was* part of the sidewalk. A living, breathing part of the sidewalk.

What the hell was he going to do now?

Give me your hand, the statue-man told him. His voice was thick and blurred, as if he had a mouthful of fine wet sand.

Officer Spanier shifted the tire iron to his left hand and offered his right. The statue-man reached up and clasped it. Tight. Tight like steel.

"Okay, mister, *up!*" Officer Spanier demanded.

No, my friend. It is you who are coming down.

Officer Spanier tugged at the statue-man's hand. But his strength was extraordinary. Officer Spanier had never felt anything like it. He tried to twist his hand free but he couldn't.

"Hey! Let go of my . . . !"

But the statue-man suddenly twisted in the sidewalk, with a smile on his face, and plunged into the concrete and disappeared. Officer Spanier yelled out, *"Stop!"* but then he was pulled down into concrete, too.

He had dived into Lake Michigan on a February morning to save a drowning woman. He had dived through fire to rescue two small children from a blazing apartment. He had dived through a plate-glass window to avoid being shot at by a crack-crazed Polack with a sawed-off shotgun. But nothing could have prepared him for being forced headfirst into the solid sidewalk of Lisbon Avenue. He was smashed into the concrete with such force that he felt as if his soul were coming apart. It was impossible for a human body to penetrate concrete, yet he felt the statue-man dragging him deep inside it, stripping away skin, unraveling arteries—sieving his flesh into bright red pulp.

He felt death closing in on him, like the closing shutter of a camera. *I'm dying, I can't believe it, this is the end of my life.* He thought he could hear himself screaming, but it was probably nothing more than the atoms of his brain, splitting apart like a supernova.

Officer Spanier disappeared into the sidewalk like a man sinking into a swimming pool. Lisbon Avenue remained silent and deserted. Officer Spanier's abandoned Oldsmobile stood with its door still open, the keys still hanging in the ignition.

Then, after a quarter of an hour, a dark wet stain appeared on the sidewalk, following the cracks in the concrete.

The stain grew wider and wider, and then suddenly a thick tomato soup began to gout out of the ground, quarts and quarts of it.

The soup was Officer Spanier—liquefied flesh, blood, and pulverized bone. He poured across the sidewalk and into the gutter, and then began to drip down the drains.

Early the following day, in Room 516 of the Hyatt Regency Hotel, on Milwaukee's Grand Avenue, a nineteen-year-old psychology student called Rhoda Greenberg opened her eyes and lifted her head off the pillow and frowned toward the window and wondered where the hell she was. Then she heard snorting, and so with all the fastidiousness of a mortician, she picked up the tangled blanket and inspected the gray-haired man sleeping heavily beside her, and she remembered.

You've done it again, Rhoda, you whore.

She tiredly dragged aside the blanket and climbed naked out of the bed. She went to the window, yawning and scratching her thick black curly hair, and noisily tugged open the drapes. Outside, downtown Milwaukee lay ghostly in the mist from Lake Michigan—the bell tower of city hall with its distinctive green roof rising above the haze like the tower of some Eastern European capital. The clock on the bell tower told her that it was five after six in the morning. Her mouth tasted of sour red wine, and her head pounded.

She looked toward the bed. One fat arm, skin white as liver sausage and thickly covered with gray hair, lay exposed on top of the blanket. It wore a steel Seiko wristwatch and a wedding band. Rhoda didn't know whether she felt disgusted with herself or not—or, if she did, how much. She had done this so often now that it was difficult to evaluate her sense of guilt. She knew very well that she would do it again, when the mood took her.

She stood by the window for a long time, in the pearly-colored light. She was not at all pretty. Her nose was hooked and far too large; her lips were thick and her chin was as weak as Olive Oyl's. She had photographs at home of her grandmother back in Breslau when she was young, and she could have been the same girl.

What she did have, however, was a spectacular figure. Her breasts were huge and rounded and firm, her waist was so narrow that most men could close their hands around it. Her legs were long, with slim thighs and perfect ankles.

She had learned when she was thirteen that men lusted after her. They didn't want to be seen with her; they didn't want to take her dancing. She was too plain and toothy and frizzy-haired and she brayed when she laughed. But men used to go out of their way to touch her breasts and to slide their hands up her skirt. She had even caught her father once, staring at her in appalled fascination through the crack of the bathroom door, one hand on his heart, whiskey on his breath, his eyes the color of Spam.

Rhoda ached for friendship, companionship, love, and affection, just as much as any other girl. Just because she didn't have the face of a prom queen, that didn't mean she didn't have emotional needs. But when men looked at Rhoda, they never looked at her face; and she had never once been taken to a party. She had decided at the age of fifteen that if men weren't prepared to give her what she wanted, she would just have to take from men whatever she could get.

She had openly chased (and laid) every single boy in her senior class at High School, except for two, who were gay; and she had gone to bed with three of her teachers, too. Now that she was studying psychology at the University of Wisconsin Milwaukee, she had taken to spending her few spare evenings at the Hyatt or the Sheraton, or around the stores on Grand Avenue, picking up lonely businessmen. Cosmetic and jewelry counters and lingerie stores were always good places to find them, as they clumsily tried to find gifts to take home to their wives.

Rhoda was always so sweet and helpful. "Do you know what *I* would buy her, if I were you . . . ?"

Back in their hotel rooms, however, she humiliated them; she made them crawl. She called them filthy and degrading names and made them perform the most disgusting acts she could think of. And the extraordinary part about it was, they always did what she told them. Some of them adored her so much they wanted to set her up as their regular dominatrix, in an apartment of her own.

She always refused. She didn't want to be owned by anyone. But she made thousands of dollars, and she always expected each man to give her an expensive gift. Jewelry, or perfume, or dresses.

She left the window and walked through to the bathroom without giving the sleeping man on the bed another glance. She couldn't even remember what his name was. All she remembered was that he was short and hairy, and that he had burst into tears after they had finished having sex. She never thought of what she did as "making love."

She switched on the bathroom light and looked at herself in the mirror. Dark circles under her eyes. She would have to catch up on some sleep this weekend. She brushed her teeth, spat, brushed them again.

As she was rinsing out her mouth she heard a noise

behind her, like somebody brushing against the shower curtain. *Sssh.*

She looked in the mirror, but there was nobody standing in the bathroom behind her. She filled the washbasin with cold water so that she could bathe her swollen eyes. She wished that she wouldn't drink red wine; it always gave her such a paralyzing hangover.

Then she heard the noise again, longer and slower this time. *Sssshhh—sssshhhhh.*

She turned around, frowning. The bathroom was empty; the shower curtain hadn't stirred. She went to the door and looked into the bedroom, but Short 'n' Hairy was still fast asleep, and snoring.

Oh, well, maybe it's the plumbing, she thought. *You know what these hotels are like. Every time somebody goes to the john, everybody else can hear it in graphic detail.*

She washed her face, patted it dry, and then opened up her makeup bag. She always liked to use plenty of makeup. False eyelashes, garish red lipstick. It was better to look like a hooker than a mouse.

She squeezed glue on to the first of her false eyelashes. She smiled at the memory of one of her men, who had discovered her eyelashes on the bathroom shelf and squashed them up in toilet paper and flushed them down the john, because he thought they were centipedes.

She was still smiling to herself when the water in the washbasin abruptly emptied of its own accord and gurgled away.

She jiggled the lever that operated the plug. Then she filled up the basin again; but again the water emptied itself out. She peered down at the plug. Maybe it wasn't straight.

She was still trying to work out what was wrong with the plug when she felt something catch at her hair. *Damn it,* she breathed, and tried to lift her head out of the basin; but somehow her long curly hair had become entangled in the drain, and she couldn't pull it out.

Carefully she attempted to unwind her hair from the plug. She couldn't work out how it had become so hopelessly snarled up. The more she tried to disentangle it, the more wound up it became. Her head was now being pulled quite painfully down into the basin, until her forehead was pressing against the cold ceramic.

"Oh, for God's sake," said Rhoda, not just impatient now, but panicky. She didn't want to cut her hair to get it free, but she couldn't work out how she had gotten so hopelessly ensnared.

"Hey!" she shouted out, trying to wake up Short 'n' Hairy in the bedroom. "Hey, give me a hand here, will you? Hey!" She wished that she could remember what his name was. Something like Herman or Harry or Herbert.

"Hey, Herman!" she called. "Herman, I'm stuck! Herman, get me out of here!"

As soon as she had said that, however, her hair was forcibly wrenched downward into the drain, as if somebody had actually snatched hold of it, and pulled it. Her forehead was knocked against the basin, and she cried out in fear. "*Help me! Help me! For God's sake, Herman, help me!*"

Rhoda's face was pulled harder and harder against the washbasin. She felt the skin crackle all over her head as her scalp was being lifted away from her skull. She screamed again and again and again, but the relentless pulling continued.

"What the hell's the matter, what the hell are you screaming for?" She heard Short 'n' Hairy Herman's voice, close beside her. She opened her eyes and saw his worried face, upside down.

"I'm caught, my hair's caught, get me out!"

Herman grasped her head and tried to yank it upward. Rhoda screamed even more piercingly, and he let her go.

"Not like that, you stupid bastard!" she raged at him, her eyes filled with tears. "The plug, take out the plug!"

Herman wrestled with the plug for a while, rattling the

lever up and down like a child pretending to drive a train, but then he gasped, "I can't. Your hair's all knotted up, it won't come out."

"For God's sake it's pulling me down!" Rhoda sobbed.

She glimpsed the ruffles of fat on Herman's big white bottom; his fist clenched in indecision. "Maybe I should try scissors," he suggested in a windy voice. "Do you want me to try scissors?"

"Just get me out!" she begged him. Her hair was being dragged with such force into the drain that she thought that it was going to be ripped out by the roots. Then it was tugged, and tugged, and tugged, as if in furious impatience; and the pain was so intense that it surged way beyond anything she was able to bear, and she started screaming again, blind purposeless screaming, against the cold ceramic of the washbasin.

Herman backed away. "Listen," he said, "I'd better find somebody to help. Can you hold on? Can you just hold on?"

He hurried back into the bedroom to find his clothes. "Jesus H. Christ." Rummaged wildly around for his shirt and his socks. "What the hell did I do with my necktie? Jesus, stop screaming, Jesus."

Rhoda took a deep trembling breath before screaming again; but this time she didn't scream at all. Two glistening white hands emerged smoothly from the washbasin and grasped her head on either side and pulled it downward, into the ceramic itself.

Herman reappeared at the open bathroom door, half-dressed, his cheeks stiff with fear. He saw Rhoda's naked body, bent over the washbasin, shuddering as if she were being electrocuted. The washbasin itself was brimming and slopping with blood.

Herman stared at Rhoda for a very long time. He had never seen anybody killed. It didn't even occur to him that Rhoda was dying in a way that defied all the laws of the natural world. Last night she had forced him to crawl across the carpet. Now she was bent over in front of him, her knees and elbows rigid with agony, right on the point of death.

He felt an extraordinary sexual excitement. She was naked and she was being killed and he couldn't look away.

At last, with an awkward little genuflection, he caught hold of the bathroom doorknob and closed the door. He breathed deeply. Then he took out his handkerchief and wiped the doorknob clean. He had probably left thousands of fingerprints all over the room, but somehow this one token gesture made him feel safer. It erased at least the fact that he had watched her dying. He went back to the bedroom, trembling, and sweaty, and very white, and packed his suitcase.

When he was packed, he went back to the bathroom door and listened. All he could hear was a slow, thick dripping. He wondered if he ought to take a last look, but he decided against it. If anybody asked him, he would deny that he had ever seen the girl before—she must have broken into his hotel room after he had checked out, and committed suicide. It was obviously suicide. Cut her throat, in the washbasin.

He knew that his wife Marcia would stand up for him. He could almost hear her now. "In thirty-seven years of marriage, my Herman has never been unfaithful once." That tight gray permanent wave nodding. He was sweating like a pig and he was so short of breath that he had to lean against the wall and tell himself: *Breathe, breathe, for Christ's sake, breathe.*

At last he managed to stop gasping. *You're all right, all you have to do now is to check out, and smile, and take the plane back to Indianapolis, and nobody will ever be able to prove that you had anything to do with it.*

He picked up his plaid valise and turned toward the door.

He was chilled to the spot, in a greater terror than he had ever experienced in his life.

The door itself had bulged out, into the shape of a short, muscular man. The man was staring at him and smiling, his face streaked like war paint with the brown-and-gold patterns of the wood veneer.

Herman stood and looked at the man in the door and didn't know what to do. He didn't dare to reach for the door handle.

"What do you want?" he whispered at last.

The man in the door continued to smile, continued to stare, and there was something about his smile that convinced Herman beyond any possible doubt that he would never be allowed to leave this hotel room alive.

It happened all over Milwaukee, and Wauwatosa, and Cudahy, and Whitefish Bay. On East Kilbourn Avenue, three-year-old twins were found crying in their baby buggy, apparently abandoned by their mother in the middle of shopping. On North Sixth Street, a well-known brewer vanished from his car while waiting at a traffic light, with no indication of where he had gone but the car's violently torn-apart seats.

Right beside the Domes at the Mitchell Park Horticultural Conservatory, three members of a wedding party were dragged into the pavement in front of a hundred horrified but helpless witnesses as they posed for photographs.

A thirty-two-year-old architect was coming back from the men's room at Mader's Restaurant when he disappeared without any trace at all.

Jack listened to the television news all day, trying to keep track of how many people were disappearing. By midafternoon, it was dozens, and he could tell by the news reports that a strong feeling of panic was beginning to sweep through Milwaukee. Governor Earl had already declared a state of emergency in the area, and the National Guard had been alerted.

"But the plain truth is that we have no idea of what we're trying to combat here . . . whether these disappearances are due to some kind of natural phenomenon, a variety of seismological disturbance . . . or whether they're part of some criminal conspiracy. . . ."

Jack looked at Geoff Summers and Geoff Summers shrugged. "Should we tell them?" asked Jack.

"Do you think they'd believe us if we did?" Geoff replied.

"Not for a moment."

"Then we're better off keeping quiet and trying to work out some way of stopping them before it's too late. I'm a great believer in doing things for oneself. The minute you start bringing in officialdom, you're lost."

Geoff had arranged for them to stay in a small back-street house on the outskirts of Madison, with a veranda overgrown with gourds and a rocking chair and a scruffy overgrown vacant lot next door. The house belonged to a professor of physics who was lecturing in Scandinavia for two years, and Geoff had a key because he was supposed to water the ferns. Geoff thought it would be unlikely that anybody would find them here.

It was a dull, headachy afternoon, with the sky dark and low over the treetops and a smell of impending rain in the air. They were sitting on bean bags in the physics professor's front parlor, drinking coffee out of Garfield mugs. Jack was close to giving up. He had let loose an uncontrollable horde of violent criminals, and every life they claimed was his responsibility. He was beginning to believe that even Geoff and Karen blamed him now.

"If only we had some way of tracking them down," he said. "Some way of finding out where they are, *before* they reach out and snatch people."

Geoff was leafing through a huge musty-smelling book called *Ritual and Magic in Pre-Christian Times*. "I've been trying to find the ritual the Druids used to use for getting inside the ground. I thought that perhaps we could hunt them down that way."

"You mean, go into the ground *ourselves*?" Jack asked him.

"How else are we going to locate them?"

"God knows," Jack replied.

Karen said, "Hold on—this is the news." She lifted the television remote control and turned up the sound. On the screen were several utility workers in hard hats, talking to the police and to TV reporters.

One of the utility workers was saying, ". . . digging here to lay new electric cables, right? And all of a sudden my divining rods go haywire. So Louis here says what the hell's happening, excuse my French, and suddenly he falls right into the pavement, and that's it, he's gone."

"You mean he fell right into your excavation?" the TV reporter asked him.

The utility worker shook his head emphatically. "No, lady. He was nowhere near the excavation. He fell right into the road. He disappeared into solid pavement."

The TV reporter turned to face the camera. "And so here on East Wisconsin Avenue yet another unaccountable disappearance, the eighteenth in the Milwaukee area in just twenty-four hours. A utility worker vanishes into the solid roadway, leaving his coworkers mystified. The police so far are 'keeping an open mind.' But there have been calls already for a special investigation, and hundreds of Milwaukee residents are leaving the area by road or by air until the disappearances are satisfactorily explained and stopped. All roads to General Mitchell Field—"

Jack reached over and turned off the sound. He turned to Geoff with a serious face. "You know what we're going to get now? We're going to get a major hystera. We're going to have to think of something quick."

But Geoff was looking thoughtful. "Did you hear what that utility worker said?"

"Sure. His friend disappeared into the solid pavement."

"Yes, but before then."

"I don't know. Just that they were laying electric cables."

Geoff closed his book and put it aside. "He said 'my divining rods went haywire.'"

"Oh, yes?" asked Jack, still baffled.

"Listen—" said Geoff, "the utility services use divining rods before they excavate the highway so that they can locate water and gas pipes and dig into the ground without damaging them. But the Druids used to use divining rods, too—to locate ley lines. Actually the Druids used hazel twigs . . . but they worked on exactly the same principle."

"So what are you trying to suggest?" said Jack.

"Well, if Quintus Miller and his chums make divining rods go haywire whenever they're around, perhaps we can recruit somebody who knows how to use divining rods to track the buggers down."

Karen said, "How about that guy on the television—the utility worker?"

"Good thinking," said Geoff. "Jack, why don't you call the electric company; see if you can find out who that chap was."

"And what are you going to do?"

Geoff picked up his book again. "I'm going to try and find out how we can deal with these maniacs once we've found them."

"I thought we had to bend them double or something," put in Karen.

"That's right . . . but we have to do it in strict accordance with Druidic ritual. Once they've traveled through the ground, remember, these people are not quite human anymore. They're rather *more* than human. We have to make sure that when we sacrifice them to Awen, they stay sacrificed. Otherwise they may return in an even more savage form and track *us* down."

Karen shuddered. Jack picked up the phone.

T·E·N

*T*hey met Otto Schröder in Watertower Park, underneath the 175-foot Gothic water tower that gave this part of Milwaukee's east side an incongruous similarity to Disneyland. The sky was brilliantly blue but the wind was piercing, and Otto Schröder was wearing a speckled woolly hat pulled over his ears and a leather USAF jacket with a lambswool collar, and he was jogging in place to keep himself warm.

"I feel the cold," he told them. "I should've had an inside job, you know? Bad circulation. But it's too late now."

Jack said, "Come and have a cup of coffee."

"It's okay. I just had lunch. I'm not supposed to be meeting you guys anyway. My foreman said not to talk to anybody."

"Well, we're not just anybody," Geoff told him. "We happen to know exactly what happened to your friend."

Otto Schröder sniffed and wiped his nose with the heel of his hand. "He went straight into the blacktop. He just vanished. I don't know whether the cops believed me or not."

"We believe you," said Jack. "What's more—we can probably find the people who did it."

Otto Schröder looked at Jack suspiciously, one eye closed against the cold. He was stubby and broad-shouldered, at least four inches shorter than Jack, with pugnacious wind-stung cheeks, and bright gray eyes, and the bluntest of Germanic noses. "Nobody *did* it, mister. Norman just disappeared."

"You didn't see anybody else there?"

Otto Schröder shook his head. "No, sir. Nobody. There wasn't a single person inside of ten feet of Norman when he went."

"Did you see any hands holding him?" asked Jack.

"What do you mean? I just told you. There wasn't a single person inside of ten feet of him."

Geoff said, "What Mr. Reed means is, did you see any hands coming out of the concrete?"

Otto Schröder looked from Jack to Geoff and back again. "What is this, some kind of stupid joke? Are you guys nuts or something?"

Jack said, "We're totally serious. The truth is that there are some very dangerous people who have found a way to move around under the ground. They can go through walls, they can go through doors, you name it. Brick, concrete, rock. As far as they're concerned, it's all the same."

"You *are* nuts," said Otto Schröder. He stuffed his hands in the pockets of his jacket and started to walk away.

"Mr. Schröder, will you please wait?" Geoff begged him.

"You're nuts," Otto Schröder repeated. "I took an early lunch, I wasted almost an hour, and you're nuts."

"But you saw what happened for yourself. You saw your friend disappear right in front of your eyes."

"An optical delusion," Otto Schröder told him. "That's all it was."

Jack reached into his wallet and took out two hundred-dollar bills and pushed them into Otto Schröder's top pocket. Otto Schröder stopped walking, and took the bills out, and carefully uncrumpled them.

Jack said, "There's a thousand in it if you help us. You can go on thinking we're nuts. To tell you the truth I don't give a coffee-colored shit what you think. Those people took your friend and they've taken dozens of other people, too, and they're going to take more. They also took my nine-year-old son."

Otto Schröder looked toward Geoff. Geoff said, "It's true, Mr. Schröder. That's why we wanted to talk to you."

"What can I do?" asked Otto Schröder.

"You know how to use divining rods, right?"

"Sure. My grandfather taught me. It's nothing special if you got the feel for it."

"Just before your friend disappeared, you felt the divining rods go out of control, right? Your exact words were, 'they went haywire.'"

Otto Schröder nodded, still suspicious.

Geoff said, "Now—whether you believe it or not—the *reason* your rods went haywire was because one or more of those people were under the ground and they were disrupting the magnetic currents close to where you were working. What exactly did the rods do?"

"They spun. They kind of spun around. Like, the left one going clockwise, and the right one going anticlockwise."

"Did you notice any change in the rods' behavior at the moment that your friend disappeared?"

"I guess I did." Otto Schröder nodded. "They stopped spinning. They stopped dead. I never saw them do that before. And they touched together at the end, just kind of kissed each other, and I got this strong feeling that there was something there. You can't explain it to somebody who doesn't dowse. But it was the same kind of feeling you get when you're close to something very big, like an underground water tank, or a tunnel."

Jack said, "Otto—it's okay if I call you Otto?"

"For sure."

"Otto, there are one hundred thirty-seven of these people. They're all maniacs, criminal psychotics. We have to find them as quick as we can, before they do to more people what they did to your friend. At the moment they can't leave the ground, or the walls—they can't walk around in the air, the same way that we can. But if they manage to kill enough people—well, they'll get out . . . and then we won't be able to stop them at all."

Otto wiped his nose again. "What do you plan to do with them once you've caught them?"

"The truth is, we're going to have to—" Jack began, but Geoff interrupted him.

"We have a special way of dealing with them," he said, with reassuring smoothness. "That's all you have to know. You don't have to be involved in that part of it in any way. Now—are you willing to help us, or not?"

Otto hesitated for a very long time. "This is on the level?" he asked them.

Jack nodded. "You want more money, I'll pay you twice as much. And look at it this way—if it's *not* on the level, and there's nobody there, what do you have to lose?"

"I guess you have a point there," Otto agreed.

Geoff smiled and slapped Otto on the back. "That's marvelous. And I'm especially glad that it's going to be you, because there's something else that we need."

"Oh, yeah?" asked Otto.

"A compressor and a jackhammer," said Geoff. "Your company wouldn't mind if you borrowed one for a while, would they?"

"A compressor and a jackhammer? What the hell do you need those for?"

"Digging," said Geoff succinctly. "Once we've found them, do you see? We're going to have to dig them out, like potatoes."

They met Otto again at six o'clock that evening, under the East-West Freeway, after they had taken Karen home. Geoff parked his limping Valiant opposite Otto's bashed-up GMC compressor truck and tooted his horn. Otto climbed down from his cab and came across the street.

"I don't know why the hell I'm doing this," he shouted over the noise of the freeway traffic as he climbed into the back of the car and slammed the door. "I must be out of my goddamned mind."

"Would you not slam the door, please?" Geoff asked him. "Diana is rather delicate."

"Diana?" Otto frowned.

"The car," Jack told him. Then, to elaborate, "He's British."

"Oh," said Otto, as if that explained everything.

Geoff remarked, "That truck looks pretty run-down."

"Yeah, sorry. It's the only one the foreman would let me borrow. I told him I was digging a swimming pool in my backyard. He said I was crazy. I agree with him."

"You've brought your divining rods?" Geoff asked him, unabashed.

Otto reached inside his leather jacket and produced two foot-long copper rods with bent handles. "Beauties, aren't they? Made them myself. Some people use iron or brass, but my grandfather used to swear by copper. Said it was much more sensitive than anything else.

"I'll tell you something—with these rods, I can locate a half-inch pipe within an inch of error. And that's something that nobody can do with a hazel twig."

Jack said, "Could I look at those?" and Otto handed them over. Jack swung them in his hands, but he couldn't feel anything at all. "Do you know how they work?" he asked Otto.

Geoff said, "Scientifically inexplicable. They do work—even the most skeptical of scientists have to admit to that. But nobody knows how, or why."

"How about you, Otto?" asked Jack. "Any ideas?"

But Otto shook his head and said, "Search me. It's a feeling, that's all. Kind of a buzz."

"It's something to do with the earth's natural magnetic field," Geoff added. "I was reading up about it this afternoon. The Druids used to use divining rods made out of willow or rowan branches to find out where ley lines ran. And I discovered something else interesting. Right up until medieval times, divining rods were used to track down murderers. Apparently, killers have measurably more natural magnetic charge in their bodies than the rest of us. Nobody knows *why*—but it could help us to hunt down Quintus Miller and all the rest of his maniacs."

"How are you planning on doing it?" asked Otto, taking back his divining rods and carefully polishing the handles with his handkerchief.

"We have the location of the last reported disappearance," said Jack, opening out his street plan of Milwaukee. "We'll start there . . . just to see if you can pick up any vibrations."

"And what if we do?"

"Then we circle the area with holy water, and we recite the prayer of exorcism that prevents evil forces from leaving a particular location. That should stop our murderous friend from getting away."

"Then what?"

"We dig the bastard up," said Geoff, rubbing his hands together with relish.

"And then?"

"You don't need to know the rest," Geoff told him. "You can look the other way."

"Hey—I'm not having no hand in no murders," Otto protested.

"Think about your friend Norman," Geoff reminded him. "Have you talked to Norman's widow?"

"He wasn't married. I talked to his sister."

"Well, in that case think about his sister. And think about all the other people who are going to be killed the same way, unless you and I and Jack here do something about it."

Otto sat back in his seat with a deeply unhappy pout on his face. "My wife thinks I'm bowling. I never told her a lie before. Maybe I should forget all of this maniac stuff and *go* bowling."

"Otto—this is your chance to be a hero."

"I don't want to be a hero. Did I say I wanted to be a hero?"

Jack checked his watch. "It's ten after six. We'd better get moving. The first location we're going to try is North Fifth, a block north of MECCA."

Otto hesitated, but Geoff said, "Come on, Otto! Give it a try! You never know, you might enjoy it!"

"I'm dowsing for psychos," Otto muttered as he eased himself out of the car. "I don't believe it. I don't even *half* believe it."

Geoff called, "Don't slam the—" just as Otto gave the door a hefty bang behind him.

"Door," Geoff finished quietly.

For almost ten minutes they paced up and down the sidewalk on North Fifth Street while Otto held his two copper divining rods out in front of him, searching for the tiniest tremor that would tell him that one of the maniacs from The Oaks was somewhere near.

The wind was growing raw, and Jack was beginning to wish that he had brought an overcoat. He was also beginning to wish that he had picked a location that was less conspicuous. They were catty-corner to the Milwaukee Exposition and Convention Center and Arena (MECCA for short), and eleven busloads of conventioneers were arriving for the Midwestern Bakers & Confectioners Jubilee Bake-off. Several conventioneers and homegoing business people and shoppers stopped to watch Otto with guarded fascination as he crisscrossed the sidewalk with his divining rods swinging from side to side.

"Anything?" Jack asked him.

Otto sniffed. "There's a sewage duct that runs across *here*, and a telephone cable that runs across *here*. But nothing else. Nothing moving. Nothing that's what you might call *alive*."

"Keep trying," Jack urged him.

"And if I still don't find nothing?"

"Then we try someplace else."

A man in a gray suit and a snap-brim hat and horn-rim spectacles came up to Jack and said, "Pardon me, sir?" He looked as if he had just arrived from 1962 without stopping to change. "Pardon me, sir, can I ask what your friend is doing?"

"Oh, sure," said Jack. "He's field-testing a new kind of shopping cart. Well, just the handles. The rest of the cart isn't ready yet."

The man watched Otto with grave and respectful interest. "You research people sure go to some lengths," he said at last, and then walked off.

Soon, however, Otto declared, "This location is stone-cold. There's nothing here at all."

"What do you think?" Jack asked Geoff. "Give it up and try the next one?"

"All right," said Geoff reluctantly. "I was just hoping that we could find some trace—you know, even after they're long gone. I was hoping they might leave some sort of natural magnetic footprints, as it were—something to track them by."

"Nothing," said Otto emphatically.

They climbed back into their vehicles and drove east across the Milwaukee River and then south toward the large white sculptured blocks of the Performing Arts Center. A twenty-seven-year-old actress called Millicent Horowitz had vanished from the rooftop parking lot just after three o'clock that afternoon.

They parked the compressor truck and the Valiant side by side, backed up against the parapet that faced the river. Then they crossed the roof to the spot where Millicent Horowitz had disappeared. The area was still cordoned off with fluttering tapes that read POLICE LINE DO NOT CROSS, but there was nobody around to stop Jack and Geoff and Otto from ducking under the tape and approaching the actual point of her disappearance, which was marked with a cross of red adhesive tape.

"I never tried dowsing on a roof before," said Otto, taking out his divining rods again. He stood over the red tape across and moved the rods gently from side to side.

Jack said, "They said on the news that she was walking across here with her boyfriend. He turned around to look at a boat on the river, and when he turned back she was gone. Totally vanished. At first he thought that she had thrown herself off the roof."

Otto said, "I got something."

Geoff stood with his hands on his hips facing the wind. "I don't know—I'm beginning to think this dowsing wasn't such a brilliant idea after all. Especially with somebody who's only sensitive to sewer pipes. Maybe we'll have to try chasing our maniacs underground."

"Any more luck with the ritual?" asked Jack.

"I've found *part* of the ritual. I have a friend at Harvard and he found Nestor Druggett's book *Druidism and the Significance of the Megaliths* in the Harvard library. It's one of the oldest and most comprehensive texts on Druidism that exists. He read me all the relevant passages over the phone. Apparently the Druids used to draw a large pentacle in blood onto a vertical rock, then they used to recite the sacred name of Awen in all its forms, but I can't discover what they did next—what it was that actually caused the rock to open up and admit the Druids physically to the underworld. All that Druggett says is that 'they played the king and thus entered their underground kingdom.'"

"I got something," Otto repeated, his voice thick with excitement. "Here—here, I got something!"

Jack said, "What? What is it?"

The divining rods were visibly vibrating. They were pointing toward the far corner of the roof, but as Jack watched them they began to swing to the left, as if they were tracking something moving.

"What can you feel?" Geoff wanted to know, laying his hand on Otto's shoulder.

"It's like nothing I ever felt before. It's like *circling,* around the roof. Circling all around us. Like it's watching us or something. You know, like a shark circling around somebody swimming."

"Can you tell if it's human?" asked Geoff.

Otto grimaced. "I'm not too sure about that. But it's moving through the ground. It's making kind of a noise. Like a gritty kind of a noise, do you know what I mean? Like when you get sand in your mouth, down on the beach, and it crunches in between your teeth."

They watched in dry-mouthed apprehension as the divining rods swung all the way around in a complete circle. There was no sign of any rippling in the concrete floor of the parking lot, but Jack knew that one of the maniacs was there, circling and circling, watching them, and waiting.

"I feel like a goat, tied up to catch a tiger," Geoff remarked.

"It's coming in closer," said Otto. "It's got this real deep vibration. Like the bottom note on an organ, you know? I never felt anything like this before. It's deep, and it's cold, and it's making this gritty crunching noise."

"I wish to hell I could feel it for myself," said Jack.

"Believe me, you don't," Otto replied. The divining rods swung around again, their tips shuddering closer together, as if they were pointing towards something which was coming nearer with every revolution.

"You've got the prayer ready?" asked Jack.

Geoff nodded, staring at the concrete. "I've learned it by heart, it's only a couple of lines." The relentless approach of the maniac was audible now. That hair-raisingly familiar *sssssshhhhhh—sssssshhhhhh—sssssshhhhhh* that he had first heard at The Oaks.

"You've got the holy water?" asked Jack.

Geoff patted the side pockets of his coat. Then he patted his breast pocket—then his inside pocket. "Oh shit, I've left it in the car!"

"Well, get it, for Christ's sake!" Jack shouted at him. "That lunatic's going to be hitting us any second now!"

Geoff glanced at the divining rods. They were pointing to the right, to the opposite corner of the parking lot. Immediately he made a dash for the police cordon off to the left, ducked under it, and began to run across the roof toward his car.

Immediately the divining rods swung to the left, too, as if the maniac under the floor had been alerted by the vibration of Geoff's running feet.

"Geoff!" yelled Jack. "It's coming after you! Make it quick!"

Otto said, "Holy Moses, look how *fast* it's going!"

Geoff reached his car. The rubber soles of his sneakers skidded on the concrete floor. He wrenched open the driver's door and reached across for the Perrier bottle he had filled up with holy water. But at that instant, a fist burst through the passenger seat of the car with an explosion like a grenade going off and seized his wrist.

"Jack!" Geoff yelled out, in panic. *"Jack!"*

Jack swung under the police line and pelted across the roof toward Geoff's car.

"It's got my wrist!" Geoff shouted.

Jack dodged around to the passenger door and pulled it open. Even though Geoff was bracing himself against the door frame, his hand was already being dragged down into the seat, and his skin was being lacerated by the broken springs. Jack hesitated for a second, then bent his head forward and bit into the side of the maniac's thumb, his teeth crunching through muscle and skidding against bone.

The hand released its grip for only one split second, but it was long enough for Geoff to pull himself free. Jack retreated from the car, spitting out blood.

"The water!" he shouted to Geoff. "Pour the water around the car!"

Geoff unscrewed the Perrier bottle and shook holy water all the way round the car, his face still white with shock. As he walked around he recited the words of the prayer of exorcism, *"Ab insidiis diaboli, libera nos Domine; ut Ecclesiam tuam secura tibi facias libertate seruire, te rogamus, audi nos; ut inimicos sanctae Ecclesiae humiliare digneris, te rogamus, audi nos."*

The concrete beneath the car shuddered with every word, as if somebody were beating against it with a sledgehammer. But when Geoff had finished his prayer, the disturbances stopped, and they could hear nothing but the wind whistling across the parking lot from Lake Michigan, and the hooting and turmoil of traffic.

Otto came over, with his divining rods still held out in front of him.

"What's happened, you got him trapped?"

Jack said, with grim satisfaction, "You bet your ass we got him trapped. Let's shift that car off there and start digging. It could be Quintus Miller himself."

Geoff climbed cautiously back into the Valiant, started the engine, and steered it across to the opposite parking area. They stood around and looked at the concrete where the car had been standing. It had been crushed into lumps where the maniac's hand had forced its way upward, but there was nothing else to suggest that the maniac was still down there.

Otto said, "That's reinforced concrete, solid. It's going to take a hell of a lot of jackhammering to break into that."

"In that case, we'd better get started," said Geoff.

"Supposing somebody asks what we're doing?" Otto asked him. "Like the cops, for instance."

Geoff said, "Urgent maintenance. This is an official utility-company truck, right? And you're an official utility-company employee."

"Jesus, this'd better be worth it," growled Otto. He went around to the back of the truck and hefted down the jackhammer. Then he started up the compressor, covered his ears with mufflers, and began to hack away at the concrete flooring.

The noise was earsplitting, and the vibration made Jack's vision blur. But Otto made faster progress than Jack had expected. The broad-bladed jackhammer chopped into the concrete and broke it into lumps, which he and Geoff cleared away with their hands and stacked against the parapet. Within a quarter of an hour, Otto had cut an oval that roughly followed the perimeter that Geoff had sprinkled with holy water. Within thirty minutes, he was clearing out the edges of the oval, and after an hour's work he was beginning to drill right into the center.

Considering the hellish noise they were making and the racketing echoes of the jackhammer from the white concrete walls of The Performing Arts Center, it was remarkable that nobody came up to ask them what they were doing. Dozens of people drove their cars up onto the roof to park—the Milwaukee Ballet was performing *Swan Lake* tonight—but nobody gave them a second glance. Anybody breaking up the ground so noisily and so blatantly must have had official approval.

But as they reached the center of their rough-and-ready excavation Otto stopped the jackhammer and took off his mufflers and said, "Damned if there's anything here. We're just digging this up for nothing."

Geoff looked across at Jack and said, "What do you think? Do you think we've missed him?"

But Jack kicked at the last remaining island of concrete and said, "This is big enough for a man to hide in, if he curled himself up. Come on, there's a chance, let's keep at it."

"You're the boss." Otto sighed and fitted his mufflers back on.

The jackhammer knocked away one chunk of concrete after another, and then suddenly Jack felt his scalp prickle in fear and excitement. Protruding from one side of the concrete island was the back of a man's bare heel. He swung himself down into the excavation, and tugged at Otto's arm, and pointed out the heel to him in jubilation.

"Got him!" he yelled over the roaring of the compressor. "Got the bastard cold!"

Otto took two or three steps back. "Holy mother of God," he mouthed.

"Come on, dig him out!" Jack urged. "Come on, Otto, before it gets dark!"

But Otto shook his head. "You want him dug out, you dig him out yourself. Jesus. I never saw anything like that, never." He laid down the jackhammer and took off his mufflers and climbed out of the pit.

Geoff said, "Come on, Otto. Be reasonable. You've come this far."

"Sure I have," Otto retorted. "And I'm the one who's been taking all the risks. Borrowing this truck, digging up city property. Who's going to fill this hole in, huh? Answer me that! And who's going to take the rap for digging it? You? Somehow, from where I'm standing right now, I just don't see that."

"All right then, for God's sake, I'll do it," said Jack. He pressed the mufflers over his ears, and hefted up the jackhammer, and squeezed the handle. With a shattering *brrr-brrrr-brrrr-brrrrrrpp!* the jackhammer jumped sideways, almost tugging itself out of Jack's grip, and fell sideways onto the ground.

Jack was bending over to pick it up when he heard Geoff shout out, *"Jack!"*

He looked up. From the surface of the concrete island, with a thick grating sound, a concrete-colored head was emerging, followed by concrete-colored shoulders. The head swiveled around and stared at him, blind-eyed, and he recognized it almost at once. Lester—who had first demanded that he bring him Father Bell.

You bastard, spat Lester. *Quintus will kill you for this.*

Otto stared at Lester's head in total disbelief. "That's a head," he said, at last, swallowing hard. He pulled at Geoff's sleeve. "You see that? That's a *head!*"

Geoff said, "It's okay, Otto. Don't panic. This is what we came here for." All the same, this was the first time that Geoff had seen with his own eyes any of the lunatics from The Oaks, and he was stiff with apprehension, too.

Let me free, Lester demanded. *Let me free, or Quintus will kill your son.*

"You mean he's still alive?" asked Jack.

Of course he's alive. He's a prize, your son! He's our final sacrifice, the innocent one who was demanded by the ancient gods! The one whose life will set us all free!

Jack stood up, grasping the jackhammer in both hands. "You're not going free, Lester. You can threaten me all you want. But you're not going free. I'm going to jackhammer your stupid head off."

Lester said wildly, *You can break up my body, my friend, but not my soul! Quintus will restore me! You wait! As long as my dust is still on this earth, Quintus will restore me! And Quintus will crush your son, believe me! Quintus will crush your son like a fledgling crushed in its nest!*

At that moment Geoff called, "Jack?" Then he turned to Otto and said, "Turn off the compressor, would you, Otto? We won't be needing the jackhammer anymore."

The compressor chugged to a stop, and suddenly the rooftop parking lot seemed very hushed. The wind blew soft and chilly, the way it had once blown across Stonehenge, and Easter Island, and the stones of Carnac. Most of the parking bays were taken, but there was nobody around. Tonight's performance of *Swan Lake* must already have started.

Geoff said to Jack, "I want you to trust me now, Jack. Quintus Miller won't touch your son, not yet—he daren't —not if Randy's already been singled out for the final sacrifice. Those maniacs can't be finally free until they make that sacrifice, that's what it says in Druggett's book, anyway. And once they've chosen a child, that's the child they have to stick with, no changes of mind. That child's

protected, until sacrifice day. Randy's safe, for the time
being, anyway."

*If you lay one finger on me, you filth, Quintus will have his
revenge on you,* Lester snarled. *You'll wish that your mother
had never parted her legs to let you out.*

Geoff replied, "I'm not too sure about that, old chap.
From the way that Quintus Miller has been lording it over
you, I'd guess that he's a classic schizophrenic. He's
obviously quite convinced that he's Awen, the god of the
Druids. Awen was a cruel god, and an extremely unforgiving god. I don't think Awen will care too much what
happens to you."

I am immortal, Lester whispered. *Whatever you do to
me, you can never destroy me.*

"Well—I very much hope that you're wrong there, too,"
said Geoff. He wiped his hands nervously on his jeans, then
turned to his Valiant and unlocked the trunk. "Give me a
hand here, Jack," he asked. Jack could tell that he wasn't
quite as confident as he was trying to appear.

Out of the back of his dilapidated car, he wrestled a
triangular wooden frame, three five-foot lengths of heavy
oak, roughly sawed and nailed together. Jack helped him to
lower it to the ground. It weighed nearly three hundred
pounds.

"What the hell is *that*?" Otto asked suspiciously.

"The university carpentry shop made it for me." Geoff
smiled. "It didn't take them long. It's an exact replica of a
Druid's sacrifical rack. As near as we've been able to make
it, anyway."

"It's a *what*?"

"A sacrificial rack. The Druids bent their victims backward over one side of the triangle—see here?—and lashed
their wrists and their ankles together. Then they tightened
the lashings with tourniquets, tighter and tighter, until the
victim was bent back so far that his spine broke. Then the
Druids spoke the sacrificial words, and that guaranteed

that their victim's spirit was obliterated, as if it had never been."

Jack turned to stare at Lester's head, rearing out of the broken-up concrete. Lester was watching them intently.

"It was difficult finding the sacrificial words," said Geoff. "But they're all in Druggett's book on Druids. They were found on a sacrifical stone in Wales.

> *"Caimich mi a nochd*
> *Eadar uir agus eare,*
> *Eadar run do reachd,*
> *Agus dearc mo dhoille."*

As soon as Geoff had completed his recitation, without any warning at all, Lester screamed. His scream wasn't audible, but it pierced their heads like a knife blade dragged across slate.

"You see?" said Geoff triumphantly. "We've got them! We've sussed them out! We've caught the bastards!"

Lester's head submerged into the concrete. But Geoff jumped down into the excavation, and pounded on the concrete with his fists, and shouted out, "You hear me! We've got you now! *A Righ nan reula runach!*"

Almost immediately Lester's face reappeared, screaming at them even more piercingly.

"Got you!" Geoff shouted back at him. He was almost hysterical with the magic and the strangeness and the terror of what they were doing. "Got you, you murderous shit! *A Dhe mheinnich nan dula!*"

Lester, concrete-faced, gibbered, *Don't, don't! Smash me up if you want to! But sixty years! Sixty years waiting! I want to get out, I want to be free!*

"Oh, there's only one way you're going to get free, chum," Geoff told him. "And that's if you tell us all about Quintus Miller, and all about your lunatic friends. Because if you don't, it's the rack for you, and absolute extinction, courtesy of Awen, the sacred name, and Bel, the sun god, for ever and ever amen."

You can have them! You can have them! I can tell you how!

"Make it quick, then," Geoff demanded. "I'm not feeling particularly patient this evening, and I've got an appetite for extinguishing mental deficients like you."

It was all in the books . . . in Krüger's library . . . and there were diaries, too. Krüger had been studying Druids all his life. Quintus broke into the library and stole them . . . and he told us that we could all escape. We planned it for months. The hardest part was finding a flute, the right kind of flute. But we pretended we wanted to start our own folk-music circle . . . and in the end Mr. Estergomy bought one for us.

"Flute? What are you talking about?" Geoff asked him.

To play the ritual music, to open the pentacle . . . so that we could all escape. And we did escape. . . . Quintus went first, and then came through the walls and played the music and we escaped, too. One to play and the rest to follow, that was the ritual. And we did it! Right into the walls!

Geoff stood quite still, the early-evening wind blowing back his hair. "One to play and the rest to follow," he said quietly. And then he recited,

> *"However he turned from South to West,*
> *And to Koppelberg Hill his steps addressed,*
> *And after him the children pressed. . . .*
>
> *"When, lo, as they reached the mountainside,*
> *A wondrous portal opened wide,*
> *As if a cavern were suddenly hollowed;*
> *And the Piper advanced and the children followed."*

Even Otto knew what that poem was. "'The Pied Piper of Hamelin,'" he said in a throaty voice. "Holy Moses, the damn thing's true; and I'm seeing it here with my own eyes."

"Yes," said Geoff. "The damn thing's true; and it's happened again and again throughout history. There aren't any such things as ghosts, or poltergeists, or demons, but there are earth-walkers, and wall-walkers—people who inhabit the real underworld."

Let me free, Lester insisted. *I've told you everything I know. Let me free.*

"Jack? What do you think?" said Geoff.

Jack looked at Lester's face in the concrete and thought of Randy, and of Father Bell, and of Essie Estergomy and Daniel Bufo and Joseph Lovelittle. He felt capable of smashing Lester's face apart with the jackhammer. In fact, he would have done so, except that it wouldn't have guaranteed the extinction of Lester's unbalanced soul.

"I vote we sacrifice him," he said. "Let's show Quintus Miller we really mean business."

You gave your word! Lester protested.

"And Father Bell died in the worst goddamned agony that anybody could ever imagine," Jack snapped back.

He wouldn't give in! He wouldn't let us go! It wasn't my fault!

"How do we get him out of the concrete?" Jack asked.

Geoff held up the holy water. "Exorcised water mixed with exorcised salt. That's the way the early Christians finally overcame the Druids. The way of the spirit versus the way of the flesh."

No! screamed Lester. *No, don't take my soul!*

Geoff unscrewed the cap of the Perrier bottle and lifted it up.

No! shrieked Lester. *I'll tell you how to find them! I'll tell you how to find them!*

Jack went right up to the concrete block and stared Lester directly in the face.

"Jack—don't go too near," Geoff warned him. But Jack was too angry to listen.

"All right, then, Lester," he said. "You tell us how to find them and we'll let you go. But I'm warning you, buddy. If you cheat us . . . I'm going to track you down, personally, and I'm going to break your back on that rack, and I'm going to take my time doing it."

Listen, will you, I'm telling you the truth. . . . You have to go back to the gateway . . . to the place where Quintus first went into the wall. . . . You have to play the music . . . the music will draw them all back. They have to follow the music, they don't have any choice. You know it, it's the summoning music for Grian-stad. . . .

"*Grian-stad?*" Jack asked. "What's *Grian-stad?*"

"It's Celtic for 'midsummer night,'" put in Geoff. "I don't know whether our friend here is telling us the truth, but he knows his Druidic lore. On midsummer night the Druids would play music to call everybody to the holy places."

"So we don't have to track them down individually," said Jack. "We can call them all back to The Oaks, and then we can deal with them there."

He had no idea how he and Geoff were going to be able to "deal" with one hundred thirty-six criminal maniacs, but maybe Druggett's book on Druidism would help them. Even if they couldn't destroy them—even if they couldn't do anything more than imprison them back in the walls of the building, the way they had been imprisoned before— that would be better than having them roaming the city, tearing innocent people into the ground.

Geoff said, "This music—what kind of music is it? Is it a special tune?"

Pipe music, said Lester. *Pipe music, played on a whistle. It goes like—*

"All right," said Geoff, "it's pipe music, but what does it sound like?"

But at that instant Lester screamed even louder than he had before. A harsh, grating screech of terror and total despair. Two massive hands rose out of the concrete on either side of his head and dragged him into the ground.

They saw one of Lester's hands lifted desperately for a moment out of the concrete, clawing at the air. Then that was dragged down, too, and Lester was gone.

"What happened?" said Jack in bewilderment. "Where did he go?"

Geoff shouted, "Otto! The rods!"

"What is it?" asked Jack.

"Get out of the pit!" Geoff ordered him. "Ten to one it's Quintus Miller!"

They scrambled out of the concrete excavation and backed toward the compressor truck. Otto was fumbling with his divining rods, trying to hold them parallel, saying, "Nothing but goddamned trouble. Wish I'd never come." Jack looked quickly around the parking lot, searching desperately for any furrowing of the concrete, any arms lifted like sharks' fins.

Otto said, "They're crazy! They're going crazy!"

The divining rods were swinging around and around and around, like compasses over the North Pole. Otto was trying to keep them still, but he couldn't. "It's too strong! It's everywhere! I just can't stop them from spinning around!"

Abruptly the divining rods stopped rotating and touched each other. There was a loud, sharp crackle of electrical discharge, and Otto was flung rigid against the side of his truck, knocking his head with a dull crunching sound like a run-over squirrel. He fell to the ground, quivering and trembling and muttering.

Jack knelt down beside him. His woolen hat was matted with blood, and his eyes were rolled up into his head.

"Don't touch him," Geoff warned. "He's been hit by natural magnetism . . . and a hell of a lot of it, too. You'd probably get a serious shock yourself if you touched him."

"You got that holy water?" Jack asked him, his eyes darting from one side of the parking lot to the other. His heart was pounding against his rib cage with the same ferocity that Lester had pounded against his concrete tomb.

"I've got it, sure—but I'm not sure how much *good* it's going to do us," Geoff replied. "Whoever pulled Lester down into the ground . . . he must have broken right through the circle."

"You're not a priest, remember," said Jack. "Maybe that had something to do with it. Maybe you don't have enough power."

"All right, I'm not a priest," Geoff agreed quite angrily. "But, damn it, I'm not that much of a sinner, either."

"Maybe we'd better get out of here," Jack suggested.

"I think you're probably right. Total cowardice occasionally has a great deal to recommend it."

They stood up, and cautiously backed toward Geoff's Valiant. Almost instantaneously, however, they were deafened by a shattering explosion. The concrete island in which they had trapped Lester was blasted apart, in a blizzard of grit and gravel and blinding dust. Chunks of concrete rattled and banged against the automobiles parked all around them, smashing windows and denting bodywork.

Shielding his eyes against the dust, Jack looked back toward their excavation. The central concrete island had been completely blown away, but standing in its place was a naked man, flayed of every inch of skin, glistening and scarlet and throbbing with fanlike traceries of veins.

In the dying light of the day, he looked almost beautiful, like a work of surrealist sculpture. Muscles, sinews, tendons; and arteries wriggling across his body like snakes. In spite of the rawness of his face, Jack immediately recognized him as Lester.

Lester tried to move, tried to cry out, but the pain that he was suffering was too intense. He uttered a single strangled bleat that sounded more like a slaughtered animal than a man. Then a hand reached up from out of the concrete

beneath his feet and snatched his ankles and pulled him
down into the ground in a grisly detonation of blood and
flesh.

"God almighty," Jack whispered.

"Jack, the car!" Geoff urged him, in a voice so shocked
that it was almost transparent. "Let's get out of here,
quick!"

They ran the last few steps to the Valiant, tugged open
the doors, and climbed inside. Geoff pulled his keys out of
his pocket, but dropped them on the floor.

"Shit!" he panicked, reaching down and scrabbling
around for them.

As he did so Jack heard a thumping noise and turned to
his right. The car at the far end of the line in which they
were parked was heaving upward three or four feet. Then it
dropped down again. Then the next car was lifted up,
colliding noisily with the car beside it, and the next car and
the next. It looked as if something huge and powerful were
making its way toward them under the ground—a tidal
wave in solid concrete—lifting up each car as it approached and dropping it again.

"Geoff, get this heap of scrap iron out of here!" Jack
shouted at him.

Geoff found the keys and jabbed them into the ignition.
As he did so, however, they felt the Valiant shaking, and
metal breaking apart underneath it. His mind blotted out
with thoughts of Daniel Bufo, Jack kicked open his door
and jumped right out of the car. Geoff followed him.

The car stopped shaking almost at once. They backed
away two or three paces farther, then hesitated.

"This one's strong," said Geoff, wiping his forehead with
the back of his hand. "This one's Quintus Miller, no doubt
about it."

In front of their eyes, the windshield of Geoff's Valiant
began to bend and distort. A face appeared, molded out of
glass; visible only because the lights from MECCA were

reflected on its cheeks and on its nose and on its lips. It was a strong, cruel face; exactly the face that Father Bell had described to Jack up at Green Bay. *A face like a rock. Hard eyes, eyes like nail heads, completely without expression, completely without compassion.*

"Quintus Miller," Jack whispered.

That's right, said a harsh, cultured, midwestern voice. *Quintus Miller in person. Pleased to make your acquaintance.*

"I want my son back," Jack told him. "You hear me? I want my son back! I want him back here and now, or else by God I'm going to give you the kind of hell that people only dream about."

Your son is very important to me, Mr. Reed. Not just important to me personally, you understand, but to my faith. Your son is going to go down in history as the most momentous sacrifice in pagan religion in two thousand years. History, Mr. Reed! Not many boys get the chance to make history. Not so young. Not so tender.

"I want to see him," Jack demanded.

You can see him, if you wish.

The windshield began to rise, as if it were being fashioned by an expert glassblower. The head and shoulders of a powerfully built man appeared, formed out of glass. Across the man's shoulders, apparently tied or handcuffed, slumped a glass boy who looked exactly like Randy. His eyes seemed to be closed, but as Jack slowly approached the Valiant he could see that the boy was still breathing. He must have been sleeping an exhausted sleep.

"Randy?" he said. "Randy?"

"Jack, keep well away!" Geoff cautioned him. "He wants to kill you—he wants to kill both of us!"

Jack stopped, hesitated, biting his lip. Quintus Miller's glass lips were curved in a shining smile.

Come closer if you want to, Mr. Reed; or can I call you Jack? It won't make any difference, now or later, I'm going

*to kill you, and you can be sure of that. Just the same way
that Lester died, trying to tell you our holy secrets. Nobody
betrays Quintus Miller, Jack. Nobody stands in his way.
They named me after the Quintessence, and that's what I
am. Killed my brothers, all four of them, poked out their
eyes with a black-hot poker.* What are you looking at me for,
nobody looks at a god, not like that! *That's what I told
them. And while they were sleeping . . . one by one. My
father's leather razor strop jammed between their teeth to
stop them from making a sound . . . then the black-hot
poker right through the eyelid into the eye. Sizzle? You bet
they sizzled! You ever hear optic fluid frying, Jack? That's
what I heard! Eight times! Each brother blinded, dead and
blind; and then my mother, too, I cauterized her, same
black-hot poker, cauterized her right where she'd birthed
me, sealed and purified, so no woman could ever boast that I
was her whelp.*

Jack's glance slipped sideways. One of the chunks of
concrete that had been blasted from Lester's tomb lay right
beside his foot. He looked back at Quintus Miller, at the
glass man rising from the Valiant's windshield, and he
calculated that he could scoop up the concrete, swing
forward and smash Quintus Miller's head, quicker than
Quintus Miller could stop him.

One second. Less than a second. Scoop, swing, smash.

*My father wasn't there . . . that was my mistake. I was
planning to purify him, too. But he was away that night,
without my knowing it . . . without my mother knowing it,
either. He was sleeping with another woman, on the other
side of town. Said he was walking the dog, but I knew better!
Rutting, that's what he was doing! He was strong, my
father . . . strong as a bull, like me. Big cock on him, I'll
always remember his cock. It used to frighten me when I was
small. I wanted to exorcise that cock, exorcise that memory
altogether. . . . But he wasn't there . . .*

Jack scooped up the chunk of concrete. Swung. Smashed.

. . . opened the door and—that dog!—

Quintus Miller's head burst open like a broken light bulb. Fragments of glittering glass fell into the driver's seat.

But to Jack's horror the smashed face continued to smile, and a glass hand came lunging out of the windshield to catch hold of his hair at the back of his head. He grunted, tossed his head, and pushed against the Valiant's fender, but Quintus Miller's grip was too fierce and too tight. Gradually he was pulled nearer and nearer to the broken windshield, until he was face-to-face with a glass mouth and a smashed-open head.

Now then, Jack . . . you've disappointed me now. I wanted a hunt. I wanted to pit my wits against you, instead of my strength. All I have to do now is pull your throat across this glass, and that's you done for . . . and don't believe I'm not going to do it, because I am. I'm not so stupid that I put the hunting before the catching . . . .I've caught you, Jack, and now I'm going to do for you.

Jack pulled his head back as far as he could. But even though his hand was made of glass, Quintus was unbelievably powerful, and Jack found himself inched closer and closer to the broken edge just above Quintus's lips.

You ever see somebody's throat cut, ear to ear? That happened back at The Oaks once, one of the crazies broke a coffee cup, cut himself open right in front of Mr. Estergomy . . . nothing sharper than broken porcelain, cuts like a razor, cuts real straight . . . but glass is good, too, except it cuts wavy. . . .

"Uh," Jack grunted, trying harder than ever to pull his head away. But the glass fist clutched his hair so tight that he couldn't break away, and the glass mouth smiled at him in total dispassion, glad to witness him die.

His throat was less than inch away from Quintus Miller's broken head when Jack heard a sharp shattering sound, and Quintus's grip was released. He dropped, knelt, half rolled back onto the ground, and found himself lying with his cheek against the concrete, right next to the curved pieces of Quintus's broken glass arm. Geoff was standing over him with a lump of concrete in his hand. He must have smashed Quintus's arm at the elbow.

"Let's get the hell out of here," said Geoff, helping him up. The Valiant's broken windshield suddenly collapsed into thousands of pieces, a heap of artificial diamonds piled up on to the seats. Together, Jack and Geoff ran down the exit ramp, glancing quickly behind them from time to time to make sure that the concrete wasn't furrowing up, and that Quintus Miller wasn't in hot pursuit.

They ran across East Kilbourn Avenue, gasping and puffing. At last Jack said, "Got to stop, Geoff. Sorry. Out of condition."

Geoff nodded and bent forward to touch his toes. "You and me both. All that pipe smoking. Should have kept up my squash."

"Jesus," said Jack, "I could use a drink."

They hobbled slowly together along the sidewalk, still sweating and panting. "Do you think Otto's dead?" Jack asked Geoff.

Geoff nodded. "He certainly looked as if he was."

"This whole damned thing was my fault," said Jack. "So many people have gotten killed."

Geoff gripped Jack's shoulder reassuringly. "Listen . . . that's the story of the human race, from beginning to end . . . you meant well."

"Meant well? Jesus!"

They crossed East Kilbourn Avenue, still keeping a weather eye open for cracks in the sidewalk.

"He's going to do his damnedest to kill us, you know that."

"You're not kidding. If you hadn't broken his arm back there, he would have sliced me up like a family pack of Farmer John's bacon."

"At least we're certain that Randy's still alive."

Jack said, "Yes, thank God. And I want him back."

They were still panting and talking and hobbling when a

police car suddenly pulled to the curb beside them, its lights flashing. Two policemen climbed out of the car and came running across the sidewalk.

"Police! Put your hands up! Put your hands right up where we can see them!"

Jack and Geoff slowly raised their hands. One of the officers kept them covered while the other cautiously approached them.

"You're Jack Reed, right?" he asked Jack. He was young and pimply, with a sparse black mustache.

"I'm Jack Reed, that's correct. What's this all about?"

"You're under arrest, for violating an order of the district court. I have to read you your rights."

"What are you talking about? I haven't violated any orders."

"Something to do with your son. Randolph Reed?"

Jack took a long, deep breath. "Is it all right if I put my hands down now? It wasn't reported as armed violation, was it? And—you know"—he glanced around the crowded sidewalk—"people are staring."

"Prefer it if you kept them up, sir. You have the right to remain silent, you have the right—"

Jack looked across at Geoff in desperation. If the police arrested him now, then he would have to come up with some explanation about what he had done with Randy. And what the hell could he tell them? That Randy had been abducted by a maniac who walked inside walls? That the Druids had taken him? That he knew Randy was safe, because he had seen him, fashioned out of an automobile windshield, a boy made of glass?

"—can and will be used in evidence against you."

E·L·E·V·E·N

Shortly after one o'clock the following morning, Geoff was allowed to leave Milwaukee police headquarters at 749 West State Street and return to Madison. Jack was detained in a cell on the second floor, next to a drunk who kept singing over and over again, *"Oh baby, baby, it's a world wide. . . ."*

Jack chewed gum that had surrendered the last of its flavor an hour ago, and paced up and down the floor. He was physically and mentally close to collapse, but he couldn't allow himself to slow down. He wasn't a bright or an educated man, he had no intellectual reserves on which he could draw. He couldn't theorize about the moral significance of what he had done or the religious significance of the Druids. He couldn't even quote *The Song of Hiawatha* to keep himself occupied.

But he had a native Wisconsin stamina, an unpolished energy that came from raw Lake Michigan winters and building your own business and fighting for your emotional survival.

He was going to see this through. He was going to beat this shit. He didn't believe in people who walked through walls. At least he didn't believe that anybody *should* walk through walls. It was old magic, something that ought to have been dead and buried centuries ago. This was the twentieth century, almost the twenty-first.

Most of all, he didn't believe that people should steal other people's children and put them through the goddamned emotional wringer.

"*Oh baby, baby, it's a world wide. . . .*"

"It's not a 'world wide,' it's a 'wild world'!" Jack shouted at him.

"What?" came the slurred reply.

"It's a 'wild world'!"

Long pause—and then the cheery rejoinder, "You're damn right it is!"

Jack sat on the edge of his bunk. His greatest immediate fear was that Quintus would discover that he was here, and penetrate the police headquarters, and drag him into the reinforced concrete floor of his cell. He was also afraid that after their confrontation in the parking lot, Quintus would find renewed blood lust to slaughter all the eight hundred people he needed to return to the real world, and that Randy would then be sacrificed as his final offering to Awen.

He rubbed his eyes. He had called his lawyer, Maurice Lederman, but Maurice was out of town (Miami, fishing, for God's sake) and his wife wouldn't be able to reach him till the morning. Meanwhile Jack had been formally charged with violating the court order that gave Maggie regular access to Randy, and he was being detained until Randy's whereabouts could be established.

At about three o'clock in the morning, his cell door was unlocked, and a neat-looking dark-haired man with a three-o'clock-in-the-morning shadow and a wide-shouldered gray suit came into the cell with a clipboard under his arm and two Styrofoam cups of black coffee.

"How're you doing, Mr. Reed? My name's Sergeant Charles Schiller. Thought you might care for some coffee."

Jack said, "If you're thinking of asking me any questions, you're going to have to wait until tomorrow. My lawyer's been catching marlin off Miami."

Sergeant Schiller said, "Yes, Mr. Reed, I know."

There was a sharpness in the tone of Sergeant Schiller's

voice that made Jack look up. Sergeant Schiller was
looking at him with an intent, cold expression that was
close to being contemptuous.

"Something wrong?" Jack asked him.

"Something *wrong*?" replied Sergeant Schiller. "Well
. . . let me put it this way. I've lived in Milwaukee all my
life and I'm proud of Milwaukee. Milwaukee has warmth
and friendship, do you know what I mean? *Gemütlichkeit*,
that's what my father used to call it. And up until now,
Milwaukee has one of the lowest crime rates in the country."

He paused for a moment, stirring his coffee with a plastic
stick. Then he said, "We've had a bad time this week,
people disappearing right, left, and center. People are
beginning to say that Milwaukee isn't safe anymore. People
are getting panicky, and aggressive, and suspicious. That
isn't *Gemütlichkeit*, Mr. Reed. That's seriously antisocial
behavior. And I don't much care for people who indulge in
seriously antisocial behavior."

Jack said tiredly, "I'm accused of violating a court order
in respect of my wife's access visits to my nine-year-old
son. That doesn't exactly rank me with Al Capone, does
it?"

"Can you tell me where you son is now?"

"Not until I talk to my lawyer."

"Is your son alive?"

"Of course he's alive. What the hell do you mean, is he
alive?"

"How about Miss Olive Estergomy, of Sun Prairie. Is she
alive?"

Jack swallowed dryly. He had been afraid of this. It
looked as if the grisly events that had taken place at The
Oaks had caught up with him at last.

"You do *know* Miss Olive Estergomy?"

"I have to talk to my lawyer first," Jack told him.

"But you do *know* her?"

Jack said, "Yes, I know her."

"Do you know where she is now?"

Jack shook his head.

"Is she alive, Mr. Reed?"

"I have to talk to my lawyer."

Sergeant Schiller sipped coffee and leafed through his clipboard. "All right, then," he said after a while, "how about Mr. Daniel Bufo, of Madison? Is he alive?"

"I can't answer that," Jack replied.

"Do you know where he is? We'd really appreciate knowing where he is."

"I can't help you, I'm sorry."

"All right, then . . . how about Mr. William Bell, of Bay Park Retirement Home, Green Bay? Is he alive?"

Jack said, "You want to explain to me what this is all about?"

Sergeant Schiller put down his clipboard. "Surely. The fact is that your son Randy and Miss Olive Estergomy and Mr. Daniel Bufo and Mr. William Bell all have two things in common. The first thing they have in common is that they are all missing. The second thing they have in common is that the last known person to see them was you."

"What does that prove?" asked Jack.

"It doesn't prove anything," said Sergeant Schiller. "But it does suggest that any line of inquiry into their mysterious disappearance ought to begin with you; and maybe end with you, too."

"Are you going to charge me?"

"Not yet. We have officers coming over from Madison tomorrow morning, and I want to talk to your lawyer, too, and to the district attorney's office. But I want to make it clear to you here and now, Mr. Reed, that if you know where these people are, the sooner you tell me, the better it's going to be for you."

Jack said, "Can I make a telephone call?"

"You want to make a telephone call *now*?"

A uniformed officer escorted Jack down the hall to one of

the interview rooms. Jack dialed Geoff's number and waited and waited while it rang. The uniformed officer stood by the door and yawned. At last Geoff answered groggily, "Hello? Who the devil's this?"

"Geoff, it's Jack."

"Oh, God. How are you, Jack? They haven't started beating you with rubber truncheons yet, have they?"

"Almost. Things have gotten a whole lot worse. They've been asking me questions about Olive Estergomy and Daniel Bufo and Father Bell."

"Jack—" Geoff warned him. "Be careful what you say. They'll almost certainly have this call tapped."

"I don't give a damn if they do. You've got to help me, Geoff. They're not going to let me out of here for days, the way things are going. It could be too late then. It's certainly going to get worse out on the streets. Geoff—come on, this is all down to me. I need to be out there, fighting it."

"What's your lawyer done to get you out?" Geoff asked him.

"My lawyer's still on his way back from Miami. Besides, I don't think that he's going to be able to get me released on bail. Not until I've managed to produce Randy, and show the court that he's safe and well. And if the police charge me with abducting all these people—well, maybe not at all."

Geoff said, "I don't see what more I can do, Jack. I'm going to try tomorrow to find out everything I can about the rituals . . . but, you know, this all happened more than two thousand years ago. Most of it's legend, and a lot of it makes no sense whatsoever."

"All right," said Jack. He felt a sudden wave of nausea and tiredness. "I'll talk to you tomorrow, if they let me. Right now they seem to think that I'm a cross between Son of Sam and Bruno Hauptmann."

Jack was escorted back to his cell. When he got there, he found that Sergeant Schiller was still waiting for him.

"How about a bedtime chat?" asked Sergeant Schiller.

Jack shook his head. "My lawyer's going to be here in the morning. Until he arrives, nothing."

Sergeant Schiller gave him a small lipless smile, like the mark of a very sharp chisel in freshly planed pine. "I'll promise you one thing, Mr. Reed. I personally believe that you were actively involved in the disappearance of all of these people, including your son. I also believe that all of them are dead, and that you killed them. And the promise is, I'm going to nail your ass to the wall, Mr. Reed."

He went to the door of the cell and opened it. "You, Mr. Reed, are going to be locked up forever."

Jack said, "Good night, Sergeant. I expect I'll see you in the morning."

"Oh, don't worry about that," said Sergeant Schiller. "You can count on it."

Jack slept for a little over two hours, and woke up at 5:15. He lay on his bunk listening to the echoing noises of the police headquarters, the distorted shouts, the constantly slamming doors, the whistling, the abrupt bursts of laughter.

In the distance he could hear ambulance and police sirens, and he dreaded to think what emergency they were rushing to deal with. More innocent people, pulled down into the sidewalks, or smashed into solid walls. More souls sacrificed, for the grisly and glorious resurrection of Quintus Miller.

He eased himself up off his bunk and splashed his face in cold water at the tiny corner washbasin. In the plastic mirror he looked white and big-nosed and distorted, a ghost who had once been Jack Reed.

If only he could walk right out of here, right through the walls, the same way that Quintus did.

He sat down again. Supposing he *could* walk through the walls. Supposing Geoff could discover the full Druid ritual. Quintus Miller had managed to do it, after all, and Quintus

Miller was a lunatic. *You have to play the music;* that's what Lester had said. *You have to play the ritual tune.*

It was a puzzle, a puzzle with pieces. Some of the pieces fitted neatly together—the way in which Quintus had found out about Druidism, for example, and the story of the Pied Piper. But there were so many unanswered questions. So many pieces that *felt* as if they ought to fit, but didn't.

Jack lay back and tried to catalog all the outstanding pieces of puzzle that he couldn't understand.

They knew most of the ritual that would take them into solid rock. But they still didn't know what the sacred tune was, the tune that the Pied Piper had presumably played to the children of Hamelin, as they walked into Koppelberg mountain.

In an odd way Lester had seemed to assume that he and Geoff should already know what the ritual tune was. *You know it,* he had said. But how could they, when they had never heard it—never seen it written down? But then Jack suddenly thought of another piece of the puzzle, another unexplained fragment.

Geoff's friend at Harvard had read him excerpts from Druggett's book on Druidism, and what had he said about the climax of the ritual when the Druids walked into walls? *They played the king.*

But Geoff had *heard* this excerpt over the telephone, rather than reading it for himself. Supposing the Druids hadn't been playing at being royalty, which is what the ritual sounded like. Supposing they had been playing "The King." A tune called "The King."

And where, recently, had Jack heard a tune about a king?

It came to him with a shiver. The distant echoing voice which he now knew to be that of Quintus Miller—in the abandoned corridors of The Oaks. That simple childhood tune that he had repeated over and over, until Jack hadn't been able to hear it without a deep feeling of dread.

Lavender blue, dilly-dilly;
Lavender green.
Here I am king, dilly-dilly;
You shall be queen.

Jack slowly sat up. The way he remembered it, Quintus hadn't sung the tune exactly right. Well—not the way it was supposed to be sung at nursery school. One or two of the notes had been different—off-key, more barbaric.

That was the tune, he was sure of it. Why else would Lester have assumed that they knew it? Why else would Quintus have sung it so often?

Because he's crazy, a small dissenting voice told Jack, inside his mind. *Crazy people never do anything for the same reasons that we do; and they never do anything predictable.*

All the same, Jack didn't have anything else to go on. He could try it, at least. All he needed were some pipes, and a razor blade to cut himself with so that he could draw on the wall the ritual pentacle of fresh blood, and a list from Geoff of all the sacred names that he was supposed to recite.

God, if it worked, Sergeant Schiller could stick his suspicions where the sun never shone.

He went to the door of his cell and called out, "Guard! Guard!"

The door at the far end of the corridor was noisily unlocked, stirring up moans and hungover groans from all the other cells nearby. A young officer with squeaky crepe-soled shoes came walking along the polished floor.

"Anything wrong?" he wanted to know.

"I need to use a telephone," said Jack.

"I have to call Sergeant Schiller, just as soon as you're awake."

"Look, all I need is to use the telephone, for two minutes."

"I have to call Sergeant Schiller, sir."

It was twenty minutes before Sergeant Schiller appeared.

He had shaved, and washed, and changed his shirt, and he smelled of toothpaste and Grey Flannel after-shave, but his eyes were still swollen like overripe plums and face was gray with fatigue.

"How did you sleep?" he asked cuttingly.

"How do you think?" Jack retorted. "Is there any objection to my using the telephone? I need to talk to my friend in Madison for a couple of minutes."

Sergeant Schiller said, "Your friend Geoffrey Summers, the college professor, is that who you're talking about?"

"Geoff Summers, that's right."

Sergeant Schiller looked down at his clipboard. "Geoffrey Summers is currently not at home. Geoffrey Summers is wanted for questioning in connection with the death of one Otto Schröder on the rooftop parking lot adjacent to the Performing Arts Center, yesterday evening at approximately seven o'clock."

He raised his eyes. Calculating as spirit levels. "According to four independent witnesses, Otto Schröder was in the company of two men yesterday evening, one of whom has positively been identified from police photographs as *you*, Mr. Reed. The other man was tall and bearded. A vehicle found damaged and abandoned on the rooftop parking lot belonged to Mr. Geoffrey Summers, the friend whom you wish to telephone this morning. Mr. Geoffrey Summers, as you probably know, is tall and bearded."

Jack said nothing, but waited for what he knew was going to come next.

"Mr. Reed—you're charged with murder in the first degree of Otto Cornelius Schröder. Your rights have already been read to you, in relation to the charge of violation of a court order for access to your son, but in relation to this charge, I'd like to remind you that you have the right to remain silent—"

Jack closed his eyes while Sergeant Schiller recited his rights. He felt that he deserved this punishment, almost, for all the people who had died since he had first found his way to The Oaks. But nobody could stop Quintus Miller and his troupe of maniacs; nobody except him.

Sergeant Schiller said, "Your lawyer should arrive at General Mitchell Field at eight-oh-five. Then you and I can start talking, yes?"

Jack said nothing, but ran his hand through his hair and looked toward the wall. He was sleeping deeply, dreaming of rain, when somebody shook his shoulder and said, "Hey . . . your sister's here to see you."

"My sister?" He frowned, trying to focus. A ginger-haired police officer was peering into his face from less than six inches away. He could chart every freckle on the officer's nose.

"Sure. Edna-Mae? She's waiting for you in the interview room. Sergeant Schiller says five minutes only."

Jack swung himself off his bunk. His sister? He didn't have a sister. But he mutely permitted the ginger-headed officer to handcuff him and then lead him along to the interview room at the end of the corridor.

When he was ushered in, he found Karen sitting at the table, fretful and uncomfortable, in a tight turquoise sweater and a short white skirt, and a bouffant blond wig whose falseness bordered on the absurd. When Jack had sat down, she glanced all around her like a nervous chipmunk, and then she said, "They called Mike Karpasian. They told him you were under arrest for homicide. I came right away. Oh, Jack!"

"You shouldn't have come," Jack whispered at her fiercely. "They'll be looking for you, too, if they haven't started looking for you already."

"I told them my name was Edna-Mae Schultz. I went to grade school with a girl called Edna-Mae Schultz."

"I like the store-bought hair," said Jack. He couldn't help smiling. "You look more like Dolly Parton than ever."

"Geoff called me," Karen told him, still serious.

"What did he say? Him and me, we're supposed to have killed that poor guy Otto Schröder."

"I know. Geoff—" She glanced around again, and then she whispered hoarsely, "Geoff called me. He's hiding someplace. I won't tell you where, in case they're listening. But they won't find him."

"Are you okay?" Jack asked her. She didn't look pretty today, and it wasn't just the wig. She looked exactly what she was, a onetime trucker's wife with big breasts and good legs and all the tiredness and cynicism that eventually overtakes any woman who has to live in a single-story clapboard house on the outskirts of Milwaukee, rearing a spoiled abandoned daughter and watching countless hours of television and knowing that her girlhood dreams will never come true.

Come on down, the price is right!

But, Jack decided, in the bald light of this bald interview room, he would rather spend the rest of his life with a woman like Karen than all the Maggies you could gather together in the Pabst Theater. She was sexy, friendly, spirited, devoted, and completely individual; and that's what made her so feminine. More than anything else, she had taken the trouble to visit him when he was in trouble.

"Are you okay?" Jack asked her.

"Sure I'm okay."

"And Sherry?"

"Sherry's okay."

Jack leaned forward as close as he dared. He could see the ginger-headed officer watching him intently, to make sure that Karen didn't pass anything over the table. "I think I know how to get into the walls," he told Karen.

"What?" She frowned at him.

"I think I know how to get into the walls . . . the same way that all of those lunatics did. I think I've worked out the secret."

"What good will that do?" Karen asked ingenuously. "You're locked up in here."

"Karen, *think* about it. If I can get into the walls, then I can get *out* of here."

Realization suddenly dawned. Karen pressed her hand over her bright red mouth. "You'd really *do* that?"

"My lawyer was here earlier. He said I had about as much chance of getting out of here on bail as he did of being elected pope. Optimist of the year, huh? The trouble is, Otto Schröder was killed by a huge charge of natural energy—you know, like a massive electric shock—right out of nowhere. Quintus Miller must have done it somehow, God knows how. Otto hit his head when he fell. Geoff and I weren't even anywhere *near* him. I mean, we were about as far away as that cop standing by the door. But as far as the police are concerned, we slugged him with a lump of concrete, and he died of a fractured skull."

He paused and sat back in his chair. "Apart from that, they think that I killed all those other people—Father Bell, Olive Estergomy, Daniel Bufo. And I still won't tell them what's happened to Randy. I still *can't* tell them what's happened to Randy. So I don't have any choices. Either I stay here, or else I try to get into the wall."

Karen said, "I *know* you didn't take Randy, and I *know* you didn't kill Daniel Bufo. I was there, I can tell them."

"I know you can, but don't. It won't do any good, and they'll haul you in, too, for being an accessory. I don't think you should come here again, in any case. Find someplace you can hide for a while."

"Oh, Jack . . ." said Karen. "If anything happened to you . . . if anything went *wrong*. I mean, supposing you go into the wall and you can't get *out* again?"

"What else can I do? I can't sit here and let Quintus Miller drag a hundred thousand people into the ground, can I? And what about Randy? Karen—I *saw* Randy, he was tied around Quintus Miller's back, and he was still alive!"

Karen said, "What are you going to do?"

"I can't do anything without your help. I know this sounds weird, but I need a flute . . . the kind of flute the

Druids might have used. Ask Geoff about it. I need a list of names, too. The names of the Druid god Awen."

"Jack—" said Karen.

He could tell what she was thinking: that he had succumbed at last to the stress and the shock of the past few days, that he was exhausted beyond all reason, that he was almost as nuts as Quintus Miller.

"Karen," he told her. "You've been brave and you've been good. I love you, do you know that? I really do. I don't know what the hell's going to happen to me. I'm scared to death. But I have to try every possible option. Do you understand me? Every possible way out, even if it sounds screwball.

"The flute, Karen, please; and the list of names. Give them to my lawyer, Maurice Lederman, his office is in the First Wisconsin Center, ninth floor. Lederman, Pfister and Lederman. Tell him they have to be delivered to me urgently."

Karen swallowed, as if she had no moisture in her mouth at all. "Okay." She nodded. "I'll try to do it today." She leaned over the table and kissed him. "I love you, Jack."

"Hey, cut out that kissing!" snapped the ginger-haired young officer.

Karen scraped her chair back noisily and pranced toward the door with her usual walk that made her body look as if it were bouncing in five different directions at once. She lifted her nose to the officer and said, "Sir, you wouldn't know what kissing was if two elephants came up and sucked you on the ass."

She *click-clack*ed off along the corridor. The ginger-haired young officer watched her go and then stared at Jack in stupefaction.

"What did she mean by that?" he demanded.

"Who knows?" said Jack. "But it sure shut *you* up, didn't it?"

✳   ✳   ✳

He spent a long morning doing nothing but thinking. Maurice Lederman his lawyer came to see him again at three o'clock and talked to him for over an hour about preliminary hearings and finding the right kind of trial lawyer. Maurice made no secret of his annoyance at having been called back from his fishing vacation. It was the first time that he had been able to get away from his wife Sheldra for nearly nine years. He hated Sheldra. He called her the *Rebbitsin*, which meant rabbi's wife, because she spent so much time at the synagogue running around the rabbi.

Maurice was irredeemably overweight, with furrowed gray hair and a furrowed forehead and deep-set, close-together eyes that always reminded Jack of prawn's eyes. The prawn effect was enhanced by his scorched, half-completed sunburn. His skin kept flaking onto his notepad, and from time to time he had to flick it off.

"It's keeping your mouth shut that's doing you no good, Jack," he complained. "If you give the police some basic cooperation, we might be able to work out some kind of a deal. It wouldn't hurt if you gave *me* some basic cooperation."

"Maurice, I didn't touch any one of those people, and the police don't have any evidence that I did. Now that's all I'm going to say."

Maurice took a Dristan inhaler out of his shirt pocket and squeezed it sharply up each nostril. "They have a witness—Mrs. Yvonne Cropper, a supervisory nurse at the Bay Park Retirement Home, who will testify that you took Mr. William Bell out for dinner on the last evening that he was seen alive. You were also seen by serving staff at the Ship's Lantern restaurant, Green Bay, in Mr. Bell's company, talking and arguing with some animation."

"Animation? What's that? Cartoons?"

Maurice fixed him with his dull black prawn's eyes. "Damn it, Jack, this is serious. These are charges of abduction, kidnap, and multiple homicide."

"Maurice, I'm innocent. I didn't do any of those things. I took an old guy for dinner. That doesn't prove squat."

Maurice took a deep, wheezy breath, hesitated, but then continued. "They also have a witness, Miss Helena Manfield, who says that she introduced you at your specific request to Miss Olive Estergomy. Miss Manfield says you exhibited an unusual and even morbid interest in the Estergomy family, who used to run The Oaks when it was an institution for the criminally insane. She says that on the night that Miss Estergomy was last seen alive, Miss Estergomy telephoned her and said she had been trying to contact you, and had been told that you were probably out at The Oaks. Miss Estergomy's car was found abandoned at The Oaks.

"They have a witness, Mr. Ned Pretty of Capitol Realtors, who says that the following day Mr. Daniel Bufo went to The Oaks to inspect the premises for insurance revaluation. He was also hoping to meet you there because he was concerned about the slow progress of his sale, and in fact had come to the conclusion that you were no longer seriously interested in buying the property. Mr. Daniel Bufo never returned from this meeting and later *his* car was found abandoned at The Oaks with serious damage to the interior, and shreds of Mr. Bufo's clothing and skin were found in the vehicle.

"Your own station wagon was also found at The Oaks at the same time, seriously damaged in a similar way."

Maurice paused, as if he expected Jack to say something, but all Jack could do was to shrug.

"Jack," said Maurice, "can't you get it through your head that this is real life-or-death heavyweight stuff. They could lock you up till Judgment Day."

Jack said, "Maurice—I met those people, sure. I'm not denying it. But I didn't touch them. I didn't touch Otto Schröder, either. No judge in the world is going to lock me up just because I *met* them."

"That's where you're wrong, Jack," Maurice replied.

"This isn't 'The Defenders' or 'L.A. Law.' The police have witnesses who saw you and Geoffrey Summers in the company of Otto Schröder literally *minutes* before Otto Schröder was killed by a blow to the head. They have enough circumstantial evidence to tie you in conclusively with every one of these other disappearances. Jack, they don't need eyewitnesses to prove homicide. They don't need smoking guns or bloody lumps of concrete or whatever you used to kill them. They don't even need bodies."

Jack retorted, "What about all these other disappearances and murders? They've been happening all over Milwaukee! They're *still* happening! Haven't the police considered that there might be some connection?"

Maurice sniffed dryly. "I wouldn't push *that* line too hard. They might decide that the connection between all of them is *you*. Anyway, do you have any evidence that they're connected? Do you have any evidence that you didn't kill any of these people you've been charged with killing? What have you done with Randy? Come on, Jack, I've known Randy ever since he was born. If he's still alive, where is he now?"

Jack was silent. He lowered his head.

"You're going to help me, or what?" asked Maurice.

"I can't, Maurice, not just yet."

"Not just yet? They've got you trussed up like a Thanksgiving turkey, oven-ready already, and you tell me 'not just yet'?"

"I'm sorry, Maurice, that's it. I can't tell you any more. You wouldn't believe me anyway."

Maurice swept away more flakes of sunburn. "Well, then, before we do anything else, we're going to have to find you a first-class trial lawyer. I want to talk to Gerry Pfister, back at the office. I was thinking of Saul Jacob, if we can get him."

Jack looked up, startled. "Saul Jacob? Saul Jacob defended the Black What's-his-name—that guy in Minneapolis who machine-gunned all those people in that Burger King restaurant. The Black Avenger, or whatever."

"Sure, and he got him off, too."

"Got him off? Jesus, Maurice, he pleaded insanity! The guy got sent to the funny farm! I'm not insane!"

Maurice pouted his sun-sore-encrusted lips and drummed his fingers on his legal pad and wouldn't look at him straight. Jack stared at him with one elbow on the tabletop and a slowly dropping sensation in his stomach. *Saul Jacob?* Saul Jacob specialized in hopeless homicide cases; in death-row appeals and stays of execution. Saul Jacob had kept Mad Frank Maharis out of the electric chair for nearly six years, and saved the life of Don Castigliani. Maurice would only think of briefing Saul Jacob if he were quite convinced in his own mind that Jack was guilty— that he *had* killed Essie Estergomy and Father Bell and Daniel Bufo and Otto Schröder—and that he had probably killed Randy, too, for good measure.

"You think I did it," he told Maurice. "You son of a bitch. You think I did it."

Maurice still wouldn't look at him. "What I think isn't important. It's what the jury can be persuaded to think."

"Christ, Maurice, you think I did it. You've known me all these years."

"Well, everybody has their hidden side. I found out only last week that Gerry Pfister was gay."

"I suppose that made a difference?"

"I had the coffee machine changed to disposable cups. Apart from that, he's gay, who cares?"

"You know something, Maurice, you're a *schmo*. And that's the nicest thing I can think of to say to you."

Jack felt—unexpectedly—cornered. His only consolation was that if Karen could bring him the pipe, and the names of the Druid god, and if the ritual of disappearing into the wall really worked, then it wouldn't matter what Maurice believed, and it wouldn't matter what Sergeant

Schiller believed, either. He would have vanished, beyond capture, and beyond the law.

"All right," he agreed. "You go talk to Gerry Pfister; whatever you think best."

"I'll be back later," said Maurice, "maybe you'll feel more forthcoming. I can't help you, Jack, if you won't tell me what really happened."

"You want me to confess to murder?"

"Anything . . . just so long as you tell me *something*."

Jack dry-washed his face with his hands. "Okay, Maurice, whatever. By the way . . . somebody should be leaving a package for me at your office, possibly sometime today. Could you make sure that you get it around here as soon as it arrives?"

"Depends what it is. They won't let you have drugs, or alcohol, or food."

"A flute, Maurice, that's all. Something to tootle on, to pass the time."

Maurice stared at him incredulously. "You want to play the *flute*?"

"I used to play the tenor sax at school."

Maurice slowly shook his head, then went to the door and knocked for the guard to let him out.

Jack said, "So long, Maurice," but Maurice hurried from the room without even turning to look at him.

At a quarter after five they let Maggie in to see him. She was red-eyed from crying, and shivering, and highly distressed, and Jack was convinced that Sergeant Schiller had sent her in to try to shame him into admitting that he had murdered Randy.

"Hello, Margaret-Ann," he greeted her.

She sat down, twisting a damp-looking handkerchief. She was wearing the wide-shouldered orange suit he particularly disliked. It always made her look pasty and unwell, even when she wasn't. What was worse, she thought it made her look like Krystle, in "Dynasty," and it made her behave that way, too. Saintly and dewy-eyed and irritatingly practical.

"Hello, Jack," she whispered, and then abruptly cleared her throat.

"How are you?" he asked her.

"Upset, what do you think?"

"How's the blessed Velma?"

"I wish you wouldn't call her that."

"All right, how's the plain and ordinary Velma?"

"She's quite well, thank you," she said, with all the politeness of true hatred.

"Herman, too?"

"He's quite well."

Jack nodded broadly. "That's excellent. Herman and Velma, a marriage made in heaven. Well, Manitowoc, anyway; and I guess that's close enough."

Maggie swallowed, and then she suddenly rushed out in a sibilant, steady monotone, "Jack, I know you don't love me anymore, I'm quite prepared to deal with that, I *can* deal with that, I have my sister and my consciousness-raising classes and plenty of supportive friends, but I have just as much right to Randy as you do and I need to know where he *is*."

Jack said, "I can't tell you where he is."

"But why? I have a right to know! He's my son! I love him!"

Jack repeated, "I just can't tell you where he is, that's all. I'm sorry." He was sorry. Whatever he thought of Maggie, he knew that she was suffering the same fears and the same uncertainty about Randy as he was; and it was an agony he wouldn't have wished on anybody.

"Is he safe?" asked Maggie.

Jack nodded. "I believe so."

"What do you mean, 'you believe so'? Don't you know for sure?"

"No," said Jack. "If you want the truth, I don't. But I'm doing everything I possibly can, believe me."

"Locked up in here? What can you do locked up in here?"

"I'm not too sure. But I have a couple of ideas that I'm working on."

"Jack! Listen to me! I'm *ordering* you! You have to tell me where he is!"

"Sorry, Margaret-Ann," Jack replied.

Maggie was silent for a moment or two, twisting her handkerchief and biting at her lips. Then suddenly she lunged at him, smacking his face and wrenching at his shirt.

"I hate you!" she screamed. *"I hate you! I hate you!"*

The door of the interview room was flung open immediately, and a uniformed policewoman caught hold of Maggie's arm. Maggie backed away from Jack, her face a mess of tears. "If you've done anything to harm our son," she sobbed at him, "I'm going to kill you!"

Jack turned his back on her. There was nothing else that he could do. He heard her sob once or twice more, and then leave the room, with the policewoman comforting her.

When she had gone, Sergeant Schiller came in. He stood beside Jack for a while, and then he held out something that he had been holding behind his back. A plain wooden flute, and several sheets of paper with handwriting on them. Jack glimpsed the name "Awen."

"You want to tell me about these?" he asked. "They were just delivered by your lawyer's clerk."

"Folk music," said Jack.

"*Folk music?* You've been charged with kidnap and homicide and you want to play *folk music?*"

"What's it to you?"

Jack found it quite unnerving to act so hard-boiled, but he knew that if he told Sergeant Schiller anything at all, he would forfeit any chance of stopping Quintus Miller and of

rescuing Randy. Sergeant Schiller would never believe that
human beings could run through walls and walk through
the earth—not until it was too late, anyway; and he would
never allow Jack to follow Quintus Miller.

Sergeant Schiller said, "How about telling me where you
hid your boy? Then you can have the flute."

"Keep the goddamned flute," Jack told him, trying to
sound as if he couldn't care less about it.

"You're going to have to tell me sometime," Sergeant
Schiller warned him.

"I can't tell you something that I don't know."

"You killed him, didn't you? Come on, it's understand-
able. You were under stress. Your marriage was breaking
up. You were tired of the responsibility of taking care of
him, he reminded you so much of your wife, so you took
the easy way out, and you killed him."

Jack turned around and stared Sergeant Schiller directly
in the eye. "That," he said, "is bull."

Sergeant Schiller stared back at him for a moment, then
handed him the flute. "I've turned over a lot of stones in
the past eleven years, Mr. Reed, sir, and I've uncovered all
kinds of pretty disgusting creatures. But I never uncovered
anything quite like you."

With that, he snapped his fingers to the guard at the
door, to order him to escort Jack back to his cell.

That night, the sacrificial blood lust of Quintus Miller and
his maniacs raged throughout Milwaukee and Madison
and along the ley lines that ran between them.

Thunder bellowed out of the sky; unnatural lightning
stalked on stilts along the ley lines; and the air was thick
with the tension of approaching catastrophe.

Close to Dousman, a fifteen-year-old farm girl called
Sarah Lee Kodiak was dragged into the depths of a dark
green kale field. She was screaming at an unearthly high
pitch as she was pulled two hundred feet across the field,

deeper and deeper, thigh-deep, waist-deep, neck-deep, until she was swallowed up into the rich black soil with her father and her brother still running desperately toward the spot where she had vanished.

By the light of their tractor's headlights, with rain smearing their hair against their faces, her father and brother dug with spades and picks for over two hours, sobbing with grief and exhaustion, but they couldn't find her. Black soil, stains of crimson, but no Sarah Lee.

A fifty-five-year-old banker named Lincoln Winter was pulled into the sidewalk as he stepped out of a taxi in The Avenue, Milwaukee. He opened the door, stepped onto the sidewalk, and as he did so his foot was wrenched straight into the concrete. He shouted out once, but nobody saw him, and when the mystified cabdriver climbed out of the taxi to collect his fare, Lincoln Winter had disappeared. The cabdriver didn't look down—or he would have noticed four well-manicured fingertips scraping in agony at the sidewalk, like four wriggling pink chrysalides, just managing to tip up a discarded Mcdonald's carton before they disappeared, too.

Heidi Feldman, an auburn-rinsed waitress from Karl Ratzsch's restaurant, in Milwaukee, was caught by the maniacs as she went up in the elevator to her fifth-story apartment in West Allis. She was leaning toward the mirror on the back wall of the elevator to pluck out a stray eyebrow hair, when two powerful hands shattered the glass and dragged her headfirst into the brick wall of the elevator shaft, while the elevator continued to whine on upward.

In the last instants of her life, Heidi Feldman felt as if her head were being ground like corn between two massive grindstones. Her husband opened the elevator door at the fifth floor with a smile and a large martini and found the elevator car torn open and empty.

A thirty-five-year-old television engineer named Roy Truesho was sleeping next to his wife in his duplex house in

Monona, southeast of Madison, when a glistening hand emerged from his laminated wood headboard and reached quivering like a praying mantis toward his wrist. Roy was tugged, inch by inch, into the headboard, with a slow churning splintering sound. He didn't cry out. His wife opened her eyes just in time to see his left foot disappearing into solid wood, its toes stiff with pain.

Then she was alone, widowed, with two small children sleeping across the landing.

Rain swept like warm blood all the way across Green, and Dane, and Jefferson Counties.

In his cell at the Milwaukee police headquarters, Jack was sitting uncomfortably cross-legged on his bunk, waiting for midnight to pass, when the moon would rise to its zenith, even though it was hidden behind the rain clouds. *About 1 o'c,* Geoff had written, *ley-lines will be magnetized 2 their utmost—easier 4 U to penetr8, hopefly.*

The note had ended, *Meet you at the pentacle, Q's room, soonest.*

Jack closed his eyes and breathed regularly and deeply, but he knew that any attempt to sleep was futile. The trouble was, when it came down to the bottom line, he didn't believe for one moment that he was going to be able to walk into the wall at all, let alone make his way to The Oaks and emerge from Quintus Miller's pentacle with all the ease of a man stepping out of a subway. He had practiced Quintus Miller's off-key version of "Lavender Blue" over and over again (much to the fury of a vociferous and spaced-out punk in the next cell but one); he had recited the rituals and the names. It all sounded more like hocus-pocus than ever. If he hadn't seen the maniacs rising from the ground with his own eyes, if he hadn't seen Father Bell's fingers burning and Essie Estergomy dragged down into the gravel, he wouldn't even have tried.

Just before twelve, he had taken up the flute again, to

play yet another reprise of *"Lavender blue, dilly-dilly; lavender green"* when Sergeant Schiller came in and stood in the doorway with his hands in his pockets and looked at him. "End of my shift," Sergeant Schiller said at last. "I'm going home now. Wondered if you felt like telling me anything that might help me sleep."

Jack looked back at him for a long time without saying anything.

"Oh well, please yourself," said Sergeant Schiller, and turned to go.

"Sergeant!" Jack spoke up.

"What is it?"

"Just to tell you, I won't be bothering you too much longer. I promise."

"What kind of a promise is that?"

"You'll see. At least I hope you will."

"You're a genuine one-hundred-percent sicko, Mr. Reed, sir. Get some sleep."

At a quarter after one, when police headquarters was comparatively quiet, only echoes and footsteps and winos and addicts moaning in their sleep, Jack lifted his head and looked around and listened. After two or three minutes, he rose quietly from his bunk and padded on stockinged feet toward the end wall of the cell. It was still raining outside. The rain sprinkled softly and suggestively against the window.

Jack thought: *This is it, at last. This is where I trust in history and ancient magic. Oh God, I hope it works. Oh God, I hope it doesn't work.*

Grimacing, he took the tiny sliver of razor blade that Geoff had secreted behind the reed of his flute and drew it across the ball of his thumb. Blood flooded out: he could hear it dropping glutinously onto the ceramic-tiled floor. *Split, splat, split, splat.* He approached the wall, holding his wrist, his thumb still dripping. He was quaking with the enormity of what he was about to do. Or perhaps with the madness of it.

It's not going to work, it's not going to work. It's far too late.

He hesitated, sniffed—then described in blood two huge triangles, one upright and one inverted, the Hexagram of Solomon. Earth and water, air and fire—and where they met, the Quintessence, the fifth element.

He stood in front of them and touched the wall, and outside the window of his cell the lightning flickered, and thunder ripped across the sky like a thousand torn bolts of broadcloth, and rain clattered onto the rooftops of Milwaukee as if God was determined to drown it, and commit it to the lake.

He lifted the scribbled papers that Geoff had sent him and began to recite the Druid rituals. *They're wrong,* he thought. *It was too long ago. How could anybody hand down these rituals for two thousand years?*

But Quintus Miller had managed it, hadn't he? Quintus Miller and all of his lunatic followers? And if Quintus Miller had managed it, then he could, too.

> *"Dia dha mo chaim,*
> *Dia da mo chuairt,*
> *Dia dha mo chainn,*
> *Dia dha mon smuain!"*

He felt like a fool. He felt like a total fool. His pronunciation was probably appalling. Even if there *were* any Celtic gods—even if there *were* any Druidic influences—they probably wouldn't be able to understand him anyway.

But he recited everything that Geoff had written for him, faithfully, down to the very last word. And then he read the list of the fifty names of Awen—Da and Yoghan, Mabo and Mabona, Lu and Lew, mab-Moi and Mabinos.

He hesitated, licked his lips, and then he played his flute, the tune that sounded so much like "Lavender Blue, Dilly-Dilly," and spoke the final ritual words that were supposed to take him into the wall.

> *"Caimich mi a nochd*
> *Eadar uir agus earc,*
> *Eadaer run do reachd,*
> *Agus dearc mo dhoille.*
>
> *"Bury me by night,*
> *Amid the pastures and the herds,*
> *Amid the mystery of thy laws.*
> *My unseeing eyes."*

As he recited these words, Geoff's paper trembling in his hand, he approached the pentacle on the wall of his cell, closer and closer, until his face was pressed against the gray-washed brickwork. *Bury me by night,* he whispered. *Bury me by night.*

He heard footsteps squeaking down the corridor outside his cell. The guard was coming. He heard keys jingling, and one of the winos calling out, *"Mother! Mother! Come and get me, Mother!"*

He closed his eyes. *Thou Being-of-Laws-and-of-the-Stars, help me. Bury me by night amid the mystery of thy laws.*

The cell door opened. The guard said, "You've been playing that goddamned whistle again, you're driving everybody bananas."

Jack stepped into the wall.

T·W·E·L·V·E

*H*e felt as if soft dry sand were pouring over him. He couldn't open his eyes, because the brick was pouring over his face, but he found that he didn't need to open them. He could visualize where he was going inside his head, almost as clearly as if he could actually see it. The walls of police headquarters were like the dark narrow pathways of a maze, and he could walk along them, swiftly and smoothly, his own molecules passing through the molecules of brick with a deep *sssssshhhhhh*ing sound.

He walked all the way along the corridor of the cell block, through the wall. Whenever he reached one of the metal doors, the sensation of passing through it was markedly different. It felt almost like being caught by a lawn sprinkler, a sudden smack of ice-cold water. He reached the stairs, but then he realized that he probably didn't need them. The maniacs had *swum* in their earthly environment rather than walked in it. Jack tried to imagine that he was swimming; and as he did so he allowed himself to sink down through the darkness of the walls, down to street level, then *below* street level.

With the awkward grace of an inexperienced aqualung diver, he surged his way through concrete and brick and rock. Every now and then he passed through a sewer or a gas pipe or an electricity cable. He had no way of knowing it, but when he passed through telephone cables, his passing caused a sudden shadowy-sounding frizzle that could be heard by people talking on the line.

He was fascinated when he raised his head to realize that he could see or at least *visualize* everything above the surface of the sidewalks, in the same way that a swimmer can see above the surface of a pool. He could see underneath automobiles; he could see the soles of people's shoes. Their images were distorted, in the same way that the images seen above water are distorted; but when he considered that he was looking out of a very dense medium into a far less dense one—well, he couldn't remember all of his high-school physics, but he guessed it was scientifically logical.

He felt the vibration of Milwaukee's scores of public clocks striking 1:45. He was going to have to find himself a ley line: one of the main connecting lines that would enable him to make his way speedily back to The Oaks, a Druidic highway. He could sense the magnetism of the ley lines around him, in the same way that he could usually sense an electric storm approaching. It was a strange, tingling, cat's-fur feeling; and it made the hair prickle on the back of his neck, and the nerves prickle in the palms of his hands.

He went deep beneath the Milwaukee River, sliding through silt, heading eastward. It was very much blacker and colder down here, and he could feel the weight of the earth enfolding him. Curiously, however, he didn't feel imprisoned or claustrophobic, even though he usually panicked in confined spaces. He felt calm and determined and increasingly capable of surging his way through the earth.

At least he had escaped from police custody. Sergeant Schiller would go crazy! Jack wondered whether the guard had seen him disappearing into the wall. Even if he had, Jack doubted if the poor man would have believed what he had witnessed—or even if he did believe it, if he would have the nerve to tell Sergeant Schiller.

Jack was close to the foundations of the East-West Freeway. He passed through the concrete piers that supported the overhead roadway with a sharper *ssshhh!*

ssshhh! ssshhh! like somebody chopping a shovel into wet cement. He could sense that he was close to a ley line now. He felt as if he were being *tugged* through the earth, his whole nervous system effervescent with natural magnetism. Southwestward, under the freeway, in the rough direction of the Wisconsin State Fair Grounds.

He was awed by the powerful forces that existed beneath the surface. He had always understood, of course, that the ocean's tides were controlled by the gravitational pull of the moon. But the vibrant patterns that ran through the soil were equally strong, if not stronger. They were capable of turning him from a man of flesh to a man of rippling soil; they were capable of dragging him along with all the force of a major river.

Jack understood now why so many legends claimed that man had been formed out of soil. When he was a kid, he had read in one of his old Buffalo Bill books that Gitche Manitou, the great god of the Indian peoples, had baked the first man out of clay—the first was burned, and became a black man; the second was underdone, and became a white man; while the third was perfect, and became a Red Indian.

Even the Bible said, *The Lord God formed man of dust from the ground.* And it was true, it had actually happened. The Druids had understood it, and so had dozens of other ancient cultures. All that Jack had done tonight was to reverse the process—not dust into man, but man into dust.

It was a transformation as ancient as the world itself: a transformation that defined man's bond with God and with the earth that God had created. God and man were one and the same substance—earth, air, fire, and water, and everything that those elements embraced and implied, melded together into the mystical and ubiquitous Quintessence.

Jack knew that even if he survived this transformation— even if he found and defeated Quintus Miller—he could never be the same man again. He had understood the meaning of Genesis; he had understood what Adam had been. He had understood the very substance of himself.

It gave him a sensation of terrible fear, yet also of limitless power. Man had lost faith with the earth on which he lived. But men like Adolf Krüger had discovered it again; and so had Quintus Miller. No wonder the early Christians had feared the Druids. No wonder they had fought so hard to destroy them.

Jack flowed his way nearer and nearer to the ley line, and at last he reached it. He could feel it all around him, a singing, reverberating river in the earth. His eyes were still closed, but he could sense the ley line running ahead of him, relentlessly straight, all the way across Wisconsin, all the way into the northlands, into the polar ice. *This* was how the Celts had traveled across the earth, bringing their Druidic culture to North America, in countless centuries gone by. Not by boat, not by coracle, not by crossing the northern straits on foot.

All Jack had to do was to follow the ley line, and he would arrive at The Oaks. Almost certainly, it would be there that Quintus Miller would perform the final sacrificial ceremonies that would release him and his followers from the earth, and let them live again.

He traveled along the ley line, running, like a man running in a dream. The soil and the rocks poured around him, poured *through* him, as if he had no physical substance at all. Yet he could feel the power of his body, and he could feel the power of his mind. He was back in the element from which man had first gained his shape, and first gained his strength.

He couldn't tell how fast he was running, but it was impossibly fast compared with the speed that a man could normally run when he was out of his element. He lifted his closed eyes to the sky, and the night's thunderclouds roiled past him like the speeded-up thunderclouds in *Close Encounters of the Third Kind.*

All he could hear was the thick rushing noise of soil,

sssshhhhh—sssssshhhh—ssssshhhh, and the easy panting of his own breath.

He passed Okauchee, Waterloo, De Forest, and Morrisonville. He wasn't more than twenty miles distant from The Oaks when he became conscious of another sound. Footsteps, pounding behind him. Somebody else, rushing through the earth. Somebody fast and powerful and determined to catch up with him.

He turned his head. Less than a mile away, he could visualize a man running after him. Two men—three. They had their heads lowered and they were running with frightening doggedness. *We're coming to get you, you bastard. We're going to tear you to pieces.*

Jack recognized the voice. Gordon Holman, the maniac who had nailed his wife's tongue to a table and his own penis to a tree, and who had set fire to Father Bell's hands. Gordon Holman was after him, and Gordon Holman was almost as mad as Quintus Miller.

Jack took a deep breath and ran harder, as hard as he possibly could. It didn't strike him as strange that he could breathe; but then fish could breathe in water, and he was using the air in the soil in almost exactly the same way. He felt the soil pouring over his face. He was running so fast now that occasional rocks and pebbles hit him and stung him nearly as viciously as if somebody had thrown them at him.

But Gordon Holman and his two companions were gaining on him. They had lived in the earth longer; their bodies were imbued with more of the earth's natural strength. Jack began to feel the vibrations of their running through the soles of his feet. They were after him, and they meant to bring him down.

This is our *day!* Gordon Holman roared at him through the thickness of the earth. *This is* our *day!*

Jack could feel that he was nearing The Oaks. The current of the ley line ran faster, like a river coming close to a precipitous waterfall. The soil rushed past, the sky rushed past, the world rushed past. Jack began to feel that he was being helplessly swept along, running down a mountain, unable to stop.

Our day, you bastard! Our day! Our day!

At The Oaks, ley lines intersected from the west, from the east, from the southwest, from the north. The spot where The Oaks had been built drew in power from all four quarters of America; but it *radiated* power, too. It was like a sun, below the ground, with a huge gravitational-pull, and yet beaming out energy everywhere.

Jack sensed that The Oaks was very near. He was running through woods. The roots of the trees wriggled darkly down in the soil, like jellyfish tentacles floating in the ocean. He could *hear* The Oaks humming as low and as powerful as a dynamo. But at the same time he could feel Gordon Holman less than thirty feet behind him. He thought: *Turn—face him—hit him hard—you're as strong as he is now, you're fighting in the same element.*

But as he turned, and stopped, something jumped up on to his back, something heavy and soft, and then somebody clutched at his arms, and somebody clutched at his legs, and before he knew it he was being pulled to his knees. He twisted his head around, fighting desperately, and then he visualized them. Women, ten or eleven women, with wild expressions and wilder hair, some of them dressed in plain institutional smocks, some of them wearing cotton skirts, but bare to the waist, some of them completely naked.

They forced his head forward until his face was pressed between his knees and his arms were stretched upward and backward behind him. He tried to sink further down into the earth to escape them, grunting with the effort of it, but one of them wriggled underneath him—a big naked woman with fat shoulders and huge breasts and blisters between her legs where she had set fire to her own pubic hair.

Come down, my darling! she said, grinning at him with a toothless gummy grin. *Come down, if you want to!*

Jack twisted, heaved, but couldn't get free. It was then

that Gordon Holman arrived and stood over him, naked
except for a straitjacket tied around his waist like an
off-white kilt. His two lieutenants stood a little way behind
him, one of them constantly nodding his head, and the
other motionless, with a crown of brambles around his
brow, smiling at nothing at all with an empty beatific smile.
St. Out-to-Lunch. But the strangest thing of all was that
this confrontation was taking place twenty feet beneath the
surface of the woods, in the darkness of the root-wriggled
soil, between Lodi and Okee, not too far from Lake
Wisconsin.

Quintus said you wanted to stop our sacrifice, said
Gordon Holman. *Quintus said you wanted us earthbound
for ever.*

Jack said, *Quintus is crazy. That so-called sacrifice, that's
my son.*

*Quintus said he wanted you dead. Dead, that's what he
said, and hung out to dry! Bring me that man's skin, that's
what he said! Bring me that man's liver!*

The fat woman squirmed lasciviously beneath him and
licked at his eyelids and his lips. He twisted his face away in
disgust.

I want to make love to you while you're dying, she
whispered. *I want to have you inside me while they're
killing you.*

One woman laughed, and shrieked, and called out,
Pandora! Pandora! Pandora! over and over again, until
another woman wrenched at her hair.

Let him go, ordered Gordon Holman.

The women hesitated at first, but when Gordon Holman
took a warning step forward, they released Jack's arms and
shuffled back and left him crouching where he was. Only
the fat woman beneath him remained, in case he should
dive for safety deep beneath the substrata of the soil.

Do you have a prayer that you want to pray? asked
Gordon Holman.

Jack remained where he was, hunched up, desperately

thinking. What were those ritual words? The words of
transformation and sacrifice? When Geoff had recited
them to Lester, on top of the parking lot, Lester had
screamed like crazy.

> *Caimich mi a nochd*
> *Eadar uir* something,
> *Eadar run do reachd,*
> Something something something

He was amazed that he could remember as much as that.
Usually, his memory was appalling. People would call him,
and he would promise to call them back within two or
three minutes, and that was it—he would have forgotten
about it instantly. So how could he remember Gaelic—
especially Gaelic that he had heard only once and read only
twice, and in the most stressful of circumstances?

> *Caimich mi a nochd*
> *Eadar Uir agus eare,*
> *Eadar run do reachd,*
> *Agus dearc mo dhoille*

There was overwhelming silence beneath the ground.
Jack remained crouched with his head bent forward. At
first he thought that Gordon Holman was simply waiting
for the right moment to kill him. But then he felt a
quivering through the loamy soil, and cautiously raised his
head; and there was Gordon Holman, trembling all over,
palsied with what appeared to be total terror.

He turned around. Most of the women had fallen to their
knees, and they were trembling, too. St. Out-to-Lunch was
frowning now, instead of smiling, and the head-nodder was
nodding so violently that Jack thought he might be in
danger of shaking his head off his shoulders.

The sacrifice, the transformation. The end of one life, the

beginning of another. That was what frightened these pathetic lunatics so much. Those words heralded death, and change, and insecurity—the superiority of magic over human will. Those were the words that the Druids had spoken to their followers at Stonehenge and Carnac and Mystery Hill, when all the world had been ruled by magic.

Jack himself could feel the potency of what he had just said. He could feel the power of the ley line gathering itself around him in preparation for the ritual that he had already set in motion.

But now what? thought Jack. *Do I make a run for it? Will they follow me? Will the effects of the prayer wear off, as soon as I move?*

Slowly, cautiously, he stood up. Still trembling, eyes still closed, Gordon Holman watched him, but did nothing to stop him.

It's not time yet, said Gordon Holman.

What do you mean, it's not time?

I haven't taken my full eight hundred. No more than fifty! It isn't time! *It can't be time!*

Jack looked up and visualized lightning crackling through the trees. It was raining hard. He could feel the bone-cold water dripping from the branches and seeping through the black hairy roots of the oaks.

Besides, said Gordon Holman, more optimistically, *Quintus hasn't called us yet. Quintus hasn't called us back. Quintus will know when it's time! Quintus will know when we've all taken eight hundred each.*

Gordon Holman laughed, and the women laughed, too, although fearfully still, and with less conviction. Jack had spoken the first words of the sacrifice. What had already been set in motion wouldn't be easy to stop, not without a sacrifice, not without death. The sacrificial ritual that Geoff had begun on the rooftop parking lot had only been concluded by Quintus Miller's slaughtering of Lester. Blood was called for, human clay.

But Gordon Holman snuffled and bayed like a hound. *Don't fret! Don't fret!* he cried out to his lunatic companions. *Quintus will call us when it's time! Quintus will play his music, and then we'll know! Quintus will call us with his pipe! The calling! The calling! We haven't heard the calling yet! If we'd heard the calling, we wouldn't have had no choice! We'd've had to go! But it isn't time! Don't fret! It isn't time!*

Jack thought, *What's he talking about, the calling? Quintus has to call them with pipe music when it's time for the sacrifice?*

He held up his own pipe. Just a smooth straight cane, with holes burned into it. Maybe the music was the answer. Maybe the music was critical. It had been a critical part of the ritual that had taken him into the wall. Maybe it was a critical part of the sacrificial ritual, too.

Quintus would play pipe music when it was time for the lunatics to assemble at the sacred place . . . and they would follow. Judging from what Gordon Holman had said, they would be *compelled* to follow, whether they wanted to follow or not. The same way that the children had followed the piper in Hamelin, straight into the hillside. Because from what Jack could work out, the piping was much more than music—much more than a simple signal. It was a direct summons from the Being-of-the-Law-and-of-the-Stars, God the Quintessence, a summons that called on the body just as strongly as it called on the sense of devotion.

Jack thought, *You don't turn down an invitation from God the Quintessence, even if it means that your whole life is going to be torn apart from top to bottom, and that everybody you know is going to be tortured on frames, and bent back double so that they lost their eternal souls for ever.*

You go—because you have no choice.

Jack hesitantly lifted his pipe. He didn't know if it would play beneath the ground, but he blew into the reed, and the air flowed thickly through the stem, and something that was less than a musical note but more than a musical vibration came quivering out of it, and through the soil, *Lavender blue, dilly-dilly; lavender green; here I am king, dilly-dilly—*

The effect on Gordon Holman and the rest of the lunatics was immediate and frightening. They rose up, and crowded around Jack, holding out their hands in blind supplication. They didn't speak, but their begging hands made a rustling sound like the pigeons clustering on the roof of The Oaks, and their bodies pushed through the soil with that terrible familiar *sssssshhhhhhh.*

Jack retreated, along the ley line, back toward The Oaks. He turned. The lunatics weren't following him. They were standing in the same place with their hands outstretched, their eyes closed, their faces desperate with longing.

What is it that somebody can long for so desperately? thought Jack. *What is it that means more to them than anything at all?*

He walked farther, then stopped. Still the lunatics remained where they were. He hesitated, then lifted up his pipe again and began to play the same tune, over and over and over.

This time they followed him. They seemed blind, as if they had lost the sharp sense of visualization that allowed Jack to find his way through the blackness of solid earth. They shuffled pale and anxious and mad, like medieval lepers. Even though Jack knew that they probably wouldn't hurt him, they looked so distorted and irrational and strange that he stepped back more and more quickly, still playing his flute, but anxious that they shouldn't catch up with him.

Lavender blue, dilly-dilly . . . the music penetrated the soil and ran along the ley lines; and where one ley line intersected with another, the music ran off again, as soft and as bright as quicksilver.

The music reached The Oaks and spread swiftly out in

all directions, as high and as vibrant as the song sung by a spiderweb touched by the wind. To Janesville and Watertown and Mineral Point, to Monona and Waukesha.

All over southeast Wisconsin, deep beneath the soil, deep beneath the concrete sidewalks, fast secreted in walls and ceilings and furniture, the remaining scores of maniacs lifted their heads, and listened, and frowned.

The calling. But the calling was far too early. Thousands more lives had still to be taken, eight hundred each. That was the law; that was the price of escape.

But no matter how many misgivings the lunatics had about how soon the calling had come, there was no question of resisting it. *The calling.* That same plaintive pipe tune, played over and over. *Lavender blue, dilly-dilly* . . . The oldest of sacred hymns to the Being-of-the-Law-and-of-the-Stars, Awen, the great creator.

The tune was a mystical arrangement of notes in the same way that the pentacle was a mystical arrangement of symbols. Those who heard it were physically drawn through the soil, along the ley lines, just as the bluestones of Stonehenge had been physically drawn from ancient Wales to Salisbury Plain. They came because they had no alternative. They came because they had been commanded.

They came because they were *called.*

One hundred thirty-six of them, drawn back toward The Oaks, some of them leaving furrowed paths across fields and highways, some of them passing invisibly but audibly through stores and walls and apartment buildings. Not dancing, not chattering, the way that the children of Hamelin were supposed to have danced and chattered after the Pied Piper. But running, with their eyes closed, running as if their lives depended on it.

By the time he reached the foundations of The Oaks, Jack already realized what had happened, and that he had called them all. He could visualize them all around him, as if he were standing on a rise in the ground, and they were approaching through the night from all directions—running, their faces grim. He had gained enough confidence over the last few miles to turn his back on Gordon Holman and his horrifying friends and to march forward at his own pace, looking ahead of him for Quintus Miller.

Above the surface of the ground, thunder cracked across the sky, and rain fell on to The Oaks relentlessly, so that its broken gutters spouted water, and the swimming pool overflowed, carrying its sickening black flotsam halfway across the flooded tennis courts.

Beneath the cellar floor, Jack stood at last in the center of a silent circle of The Oaks's last residents—all there, except for Quintus Miller.

You called and we came, said a tall man with a huge encephalitic head. *Where is the sacrifice?*

I called you because we must pay homage tonight to Awen, Jack extemporized, trying frantically to sense where Quintus Miller could be.

Does this mean a sacrifice? asked a black man with a dramatically sloping forehead. *Does this mean that somebody has to die?*

Well—ah—that's right! said Jack. *Somebody has to die. One of you—to show Awen that you're not afraid to give up anything for her—including your lives, right? Including your souls.*

There were hair-raising screams of dread throughout the assembly of lunatics. They sounded like the passengers of a falling airliner. They were not afraid of sacrificing their physical lives. They were clay, after all, in their present condition, they were nothing more than soil, and just like clay their physical presence could be restored . . . provided their soul had survived. But if their soul were annihilated, there would be nothingness, and worse than nothingness. There would be the never-ending *consciousness* of nothingness . . .

Jack said, *My friend knows all about the sacred traditions of Druidism . . . and my friend says that by sacred tradition, your leader should be sacrificed. If you don't, you'll never know what it is to walk around in the air, ever again. You will never be given Awen's blessing to escape from out of the ground. You hear that? Your leader represents all of you . . . if you sacrifice him, then Awen will know for certain that you all worship him . . . that you are all devoted to him.*

He was breathing deeply. The air from the soil was sour and damp, and he could smell that vinegary odor that permeated The Oaks. A hundred thirty-five ill-assorted faces watched him with their eyes closed, not seeing, but sensing. Some of the faces were impossibly beautiful. Others were grotesque, like gargoyles. Others had an un-hinged plainness about them, so ordinary that Jack could tell that they were dangerous.

All right . . . he said, raising his arms. *What we have to do is to locate Quintus Miller. You understand that? And when you've located him, you're going to have to sacrifice him. Otherwise you don't stand a chance. You'll be trapped in the ground forever.*

The man with the huge head said, *What about the eight hundred lives we're supposed to take? I've taken only six so far. People aboveground aren't easy to catch.*

Forget about the eight hundred lives. It's Quintus Miller you have to go for first.

A woman stepped forward. Her long ash-blond hair trailed through the soil like the hair of Botticelli's Venus, except that this was a child of the earth rather than the sea. She seemed to be barely thirty: in truth she was nearer ninety. She held out her arms and whispered, *How can we trust you? We have always trusted Quintus. You want us to sacrifice Quintus, but is that because Quintus intends to sacrifice your son? What guarantee do we have that you're not deceiving us—that we will never escape?*

Jack said, *You trusted Quintus, and what happened? You spent sixty years trapped in the walls. Quintus will save himself, believe me. Quintus doesn't care about you.*

Quintus wants out, and as far as he's concerned that's all that matters.

The ash-blond girl said, *He's here.*

What do you mean, he's here? Where? I don't see him.

He's here, in the building. He's here at The Oaks. Upstairs. I can sense him.

Jack's skin prickled. So Quintus was already here. But why? Jack would have thought that Quintus would have been scouring the streets for more and more people to kill so that he could walk in the real world once again. He looked up through the main supporting wall above his head, but he couldn't see anything except darkness.

Wait here, he told the assembly of lunatics. *Make yourselves ready for a great sacrifice to Awen. Pray. Think of the days when you used to walk around in the real world, okay? Those times are going to come back. But don't go away, do you understand me? I'm going to need you here to help me.*

Where are you going, piper? asked Gordon. His voice was strangely expressionless and spaced out, as if he were still under the influence of the music.

Up, said Jack. *I'm going up.*

He pushed his way up through the dark gray brickwork of the walls, like a diver rising toward the surface of a thickly silted pond. His cupped hands pulled him *sssssshhhhhh—sssssshhhhh—sssssshhhhh* through the cold, damp cement. An occasional splintering pine-needle prickle as he penetrated a wooden door.

He was heading for Quintus Miller's room, where the pentacle was drawn on the wall. He had a feeling that if Quintus were anywhere, he would be there, searching for a way out.

The walls of The Oaks were deceptively complicated in their construction. Every time Jack forged directly toward the second floor, he seemed to find himself confined to walls that curved over into archways and took him back down to the first floor again. Every time he turned toward

Quintus Miller's room, the walls led him emphatically and quickly away.

He stopped at the end of the second-story corridor, trying to sense the whole building, trying to feel its symbolism, trying to feel its totality. *The Maze,* Adolf Krüger had called it; and it *was* a maze.

Jack thought to himself, *You're a businessman, you run a highly successful muffler and tire outfit. Use some business know-how. Use some practical thinking. These Druids lived thousands of years ago, they couldn't have thought of something that good old U.S. business acumen couldn't lick.*

He tried heading *away* from Quintus's room, the way that Alice had walked in the opposite direction when she was trying to find her way through the Looking Glass garden. But he found himself on the opposite side of The Oaks, in one of the dingiest corners, next to the broom closet.

No, he decided, the trick was more elaborate than that. He tried rushing directly back to Quintus's room, but again he found himself way beyond it. He felt as if he were taking one step forward and two steps back.

Maybe that was it. One step forward and two steps back. He tried it, and to his surprise, he managed to reach the corner of the second-story corridor. He tried it again, but this time he was farther away than ever. Maybe it was progressive. One step forward and two steps back. Then two steps forward and three steps back. Then three steps forward and *four* steps back.

After four or five more minutes, he suddenly cracked it. One step forward, two steps back. Two steps forward, one step back. He repeated the same pattern again and again, turning right and left as he went, until quite abruptly he arrived in the wall of Quintus Miller's room, opposite the hexagram.

He couldn't stop himself from letting out a suppressed grunt of shock.

Quintus Miller was already there, and so was Randy.

Quintus Miller was crouched inside the wall in the far corner of the room, not looking in Jack's direction, and too preoccupied to stop what he was doing.

Jack stayed where he was, rigid with alarm, trying not to breathe too loudly. Quintus hadn't yet sensed that he was there—or if he had, he was so contemptuous of Jack's ability to stop him that he simply didn't care.

Jack had found Quintus unnerving enough when he had appeared in the glass of Geoff's windshield. But here, in the wall, his appearance was even more daunting. He was short, big-headed, bull-necked, with slashed-back hair and a face as cold as a painted steel mask. He wore soiled gray flannel pants, and a heavy Sam Browne belt with hammers and pliers hanging around it. Quintus's back was thick with graying woolly hair, and his elbows were raw with pink-and-white eczema.

What he was doing was even more frightening. He had forced Randy to stand naked inside the wall, behind the blood-marked hexagram, with his arms and his legs spread apart to correspond exactly with the star shape of earth and water, air and fire. He had fastened Randy's wrists and ankles by forcing them through to the real world outside, small hands and small feet protruding from the plaster.

Randy had his head bent forward, resting against the inside of the wall. He looked dirty and tousled and exhausted. If Jack hadn't known just how dangerous Quintus Miller could be, he would have rushed forward then and there and taken Randy into his arms.

There was another thing: Jack didn't yet understand how Quintus and the other maniacs could reach out of the walls and the floors, while Father Bell and Randy had obviously been trapped when their hands were forced from one element into another. And Jack had seen for himself what had happened to the people whom the maniacs had dragged right into the ground.

Maybe Quintus and his followers had acquired more of the earth's natural power, from all of the years they had spent in the walls of The Oaks. Maybe they had entered the walls with a different kind of a ritual. Geoff had told him that there were scores of Druidic rituals for moving from one element to the other, most of which had been lost. Maybe Quintus had discovered one of them in Adolf Krüger's books, the books that were now burned to ashes.

Jack didn't move. He wasn't at all sure what he was going to do now. He wondered if it would be feasible to lure Quintus down to the floor below the basement, where the rest of the maniacs were assembled, ready for a sacrifice. The trouble with that idea was that he was still unsure about making his way around the maze of walls, and Quintus would inevitably catch up with him. Even if he *did* manage to lure Quintus to the basement, Jack had no guarantees that once they saw him, his followers would not remember their long-standing loyalty to their leader and help him to tear Jack apart.

His only defense was his flute, and he wasn't certain how long the influence of "Lavender Blue" could last . . . especially since he didn't know any more Druidic music, or any more Druidic rituals.

He was still standing stock-still in the corner of the room when Quintus bent forward so that his head was touching the floor and began to chant a long, muffled litany. Jack could only catch a few words of it, but it was definitely Gaelic.

> *"Failt ort fein, a gheallach ur,*
> *Ailleagan iuil nan neul!"*

Randy whimpered and moved his head listlessly from side to side, his eyes closed just as Jack's were, and just as Quintus's were.

> *"Failt ort fein, a gheallach ur—"*

Ohhhh . . . moaned Randy.

> *"Ailleagan iuil nan neul!"*

While Quintus was reciting, Jack heard a noise in the corridor outside the room. Not inside the walls, but in the corridor itself. Footsteps, voices. He glanced back toward Quintus, visualizing his crouching figure, but Quintus was too deeply involved in his chanting to have heard.

Jack suddenly recognized the voices, and the tap-tapping of high-heeled shoes. It was Geoff and Karen, at last, thank God!

Geoff was saying, ". . . no way of knowing if he got away. I can't exactly call Sergeant Schiller and ask him outright."

"He'll get here," Karen insisted. "If there's any way that he can do it, he'll get here. He's that kind of a guy."

"Well, anyway, let's take a look in here," suggested Geoff as they reached the door of Quintus's room. "The pentacle is the entrance and the exit to the maze. If he's going to come out anywhere, he's going to come out here."

"But how come *Jack's* going to be able to come out, when Quintus Miller can't. Leastways, not without killing all of those people?"

Geoff opened the door and stepped into the room and quickly shone a flashlight around. "Don't know for sure, to tell you the truth. But Druggett's book says that the rule was, one sacrifice for every lunar month spent in the earth. Awen demands it. Kind of compensation, I suppose, for all the power and energy that one person draws out of the soil when they're living inside it. The earth's magnetism has to be replenished, the same way that its minerals do. Awen is the earth's protector, and as far as Awen is concerned, the earth is more valuable than individual human lives."

"You're making me shiver," said Karen.

Jack raised his hand and pressed it against the inside of the wall, tried to press it *out* of the wall, to attract Geoff's attention. But the wall was too hard; he was not yet strong enough to push his way through the mystical meniscus that separated the world of earth from the world of air.

He hesitated. Quintus was still softly chanting and nodding backward and forward, as if he were slowly going into a trance. Maybe if Jack called out to Geoff, Quintus wouldn't hear him.

Randy moaned and tossed his head back, and at the moment he did so, he flapped his hands and his feet, and Geoff shone his flashlight toward the hexagram.

Because Jack had been able to visualize everything around him with his eyes closed, he had almost forgotten that it was still dark and that Geoff needed a flashlight to see what was happening. The flashlight crossed the wall in front of Jack's face and momentarily dazzled him—not the light itself, because the light couldn't penetrate the wall—but the ionized particles that streamed out of the flashlight.

"Karen!" called Geoff. "Look at this! Hands, and feet, at each point of the hexagram! A child's hands and feet!"

Geoff! Jack hissed. *Geoff, for Christ's sake!*

But Geoff didn't hear him. He knelt down in front of the pentacle, and took hold of one of Randy's bare feet, and said, "It's Randy! It must be! There weren't any juvenile patients at The Oaks!"

"But why are his hands and his feet sticking out of the wall?" asked Karen. Jack caught the blond nylon shine of the wig she had bought to pretend to be his sister Edna-Mae. "Is he *in* there?"

"Yes, he is," said Geoff, worried. "And the reason he's been arranged like this is because he's going to be sacrificed. This is the final child sacrifice that allows an earth-walker to emerge from the wall."

"But they haven't killed enough people," said Karen. "The news said two hundred sixteen, that's all. That isn't enough to let *one* loony out of the wall!"

Geoff! called Jack, louder this time.

Quintus Miller had stopped chanting, halfway through his ritual, and he was rising slowly to his feet. His face was expressionless, his eyes unblinking, but Jack could tell how angry he was at being interrupted. The muscles across his shoulders and back were bunched up and wriggling with swollen arteries, and the sinews in his huge neck were as taut as braided steel cables.

"Can you get Randy *out*?" Karen was asking Geoff.

Geoff! screamed Jack. *Quintus Miller is here! Get away from that wa*—

Without any hesitation, Quintus thrust his arm out of the wall and seized Geoff's beard, pulling Geoff facefirst into the wall.

Geoff roared out in pain. Karen screamed. Immediately Jack ran around the walls of the room and snatched hold of Quintus Miller by the shoulders, shaking him as hard as he could.

Quintus released Geoff, who fell back bloody-faced into the room. He turned on Jack and this time his eyes were open, they were gleaming like steel studs. His chest rose and fell with fury, and now that he was facing him, Jack could see the full horror of the tattoo on his abdomen.

Two tattooed hands appeared to be reaching around Quintus's waist and dragging open his skin and his flesh, so that all his internal organs were exposed. Whoever had created this grisly trompe l'oeil, he must have been an obsessive but consummate tattooist, because Jack had to look twice to make sure that Quintus hadn't really been disemboweled.

The dark mauve liver, the glistening beige pancreas, the pale loops of large intestine—everything had been depicted in meticulous detail.

Quintus said, in a tensile voice, *I warned you. You meddling malicious bastard. I warned you.*

I want my son, Jack demanded.

Quintus came closer, and Jack backed away. *Your son belongs to me now. Your son is my passport.*

I won't let you take him, Quintus. You'll have to kill me first.

With pleasure. Quintus grinned and swiftly advanced.

Jack thought, *Shit, this is it,* and braced himself. But Quintus was even stronger than he had expected. Quintus came at him with the unstoppable force of a speeding truck, seizing both of his wrists, and head-butting him so hard that he was momentarily dazed. Then Quintus punched him twice in the stomach and once in the chest. He heard a rib snap, but his lungs were empty of air, and he couldn't even cry out.

Quintus lifted him up bodily and flung him the entire length of the wall, so that he landed on his shoulder right next to Randy.

Now I'm going to tear your arms off, Quintus promised. *I'm going to tear your arms off and stuff them down your throat.* He came toward Jack with both hands raised and a look of calculating madness on his face that turned Jack's spinal column to ice water.

Quintus grabbed hold of Jack's right arm, but as he did so he flinched and turned around in fury. Then he flinched again, and smacked at his shoulder as if he had been stung, and let Jack go.

Stunned, winded, Jack looked into the room and saw that Geoff was standing in the middle of it with his Perrier bottle of exorcised water, spraying the walls.

"Ab insidiis diaboli, libera nos Domine!" he was calling out, through swollen and bloodied lips. *"Audi nos!"*

Quintus bellowed in anger, a harsh throat-tearing sound that made Jack involuntarily jump.

The Christian priests had used the powerful rituals of the Holy Church to supersede the Druids, and now Geoff was using the same rituals to hold back Quintus Miller.

Each splash of exorcised water sizzled on Quintus Miller's flesh like acid. The hair on his back shriveled and burned. But he advanced on Jack yet again, keeping up that steady and terrifying roaring. *Pieces! Damn you! Pieces! That's all that anybody's ever going to find of you! Pieces!*

Quintus's outline must have bulged from the surface of

the wall, because now Geoff was sprinkling the exorcised water directly onto him, a shower of holy brine. Quintus's face blistered, his earlobe sizzled, skin twisted and scorched on the side of his arm.

"Ut inimicos sanctae Ecclesiae humiliare digneris, te rogamus, audi nos!"

Quintus gripped Jack's arms with fingers that quivered with power and pain. He stared Jack straight in the face and Jack believed in that instant that he was going to be killed. But then the exorcised water lashed down again, a cat-o'-nine-tails across Quintus's back, and Quintus threw Jack away from him with a hideous screeching shout.

Jack tumbled backward, overbalanced, but just managed to catch hold of Randy's arm as he somersaulted.

The two of them exploded out of the hexagram on the wall, and rolled arms and legs across the floor.

Behind them, the plaster gray bas-relief figure of Quintus Miller, still imprisoned, roared and raged at them in frustration. Geoff stepped up to him, spraying him again and again with the sign of the cross, until he suddenly vanished.

Karen, down on her knees, held Jack tightly in her arms and shuddered with shock and relief. Jack kept his arm around Randy, covering him up with his dusty shirt. His face and his hair were thick with dry plaster, and there was black soil under his fingernails.

"You made it, I can't believe it!" Karen sobbed. "You went through the walls and you made it!"

Jack looked up at Geoff. Geoff was holding a blood-spattered handkerchief to the side of his face, but he was smiling.

"Thanks to you, good buddy," Jack told him.

"You had the guts to do it, old chap," Geoff replied. "And you saved your son, too."

"That hurt?" asked Jack as Geoff dabbed at his cheek.

Geoff shook his head. "It's not much more than a scratch."

Jack said, "Randy? How are you feeling? Do you feel okay?"

Randy coughed, and rubbed his eyes, and stared up at his father numbly. He couldn't understand yet that he was free. "Do you have a root beer?" he asked.

Karen squeezed him. "Honey, I wish we had. But we'll get you some water."

Jack eased himself painfully up. "I think that son of a bitch broke one of my ribs. I was lucky he didn't kill me."

Geoff said, "I think we ought to get out of here as quickly as we can. Quintus needs a last sacrifice to get out of the walls, preferably Randy, but Karen would make a reasonable second-best, and he'd use one of us at a pinch—so don't believe that he's going to let us go easily."

"I thought he had to kill eight hundred people before he could get out of the walls," said Jack.

"Well, me too," Geoff agreed. "Lester said so and Druggett's book said so. But it seems as if he's ready now. And, believe me, he won't stop at anything. I've seen some of his medical records. I've been hiding here at The Oaks ever since the police started looking for me. I went through Elmer Estergomy's files and found quite a few references to Quintus Miller. His personal file's gone . . . the police must have destroyed it when the patients first disappeared. But Estergomy made lots of peripheral notes, and he kept a daily diary, too, which is pretty revealing."

Geoff helped Randy on to his feet. Then he struggled out of his hairy brown pullover and tugged it over Randy's head. "There? How about that? That should keep you warm till we get to the car."

They left Quintus Miller's room and started to walk back along the darkened corridor, following Geoff's darting flashlight. Jack kept one arm around Karen and the other arm around Randy. He was determined not to lose either of them—especially not to Quintus Miller.

As they went he told Geoff as much as he could about his

surrealistic journey along the ley lines, and the way that he had summoned the maniacs back to The Oaks.

"They're down there now, as far as I know, still waiting."

"In that case," said Geoff, "we'll do what Father Bell did, and circle the building with holy water, and hope that they don't get out a second time."

"It's Quintus Miller we have to deal with," said Jack.

"Yes," Geoff replied. They were nearing the landing now. "Elmer Estergomy's notes on him were fascinating. Quintus is a classic paranoiac who came to believe from reading Adolf Krüger's books on Druidism that he was the only true son of Awen, the Druid god. He had delusions of grandeur, but he also had delusions that everybody was persecuting him. That's why he took revenge on his family, by blinding them and stabbing them.

"He was very charismatic, too, according to Elmer Estergomy—although of course he didn't use that actual word. He always commanded attention from the staff and his fellow patients, and his charisma occasionally went beyond that. Some of the staff were supposed to have seen him roll pencils across the table by the power of his mind alone, and once he was supposed to have torn up sheets of newspaper just by staring at them. Strange, huh? Elmer Estergomy wrote again and again in his daily diary that Quintus was probably the single most dangerous patient he ever had to deal with."

Jack grimaced and pressed his hand against his ribs. "I'd agree with that. But what about weaknesses? Doesn't he have any weaknesses? Karen suggested we should find out what he's afraid of, if he's afraid of anything at all, and play on that."

They had almost reached the landing, and Geoff cautiously played the flashlight from one side of the corridor to the other.

"From what I could read from Elmer Estergomy's diaries, Quintus Miller is morbidly afraid of dogs. He tore all pictures of dogs out of magazines and shredded them up, and if anybody talked about dogs he went into a fit. Elmer Estergomy guessed that it was something to do with the night he killed his brothers and his mother. His father came home and found him and set the family watchdog on him . . . apparently he was almost killed. He had himself tattooed to cover the scars, and also to taunt his father that he had nearly been ripped open. But that's the only specific phobia Estergomy mentioned."

Jack said to Karen, "That's probably what kept Joseph Lovelittle alive for so long. Quintus Miller didn't want to come anywhere near him, not with that Doberman of his."

They reached the landing. Jack recognized the pale blind statues and the skeletal hanging lamp and the dull gleam from the marble floor. God, he hated this place, and feared it, too. He had never hated any building the way that he hated The Oaks. Somewhere, he could hear rain clattering through the ceiling on to the floor, and the distant grumbling of thunder.

They were just about to start down the staircase when a flashlight dazzled them from down below in the hallway, and a woman's voice said sharply, "Who's there?"

Jack frowned into the darkness. "Geoff," he said, "give me the flashlight."

The woman's voice repeated, "Who's there? Jack? Is that you?"

"Jesus Christ," said Jack. "It's Maggie."

T·H·I·R·T·E·E·N

Maggie walked smartly across the marble floor until she reached the foot of the staircase, her Burberry raincoat rustling. She prodded the beam of the flashlight up the stairs, first into Jack's face, then into Karen's face, then down at Randy.

"Randy!" she cried out. "Thank God you're safe!"

She ran up the stairs, her court shoes tapping, and knelt down and hugged him tight. Randy burst into tears.

"What have you *done* to him?" Maggie snapped. "What have you done with his clothes?" She stared fiercely at Karen and said, "I might have known that *you* would be here!"

Jack retorted, "What I'd like to know is what the hell *you're* doing here. What time is it? It isn't even light yet!"

"Sergeant Schiller called me, as a matter of fact, to warn me that you'd escaped, and that you could be dangerous."

"Well, thanks. I've just saved Randy from being sacrificed alive and now I'm supposed to be dangerous."

"I never believed that you'd killed him," Maggie replied. "I may not love you, Jack. In fact I think I probably hate you. But I know you better than that. It just occurred to me that you might have *hidden* Randy someplace, and that if you'd escaped you'd be going to get him so that you could take him away. The only place I could think of where you might have been able to hide him was here. I knew that I would have to be quick, so I drove here at once."

Geoff said, "Mrs. Reed . . . this building is extremely dangerous. We have to leave here right away."

"Who's this?" Maggie demanded. "I warn you—I'm going to call the police!"

"At this moment, Mrs. Reed, the police are the least of my worries. Now, shall we go?"

"If you think I'm going to let you get away, you've got another thing coming," Maggie told Jack. "You've put me through absolute hell!"

. She took hold of Randy's hand and began to march down the stairs with him, swinging her flashlight. Geoff looked at Jack and raised his eyebrows, and Karen said, "If she calls the cops . . ."

But Maggie was only a third of the way down the staircase when she screamed, and Randy screamed, too. Geoff flicked his flashlight toward her, and to Jack's horror, he saw that two gray, blistered hands had thrust themselves up from the stairs and were pulling Maggie and Randy into the marble treads.

"Maggie, hold on!" Jack shouted. Both he and Geoff ran down the stairs, and while Jack kicked viciously at Quintus Miller's fingers, Geoff shakily opened up his bottle of exorcised water and sprinkled it all around. Maggie screamed and screamed and clutched Jack's leg, but then the water sizzled into Quintus's flesh and his grip relaxed, and Jack was able to drag Maggie back up the stairs. Randy came running up, too, weeping and shaking.

Geoff was still spraying water around when another hand reached out of the stairs behind him and grabbed at his ankle.

He turned, slipped, and almost lost his balance. The Perrier bottle fell out of his grasp, bounced once, and rolled away.

"We'll have to make a run for it!" Jack shouted. "Down the stairs, across the hall, and out through the lounge, as fast as we can!"

Geoff said, "Come on, then! The quicker the better!"

He launched himself down the staircase, but just as he reached the bottom stair a forest of marble hands rose from the hallway floor, clawing blindly at him. The lunatics had left the basement and had risen through the building in search of their promised sacrifice. The hallway looked like some hideous asparagus bed of pallid arms.

"Up!" Geoff yelled, and came running back up the stairs again. As he passed the place where Quintus Miller's hands had emerged the marble steps suddenly cracked and exploded, and a thunderously splintering furrow came chasing up the stairs after him.

Geoff snatched hold of Karen and Maggie and dragged them forcibly along the corridor at full tilt. Jack came hop-hobbling behind them, his broken rib jabbing into him with every step, tugging Randy along as fast as he could run.

Only feet behind them, the linoleum floor of the corridor was ripped furiously open as Quintus Miller relentlessly pursued them, mad for revenge, mad for sacrifice, mad to tear them apart.

"We'll have to go up!" Geoff gasped as they reached the landing outside Elmer Estergomy's office. "Then along the top corridor—down the other staircase!"

Maggie screamed, "What is it? Jack, what is it?"

But Jack shouted back at her, "No time! Get up those stairs!"

"But what *is* it?"

"Maggie!" Jack bellowed as the floor burst apart all around them. *"Get up those fucking stairs!"*

They scrambled up, hands and feet, like scampering children, and right behind them the stairs split and the banisters burst open, and the steel mesh over the windows rattled and vibrated.

"I can't—I can't run any further—" Karen panted. But Jack said to Maggie, "Take Randy's hand!" and hefted Karen up in his arms. The pain in his rib was excruciating, but he staggered up the next flight of stairs, with Chinese whiskers of blood running from the sides of his mouth, until they reached the very top landing.

Behind them, the stairs were furrowed up in a relentless *crickle-crackkle-crikk-crackkle* and plaster showered off the walls in a blinding gray fog.

Jack dropped Karen back onto her feet. Then he gasped, "Okay—we'll run along here—to the other end—then down again—see if we can't—"

But Karen cried out, *"Look!"* and pointed along the corridor ahead of them.

Surging toward them at a steady walking pace came the head of Gordon Holman, the tongue nailer, his face breaking the surface of the floor like a buoy being dragged behind a boat. Geoff shone his flashlight toward him, and for a second Gordon Holman's eyes gleamed over the crest of the rippling floor, as red as the eyes of somebody caught in a surprise-party photograph.

Jack twisted around. Quintus had almost reached the head of the stairs. There was no way back down, in either direction.

"There!" Jack said, pointing toward the ceiling. "Geoff, there must be a loft up there!"

Set in the ceiling, right above the head of the staircase, was a small square trapdoor. A frayed cord hung down from the catch, but when Geoff reached up for it, he found that it was four or five inches out of reach. He jumped, and flicked it, but he still couldn't get a grip on it.

The top stair cracked apart, and broken banisters tumbled down the staircase with a hollow ringing noise. Gordon Holman's head was only a dozen feet away from them, along the corridor, and surging closer. One of his hands suddenly emerged from the floor, ready to snatch at their ankles.

Jack swung Randy up in his arms and said, "Grab it, Randy! Grab the cord!"

Randy tugged the cord but nothing happened.

"Again, Randy!" Jack shouted.

This time the trapdoor abruptly came free, and a wooden ladder came banging down with it; but at the same time they were drenched by a heavy slippery torrent of black putrescence, smelling so strongly of vinegar that Karen retched out loud.

"Jesus, what is it?" screamed Maggie.

"I don't know! Up!" Jack ordered her.

"Up *there*? I can't! Oh God I can't!"

But Geoff suddenly shouted out in pain, and they looked around to see that Quintus Miller's hands had risen out of the linoleum and seized his right ankle.

"Up!" Jack shouted at Maggie. "You, too, Karen! And take Randy!"

Maggie closed her eyes for one split second, then pushed Randy ahead of her up the wooden ladder. The rungs of the ladder dripped with black loops of decomposing mush, and as they climbed up, more strings and bladders of unidentifiable slop came dropping on to the floor.

Jack kicked viciously at Quintus Miller's hands, but this time Quintus was determined not to let go.

Geoff held on to Jack tightly, his eyes wild. "Jack—for God's sake—save yourself! Just make sure—make sure he doesn't sacrifice me—don't let him—not the ritual—otherwise—he'll be *free*, Jack! Don't let him get free!"

Quintus dragged Geoff's right foot deep into the solid floor. Geoff screamed, and his ankle welled with blood. But he stiffly took his hands away from Jack and said desperately, "Save—yourself—Jack—"

Jack turned. Gordon Holman had almost reached him, his eyes gleaming with blood lust. Karen was disappearing up the slithery ladder into the loft.

Geoff gave him a rictus smile, and a rigid shake of his head, and then threw himself backward and sideways with all his strength. He tumbled over the banisters, blood spraying from his ground-up foot, and fell all the way down to the landing two floors below. Jack heard a terrible smashing noise as he landed.

He almost gave up there and then, and threw himself after Geoff. But he turned, with tears of frustration and fury filling his eyes, and kicked Gordon Holman straight in the forehead. Then he grabbed hold of the slippery stinking ladder and climbed quickly up into the loft.

The scene in the loft was appalling beyond anything that Jack could ever have imagined. It ran the entire length of The Oaks, apart from the spires at either end, and it was illuminated only by Maggie's flashlight and by occasional shivers of lightning through the tiny eye-curved windows. The noise of the rain falling on the wooden shingles directly above their heads was deafening, and it was accompanied by the spouting of broken gutters and the persistent *trickle-click-trickle* of water running through corroded flashings.

Maggie and Karen and Randy stood in the middle of the loft in complete horror. The floor was a foot deep in decomposed human remains, some of them mummified, so that they crunched underfoot, others much more recent, but decomposed to the point of liquefaction. The air was almost unbreathable. Vinegar had been emptied in gallons all over the bodies—presumably to mask their smell. Jack guessed that vinegar was all that Quintus had been able to find in a long-abandoned asylum—but the combined stench of vinegar and human decay was numbing in its intensity.

Jack waded across the slithery floor. He saw a bag or a sack of some kind lying in the ooze and picked it up, allowing it to spin around slowly in the light from Maggie's flashlight. He read the name on the stained label. "Gale McReady, University of Wisconsin La Crosse." Then he let it drop. "You see what Quintus has done here?" he said, his voice hoarse with awe. "He's already taken his eight hundred lives, or most of them, anyway. In sixty years, he's been killing anybody who's visited The Oaks—bums, hitchhikers, who knows—anybody who crashed out here or squatted here, or came to take a look around. He's killed them all. And he's probably enticed some here, too, with that little gray child of his, that little gray child who's nothing but newspaper."

He tried to swallow, tried to breathe, but he couldn't. "He could do that, you know. Tear up paper without touching it, make things move. That was the way he brought me here to The Oaks. The only way he could reach me."

He looked around, and he was crying so much from grief and disgust that he could hardly see. "He must have been so damn close to taking his eight hundred lives . . . maybe the other crazies knew, maybe they didn't. But Quintus himself—Jesus, look what he's done!—Quintus was almost ready to break himself out of here—into the real world. That's the only reason he didn't kill me, too. That's the only reason that *I'm* not lying here. Somebody to be sent off to find Father Bell. Some poor gullible bastard."

Maggie staggered toward Jack with her arms outstretched, choking with fear. "Jack—you have to get us out of here. *Jack! You have to get us out of here! I can't stand it! I can't stand it! I can't stand it!*"

He took hold of her wrists, steadied her. "Don't drop the flashlight, whatever you do. Look—there's a larger window over there. We can climb out on to the roof—then maybe we can climb down the drainpipes."

"I can't stand it, I can't do it! Jack, you have to get me out of here!"

Jack dragged her over to the semicircular window. Its glass was thick with grease and dust, but when he wiped it with the edge of his hand, he could see the parapet of the mansard roof outside, brimming with water. The rain was cascading down on all sides, and lightning flickered over the distant treetops like serpents' tongues. Jack made a point of not looking down to see what he was treading in, but it felt like a greasy heap of rubber gloves.

He tried the window catch. It was an old-fashioned brass lever, dulled to green. It was stiff, and he had to force it down with both hands, but to his surprise it actually opened, and the window groaned open sideways, and he was spattered in the face with cold refreshing rain.

He leaned out, his eyes squinched up against the wind and the rain. The parapet had flooded because the drains were blocked with sixty years of leaves and pigeon droppings, but if they balanced ten or twelve feet to the corner of the east tower, there was a vertical pipe in the angle between the tower and the main wall that looked as if it would be comparatively easy to climb down. Brackets every four feet, and plenty of handholds. He turned back to Maggie. "You see that? You see that drainpipe?"

"What?" she asked him, her hands over her ears, her eyes tight shut.

"Maggie, look at me! Listen! Do you see that drainpipe? There—in the corner?"

She glanced quickly and then nodded.

He took hold of her shoulder and said, "What you have to do is—climb along the parapet—okay?—keep your hand on the roof for support—then climb down the pipe to the ground. Then run. Do you understand me?"

Maggie nodded, her eyes still shut tight.

"Maggie, for God's sake, do you understand me? You have to climb down the pipe!"

"Yes! Yes! *Yes!*" she shouted at him. "Yes, I understand!"

"All right, then, go! Randy will come right after you, then Karen."

Maggie opened her eyes and stared at Jack wildly. The pupils of her eyes were tiny with shock. *"I can't do it!"* she screamed. *"How can you expect me to do it?"*

Just then, however, Karen said, "Jack—there's something moving in here. Jack, hurry, please! There's something moving."

Jack grasped Maggie's wrist and half helped, half heaved

her out of the window. She stood on the parapet ankle-deep
in rainwater, her Burberry flapping in the wind, her eyes
closed, her hands pressed against the tiles of the roof.

"Edge your way along!" Jack shouted at her. "Edge your
way along to the corner—then climb down the pipe!"

Maggie nodded, dumbly, and began to make her way
along the parapet, shuffling one step sideways at a time,
groping with her hands. Jack watched her with crushing
impatience as she made her way gradually to the corner of
the tower. There she paused, reaching behind her with one
foot, her eyes still closed.

"Kick your shoes off!" Jack shouted at her. "And for
God's sake open your eyes!"

He turned to Randy, who was white and shivering in
Geoff's huge brown sweater. "What do you say, spaceman?
Think you can do it? Along the ledge till you get to the
corner, then climb down the pipe. All you have to do is
watch what you're doing and hold on tight."

"Yes, sir," Randy said, quivering. Jack lifted him out of
the window, and he followed his mother into the rain, his
feet splashing in the flooded parapet.

God, that's my boy, Jack thought. *Sure of himself, knows
what to do.*

He shone the flashlight back into the loft. He tried not to
focus on any of the grisly heaps of shining flesh. Karen was
balancing her way toward him, her nose wrinkled in
disgust, her legs streaked with putrefying ooze.

He reached out his hand for her. "Come on, honey, we're
going to make it now. Quick as you can!"

But ten feet behind her, the piles of human detritus
suddenly shuddered. Something was forcing its way up
from underneath them. Coils of shining intestines snaked
swiftly and sulkily off to one side; jellified flesh slithered
apart; skulls rose and fell as if they were floating on the
tide. The floor of Quintus Miller's slaughterhouse almost
seemed to *boil* as a powerful wave of energy forged its way

toward them—a wave that could only have been caused by the vengeful and unerring form of Quintus Miller, swimming his way through the floor.

"*Faster!*" shouted Jack. Karen turned around, and uttered a short single "*Ah!*"

"*Faster!*"

Karen reached out for him—"*Jack, please*"—her hands quivering in panic and desperation. Her blond wig had skewed to one side; her face was distorted with fear. She had almost reached him when she slipped, stumbled, and fell to her knees.

Instantly, voraciously, Quintus Miller's hands surged out of the bloody mass of decomposed bodies, and seized her ankles, and yanked her away.

"Karen! Hold on!" Jack shouted, and waded through the flesh toward her.

Karen screamed and thrashed. But Quintus kept dragging her farther and farther away. Jack yelled, "Hold on! Keep kicking!"

At that moment, however, Randy appeared at the window, white-faced, his hair dripping with rain, his sweater black and soggy. He let out a piercing shriek, "*Daddy! Daddy! Mommy's falling! Daddy, come quick!*"

Jack looked in horror at Karen, then back at Randy.

"*Please, Daddy—Mommy's falling! She can't hold on!*"

"*Ja-a-a-cckkk!*" screamed Karen.

Jack took two or three heavy, sloshing steps toward Karen. She was being pulled face down across the floor now, toward the trapdoor. She raised her head from the glutinous mire and her face was a rigid mask of absolute terror.

"*Daddy!*" Randy wailed. "*Daddy, please!*"

Jack turned to the window, then turned back toward Karen, then turned to the window again. He covered his face with his hands and roared out loud in anguish.

He didn't know why he decided to keep his back turned

on Karen. It wasn't a conscious decision. But the next thing he knew, he was wading his way back to the window.

He grasped the window frame and was just about to lift himself out when he heard Karen utter a hopeless gurgle, and then a last compressed cry of *"Jack! Save me!"*

Trembling, he climbed out onto the flooded parapet and balanced his way toward the drainpipe at the corner of the tower. The rain lashed at his face like cold steel wire, but he almost welcomed it. It concealed the tears that coursed down his cheeks, and it gave him an excuse to shiver.

Randy followed just behind him, saying, "Quick— quick, Daddy, quick!"

Jack knelt down and looked over the edge of the roof. Maggie was only six or seven feet below the parapet, clinging to the drainpipe and moaning in fright.

"It's okay!" Jack shouted. "Maggie, it's okay! I'm coming down! Just hold on tight and stay where you are!"

He heaved himself over the parapet, his broken rib digging into his lung, and carefully climbed down to the place where Maggie was huddled.

"I'm going to climb over you—you got me? I'm going to climb over you so that I can get underneath you—then I can help you down!"

Maggie didn't reply, but continued to shudder and to moan.

"Margaret-Ann!" Jack screamed at her. "Hold on tight, I'm climbing down over you!"

Carefully, keeping one hand pressed against the side of the tower, Jack climbed over Maggie, until he was right behind her. The drainpipe creaked threateningly, and one of the brackets began to ease itself out of the brickwork.

"Oh God, I'm terrified," said Maggie, with her eyes closed. Her wet Burberry kept wrapping itself around Jack in the wind, and he found it almost impossible to get himself free.

"Listen," he told her, "I'm going to climb down just

below you. I'll guide your feet with my hands. Just hold on
tight and keep on coming and you won't fall."

"Oh, God," she prayed.

*"Margaret-Ann, do what the hell I tell you and climb
down!"* Jack shouted. *"Otherwise, God help me, I'm going
to leave you here!"*

"I'll climb down, I'll climb down," Maggie promised
him. "Don't shout at me anymore, Jack, I'll climb down."

Inch by painful inch, they descended the drainpipe. As
soon as Maggie was well clear of the parapet Jack called up
to Randy to climb down, too. Randy had climbed trees that
were almost as high as The Oaks, and he came down
without any difficulty. Maggie prayed and moaned all the
way to the ground, and when Jack guided her last step on to
the gravel, she turned, and she flung her arms around him,
and smothered his unwilling face with wet kisses, and cried
hysterically.

Jack pushed her aside and held her arm so that she
stayed well away from him. He watched and waited until
Randy had jumped down, and then he said, "Where's your
car?"

"Back by the gates," Maggie told him. But then she
looked up toward the rooftops, and said, "Where's Karen?"

"Never mind about Karen, run to the car, take Randy
with you, and get the hell out of here. Go home, don't
stop."

"But I thought Karen was right behind us!"

"Maggie, go home! Now!"

Dazed, Maggie took Randy's hand, and the two of them
walked quickly down the avenue of oaks toward the gates.

"Run!" Jack shouted, and they started to run.

Jack stood watching them go with emotions so strong
that he could scarcely breathe. Then he turned back toward
the dark spires of The Oaks. He had the most vengeful of
all scores to settle with Quintus Miller.

* * *

He skirted around the kitchens and around the back of the house to the conservatory. The heavy rains had brought down more of the glass roof, and water was splattering noisily all over the tiles. He hesitated for a moment, then stepped inside, leaving the door wide open behind him.

He made his way through the darkened lounge until he reached the hallway. The two blind statues watched him without opening their eyes. There was no sign of the clutching hands that had risen from the marble floor. No sign of Quintus Miller or Gordon Holman or any more maniacs.

The hallway stood silent.

Jack darted the beam of his flashlight all the way around the perimeter of the hallway. At last he caught the flash of green glass. Geoff's Perrier bottle of exorcised water. He waited, and listened, straining for that telltale *sssshhhh—sssshhh—sssshhhhh,* but all he could hear was the rain. Maybe Quintus was resting, after his orgy of violence.

Karen, he thought, with a sudden pang of grief.

He tiptoed across the hallway and picked up the Perrier bottle. Then he retreated, whipping the flashlight this way and that, nervously searching for hands or faces coming out of the walls.

The exorcised water made a soft slopping sound in the bottle. He prayed that it would work, the same way that it had worked for Father Bell. He didn't know any of the prayers of exorcism, but he hoped that the sincerity of his determination to rid the world of Quintus Miller and all of his homicidal maniacs would prove to be exorcism enough.

To his relief, he reached the conservatory doors unmolested. He stepped out into the rain, and unscrewed the top of the Perrier bottle, and began to circle The Oaks, sparingly sprinkling what remained of the holy water and reciting his own version of a prayer to keep unclean spirits imprisoned for ever.

"Oh God, if You love the world . . . if Thou lovest the world . . . if Thou lovest life, and happiness . . . keep these people locked up inside this circle for time everlasting . . . the power and the glory, amen."

He had almost finished his circle when he began to hear a pummeling deep within the ground, almost like the engines of the Morlocks thumping in *The Time Machine*.

Then he heard a high keening sound, and he stood alone in the rain and realized that it was the lunatics, crying inside the walls. He had trapped them all back in The Oaks. He had caught them; and this time they would never escape, because *he* had imprisoned them, and the only person who could let them out was him. Either him, or a trio of cardinals.

"Bastards!" he screamed, up at the sky. *"Bastards!"*

He stepped back across the gravel and looked up at the sinister neo-Gothic skyline of The Oaks, and wished he could raze the whole building to the ground.

He was still blinking against the rain when he heard a deep *sssssshhhh* sound in the gravel off to his right, close to the bathhouse. He pointed the flashlight in the general direction of the noise, but at first he couldn't see anything.

Then he heard it again. *Sssssssssssssshhhhhhhhhhhh*—quicker and quicker, building up toward a crescendo. *SssssssSSSHHHHHHHHH* . . .

He flicked the flashlight from one side of the gravel path to the other. Suddenly he saw the huge tidal wave in the shingle, bearing toward him faster than a man could run.

He didn't have to see who it was. He *knew*. Quintus Miller must have left The Oaks before he had sprinkled his circle of holy water. And now Quintus Miller was blasting through the ground toward him with limitless rage and unstoppable power.

The gravel seethed and sprayed apart. The turf sprayed apart. Two stone urns detonated like bombs. Then Jack was running down the slope toward the tennis courts, pursued by a huge furrow of bursting grass and earth.

Quintus Miller was so close behind him that Jack didn't

dare even to stop, and turn, and confront him with the holy water.

He ran and ran until he was running so fast that he couldn't have stopped even if he had wanted to. He crossed the flooded tennis courts, his shoes splashing in the puddles. The asphalt was ripped up only three feet behind his heels. He reached the edge of the overflowing swimming pool, tried to avoid it, slipped, arms whirling, *Hold on to that holy water, whatever you do,* then fell sideways into the murky, cold, repulsive depths of the deep end.

He gasped with the cold, struggled—lost his flashlight—saw it falling dimly to the bottom.

Then the tiled sides of the pool were smashed open, and Quintus Miller came surging into the water in a massive explosion of bubbles and dirt and churned-up filth. Jack screamed underwater, thrashed to the surface, sucked in air. But Quintus immediately seized at his ankles and dragged him back under again.

Jack kicked and twisted, but this time Quintus was determined not to let him go. He grabbed Jack around the waist, and then around the chest, and bent him backward. Desperate for breath, Jack felt Quintus's powerful fingers digging into his face, searching for his eye sockets.

He hit back at Quintus with the Perrier bottle, missed, and lost his grip on it. In retaliation, Quintus seized hold of his throat, forcing his thumbs underneath his jawbone, gradually pushing it apart. Jack's eyes bulged and bubbles of air began to leak out between his tightly clenched teeth. He felt as if Quintus were going to break his whole face in half.

Jack thrashed his arm out—and touched something repulsively familiar. The sack containing the decomposing remains of Joseph Lovelittle's two-headed German shepherd. Instinctively he pulled it toward him.

He's frightened of dogs—his father set the family dog on him after he had killed his brothers and his mother—almost killed him—frightened of dogs—

Sniffing in nostrilfuls of water, Jack brought up his knee and hit Quintus sharply in the chest—once, twice, three times. Quintus released his grip on Jack's face, but came circling around to grab him around the waist and bend him backward.

Jack pulled open the neck of the sack, fumbled disgustedly inside, and then dragged out the two-headed dog by the sodden scruff of its neck. He couldn't see it, in the filthy darkness of the swimming pool, but Quintus would be able to visualize it as clearly as if it were floodlight.

There was a split second when Jack believed that it wasn't going to work. But then Quintus convulsed, and convulsed again. He churned away from Jack, but Jack could still feel his epileptic spasms through the water, and a bubbling screech of abject terror.

He kicked himself to the surface of the pool, still clutching the monstrous dog. He could see which way Quintus had gone by the shuddering ripples that led to the edge. The sky was beginning to grow lighter now, even though it was still raining.

The tiles at the far side of the pool cracked and splintered as Quintus convulsively left the water and crept back into the earth. Jack struck out after him and reached the ladder. As he did so he heard something clinking close beside him. It was the Perrier bottle, floating on the surface. He lifted it out, and he could have kissed it.

Heaving himself up the ladder, with water draining from his clothes, Jack followed Quintus's progress across the grass. He held the corpse of the two-headed dog up in front of him, like a shield, like a grisly talisman.

Quintus reached the low brick retaining wall that separated the lawns from the woods. From the shifting and the shuffling of the brickwork, Jack could see that he was creeping into one twelve-foot section of it, between two sets of stone steps, in the same way that a man suffering from chronic influenza creeps into the warmth of his bed.

Jack dropped the dog's body close by, and then purposefully unscrewed the bottle of exorcised water, and walked all the way around the section of wall, reciting his prayer and sprinkling his water.

"Quintus!" he shouted. "Can you hear me, Quintus? You're trapped now, you can't get out!"

There was no reply, but the bricks dryly rubbed against each other, like somebody with a mouthful of sand grinding their teeth together.

"Quintus, where's Karen? What have you done with her, Quintus? I'm not going to let you sacrifice her, Quintus! Do you hear me?"

You pathetic idiot, Quintus's harsh, midwestern accents suddenly replied. *I couldn't sacrifice her because she's dead. You didn't even give me time, you and your holy water and your half-assed prayers! I killed her because of you!*

"You're lying!" Jack shouted at the wall. "You've got her hidden!"

I wish I had. But she's dead, Mr. Reed. Tomato puree.

Jack took two quick, quivering breaths. "O Lord keep this sinner trapped in this wall, because he deserves everything that's coming to him, amen."

He turned stiffly and trudged back toward The Oaks. He was too exhausted to run. Close to the back of the conservatory, he had seen a gardening shed, and where there was a gardening shed, there were usually tools.

The shed was padlocked, but so dilapidated that he kicked the door off its rusted hinges. Inside, he found stacks of flowerpots, a petrified lawn mower, gasoline cans, bunches of garden canes, and just what he was looking for—a pick.

He walked wearily back down the lawns to the wall in which Quintus was imprisoned. A weak sun showed its face behind the clouds and glistened on the rain-soaked grass.

He lifted the pick and hacked away two of the top layer of bricks. Then more, and more, until the wall began to collapse onto the grass.

Quintus began to rage at him. *Stay away, you bastard! Stay away! I'll kill you for this, I'll tear you to pieces!*

But Jack didn't reply. He was too tired to reply. He kept on swinging the pick and chopping down more of the wall, until Quintus was crowded into the very end of it.

No! screamed Quintus. *You touch me now, and I'll kill you!*

Jack swung the pick again. *Clokk.* And the bricks barked against each other as they rolled across the lawn. "You don't have anyplace left to go, Quintus. This is it."

Quintus shrieked. A sound so piercing that Jack could hardly hear it.

He swung the pick, and the bricks dropped away, and there was Quintus's face, his eyes wide open, his mouth stretched in a scream of paranoiac agony.

Jack swung again, revealing Quintus's shoulders, then his chest. Then there was nothing but a half-naked trembling man crouched amidst the scattered bricks.

Quintus raised his eyes. Metallic, unforgiving, expressionless.

You shall be damned forever and ever for this.

Jack said, "God forgive me," and swung the pick, and the point hit Quintus straight in the forehead.

Quintus broke apart, like two halves of a statue, and then collapsed into lumps. Jack bent forward and picked up one of the lumps, and that was brick, too—brick that crumbled between his fingers, into dust.

He stayed where he was by the broken wall for a very long time, while the sky cleared, and the rain began to dry, and The Oaks behind him was shrouded in mist. Then he dropped the pick and began to walk back up the hill.

Two of the gasoline cans were still three-quarters filled with gasoline. Jack hefted them out from the back of the shed and carried them over to the conservatory door, his back hunched because of the weight.

He knocked off the lids and threw them into the reading lounge. They banged and echoed and tumbled over; then all he could hear was gasoline glugging onto the floor.

He had no more prayers, no more cries of furious revenge. He took out a book of matches with shaking hands and tossed three flaring matches into the lounge, one after the other.

The first two fizzled, but when he threw in the third, the lounge suddenly *whoomphed* into flame.

The burning of The Oaks was spectacular. Floor by floor, window by window, fire raged up toward the roof.

The lunatics trapped inside the building's fabric must have risen higher and higher through the maze of the building's walls, because it was only when the fire reached the third story that Jack heard screaming.

He stood on the lawn, his hand shielding his face against the heat, while the Gothic outlines of the massive building pulsed with sparks, and fire waved in the early-morning wind like a huge orange flag.

They screamed in panic and anguish and pain, and in the total despair of having survived for sixty years only to die like this. *Rats in a trap,* thought the man who had piped them here.

The spires collapsed; the staircases fell. The blind faces dropped from the parapets. The screaming went on and on, a hundred and thirty human spirits roasted into extinction. Jack watched and waited with hollow-eyed patience until the very last scream had died away.

He could hear sirens in the distance. He wiped his heat-reddened face with the back of his sleeve. He took one last look at The Oaks, and then he walked away through the woods.

Sergeant Charles Schiller crunched through the smoldering ashes of The Oaks, his hands in his raincoat pockets. Not far away, a demolition crew was bringing down two pale soot-streaked statues, which had miraculously been left standing when the hallway collapsed.

The fire chief came trudging over, sniffing and rubbing his hands together. "Some blaze, huh?"

"How long before our forensic people can get in here?" Sergeant Schiller asked.

"Four or five hours. Give it a chance to cool off."

Sergeant Schiller circled the demolition site, feeling the heat of the recent fire through the soles of his borrowed fire-department boots. He picked up fragments of broken marble, pieces of cracked china, a twisted fork. There were bones here, too, but he didn't touch them.

It was only when he was ready to leave that he saw something gleaming in the ashes. He squatted down and teased it out of the ground with his pen. It was still too hot to touch. He lifted it up and let it dangle on the end of his pen.

A cheap gold necklace, fashioned into the letters K-A-R-E-N.

Jack never went home. He took the last of his money out of the First Milwaukee Savings Bank and bought himself a faded beige Plymouth from a retired apple farmer in Standard, Wisconsin, and drove north undetected over the Canadian border.

His name is Jack Pontneuf these days, and he works as a foreman for St. Basile Muffler close to Quebec and speaks passable French. His drinking friends call him Jack the Dry, because three drinks is all he will drink, and he hates the rain, and he never talks much, except about mufflers, and there isn't much to say about mufflers.

He rents a room in a small blue-painted house in a nondescript suburb of Quebec and spends most of his time looking out of the window at the telegraph poles and the weather and the children playing in the street.

His landlady is a woman called Cécile de Champlain. A

widow of forty-five, plain, sweet, and sad. She places a jelly jar of fresh flowers in his room every two or three days, but rarely talks to him.

He has asked her to tell him immediately if she ever hears a rustling noise in the walls, or if she ever sees the ground breaking up for no reason, or if a small child in a gray-white raincoat ever crosses her path.

She has promised faithfully that she will.

He has also asked her (awkwardly, his eyes focused on something quite different, far away) never to sing the children's song "Lavender Blue."

She has promised faithfully that she won't.

Cécile de Champlain thinks privately that Jack probably needs some psychiatric help. They have homes for people like him.